DAHVEED

DAHVEED

YAHWEH'S WARRIOR

BOOK TWO

TERRI L. FIVASH

REVIEW AND HERALD® PUBLISHING ASSOCIATION

Since 1861 | www.reviewandherald.com

Published by Review and Herald® Publishing Association, Hagerstown, MD 21741-1119

Review and Herald® titles may be purchased in bulk for educational, business, fund-raising, or sales promotional use. For information, please e-mail SpecialMarkets@reviewandherald.com.

The Review and Herald® Publishing Association publishes biblically based materials for spiritual, physical, and mental growth and Christian discipleship.

The author assumes full responsibility for the accuracy of all facts and quotations as cited in this book.

This book was
Edited by Gerald Wheeler
Designed by Trent Truman
Cover art by Raoul Vitale
Interior designed by Heather Rogers
Typeset: 11.5/13.5 Bembo

PRINTED IN U.S.A.

13   12   11   10   09   5   4   3   2   1

Library of Congress Cataloging-in-Publication Data
Fivash, Terri L.
  Dahveed : Yahweh's warrior / Terri L. Fivash.
    p. cm.
1. David, King of Israel. I. Title.
  BS580.D3F58 2008
  222'.4092—dc22

              2008013913

ISBN 978-0-8280-2465-5

DEDICATION

This book is dedicated to
Keith and Theron and Jared
for all their help and support when I write.

ACKNOWLEDGMENTS

As always, I am indebted to many people for their help in the creation of this book.

Among them are Leona Running and Roy Gane for their expertise in biblical Hebrew; Alice Williams for her help with plotting; Ulla Hansen and Joel Griessel for their critique of the manuscript; Gerald Wheeler, my editor; and J. Amanda McGuire for steering me into those Hebrew grammar books I needed!

Thanks to each of you, and the others I couldn't mention.

TO PARENTS OF YOUNGER READERS

The story of David is one of the best known in the Bible. However, David lived a violent life, and warfare back then was very up-close and personal. You will, therefore, find a great deal of combat in this book. While I do not feel that I must wallow in blood and gore, a certain amount of it is unavoidable if I am to remain faithful to the culture of biblical times and the biblical narrative itself. Please keep this in mind if you choose to read it to your children.

Another usually ignored aspect of David's life is that he dealt with demons when he served in King Saul's court. That was, after all, the reason that the royal family brought him to the court in the first place. Again, I have tried to find the balance between portraying the reality of what this meant without going overboard on the occult aspects. I hope I have succeeded.

TO THE READER

A s with my other books, one of my purposes is to tell these stories in their proper historical and cultural context. That means I try to depict them from the perspective of the protagonist, using the mindset, attitudes, and accepted ways of the world as they were understood back in the Late Bronze Age/Early Iron Age when Dahveed lived. Details and comments in the Bible make it clear that Israel and Judah in Shaul and Dahveed's time were very much a part of the Bronze Age culture in the ancient Near East, just as we are part of our culture today. Therefore, to really appreciate much of what these stories have to say, we must forget our own ideas of "the way things should be," and put ourselves in the sandals of the biblical characters, attempting to view their lives and times through the same perspective that they had back then. And speaking of time, let's have a word about . . .

Chronology

As I've discussed in my previous books, historians argue endlessly about chronology. Ancient history has only one set date, and that is 664 B.C. (or B.C.E. if you prefer), the end of the third intermediate period in Egypt. Every date previous to that one, and many after it, are simply educated guesses. Some guesses are more educated than others, and the further back one goes, the more "guess" enters the picture. The usual estimate for the beginning of Dahveed's reign is around 1000 B.C., give or take 50 years, with Solomon taking the throne around 970 B.C., with the same margin of error.

The other very important aspect of chronology is that the Bible comes to us from an oral tradition. All the stories in the Bible originally circulated by word of mouth, and only got written down much later. The Bible authors narrated in thematic sequence, not necessarily in straight chronological order, a fact vital for our understanding of the stories. But that should not be surprising. When you are telling someone about things that happened to you over a period of several days or weeks, you don't relate everything that happened in between the relevant events! You skip those until you have presented the entire connected sequence. Then, if there is some other theme you want to discuss, you go "back in time" and begin another sequence. Scripture tells the stories of Dahveed's life in exactly the same way. It means, of course, that we don't know how much time may have passed between events in a sequence, or even how the sequences actually fit together in straight chronological order. We can only guess. Note the amount of time I have put between Goliath's death and the covenant between Dahveed and Jonathan.

English readers, however, are used to written history and stories occuring in straight chronological sequence. Again, to make it easier for my readers, I have given my best guess at the chronological sequence of many of the events in Dahveed's life. At times, however, I have followed the thematic sequence, and then gone "back in time" to pick up the story in another place. (For those of you who are curious, yes, the Hebrew does indicate such a thematic sequence, and no, I'm not going into detail. It involves the use of the Hebrew letter vav, about which Hebrew scholars argue with as much verve as historians do about chronology.) Now, let's move on to a word about . . .

Samuel or Chronicles?

I have chosen to follow the plot of Dahveed's life as outlined in 1 and 2 Samuel. Written hundreds of years before Chronicles, they are, therefore, considered more reliable than Chronicles. By the time of the composition of Chronicles people considered Dahveed a national hero, and you'll notice that in Chronicles the biblical author has purged his life of any hint of wrongdoing with the exception of his affair with Bathsheba. That got him in so much trouble that no one could ignore it, even hundreds of years later! But notice that Chronicles mentions it only in passing. I feel that the books of Samuel reflect a truer picture of what Dahveed was like, so I have used the account in Chronicles only for additional details to the narrative if I thought they might be useful.

Next, a word about . . .

Translations of the Psalms

They are my own. Don't blame anyone else for them or look for them in any Bible.

I realized when I was writing my book about Ruth that I needed to know more about biblical Hebrew in order to really understand the story. By the time I started research for *Dahveed*, I knew that I had to know a lot more about biblical Hebrew. So I sat in on Hebrew classes at the Theological Seminary at Andrews University. (And my profound thanks to the teacher for so graciously allowing my presence in the classroom!) As a result, I learned how to do my own translations.

My goal has been to reflect more of the Hebrew usage and words rather than tweaking them for a smooth English translation. Thus, if the Hebrew employs the word "voice" three times in three sentences, so do I, rather than put in a synonym as "better English usage" demands. Note Psalm 23 with its "ruts of righteousness!" "Path" is more melodic in English and flows better, but the Hebrew word is "rut," not "path." Rougher sounding in English, I know, but a much more vivid word picture. So if the psalm translations use repetitive words arranged rather oddly, leave out or add some words, and sound a bit skewed to your ear, blame it on the flavor of biblical Hebrew! I hope you like the tang, as if you've had the chance to taste an exotic food for the first time. Now that my last two sentences have thoroughly mixed that metaphor, let's have a word about . . .

Numbers

Here is where the cultural differences between our day and Dahveed's rear their heads in an unmistakable way. Today, our lives are intensely entwined with extremely accurate and precise numbers. We assume that the rest of the planet also adheres to such accurate and precise numbers. Sorry. There still exist cultures today that have two numbers: one and two. Anything else is "more."

Furthermore, we assume that past cultures must also have loved very accurate and precise numbers. After all, we received 60 seconds in a minute and 60 minutes in an hour from Babylon. But Israel isn't Babylon, and Hebrew numbers are mushy. We're dealing with a culture in which the smallest amount of time that we know they used is the hour, not the split second. And they defined the hour as a certain segment of dawn to dusk, and dusk to dawn. That meant the hour stretched and shrank according to the season of the year.

Therefore, "40 years" can mean 40 years as we understand it, or "the years from adulthood to death" or "a generation." Since the scribes who wrote down the stories for us were not concerned with our passion for absolute accuracy in numbers, they neglected to indicate which meaning they had in mind when they used the term, leaving it up to us to guess which one seems the most logical. If more than one meaning can logically fit, take your best guess.

For instance, Dahveed reigned for 40 years. Does it mean exactly 40 years to the day, or 38.5 years, or maybe 43 years and two months? If we were to ask the recording scribe which one is "right," he would look at us as if we were crazy. Dahveed reigned from his adulthood until he died. What more do you need to know? The exact amount of time that period covered was irrelevant and useless information, so no one bothered with it. Such an attitude naturally drives us Western number-oriented people right up the wall, and it's one reason that historians argue so intensely about chronology!

Now, one of the favorite units of numbers in the Bible is the *elef*. Translators render it in one of two ways—either "family/military unit" or "thousand." Here's where things get very sticky. The meaning of *elef* in Dahveed's time is "family/military unit" and very well could have had a standard number assigned to it that everyone back then understood. But by the time the Jews translated the Hebrew scriptures into what we know as the Septuagint, the number that went with *elef* had long since been lost. So the scribes doing the translating assigned a number to *elef*. They chose "thousand." It seemed the best guess to them.

For hundreds of years no one thought to question that assignment. However, modern scholars have much more to work with than did the scribes who created the Septuagint. We have thousands (our thousands) of clay tablets from numerous places in numerous languages, covering different time periods of ancient history. In addition, we have archaeological discoveries to help us interpret the documents. And the word *elef*, or its equivalent, is quite common. But translators had just one problem. "Thousand" didn't fit. Scholars therefore went back to the records, trying to understand what was going on. The essential question was "How many is a 'family unit'?"

Well, that depends. How many people are in your family? Mushy numbers, remember? Therefore, hold on to your hats! Currently, the best scholarly guess at how many an *elef* is stands at 5-14 people. (Is it safe to come out now? OK.) Naturally, this wreaks havoc with the general ideas of how many people were involved in the biblical battles, for instance. However, it does bring the biblical record into line with what we know about the general culture, the population, the amount of land available, and the size of towns, settlements, and kingdoms. So maybe deciding that the guess of the Septuagint scribes was not quite correct isn't such a bad idea.

Because we really don't know how many an *elef* is, I've used the word "unit" as a substitute. "Unit" can also be mushy, just like *elef*. How many a unit contains depends on who's counting and what is being counted. The ancients probably approached *elef* exactly the same way. (Yes, I know. If "thousand" is 5-14, how many is a "hundred?" Since "hundred" means "fraction or multiple," maybe we shouldn't go into that.)

And finally, a word about . . .

Ishvi

For those of you who have read the genealogies in the Bible that give Shaul's descendants, you may be wondering where Ishvi is. First Samuel 14:49 lists him as a son of Shaul, and as far as I know, the name never appears again. Scripture mentions a son named Abinadab as dying with Shaul, but he never shows up elsewhere in Shaul's story. Some scholars speculate that Ishvi and Abinadab are one and the same. I don't know. But in the interests of simplicity, I picked one name to use in my story, ignoring the other. I liked Ishvi better than Abinadab, and Ishvi was mentioned first. Besides, Dahveed had a brother named Abinadab, and I didn't want to confuse people more than I had to with multiple characters having the same name.

CAST OF CHARACTERS

Names in **BOLD** appear in this book of the series.
★ Before name indicates a biblical character.

Abiadan—Sahrah of Ammon, daughter of King Nahash, wife of Jesse and mother of Abigail and Zeruiah. Deceased.

Abiaz—Troublemaker in Heshbon when Ruth was a young woman.

★ Abiezer—One of Hassar Jonathan's personal guards.

★ **Abigail**—Dahveed's half sister, and full sister to Zeruiah. Daughter of Abiadan.

★ **Abinadab**—Jesse's second son by Miriam, his Israelite wife. Half brother to Dahveed.

★ **Abishai**—Dahveed's nephew, first born of Zeruiah, half sister to Dahveed.

Abner—General of Shaul's armies and his cousin.

★ **Achish**—Son of Maoch of Gath, who becomes seren of Gath when his father dies.

Achsah—Maid to Michal.

★ **Adriel**—Son of Barzillai. Marries Merab.

Ahaz—Elder of Bethlehem.

★ **Ahiam**—Habiru sworn to Daveed.

★ **Ahimelech**—High priest in Nob during Shaul's reign.

★ **Ahinoam**—Shaul's wife.

★ **Ahor**—Canaanite landowner near Shechem. Grandfather to Hushai the Archite.

★ **Aiah**—Father of Rizpah, Shaul's concubine. Lives in Jabesh.

★ **Achish**—Son of Maoch of Gath, who becomes seren of Gath when his father dies.

Ala—Zelek's sister. Half Ammonite, half Cushite, and blood cousin to Abigail and Zeruiah.

★ **Amasa**—Son of Dahveed's sister Abigail.

★ **Araunah**—Title for king of Jebus. Used as a name.

Areli—Man from Naphtali in the second unit.

* **Armoni**—Rizpah's first son.
* **Asahel**—Dahveed's nephew, third son of Zeruiah.
  Asaiah—Boy in Bethlehem, son of Telah.
  Atarah—Jebusite woman rescued by Dahveed and Ethan. Sister to Ornan.
  Balak—Man of Bethlehem who dislikes Dahveed.
  Baqqush—Envoy from the kingdom of Mari who makes a covenant with Shaul.
* **Barzillai**—Man from Jabesh in Gilead.
  Basemath—Maid to Rizpah.
  Ben-geber—Dahveed's childhood name.
* **Boaz**—Dahveed's great-grandfather. Ruth's husband.
  Bodbaal—Philistine member of Ethan's band. Mute. Brother to Geresh and Peleth.
  Bukki—Lahab's father. Landowner in Bethlehem.
  Caleb—Habiru member of Ethan's band with twin daughters.
  Carmi—homesteader north of Bethlehem.
* **Dahveed**—Jesse's eighth son, anointed to be king for Yahweh. (Dahveed is also a title.)
* **Dara**—Hassar Jonathan's shield bearer.
  David—See Dahveed.
  Debir—Adon in Jebus who stages a palace coup and becomes Araunah.
  Dishon—Commander of the eighth unit.
* **Dodo**—Father of Eleazar of Benjamin.
* **Dodo**—Father of Dahveed's childhood friend Elhanan.
  Dumah—Kin of Ornan and Atarah, who betrays them.
* **El**—Mighty One, God.
* **El Elyon**—God Most High.
* **El Shaddai**—God Almighty.
* **Eleazar**—Left-handed swordsman who becomes shield bearer to Sar Ishvi.
* **Elhanan**—Son of Bethlehem's innkeeper.
* **Eliab**—Jesse's firstborn child, his bekor. Half brother to Dahveed.
* **Elihu**—Jesse's seventh son. Trains to be a scribe. Half brother to Dahveed.
* **Eshbaal**—Shaul's fourth son, younger than Michal. Not a warrior.

Ethan—Grandson of Patah and Gaddi. Leader of the Habiru near Bethlehem, and Dahveeds' teacher.

★ Gad—Roeh Shamuel's servant.

Gaddi—Grandfather to Ethan. Lifetime slave to Boaz's house.

Gedor—Man of the second unit who dies saving Sar Malchi.

Geresh—Philistine Habiru of Ethan's band. Brother to Bodbaal.

★ **Goliath**—Traditional name of the champion of the Philistines whom Dahveed kills.

★ **Hanan**—Habiru youth affiliated with Joel's band near Keilah. One of Yahweh's Arrows.

(The) Hassarah—Title of respect given to Ruth, Dahveed's great-grandmother, from whom he inherits his musical skills, and much else.

Hod—Balak's father. A Moabite landowner in Bethlehem.

★ **Hushai**—The Archite. Grandson of Ahor, who likes Dahveed.

★ **Ira**—Great-grandson of Shamuel, who asks for a song. Brother to Hannah.

★ **Ishvi**—Shaul's second son. A sar.

★ **Ittai**—Philistine/Israelite youth bound to Dahveed through circumcision.

★ **Jaasiel**—Abner's son.

Jamin—Ethan's younger brother. A Habiru and one of Yahweh's Arrows.

Jarib—Demoted commander of the second unit. Dahveed's assistant commander and very clumsy.

Jashobeam—See Josheb.

Jerioth—Sister of Asaiah and wife of Elhanan.

Jeshua—Leader of the Gibeah band of Habiru.

★ **Jesse**—Dahveed's father. Elder and rich landowner in Bethlehem.

★ **Jether**—Abigail's husband. Ishmaelite trader.

★ **Joab**—Dahveed's nephew. Second son of Zeruiah.

Joel—Habiru dahveed of the Keilah band. Supporter of Ethan.

★ Jonadab—Second son of Shammah, and Dahveed's nephew.

★ **Jonathan**—Dahveed's uncle (brother of his mother).

★ **Jonathan**—Shaul's oldest son. The hassar.

★ **Jonathan**—Dahveed's nephew, son of Shammah.

★ **Jonathan**—Son of the Habiru Shagay. Yahweh's Arrow.

Josheb-Basshebeth—One of Hassar Jonathan's personal guard, who swears to Dahveed.

Judith—Maid to Ahinoam and wife of Balak.

Kemosh—god of Moab.

Kemosh-dan—Overlord of Moab when Ruth was a young woman.

Keren—Dahveed's mother. Becomes Jesse's wife.

Keturah—Gibeonite woman dependent on Dahveed. Sister to Naharai.

Keziah—Wife of Dahveed's half brother Shammah.

Kish—Shaul's father.

Kohath—Head scribe under Eshbaal at Gibeah's fortress.

Lahab—Vintner of Bethlehem and son of Bukki. Sets up shop with Raddai.

Leah—One of Caleb's twins. Habiru.

Libni—Commander of the tenth unit. Supports Abner.

Lotan—Man of the second unit. A Hittite mastersmith.

Malchi—See Malchi-shua.

Malchi-shua—Shaul's third son. A sar.

Manani—Cruel seren in Ekron.

Maoch—Seren of Gath.

Mari—Messenger sent to Shaul, who is murdered on the way. Also a city-state north of Israel.

Mattan—Meshullam's son and dahveed after him. Swore his band to Boaz and Boaz's bloodline.

Mephibosheth—Rizpah's second son.

Merab—Shaul's oldest child, his bekorah. Promised to Dahveed. A sahrah.

Meshullam—Habiru dahveed of Boazs time.

Michal—Shaul's younger daughter, between Malchi and Eshbaal. A sahrah.

Minelek—Philistine merchant of Chephirah, whom Dahveed appoints as Gibeonite overseer.

Miriam—Jesse's Israelite wife.

Nadab—Quartermaster of Shaul's army.

Naharai—Gibeonite man of the second unit. Keturah's brother.

Nahash—King of Ammon, and grandfather of Abigail and Zeruiah.

Natan—Newly appointed commander of the fifth unit.

Nemuel—Jonathan's boyhood friend. Killed by Philistines.

★ **Ner**—Abner's father. Uncle to Shaul.

★ **Nethanel**—Jesse's fourth son, Dahveed's half brother.

Nimshi—Ethan's youngest son.

★ **Obed**—Ruth's son, Jesse's father. Deceased.

★ **Ornan**—Jebusite youth rescued by Dahveed and Ethan. Brother to Atarah.

★ **Ozem**—Jesse's sixth son. Younger twin to Raddai, Dahveed's half brother.

Pallu—Man of the second unit. Good archer.

Pasach—Commander of the eleventh unit.

Pashur—Habiru of Boaz's time.

Patah—Old dahveed of the Habiru when Ben-geber was a child. Grandson of Meshullam and grandfather of Ethan and Jamin.

Peleth—Former Philistine slave to Hassar Jonathan, and older brother to Geresh and Bodbaal.

Qausa—Habiru from far south who killed Mari. Also accepted money to kill King Shaul.

Rachel—One of Caleb's twins. Habiru.

★ **Raddai**—Jesse's fifth son. Older twin to Ozem, Dahveed's half brother.

Ram—Commander of the first unit in King Shaul's permanent forces.

★ **Recheb**—Gibeonite from Beeroth. Son of Rimmon to whom Jonathan Hassar gives hesed.

Reu—Man of the second unit. Good engineer.

★ **Rimmon**—Gibeonite from Beeroth who tried to kill Jonathan Hassar.

★ **Rizpah**—Concubine to King Shaul from Jabesh in Gilead.

★ **Ruth**—the hassarah. Wife of Boaz and great-grandmother of Dahveed.

Samuel—See Shamuel.

Saul—See Shaul.

★ **Shagay**—Habiru and Yahweh's Arrow. Dahveed's first retainer.

★ **Shammah**—Jesse's third son, Dahveed's half brother.

Shammah ben Agee—See Shagay.

★ **Shamuel**—Roeh, seer, in Israel. Anoints Shaul and Dahveed.

* **Shaul**—King of Israel, Jonathan and Michal's father.
  Sheva—Commander of the king's guard.
* **Shimei**—Cousin to Jonathan Hassar. Banned from appearing at court.
  Shoher—Father of Ethan. Deceased.
  Sithri—Man of the second unit who can sharpen things well.
  Steward of the House of Tahat—Man to whom Jonathan Hassar
      wants to talk.
  Tahan—Man of the second unit who knows jewelry.
  Tahat—Business associate of Dahveed's great-grandfather Boaz.
  Tamakel—Son of Nahash, father of Ala and Zelek. Deceased.
  Telah—Elder in Bethlehem.
* **Yah**—Short form of Yahweh.
  Yahas—Balak's great-grandfather whom he meets in Jebus and who
      teaches him to worship Kemosh.
  Yahoadan—Jamin's daughter. Habiru.
* **Yahweh**—Israel's God. Has chosen Dahveed.
  Yahweh's Arrows—Habiru who have affiliated with Ethan and his
      band to protect and serve Boaz's bloodline.
* **Zelek**—Unfortunate Ammonite/Cushite who is forced to assassinate
      Hassar Jonathan. Brother to Ala. Blood kin to Abigail and
      Zeruiah.
  Zemirah—Head elder in Bethlehem.
  Zeri—Habiru from the Gibeah band. Yahweh's Arrow.
  Zeruiah—Jesse's oldest daughter by Abiadan. Mother of Abishai,
      Joab, and Asahel.
  Zorath—Commander of the third unit and supporter of Dahveed.

Habiru lineage:
Meshullam—Mattan—Patah—Shoher—Ethan—Nimshi

Dahveed's lineage:
Salmon—Boaz—Obed—Jesse—Dahveed

Masculine title of respect in Israel—from least to most
Geber—Adon/Baal—Sar—Nahsi—Nagid—Melek

Feminine titles of respect—from least to most
Geberet—Baalah—Sahrah—Hassarah

VOCABULARY

Pronunciations:

A pronounced "Ah." Spelled "ah"; occasionally pronounced
as short "A." Spelled "a."

E pronounced as long A. Spelled "ay"; occasionally pronounced
as short "e." Spelled "eh."

I pronounced as long E. Spelled "ee."

O pronounced as long O. Spelled "oh."

U pronounced as "oo." Spelled "oo."

AI pronounced as long I. Spelled "aye."

Italics indicate the stressed syllable.

Abbi—(*ah*-bee) my father, term of endearment, somewhat like Daddy.

Adon—(ah-*dohn*) masculine title of respect: lord.

Adonai—(Ah-dohn-*naye*) plural of adoni—used exclusively for
Yahweh.

Adoni—(ah-dohn-*ee*) my lord.

Aijalon—(Aye-yah-*lohn*) a pass from the hills into the Shephelah about
15 miles west of Jebus.

Baalah—(bah-*ah*-lah) feminine title of respect: lady.

Bat—(baht) daughter of, or female descendant of.

Bekor—(beh-*kohr*) first born, masculine.

Bekorah—(beh-kohr-*ah*) first born, feminine.

Ben—(bayn) son of, or male descendant of.

Chinnereth—See Sea of Chinnereth.

Couscous—(*koos*-koos) cooked cracked wheat.

Cuirass—(kwee-*rahs*) armored "shirt" for heavy infantry.

Dagon—god of the Philistines.

Dahveed—(dah-*veed*) probably "Beloved one." May have been used
to designate an important or "beloved" leader in war. I use it in

this context in this book, although much argument rages about the word's ancient usage and meaning.

Dod—(dohd) kinsman, uncle, indicates close kinsman relationship.

Dodi—(doh-*dee*) my uncle.

Geber—(*gehb*-behr) masculine title of respect: master or sir.

Geberet—(geh-*behr*-eht) feminine title of respect: mistress or ma'am.

Gebirah—(geh-*beer*-ah) the woman in whom the kingdom is embodied. She is also called the "handmaid." Whomever the gebirah marries will have the right to rule the kingdom. The gebirah was normally of the same clan as the royal family, if not the royal family itself.

Girdle—wide strip of cloth or soft leather wrapped around the waist to hold a robe together and to provide a place to put things.

Great Sea—ancient name for the Mediterranean Sea.

Habiru—(hah-*bee*-roo) name for bands of nomads, usually small, that roamed Israel during the time of Dahveed. They consisted of landless family units or displaced persons from the 12 tribes or any of the surrounding nations. Their main occupation was as mercenaries, but many bands simply supported themselves by robbery and murder. Habiru can refer to the entire band or a single member of it.

Hakkohen Haggadol—(hah-koh-*hayn* hah-gah-*dohl*) the high priest.

Hamsin—(hahm-*seen*) harsh dry east wind from the desert.

Hassar—(hah-*sahr*) *the* prince, hence first or crown prince.

Hassarah—(hah-sahr-*ah*) *the* princess/queen, hence most important princess/queen.

Henna—reddish stain from plants used to decorate nails and skin.

Hesed—(*hes*-ed) voluntary kindness on the life-saving level provided by the only one able to give it.

Jebus—ancient name for the city that became Jerusalem.

Leben—(*leh*-behn) curdled milk, churned in a skin bag and used for food.

Ma'at—Order, harmony, peace.

Mashiah—(mah-shee-*ah*) anointed one.

Meil—(may-*eel*) expensive, richly embroidered tunic worn only by royalty.

Melek—(*mel*-ek) king. Dahveed was anointed as melek.

CULTURAL NOTES

Ages of Dahveed and Jonathan—Nearly everyone assumes that Dahveed and Jonathan were close in age. Nearly everyone is wrong. First Samuel 13:1 tells us that Shaul was 30 years old when he began to reign, and that he reigned for 42 years. Verses 2 and 3 indicate that Jonathan was, at this time, old enough to lead the army, therefore in his late teens at the youngest. If Dahveed at 30 (2 Samuel 5:4) took the throne in Hebron when Shaul and Jonathan died (2 Samuel 2:7), then Shaul must have reigned at least 10 years before Dahveed's birth, making Jonathan in his late 20s or older at the time. Jonathan is, therefore, old enough to be Dahveed's father.

Bloodguilt—The murder of a person always brought the curse of bloodguilt, which could be cleared only with blood. If a family member was murdered or killed by someone, the family would appoint a "redeemer (*goel*) of the blood" to track down and execute the person responsible. This was the reason for the cities of refuge. A person who caused accidental death could flee to them and be safe from the avenging Goel of the Blood. If a person was found murdered out in the forest or on the road somewhere, the land itself had incurred bloodguilt, and there was a specific sacrifice and ritual associated with cleansing the land of the murdered person's blood, thus removing the curse from the land and/or any nearby towns. Curses were terrible punishments and greatly feared since the gods or Yahweh enforced them, and there was no protection from Yahweh's curse. For that matter, there isn't any today, either.

Casement walls—Builders created casement walls by constructing two parallel walls out of the largest stones manageable, then filling the space in between with smaller rocks, dirt, rubble, or whatever else was available. They would then pave the top with stone. With a large enough casement wall, you could literally hollow out a room in it.

Clothing and honor—As mentioned later under "*Fringe,*" clothing was a signal of social status. In addition, clothing literally bestowed authority. To this day, we still have investiture ceremonies wherein an individual receives the clothing (the vestments) of an office. We just don't continue to wear that clothing every day! The opposite of invest is divest, and if we divest someone of something, we strip away the associated vestments and thus the authority. The possession of a high office brought with it the obligation to wear the clothing of that office so that people would know who held what place. By wearing the clothing associated with an office, a person laid claim to its authority. Because of this, simply wearing the king's clothing could be an act of treason.

Family relationships—Family was of primary importance in the ancient Near East. However, families were organized differently then than they are today. The closest bond a person had was with siblings, not parents. Brothers and sisters were expected to look out for each other and be the confidants and advisers for each other. The husband-wife relationship was more of a business/contractual partnership than anything else. Society did not expect a wife to love her husband. People did assume that she would be loyal to him, but her supportive relationships would come from her family of origin, and she would not be counted part of her husband's family until she bore a son. The closest bond for a married woman was with her son, who was expected to stand up for her against all comers, even his father if necessary, and who would care for her in her old age. The function of a father as we understand it today was not performed by the man who sired you, but by your mother's brother—your maternal uncle. He was the one responsible for emotional support, teaching, and guidance.

Fringe—The fringe on a robe indicated status. The longer the fringe, the higher the status. A person could quite accurately place others in the correct status level simply by looking at the color, ornamentation, and material of their clothes.

Gebirah—The gebirah was the woman who owned the land, and so embodied that land. Whoever married the woman thus "married" the land and became its ruler. The idea of the gebirah had several variations in ancient times. In Egypt any woman in the palace could be named gebirah, so to be safe, the pharoah married them all. On the other hand, in Edom one woman was gebirah (and her daughter probably became the next gebirah), and whoever married her became the next king of Edom. The Hittites had a position similar to the gebirah that also carried religious duties, and the woman was appointed to the position, but held it for life independently of other political changes. The institution of gebirah existed in Israel until King Asa, as attested in 1 Kings 15:13 and 2 Chronicles 15:16. Translators render the word as "queen mother" in these verses.

Gibeonites—The Gibeonites lived in four cities occupying the heart of the territory of Ephraim west of Jebus/Jerusalem: Gibeon, Beeroth, Chephirah, and Kiriath Jearim. See Joshua 9 for the beginning of their service to the tabernacle. The genealogies in 1 Chronicles 8:29-34 and 9:35-40 give clear indication that Shaul's clan descended from Gibeon.

Grain silos—Many times the people of Bible times stored their grain in large jars called *pithoi*, which they buried up to the neck, then covered with a wooden or pottery lid. The pithoi could be six feet tall and 30 inches across at their widest point which was directly under the neck. The vessel then tapered down to a near point, at the bottom. The sides were up to one inch thick, with the surface only roughly smoothed. As the level of grain lowered in the pithoi, someone would actually have to be lowered into it—probably a child—to hand up the grain,

Harp or lyre—The ancient Israelites had two stringed instruments that scholars have been able to identify as a harp or a lyre. Unfortunately, they have not determined which Hebrew name goes with which instrument! Therefore, some scholars say the instrument Dahveed played for Shaul was a lyre; others call it a harp. Since "common knowledge" considers Dahveed as playing a harp, I chose that one.

Hesed—Most modern versions of the Bible translate this word as "loving-kindness." Some render it as "mercy," but both translations again leave out some of the important connotations of the Hebrew concept. Hesed can only come from the one person who must act in order for another's life to be preserved. This makes it the perfect word to describe what God does for us. If He didn't intervene, we'd all die, and He is the only one whose action will give us life. Therefore, He gives hesed.

Honor—Honor was the grease that made ancient society work, much as money does in Western societies. We can think of it as the respect and approval of one's community. To understand honor, think of it as a credit rating. Without honor, the avenues open to a man to support himself and his family were severely limited, much as a bad credit rating limits a person today. Anything that would make people think less of an individual or their family reduced the family honor. Keeping and maintaining honor, therefore, was of primary importance, and one had to measure every action against what people would think of it. Generally speaking, for people on the same status level, older persons had more honor than younger ones. All honor already belonged to someone, and gaining honor meant that someone else lost it. Where honor came from was very important, and being greedy about honor brought dishonor! Also, richer people had more honor than poorer ones, but only generally speaking. The most honorable man in town didn't have to be the one with the most possessions. To be rich without honor meant a person was greedy, and so the community despised such an individual. To be rich with honor meant a person was wealthy, and therefore blessed and honored.

Honor wars—Honor wars involved what we today call "disrespecting" someone. Such struggles could develop only between persons of the same status. Therefore, a householder could not have an honor war with a servant, only with another householder who held the same amount of honor in the eyes of the community. Servants could have honor wars with each other but not their master/employer. One could show disrespect in either overt or subtle ways. Deliberately not bowing low enough to someone would slight their honor. Refusing to look at someone could do the same, as well as the order in which you spoke to various people when in their presence. If an honor slight took place, the person slighted was obligated to either protest the slight or return it in some way, or else lose honor in the eyes of the community. Wars could also develop, though, over compliments and gift giving. Any gift/compliment received brought the obligation to return a gift/compliment of equal value. Otherwise one lost honor to the giver. Any social interaction, therefore, had to be carefully viewed and calculated to take honor into account.

Israel and Judah separate—People during the time of Shaul and Dahveed considered Israel and Judah as separate political entities, which is the reason so much of the Bible mentions them separately. This may hark back to Genesis 38:1, which tells us that Judah separated himself from his brothers and lived around Adullam. What was involved in this isolation, how long it lasted, and how it affected his relationship with Jacob and the rest of the family we don't know. In any case, Judah was apart from the rest, and many of the stories in Judges never mention the tribe. Archaeology tells us that at the time of Shaul and Dahveed, Judah was very sparsely populated, and people lived at subsistence level. Only around Hebron do we find some measure of wealth. The distinction between Israel and Judah continued during the United Monarchy, preserved in the differing political arrangements between the two countries and their king, who simply happened to be the same person.

Money—People in Israel in Dahveed's time didn't have money or even coins as we know them. They had pieces of precious metals, and traded them for goods, although most buying and selling actually consisted of trading for goods in kind. (For instance, "I'll give you this goat for that much grain.") Thus jewelry was as much currency as it was body decoration. In my book *Ruth and Boaz* I do use the term *gerah* to indicate pieces of gold or silver, etc., since it seemed the most convenient to do so. However, in this book, I decided that simply saying "piece" gave more of the flavor of the times.

Power—Just as today, power in Bible times brought responsibility. Much power in the Bible rested on influence, and influence was based on honor (see above). In other words, honor brought power. With death and/or disaster able to descend in so many ways, people greatly sought after anything that might protect the family, and power opened up ways to ease the family's position and provide a small cushion between the family and death. Therefore, when an individual acquired honor/power, they found themselves compelled by social norms and sheer survival to seek ways to use that power to benefit their family first, then anyone associated with with the family. Because power was connected to honor, however, one must employ it extremely carefully to avoid anything that would detract from honor, and thus lessen the power itself.

Preserving a name—The most important thing in the culture of the ancient Near East was to preserve a name and/or an inheritance. People had no belief in an afterlife, such as the Egyptians did, or in the idea of an immortal soul that lived on after the body died, such as the Greeks developed. (Christians today get the idea of an immortal soul from the Greeks.) The ancient Israelites believed that when you died, you died. The concept of eternal life was actually the concept of eternal remembrance. If a person's descendants remembered their name, that's how the individual survived death. One lived on in memory, for a person's name *was* the person. The concept made having descendants of utmost importance, since who else would remember your name? To die childless was the ultimate death. The chances of having descendants to remember greatly increased if they had land to live on, making the preservation of the family land of paramount importance also.

Prophesying—What people consider the gift of prophesy changed over time, just as did many other things in ancient times. While Samuel was alive, prophecy had little to do with foretelling the future. That definition of prophesying came into being much later. Prophecy in the time of Shaul was an ecstatic behavior, probably most analogous to what we today call "speaking in tongues." When the Bible describes Shaul as prophesying, the word may be used to indicate his external actions without any spiritual connotations. This word would probably be the closest description the ancient Israelites had for a manic-depressive state such as bipolar syndrome, which is our best guess at what Shaul suffered from.

Pure and impure—Ritual purity/cleanness or ritual impurity/uncleanness had nothing to do with dirt, grime, germs, and such. Ritual purity/cleaness had to do with *boundaries*. Such boundaries created order out of chaos (Job 26:10; Psalm 104:9; Proverbs 8:29; and Jeremiah 5:22, among other verses) and so were sacred. Therefore, anything that crossed boundaries threatened order and created impurity/uncleanness. Rituals then must be performed to restore the boundaries and thus order. Such rituals could be as simple as washing with water, or they might be elaborate, involving sacrifices and other ceremonies. Impurity could occur anywhere. Bats, for instance, were in the ancient way of thinking neither bird nor mammal. They crossed boundaries and were unclean. Blood should remain within the boundary of the skin. Contact with blood outside the skin created impurity since it had crossed a boundary. Often births and deaths, and always menstrual cycles, created ritual impurity, and that must be rectified by the counterritual of washing. Nocturnal emissions for men did exactly the same thing, and also required washing.

Shalom—We do not know the standard greeting that the ancient Israelites employed, if indeed they had one. But because modern dialogue is so used to having such a thing, I have picked the word "shalom" since it is already closely associated with Israel.

Teraphim—Teraphim were the spirits or gods who protected a house. They were part of the Elohim, supernatural beings ranging from spirits and demons up to the gods themselves. Spirits were everywhere and were capable of action for or against humans. It was wise to remain on their good side with sacrifices and gifts. Fortunately, all spirits and gods were tied to a geographical location, and their power weakened quickly when outside the geographic area. Crossing a border meant leaving the power of one god and coming under that of another. House gods— teraphim—could guard only a single dwelling, while a hill spirit could act only on that single hill, etc. A god's power was directly tied to the amount of territory he or she could operate in. Thus the more territory a king conquered for his god, the stronger the deity became. That is why war was a sacred activity.

Titles—Hebrew has several titles of respect. I have decided to use them, somewhat arbitrarily, in the following order, from that of least respect to greatest: geber (sir); adon (lord)/baal (lord); sar (prince); nahsi (governing lord); nagid (ruling prince); melek (king).

Feminine titles are as follows: geberet (ma'am); baalah (lady); sahrah (princess); hassarah (queen).

The Philistines also had sars, but for them, "sar" was the equivalent of the Hebrew "commander" The word they used for "sar" or "prince" was "seren." See Vocabulary.

In Hebrew, as in many languages other than English, the title normally follows the name rather than preceding it. But to make it easier for my readers, I have used the English convention unless the speaker employs the title in its most formal sense. Also in Hebrew, it is more courteous to call someone simply by their title. Only intimate family or very close friends would have used the personal names of respected persons. Thus, to begin with, Dahveed calls Jonathan "Hassar Jonathan," or "Hassar." For very formal introductions, or when someone meets a person in their formal capacity, Jonathan's name would be "Jonathan ben Shaul, Hassar Israel," with the title last. It will behoove the reader to pay attention to how characters use titles in the story!

Transfer of the throne—The period of Shaul/Dahveed/Solomon was extremely uncertain politically for the emerging nation of Israel/Judah. Many of the same problems occurred between the tribes as took place between the states here in the United States of America under the Articles of Confederation before they adopted the Constitution and George Washington became president. Each tribe was independent—indeed, each town and clan was autonomous and provincial in outlook. Shaul rose to power on the need for protection from the Philistines, and "ruled" through his alliances with the elders of towns and tribes who followed him only because he was the best one at keeping the invaders out of the highlands. Dahveed inherited this chiefdom and gradually shifted it toward a monarchy. The old autonomous ways, however, resurfaced after Solomon died, producing the divided kingdom.

As in every political entity, the transfer of power was vital, and since Shaul was the first "king," the people had no precedent to follow. In the ancient Near East, power normally transferred in one of three ways. When the old king died, the throne could pass by inheritance to his son, or return back to the gebirah (see above), who might or might not be the king's daughter or relative. Her husband, if she had one, became the next king. The throne could also transfer by popular acclaim, the candidate that the most people liked getting the position. This method usually disintegrated into civil war with any number of sides until one candidate slaughtered all the rest, or a foreigner with a bigger army swept in and seized the throne. If he married into the previous royal family, he could be accepted. Often, however, the fact of his foreign blood would produce rebellion against his son, or his house even generations later.

In the case of Shaul and Dahveed, it is clear that Dahveed rivaled Jonathan in popular acclaim, and married to Michal, he became a son of the king. If Michal was named gebirah, Dahveed would have a very strong claim to the throne no matter which way Shaul chose to pass it on. Hence Shaul's eagerness to remove Dahveed from the picture to assure that Jonathan, the son of his blood, would get to rule.

Units of measure—I decided to use modern units of measure for units of length since it would interrupt the flow of the story if the reader had to pause to equate ancient units of length with modern ones.

MAPS

TAMAR BAT DAHVEED

S *halom to you all! When the doorkeeper said someone was waiting for me, I had no idea there were more than one! Let me guess why you're here— for more of the story of Yahweh and my father? I thought so.*

Well, I have time tonight, and I can tell you the next part of it. But first let me call for some fruit and wine, maybe some pistachios and almonds to go with it. Yes, yes, we can have the harp out also so you can see the story written on it.

There, now, is everyone settled and comfortable? Then let's begin. Remind me, now, where did I leave off? Oh yes, with Dahveed becoming general of Israel's armies. My, was he surprised at that! And he began to have second thoughts about it the very next morning. It was all that Jonathan Hassar could do to convince Dahveed that the king would not take the general's mantle back.

Dahveed has a difficult time ahead, for if you recall, he is unused to honor, being an unclaimed son and raised as a servant in Jesse's house, with Eliab, Jesse's bekor, constantly reminding him of how little honor he can have. Then when Dahveed was about 15 years of age, Roeh Shamuel, Yahweh's seer, risked his own life by coming to Bethlehem and secretly anointing Dahveed as king for Yahweh.

Knowing that King Shaul would seek the life of the anointed one, the mashiah, Yahweh had provided his Arrows to guard him, a band of Habiru connected to Jesse's house. Barred from Yahweh's covenant with Israel because they had no land, most Habiru lived as outcasts and robbers, but Ethan's band served

Jesse's house, and they took the young shepherd under their wing, teaching him their ways and skills, and when the time came, pledging themselves to him.

The very day of Dahveed's anointing, Jesse claimed him for his son, and soon after that, Dahveed began playing his harp in the court of King Shaul at Gibeah, recommended by Balak ben Hod, who, you'll remember, never had much use for Dahveed and mentioned him to Sahrah Michal, Shaul's daughter, only because he thought it might advance his own position in the court.

But the music Dahveed could bring from his great-grandmother Ruth's harp was more powerful than anyone expected, and after Dahveed drove away the demon tormenting the king, the royal family took him to their hearts. But it was when Dahveed was about 18, and nearly died defending his sheep from a lion, that Shaul's oldest son, Jonathan, realized how much the zammar, or singer, had come to mean to him, although the crown prince was older by at least 22 years.[1]

Then came summer, and the war season, and the Philistines brought the giant of Gath with them to Israel. King Shaul, knowing that Yahweh had rejected him, was afraid to fight for Israel and, fearing that Jonathan would be killed, he forbade his son from entering combat also, opening the way for another champion. That's when Dahveed understood why he had received the gift of Yahweh—that ability to become more than himself when danger threatened—to be the vessel that Yahweh fought through to save His people. Adonai entered into him there in the Valley of Elah, and Goliath died, his sword and severed head carried to King Shaul as a token of the shepherd lad's victory.

Dahveed's triumph was very short-lived, for King Shaul asked him to pledge loyalty to him that day. But as mashiah, Dahveed could not give his loy-

alty to anyone, let alone the man rejected by Yah for treason against Him! So, although the king had favored him greatly and Dahveed loved him, he refused to pledge. That roused the king's anger to the extent that he nearly killed Dahveed, and only the intervention of Hassar Jonathan saved him from death.

Yahweh had a special spot in his heart for the king's oldest son, for Jonathan, too, placed Yahweh and Yahweh's honor before everything else, and he had seen more than the death of the champion of Gath that day. Jonathan recognized that Yahweh had given not only Goliath into Dahveed's hand but Israel and Israel's throne as well. Yet while his words saved Dahveed's life, he could not stop his father from enslaving the young man, a bitter reward indeed for saving the kingdom.

But Yahweh was not done yet, and before long, Jonathan thought of the zammar as a younger brother, and Dahveed gave his love to the king's son. You see, Adonai knew how deeply each needed the other. Dahveed has been placed in a life completely strange to him. Someone has to counteract Eliab's influence on Dahveed's life, protect the mashiah from the plots against him, and teach him how to act as a ruler.

Jonathan must shift his lifelong loyalty from his father and king to Yahweh's mashiah. Therefore, someone must provide the hassar with what he needs to safeguard Israel, protect the king's family, and counteract the sadness, shame, and pain that will come to Jonathan's heart.

Shortly after the battle in the Elah Valley, the Philistines planned an attack on the Israelite camp. Adon Manani[2], who soon became seren, or ruler, of Ekron, planned an assassination attempt against the hassar on the same night. Dahveed got in the way of both plans. Yah's gift filled him during the attack, *and using General Abner's sword, he stood like a wall in front of the king, giving the Israelite soldiers time to form up and defeat the enemy. When Shaul discovered that Dahveed had also saved Jonathan that night, he forgot his anger and gave Dahveed command of the army.*

And that's when the problems began. As proud and pleased as Dahveed was at the honor given him, he was also uncertain and afraid. He realized that he didn't know how to command an army, and he also recognized that Abner, the king's cousin whose place he had taken, was very angry over what had happened. Jonathan understood that too, and both of them expected trouble from that quarter.

What they didn't know was that the Evil One was raging over the way that Yahweh had bound their hearts together. Adonai sees far, however, and He planned to bind another of Shaul's children to the mashiah, strengthening both Dahveed's position and Jonathan's.

---

[1] See Cultural Notes: Ages of Dahveed and Jonathan.
[2] See Cultural Notes: Titles.

PROLOGUE

It was late in the afternoon when Sahrah Michal emerged from the west passage of the residence in the fortress on Gibeah's hill, dressed for the feast. King Shaul and the units with him had returned the day before yesterday from the Shephelah, much to Hassarah Ahinoam's relief. For in spite of Jonathan's reassurances, she had worried about the safety of the king now that Abner was no longer general of the army. Michal shook her head a little. Dahveed must have fought like a god for her father to promote him to the general's position, ousting his own cousin.

Yesterday her brothers, Sars Ishvi and Malchi, had also returned with the rest of the army and the demoted Abner. As she walked into the small private courtyard, she noticed, for the first time, the five bundles by the low wall.

"Have you had a chance to look in them, Sahrah?" the zammar's voice asked from behind her.

She turned around and caught her breath. Dahveed wore a fine dark-red robe, his thick chestnut-colored hair fastened with a gold band, his beard trimmed, and the blue general's mantle fastened over one shoulder with a gold brooch. For the first time she noticed how long his eyelashes were, and the red robe brought out the dark-brown flecks in his golden-brown eyes. Gold earrings glinted in the sunlight, and on his chest hung a twisted brass earring on a gold chain.

Finding it a bit difficult to speak, she shook her head.

"I wasn't certain what you'd like, but I tried to choose what you might want from the spoils for the throne room or the palace quarters."

"I'll go through them as soon as I can," she heard herself say, inexplicably finding it very important that he had thought of her out there while fighting Philistines. She couldn't stop staring, and he glanced down as he always did, then jerked his head up with a small smile.

"It's good to see you again, Sahrah. I'm glad all here is well." He moved as if to go.

"I didn't recognize you at first," she blurted out, to keep him from

35

leaving. "I mean, when I saw you from the wall, when the army re-turned, beside Abbi."

"A lot has happened since I was here last," he said wryly.

She flushed faintly, realizing that she had actually babbled at him! Taking a deep breath, she managed to control herself. "How long will you be staying this time?"

His face clouded. "As long as the king wishes."

"Then I hope he wishes it for a long time."

Dahveed smiled, and a thrill went down her spine. She felt ridicu-lously pleased that she had made the zammar happy again. Even when she tried to jerk herself back to reality, nothing seemed important ex-cept the pleasure flashing from those wonderful eyes.

"Did I hear your voice, Dahveed?" Jonathan asked, emerging from the west passage of the residence.

"You did, Nahsi," the zammar replied.

Michal quickly looked down, relieved that her brother had come before she did anything silly, yet resentful that he had interrupted. What was wrong with her?

Jonathan tilted his head to one side and raised his eyebrows as he circled the zammar, who endured his scrutiny uncomfortably. "War must agree with you," her brother said, his voice amused. "Where did you get all that?"

"Blame my retainer," Dahveed replied in disgust. "He shamelessly robbed the spoils."

"I'll have to send a reward to him, then. Ahiam obviously knows what to do with spoils!"

The hassar held out his arm, and the zammar gripped his wrist. Michal's eyes widened when her brother wrapped his other arm around Dahveed in an embrace. She barely remembered the last time he'd done that with anyone except herself and Immi, their mother.

"I heard you went through the entire attack on the camp without any armor. I also noticed you were wearing a cuirass when you came through the gates with the king," Jonathan commented.

Dahveed cast an annoyed glance toward the old storeroom that he and Ahiam lived in. "Ahiam insisted I wear that thing all day every day since the attack. He even made me eat in it!"

Jonathan laughed. "I owe Ahiam another reward for that!"

The zammar groaned.

"The king tells me you did an excellent job leading the army," the hassar went on, a sly look in his eyes.

"Everything was pretty much over except a raid or two," the younger man shrugged.

"That's all war is, you know. Raid and counterraid. It's been years since we've had a pitched battle like the one you won for us."

His expression gradually growing irritated, Dahveed stared at him. "You could have told me!" he fumed.

"I did. But after that first night, you were too upset and nervous about taking Abner's place to believe me. What calmed you down?"

Dahveed flushed. "Once I figured out that I was simply a messenger between the king and the commanders, I could relax."

An odd expression crossed Jonathan's face.

"Is Abner coming to the feast tonight?" Dahveed asked, his voice anxious.

"Don't worry, Dahveed. Abner will honor the king's choice of general."

"Only as long as he's forced to. Although it may be easier for him once I return his sword."

"And what about my mule?" Jonathan added, smiling.

The zammar flushed. "Ahiam brought word that Ethan found it."

"Good. Now all I have to do is figure out how to pay that Habiru for his efforts," the hassar laughed as they walked away.

Michal watched them leave. The zammar turned back briefly, flashing a smile. The sunlight glinted on the gold band, and she gripped her sides. She'd never felt like this before. He was . . . he was . . . she searched for the right word. He was a man. That was the difference. He'd left here almost six months ago as a youth, and he had returned as a very handsome, attractive man, and she wanted him. Her cheeks burned, and she had to sit down.

He was more than 10 years younger than she was—a southern hill man and a *shepherd* of all things—and she was Michal bat Shaul, Sahrah Israel, but one look at him dressed as an adon, and she was lost. Clenching her hands, she tried to contain the feeling flooding over her. She wanted Dahveed more than she had ever desired anything in her life, and Merab was promised to him. Merab, Shaul's bekorah, his firstborn, not Michal, the second daughter.

She closed her eyes. Merab wouldn't know what to do with him. Dahveed needed someone who would challenge him and engage him, and make his eyes go dark and smoky as her father's had when he had looked at Ahinoam yesterday in the court and taken her to his room.

But Merab would be daughter to the king and the general's wife. Her sister didn't even want that much status, but Michal did. Slowly she relaxed and stared at the bundles across the courtyard against the low wall. "You're mine, zammar," she whispered. "I want you, and you'll be mine, one way or the other."

JONATHAN AND GIBEAH

CHAPTER 1

Sitting on my usual three-legged stool at the corner of the ells of the throne room in Gibeah's fortress, I watched the people around me. Adon Abner's sword lay under my stool, and I'd already planned what to say when I returned it. I hoped my speech would soothe his honor[1] enough to deflect his anger for the way that I had snatched it from his waist and gone charging off to meet the Philistines on Hassar Jonathan's mule. The fact that the attack had happened because of Abner's stubborn penchant for ignoring warnings brought by Habiru didn't make matters any easier.

I cocked my head, listening to the sounds around me. The guests with less honor, sitting at tables toward the outside of the room, wore robes in shades of brown and gray. The colors got brighter on the guests sitting closer to the long table, culminating in the riot of color mixed with gold and silver thread flashing off the embroidery on the *meils*, or royal tunics, that Shaul's family wore. I smiled at how carefully Sar Malchi had dressed. Shaul's third son was as tall as his abbi, but his shoulders were broader, although the king still had a longer reach.

Jonathan laughed at something Bekorah Merab said, but I could tell by the set of his shoulders that he wasn't completely relaxed. The occasional white hair showed in the black mane flowing down his back. He'd had shadows in the back of his eyes today, and it hadn't taken me long to realize that he and Abner were not speaking to each other. I sighed. Chances were that whatever had come between them involved me.

Farther down the long table, Sar Ishvi[2] listened closely while Sar Eshbaal outlined the reorganized court procedures instituted over the summer. Rumor had it the hassar was less than pleased at the changes his brother had made, but he had accepted them when he realized how much smoother and quicker court business flowed, and Sar Eshbaal was now Jonathan's foremost assistant.

To my right, in the small west ell, two scribes discussed the number of judgment cases involving Gibeonites lately. Beyond them, Balak ben Hod directed the servers, stationing himself by the door on the west wall at the end of the room, where he could coordinate everyone. In spite of the dislike between us, I recognized the excellent job he was doing tonight. From the approving looks Sahrah Michal had given him, she did, too.

Just then, King Shaul rose, and Jonathan escorted him to the throne on the dais. The royal headband gleamed against the king's dark hair, the light reflecting off the engraved openwork of the band, matched by the armband that he wore on his right arm. The room quieted. Lined up at the back of the dais were the gifts that I'd chosen for each man. Abner had never bothered honoring anyone in this manner, deeming that a reward given by a unit commander was sufficient, but I knew well what public recognition could mean to a person. And as Jonathan called each name, describing what the man had done, the expressions on the men's faces assured me that they would never forget the moment they received their reward from the hands of the king himself.

When the presentations were more than half finished, I heard the faint sound of bowls crashing to the floor in the anteroom below. Moments later, the door next to me opened slightly. "General, you're needed in the anteroom," a voice said softly.

I glanced in its direction. "I'll come down when I can," I replied just as quietly. If I didn't get that sword back to Abner in this public venue, he'd never forgive me for taking it.

Cheers erupted as Jonathan described what Commander Zorath of the third unit had done during the attack.

"It can't wait," the man insisted. "General, you must come now!"

Something in his voice caught my attention, and I noticed how white his face was against the dark cyprus wood of the door. He pushed the door open another couple inches. I glanced at the dais again. The next two presentations were longer ones.

"Please, General, hurry."

I followed him down the stairs. Two men sprawled on the floor, hands bound behind them, and one of the two guards standing over them had blood running down his arm, while another had an eye that would probably be swollen shut before very long. Those on the floor lay facedown, so I couldn't see what they looked like.

"What happened?" I asked.

The guard reached down with the tip of his sword and flipped up the robe of the nearest man. The man's thigh had a battle dagger strapped to it.

Assassins! A chill went over me. More cheering drifted down from the room above, letting me know there was only one more presentation before mine. I wouldn't be able to live with Abner if I missed this chance to honor him, but an attempt on the life of the king couldn't be ignored. Inwardly I groaned. I had neither time to, nor any idea how to, handle this!

"The hassar will want to know," the man who'd brought me down said quietly. He was one of the new scribes appointed by Sar Eshbaal during the summer.

Another round of cheering began in the throne room. I needed to be up there *now*.

"Take them to Commander Sheva's chamber on the wall," I said hurriedly, one ear cocked to hear what was happening above. "Wait there. I'll bring the hassar after the feast."

The guards nodded and reached down, yanking the two assassins to their feet and shoving them toward the door. "Clean up the mess here as best you can, and follow them," I added to the scribe. "Make sure no one else comes into Sheva's chamber."

The cheering above began to die down, and I took the stairs two at a time, slipping back into the throne room just as Commander Ram, the last man to be rewarded, sat down again at his place. Jonathan's quick eyes saw the door closing behind me even as I bent to retrieve the sword under my stool.

Taking a deep breath, I adjusted my clothes as King Shaul said, "Adon Abner, if you would come forward?"

His face carefully blank, the king's cousin left his place at the table and walked to the dais.

"I believe the dahveed has something for you," Shaul said, a small smile on his face.

Holding Abner's sword, I approached the dais, and Abner faced me, a wary look in his eyes.

I cleared my throat. "Most of the men here today have been honored for their part in the defense of the king when the Philistines attacked our camp. But I doubt any of them know the help you gave to me, adon." The room got very quiet as I knelt, and everyone strained to see. "I could have done nothing against the Philistines during that attack without the use of a good sword, and I wish to thank you, Adon Abner, for lending me yours. It is the best blade that I have ever had the honor of using." Head bowed, I presented it to him across my arm, hilt first.

After a moment of startled silence, the room erupted in cheers as Abner accepted the sword and returned it to its sheath. The cheering continued until the king's cousin, looking flushed and gratified, nodded to everyone, and I got off my knees. Abner managed to nod at me, and I hoped this would end the matter.

King Shaul smiled, touching my shoulder before turning to his cousin. Jonathan took my arm and smiled also. "Is anything wrong?" he whispered.

"Come to Sheva's chamber as soon as you can," I replied, smiling and bowing to him as the servants brought in bowls of parched grain and fruit to end the feast.

"What happened?" Jonathan demanded as he topped the stairs by Sheva's chamber later that evening.

"We had visitors," I answered, opening the door.

The two guards sat on the rough wooden benches, and I noted that someone had tended the cut, and that the other man's eye had swollen completely shut. The prisoners lay on the stone floor, one, who was obviously the younger of the two, shaking like a poplar leaf.

Jonathan looked them over, then shoved up the younger one's robe to expose the empty knife sheath strapped there. His gaze chilled. "Bring Eshbaal," he said to me curtly.

"Sar Eshbaal?" I asked, to be certain that I'd heard correctly.

The hassar nodded.

I left, my stomach tight with apprehension. If Jonathan was excluding Abner from any knowledge of an assassination attempt, whatever had happened between them must be very serious.

When I returned with the king's youngest son, the hassar said, "Take down what is said here, Eshbaal." As the young sar moved to obey, he saw the sheath on the man's thigh. His eyes widened, and he sat down a bit shakily, then waited for the hassar to continue.

Jonathan turned to the scribe. "What happened?"

"I was working late in one of the scribal chambers behind the anteroom, and I had come into it looking for a blank papyrus when these two appeared, carrying bowls of fruit for the feast. I knew food was supposed to go to the west door on the wall, and I nearly said something when I realized they were strangers. I didn't know if anything was wrong or not, but they didn't look right, somehow, so when they walked by, I knocked the bowls out of their hands. The guards outside the door heard the crash and rushed in. One of the men tried to grab me, and then the guards attacked, and I don't remember much except fighting for a while." He stopped, his composure shaken. "Once they were bound, I went to the throne room and brought General Dahveed. He sent us here."

"Get him up," Jonathan ordered, indicating the older one.

The guard hauled the man to his knees.

Jonathan studied him. "You're a Gibeonite," he stated, his voice tired. "Which town?"[3]

The assassin refused to answer, simply staring at the hassar with bitter eyes.

"I know the king has treated your people with contempt," Jonathan said, "but murdering him will not do them any good."

"The king?" the man spat. "It's you I want. After that message you sent in reply to our complaint, did you really expect us not to protest?"

Jonathan stared at him. "I haven't sent any message."

The man laughed harshly. "It had your seal on it, and you personally delivered it to the elders just as we left the fortress."

"That was months ago! You Gibeonites from Beeroth complained that the overseer for the tabernacle was using you as laborers on his own estate without pay."

"Yes, and when the elders got back with that message and delivered it to the overseer, he waved it in our faces and said it gave him permission to use us as he would. And he has! He—"

"He said what?" the hassar asked very quietly, his voice like oil.

The man stopped.

"I told you, Abbi! I told you," the younger one sobbed. "The hassar wouldn't do such a thing."

"That letter I sent told him to do absolutely nothing further until the king reviewed the case as he said he would."

"But the king will never review the case," the man said bitterly.

"Precisely. Therefore, that overseer is barred from using you any longer. So how are you called, and just what has this man been doing?"

The assassin looked away.

"I told you, Abbi!" the younger man said again. "The hassar will avenge us!"

The Gibeonite stared into Jonathan's hard eyes. "I'm called Rimmon," he said at last.

The people in Beeroth had suffered much since the letter had come, he explained, the overseer indeed doing whatever he wished. Rimmon's wife had died as a result of the man's abuse, and the bitterness had festered in Rimmon until he had determined to kill the hassar.

When he finished the recital, Jonathan's face was white with rage. He turned his back. "You know I cannot let you live," he said flatly.

"Had I wanted to live, I wouldn't be here, Hassar. But Recheb is here only because I forced him to come. If there is any hesed, grant it to him."

"Jabesh in Gilead is a convenient town."

"I'm sure my son will do well there. Recheb, you will go there, and you will not leave."

"Yes, Abbi," his son replied, still shaking.

Jonathan took a deep breath. "For you, Rimmon, I can do this much. I will grant you the right to take your own life after we visit the overseer in Beeroth."

Rimmon looked at the hassar's back. "When will we go?"

"In the morning."

"I shall see your vengeance, and the overseer will know that I watch?"

"If you wish."

"Then I will die happy, and my family will not hold bloodguilt against you, Hassar."

As Jonathan turned around, his gaze fell on the two guards. "How is it that two strangers walked into the king's court, and you did not stop them?" he demanded.

"Adoni, we have only started our duties here three days ago, and we don't know who belongs and who doesn't," one said, dropping to his knees. "General, uh, Adon Abner was at the practice ground today. He asked which unit had been assigned to help the king's guard with the feast tonight, and when he discovered none had, he made the assignment right there," the guard continued, giving me a guilty look. "He ordered us to stand outside the anteroom door, and said to be certain that anyone who went in took no weapons. No one came until these two, and they had no weapons in sight. No one told us to search anyone."

My heart sank. I'd had no idea that army units helped with guard duty during feasts. Abner would have been furious with my lapse, which underlined another reason I shouldn't be general.

"So Abner explained the rules just to you?" the hassar asked.

"Yes, adoni."

"Now that's the most interesting piece of information I've heard yet." Jonathan's eyes glittered, and he stared at the wall for several seconds.

I cocked my head, having never heard the hassar purr before. I wanted to run at the sound, and I knew the shaking guard wanted to do the same.

"You two will come with us in the morning," he said a moment later. "After we visit the overseer in Beeroth, you will escort Recheb ben Rimmon to Jabesh in Gilead, and remain there for a year and a day. You will return only if *I* send for you. After that time you may go or stay as you want."

"Yes, adoni. Thank you, adoni." Both guards bowed to the ground.

He turned to the scribe. "Since Beeroth will need a new overseer after tomorrow, you will take over those duties. You showed exemplary presence of mind and discretion tonight, two things I imagine that you will need to straighten out the mess we've just uncovered."

"I will do as you wish, Hassar."

"Did you get everything down, Eshbaal?" Jonathan asked.

"Yes, Hassar."

"I'll keep the records." He held out his hand, and Eshbaal rolled the papyri and handed them to him. "This is not to be mentioned by anyone unless I personally give permission."

"Yes, Hassar," we all said.

---

¹ See Cultural Notes: Honor.
² See Cultural Notes: Ishvi.
³ See Cultural Notes: Gibeonites.

CHAPTER 2

There, that should do it," Judith said, standing back after adjusting Balak's girdle to her satisfaction. "Let's go. We don't want to be late. Hassarah Ahinoam has been so upset since Jonathan got back yesterday. His robe was soaked with so much blood that she burned it outside of town. Basemath, Baalah Rizpah's maid, says the guards that went with him won't speak of what happened. They just turn white and walk away. Where could he have gone, do you think? And the morning after a feast like that?"

Out of habit Balak ignored Judith's voice as they left their small house. The only redeeming factor in his marriage to her was that she was kinswoman to the king. Otherwise, she was totally unsuitable as the wife of the adon that he intended to become. He'd never taken her to meet his family in Bethlehem, or his relatives in Jebus. Her penchant for talk would spread his Moabite ancestry all over Gibeah, and Shaul's dislike for foreigners was becoming more pronounced every year. His position as the king's personal attendant was his best chance to erase the disgrace that he had brought on his family at Bethlehem's gate—no, he corrected his thinking, the disgrace forced on his family by Hassarah Ruth at Bethlehem's gate—and if King Shaul knew he was not of Israel, he would likely be dismissed. If he succeeded here, Abbi would be proud of him again.

He arrived at the throne room just before court opened for the day.

"I didn't see any petitioners," King Shaul commented to Jonathan.

"No, adoni. Petitioners will arrive after the noon rest. Sar Eshbaal reserved this morning for court business."

"Good. I want to reward the zammar for killing the Philistine champion."

Balak kept his face expressionless as he filled the wine pitcher from the corner jar, but in his opinion, Dahveed had received more than enough rewards already.

"How would you like to reward him, adoni?" his oldest son asked, motioning Eshbaal to bring a papyrus.

The king smiled with anticipation. "We can make a proclamation announcing the marriage to Merab, and have a feast to celebrate it, and call him in to give him the house and servants and land and tax exemption."

Irritation at King Shaul's litany of rewards rose in Balak, and he nearly spilled the wine. Setting the jar against the wall again, he glanced toward the king and caught the intent, nearly desperate look on Michal's face. What could be bothering her? Hadn't Judith said something about the sahrah just yesterday? As he carried the pitcher back to its place, he frantically tried to remember. When he did, he nearly lost his grip on the pitcher, but another glance at Sahrah Michal convinced him that Judith's gossip had been right. The sahrah wanted to marry Dahveed. "Sahrah, if I may speak?" he said quietly.

"What is it?" she replied, her mind clearly elsewhere.

"Didn't the king find the zammar rather difficult to reward the last time he called him in? He seems to have a way of slipping out from under what the king would like to do."

Michal gave him a strange look. "Yes, he did."

"Wouldn't it work better if he did the same thing as before? If Dahveed protests a reward, he gets a bigger one?"

Her eyes widened slightly, and she stared at him a moment.

"What's that you said, Balak?" Shaul asked, turning from the throne.

The attendant hastily bowed, repeating his comment.

Shaul chuckled. "That did work well! The zammar stopped arguing then. Let's do it," he decided. "What should we start with? Merab?"

"Merab will make a most effective threat, adoni," Michal cut in offhandedly. "Once the zammar has accepted other honors, he won't be so opposed to accepting one as great as the bekorah."

"That sounds good, doesn't it, Jonathan?"

The hassar switched his steady gaze from Balak to his sister. "It will undoubtedly work better than trying to give him everything at once. Which part of the reward do you think he will find the least objectionable, Sahrah?"

Satisfied, Balak eased back to his duties. Apparently Sahrah Michal did want Dahveed enough to fight with her oldest brother about it.

"Perhaps the king could begin with rewards of gold and clothing," she said meekly enough. "Dahveed has accepted those before, although not very much. Later, if he received the tax exemption for his family, he could hardly refuse that. And having brought that much honor to his house, he will need to uphold his new status, and—"

"Well thought out, daughter," Shaul interrupted, delighted. "I'll begin today. Send for the zammar."

While Eshbaal sent a messenger to bring Dahveed to the king, Michal flushed under the hassar's unreadable stare. She murmured something about finding more sweet Tekoa figs and fled from the room. Balak kept himself busy at the far end of the west ell, his mind racing over what more might develop from the situation.

That evening Jonathan surprised Michal by coming to her room. He silently handed her her cloak and led the way out to their favorite place on the southeast battlements. What was she going to say about Dahveed, she wondered as she climbed the stairs. That she'd suddenly found herself wanting the man promised to her sister?

Once in their corner, Jonathan lounged against the wall, staring south toward Jebus.

Michal shifted restlessly, expecting questions, but he remained silent.

"What did Dahveed take for his reward?" he finally asked.

"He didn't take anything. Ahiam did. Dahveed left in the middle of it all, too horrified to stay!"

Jonathan chuckled. "I wonder what will have to happen for him to accept his new status."

"Something a bit more shattering than an earthquake."

Sighing, Jonathan looked up at the stars not yet covered by the drifting clouds. "It will have to be addressed soon—it's becoming a problem. And what were you and Balak up to today in court?"

She scuffed her sandal on the stones. "Nothing, really. His suggestion just showed a way to make it easier for Abbi to give Dahveed what he wants him to have."

"And?"

"Does there have to be more?"

"There is more."

She chewed her lip again, shifting uneasily. "Do you think he really wants Merab?" she asked at last.

"The king promised Merab. What else is there to discuss? Would you want the king to break his word, Sahrah?"

Michal knew that she didn't dare say yes, so she said nothing at all. "Sahrah?"

At her continued silence he took her arm and pulled her closer, putting his hand under her chin and forcing her to look at him. Her eyes widened. She'd never realized how strong her brother was, and for the first time she felt a hard edge to him. "Jonathan, you're hurting me," she gasped. For a moment she didn't think he would respond, but then his grip loosened. What had she touched in him?

"What did you want with Balak when you stopped him in the street late this afternoon?"

"Nothing," she said again, looking away. She hadn't thought that anyone had seen her, but she was desperate enough about Dahveed to use even Balak, who still made her vaguely uncomfortable whenever he was around. Then she glanced back at her brother.

Jonathan stared at her, his eyes suddenly remote and distant in the dim light from the partially obscured moon. She shivered. He'd never looked at her like that. Somehow he wasn't her brother anymore, but someone very frightening.

"You're lying, Michal. Don't make me act the hassar with you."

Tucking her hands into the cloak to hide their shaking, and with her stomach in a knot, she looked down. She'd never encountered anything like this in Jonathan before.

After a moment he turned and stared out over the wall.

Not wanting to see any more of what he might be like as hassar, she began slowly. "It's rather jumbled. I can't explain it to myself, let alone you."

"But you spoke to Balak about Dahveed?"

"Only to hint that anything he could say that would keep Dahveed's rewards within reason would be useful."

"Do you wish Dahveed harm, Michal?"

She stared at him in astonishment. "Of course not! Whatever gave you that idea?"

"The fact that you involved Balak."

"Balak has the ear of the king at odd moments, and that may make it easier to keep Abbi from piling more on Dahveed than he should. Given what some of those allied northern adons will think of a southerner replacing Abner, that would be a good thing for everyone, Jonathan."

Her brother slowly relaxed, and the hardness disappeared. Taking her hand, he drew her gently to his side, hugging her tightly. "I didn't want to frighten you, Michal," he apologized. "But I've found too many who shouldn't wish Dahveed harm, but do."

"It seems you've become very careful of him," she said cautiously.

"And I will do whatever it takes to safeguard him, Michal."

Much later, lying in her bed, she stared at the narrow poles that lay across the beams above her and formed the ceiling. There was something very different about the way that Jonathan now regarded the zammar. What puzzled her was his willingness to do whatever it took to protect the young shepherd.

Putting her hands behind her head, she frowned into the darkness, listening to Merab's soft breathing. She had never known Jonathan to deviate from the king's wishes in the slightest since the battle at Michmash. Of course, she suspected that he'd warned Roeh Shamuel of Shaul's spies during the night he had disappeared from the fortress four years ago, but he did that only because his loyalty to Yahweh came first. Was it possible that was the case again?

Sitting up, she wrapped her arms around her knees. What had Jonathan said about Dahveed when he first told them the king had asked for the southerner's loyalty? "He had to refuse." She squeezed her knees tighter. What could Jonathan mean: "He *had to*?" Only Yahweh's honor was greater than Shaul's, and as king, her abbi had every right to demand, and receive, loyalty from those with lesser status, to say nothing of the way he had favored Dahveed.

Michal chewed her lip. Yet Jonathan apparently took it for granted that Dahveed *must* refuse, and had then publicly disagreed with his father. Only his loyalty to Yahweh would make the hassar place anything higher than the king's honor. But wasn't that saying Dahveed had more honor than Abbi? How could that possibly be? Who could have more status than King Shaul?

The thought that exploded in her mind made her shiver, and she pulled the bedclothes closer around her. Whoever was anointed in Shaul's place would hold higher honor under Yahweh than anyone in the kingdom. But Dahveed, mashiah? A shepherd to be king? And a rustic *southerner* at that? What could Yahweh be thinking?

On the other hand, if Dahveed *was* the mashiah, everything that Jonathan had done fell neatly into place. Michal gripped the bedclothes so hard that she nearly tore them. Only for the mashiah would Jonathan defy the king and do "whatever it took."

The king's zammar would assume the throne, and the hassar would help him. Would she?

TAMAR BAT DAHVEED

Much is happening now. Yahweh never asks for a change without having a reason, and Jonathan's shift in loyalties was necessary because his father's part in Yahweh's plan is nearly over. Shaul's task was to free the Israelites from the domination of the Philistines and bring about the birth of a kingdom. While he has not always followed Yahweh's will in the method, the result has come about. The need for Jonathan's complete loyalty to his abbi is over, for Israel is about to be recognized as a kingdom. Shaul's concerns can take second place as the hassar guides the fledgling realm during its first shaky years while Yahweh fully prepares the anointed king for the responsibilities of rulership.

However, the Evil One has planned well in his turn, and Dahveed has already lost his way. Yahweh will do all He can to show Dahveed the path that he should follow, but the Evil One has used the past with devastating effect.

Since Yahweh ever leaves His servants free to choose, it's up to Dahveed, Mashiah Israel, and Jonathan, Hassar Israel, to decide how committed they will be to Yahweh's will and Yahweh's timing.

CHAPTER 3

W hat's worrying you, Jonathan?" Michal asked, gathering her cloak around her in the midwinter chill as she joined her brother on the battlements.[1]

"Dahveed," the hassar said with a sigh. "And what are you doing out in this wind? Immi will be upset if you get sick."

"Not half as upset as she will be if you do. What's the matter with the zammar?" She turned her face up to the weak afternoon sunshine.

"Haven't you noticed anything?"

"I haven't had the chance. Immi's had me overseeing inventories at our estates in Zelah. Eshbaal's changes here made things so much easier that she's extending them to our personal estates." She thought for a moment. "Dahveed does seem rather subdued though."

"*Rather* subdued? He hasn't laughed in weeks! Nor will he permit me a private moment to ask why. I've been using him as a courier again to get him out to the god-places, and I know he's gone to Roeh Shamuel in Ramah at least twice. Usually he seems better after that, but it doesn't last for long. He was so pale that Merab asked him the other day if he was sick." Her brother glanced at her. "You know that Abner has taken over all the duties of general again?"

"No. How did that happen?"

"So gradually I didn't notice until it was too late," Jonathan said sourly. "As near as I can tell, our esteemed cousin simply encroached on Dahveed's authority a little at a time. He was always quick to defer to Dahveed at first, or consult with him if forced by circumstances. Dahveed never protested, and now Abner simply ignores him."

The sahrah remained silent for some time, while the constant wind whipped her cloak around her. "Abbi must know this, and he obviously doesn't mind," she said slowly. "The servants think the king made Dahveed general to raise his status so that he can marry a king's daughter. No one expects him to be more than a figurehead. Why won't that arrangement work?"

"Because of the army. Remember, half the commanders and professionals were with us in the south. They fought with Dahveed, felt what emanates from him during a battle, and experienced how he leads.

Dahveed shared out honor in a way that Abner has never dreamed of doing. You saw the reaction here in town to singling out commended men and inviting them to feast with the king. And that was just one thing of several. But the other half of the army can't imagine a zammar knowing anything about war.

"Our professional force is split down the middle, with Ram and Zorath leading the support for Dahveed against Libni and his friends. Since Dahveed says nothing and does nothing, Abner's supporters simply scoff at him. We've had several serious injuries during sparring because of this. I don't know what to do."

"Surely Abner can see the danger! Can't you speak to him?"

"He thinks I could have saved him the disgrace of giving up the general's mantle, and that I deliberately didn't," Jonathan replied heavily. "If I publicly support Dahveed, we could have a clan war on our hands, and that would be disaster for the kingdom."

"No wonder he isn't speaking to you!"[2] Michal groaned. "Could you have changed Abbi's mind?"

"No. Besides, I thought the appointment would be only temporary. But since then I've found out that Abbi thinks having Dahveed as general will force Yahweh to grant Israel victory, and that way he cannot lose the kingdom."

"And so circumvent the roeh's prophecy," Michal added quietly.

Grimly the hassar nodded. "Meanwhile, Dahveed's apathy makes mockery of his appointment, which disgraces the king. If I just had a good enough excuse to deal with Abner, I might be able to hold things together. But as long as Abbi thinks he will keep the kingdom with Dahveed as general, he will not transfer that mantle back. And since we haven't had that shattering earthquake required to shake Dahveed into action, nothing will change."

"What *are* you going to do?" she asked, suddenly frightened.

"I'm trying to figure out how to defend Israel next summer with only half the professional force available to fight at any one point."

"And if you can't?"

"Know any good ways that I can cause a shattering earthquake?"

The damp air bit through my cloak, and I was thankful for the warmth of the cuirass Ahiam insisted that I wear. I still felt as if it restricted my movements, but I was getting used to it. As always, I had my leather sling wrapped around my wrist.

Glumly I stared at the muddy road. The arrival yesterday of the blade that I had found in the spoils was the one cheering event of the week. The new hilt, without decoration and wrapped in leather, fit my hand perfectly. The balance was impeccable now, and the blade's edge honed razor-sharp. The new bronze sheath was wrapped in leather also, and balanced at the perfect angle so that I could flip the sword and shove the point in without looking.

I wore the arm guards and war dagger the hassar had chosen for me, so I could participate in the mock battle planned for this afternoon. The rain had stopped today, and the sun shone pale through a haze of clouds, illuminating the army training ground south of Gibeah. I went to my usual vantage spot, arriving when the exercises were well under way.

Across the training ground, Sar Malchi, dressed in cuirass, greaves, and a leather kilt, examined spears. The hassar was here again, working with the archers.

Abner was sparring with a new man, who seemed painfully self-conscious, flushing whenever anyone of any rank looked at him. The soldier faced Abner nervously, sword gripped much too tightly in his right hand. He performed adequately until Abner increased the pace; then his first reaction was always to raise his shield, the sword staying still. After a few minutes the former general stopped in disgust. "You're reassigned to the second unit," he said curtly, walking away.

That unit had always been the worst of the professionals, but after the Philistines had staked down their tent flaps during the attack last summer, the unit was simply laughed at. For a moment the man looked as if he would protest, but when he saw Libni watching him, he swallowed his humiliation and went to where the second unit watched the exercises, doing nothing.

"I've b-been assigned to you, Commander," he stammered to Jarib, flushing.

"All right," the officer answered with a sigh. "Join the others, I guess."

The soldier obeyed, going off to the side where he would be half hidden.

As I watched him take off the shield and adjust his dagger, a possible reason for the man's trouble came to my mind. Taking a wooden sword from the pile by Jarib, I walked over. "How are you called?" I asked.

He jumped to his feet. "Your pardon, sa—uh, comman—uh, g-geber," he sputtered, looking at me frantically to discover my rank.

I grinned. "I'm a servant of Shaul, like you, geber."

Relief flashed in his eyes. "I'm called Eleazar ben Dodo, from Benjamin."

"If you're left-handed like most of your kin, would you spar with me? I need some practice against a left-handed man." Then I nodded my head toward a cleared space in back of everyone else.

He grinned back and quickly fastened his shield on his right arm, his shoulders relaxing. I struck with no warning. That left hand flashed up, and his blade met mine solidly. By the time we finished the standard drill, his eyes were sharp with concentration, and he was moving easily around me, instinctively circling, advancing, and retreating as he went through the motions.

"Why didn't you tell Abner you were left-handed?" I asked when we paused.

His eyes got big. "He said we needed more swordsmen and put me with the right-handed men. It isn't my place to question the assignment, geber!" he gasped.

We began again, and when he had his concentration, I picked up the pace. His blade still met mine firmly. He was very good with that sword, but what interested me was his shield, staying like a wall in front of him, and I'd never get around it unless I was under Yahweh's hand.

"Where did he come from?" Dara, Jonathan's shield bearer, asked behind me during a pause in our work.

"I've noticed him only for the past couple weeks. Abner just put him into the second unit," I replied. "Sar Ishvi needs a shield-bearer if I recall. He can have Eleazar here if he wants him."

Dara gave me an odd look. "Only the general can reassign the men," he said in a low voice.

"I am the general," I said absently. "Do you want to try him out?"

"Yes," Dara said with another odd glance at me.

"Keep him concentrating. He's shy of rank," I warned as I stepped back.

"He'll have to get over that," the shield bearer commented as he approached, and Eleazar advanced to meet him.

I sent a soldier for Sar Ishvi while I watched. More men drifted over as Dara tested Eleazar's use of the shield from different angles.

Sar Ishvi arrived beside me. "He looks Benjamite. How's he called?" he asked, studying the way the man moved around Dara.

"Eleazar ben Dodo, and he stumbles over himself when a commander looks at him, let alone a sar."

"I'll keep that in mind." Ishvi took the spear that Sar Malchi held out to him and reversed it to spar with the pointed metal counterbalance on the end of the shaft. Nodding to Dara, he stepped in at the right of Eleazar and slightly behind. "I'm standing with you," he said quietly. "But I don't have a shield, so you'll have to use yours for both of us."

Eleazar's head jerked around, his eyes widening. "Geber—uh, comm—"

"Watch out!" Sar Ishvi exclaimed as Dara lunged forward and whacked the flat of his blade on Eleazar's leg hard enough to make the man cry out and instinctively turn to the attack, driving Dara back.

"I'm still here, Eleazar," the sar reminded him.

"Yes, geber." The man backed up, without taking his eyes from Dara this time.

"Let him come to us," Sar Ishvi advised. "I'll hold him off with my spear. You just concentrate on the shield."

Eleazar obeyed, and even though he held only a small round personal shield, Dara couldn't break through.

Then the hassar stepped out with a spear, handing Dara a personal shield.

As soon as Jonathan appeared, Eleazar backed up, his steps uncertain. "Watch carefully now," Ishvi warned him quickly. "That soldier has a spear, and it can reach us both. Be sure to keep blocking him with that shield."

Eleazar relaxed at the word "soldier." "Yes, geber." His intent gaze went from Dara to the hassar, who circled first one way then the other as Ishvi coached Eleazar. Jonathan tried several strikes, but the shield always met them. As they settled down to a mock battle, everyone at the training ground gathered to watch.

Abner stood with his arms folded, staring sourly at the man that he'd just sent to the second unit. His icy stare landed on me more than once, and I knew he blamed me for making him look foolish. Although it left me feeling uncomfortable, I decided that I wouldn't back down. Sar Ishvi needed a shield bearer.

In spite of his mistakes Eleazar managed to hold his own, and that shield stayed right where it was supposed to. Then, for a short time, he and Ishvi worked like one man. The sar quickly pressed the attack, forcing Jonathan to the left. "Strike, Eleazar," he called.

Jonathan jabbed the spear, and Eleazar's sword flashed up with the same lightning-like sweep that Dara had, snaking around and sliding up the spear handle, the wooden point clanging into the hassar's cuirass below his arm.

A shout filled the air, and Eleazar jerked back, his concentration finally broken, staring at the man he'd just hit. Abner turned on his heel and walked away, his face hard with anger.

"Dara, you're supposed to stop those," Jonathan grumbled, rubbing his side.

"That was on *your* side, Hassar," his shield bearer reminded him.

Shaking, Eleazar dropped to the ground.

I went to him, knowing what he felt like. "You did very well," I said, putting my hand on his back to get his attention. "It's rare for someone to score a strike on the hassar when he and Dara take the field. Sar Ishvi was practically jumping up and down."

Finally Eleazar sat up. "I was shielding for a sar?"

"And doing a magnificent job. Sar Ishvi's shield bearer was badly hurt from a fall this past summer and will not be able to carry the shield for him again. After what you've just done, he'll be asking you to take his place."

"I couldn't. Not a sar!"

"Why not?" I said, grinning. "Just think of him as a little brother you've got to keep out of trouble."

The ludicrousness of that suggestion jerked the man from his daze.

"Here he comes now," I added. "Stand for him. None of the sars like groveling, Ishvi least of all. Look him in the face. You are related to him, after all."

Eleazar was on his feet when the sar stopped.

"You are an excellent left-handed swordsman, Eleazar," Ishvi said. "Would you be willing to train as my shield bearer? In year or two we'd be able to pry Dara and Jonathan apart."

The soldier gave me a desperate look.

"He's your kin," I said.

"I would be honored to, Sar," the man finally managed to say.

Balak watched the professional soldiers disperse for the noon meal. Returning from a visit to Jebus, he had paused to view the spear bout. Various comments from the soldiers explained Abner's obvious disgust, and Balak watched the former general closely, gauging his mood.

He'd kept everything he had said to Adon Abner the past couple months casual and short. Abner had shown his dislike of the general too plainly during the past war season, and now that Kemosh had turned the king's cousin into an ally against Dahveed, it behooved Balak to get back on the man's good side. Thus he had begun by informing the former general that Dahveed would not protest encroachment on his honor, and Balak had to admire the smooth way in which Abner had slid into Dahveed's place as a result.

"How long has Dahveed known this Eleazar was in the army?" Balak asked the man next to him.

As he'd hoped, mention of Dahveed's name made Abner turn and listen.

"He's new, I think," the soldier replied. "I've noticed him only for the past couple weeks."

"I wonder when Dahveed realized that man would make a good shield bearer for the sar? Today seems a rather odd time to show him to Sar Ishvi," Balak mused. He walked away, but not before seeing the glint of suspicion in Abner's eye. Given the officer's anger over his demotion, he'd have no trouble convincing himself that Dahveed had plotted for weeks to disgrace him this way!

After the noon rest the whole town gathered in the meadow on the other side of the Jebus highway from Gibeah's hill. The midwinter mock battle was always well attended, everyone cheering for their favorite soldier or unit, while the king checked on how the training of the newer recruits had progressed.

Abner made unit assignments, and when he came to the second unit, he glanced at me. "Would you stand with them and try to give them a little backbone?" he asked sarcastically.

"If that's your wish."

"It is."

As the second unit lined up on the extreme right of the battle line, I heard some quiet comments from the seventh unit, opposite us, wondering what the king's zammar was doing in a mock battle. The eleventh unit, which was one of the best and had also been north the previous summer, was on our left, and already planning how to engage both the unit in front of them and the one in front of us. They too looked at me askance, and I sighed inwardly, reminding myself that I had honor from Yahweh and didn't need it from anyone else. Sar Malchi judged our end of the line, with the hassar in the middle, and Sar Ishvi worked the other end.

The hassar gave the word, and the exercise began. Using a dulled wooden blade like everyone else, I sparred easily with the man facing me. It didn't take long for Sar Malchi to begin pulling out men who would have died if it had been a real battle. Mostly they came from the second unit, even though the seventh wasn't really trying. No one paid any more attention to me than to the others, which gave me an idea.

"Eleazar, to me!" I ordered, stepping back from the line.

He dropped back.

"On my left," I panted. "Come on."

Going to the end of the line, I faced the soldier there, quickly knocking him out, then turned at right angles and walked into the flank, Eleazar with me. My concentration sharpened, and I drove forward, picking up my sparring, the flat of my blade slapping three men in quick succession.

Sar Malchi waved for them to leave, and I looked at the man beyond Eleazar. "Turn!" I yelled, moving forward again. Eleazar took out two more, and another man in the second swerved with us. In moments the unit was fighting as it never had before. I called encouragement, my sweep bunching men as more of the second unit turned on the flank.

Feeling the connection between me and the men on my side, I coached and shouted instructions as I drove forward. Pasach, the commander of the eleventh unit, didn't care about the tension between Abner and me, and he gleefully joined the drive into the flank. He sent a messenger to the center, and Commander Ram stepped back in time to see the seventh and eighth units crumbling under our combined charge.

The commander next to Pasach shoved his men in also. Ram instantly ordered the first unit to fall back, and the men obeyed. Libni, opposite him, carelessly pressed his unit forward, eager to rout his rival.

Abner looked up too late, and suddenly found himself and Libni in danger of being surrounded since they now faced two fronts at right angles to each other. I anchored the line, Eleazar shielding like a rock beside me.

Sar Malchi's voice roared constantly, calling out man after man, and Abner struggled to bring order from chaos, dismayed to discover all his unit commanders called out. Most of the second unit cheered madly on the sidelines, and Ram's men stood solidly, having sucked the tenth into a neat trap.

Pasach waved his hand and shouted, "Forward, Dahveed!" I plunged again, facing the determined resistance of units now fighting to stay in the battle. The sounds around me faded, and the desire to defeat any who stood against me grew stronger. Eleazar remained beside me, the sword in his left hand still flashing up with incredible speed, stopping blows as did the shield in his right. And then I ran into a man who refused to be defeated. I whipped the sword out of his hand, and he jumped away, so I turned to another.

"Forward, Dahveed," someone yelled just as Eleazar was called out. I tried, but that man returned, blocking my way. Maneuvering him in front of me, I drove him back step by step. He panted hard and sweat poured from him. His hand slipped on the sword grip, and I twisted it away a second time. Jumping back, he looked wildly around. Then, ducking a swing from someone else, he grabbed a sword from the ground.

Impatiently I turned to him for the third time. Switching the sword to my left hand, I blocked his blow, forcing his sword up and out, then whirled under our arms, bringing my blade back to land the flat surface solidly in his back and side when he was too slow to turn after me.

"Down and out!" Sar Malchi said, pointing straight at him. I turned back to the rest, glad to be rid of him.

"*Dahveed!*"

Sar Malchi's shout hit my ears the same instant I caught movement in the corner of my eye. As I leaped to the side, a searing pain burned on the back of my right hip. The pain jarred again when I landed, and I whirled, shouting my protest.

As there was nothing dulled about the blade slashing at me now, I hurled the wooden sword away. I remember giving a battle cry, and the hassar's voice thundering, "*Ishvi, Malchi, get the men back!*" As I pulled my new blade from its sheath, Yahweh's gift flooded me, and I knew the blood on the sword flashing in front of me was my own.

Batting it aside, I stabbed forward, following the man back as he retreated, swatting and stabbing, turning his backswing to the ground and driving forward again, straight for his stomach, some part of my mind telling me this was no mock battle. He jumped away, and I lunged, determined that he wouldn't get the chance to touch me again.

His breath whistled in his chest, and he desperately tried to keep his sword in front of him, but I refused to back off, knowing that I must finish this quickly, but unable to remember why. I kept turning his blade to the side, down, up, anywhere but in front of him, and always I stabbed, faster and faster until I felt the blade hit home, and he cried out, falling backward.

I paused.

"*Malchi, no,*" someone shouted, and then a spear point stabbed at my face. I *hated* spears! Jumping back, I snatched a fallen helmet from the ground, and when that point lunged at me again, I jammed the helmet on it, shoving back and turning the warrior's side to me as I brought my sword down on the shaft as hard as I could, slicing it cleanly in two, giving me a split second to retreat.

His sword flashed in the light, and I met it. I wasn't expecting the twist up and around, and I couldn't resist the powerful flip as my sword spun from my hand. His point swung up toward my throat, and I leaned back, swinging my arm over it, jamming the blade among the bronze scales of my cuirass. My thumb dug savagely into the muscle of his arm, and his hand popped open. Then whipping myself around, I slammed my shoulder into his chest as the sword landed on the ground.

I felt as if I'd hit a wall, but his weight shifted, and pain lanced from my hip. Crying out, I reached for his dagger, finding his hand already there. Forcing it down and around, I twisted it behind his back. But turning like a snake into the twist, he brought his opposite elbow smashing into my jaw. I let go, dropping to the ground and spinning, sweeping his legs from under him, and he hit full on his back right beside me. Still on my knees, I snatched the sword from the ground, tucked it between his cuirass strips, and leaned just a little against it.

He froze, staring at me, sweat forming on his face, then running down it. Slowly he let go of the dagger.

Fighting to remember what this was all about, I eased up a bit. Pain from my jaw and the hassar's voice hit my mind at the same time.

"Dahveed?"

I relaxed the pressure on the sword again. If the hassar was here, things had probably gone far enough.

"May I have my brother back now?"

Struggling to find my way out of the gift, I looked up. Someone stood six feet away, arms folded, his eyes amused, especially when he looked at the man on the ground.

"Who am I, Dahveed?"

My voice returned with the pain in my hip. "Nahsi," I managed to get out.

"If you would let Malchi have his sword back, we can take care of that hip for you."

"Sar Malchi?" I croaked, looking around.

"Down there, Dahveed," the hassar said, pointing to the man under my sword.

I looked down into the sar's wide eyes. The tension drained from me, and I swung the sword away from him and pointed it toward the ground.

Sar Malchi rolled to his feet, taking the sword from my stiff hand and sheathing it. As soon as he stood, cheers filled the air. Nearly every man in the professional forces and the townspeople clapped and yelled wildly, many shouting my name. King Shaul, his face angry, watched from where he stood by someone lying on the ground. Ahiam helped me up, and I winced.

"What hurts?" I gasped.

"You've got a slice on your hip," Ahiam said. "You'll be sleeping on your stomach for a while."

"Then how come my jaw hurts?"

"Sar Malchi hit you with his elbow."

"Referees aren't supposed to fight."

"You attacked him."

"Why did I do that?"

"He jumped between you and Abner, trying to save him from you."

"*I fought Abner?*"

"If you can call what happened a fight."

* * *

As Balak attended the king later that evening, he tried to keep an impassive expression as befitted a servant. On the good side, Abner had certainly reacted to the suggestion that Dahveed had deliberately dishonored him. On the bad side, the king's cousin had pushed the dahveed into showing what he could do, and now the entire town could talk of nothing but the encounter.

He glanced at the king's troubled face. "Adoni, you seem upset about what happened this afternoon," he said respectfully.

"There has been dishonor done," Shaul replied shortly.

"I saw it, adoni. I suppose tempers cannot always be controlled even in a mock battle."

"That is not an excuse for one of my house to attack from behind!" the king said icily.

"Of course not, adoni," he said, looking abashed. So it was Abner the king was angry with. He waited a moment. "But maybe the incident could have been passed over if Dahveed had controlled himself." He cast another glance at the ruler, but Shaul said nothing as he took off his girdle.

"Dahveed simply defended himself," Shaul finally commented, but he frowned.

Balak said nothing more. The king might be angry with Abner, but he didn't look very pleased with Dahveed either. After all, Abner was kin, and he was quite seriously wounded.

---

[1] See Cultural Notes: Family relationships.

[2] See Cultural Notes: Honor wars.

CHAPTER 4

With Abner confined to his bed by his wound, I became general in practice, not just name, and I suddenly found myself with more duties and responsibilities than I'd ever had before.

The older sars' matter-of-fact acceptance of me smoothed my way everywhere, but especially with the unit commanders. Only Libni treated me coolly, and one or two others remained neutral. Because I couldn't move around much at first, I paired the men off for sparring as the Habiru did, making it easier for me as I wandered among them, leaning on Ahiam for support. I gave suggestions and hints, depending on the weaknesses that I saw. A few men grumbled about the change, but performances improved.

The same few also muttered about the cross-training I started. Following Ethan's example, I wanted to be certain that any man in the Israelite professional forces stood a chance at surviving so long as he had something to fight with. The protests stopped the day they saw Sar Malchi working on the archery range, and the hassar practicing with a sling.

The king did not give me more of the rewards that he had promised, much to my relief. The fact that I had wounded Abner displeased him. I was content to remain a place-holder, and serve the king as zammar, for Shaul had three bouts of prophesying during this time. As previously, the sars led him to his room, Hassar Jonathan returning to the throne room to continue court, Sar Ishvi remaining with the king.

While I played, Shaul stared fixedly, his eyes blank, words spilling from his mouth so swiftly they disintegrated into meaningless sounds. Other times he would lecture the pillars about how to arrange the bedclothes when the moon was shining, or the importance of taking no more than six fleas off a dog in any one day. Eventually, the music would stem the torrent of words, and the king would sleep. Every day I prayed for Yahweh's healing on him, for he had done more for me than I could ever repay. Since I could not give him my loyalty, I gave him my love instead, determined to serve him with the best that I had.

I also returned the earring to Jonathan when he got impatient with one of the men on the training ground who had been overawed by him. Not long after, Zorath let slip that the men had a betting pool among themselves about how long each of us would have to wear the thing.

My wound healed quickly, and I was soon back to normal activities. As the weeks passed, however, I grew impatient for the king to give the general's mantle back to Abner. Even though Abner's wound was slow to heal, I couldn't imagine that the king planned on me actually leading the army during the next war season.

◻◻◻◻◻

"Is there anything else today?" King Shaul asked as Kohath, the new head scribe for the fortress, left the throne room.

"Only the matter of Abner's attack on Dahveed, adoni," Jonathan replied.

Shaul frowned. "You attend to that," he said, making Michal look up quickly.

"Do you wish *me* to pass judgment on Abner?"

"Do as you wish," his father answered, looking at Jonathan steadily.

"And if Abner insists on seeing you about my decision?"

"If you handle it well, that will not happen."

Jonathan straightened. "As you wish, adoni."

Because of the grim set to her brother's face, Michal wondered what was in store for the king's cousin. This was not the first time that Shaul had shifted part of his authority to Jonathan, but it was the most important matter he had passed on, and Michal knew that if Jonathan handled it to the king's satisfaction, he would be coruler for all practical purposes. And if *that* happened, perhaps a lot of things would change.

Her mind still toyed with possibilities as she left the residence for the afternoon check on Abner's wound. If Jonathan became coregent, maybe he'd find some way to help Dahveed. She'd watched the zammar that afternoon, and Jonathan was right. Anyone who saw Dahveed's hesitant, diffident manner would scorn him for not upholding his appointment by the king, to say nothing of dismissing his abilities as a fighting man. If he remained general, that could easily translate into more attacks on the kingdom. *Something must indeed be done*, she thought as she entered the courtyard of Abner's house in town.

"How is that wound today?" she asked, walking up to the awning in the courtyard where Abner rested against some cushions.

"The same as always," he grunted.

"Has it been cleaned recently?"

"It's fine, Michal. Don't go poking around in it." He stirred fret-fully, and Michal stepped back.

The gate opened again, and Jonathan strode in. "Good, you're here, Michal," he said, walking over.

Abner glared at the hassar. "What are you doing here?"

"I have business to discuss with you, adon, regarding the position of general."

"I am Shaul's general."

"The king made Dahveed general."

"A temporary appointment, at best," Abner snorted.

"It may now be permanent because of what you did in that mock battle. The king is very displeased, Abner. So much so that he left your case up to me. And I wish to make it very clear that Dahveed is now the king's general."

The officer laughed harshly. "So *you* say. Well, I'll see to it that no one follows his orders!"

"I am Hassar Israel, Abner. Remember that when you speak to me."

"And I turned you over my knee more than once, Jonathan. Remember that when I speak to you."

Wishing that she could leave, Michal stood motionless.

Jonathan stared at Abner until the man's eyes shifted away. "I have remembered, Abner. That's the only reason you still live. But unless you show more honor to the king, not even that will save you. You attacked your superior officer *from behind* before the entire professional forces and most of the town. Even if he had been only the king's zam-mar, please explain how those actions honor the king."

The older man flushed a dull red, and Michal pressed her hands together to keep them from trembling.

"He is nothing but an ungrateful slave who refused to swear loy-alty! And when he worms his way into the king's favor and takes my position out from under me, am I supposed to let that go unanswered?" Abner demanded in a shaking voice.

"He did not take your position, Abner. The king, *as is his right*, gave him that mantle," Michal's brother said, folding his arms across his chest.

"Michal, there's no need for you to remain. Go back to the fortress," Abner growled at her.

She turned immediately to leave.

"Michal Sahrah, stay."

Jonathan's tone rooted her to the ground. His eyes were distant and remote, and the hardness in him frightened her. He was the hassar now, and not her brother or Abner's younger cousin, but a judge and executioner if necessary. She knew that he held something back, and she didn't want to know what it was.

Slowly she took a deep breath. "As Michal Sahrah, king's daughter, please tell me why I must be here. I would leave you alone with Abner if possible."

"Your presence is required as a witness, Michal Sahrah. That way Adon Abner will know that I am willing to grant hesed for his neglect only once."[1]

Michal swallowed, and Abner struggled to raise himself from the cushions under the awning.

"If you don't have something to prove that accusation, I'll cut you down myself," he threatened, then fell back gasping.

"How many witnesses will be sufficient? Four? Or shall I bring all five to court?"

Abner stiffened in amazement.

"Remember that feast for the honored men just after the king returned? Two assassins pretending to be servers made it into the anteroom. By sheer chance a scribe was in that room, realized something was wrong, and gave the alarm. If they had made it into the throne room, I would be dead."

"Who let them in?"

"The guards at the anteroom door. That night was only their third in the palace, everyone was a stranger to them, and they had no way of knowing that those two were not servants in the fortress or even residents of the town."

"Which commander assigned two new men to those doors? I'll kill him for that!"

"Draw your own dagger. You assigned them yourself, out on the training ground, and you carefully informed them—and them only—of the rules pertaining to weapons in the presence of the royal family. Do you know what that means?"

Abner sucked in his breath.

"You've been so busy protecting your honor from someone who doesn't threaten it that *I nearly died, Abner.*"

During the long silence Michal continued to remain motionless, doing her best to keep from trembling. Neglect of such caliber was tantamount to treason.

"I look at all you've done, and I know what I should do," the hassar continued. "And then I remember that you are of my blood, the one rock that Abbi will always lean on, the man who taught me everything I know about war, and I remember the times when I was a child. When the king placed this case in my hands, I decided to speak to you with only one witness, Michal Sahrah, whom I know can be trusted. You know what sentence I should pronounce."

Breathing hard, his face twisted with pain, Abner slumped backward again. "Yes, Nahsi," he said at last.

"Because you are of my blood, Abner, I will give you the chance to handle this yourself. I would prefer that you choose exile over death, and I believe the king feels the same. If you have not decided in a day's time, I will pronounce sentence."

Jonathan held out his arm to her, and Michal walked with him out of the gate. Once they were away from the house, the tension rushed from her brother, and the drawn, haggard expression on his face told her how hard it had been to speak thus to his kinsman. She moved closer to him, and he put his arm around her, leaning on her for support as they returned to the fortress.

In the morning Abner was gone.

"How can Abner be gone?" Balak asked quickly, turning to Judith as she placed the dishes with the noon meal in front of him.

"He's gone," she repeated. "Basemath says there's not even a servant left at the house in town. He left during the night, and no one knows why."

"Surely someone must know something," Balak persisted, trying to adjust himself to the news.

"Well," Judith continued, sitting down by him, "Achsah said Sahrah Michal went to see him as usual, but stayed ever so long, and when she came back, Hassar Jonathan was with her, and both of them went to their rooms and never said a word."

The hassar! He might have known. "Does anyone know what went on?"

"Nooo, but there are a lot of rumors. Someone claimed the hassar killed him and spirited the body away, but no one believes that. Another said that Michal bewitched the adon, and Jonathan couldn't stop her, and—"

"Hasn't anyone said anything sensible?" Balak demanded, irritated.

"Well, the servant of the neighbor of the recording scribe from yesterday says the scribe told his wife, who told the neighbor's wife, and the servant overheard, that Jonathan sent him away and not even the king knows how."

Hiding his frustration, Balak ate while he listened to Judith's speculations. Why did Abner have to get himself banished just when he was becoming extremely useful?

After the noon rest he returned to the fortress a little early and headed for the alcove in the wall of the passage where he used to stay. He needed to think.

"Balak!"

He turned irritably at the call.

Peleth, the Philistine servant, hurried toward him. "I was just going to get you. Hassar Jonathan wants to get an early start on afternoon court. He wants you to waken the king now."

Seething silently, Balak nodded. Waking the king wasn't a chore that anyone wanted, since no one ever knew what state of mind Shaul would be in after he slept. Since he was the king's personal attendant, the job now fell to him, and he'd quickly discovered that waking the king early was not to be done unless absolutely unavoidable.

When he quietly entered the king's chamber, Shaul's breathing was deep and even. Good. He'd slept well, then. As he laid out the king's purple mantle and got some jewelry from the chest, he let the sounds of his movements rouse the king.

"It is time to waken, adoni," he said, standing by the wide wooden platform set in the wall that served as both seat and bed for the room.

Shaul opened his eyes. "Balak?"

"Yes, adoni. It is time to rise."

"Not yet," the king said fretfully, and closed his eyes again.

Balak clenched his teeth together, wishing he could yank the king from the bed and throw him out the door. A smile flickered across his face. Maybe he would some day. Who would know? He was alone in here, after all.

Suddenly the world seemed to become motionless. He *was* alone in here! *Every single day* he had time completely alone with the king! Who knew what he might be able to do?

"But, adoni, Hassar Jonathan has asked to begin a little early," Balak said, trying to keep his voice steady and watching closely to see the effect of his words. "You know it must be something important for him to ask that."

With a sigh Shaul opened his eyes again.

"Surely you want to rise and see what is on the hassar's mind," the servant coaxed softly.

"Yes, I suppose I do." Shaul started to sit up.

"Except, of course, it if involves Abner," Balak dared to say. "You don't want to talk about him today, do you?"

The king frowned. "No, I don't. Jonathan says he is gone. We don't need to discuss him again."

"Except to find out how his wound is," Balak added offhandedly as the king stood.

"That, of course. He is our cousin, after all."

"Here, then, let me comb your hair out again, adoni." Balak picked up the comb, and the king obediently sat down on the chair.

That night, after Judith fell asleep, Balak took the baked clay shrine from the wall niche and went out into the courtyard. He carefully set the six-inch bronze statue of Kemosh in the boxlike shrine and knelt before it.

"It is I, Balak, your servant, who comes to you again, O Kemosh," he whispered. "What a boon you have given to me! You have defeated Yahweh, your enemy, even though Yahweh took away the ally you sent to me, for you have placed me closer to the king than even Dahveed! Soon all will know what a mighty god you are. May all who oppose me wish they had never come against so powerful a god as you!"

⬛▭⬛

My mind refused to sleep, filled with discouragement and near despair. Even though I wore the general's mantle to the training ground every day, I knew that people thought me a fool, and that Abner's opinion of me—that of an ungrateful slave—was causing arguments about whether or not I deserved the honor of the generalship. Plainly, I had taken inappropriate honor when I accepted that mantle, and I'd disgraced myself and my family just like Eliab always said I would. I cringed inside every time I thought of it.

Consequently, I left everything connected with the army up to the commanders. They knew more of what Abner would want than I did. I could only pray that King Shaul would recall his cousin before the war season.

It didn't help that in court I never knew how the king would treat me anymore. Some days he was pleasant and relaxed. Others, he looked at me coldly, his eyes angry as they had been after the mock battle. And buried under it all was the ever-present knot of aching loneliness for home that I could no longer ignore. I had heard nothing of my family since last war season, and the fear that Abigail had died after her miscarriage in Damascus ate away at me until the pain never left.

I twisted and turned on the bedroll for what seemed like hours before I finally dressed and climbed the ladder to the roof of our little room, going from it to the fortress wall. There I paced above the hidden door that led out of the fortress, fighting down the need for the god-places, the wild forest, and the stirring of wind in the pines of a hilltop. I knew that if I left, my feet would take me south whether I wanted them to or not. Eventually, I found myself at the southeast battlements instead, staring into the darkness toward Jebus, my hands gripping the stones, thankful the sentries didn't seem interested in walking by.

If only I could return to the pastures and Abbi's sheep, back to when I'd known my place, and had Eliab to keep me in it, and didn't have conflicts and mistakes staring at me everywhere I turned. That he-lamb hadn't cared whether I wore a blue mantle or not when I slung the stone that stopped the bear. The picture of the pasture with the old hollow oak rose before me vividly, and the overwhelming yearning for home crashed over me. "Immi, I cannot go home!" I heard myself cry as my knees hit the hard stone under me. I'd never known a pain like this, cut off from my family and clan, denied the land where my fathers were buried, the very thing that bound me to both Abbi and Yahweh. Who was I without that? Even as a servant in Jesse's house, I had had some claim to his honor, and some place before Adonai, who owned the land that gave us our living.

But what did I have now? Certainly nothing here, for I had for-feited all rights by my inability to keep to my proper place. And if I could not go back to the place of my ancestors, would I be abandoned and forgotten? The oil of my anointing had dripped on the floor of Jesse's house, had fallen from my hair and hands as I ran to the god-places, and the robe rested even now in Yahweh's presence in the upper room of Hassarah Ruth's forest house near Bethlehem. But if I could not return to my family and land, how could I remain before my God? Who would there be to speak my name before Him and keep my life in His memory since I now had no place where I could go?

I knelt on the rigid stone, pressed against the cold, unyielding hard-ness of the wall. "Do not forget me," I whispered. "Adonai Yahweh, *do not forget me!*"[2]

Not long after Dahveed had left the battlement, Jonathan detached himself from the corner where he had stayed in absolute stillness while Dahveed mourned.

I barely made it through the next two days, performing my duties automatically, and knowing little of what went on. Somehow I was aware that a message had arrived from the king of Mari, stating that an emissary was on the way. I'd also seen Sahrah Michal talking to Ahiam, and I could hardly stand the thought of more clothes or jewelry coming my way.

On the third day, when court dismissed for the noon rest, I hurried down the stairs, but the hassar's voice caught up to me in the anteroom. "Dahveed, I wish you to attend me."

Reluctantly I turned back.

He took me through the door at the bottom of the stairs into the back passage under the throne room. "A guest is here whom you can help me entertain," he said quietly.

My heart sank. "Adoni, why must it be me? I—"

His cold, remote look cut the words off in my throat. "Because you are my servant, and I said to."

I flinched. Had he used a whip, he could not have cut more deeply. Would I never learn my position? "As you wish, bekor," I said in a daze.

He entered one of the scribal rooms, and I followed him.

"I trust you had an easy journey?" the hassar asked.

"Yes, adoni," my brother Ozem's voice replied, shaking a little with nervousness.

My head jerked up so fast that I nearly snapped my neck.

"I hope that Yahweh has blessed your house with peace," my brother went on, not daring to look at me yet.

"He has. I am pleased that you have arrived so quickly. What did you bring?"

"I know that you requested a fleece," Ozem gulped a little, "but we don't have any just now. A while ago, a ewe died, and we skinned it for a pelt. I brought that. I hope it will be all right."

"Yes, that should do just as well," the hassar said. "Spread it out."

I swayed slightly, my head spinning as Ozem opened out the white pelt splotched with black. Jonathan buried his fingers in the long, kinky wool, giving a faint whistle under his breath. "Ahiam was right! This is the equal of Dibon wool."

"It is Dibon," Ozem said a little proudly.

"How much will you shear out this year?"

"Close to 100 pounds, adoni. Most of it will have the long fibers you see on the pelt. We can shear close. Our sheep are not bad-tempered."

"Just what I needed to hear," the hassar said with satisfaction. "Now, I would imagine Dahveed here hasn't quite recovered his voice yet, so I'll ask the first question. Did Abigail recover from her miscarriage?"

Ozem's mouth opened, but no sound came out as he switched his gaze from Jonathan to me and back again.

"Uh, well, uh, y-yes," he managed to stammar.

"She's alive, then?" I whispered.

"And nearly back in good health," my brother replied, reaching his hand out to me.

Tears flowed as I hugged him, and Jonathan quietly slipped out the door, pulling it firmly shut.

As the talk of home poured from Ozem, I drank it in hungrily, one part of my mind still stunned at what Jonathan had just done, since I knew full well what the king would think of this visit. I would let Jonathan Hassar treat me any way he wanted after this!

Abigail was indeed fine, Ozem assured me, but her husband, Jether, was more careful of her than ever, and it frustrated her. My other half sister, Zeruiah, worried about her son Joab, who was in trouble constantly. Most of the family found themselves spending much of their time trying to control him. His older brother, Abishai, stayed home, helping Zeruiah, and the youngest, Asahel, had won three more footraces.

Of my half brothers, Eliab had recovered from the sword wound, although he limped, and the leg ached in the evenings. Abinadab's carpentry business was flourishing, and Shammah was working with Zelek, Abigail's Ammonite cousin, training mules.

Nethanel was thinking of asking for a wife, and had taken oversight of the olive grove as well as helping Jesse in the fields. Blight struck several fields, and we had lost considerable grain to it. However, the grapes were coming along fine, and so were the olives.

Raddai, Ozem's twin, had gone into partnership with Lahab ben Bukki and spent most of his time in the vineyards and the wine shop they set up.

Ozem confessed that he had taken over breeding the Yidla-Dibon cross that Grandmother Ruth had developed, pairing the Yidla good temper with the long Dibon wool. He had several questions to ask about that, and we discussed it for some time.

Elihu was home for harvest this year, and had received much praise from his tutors at the scribal school in Beth-shean.

"You mentioned Zelek. Ethan must have found both him and his sister, Ala?" I asked, referring to my two Ammonite half cousins.

"Yes, although Abbi was dubious about taking them since it was clear they hadn't come because they wanted to. If he'd known that Zelek had tried to kill the hassar, he wouldn't have allowed them to stay.

"But it turned out that Zelek's abbi raised mules and chariot horses for King Nahash of Ammon. Once he saw Shammah's mules, they struck up a partnership right then, and Keren was happy to have Ala help around the house.

"I brought several mules with me today, as well as this pelt," he concluded.

I chuckled. That explained why Jonathan had left so quickly.

"Oh, and your friend Elhanan has a new little son!"

I don't know how long we talked before Ozem reluctantly rose to go.

"Tell Immi I love her and think of her every day," I said as we stood at the door.

"I will, and she always worries over whether you have your sling with you."

I smiled through the tears gathering in my eyes. "I never go out of the gates without it. Tell her I will come to her when I can."

"I will, Dahveed. And one more thing. Abbi called your name first at this year's new moon feast!"

I didn't know what to say. I was first in clan honor at home? Ahead of Eliab?

"Tell Abbi I am grateful," I managed to stammer.

Ozem gave me one more embrace and then left.

Too full of conflicting emotions to think straight, I sat down on the floor. Foremost in my mind, however, was the risk that Jonathan must have taken to arrange such a visit. What could I ever do to repay this man whom I loved as fiercely as I had loved Hassarah Ruth?

It was some time before I regained my composure and the door opened again. Jonathan stepped in and put the earring around my neck. "I ought to make you wear it to the end of your days for not telling me how much it pained you to hear nothing from your family. How am I supposed to be your older brother if you don't trust me with such things?" he said in exasperation.

"What kind of a friend would I be if I asked you to go against the king?" I retorted in surprise.

"You let me worry about what can and cannot be done concerning my abbi."

"Yes, Hassar," I said, relaxing against the wall.

"And if you ever call me 'bekor' again, I'll—I'll load you down with fringes and gold and parade you through Jebus on my own mule!"

"Yes, Hassar."

"I won't have you speaking to me as if you were Ben-geber."

"Yes, Hassar."

You say that just to provoke me, don't you?" he demanded, folding his arms and staring at me.

"Yes, Hassar."

Without a word he stomped out, slamming the door so hard against the threshold that it popped open again.

"Did you find him? Malchi wants to know if he'll be at the training ground at all this afternoon," Sahrah Michal asked just outside.

"Of course I found him," Jonathan roared. "He was right where I left him, and still the most irritating example of a hill man in the entire land!"

Chuckling, I wiped my face on my sleeve one last time and went to see what Sar Malchi wanted.

---

[1] See Cultural Notes: Hesed.
[2] See Cultural Notes: Preserving a name.

CHAPTER 5

Just before the beginning of harvest, the emissary from Mari, Baqqush by name, arrived. It was nearly noon by the time that everyone had observed the official greetings and carefully correct courtesies, and Shaul ordered food brought so the emissary could eat while his retinue set up camp. The two men seated themselves at the long table, and the elderly emissary looked around with sharp eyes, taking in the dais, throne, and orderly functioning of the court around us. Sahrah Michal and her maid, Achsah, brought in the unleavened bread, goat cheese, dried apricots, sweet Tekoa figs, and wine.

The figs brought a pleased expression to the envoy's face, and he ate several. The wine surprised an exclamation from him, and he looked in his cup respectfully. "This is quite a vintage."

"Yes, my oldest son obtained it, and we've been very pleased," the king responded.

Baqqush turned to the hassar, who stood by, serving his father. "And where did you import it from?"

"Not far south of here," Jonathan replied. "The vintner warned me that this pressing might not come up to his usual standards, but I'm inclined to think he was being unjustly dubious of it."

The envoy sipped again. "It has an excellent flavor."

"Would you like a little to take home with you, as a gift to your lady wife, perhaps?" the hassar offered.

"Regrettably, my wife is dead," the envoy sighed.

"Then I shall insist that you take some, if only for comfort in your misfortune. You must accept some, adon."

"You are very kind, Hassar."

Talk drifted to other subjects as the meal progressed. Sahrah Michal had whispered to me to stay in case the king wanted me to perform, and I waited on my stool. Once the food was gone, King Shaul looked in my direction. "Play for us, zammar."

I played a song about a traveler that I'd composed soon after my arrival in Gibeah, and when I finished, the envoy nodded his head at me. "King Shaul, that zammar has a voice to grace any monarch."

"He pleases me."

"As I hope my reason for coming will," Baqqush went on. "My adon feels it would be well to have friendship between our country and your house. We have lately received occasional goods from caravans with prices that please my adon very much.

"He requested that I investigate this, and it was only with great difficulty that I was able to persuade the steward of the House of Tahat to set me on my way. The steward mentioned to me that it might be worth my time to travel in the hill country, as he had always found it, ah, satisfying, I believe he said." Baqqush paused significantly. "After tasting the vintage you set before me, I will admit that I have found it so as well. If more of such wines could find their way north, my adon would express his gratitude for the circumstance. He can be very generous, and he has empowered me to make arrangements with you."

Jonathan's eyes lit up.

"Indeed, I would expect nothing less than generosity from an adon as honorable as yours," the king replied. "Is there any other particular item that your adon might also find, ah, satisfying, shall we say? Perhaps a small token to take along with the wine?"

The envoy studied his cup. "Now that you mention it, I do believe my adon's house steward expressed an interest in some wool that came his way. The steward of Tahat said that he had found the product from the Jebus area as fine as that from Moab, but I would have to see a sample of it," Baqqush ended doubtfully.

The king looked at Jonathan.

"I may have a sample for you, which recently arrived. It won't disappoint your adon," the hassar added.

I smiled to myself. *Grandmother Ruth, how far you saw!* I thought. Breeding the bad temper out of the Dibon sheep was paying off handsomely.

"He will be pleased. Very pleased," Baqqush said, nodding.

"Then it seems we will have things to discuss," Shaul said. "We will do all that we can to see that you and your retinue are comfortable. Play for us again, zammar." I entertained them for another half an hour before the king rose, and the emissary took his leave.

I had expected the king to be closeted with the emissary while they worked out a trade covenant between the two countries, but instead, for the next three days after the official greetings each morning, Baqqush and Jonathan went off on some jaunt or other, usually involving hunting. They did spend the afternoon of the third day in Jebus at the Brass Lion, however, and the hassar returned with a gleam in his eye. Word soon spread that the king and Baqqush would formally cut a covenant the next morning and that a feast would take place in the evening.

Some of the servants wondered if there would be a full cutting ceremony, but I doubted it. I didn't know of anyone who performed the ancient ceremony in full anymore. People didn't have heifers, she-goats, rams, and other animals to spare for it. The animals had to be slaughtered, the carcasses divided in two so the covenant participants could walk between the pieces, asking the gods to cut them up like the animals if they failed to honor the covenant being made. Nowadays people simply called the gods to witness the covenant and had some symbol of death with them to represent the divided animals.

The next day, Shaul and Baqqush swore to the covenant in the throne room, using a dagger, and then pressing their seals into the clay tablets, each participant keeping one. The feast lasted long into the night, and I was exhausted and my throat sore by the time it was over.

The next morning was unseasonably chilly as the entire royal family, dressed in their best clothes, gathered to send the envoy on his way. Shaul had on the openwork royal headband and armband, along with his meil, and the hassar wore his ceremonial sword and dagger (the matched set), and the ceremonial cuirass over his best meil (the dark-blue one with gold and silver in the embroidery). Baqqush took his leave with much pomp and assurances of the friendship that his adon would feel toward the king when he saw the covenant.

I'd never seen Jonathan so elated before. When the last of the envoy's retinue had vanished, he grabbed the arm of the nearest servant and sent him to the fortress at a run. Then he grabbed me, hauling me along after him, and strode swiftly down the road to the path that entered the forest west of Gibeah. "We're going hunting," he announced, his eyes sparkling.

I could hardly keep on my feet. "Hassar, please," I gasped. "Give me a chance to catch up!"

Laughing, he turned back. "What? The hill man caught off guard? This must be a first, zammar. I should enter it into the royal records."

"That will hardly be necessary," I said, steady enough to keep up with him now. "And you'll spoil those clothes if you don't change," I predicted, eyeing him.

"Only if you make me do my own dirty work," he retorted.

At last Dara appeared on his mule, bringing the hassar's best bow and quiver, along with mine, carried by a new arrow boy. I started to chuckle as soon as I saw him.

Jonathan raised his eyebrows. "Who is this?" he asked.

Nimshi stuck his head around Dara's shoulder. "Shalom, geber!"[1] he replied, his eyes sparkling.

"Do you know what you're doing, Dara?" the hassar asked skeptically. "Every time I'm with this scamp, he takes me to places I don't ask to go."

"Yes, I'd noticed that he was a saucy one," Dara replied, giving Ethan's youngest son an arm down so he could deliver the bows and quivers.

"Shalom, Dahveed," Nimshi said to me.

"Shalom. Ethan decided to let you serve the hassar, did he?"

"He thought that since you and Ahiam were here, it would be all right."

"Ahiam and Dahveed!" Jonathan exclaimed, irritated. "Hassar Israel is not competent to take care of you?"

Nimshi's brown eyes widened. "Take care of *me?* Geber, my abbi told me very plainly that I was to take good care of *you*. He said I was to be sure that you never got lost, and that you always ended up where you wanted to go, because if he ever found you wandering around in the hills now that I was with you, he'd make me answer for it. And geber, *nobody* wants to have to answer to my abbi for something."

The hassar stared, speechless, at his new arrow boy, and I coughed to hide my laughter. Shoving Jonathan's bow and quiver into his arms, I turned him around, propelling him down the path. "I believe, Hassar, that we were going hunting. If we stand around here much longer, your escort will probably want to come along, so maybe we'd better get started."

"Did you hear what that impudent guttersnipe said to me?" the hassar fumed, striding along the path. "Find me wandering around in the hills indeed! I've been hunting these hills since before he was even thought of!"

Once we were out of sight of the town, Jonathan quieted, and he didn't seem in any hurry to begin our hunt. We were very close to the Ezel stone before he strung his bow and we started looking for deer. Neither of us was ready when we surprised one, and Jonathan's arm got tangled in his cloak when his hand flashed back for an arrow.

I hid my smile at the exasperation on his face as the deer vanished in the trees. He looked at me and saw that my cloak was folded back

GIBEON HABIRU
TRAINING GROUND AND EZEL STONE

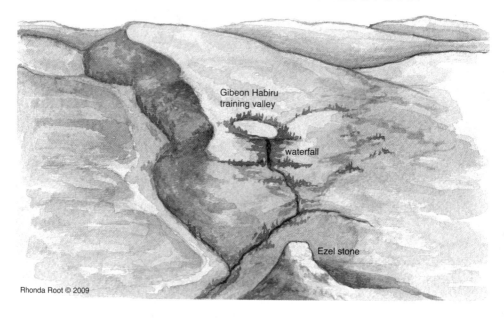

Gibeon Habiru
training valley

waterfall

Ezel stone

Rhonda Root © 2009

SECOND UNIT TRAINING GROUND

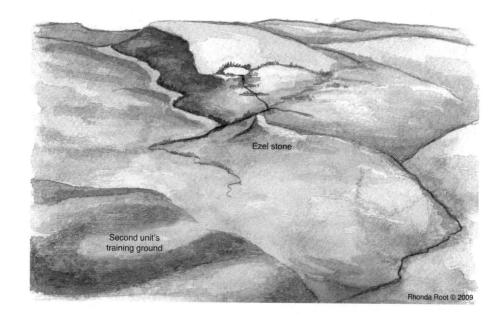

Ezel stone

Second unit's
training ground

Rhonda Root © 2009

over my shoulders so that I'd have free access to my quiver.

"Don't say a word," he growled.

We wandered for a while longer, but I soon realized that hunting was just an excuse for him to get away. I led him around the east way to the cup valley where Jeshua's band trained, knowing it would be empty at this time. Once there, I squatted down on the warm grass in the sun. Red, white, and yellow flowers nodded at the edge of the trees, and the seasonal brook behind me was half full, creating a tiny waterfall over the rocks as it joined the one in the lower valley.

A faraway look in his eyes, Jonathan paced back and forth a while. "What do you know of this House of Tahat that Baqqush mentioned?" he eventually asked.

"I've never heard of it, but I don't necessarily know the trade houses on the caravan lines. Abigail would. So might Ethan."

"I'll have to see what I can find out. This is important, Dahveed."

I stared at him, a bit puzzled. "Why, adoni?"

"We've been recognized as a separate kingdom, Dahveed," he said, elation in his voice. "That envoy came after a treaty for wool. The wine was a surprise to him, and we worked in those Tekoa figs, as well."

"But there isn't much of any of those products now. Maybe in a few years there could be," I said, still trying to understand his excitement.

"What's important is the fact of a covenant, Dahveed! It's just a beginning. Here, look . . ." Dropping down by the little brook, he used his dagger to make some swift lines in the sand.

"What is it?" I asked.

"It's our land. Here's the Great Sea," he explained, pointing to a curve on the side. "This is the Jordan, with the Chinnereth Sea on the north and the Salt Sea on the south, and here's the desert on the east. Dan is here by the Chinnereth, and Beer-sheba is down here, close to the border of Egypt, which is here," he went on, stroking in another line. "And here we are," he added, making little humps to represent hills.

"Our land is a passageway between the sea and the desert," I said slowly.

"That's exactly what it is. And there are three paths through this land. One is the Way of the Sea." He drew a line along the curve. "The middle path is in the Arabah, the valley where the Jordan flows, and the third is the King's Highway by the eastern desert. I hadn't considered the Arabah before," he ended thoughtfully. "But it's right down the middle, and it goes all the way."

He added two spots in the south. "Amalek and Edom," he muttered. "Edom is the key. If we have Edom, then Moab, Ammon, and Bashan over here on the east of Jordan won't matter."

"What's in the north?" I asked, intrigued. I'd never seen a map of Israel before, and it gave me a different perspective.

"Aram is northeast of Dan, with Damascus about here. The country of Zobah is directly north of Dan, and the Phoenicians control the coast. Hamath is above Zobah and Damascus, and stretches east to the Euphrates, which runs southeast this way, making a crescent moon shape. The desert is the dark of the moon."

He put another dot on the crescent. "Mari is about here. That steward, or whoever, of the House of Tahat could be using the Arabah. Baqqush kept hinting at how low the House's prices were, and I started wondering if the steward had found a way to avoid the Egyptian road taxes. But he could do that only by using the Arabah, where all those gorges are. It must take forever to get his goods north."

"It shouldn't be that much of a problem," I mused. "By the time the rivers get to the Jordan, the canyons aren't that deep anymore, and in the dry season most don't have much water, if any."

Jonathan looked thunderstruck. "That's how he's doing it! If he transports his goods seasonally when the Arabah is driest, he won't have to use either the Way of the Sea or the King's Highway! He can collect his goods up near Chinnereth and then move them from there!"

"What are we talking about, Jonathan?"

"Trade! Look at it, Dahveed," he said impatiently, gesturing toward the sand. "Who's in the middle? Who's the heart of this whole thing?"

"We are," I said, staring at the map. "We could—why, we could have it all!" I exclaimed in amazement.

"Yes, we could," the hassar repeated with the wickedest grin that I'd ever seen on his face. "We straddle the only trade routes between Damascus, Egypt, and Edom. And we don't even have to control much more land than we have now. We must hold the Jezreel Valley in the north, which will be a constant weak point, but it can't be helped. In the south we must control Edom. Then everyone else has to covenant with us, or we block all their trade."

Jonathan was nearly bursting with excitement. "Israel could control the trade of the world! And now I know how to get started."

"How?" I demanded, as caught up as he was.

"In order to succeed, we must have good internal trade under a central authority that can take grain from Jezreel south and bring wine, oil, and such north. When Baqqush told us about this House of Tahat, he let slip that someone is already operating an internal north/south trade route within Israel. If I can interest the steward in this, the job is half done!"

I studied the map. "You've thought about this a lot, haven't you?"

He nodded. "But it's taken longer than I expected to drive out the Philistines and be recognized by the surrounding kings. To most of them, we're still just troublesome hill people who don't know what's good for us. But if we could unite the tribes of Israel with Judah and drive the Philistines out of Jezreel, that alone would be a good base for you to work from." His voice trailed off, and he absently stared down at the map.

I looked at him, startled. What was it he had just said?

"And now that the king of Mari has recognized us, others will," he resumed, his eyes far away. "Just think of it, Dahveed, the whole world coming here to trade! Remind me to have you with me the next time we cut a covenant. You'll need to know how to understand all the double-talk when you're king."

An icy chill washed over me. When had the hassar found out about my anointing? I inched backward, knowing that as hassar, it was Jonathan's duty to kill me and all my house. I had to get away, to warn them if nothing else!

He turned just his head. "What did I say?" he asked, puzzled.

My thoughts racing, I hesitated. Had this been a simple slip of the tongue? Did he truly not know what he'd said? But could I risk that possibility?

"Yah, what am I to do?" I silently cried. Yahweh's presence sparked in my heart with that calm, warm feeling, and nothing else. I must not be in immediate danger then, or my gift would be humming through my veins.

I took a deep breath and looked at the hassar. "Your words came out tangled, and it startled me," I shrugged.

He turned, and I jumped away.

"Tangled words don't suddenly make you that edgy. What did I say?" he persisted, without moving.

When I didn't reply, he stood smoothly, and I moved with him, backing several feet to stand within reach of the trees and safety.

Fists clenched at his sides, he turned his back to me. "What is it going to take, Dahveed?" he continued, his voice rough with bewildered pain. "After all that has happened, why won't you trust me?"

I wanted to, more than anything, but I didn't dare. He was Hassar Israel, the charismatic, beloved son of Shaul with no rival for his father's throne. The king expected him to sit there, and so did the people, despite the declarations of Roeh Shamuel to the contrary. Why should he give that up just because a hill man from Bethlehem claimed that he'd been anointed? And why would he believe me if I told him I didn't want the throne, even though Yahweh said it was mine?

Yet he had done more for me than my blood kin, making my exile from home bearable, honoring me with his friendship and loyalty, even defying his father to bring me news of my family.

"Please, Dahveed," he pleaded. "*What did I say?*"

"Don't ask, Hassar," I replied. "I don't know how else to answer you."

"But Dahveed," he said, putting more space between us before he slowly faced me, "we were only talking about trade, and uniting the tribes, and treaties, and what needed to be done." He paused, then closed his eyes and sighed. "And then I probably mentioned something about you being king, didn't I?" He drove his fist into his thigh. "And that can't be ignored now that it's been said."

"No, Hassar," I replied, my voice unsteady. "Let me go, adoni. I can leave now."

"If you run, you go against the king's command, Dahveed. Would you outlaw yourself just because I let slip what I've known for months?"

Months? How come he hadn't done anything? I was a threat to him, to his father, to the life of every one of the royal family!

"Maybe even longer than that," he went on. "Sometimes I think I've known from the first time I saw you, when you appeared like a spirit on the stool in the throne room and made Yahweh's music with that harp.[2] Maybe that's why I gave you permission to wear that belt knife in the king's presence."

What kind of a man was he? "Why would you have suspected?" I asked. "I'm nobody, a shepherd from Bethlehem."

He ran his hand through his hair. "It was knowing that you were from Bethlehem that alerted me. I knew the roeh had gone there to anoint someone at the new year's feast four years ago. Abner had stopped him outside Gibeah, and I hid the anointing oil for him so that Abner wouldn't find it."

The hassar had done that, knowing what the oil would be used for? Was it possible I really could trust him?

"So all along you knew?" I choked out.

"Shall we say I wondered?" His face suddenly looked tired.

"But then when you sang and brought Yahweh down to drive the demon from Abbi, I wasn't sure. I thought maybe Yahweh had chosen you to protect the king, and nothing else. I could account for your actions that way. You held my life in your hands more than once, and you never seemed tempted to kill me. You certainly had the perfect opportunity that first day."

"Why would you think I'd do that?" I said, astonished.

"Dahveed! I woke up with my shoulder on fire, and someone at my throat. What else would I think? And I do not like waking up thinking that someone is trying to murder me in my sleep!"

I smiled in spite of my uncertainty. From the way he stood and talked, I knew he was fighting for my trust, but I also knew how persuasive this man could be and how much I wanted to give in to him. When I glanced at the forest again, that calm reassurance from Yah remained steady and clear.

"I didn't start thinking that way again until after you beat me here, in mock battle," Jonathan continued. "The way you fought, the presence that I felt with you, made me wonder. The king of Israel must be a warrior to keep the people safe, and I realized you were just that. But out there on the battlefield with Goliath, I knew."

I still struggled to understand. "But you protected me after that. You saved me from your abbi!"

"Will your stubborn hill mind never understand, Dahveed?" he asked almost angrily. "Don't you think I know what happened that day? Yahweh didn't just give you the victory over Goliath—He gave you the kingdom, and all of us along with it. It's yours!"

"But I don't want it!" I exclaimed. "Hassar, please believe me. I don't want it!"

"I know," he said wryly, "and that's what *I* don't understand."

A thousand things ran through my head, suddenly weaving together into a complete picture, climaxed by the hassar's enthusiasm for the trade opportunities and what they could mean for Israel, and the way he ground his fists into his hips right now. I couldn't have stayed standing if my life had depended on it. Collapsing to the ground, I watched him from where I sat on my cloak.

"You do want the throne, though, don't you?" I whispered.

He nodded.

The irony of it brought a short laugh from me. "Take it, please! Let me go back to my father's sheep."

A smile twisted his mouth, too. "You're very generous, Dahveed, but is it yours to give?"

"No."

"Nor is it mine to keep. It's Yahweh's, and I will not go against my God."

I looked up at him. Could it be that simple? Were we just two friends that both put loyalty to Yahweh and His will above all else? It would explain so much about the way that Jonathan had treated me, what he asked of me—and didn't ask.

Just then he stepped toward me, and I stood up, unable to keep myself from edging a little closer to the trees.

Pausing, he studied me for a long time. "Is it really this hard just to trust me, Dahveed?"

I didn't know what to say. Why should he let me live? Especially now?

"But then, how can you?" he finally went on. "And what I had to do a few days ago didn't help. I knew as soon as 'bekor' came out of your mouth that you thought I had turned on you and thrown you out as Eliab did. If that's the kind of treatment you've had all your life, how am I ever going to get you to believe me?

"But I am going to get a five-pound brass earring made and shackle it to your neck if you keep lowering your head like that," he finished, his voice angry.

I jerked my head up.

"At least you believe that much of what I say," he said, noticing my reaction. "Have you concluded yet that I'm not going to execute you in the next three seconds?"

Flushing, I nodded.

Curiosity appeared in his eyes. "Why? You seem convinced that I might turn on you tomorrow. Why not now?"

I took a deep breath. "Yah keeps saying you're not a danger."

"How is it that you've come to trust Him in the face of everything else?"

"He wishes to use me. I'm no good to Him dead."

Jonathan shook his head. "What could be more simple?" He stared at me, and I got more and more uncomfortable while I tried to keep my head from bobbing up and down.

Every time it lowered, I saw that earring. At the same time, I knew he was angry that I had not trusted him, and the only way I knew to appease him was to humble myself as I always had to Eliab. But doing that disturbed him more. I was so twisted up inside that I didn't know what to do, and the memory of what I felt when I thought he had cut me off made me shudder.

"From the way you're fighting to keep your head up, you believe my threats about what will happen if you don't," Jonathan mused. "But why don't you believe me when I say that I will not go against my God? Isn't my duty to Him higher than my duty to you?"

I looked down again, then jerked my head back up and glanced away instead, too knotted up inside to speak.

"Answer me, Dahveed."

Trapped, I looked around desperately, trying to still my shaking. "I don't understand, adoni," I said, fighting for some way out of this mess.

"You understand perfectly, Dahveed," he told me, eyes narrowed. "Either you are questioning my honor, or you are not."

"I am not, Hassar."

"For any reason?"

"No, Hassar!"

His gaze bored into me. "I think I'll hold you to that," he said slowly. "It's time you stop denying who and what you are."

Setting the end of his bow against his instep, he bent it, unstringing it. Then he took the quiver off his shoulder and held them out for me to take. The gesture was so natural that I responded without thinking, approaching and accepting them. Then he unfastened his cloak, letting it drop, and went fishing for the ties to the decorated ceremonial cuirass he had on.

Knowing how hard they were to deal with, I asked, "Want some help?"

"It would be easier," he said, holding out his arms as he did for Dara, and I untied the straps, assisting him out of the armor. Again he handed it to me. I jerked a little when his hands went to his sword, but he just unfastened it, along with the matching dagger, and held those out to me also. Taking them, I put everything on the ground. As he stripped off the sar's meil and handed that to me, I took it slowly, wondering what was happening. When his girdle followed, I didn't know what to think.

For a moment he stared at the belt knife in his hand. "If you don't mind, I'll keep this."

"As you like, Hassar," I said, completely lost. I glanced at the clothing in my hands and down at the weapons and armor on the ground. By the time I looked back, he was halfway out of his robe. "What are you doing, adoni?" I gasped.

"Showing you who Yahweh says that you are, and who I am," he said, tossing his robe into my arms. "Those belong to you."

The sunlight glinted off the gold on the sword and dagger hilts, and blazed on the embroidery of the meil. The fringes on the robe shook[4] because I did, and the colors swam before my eyes. "Hassar?"

"I am called Jonathan," he replied, standing in his cotton undergarment, arms to his sides, watching me steadily.

As I swayed, something twisted in my stomach. Jonathan had just given me everything that marked him as Hassar Israel, literally stripping himself of his status and honor and giving it to me, making me into what he had been.[5] He waited as I fought to deny what had happened. Dazed, I raised my eyes. "I don't understand. Why are you doing this?"

"Because *you* are Yahweh's mashiah, adoni. Not I."

I could hardly breathe, let alone think what to answer him. "I'm not—I'm not your adon, Hassar," I managed to say, unable to meet his gaze.

"I am called Jonathan, and as the mashiah, you are adon to my father, let alone me."

"Shaul is mashiah. You are his son. You want the throne! I don't!" I protested wildly.

"Yahweh has rejected Shaul, and Israel's throne is His to give to whom He wills. I do not go against my God!"

"Why are you doing this to me?" I repeated, trying to control my voice.

"Because I seem to be the only one able to provide a shattering enough earthquake to get your attention! If you were anointed as nagid for Israel like Shaul, then you need to—"

I turned my head away, then cursed myself as Jonathan broke off to study me.

"You were not anointed as nagid, were you? What were you anointed as?"

"Hassar, please don't—"

"I am called Jonathan," he said for the third time.

"Adoni, I—"

"I am not your adon."

He was relentless. I could hardly hold on to the garments in my arms. Cold sweat broke out all over me, and I looked longingly at the trees just steps away. I did not want this to happen! Didn't he understand that? "What do you want of me?"

"I want you to acknowledge who you are, who *Yahweh* says you are. Tell me, Mashiah."

I couldn't. I couldn't even look at what I held in my arms, let alone him, stripped as he was. Didn't he understand that I didn't want to face the knowledge he was forcing on me? To outrank the hassar? The king? So long as I hadn't spoken it, I could go on being what I was used to, staying where I was comfortable. Fighting against the admission with everything that I had, I fell to my knees.

"*Get up!*" Jonathan's voice lashed at me. "Don't you ever do that again," he raged as I sprang to my feet. "You are Yahweh's mashiah, second only to Him! How dare you dishonor what He has done for you! You are *not* Ben-geber! Who are you, Mashiah?"

Shaking my head, I backed away like a ram pulling against a tether. Why did he demand this? What difference could it make? Shutting my eyes to beg Yah to stop this somehow, I got a sudden picture of the dragonfly writhing as it fought to break the last tie to its old shell. The image froze me. Is that what was happening here? What Yahweh wanted to happen? Was I fighting to *remain* bound in the shell of my childhood, in the confines of Eliab's idea of where I belonged?

"*Tell me who you are, Mashiah!*" Jonathan commanded.

Memories welled up inside, bringing again the incredible filling that I had experienced as my God took possession of me at my anointing. I tightened my hands on the clothing. Before that powerful Presence, Jesse's bekor faded into insignificance. I looked directly into Jonathan's challenging gaze. "I am the dahveed, anointed king for Yahweh."

As I said the words, a dazzling light blinded me for a moment, and it seemed as if the last pieces of a confining prison fell away, and I could finally stretch and grow as I must in order to take the place that Yahweh had set before me.

Jonathan held my gaze as he knelt to me. "In Yahweh's name, cut a covenant with me, Mashiah."

Clinging to Yah's presence, I looked away. I had claimed my status. Why did Jonathan want more?

"Adoni, swear there will be Yahweh's hesed and friendship between you and me," he insisted.

I shifted on my feet, shying away from the thought. Why did he want something so irrevocable as a covenant, marking me forever as his superior?

"Grant me my request, Mashiah. Cut a covenant with me." He was not going to let me refuse.

"I will cut a covenant if you will still be my older brother," I said finally, perversely trying to keep as much the same as I could while I dealt with this new change.

"If my acting as older brother is commanded by you, adoni, I will, of course, obey."

"If that's what it takes," I sighed, then noticed the wicked gleam in his eyes. "Oh, get up, Jonathan." Irritation swept through me. "You're as impossible as Ethan! He made me do the same thing."

"Ethan knows?" he asked as he stood. Then he chuckled. "His whole band knows, don't they?"

"Yes. When I left the roeh's presence, I ran to the god-places. The scent of the oil is unmistakable. I assume that you won't require the full cutting ceremony?"

"The usual will do, once you get dressed," he replied coolly, taking the clothing from me and holding out his robe.

"The girdle and the meil," I bargained. "The robe and cuirass are too big, and I don't need them any more than I needed your father's armor in the Elah Valley."

"All right."

I dressed in Jonathan's girdle and meil, adding his sword and dagger upon his insistence. Collecting my belt knife, I slipped it in place, then stood back. "Are you satisfied?"

He looked me over. "Now we can swear."

"Not until you're ready." Picking up his robe, I held it out to him.

"Adoni, that is yours."

I gave him his own stare. "And if I want you to wear it, are you going to argue?"

The corners of his mouth twitched. "It would seem, on occasion, that southern hill men really can learn with reasonable speed!"

Once he had his robe tied with my girdle, I helped him into the cuirass again, then stepped back. "*Now* we're ready," I said.

Taking out the dagger, I knelt, and Jonathan did also. Placing it on the grass with the point toward me, I began, "I, Dahveed ben Jesse, swear in Yahweh's name this day that I will forever hold Yahweh's hesed and friendship toward Jonathan ben Shaul to preserve his life." I hesitated a little, and then went on. "I also swear this day that I will never stretch out my hand and *take* that which has belonged to Jonathan or his house. May Yahweh my God require this of my hand and make me slaughtered as an animal if I ever do not do as I have sworn."

Then I turned the dagger point toward Jonathan.

"I, Jonathan ben Shaul, swear in Yahweh's name this day that I will forever return Yahweh's hesed and friendship to Dahveed ben Jesse to preserve his life. I also swear this day that I will never *withhold* from Dahveed and his house whatever has belonged to me that Yahweh shall give him. May Yahweh my God require this of my hand and make me slaughtered as an animal if I ever do not do as I have sworn."

"Let Yahweh witness what we have sworn today," I said, taking up the dagger as we stood. Jonathan held out his arm, and I gripped it, turning to him as we embraced.

When we separated, I started to take off the meil, but Jonathan stopped me.

"No. It's yours."

"As you wish, Hassar," I said, bowing slightly. "Keep what I have given you, also."

"I will, Dahveed," he replied, bowing as I had.

We picked up our cloaks, and both of us fastened them fully. Then I handed Jonathan my bow and quiver and took his, and we went back to Gibeah.

---

[1] See Cultural Notes: Shalom.
[2] See Cultural Notes: Harp or lyre.
[3] See Cultural Notes: Fringe.
[4] See Cultural Notes: Clothing and honor.

CHAPTER 6

Michal climbed the stairs to the battlements in the darkness, her thoughts tumbling over one another. What had happened out in the hills today between her brother and the zammar? They had looked so odd coming through the fortress gate, but she couldn't figure out why. And she could have sworn that when Jonathan left this morning, he'd had on his ceremonial sword and dagger set. But they weren't there when he'd greeted her upon his return.

Something made her look down the wall, and she saw two figures slipping toward the northeast storerooms. She faded back into the shadows of the corner just as the clouds uncovered the moon. The zammar and his servant hesitated a bit, then disappeared into the shadows as they'd done last time. On impulse she hurried to the north wall. Not long after, she saw a flicker of movement at the northeast corner of the town. Michal frowned. Whatever had happened had sent the zammar to see the roeh again. Below her in the king's private courtyard, she thought a door closed, and she waited, certain that Jonathan would join her before long.

She resumed her pacing. Half an hour later, still alone, she glanced south, and the moonlight shining around the edge of a cloud flickered off something across the narrow valley on the training ground. *That's where Jonathan has gone.* Quickly she headed down the stairs to the gates.

Accompanied by a sentry, she hurried along the road to the training ground. Once there, she dismissed the guard at the circle where the swordsmen trained, going on to the archery range.

Jonathan stood with his right side to the target, sighting down an arrow. She waited until he let it fly. It hit very close to the center.

"Good shot," she said softly.

"It's a good bow. What are you doing out here at this hour?"

"Same thing you are."

He pulled another arrow from the quiver and shot again.

"Having trouble sleeping?" she asked.

"Not because of Nemuel," he replied, referring to the nightmares that he sometimes had about the death of his childhood friend. Another arrow flew to the mark. "How long have you been up?"

She glanced at the moon. "More than an hour."

"Did Dahveed leave?"

"Not long after I came out."

Jonathan lowered the bow. "Good. He needs someone to talk to."

"And you don't?"

"Michal Sahrah, I don't want to rob our mother of her youngest daughter."

"Jonathan Hassar, Yahweh appears to have chosen us both to keep the king from more dishonor toward Israel's God."

For a long time he didn't speak. Then he put his arm around her and pulled her to his side. "What would I do without you, Michal?" he said, his voice breaking.

Michal bit her lip. Jonathan was suddenly shaking beside her, and the pain in his voice tore her heart. What could have upset him so badly? It felt as if a dam inside him had burst, and the emotion in him rushed out.

He doubled over, then eased himself to the ground, and Michal crouched down beside him, thinking frantically. It had to be connected to the zammar. But Jonathan was acting as if he had betrayed the king!

What was this about? Searching her memory, she saw again in her mind the zammar and her brother returning from their hunt. She caught her breath. *The zammar had come through the gate first.* And when she had accidentally bumped into him after greeting Jonathan, she had felt a sword underneath the cloak. That's why their cloaks had been closed! If Dahveed had been wearing Jonathan's sword, he probably had the meil as well. Which meant . . .

"You bowed to him, didnt you?" she whispered, her voice trembling.

"What makes you say that?"

"I figured out quite a while ago that he's the mashiah, Jonathan."

Her brother barely nodded. "It was the only thing I could do. My tongue betrayed me."

"Did he threaten you?" Michal asked unsteadily.

Her brother laughed. "Quite the opposite! It was all I could do to convince him I wasn't going to cut his throat if he got within my reach. I told him I knew he was Yahweh's mashiah, and then—What else could I do, Michal?" he finished savagely.

"Nothing, Jonathan. We both know that. What will he do?"

The hassar shrugged. "I'm beyond caring tonight. If he killed me right now, I'd thank him for doing it. How can I face Abbi tomorrow? He trusts me now more than he ever has. If the king knew what I've done, he'd kill me. And this time I deserve it."

Tears wet her brother's cheeks, and she sat beside him, pressing as close as she could, her heart breaking for him. Why was he the one who had to be torn apart by what was happening? Why didn't Yahweh pick on someone else?

Jonathan put his arm around her again, his shaking finally subsiding. "You know, at first I thought I'd hate whoever was anointed in my place. But I love Dahveed, Michal. Since I can't have the throne, there's no one else I'd rather see there.

"He's become my brother and more. That eases my heart after days like today. That and having the best sister that Yahweh ever made."

Her brother's arm was tight and hard with his grip across her shoulders. "Don't worry so, Jonathan," she said softly. "You may have done things that would make Abbi angry if he knew, but in the end, they will bring good to us, because you have always honored Yahweh first. Surely He can see your heart and will honor you so that our house will not be forgotten."

The hassar sat motionless beside her. "Yahweh, grant us hesed as You promised," he murmured, and they sat in silence, watching the clouds play with the moon.

Another cloud drifted by. They were getting thicker, and I waited in the darkness in Roeh Shamuel's private courtyard, wondering if I'd ruined everything by my actions that afternoon.

Minutes later, Ahiam and I rose at the same time, both of us hearing the roeh's door opening. A torch appeared, and the Habiru and I drew back even farther into the shadows. My retainer knew what had happened today, and the look on his face when I took off the cloak and he saw me in the hassar's meil and with his ceremonial weapons was indelibly imprinted in my thoughts. I didn't have to tell him not to reveal this to anyone, not even Ethan, but I did anyway. He just nodded, too dumbfounded to speak.

The roeh said a few words of farewell and urged the man to take the torch with him. When his visitor had disappeared down the street and the light from the torch had disappeared between the houses, a voice commented from the darkness, "You are a very patient man, son of Jesse. Come in."

Ahiam and I approached the door, both of us instinctively staying in the shadows. On occasion Shaul still had spies watching Roeh Shamuel.

Shamuel preceded us into the house, and Ahiam shut the door as we entered. I followed the dim light coming from the single oil lamp illuminating the room where Shamuel received visitors.

He waited for me, sitting on the cushions as always, the scent of incense still lingering in the air and the lamplight winking off the embroidery of his meil. The sight of the old prophet, his knowing eyes questioning mine, brought the events of the day crashing down on me, and I nearly fell as I bowed to the floor, tears streaming from my eyes.

"Something indeed has happened," he said, his deep voice soothing. "Come near, Dahveed. There is wine here and some of the dried Tekoa figs you love so well. Tell me what has you in such confusion."

After taking the place opposite him on the cushions, I steadied myself enough to drink some of the wine.

"Now, what happened?"

"The hassar commanded me to tell him who I was, and I did," I said, my voice shaking with the memory of Jonathan handing me his life.

Shamuel's eyes widened.

"I—I made a covenant with him, too," I confessed, wanting to get everything over with as quickly as possible.

"Did you? In Yahweh's name?"

Wondering how big a mistake I'd made, I nodded.

"Hmmm. Start at the beginning, Dahveed."

After I'd told him everything I could remember, he stroked his beard and stared at the flame in the lamp. "What do you think about what you've done?" he asked, the coil of his long hair shifting down his back as he turned to me.

"I'm afraid, Roeh. Has the hassar really known who I was for so long? Can I truly trust him? Is this of Yahweh, or have I strayed from the path He set for me? I know my highest loyalty must be to Him and the task He has given me to do. I don't know if what I've done has helped or hindered."

Shamuel smiled gently. "As to your first question, I'd say most likely. There isn't much of importance in this kingdom that doesn't reach the hassar's ear sooner or later. He's a canny man. As to your second, Yahweh Himself answered it earlier. As to the last, did this covenant interfere with your duty to Yahweh?"

"I don't think so, Roeh."

"Then what is really the problem, Dahveed?"

"He gave me his station and honor. Made me his superior!" Again I trembled, clenching my teeth to keep them from chattering.

"You *are* his superior, Dahveed. When Yahweh took possession of you as His king, He raised you to the highest rank in the land. You knew this had to happen sooner or later."

Not the roeh, too! I froze inside, putting my head in my hands and rocking with the distress tearing at me. "But I don't want to be! I can't!" I burst out. Tears spilled down my cheeks again. I bent my head and let them fall. What was I going to do?

"So that is the trouble. You were not ready. Well, perhaps because of the hassar's slip of the tongue, this was a bit premature, but I don't think by much. Dahveed, tell me this. How does knowing that the hassar realizes your place really change anything?"

I looked at him in amazement. It changed everything! It had to.

Shamuel stroked his beard again, eyes intent on my face. "Remember, *he* hasn't gained any new knowledge—only you have."

But—but— I stumbled around in my thoughts. Surely this must change something, mustn't it?

"Things might actually be easier now" Shamuel went on, still watching me. "You can learn from him without concealing why, and he can teach without inventing a reason. If you are to fulfill Yahweh's task, you must accept the place that He has for you and conduct yourself in such a manner as to bring honor to the One who gave it to you. There's no one better than the hassar to teach you this. And if I know Shaul's oldest son, he will do a very thorough job."

"Of that, you can be sure!" I laughed a bit shakily. My breath came easier, and I rubbed my eyes with my palms, relief spilling through me. "Yahweh's time is not yet, then. I am still to wait and learn."

"Yes."

Now that it had been pointed out to me, I did see that the only change was in my knowledge of how much I owed the hassar. Like a silly sheep I had been frightened by something that had been there all along. "Thank you, Roeh," I said, feeling a little foolish. "I should not have taken up your time with such a little thing."

"The little thing was useful in that it brought you to me with the big thing. You made a covenant in Yahweh's name, Dahveed, and you made it as Yahweh's mashiah. That is a very big thing." Roeh Shamuel's eyes grew dark and serious. "Do not *ever* even think to break that covenant. Only Yahweh Himself can overrule what you pledged to Jonathan Hassar. You have bound yourself, forever, and Yahweh is a God who will hold everyone to account, especially His mashiah."

His voice made me shiver.

"Given how much you need to learn, I would discourage you from making any more covenants," he added.

I paled. "Do you think I have hindered Yahweh's will?"

Shamuel considered. "Because of the hassar's integrity, I don't believe so. But the next person who tries to maneuver you into a binding agreement might not be as dedicated to Adonai's plans as the hassar."

"Yes, Roeh."

The lamp sputtered, nearly out of oil. "We have talked long, and you must go, Dahveed. Come here and let me bless you."

I knelt before him, and as he put his hand on my head, that welcome assurance of Yahweh's presence stole over me, bringing a sense of peace. With my God's help, I should be able to survive the newest changes in my life.

But the next day, I wasn't so sure. My troubles began when I was dressing and trying to decide how soon I could send the weapons and clothing that Jonathan had given me south to the forest house for safekeeping. The door opened, and Ahiam stepped in. "He will expect you to make some acknowledgment of his gifts, geber," my servant said, seeing all of Jonathan's things still on our small three-legged table. "Where honor is rightly given, it must be accepted. You know this, Dahveed."

I sighed. "But if I wear these, I am laying claim to the hassar's place, and the first man who sees me will kill me."

"No, you can't wear the meil or sword and dagger, but the girdle is acceptable."

"But that will bring me a sar's status, and people will grant me equal authority with them!"

"I think that was the point, Dahveed," Ahiam observed dryly.

I sat down on the clothes chest, my hands stroking the fine dark-blue wool of the girdle. Single twining strands of gold and silver thread decorated its full length, complementing the magnificent, colorful embroidery of the matching meil. Long tassels hung from the ends. "I just can't believe I deserve this, Ahiam," I admitted in a low voice.

The Habiru warrior's face darkened. "There are times, Dahveed, when I could curse Jesse's bekor for pounding into you your lowly status, which, I might add, was never your true place. Would you disgrace the hassar—and Yahweh—by refusing this?" He stalked out the door, shutting it with great care behind him.

Unbidden to my mind came a picture of a sheep, balking at going past a tree for no reason at all. I bowed my head. "Be with me, Yah," I whispered. I tied the girdle around my waist, folding and tucking the ends to at least hide the tassels.

Slinging the harp case over my shoulder, I left the private courtyard just as a man came through the fortress gate, looking even more uncomfortable than I felt. The guard spoke briefly to him, gesturing toward the throne room, then turned to someone else. The geber walked away uncertainly. Then he cast a quick glance at me, and I smiled in return, walking up to him. "How may I help?" I asked, noting he was close to my age.

"Please, geber, if you could direct me," he began, and then he saw the girdle and turned a fiery red. "Pardon me, adon—sar," he stammered. "I mean to bother—uh, *didn't* mean to bother . . ." He trailed off into confusion, obviously wishing the daily wind across Gibeah's hill would blow him away.

"Think nothing of it, geber. You are looking for someone?"

"No, adon—I mean yes, adon. I mean—I'm looking for my abbi." His face reddened again, and I had the feeling that he'd be scuffing his toe in the dirt if he hadn't been too terrified to move.

"And his name is?"

"Whatever you say, adon."

I blinked. The man had his teeth clenched and was staring at the girdle and looking more embarrassed every second.

Here was exactly the kind of thing that I'd been afraid would happen if I wore this thing, and I didn't have the slightest idea what I could do. Then something I'd seen Sar Ishvi do came to mind. Casually I put my hand on his shoulder and waited. The physical contact jarred him into looking wildly at my face, and I held his gaze.

"I do not normally eat visitors at first meeting," I said gravely.

After a second of astonishment, the corners of his mouth twitched, and he recovered some of his poise. "Yes, adon. Please forgive my confusion and ignorance."

"There is nothing to forgive. We all have to learn our way around at first, and the hassar doesn't take kindly to those who make things difficult for others."

"No, Jonathan wouldn't," he agreed, straightening as I took my hand from his shoulder. "I'm called Adriel ben Barzillai, and I have a message for my abbi, who is to meet with the king today."

"Then we should check with the scribe in the anteroom," I said, moving through the crowd toward the door. "Where are you from?"

"Gilead, north near Jabesh."

"Then you've had a good two-days' journey," I commented, wondering why the crowd parted so easily until I remembered the girdle. "The king's concubine, Baalah Rizpah, is from that area. Do you know her family?"

"Yes, adon. Her abbi, Aiah, heads another branch of our clan, and Hassarah Ahinoam is my father's cousin."

The guard at the door greeted me respectfully, then bowed, his eyes wide as he noticed Jonathan's girdle. I continued into the room, the scribe at the low table by the hangings quickly becoming expressionless when he saw what I wore.

"May I serve you, adon?" he asked.

"This geber is looking for Barzillai of Jabesh-gilead. Has he gone before the king yet?"

"He remained in the throne room after the meal. Some elders are with the king now. You can go in when they leave, adon."

"All right. We'll wait outside."

While we waited, Adriel and I sat on the stone bench on the west wall. The Gileadite studied me, his quick eyes noticing several scars. "I would appreciate knowing your name, adon. You have been most kind to me."

I swung the harp case from my shoulder and set it on the ground in front of me. "I'm the king's zammar," I said casually. "And during my first days here, I tripped over myself before the sars or Sahrah Michal so many times that I came near to being the jest of the court."

Adriel grinned crookedly. "Somehow that does make me feel better. Is that Merab?" he asked, glancing up.

"Yes," I replied, as Shaul's bekorah walked across the courtyard with her immi. Something about the way Adriel said her name made me examine him closely. There was a wistful expression in his eyes, quickly banished by an ironic smile. That brightened into a welcome as the two women noticed us and hurried over.

"Adriel, I can't believe it!" Merab exclaimed, holding out her hand to the man.

We both stood, and he took the hand, bowing gracefully. "Bekorah, you are truly the most beautiful woman in the land."

"Oh, you wicked boy!" she protested, laughing, and giving him a hug. It was followed by one from Ahinoam. I looked away, the longing for my sister Abigail and my own immi sweeping over me suddenly despite the fact that I'd had news of home recently.

"I see you've met the zammar," Ahinoam said.

"Yes, he has been guiding me through the intricacies of the court." He sighed. "I'm afraid I'm a burden to him."

"Then come and be a burden to me," Merab said, resting her arm affectionately on Adriel's. "I haven't heard the news from Jabesh for so long, I hardly know who to remember anymore. Can you talk now?"

Adriel shook his head. "No, I have a message I must get to Abbi."

"I hope you don't have to wait too long," she commented. "Abbi started court later than usual. Barzillai and Jonathan were back at their old feud, trading outrageous stories, and you know how they can get."

Just then, I saw a guard look around the corner and start our way.

"I think we can go in now," I announced. "If you will excuse us, sahrahs?"

"I'll look for you later, Adriel," Merab said.

"I'll come. Shalom, Hassarah," he added to Ahinoam.

As the two women left, the wistful look returned to his face.

I guessed that he loved Merab, and the fact that the bekorah had been promised to me was a complication I thought the geber could live without, so we walked in silence.

Once in the throne room, I sat down on my stool, wishing I had worn a mantle or cloak to hide the girdle that drew stares from every eye in the room and made me feel extremely conspicuous. But the look in Jonathan's eye implied that I'd have to wear it for a few days at least. I sighed.

CHAPTER 7

Standing at her favorite spot on the battlements, Michal chewed on her lip. The wind swirled around from the east, and she shivered, pulling her cloak closer. Beyond the east wall houses hugged the hillside, and a rocky ridge like a finger bridged the valley to the steep ascent across it. She fretted in vexation. Merab was destined to marry a warrior though she hated violence and killing, and she was herself doomed to watch the man she loved go to her own sister. Just thinking of that set every bone in her body aching with protest, and, if she was honest, other parts of her, too!

"If that's Your plan, I don't think much of it, Yahweh," she muttered, beginning to pace. Even though she'd managed to delay Merab's wedding, she still hadn't come up with any way to convince the king to give Dahveed to her.

If only her sister were already married! She nearly kicked the wall in frustration, swinging sharply around to stride in the other direction. But who would marry the bekorah, knowing the prowess of the man they would be taking her from? Not that Dahveed would take offense. He should, since it would be a grave insult, but after watching the way he kept the hassar's girdle all tucked up whenever he wore it, she knew that he wouldn't! She would make certain *that* changed once she married him. *If* she married him.

Whipping around, Michal stared again at the fortress residence. If Merab married the dahveed, she'd have to stay here and endure the torment that overwhelmed her every time their father started prophesying,* something that would send her sister to an early grave. She needed a nice rich farmer from far away who wanted lots of children and had lots of servants to make the work lighter.

A firefly that she had disturbed lit up next to her hand. She turned away, looking longingly toward Jebus. If they ruled from Jebus, her father wouldn't have had to fight the Philistines and thus would never have promised Merab to Dahveed. And likely she could marry whomever she wanted, for the Araunah was the most powerful ruler in the land. Only because he let him, could Shaul rule anything at all. Jonathan might laugh at the very thought, but Michal knew that someday Dahveed would conquer Jebus, and if she was married to him, she would know exactly what it was like to look at the world from the most perfect fortress ever built.

She stared at the corner of the wall, realizing that she was right back where she had started. How was she going to persuade her abbi to let her marry the dahveed? If only Jonathan would help, Abbi would be much easier to handle, but she probably shouldn't count on that. He thought the king should have given Merab to Dahveed the previous fall.

There was always Balak, she thought reluctantly. Even though Jonathan had not been pleased when she spoke to him the first time, the servant might be useful if he went with the king to war again.

But what if the king stayed here? She eyed the stone parapet beside her. Abbi was getting older, and Immi would be very relieved to have him stay home during the war season. Not only would it give Dahveed a chance to prove himself on his own, but she would have more time to work on her father and come up with someone else for Merab to marry.

Immi might even help. Talking to Barzillai had been so good for Merab tonight. She had come alive, hearing all the news about crops, goats, children, and weaving. Too bad Barzillai was married. He'd be perfect for Merab. His home was two days north, and he was rich and lived exactly the kind of life that Merab longed for.

Michal suddenly froze. Not Barzillai—Adriel! He could take Merab far away, give her lots of children, was wealthy enough to have several servants, and would be protected by his father's reputation. Adriel would certainly be delighted to have her. After all, he had loved her all his life, something she was astonished that Merab hadn't noticed.

"Thank You, Yahweh," she whispered. "Adriel will be perfect." Her thoughts raced, sorting through the options. But she kept running into the same obstacle—Jonathan. He would be more protective of the zammar's honor now than even the king's, and it would be impossible to do what she planned unless he consented.

Whirling around in exasperation, she took one step and ran full tilt into Jonathan. His quick reactions saved her from a fall as she bounced off him.

"I must have really interrupted something! You haven't bounced off me like that in years," he chuckled. "What are you doing up here, Michal? It's past midnight."

"Then why aren't you in bed?" she snapped, her exasperated thoughts spilling over into speech. There was just no way around her brother.

"I *was* in bed," he informed her. "Then Immi found Achsah fast asleep in your room, waiting for you to come. What's had you fretting up here for hours?"

She was going to have to tell him, and she was desperate enough to get down and beg if it came to that.

Suddenly she found herself shaking, squeezed tight against

Jonathan's side.

He looked down at her. "Are you cold?"

"No."

"Then what is it?"

"I love him, Jonathan."

"What do you mean?"

"Dahveed. I want to marry him, so much that I can't think of anything else. Merab will be miserable with him. He'll be fighting most of his life just like you and Abbi. And Merab would hate it!" Michal couldn't stop the tears, much as she tried, and her brother pulled her close again while she sobbed into his cloak.

"So that's why you have been thinking up all kinds of delays for the marriage," he said gently. "When did this happen?"

"When he came back from the war season last fall. He was dressed for the feast in that dark-red robe, and I've never felt anything like that before."

"No, I don't imagine you have."

The hint of amusement in his tone irritated her. "Don't you dare laugh at me, Jonathan!" she said, punching him.

"I'm not," he replied, catching her wrist. "But you do have to admit that the idea of you feeling that way about any man takes getting used to."

"You don't have to tell me that. I still don't know what to do with it, except marry the man!" She dried her face on her cloak and sighed.

"What do you want from me?"

"Help me convince Abbi to marry him to me, not Merab."

"But, Michal, the king promised his bekorah to the man who killed Goliath."

"Does that mean everyone has to be miserable for the rest of their lives? Merab will be, and she's old enough to be Dahveed's mother! How would you feel if you were going to marry someone Immi's age? I'm at least somewhat close to his years. And like Dahveed said, a reward needs to be something the receiver appreciates, too! Please, Jonathan, you've got to help me!"

"But the king said—"

"The king has said lots of things, and you've quietly changed things a bit to make it better for everyone. That's all I want. Just switch daughters. Please, Jonathan."

The hassar sighed, shifting restlessly. "Well, he does seem to pay more attention to you than Merab."

Michal sensed her brother was weakening. "He always has. Immi will feel better about it too. You know how worried she's been. She'd like to see Merab away from here. That won't happen if Merab marries Dahveed."

"Well—"

"Please, Jonathan," Michal pleaded, pressing closer to him. "Immi will be much happier, you know Merab will, and so will I and Dahveed. I've never really asked you for anything before, but I just have to have this!"

"I don't know, Michal."

"If you don't want to say anything to Abbi, I won't ask you to," Michal continued, seizing her advantage. "Just let me see if I can persuade Abbi to give Dahveed to me. Can't you just stand back and give me a chance?"

"I—"

"Please, Jonathan?"

"All right," he gave in with a sigh. "You can try to persuade the king to give you to Dahveed. But be very certain that you don't bring dishonor on the family or Dahveed in the process."

"I'll be careful."

"I hope so. You can be very single-minded sometimes, Michal."

Balak looked up as another messenger entered the throne room, still breathing heavily from his run. With a sigh the servant filled a cup of wine to take to the man, something it seemed he had done today every time he turned around. Court had started late because the royal family had lingered over their good-byes to Barzillai's people, and since an emissary from Hamath was expected that afternoon, everyone was scrambling now to get the essential judicial business done before the noon meal.

"What is that you read?" Shaul asked, his voice loud.

Everyone glanced up, surprised at the king's angry tone.

"Who dares excuse Gibeonites from their labor at the tabernacle?

Which town was it?"

"Chephirah, adoni."

"Look into this, Jonathan. The Gibeonites should not be excused! Look into this today! I want a report in the morning."

"Yes, adoni."

Balak saw the hassar clench his teeth as he made his way to Eshbaal's table. "Who's available for something like this?" Jonathan asked.

"We really don't have anyone," Eshbaal said doubtfully. "I suppose we could send one of the army commanders, but this really isn't a military question. It's harvest, so most everyone is at his estate."

"I'd better go, then," Jonathan decided. "Abbi is too upset to send just anyone."

"But the emissary," Eshbaal protested.

"Ishvi can take my place until—"

He didn't get to finish, for everyone heard the command to clear a path from the messenger running through the fortress gates.

"Open the south door," the king ordered the guard, who jumped to obey, and motioned the messenger to come up the outside stairs.

"Adoni Shaul," the man panted. "The emissary from Hamath approaches. He is nearly here on the Jebus highway."

"Here?" Shaul gasped.

"Go tell the hassarah to start preparing a meal," the hassar snapped to the scribe at the door. "You get the sars from the training ground," Jonathan continued, pointing to the messenger. "Balak, lay out what the king needs to wear. Michal, bring dried fruit, some of the good wine, and parched grain."

Everyone rushed to obey the hassar's orders, but Balak paused a moment to glance at the king to see what Shaul wanted to wear.

"Chephirah?" he heard Sar Eshbaal say in a strained voice, holding up the papyrus that pertained to that problem.

"Oh—send—send Dahveed," the hassar replied hurriedly. "Have a messenger give him the papyrus and tell him that he's the king's representative in this matter. King Shaul wants to know why these names were excused from their labor. Then get changed into your best robe and meil."

The hassar turned away from Sar Eshbaal. "Balak, bring a comb when you return to the throne room. My hair, at least, will need attention." The hassar took Shaul's arm, and they both hurried from the room, leaving Sar Eshbaal looking around frantically for a messenger.

"I'll find one," Balak offered, taking the papyrus.

Nodding gratefully, the younger sar hastily followed his brother out the door.

Balak hesitated just a moment more, thinking rapidly. Dahveed wouldn't know what to do as a king's representative, and that would only bring dishonor on Shaul, something Hassar Jonathan would have realized if he'd thought of it. Better to send Dahveed in a way that he was already used to. Let him just go as Shaul's general. At the door of the west ell the servant shoved the papyrus into a soldier's hand and said, "Give this to General Dahveed. He's to find out why these people were excused." Then he raced down the wall stairs, running through the private gate to the residence just as the king and the hassar pulled away from the knot of people at the anteroom door, Jonathan still issuing orders.

⊡⌁⊡

"You handled things smoothly tonight, Balak." Sahrah Michal smiled tiredly as she checked the passage by the storeroom to be certain that everything had been put away.

"Thank you, Sahrah," he replied, bowing slightly. The frantic preparations to entertain the emissary properly had been barely controlled chaos from his point of view. Kemosh had obviously blessed him again.

As he followed her outside, he saw Dahveed come through the fortress gate, trailed by Ahiam. The skirt of the general's robe was soiled and slashed open in front, and he was on foot. In the torchlight he looked as if he'd returned from a wine shop brawl, not an errand for the king.

"Dahveed, I was wondering when you'd . . ."

Balak jumped at the sound of the hassar's voice. He hadn't realized that Shaul's son was standing in the shadow of the anteroom.

"I believe I'll take your report in the anteroom now, Dahveed," Jonathan said smoothly after a short silence.

Balak shivered at the suppressed anger in the hassar's tone.

"Yes, Hassar," the young general replied, his body tense as he followed Jonathan through the door.

Balak heard the bar drop into place on the inside. Eyebrows raised, he loitered near the anteroom, ears cocked for any sound. But he heard nothing, and gradually the silence deepened until even the buzz and shrills of insects ceased. Uneasy, he glanced toward the fortress gate. The torches still burned, but the shadows seemed much darker than before. He edged toward the light, looking overhead, expecting to find that clouds had covered the sky. The stars gleamed back, but the anteroom seemed blanketed by an eerie black stillness.

Heart unaccountably pounding, the servant hurried from the gate, taking the steep path down the west side of the fortress hill instead of the road. Nearly running when he reached the street again, he shivered. Darkness seemed to spill over the fortress wall towering above, its coldness swirling around his feet as he rushed to his house and barred the door after himself. It was a long time before he could relax enough to get to sleep.

He woke the next morning relieved to hear the normal sounds of Judith moving around in the courtyard, preparing a quick morning meal. Her usual chatter on the way to the fortress soothed the last of the uneasiness from his mind even though he had no idea what she said to him.

Entering the anteroom, he stopped a moment, his hand still on the door, the excited murmur of tense conversation alerting him to something unusual. "What happened?" he asked the scribe at the table.

The man looked around and lowered his voice. "It's Dahveed. A messenger has just gone for Dara. They say Hassar Jonathan beat him so badly that he cannot rise from his bed! No one knows exactly why, but something happened last night. It looked as if there had been a battle in here when I arrived this morning!"

The hoofbeats of a hard-ridden mule pounded on the road outside the gate. Balak hurried to look outside. Dara leaped off the animal, which was heaving for breath from the run up the steep grade. Hassarah Ahinoam greeted him at Dahveed's door, and Sar Ishvi arrived shortly after. Reluctantly Balak went up the stairs to the throne room. Sahrah Michal was not in attendance, and he quickly filled the king's wine cup and added more fruit to the bowl by the throne. As he worked, he noticed that the hassar moved as if every muscle in his body was sore. And why was he wearing those two wide silver bracelets?

A scribe was halfway through a report when all sounds from the anteroom ceased. Balak clearly heard the footsteps as someone climbed the stairs. Hassarah Ahinoam appeared in the doorway, her back very straight and a white spot on each cheek. She nodded to the king and turned to her son. "Jonathan Hassar?"

"Yes, Hassarah," he replied, bowing a little.

"You will close court immediately. The king will be leaving shortly for Zelah." Her voice was uncompromising.

In amazement Balak glanced at the throne. Shaul had one hand up covering his lips, his interested eyes going from his wife to his son.

"But we have—"

"*Immediately, Jonathan ben Shaul!*"

"Yes, Immi!" her son agreed instantly, with the most bewildered look on his face that Balak had ever seen.

★ See Cultural Notes: Prophesying.

CHAPTER 8

Every muscle protesting, Jonathan climbed the outside stone stairs to the upper room of his private house near Zelah. He'd managed to stay on the mule during the ride only because the animal had the smoothest gait in the land.

"Shalom, geber," Nimshi greeted him from the doorway.

"What are you doing here?" Jonathan asked his newest arrow boy in surprise.

"I came ahead with the servants, geber." The boy's gaze was direct and grave, not filled with mischief as it usually was. The hassar wondered what was the matter. Everyone but his abbi had pointedly ignored him on the way here. Even the servants refused to look at him. If Nimshi was upset, too, it must be connected with Dahveed.

Jonathan walked into the coolness of the house and took off his sword. Nimshi hung it on the wall as Jonathan sat down and reached for the wine on the table. After a swallow or two, he put the jug back, his finger tracing the brown band around the white background. "Nimshi, is there anything wrong with the dahveed?"

Shifting his feet, the lad studied him doubtfully. "Don't you know?"

"I haven't seen Dahveed today."

"Is it true that you beat Dahveed last night?"

Jonathan's eyebrows shot up, and his head jerked around, making him wince. "Did Dahveed say I beat him?"

"I don't think so. But Sahrah Michal said you must have, because no one else could do that to him."

The hassar straightened in the three-legged chair. The core of last night's events would never leave him, but the details were getting hazier by the hour. It was only Yahweh's hesed that either of them had survived the battle that had overtaken them.

"Tell me about this, Nimshi," he commanded.

"Ahiam found him this morning so bruised all over that he couldn't get out of bed. One knee was swollen, he had a big lump under his left eye, and a cut inside his mouth. Dara said he might have broken ribs, too."

Jonathan leaned back in the chair, his heart sinking. He'd guessed right. Dahveed had tried to protect him far longer than he should have before yielding to his gift. "You have done well to tell me this, Nimshi."

The young Habiru left, and Jonathan stared after him. Then he eased off the wide silver bracelets he wore and stared at the swollen red marks of Dahveed's hands on his wrists. A shudder went through him at the fragmentary memories of the howling evil that had reached for him last night, and the searing light flashing forth to combat the darkness.

Later that evening, Grandfather Kish welcomed his son Shaul and grandsons to his estate, and the hassar was able to hide his own discomfort and worry in the general rejoicing of the clan. Kish had 10 uncles, so most of the countryside was related to Shaul one way or the other. Abner and his son, Jaasiel, had come with Dodi Ner, but Shaul didn't seem to notice. Once the meal was over, Jonathan couldn't stand the fawning attention of his cousin Shimei another minute, and he managed to pass the man on to Ishvi. Shimei was clearly delighted to be related to Israel's king, and Jonathan cringed when he thought of how the man must act around other people. Slipping outside for a moment, he found his grandfather in the courtyard.

"You are a fine man, Jonathan," Kish said, patting his hand when he walked over. "Shaul is blessed indeed with such sons. I questioned whether Ahinoam was a good choice for Shaul, but she has raised sons who know how to carry the honor given to them."

"Immi will be glad to know that, Grandfather."

"Too bad Shimei's mother didn't do the same," Kish went on. "He is nearly shameless with his posturing and demands. Shaul was wise to bar him from the court."

"Oh?"

"It was quietly done, a word only to the man's father, but it was enough. Now, what has happened between you and Abner?" Kish looked searchingly at his grandson. "You do not speak, and even Shaul has hardly acknowledged him."

"Abner let his anger bring dishonor to the king," Jonathan replied carefully. "At my father's request, I reminded him of his duty."

The older man's eyes sharpened. "Will Shaul ask him to lead the army this season?"

"I don't know. The king was very displeased."

"Will you stop talking to me as if I'm an ambassador and you're the hassar?" Kish said impatiently. "Sit down, lad, and answer my questions!"

"Grandfather, I cannot!" Jonathan protested.

"Pish-posh. If I keep Shaul up all night asking him, no one will thank me. Sit down."

Looking bemused, Jonathan sat. He gave his grandfather a rough outline of the situation, reserving many of the details, which he suspected the shrewd old man filled in anyway.

"More fool, Abner," Kish snorted when Jonathan finished. "At least he had the wit to take himself away. Well, when Shaul's anger cools, he'll have him back again."

"Yes," Jonathan said, hiding his private skepticism on that point.

"You look tired, Jonathan."

"I am, and with your permission, I would like to go."

"Only because I know you'll be back. Sleep well, lad. Shalom."

"Shalom, Grandfather."

He arrived at his own house before the night was half done, so bone-weary he could hardly stand, but his uncertainty would not let him rest. He was beginning to understand Dahveed's talk of the god-places. Something in him tonight sought to lead him away from the house, pulling him toward a dimly remembered oak higher in the hills to the west. He wanted to be alone, to ask for wisdom as he walked the thin line between duty to his father and loyalty to his God.

The oak was still there, the stump of a smaller tree at its foot offering a seat. Jonathan sat down, setting aside his bow and quiver. He got out the ashes he'd brought in a small pouch and smeared some on his forehead and the backs of his hands to begin his fast. Then he stared up at the stars.

"Grant me understanding of Your will, Yahweh."

The next morning was half gone when Jonathan heard someone approaching. He held still, hoping to be passed by, but the footsteps came directly to him.

"I see you remembered my oak tree," Immi said.

"Just barely," Jonathan admitted. Rising, he seated her where he had been. Then he eased down beside her, resting his head against his immi's knee, and she stroked his hair just as she used to after Nemuel died and his nightmares had been the worst.

"What happened about Chephirah?" she asked.

Leaning forward, Jonathan sighed, glad that he could confide in someone. "I lost my temper, Immi," he confessed. "I sent Dahveed to Chephirah as a king's representative, and he didn't even have the sense to ride there! He ran the forest trails like a Habiru, so of course when he arrived, no one believed he was on the king's business. The elders tried to arrest him, and he got into a brawl at the city gate before someone recognized him as Dahveed. Then he spent the rest of the afternoon wandering around the town in a torn robe, helped by a Philistine merchant! I exploded at him!" After staring off into the forest for a moment, he took a deep breath and chose his words carefully. "We are just now getting the tribes to work together. They will fall apart again if the king loses his authority. I didn't dare let the king's honor be treated lightly.

"What I don't understand is how Dahveed could have been that careless!" Jonathan added in exasperation. "He's always been so respectful. What happened?"

Immi stroked his hair again. "Dahveed has been a servant all his life, Jonathan. Showing respect to another is something he can do without thinking. Now suddenly he's on the other side of the situation. How would he know how to act?

"Think, Jonathan. Dahveed was a shepherd when he came to us, spending every day out in the hills with his sheep and the Habiru. He grew up in two worlds—on the outside of honor in one, and in another without honor as we know it. Then we thrust him into a third world, confined him inside walls, and put restrictions on his actions and words everywhere he turned."

Ahinoam sighed and gazed toward the forest. "Is he supposed to drop the habits of 18 years in a few months? You asked too much of him, Jonathan, and then condemned him when he failed. Yes, the dishonor to the king had to be rectified—you are right in that—but the first mistake was yours. Why did you make it?"

"Because he's much more than a servant! He's more than all of us!" Jonathan said in frustration, locking his arms around his knees to keep from pounding the ground.

His mother's hand stilled on his head. "Yes, I think so too. But do not confuse what he may become with what he is now. That, I think, is where you stumbled. Perhaps Yahweh sent him to us not only because Shaul needed him, but because Dahveed needed to learn. You, more than anyone else, have that task. It took you more than 20 years to learn to be the hassar, but I don't think Dahveed will have that much time, so teach him, Jonathan. There is so much he can learn only from you. Just be careful that you do not ask more than he can give, for he will attempt anything you set him to. As he did yesterday. In spite of everything, he did find out what you wanted, didn't he?"

"Yes," her son answered. "In the process of discovering that the Gibeonites had been excused because they were dead, he also uncovered the complete incompetency of the appointed overseer, and the corruption of the scribal assistant. That scribe, by the way, vanished from the house just before Dahveed found that he had embezzled nearly everything his employer owned."

"All that in one afternoon?" Immi's eyes twinkled.

"There's more," Jonathan sighed. "He also passed judgment on the elders at the gate for their part in disdaining the king's honor when he first arrived. The fine he levied was quite proper, given the circumstances. Then he topped it off by appointing the Philistine merchant as the new overseer. The entire situation was infuriating, but since I couldn't fault the investigation itself, I confirmed the appointment, as well as the fine," the hassar admitted with a rueful laugh.

"I'm glad you value him, my son. I was afraid when he first came, you know."

"Why?"

"You have been the people's hero since Michmash, and if the throne is to be transferred* by popular acclaim or military prowess, you would have been given it the instant Shaul died. Then Dahveed arrived, and his music and battle skills drew everyone to him. I feared there would be envy between you. But Yahweh did something I never expected. Dahveed is your son, isn't he?"

Jonathan closed his eyes. He should have known his immi would see that. "Yes," he admitted. "It doesn't seem as if I will have any other, so I have made him mine in my heart."

"It is good to have treasures in your heart."

At the faraway look in her eyes, Jonathan leaned back. "What treasures are in yours?"

She smiled sadly. "I wish we never had to go back to Gibeah."

"And give up being hassarah?"

"I am the daughter of a farmer, and I married a farmer, if you recall," she said tartly. "I would like nothing better than to get back to where I started. Your brother Ishvi would too."

Jonathan grinned. "What about Malchi?"

"He loves the army," Ahinoam admitted. "He would cheerfully

serve whatever king sat on the throne, so long as he got to fight. And Eshbaal is happier than he's ever been, keeping everything organized."

"But Merab would go with you."

"Yes," Immi said seriously. "I worry about her. She loves growing things and needs little ones around her."

"And what of Michal?" Jonathan continued, intrigued by such revelations.

"Michal is more than a little spoiled." Her voice was tart again.

"Surely she doesn't get her way in everything!"

"And who would dare cross her with you doting on her?" his mother stated, bringing her knuckles down smartly on the top of his head.

Rubbing the spot, he grinned again, then sobered. "She loves Dahveed, you know."

"I've noticed it."

"What do you think, Immi?"

"The king promised his bekorah."

"Don't talk to me like I'm the hassar. Talk to me like I'm 9 years old again," Jonathan said, turning to face her. "Do you think Merab would be miserable married to Dahveed?"

"Yes," Ahinoam sighed. "And I can't imagine that your father would intentionally condemn her to that. Something needs to be done soon, though. She's sad all the time now.

"Help me up, Jonathan," she added. "It's time I got back."

Jonathan assisted his mother off the old stump. "Let me escort you back to my house at least."

"I have an escort. Nimshi is an amusing little thing!"

"Amusing like a young bear!" Jonathan snorted. "He'll grow into the terror of this land all too soon!"

◧◰◧

From the roof of Jonathan's private estate Michal watched the last of the sunset's afterglow until Jonathan returned.

"Immi talked to you about Dahveed, didn't she?" she asked as her brother joined her.

"Yes."

"And did you tell her what really happened between you and

Dahveed?"

Jonathan shrugged. "Everyone knows what happened. I got angry with Dahveed. And I'm the only one who could have beaten him like that."

"I'm not blind, Jonathan. If you had raised your hand to Dahveed, it would have torn you up inside, just like it does when you have to go against Abbi. Now, what happened?"

Her brother didn't reply for a long time. "It was a good thing Merab was at Ishvi's house that night," he said at last. "I don't remember much after the demon returned."

Michal gasped. "But Abbi was fine!"

"It didn't attack Abbi. It struck me."

"You!" She clutched her brother, heart pounding.

"Yes. Dahveed had finished part of his report about Chephirah, and I couldn't believe what he'd done. I stood there thinking I was out of my mind to hand my throne to this rude sheepherder from the south who didn't even know how to wear a sar's girdle!"

He shuddered, and Michal put her arms around him.

"That's when the demon struck. I can remember only a whirling vortex of fire, a terrible howling darkness, and something in my mind telling me to kill. That I had to keep my throne. He didn't deserve it."

Michal squeezed tighter. "How did you defeat it?" she whispered.

"I couldn't. No matter how hard I fought, it was stronger than I and kept turning me against Dahveed. Finally, there was only one thing left I could do. I threw myself into the fire." He stopped.

"Then what?"

"Then I was in the anteroom, backed up against the wall with Dahveed holding my wrists in a grip like I've never felt before, and my battle dagger at our feet. Both of us were exhausted. It took a while to sort things out." He shifted uneasily next to her. "That grip was odd. He held me off with it, and somehow he kept me here at the same time. Does that make sense?"

"It doesn't need to. Things are different around Dahveed," she said in a shaky voice.

"They are. But you know the oddest thing, Michal? I've been so afraid that when the time comes for Dahveed to take the throne, I won't be able to let it go. But now I know I will. The decision was forced on me that night, and I made the right choice."

They stood for a long time in silence before she stirred. "What did Immi say about Merab?"

"Merab deserves to be happy. If necessary, I'll speak to the king."

Michal felt a sudden warmth in her heart as she realized how much she loved this brother of hers. As they went down the stairs, she remembered something. "Oh, Abner begged Abbi's forgiveness."

"When?"

"Just after Shabbat ended. You weren't there. Abner came after the evening meal while half the clan was there, and asked pardon for attacking Dahveed. Abbi kept him kneeling for a while before he held out his hand for Abner to take. He didn't say anything though. I don't think he's quite ready to bring Abner back. But it might be because that wound still isn't fully healed. Or maybe the message tablet Abner gave him has something to do with it."

"I wonder if Abner thought this out on his own, or if Ner suggested it to him," Jonathan mused. "It would put Abbi in a bad light if he refused to reconcile under those circumstances."

"I hadn't thought of that. Abner's son, Jaasiel, was there, and I remember thinking that was odd."

"I'll wager Dodi Ner had a hand in it. Wonder what was on that tablet?"

"Probably nothing important."

---

* See Cultural Notes: Transfer of the throne.

CHAPTER 9

Balak walked down the street, his head ringing with Judith's constant chatter. Four days without relief from his wife's voice had driven him from the house. He should go to the fortress and help Kohath catch up on the court records, but he turned toward the west gate instead. In the market he saw an old stool by a stall, and sat with his back against the wall where he could listen to the elders' discussing matters and judging complaints. It was a relief to hear something discussed besides the royal family.

Then a boy appeared beside him. "Shalom, geber. The elders sent me to ask whether gifts for the royal family can be taken to the fortress if they are not there."

Balak glanced over to the gate, spotting the man with a donkey beside one of the younger elders. He followed the boy over to them and nodded respectfully to the man seated on the wooden bench. Then he turned to the traveler. "You have something for the king?"

"Yes, but now I've heard there's no one here."

"That need not inconvenience you, geber. Go on up to the fortress. At the gates, ask the sentry for Kohath, the scribe. I happen to know that he's there today, and he can accept your gift and make sure it is recorded."

The traveler's face eased into a smile. "You've been kind, geber." He moved off.

As Balak turned to go, the elder called him back. "Do you have time to stay? We've had several inquiries like this one, and no one really knows what to answer. Why don't you sit here?"

"As you wish, geber." Balak sat on the last bench, wishing now that he'd worn a better robe. Minutes later, another traveler came in, a poorer man by his looks. He stopped at the elder who had invited Balak to sit, and asked a question.

The elder turned to Balak. "This man should know," he said.

The traveler bowed respectfully. "Geber, if you could tell me when the royal family will again be in residence, I would be grateful."

"I couldn't say for certain, geber, but I doubt anyone will return until after Shabbat."

"Then I will return on my way home." Bowing again, he continued up the street.

Balak answered two more inquiries before he left for the noon meal. He also heard several snatches of conversation, not the least of which was that Sar Malchi was so out-of-temper since the mock battle that even his brothers avoided him, and people were worried about what would happen this war season with Abner gone and the sars not in accord.

Walking home, Balak decided he would make it a practice to visit the gate a couple of times a week. Not only had he received unexpected honor, but he had learned a lot.

As spring advanced, I worked hard to forge the permanent units into one army again. I found that Abner's attack against me had actually done much to smooth the way, and the commanders who supported the king's cousin had appreciated my refusal to take advantage of the former general's disgrace.

As it did every year, a subtle tension grew in the army as war season drew closer. The veteran professionals took it in stride, knowing the chance for a pitched battle was small. But they recognized the constant possibility of an ambush, and everyone drilled seriously. This year, however, the tension pervaded the entire town, keeping the elders at the gate busy with petty disputes that normally would never have caused a problem.

Out on the training ground the commanders kept a tight rein on the men, and a wary eye on Sar Malchi, who was barely in control of himself despite the time he'd had in Zelah. The situation rapidly worsened to the point that it must be addressed, and since I was general, that made it my job. I dismissed the men early one day so I could speak with the sar alone. After most of them left, I crossed the sparring ring toward him, wondering how to approach the subject.

He didn't give me the chance. "What's this I hear about your angering Jonathan by wearing his girdle?" he demanded.

I studied him a moment. In spite of his liking for combat, Malchi was usually the most easygoing of the sars, and I'd never known him to deliberately insult anyone. Whatever was eating at him had really gotten under his skin, and he didn't look very ready to confess it to me. His shoulders were tense, hands clenching and unclenching.

Hoping a reasonable answer would calm things down, I smiled ironically. "He was more annoyed that I didn't wear it, Sar. I wanted to save his gift for special occasions. But he wanted me to wear it every day."

"Gift? Why would he give it to a shepherd from the south?"

Why was he determined to stir up trouble, I wondered. Then a memory sprang to my mind. That ram that I'd saved from the bear had had an odd personality quirk. Most of the time, it was very good tempered, true to its Yidla breeding. But every once in a while it got restless, stomping around the pasture looking for something to fight. It would tackle anything, so long as its target was bigger than it was. And the look on Sar Malchi's face right now was just like that ram's!

I smiled again. "If you need a fight this badly, Sar, just ask." I whipped my blade from the sheath, and swift as I was, he matched me. He twisted his blade around, and I met it again.

As he increased the pace, I responded, cautiously testing the limits of his skill as he did mine. His superior strength and reach soon demanded my strictest attention. Malchi was more powerful than even Jonathan, and just turning aside his blows took most of my strength. But I was quicker than he and had more patience.

Soon both of us panted heavily, but I hadn't had so good a workout in ages. Annoyed that I stood up to him so long, Sar Malchi pushed the sparring impatiently until I pulled back. "You're wasting your strength, Sar. If you keep trying to beat me into the ground, I'll put you on it," I warned.

That annoyed him more, and he pounded at me harder than ever. I strained to meet his blows, harboring my strength, watching his eyes for what I knew would come. Finally he brought his sword down from above, but I simply wasn't there, instead slicing his blade off to the left, pivoting past him, my blow between his shoulder blades speeding his fall.

To my amazement he didn't land on the ground, but stumbled to his knees, recovering in a flash. The look on his face, however, made me grin.

"The hassar didn't like that one either," I drawled.

"Jonathan wouldn't," he said grimly. "But I'll beat you just like I did him."

"You and whose thousand, Sar?"

His eyes gleamed. "You'll eat those words, General."

"Not today."

Our swords crossed again, and the air rang with our blows. Not long after, chests heaving, we faced each other with just our daggers. I suddenly grinned. "Call it a draw, Sar."

"Thought you'd never ask," he gasped, both of us leaning forward, trying to get our breath back. I groaned a little, suddenly realizing how much my left side ached.

"So, you finally ran up against someone who can hold you off, Malchi?"

I looked around. Half the professional force circled the ring, watching and applauding, and Sar Ishvi regarded his younger brother with a smile.

"He did today," the sar admitted. "It might have been chance."

"Don't count on it," I replied. "You haven't matched my best speed yet."

"And I didn't bear down on you all the way, either!"

Sar Ishvi chuckled. "Save it for next time."

"There won't be a next time," the hassar broke in, striding toward us. "You'll settle this quarrel another way."

"What quarrel?" Malchi asked.

"You mean you two were only sparring?"

"Yes," we both said at the same time.

Jonathan fumed silently. At last he turned to me. "Will you share the evening meal with me, Dahveed?"

"Of course, Hassar," I managed to answer between breaths.

Muttering to himself, he walked away.

As soon as he was out of earshot, Malchi collapsed with quiet laughter.

I looked at him inquiringly.

"My oldest brother had to invite you to a meal?" he gasped. "Immi must have taken strips from his hide for the way he beat you! And now he's got to apologize. Make him work at it, will you? It's *sooo* good for him, and it happens so rarely." Malchi went off, still chuckling.

Back in my room, I washed myself off and dressed in a green robe and black girdle that King Shaul had given me. I was dubious about Sar Malchi's interpretation of events. More likely, the hassar wanted me to play for some friends or maybe an emissary from out of town. I set the harp on the three-legged table, pushing aside the bundle there, and got the case, looking for the jar of oil.

"What are you doing, geber?" Ahiam asked as he entered.

"I thought I'd oil the harp before I go. If Jonathan is entertaining friends, I need to be ready."

"Friends? The hassar doesn't have friends, Dahveed. Acquaintances, allies, relatives, or dependents, yes, but no friends—except you. Have you even looked at the gift he sent?"

As I set down the oil and stared at the bundle, I felt a sinking feeling in my stomach. "No."

"I suggest you do so."

I opened it. A dark-brown robe unfolded in my hands, fringe longer than any I'd ever worn spilled down the edges, and a wide swath of sand-colored embroidery followed it. There was a matching girdle, and a mantle the color of pine trees in the distance. Everything was the finest wool. He'd included a silver headband, earrings, and a silver brooch to fasten the mantle.

"I don't think he's expecting you to play the harp," Ahiam commented dryly.

I didn't either.

I was ready when someone knocked at the door.

"Jonathan Hassar sent me to bring Dahveed," Balak's voice said when Ahiam opened it.

I could have sunk right through the floor.

"He'll be out in a moment," my retainer replied.

I reached for my cloak, determined to cover the rich robe that I wore.

Ahiam looked at me, and I stared right back. "Well, the wind seems a little cool tonight," he finally acquiesced.

Balak bowed stiffly when I emerged, and I nodded in reply. His face was blank, but his eyes burned with anger as he turned silently and led me across the private court and up the stairs of the residence. On the first step I stumbled, then turned red at the quick look of contempt my childhood nemesis threw at me as he waited for me to regain my balance. More nervous than ever, I started up the stairs again. Who else would be here? I'd made such a mess of things in Chephirah, and I'd likely do the same thing now.

Balak knocked at the upper room door, and Judith opened it. "Come in, adon." Although her face was sober, her eyes laughed at me.

Just seeing her trying to be serious eased my discomfort, and I smiled back, coming inside.

"That will be all for the night, Judith," the hassar announced.

"Yes, adoni." She went out, closing the door after her.

My stomach in knots, I turned to face the hassar, and whoever else was here. Jonathan stood by a low table covered with food. The lamps flickered in the breeze that came through the three slits in the wall. He was alone and dressed as if it was an informal dinner at his brother's house.

The clothes I had on were entirely inappropriate. I flushed. Probably he'd meant the robe as a gift for very formal occasions, which this obviously was not. But knowing how he hated it when I wouldn't meet his eyes, I managed to do that, and he walked toward me, holding that gaze. I didn't know what to expect, and I had already made a large mistake. Clenching my hands under cover of the cloak, I shifted my gaze to a spot beyond his shoulder.

"I'm glad you could come, adoni," he said quietly.

Adoni? Was he mad? We weren't out alone in the forest, but in a room in Shaul's residence, and could be interrupted by anyone at any time. Did he want us both killed?

"Hassar, what are you saying?" I protested.

"I am called Jonathan," he replied, starting to bow.

"Jonathan, please!" I begged frantically. My mind raced as I tried to find some way to persuade him to be reasonable. The king would hang our bodies from the walls for this!

"What did you say, *adoni*?" His eyes bore into mine.

I got very still. Oh. *That's* what he wanted. "Stand up," I said, my voice a little unsteady.

He did.

"Please don't do—" I stopped as his eyebrows climbed up his forehead.

"Was there something you do not wish me to do?" he prompted.

"Yes," I managed to say. "Please—" I caught myself this time.

Jonathan looked at me, his face completely impassive.

I was too shaken to get angry. Taking a couple of deep breaths, I tried to think of an appropriate way to phrase what I wanted. "I do not wish you to bow," I said in a rush.

"Your tone leaves me with some uncertainty, adoni."

"Do not bow to me, Jonathan."

"That was very clear, adoni," he said approvingly.

"And pl—" I swallowed what I had been about to say. "And don't call me adoni," I added.

"Then how shall I address you?"

"As 'Dahveed.'"

"As you wish, Dahveed." He looked at me expectantly.

I stood there, breathing easier now that I had found the way to keep our heads on our shoulders, and waited for whatever would come next. Nothing. I looked at the food on the table, and then back at him, wondering why he didn't invite me to at least take off the cloak and eat. That's why I was here, wasn't it?

"Was there something you wish me to do now?" Jonathan prompted again.

A dim idea of what this meal was going to be like crept into my mind, making sense of the clothes I had on, the ones Jonathan wore, and why there was only one place set at the table. For a moment I closed my eyes in pained realization.

Finally I undid the fastenings of my cloak and handed it to him. After hanging it on a peg on the wall, he turned back to me, waiting. I flushed and preceded him to the low table, seating myself on the chaff-filled cushion. He stood to one side, watching me. I looked around uncomfortably. If he stood there the whole time, I'd have the worst meal of my life. And the silence was strained, at least from my point of view.

Hands shaking, I took some bread, unable to even tear it in half. I put it on the polished stone plate in front of me, acutely aware of the hassar standing to one side. When I tried to eat some of the fruit, everything tasted like sawdust.

"Something is not to *your* liking, Dahveed?"

Suddenly furious, I turned toward him. "There is quite a lot not to my liking," I snapped. "Change into some clothes fit for you; then eat with me like Hassar Israel should!"

His smile flashed, and he disappeared into the other ell of the room. He must have had clothes already there, because he shortly returned and sat down opposite me. By that time I had simmered down to simple irritation, which he soon charmed away, and we talked about anything that came to our minds while we devoured the food.

When the last of it was gone, and I was taking the final sips of my wine, I looked at him across the table. "Why did you do this, Jonathan?"

"Because I'm the only one who could," he replied seriously. "Immi pointed out to me that you are not used to status. But if you will uphold it with me, you will with anyone." He paused a minute. "Immi also drew my attention to something else. I should have seen it myself, but didn't. And it's something for which I must ask your pardon."

"You don't need to offer apologies," I interjected. "You have done nothing to apologize for, Hassar."

"I am called Jonathan," he said, eyes boring into me. "Try again."

I sighed. He wasn't going to let me brush this aside. I took a moment to phrase my question. "In what do you feel that you have offended me?"

"I sent you to Chephirah as a king's representative, knowing you had no preparation for such a position."

My head jerked up. King's representative? The message I got said nothing about that! Then I caught my breath. That soldier had said the papyrus and message had come to him from Balak ben Hod.

"I ask your pardon and that you will tell me what needs to be done to restore your honor," the hassar finished.

I fingered the goblet, the silver one that Jonathan used for formal banquets, completely at a loss. If Balak had indeed changed the message to me, he was responsible for most of that day's disaster. On the other hand, Ahiam had repeatedly tried to advise me about how to arrive and what to wear, if only to uphold my status as general. But I refused to listen to the helper Yahweh had provided until after we'd nearly gotten killed.

The silence stretched while I decided that I would say nothing about Balak's likely interference. Besides, I did owe the man for his recommendation that had brought me here in the first place. I'd now count that debt paid.

Jonathan's dark eyes were still on me, and I twisted the goblet a little, watching the light reflect off the polished silver.

"By the time I got your message, it was unclear just how much authority you'd given me," I said carefully. "Had you sent any instructions with it?"

"No, Dahveed," he admitted. "We'd just gotten word that the emissary from Hamath was nearly at the gates, and I knew Ahiam would have a good idea of what I wanted you to do."

I traced a circle on the table with the bottom of the goblet. No wonder he'd been so angry there in the anteroom. As a king's representative, the manner in which I had handled the inquiry was much more than just careless with the royal honor. I had despised it at the very least!

Then sudden resentment welled up inside. What right did he have to get angry when he knew that I was unprepared for the task he gave me? There in the anteroom, he had not even asked why I had gone as I had, or given me the chance to explain. Instead, he had simply exploded at me. Anger made me clench the hand I had under the table. How did I know he wouldn't do something similar again? Or even care if he did? He was Hassar Israel. I was a southern shepherd. Realistically, how much could I trust him? My thoughts stopped, and my hand unclenched. Yahweh had shown me exactly how much I could trust this man.

"Do you remember saying anything in the anteroom that night?" I asked without looking up, still circling the goblet around and around.

Jonathan's face stilled, tightening as if with pain, and sweat appeared on his brow. "No. Beyond the fire and darkness, the only clear thing in my memory is your grip on my wrists. I can feel it yet."

I knew his despairing plea to Yahweh for death would never fade for me. Since the incident, I'd dreamed of it more than once, seeing him again throw himself at the whirling vortex of fire, choosing oblivion rather than killing me. Finally I stilled the goblet. Jonathan might get angry with me, or laugh at me, or even beat me if I was so foolish as to disgrace the king again, but he would never betray me. He would die first. In fact, he'd already done it, in some odd, backward way.

"Any offense you have given me is rectified, Jonathan."

"Then there *was* an offense," he said softly.

I met his eyes. "I think so, but not that serious a one, so I'll ask of you the same thing Bodbaal requested when he returned the brass earring. Give me your regard, Jonathan Hassar, and we will let the rest of the country think these clothes paid a recompense."

"You are easier on me than you should be, Dahveed. Ask *something* of me."

I grinned, amused. "All right. If you ever invite me to share a meal with you again, don't send Balak to get me."

"As you wish, adoni."

When I stood, he rose also. "The meal was exceptional, Jonathan. You were kind . . ."

His eyebrows began to arch.

"Don't say it, Jonathan," I warned.

His eyes laughing, he remained silent.

"I enjoyed it very much," I corrected myself. "I would like to do it again, if it is *your* wish."

"I'll remember."

I walked to the door, reaching for my cloak.

His hand got there before mine. "You are the adon, Dahveed."

Although I glared at him, he couldn't quite hide his smile as he put my cloak over my shoulders.

CHAPTER 10

It was dark when Michal softly closed the gate to Ishvi's private estate in Zelah and studied her surroundings carefully. Her brother and Dahveed had come here several times in the past weeks, piquing her curiosity, and tonight she had finally found an excuse to visit Zelah herself, giving her a chance to see what they were doing.

Lamps burned in the upper room of the large house. If she remembered correctly, a ladder went up to the far end of that room from the storage area below. No servants seemed to be around, for which she was grateful as she slowly felt her way into the storage chamber to avoid making any noise. Stealthily she climbed the ladder until she could see through the hole into the second-story room.

"You slipped again," her brother said. "Remember, when you are adon, things are arranged to your satisfaction, you do not accommodate yourself to what you don't want. Try again."

"What did I do this time?" Dahveed asked, a note of resignation in his voice.

"You tell me."

During the silence Michal crept upward to see better. Dahveed sat on a cushion at the low table that was covered with food. Her eyes widened at the robe he had on. It was unmistakably a sar's, and the zammar looked only halfway comfortable in it. He stared at the table, his eyes unseeing.

"All I did was move the dishes to make more room," he said.

"And what do you think servants are for?"

Michal had to cover her mouth. Jonathan had on a robe that must have been in the bottom of his clothes chest for years. It barely fit anymore. He looked more like a street vendor than a sar.

From Dahveed's tight face she concluded that things had not gone well, and the glint in Jonathan's eye said most of that was purposeful. It seemed that her brother had taken steps to deal with Dahveed's hesitancy to uphold his new status! Vastly amused, Michal silently stepped off the ladder, backing up into the shadows to remain hidden.

"Move the dishes," Dahveed said, gesturing to them.

Jonathan did, along with several others, including one that Dahveed was just reaching for. The zammar started to say something, annoyed, then hesitated, got disgusted at his hesitation, and sat back completely exasperated. The succession of emotions across his face was so comical that Michal couldn't stifle her laughter, and both men heard it.

Dahveed jumped up, his face white, hand on his belt knife.

Jonathan simply turned his head. "Come here," he commanded.

Michal walked into view. "Yes, Jonathan?"

The hassar's face darkened with anger, but Dahveed's relaxed from relief, and then an expression of roguish glee crossed it that she'd never seen before.

Her brother started to say something, but Dahveed stepped forward. "Why, Sahrah, how nice of you to come." He offered his hand.

Since Jonathan was speechless, Michal gave Dahveed her hand. "I hope I do not intrude."

"Not at all." The zammar guided her to the table as if he'd been doing it for years. "Please join us."

"Dahveed, this isn't—" Jonathan started to protest.

"I don't recall asking for your opinion, Jonathan," Dahveed said, his tone cold.

The hassar blinked.

The zammar sat down beside her. "What brings you here so unex-pectedly?" he asked, turning his attention to her with a smile.

Michal gasped. The room felt hot. His dark-brown robe, she sud-denly realized, matched the dark flecks in his eyes. The flickering light of the lamp flashed from the silver band around his head, and his voice—she caught her breath. He was the zammar, the musician from the hills. She'd known him for several years now—or had she?

She looked at him again. No, this was not the zammar. Here was someone she'd never met, and he was very exciting. "A very simple thing, adon," she replied, steadying herself and meeting his gaze. "My sister and I came to Zelah to get some robes left from our last visit, and I thought I remembered that Ishvi had some of those sweet Tekoa figs in his storeroom. There were no servants about, so I went to see for myself. I heard voices and felt compelled to see who was here. Please do forgive me for intruding on you."

"There is no need to ask for pardon," Dahveed smiled. "Such com-pany as you bring would never be considered an intrusion." He picked up her hand and raised it toward his lips. Michal's eyes widened, and she felt her throat tighten. Dahveed was going to kiss her hand.

But he stopped just before it reached his lips. "I most humbly beg your pardon, Sahrah," he said, his eyes suddenly twinkling. "You daz-zled me so, I forgot myself."

The fact that her brother, Jonathan, Hassar Israel, was in the room, crashed back into her mind. Taking a moment to organize her thoughts, she glanced up coolly into the hassar's incredulously furious dark eyes.

"Yes, the proprieties must be preserved, adon," she said. "But such an immediate and humble apology certainly deserves no less than an immediate pardon. Please, think nothing of it."

"Your graciousness warms my heart, Sahrah." Dahveed let go of her hand. "It doesn't sound as if you've eaten. Is there some trifling bit here on the table that might tempt you?"

Michal had to bite her tongue. She was definitely tempted, but not by what was on the table. Taking a tight grip on herself, she sighed del-icately. "Truly, adon, those figs look very good. Dare I hope they are the sweet ones, fresh and so early?"

"They must have known you would wish to have them and ripened accordingly," Dahveed replied, picking one up and holding it to her. The gleam in his eye was positively wicked.

She cast a glance at Jonathan, standing there, every muscle taut. "Please, adon, we must remember the servants."

"Ah, yes, I had forgotten." Dahveed turned to Jonathan. "You may clear the table."

The hassar's face suddenly went blank. "Yes, adoni." He reached for a red-glazed bowl with parched grain in it.

"Leave that one," Dahveed directed.

The hassar set the bowl back down. "Yes, adoni." His voice was perfectly flat.

Dahveed looked him up and down, a frown of disapproval on his face. "I don't know what servants are coming to these days," he sighed, glancing at her in apology. Keeping his gaze on her, he placed the fig in her hand, leaving his there as he continued speaking. "Go put on some decent clothes, Jonathan."

The hassar didn't move.

Turning his head, Dahveed looked at him, the corners of his mouth twitching. "When you get back, you can flay me alive while we eat."

The hassar still didn't move.

Dahveed sighed. "Or would you prefer to pelt me with whatever comes to hand immediately?"

"I haven't decided yet," Jonathan forced out. "I'm wondering if I dare leave my sister alone with you."

At the dahveed's blank expression, Michal burst out laughing. "Oh, do go on, Jonathan. Dahveed is hungry, and you're keeping him from eating."

She watched Jonathan disappear down the ladder she'd just come up, and turned back to Dahveed. The adon she expected had vanished, and the zammar sat there instead, his eyes worried and tired.

"I offended him, didn't I?"

"You surprised him. You've never acted that way before."

"There was no reason to." He got up and went to the far end of the room.

The adon's robe looked out of place on him, and Michal bit back her frustration. He always did the same thing—giving her a glimpse of what he could be, and then retreating again into the guise of the zammar from the hills.

Jonathan appeared beside her so quietly that she didn't hear him. Dressed for a formal dinner now, he watched Dahveed.

"What happened?" he asked her in a low voice. "That royal sar I left has disappeared."

"He's afraid that he offended you."

"He may be right."

"Don't take offense on my part, Jonathan," she said quickly. "Just find out what prompted him to act like that. That's the key to what you're trying to do."

"I hope so. I was beginning to wonder if he could act like anything other than an under-scribe. Did you hear his voice when he told me to clear the table? There was simply no room for refusal in that tone."

"The point is, where did he learn it?"

"That might be difficult to dig out, unless . . ." The hassar stroked his beard thoughtfully. "Have you noticed, Michal, that Dahveed is unusually direct? If he wasn't so respectful, he'd be rude many times."

"I noticed," she said, taking a deep breath to steady herself again. The dahveed's gaze had been very direct indeed when he took her hand, but now was not the time to blush.

"Maybe that's been part of the problem," her brother muttered to himself. "I've been hinting at things I should just ask for. If he's both subordinate and superior, then I'll have to be both also."

The hassar walked past the table. "Dahveed."

The zammar whirled around. "Adoni?"

"I am called Jonathan!"

At the exasperation in her brother's voice, the zammar went rigid, looking somewhere past the hassar's right shoulder.

"I refuse to start all over again," Jonathan continued. "I walked out of here leaving a royal sar sitting at the table, and when I return only minutes later, I find a hill man dressed like a puppet in an adon's robe. What happened, Dahveed?"

"I didn't mean to offend you, Hassar."

"What did you expect when you treat me like a slave and then seduce my sister in front of my eyes?"

"Seduce your sister?" Dahveed echoed, stunned. "But that was just part of the game!" His voice trailed off, and he turned white. He looked ready to collapse on the floor.

"Don't you dare!" Michal's brother growled.

Dahveed steadied himself and waited while the silence stretched longer and longer. At last he looked at Jonathan.

"I see Jesse's bekor made quite an impression," Jonathan said tightly. "If I had known how much of an impression, I might have left parts of him scattered around his tent instead of just telling him about it."

Dahveed's eyes widened. "Just what *did* you say to him in that tent? he asked curiously.

"I wouldn't want to repeat it in front of the sahrah. Now, if you will tell me what made you suddenly do what I've been trying to get you to do for weeks, I may survive the shock of the experience."

"A game I used to play with Abigail."

"Abigail is your sister?" Michal asked.

"Yes, Sahrah. I had to stay in bed several days when I was young, recovering from an injury. Geberet Miriam, Abbi's wife, had me clean wool, and I sat by Abigial's loom so we could talk as we worked. I used to pretend to be an adon and made up the most outrageous compliments I could think of to entice her to visit me, and she pretended she was a sahrah and made up the silliest excuses she could to refuse. Hassarah Ruth heard us at it one day and laughed so hard, she nearly fell. That's what gave her the idea for the "Answering Song," about the boy and girl at the wine press."

"So you got irritated with me, and decided to pay me back for all the misery I've put you through?" Jonathan guessed.

The zammar nodded. "I had no idea it would be taken seriously. What do you require, adoni?"

"I am called Jonathan. Who did you pattern your voice after?"

"The Hassarah's."

Jonathan sighed in exasperation. "For weeks I've been pushing you to act the adon, and now I find out it's just a game to you! I suppose you could do the same thing in any situation?"

Dahveed shrugged. "I've never really tried. It was just something that Abigail and I made up to keep me from getting bored, and we had so much fun with it, we've been doing it since."

"Yahweh, give me patience. Well, Dahveed, try it right now. Suppose you had just insulted the sahrah. What would you do?"

Closing his eyes, Dahveed thought a minute; then, when he opened them, he had subtly changed again. Michal couldn't see that he'd moved a muscle, but the robe fit, and when he turned to her, his eyes took her breath away.

"Allow me to offer any apology I can for the slight against you, Sahrah," he said. "I do not entertain any thoughts of dishonor toward you or your house." Then he turned to Jonathan and bowed slightly from the waist. "Sar, I fear that some carelessness on my part has caused you to doubt my intentions. In what way may I show my regret for this circumstance?"

Jonathan bowed back, a little deeper than Dahveed had. "Coming from one as honorable as yourself, adoni, there is no need for any further recompense. Your apology has corrected any misperceptions."

"May Yahweh bless you and yours for your understanding," Dahveed continued.

"And may He bless you for your consideration."

Dahveed waited a minute. "If that takes care of everything, I'd still like to eat."

"Who is there to stop you, adoni?"

◻◻▭◻◻

Now that he'd found the way to make me do what he wanted, the hassar was relentless as usual. I couldn't imagine what all this was for, but it must be important. He had me in the upper room at Ishvi's estate every other night, insisting that I act the adon to him under every possible situation, including some that I swore would only happen if the Jordan flowed north!

"You never can tell, Dahveed," was all he said. "Try again." And constantly, relentlessly, remorselessly, he drummed into me my change in status. Sometimes the way he wanted me to act seemed awkward, not fitting what I wanted to do. I did my best, but I got more and more uncomfortable.

One day I mentioned it to Ahiam. "Why don't you do something about it, geber?" he inquired. I sighed. Obviously he would be no help.

That night the hassar grilled me again. Halfway through the evening, I reached my limit.

"No, Dahveed," the hassar said. "Looking down that way tells everyone that you are uncertain, or are yielding honor and status. You are more than adon, remember. You do not yield to anyone! You always have higher honor."

I threw the piece of bread I held down on the table, pushing myself to my feet. "If you don't stop pounding that into me, I'll start believing it myself!" I nearly shouted, turning my back on him.

"And why shouldn't you?"

"Because it's not true!" I exploded, whirling around.

"And why isn't it true?" He planted both fists on his hips and glared at me. "What makes it not true? The fact that Jesse's bekor said it isn't? Does his word take precedence over that of Yahweh of Israel? Would you believe what that self-important, greed-ridden spawn of your father told you instead of what El Shaddai made you?"

"Don't insult my family, Hassar!" I warned, my temper seething.

"*Insult* your family? Let me tell you something, Dahveed. If I have to, I'll go to Bethlehem myself and drag that honored oldest brother of yours all the way back to Gibeah behind my mule and leave him tied up across your doorstep so you have to step on him every time you go in or out."

I was shaking, whether from rage or hope at the deadly seriousness of the hassar's tone, I couldn't tell. He stepped toward me.

"What did he do to you, anyway? Probably nothing overt. That might have gotten him in trouble, but I'll wager that every time he called you Ben-geber, his tone reminded you that you didn't even have a proper name. He probably took any occasion he could to correct you, publicly, in that nice, proper tone that announced how inept you were and how wonderfully patient he was with your mistakes. And anytime you did do something right, I'll bet he took pains to caution you about taking more honor than was your due and dishonoring the family that way, didn't he, Dahveed?"

I couldn't take my eyes from his face as scene after scene from my childhood flooded my thoughts. "Yes," I whispered, turning to the wall as pain washed over me. I had tried so hard, done anything that I could to please the bekor, and he was never satisfied.

Then anger rose in me. Despite all the honor that I'd brought to the family, I couldn't even show pleasure about my victory over

Goliath because it might offend Eliab! And never once had Jesse re-strained him, even when Eliab was unreasonable. I hit the wall with my fist, teeth tightly clenched. Wasn't I Jesse's son also? Was it too much to ask that I could be recognized as such? If not by Eliab, at least by the others? Even after I had killed the Philistine champion, and brought honor to all of Israel, I still wasn't good enough, and the bekor left me to sleep outside the tent, as if I had no place at all in Jesse's house.

Shaking with the memories, I leaned against the wall, my anger finally draining into sadness. "All I ever wanted was a word or two that said I had a brother. Why wasn't I worth even that?"

"You do have a brother, Dahveed."

Bewildered, I turned around. Had I spoken aloud?

Jonathan's grip tightened on my shoulder. "You are more than brother to me, Dahveed."

I put my hand on his and leaned against him as my heart bled for what should have been, but never was. When I straightened up again, I walked to the door, and the hassar handed me my cloak.

"We can work more tomorrow," he said, opening the door.

Pausing just outside, I turned back to him. "No, Jonathan. I under-stand what I must do, and I will take what you have given me and make it my own."

I rode back to the fortress, but, unable to rest, I strapped on the harp and walked out the fortress gate. Once away from the town, I headed west, running down the paths through the forest until I came to the valley below the cup where Jeshua's band trained. The stream still ran, and I sat down near the pool formed by the waterfall from the ledge above, listening to the water, staring at the Ezel stone on the other side of the meadow.

Above me, the stars spread out like the glints of silver thread on the hassar's girdle. I studied them, wondering what my life would have really been like had I not been forced to leave Bethlehem. Constantly beaten down by Eliab's words and actions, with no one to look me in the eye and tell me that I had honor and value, how long would I have kept my faith in Yahweh's promise at my anointing?

A shooting star crossed the heavens, leaving its brief trail behind, and as I gazed, the lights above seemed to bend close to me, spilling over with some important message that I had to quiet myself to hear.

What if I had to let go of my ideas of where I belonged? What if the God who chose me wanted to take me beyond anything that I had known? I shook my head. Even with the hassar's encouragement, I saw now that I had struggled and balked and fought every step of the way.

The wind from the distant sea was cool, and I drew the cloak closer to my shoulders as I leaned back, the blackness of the night making the stars stand out even more. I listened as their silence reminded me that the One who set them in their places had also set me in mine. Ethan had told me that Yahweh would teach me all that I must know to be His mashiah, and the dragonfly had shown me that struggle was a necessary part of my transformation. That's what sorted out what I must give up and what I should keep. After all, the full-grown dragonfly looked nothing like the grub it came from, but whatever it was in the end was made from what had been there in the beginning.

Gleaming down, the stars waited for me to understand them fully. How many times had I watched them? From that first night when I had sat with Grandmother Ruth and I had asked Yah to claim me, to this night when I gazed at them again? Every night they were there, their knowledge waiting for ears to hear their unspoken voices.

"Night after night, they display knowledge, declaring the glory of El," I said, reaching for the harp.

I closed my eyes, listening to the water, reaching out for anything else that might come from the hand of God. In the dim corners of my mind I heard more. Setting my fingers on the harp, I plucked a note, bringing it from the background of my thoughts. Another came, and a third. I stared at the stars, playing the notes again. More of a melody floated down in their shimmer, and I added that.

"The heavens declare the glory of El," I sang softly, putting words to the melody, "and the skies proclaim the work of His hands. Night after night they display knowledge."

I hesitated. "Day after day they pour forth speech, and night after night they display knowledge." That fit better. The great arch of the sky seemed to go on forever. "Their voice goes to the end of the earth, their words to the pillars of the world. Their speech and language are heard in all parts of the earth."

My fingers hesitated again on the harp as I rested, listening, waiting to hear the melody as it should be, and slowly it came.

"The heavens proclaim the glory of El;

"And the firmament announces the work of His hands.

"Day to day they pour out speech;

"Night to night they announce knowledge.

"There is no voice, there is no speaking

"Without their voice being heard.

"Their voice goes forth in all the earth,

"And at the end of the land is their word."*

After playing it through several times, I sat back, contented. The song was well started, and the rest would come in its time.

By dawn I stood in the middle of the fortress courtyard, watching the day star throw its rays over the eastern height, sifting through the trees, and creeping over the walls. The commonplace, awe-inspiring splendor of its gold brought back to my mind one simple thing I had forgotten in the latest turmoil of my life.

Just like Hassarah Ruth, I held my honor from Yahweh, for the highest honor that I had came to me the night that Yahweh claimed me for His own as a child. Now I must learn to conduct myself as befitted someone with Yah for a father in whatever situation I found myself. Sometimes that might mean I should act as mashiah, the highest in the land, or as a northern adon, as Jonathan taught me. Other times I should be zammar to the king, or yes, even despised youngest brother to Eliab. Because the honor I had from *Yah* was so great, it didn't matter whether *human beings* gave me a sar's robe or a shepherd's robe to hang from my shoulders. What mattered was whether I would remain a true son to Yahweh.

"Geber?"

I turned.

The moment I met his glance, Ahiam dropped to one knee, bowing his head. "Adoni, a message came last evening from the hassar. King Shaul has decided to celebrate the harvest festival, Feast of Weeks, at Nob. The hassar sent word that you will accompany them when they go." He looked at me briefly. "Is that acceptable to you, adoni?"

His question startled me. If the hassar said it, why wouldn't it be? Then I turned and looked at the sun again, just beginning to shine over the horizon, and I smiled to myself.

"Yes, Ahiam. I will accommodate the hassar's request."

---

* Author's translation.

JONATHAN AND ISRAEL

TAMAR BAT DAHVEED

S o, at last, Dahveed has accepted the fact of his status and power, winning the battle over his past. Adonai has worked for generations for this victory, for Dahveed learned more from The Hassarah than he ever suspected. Along with her love and her music, she gave him a unique way of looking at things and the ability to put ideas together in different manners. Ethan has noticed this in connection with Dahveed's skill at arms, but it is much more pervasive than that.

Did you notice it just now in Dahveed's thoughts about honor? Most people would say that his highest honor came from his anointing, but Dahveed saw the truth. His anointing occurred in the first place only because Yahweh claimed him. Like that dragonfly, he is expanding and stretching, and Adonai is carefully nurturing Dahveed's new way of looking at things and people and himself, helped by what Jonathan has taught him.

And now Yahweh's mashiah will begin to change what is around him, and that quirky turn of mind will emerge—in some very unexpected ways!

CHAPTER 11

I stood to one side of the tabernacle entrance, watching people arrive. It was almost time for the morning sacrifice, three days into the Feast of Weeks celebrating the grain harvest. In the surrounding valleys more campsites had blossomed each day as people arrived for the festival. I had spoken to Hakkohen Abiathar briefly when I first arrived, and he had told me they expected a large crowd this year since the king and the sars would attend. The high priest, Hakkohen Haggadol Ahimelech, had called in most of his clan to handle the volume of sacrifices expected.

People gathered around, talking among themselves and hushing children as they waited for the sacrifice to begin. The king arrived with his three oldest sons. Murmuring respectful greetings, the crowd opened up to allow him to come to the front.

I wondered what Jonathan was thinking. I had sent no response to the message Ahiam brought, and a minor crisis in the professional forces had kept me away most of the time since that last night at Ishvi's estate.

The rams' horns sounded their high-pitched call as the officiating priest emerged, and the morning offering of a lamb was soon done. Incense drifted from the doorway of the holy place, and I closed my eyes. The crowd knelt when the priest approached to give them Yahweh's blessing. When he finished, I touched the strings of the harp and sang a response, my own heart full.

As the crowd got up, I stepped away, my part finished.

"Geber?"

I turned to see a little girl regarding me.

"Yes, geberet?" I said soberly.

A dimple appeared in each cheek as she smiled, her eyes dancing. "I liked your song."

"I'm pleased that you did, and it was nice of you to tell me so."

"May I touch your harp?"

"If you wish." I knelt to bring it to her level.

Shyly she put her finger on the wood. "It's so smooth," she commented. She plucked a string, and then another.

"Hannah! What are you doing?" a woman gasped, hurrying over. "Please accept my apologies, geber. Hannah, you must not bother the zammar."

I stood. "Hardly a bother, geberet. Your daughter gave me a well-spoken compliment. She is a credit to her house."

"Why, how kind of you to tell me!" the woman said, looking at her daughter with pride. Those dimples flashed at me again as her mother led her away.

"Zammar?"

I glanced up.

"That blessing—I wanted to tell you it meant a good deal to us."

An older man and his wife stood in front of me, dressed in worn clothing, the man's accent telling me he was from the south. It was good to hear. "What part of Judah are you from?" I asked, thickening my accent a little. "I'm from Bethlehem."

"Why, you wouldn't be Geber Jesse's son that came to the king, are you?" he asked.

I nodded.

Well, that is a surprise!" the woman said, turning to her husband. "We have to stop on the way home. Geberet Keren will want to know how well her son is looking, and that he sang before the taber-nacle."

"I would be very grateful if you would speak to her. I miss her, and I know that she misses me."

"That she does, and, well, seeing the king or no, you just bend down here, young zammar, and let me give you a hug for your own immi. And I'll take yours back to her."

Tears came to my eyes, and I bent down as her arms wrapped around me. I hugged her back, harder than I meant to.

"You're a good lad, and know your duty," she added.

"Please, take my greetings to my abbi as well," I said, looking at the farmer.

"And no trouble it will be."

They walked away. "Such a bearing he has!" I heard the woman tell her husband as they left. "He could be a sar! But still courteous to old folks such as us."

I had only a moment or two to consider that comment before someone else came up, wanting to thank me for my song, and the rest of the morning swept me into its activity.

After the noon rest, I rose before anyone else and wandered around, studying the people there. Most were from Benjamin or the north and east, Ephraim and Manasseh being heavily represented, with more coming in from Zebulun and Naphtali. Some Gaddites had crossed the Jordan, and a large group attended from Gilead, along with a party of Danites. I wondered if they had any connection to Ethan. His family was Danite.

A little later, the three sars left the pavilion and separated, each one covering a designated area. Malchi went down the valley toward Jebus, Ishvi into Nob's market, and Jonathan circulated in the area closer to the tabernacle. I stayed with him, keeping to the background and listening, Ahiam attending me.

"Geber, is that the hassar?" someone asked.

I turned around. "It is. Did you wish to speak to him?"

"Yes, geber, uh, adon," he replied, looking at me a little puzzled when he noticed Ahiam stopping with me and not continuing with the hassar.

"Did you have a petition for him?"

"Well, you might say so, adon." He hesitated again. "See, I've got some good wine from two years ago, and I'd heard that the hassar likes local vintages. I wondered if I could give him some."

I hesitated. While it wasn't something especially important, it might be the only chance he had to contact the hassar, and if Jonathan liked the wine, he would purchase some.

"Sar Eshbaal," Ahiam murmured, looking away.

"Well, geber, the best way for you to send a gift for the hassar's table is to deliver a small jar to Sar Eshbaal at Gibeah. He will record who sent it. Then if the hassar likes it, he'll know where it came from."

The man's face relaxed. "Thank you, adon. You've been kind."

"Shalom," I replied.

We had fallen behind, and I tried to catch up, but Ahiam laid a restraining hand on my arm.

"There's someone trying to get courage to talk to you," he said, a slight jerk of his chin, drawing my attention to an older man to one side, trailing along and glancing at me frequently.

"Adon, if I may have a moment?" someone else interjected. A slender man, he wore slightly garish robes and a practiced smile.

"Yes?"

"I noticed you walking with the hassar. Perhaps you could draw his attention to something?"

Ahiam flicked the Habiru signal for caution at me.

"That would be hard to say immediately," I said carefully. "The hassar is very busy."

"Of course, of course," the man agreed, rubbing his hands together. "I understand. I just hoped that since you are in his company, you might speak with him."

"What about?"

"Only a trifling matter, but one that might rouse his interest. Yes, indeed."

I looked at him impatiently. "What matter?"

"One can find it hard to say. But the hassar will be pleased to hear of it, and may reward you well for drawing it to his attention. Just a quick word, perhaps an introduction. A moment only of your time."

I pressed my lips together. So far he had told me nothing at all. I glanced at Ahiam, who deliberately placed his hand on his dagger, raising it slightly from the sheath.

"Perhaps your request can be considered another time." I turned to go.

"Do not hasten so, adon. I beg another moment of your time. The rewards might be great."

Ahiam slid the dagger from its sheath.

"Then again, perhaps another time," the man finished smoothly, backing away. "My request can indeed wait. There is no hurry." He moved off, rubbing his hands again, looking around alertly.

"Do you have any idea what he wanted?" I asked, exasperated.

"I would guess he wanted to invite the hassar to his brothel," my retainer said in disgust.

I started on again, keeping an eye on the individual that Ahiam had originally pointed out. He worked his way closer to me, listening again when someone asked me if I knew whether the hassar would accept a gift of special raisin cakes.

I directed that to Sar Eshbaal also.

At last the man approached us. "Adon?" he asked doubtfully.

"Shalom, geber. Was there something you wanted of me?"

"No, Dahveed," he admitted. "We'd just gotten word that the emissary from Hamath was nearly at the gates, and I knew Ahiam would have a good idea of what I wanted you to do."

I traced a circle on the table with the bottom of the goblet. No wonder he'd been so angry there in the anteroom. As a king's representative, the manner in which I had handled the inquiry was much more than just careless with the royal honor. I had despised it at the very least!

Then sudden resentment welled up inside. What right did he have to get angry when he knew that I was unprepared for the task he gave me? There in the anteroom, he had not even asked why I had gone as I had, or given me the chance to explain. Instead, he had simply exploded at me. Anger made me clench the hand I had under the table. How did I know he wouldn't do something similar again? Or even care if he did? He was Hassar Israel. I was a southern shepherd. Realistically, how much could I trust him? My thoughts stopped, and my hand unclenched. Yahweh had shown me exactly how much I could trust this man.

"Do you remember saying anything in the anteroom that night?" I asked without looking up, still circling the goblet around and around.

Jonathan's face stilled, tightening as if with pain, and sweat appeared on his brow. "No. Beyond the fire and darkness, the only clear thing in my memory is your grip on my wrists. I can feel it yet."

I knew his despairing plea to Yahweh for death would never fade for me. Since the incident, I'd dreamed of it more than once, seeing him again throw himself at the whirling vortex of fire, choosing oblivion rather than killing me. Finally I stilled the goblet. Jonathan might get angry with me, or laugh at me, or even beat me if I was so foolish as to disgrace the king again, but he would never betray me. He would die first. In fact, he'd already done it, in some odd, backward way.

"Any offense you have given me is rectified, Jonathan."

"Then there *was* an offense," he said softly.

I met his eyes. "I think so, but not that serious a one, so I'll ask of you the same thing Bodbaal requested when he returned the brass earring. Give me your regard, Jonathan Hassar, and we will let the rest of the country think these clothes paid a recompense."

"You are easier on me than you should be, Dahveed. Ask *something* of me."

When the last of it was gone, and I was taking the final sips of my wine, I looked at him across the table. "Why did you do this, Jonathan?"

"Because I'm the only one who could," he replied seriously. "Immi pointed out to me that you are not used to status. But if you will uphold it with me, you will with anyone." He paused a minute. "Immi also drew my attention to something else. I should have seen it myself, but didn't. And it's something for which I must ask your pardon."

"You don't need to offer apologies," I interjected. "You have done nothing to apologize for, Hassar."

"I am called Jonathan," he said, eyes boring into me. "Try again."

I sighed. He wasn't going to let me brush this aside. I took a moment to phrase my question. "In what do you feel that you have offended me?"

"I sent you to Chephirah as a king's representative, knowing you had no preparation for such a position."

My head jerked up. King's representative? The message I got said nothing about that! Then I caught my breath. That soldier had said the papyrus and message had come to him from Balak ben Hod.

"I ask your pardon and that you will tell me what needs to be done to restore your honor," the hassar finished.

I fingered the goblet, the silver one that Jonathan used for formal banquets, completely at a loss. If Balak had indeed changed the message to me, he was responsible for most of that day's disaster. On the other hand, Ahiam had repeatedly tried to advise me about how to arrive and what to wear, if only to uphold my status as general. But I refused to listen to the helper Yahweh had provided until after we'd nearly gotten killed.

The silence stretched while I decided that I would say nothing about Balak's likely interference. Besides, I did owe the man for his recommendation that had brought me here in the first place. I'd now count that debt paid.

Jonathan's dark eyes were still on me, and I twisted the goblet a little, watching the light reflect off the polished silver.

"By the time I got your message, it was unclear just how much authority you'd given me," I said carefully. "Had you sent any instructions with it?"

The next morning I had Ahiam show me what to wear, incorporating something simple for when I sang with something more extravagant for later. I rode beside the hassar on the way to Nob. The previous war season, I'd discovered that early morning was not Jonathan's best time of day, so I didn't feel any obligation to talk. But I hadn't realized that I'd been humming the song I'd started out in the valley until the hassar spoke.

"It doesn't sound right."

"It isn't finished."

"Will you manage to finish it before I die?"

"Certainly not with you snapping at me like an ornery mule," I said calmly.

On the other side of Jonathan, Ishvi choked a laugh into a cough, and Sar Malchi's mule crept up on my other side.

The hassar remained silent a while. "Did you decide to wear something less like an under-scribe today?" he asked mildly. "I believe you told me that hill men could learn with *reasonable* speed. Why don't you ask that servant of yours to show you some decent clothes? After all, he's raided the treasury often enough to have something worth your while to put on."

"Well, Hassar, I thought the—"

"If you can't catch on to these things faster, Dahveed, I'm afraid I'll have to load you down with a little more gold. Or maybe a ride on my mule through the streets of Gibeah with someone singing your praises would help out? What do you think?"

"I think that you should listen to—"

"I should listen? I don't know what servants are coming to these days." He kicked his mule up to join the king.

We arrived in plenty of time for the service, and I was careful to stay out of Jonathan's sight. As with yesterday, when I finished and the priest had dismissed the crowd, several people came up and thanked me. The girl Hannah returned, wanting to touch the harp.

After everyone had spoken to me, I returned to the pavilion, and Ahiam gave me some silver armbands and earrings to wear with the new gray robe I had on. I retied Jonathan's dark-blue girdle, letting the ends hang down to display the tassels. Then I took off the brass earring, and Ahiam combed out my hair, putting on the silver headband.

Finally, quickly locating the knot of people around the king, I headed for it. Ishvi saw me first, and his eyes widened. He nudged Malchi, who nearly burst out laughing. They both turned to watch their brother. I stepped up to the hassar.

"Adoni?"

He turned. "Yes, adon?" Then he froze as he recognized me.

"I believe an important piece of your jewelry got left behind on the trip here this morning," I said, holding out the brass earring.

"You've been a big help tonight," Kohath said. "I didn't know that you could read and write. Why haven't you trained as a scribe?"

"My abbi never thought of it for me," Balak replied. "It's been interesting working with you, though. I never realized everything that has to be done to keep court records. No wonder Hassar Jonathan depends on Sar Eshbaal so much now."

"Things have gotten much busier here in just the past few months. As you can see, we've had to use an entire scribal chamber to store records in." He gestured around the room. "We've already got two shelves full of daily annals, along with fortress inventories, private estate records, and papyri for the crown lands."

"What's all that?" Balak inquired, looking at the stacks of tablets and papyri sitting on three shelves on the wall left of the door.

"The Gibeonite records," Kohath sighed. "I haven't had time to even begin sorting out and arranging all of them."

"Are there judicial records?"

"Over there, under the private estate collection." The scribe pointed to the opposite wall. "Well, I think we've done enough for tonight. Will you be able to help again tomorrow?"

"I may, in the afternoon," Balak replied. He planned on going to the city gate in the morning. It was quiet there with so many people attending the Feast of Weeks at Nob, and he'd had time to get acquainted with the elders. They now routinely referred any questions about the royal family to him, and several travelers had expressed their gratitude for his advice with a piece of copper or two.

The Moabite servant followed Kohath out of the room, saying his shalom absently. His decision to cultivate Kohath was paying unexpected dividends. Now he had access to any court records that he wanted to see, and with the judicial tablets at his disposal, he could study them to see which way the hassar leaned in legal disputes.

The king had asked his opinion about some of the cases, and Balak hadn't been prepared to say much. But he would be in the future. And a vague idea hovered in the back of his mind, one that he hardly dared to start considering. But the more he knew, the more likely that idea would come to fruition. Then he'd be able to stay one step ahead of Dahveed.

---

* See Cultural Notes: Power.

CHAPTER 12

Because I was dressed in adon's robes today, many more people approached me. Again, Ahiam helped me handle each one, and by the time I retired to the king's pavilion at noon, I had a much greater appreciation for the place the sars held in society and what they did to support their father.

I woke from the noon rest hearing Ethan taking his leave of the hassar. At the entrance to the pavilion the Habiru stepped aside as Sar Malchi came out.

"Good to see you, Ethan," the sar commented, nodding. Then he stopped. "Uh, it is safe for me to go wandering around?"

Ethan laughed. "If it's Caleb's twins you're worried about, Sar, they should be tucked away near Bethlehem. Although with Rachel and Leah, you never can tell."

"I'll chance it," Malchi said with a crooked grin.

Jonathan accompanied the Habiru away from the pavilion, and when they were almost to the crowd and everyone could overhear him, Jonathan said, "Ethan, allow me to request that your band attend the festival as my guests."

The Habiru halted in his tracks, but managed to control his amazement. "Your offer is very generous, adon."

"Let me know how many can attend. Shalom, Ethan."

"Shalom, adon."

I caught up with my old friend a couple minutes later as he leaned against a tree at the edge of the forest, looking bewildered.

"Was he serious with that invitation?" Ethan asked.

"If he made it, he was."

"Then I guess I'll have to go back to Bethlehem." He paused a moment. "Dahveed, why is the hassar interested in the House of Tahat?"

"Because he suspects the House has a trading network throughout both Judah and Israel. He wants to unify *all* the tribes, Ethan. He has a vision of what Israel could be, and wants to talk the steward into helping him. Why?"

An odd expression flickered across Ethan's face. "He asked me to find the steward, or barring that, any information I could about the House. He thinks it's in the north."

"What did you say?"

Ethan chuckled. "I asked him what my fee would be! He said he didn't know, since paying me is as hard as rewarding you. I also noticed that he's wearing the king's signet ring. When did that happen?"

"Just recently. Now that Sar Eshbaal has everything so organized, Shaul is impatient with the routine and shoved it off on Jonathan."

"This will change a lot of things," Ethan observed.

The last day of Feast of Weeks, the day after Shabbat, Michal woke from the noon rest hearing a giggle. Puzzled, she opened her eyes, studying the roof of the pavilion over her head. Then she rolled over, still tired from the long morning service. Seven male lambs, a young bull, and two rams had been offered as burnt offerings in the first part of the rite. Then a male goat had served as a sin offering, and finally two more year-old lambs as a fellowship offering. Afterward the Hakkohen Haggadol had given the blessing and thanked Yahweh for the harvest just gathered, and Dahveed had led the people in two songs of praise before personally singing a final one.

A different giggle joined the first one, and curious, she got up, the sounds leading her into the trees beside the pavilions. In a small clearing Dahveed sat on the grass, holding his harp, with two or three children watching.

A little girl reached out hesitantly and touched the harp, causing a string to sound.

"Are you sure you didn't touch a string, Hannah?" Dahveed asked, a perplexed expression on his face.

The girl nodded, giggling, and touched the harp again.

The string vibrated again.

"That's odd," Dahveed said. He touched the wood. Nothing happened. Carefully he examined the harp. "This is my harp, isn't it?"

The children nodded.

"Then why won't it play for me?"

A little boy reached out his finger, touching the wood, and a bass string twanged.

"What did you do?" the zammar asked. "I can't get it to make a sound. What do you suppose this means?"

"I know," Hannah cried. "It means the harp wants to play for us, not for you."

"But it's my harp!"

"Oh, the little darlings," Merab said, slipping up beside her sister. "Where did they come from?"

"I don't know," Michal answered.

Several more children emerged from the trees, joining the first few.

"The harp wants you to play for us," Hannah insisted.

"Then maybe I'd better," Dahveed replied. "If I don't, the harp might not play the next time I go before the king, and then what do you think would happen?"

The little boy looked at Dahveed critically. "Are you really the king's zammar?" The child had a surprisingly deep voice. "You're dressed like an adon."

"Tell me something, little bass drum," Dahveed asked. "Do you like to dress up in a good robe?"

The boy looked down at the garment he was wearing and sighed. "No."

"Well, neither do I, but it's festival day, and I have to dress up."

"What do you like to wear?"

"Promise you won't tell," Dahveed cautioned, looking at all of them gravely.

They nodded.

"I like to wear a kilt!"

Giggles exploded everywhere as the children tried to imagine the richly dressed adon in a kilt.

"Habiru wear kilts," the boy said. "Are you Habiru?"

"Well, now, that's a good question. If Habiru wear kilts and I wear a kilt, then maybe I am. On the other hand, I'm not wearing a kilt, so maybe I'm not. Do you suppose it matters, Ira?"

The lad thought for a long time. "Not if you'll play the harp for us," he decided.

"Sit down, then," Dahveed directed, and they all gathered around. He played a song about a lamb out in the pasture for the first time, wondering about everything as it explored the place.

A chuckle beside her made Michal glance around.

Ishvi stood there. "Shall we join them?" he asked.

"Maybe we'd better not," Merab answered, looking wistfully at the children. "I wouldn't want to spoil this."

"I don't think we'll spoil things." Ishvi held out his hand. Merab took it, and they walked into the clearing.

Dahveed never batted an eyelash as the sahrah and sar sat down. Michal stayed where she was, having too much fun watching the expressions on the children's faces.

More children came from the trees in a group, approaching hesitantly.

"Hannah, go bring Yahoadan and her clan here," Dahveed told her. "They're feeling shy."

The child jumped up and ran to the oldest girl among the newcomers, taking her hand. "Come and sit down. If you don't, the harp might not play, and it's such fun."

Next Dahveed played the traveler's song. He invited the children to guess from the sounds that the harp made what the man had seen on his journey. As the laughter from the guesses rang out, Hassarah Ahinoam seated herself on the other side of the group, a delighted smile on her face.

More children found them, gathering quickly around. Merab's expression glowed. She had one child in her arms and two in her lap. Ishvi had a boy on his shoulders and another leaning against his side.

Finally, King Shaul emerged from the trees, Ahiam bringing a stool for him to sit on, and Dahveed began a song about a goat kid that ran away and got into all sorts of trouble before the shepherd found it.

A little toddler more interested in learning to walk than listening to the zammar, plopped down beside the king. She grabbed onto his robe, pulling herself up, and Shaul absently reached down, sitting her in his lap. She looked up at him doubtfully, but he paid no attention, listening to the zammar. The child nestled into the fringes of his robe, stuck her finger in her mouth, and went to sleep.

A few adults had gathered around the edge of the group, but Dahveed was singing solely for the children. They repaid him lavishly with laughter, shouts, and clapping.

"Here's where everyone is," Jonathan suddenly said beside Michal, Malchi with him. "How long has Dahveed been playing?"

"I don't know," she answered, "but the children are fascinated."

"They're not the only ones." He indicated the silent, intent adults.

Malchi started around the edge of the group, and muffled shrieks of delight came from a knot of children. Two girls, alike as they could be, converged on him.

"Dodi sar, dodi sar," they exclaimed, hanging on his robe and arms.

Jonathan exploded into quiet laughter, and Michal followed him over to their brother.

"Tell me it isn't so," Malchi begged. "It can't be. They're supposed to be in Bethlehem, and—and they're bigger!"

"Did I forget to mention that I invited Ethan's band to the festival?" Jonathan asked.

"Yes, you did," Malchi retorted. "Now what am I going to do? I'll never get away." He looked down at the twins tugging on his robe.

"Dahveed, Dahveed," they called. "Dodi sar is here. Play the donkey song."

"Don't mention donkeys," Malchi pleaded. "You're too old for that, aren't you?" he said to the two children.

"What song did you want?" Dahveed's voice rang out above the noise of the children.

"Dodi sar is here! Play the donkey song!"

With a roguish grin Dahveed set his fingers on the strings, while Jonathan watched inquiringly.

The zammar began a song about a little boy getting a ride on a donkey that didn't want to be ridden. The things the donkey did and the sounds of protest it made brought screams of laughter from the children.

But the effect on Michal's brothers was dramatic. Jonathan suddenly folded up in silence. Ishvi leaned against Merab, laughing so hard that no sound came out.

Malchi was on the ground, completely buried under six or seven children who sat on any part of him they could find. They completely ignored his pleas to be careful of his robe, his hair, or just plain hesed.

The song ended with the donkey trapped under a huge load and becoming a willing animal when the boy rescued it. By the time Dahveed finished, Jonathan was also sitting on the ground so helpless from mirth that he could only wipe his eyes occasionally.

Although Malchi tried to get up, the children wouldn't let him. One little boy patted his head gently and said, "Just stay still, donkey. We'll let you up when you've learned your lesson."

Jonathan exploded with laughter again, gasping and holding his sides.

"Do another one about a sar," little Ira in the front demanded.

"About a sar?" Dahveed questioned. "That wasn't *about* a sar. It was *for* a sar. There's a difference, you know."

"Can you make a song for me?" the child continued.

Dahveed smiled. "Maybe some day." The corners of his lips twitched. "But I do have another song for a sar."

"Sing it! Sing it!" the children begged.

"This one is about a sar who lived very, very, far away, and who had three brothers!" He started the song. It told of a sar who went hunting for deer with his brothers. Even though he'd never hunted deer before and his brothers gave him many helpful suggestions, he refused to listen. Finally he went off by himself. When he saw a deer, he started after it, ignoring all the suggestions that his brothers had offered, and ended up falling into a pit snare and unable to climb out.

Malchi had managed to sit up now, and his head jerked up with interest. The hassar looked at Dahveed oddly.

The snare had been set by a group of children who had never seen a sar before, and the terrible time he had convincing them that he wasn't some strange animal brought laughter to everyone. By the time Dahveed got to the part where the sar had to humbly do whatever the children said in order to get out of the trap, Malchi was holding his sides, while Jonathan regarded Dahveed with total exasperation.

At last the sar's brothers rescued him, for which he showed proper and generous gratitude.

"I'll have to send Dahveed something for that one," Malchi gasped when he could finally talk, looking at Jonathan. "Something gold."

When she turned the other way, Michal saw Ishvi wiping his eyes as he explained something to Merab.

Then Dahveed glanced at the sun and stood. He started a simple praise song to Yahweh, encouraging the children to sing with him.

As the zammar departed, Michal realized it was almost time for the evening sacrifice. The adults helped the children sort themselves out. Michal smiled at the astonishment of some parents who found their children clambering all over the royal family, especially those of the toddler, who found her still fast asleep in the king's arms.

Malchi looked almost sorry as the children departed while he stood talking to a group of people to one side, probably from Ethan's band. The twins were still with him, however, swinging from his arms at every opportunity.

On the way to the tabernacle for the evening sacrifice, Michal convinced Merab to tell her what her brothers had been laughing about when Dahveed sang. Merab related how Malchi had first met the twins when Jonathan led his brothers straight into an ambush in a Habiru camp, and they had to surrender to a bunch of children, then how the twins had cornered Malchi again at the party to celebrate Dahveed's recovery, demanding that he carry them around like a donkey. "He finally played with them like Abbi used to with us, pretending to be stubborn, and falling down and shaking them off, and all," she concluded.

"Abbi used to do that?" Michal asked in amazement.

Her sister nodded. "He and Dodi Abner, all the time. I keep forgetting how much you don't know because you weren't born yet, or were too little to remember."

Suddenly Michal laughed. "So that second song was about

Jonathan!"

"Yes, and Nimshi was the one who lured him into the ambush, and that made Jonathan ask if Nimshi could join his service."

Michal shook her head. "Trust Jonathan to find something to his advantage in any situation."

Glancing at the sun, I hurried into the pavilion to change into a kilt and cuirass for the ride back to Gibeah. I'd been gone for two days, and I wanted to check in with the town sentries and the commanders at the training ground before returning here for the feast tonight. As I rode by the clearing where I'd just sung, I noticed Abner and his son, Jaasiel, approaching the king. Maybe Shaul was ready to bring his cousin back as general. I hoped so.

My mule was climbing the hill south of Gibeah after I'd checked with Sheva's assistant in the fortress when I heard yelling and recognized Sar Malchi's voice harsh with anger. I kicked the mule into a run. Keeping Sar Malchi on an even keel was probably the oddest duty I had as general, but no one else could stand up to him, and I'd sparred with him more than once since that first time. But when had he returned from Nob?

By the time I slid off the mule at the sparring ring, Commander Libni of the tenth unit was white-faced and rigid, telling me that he hadn't deserved what Sar Malchi had just unleashed. I was going to have to find out once and for all what was bothering the sar, for I couldn't have a division commander alienating his subordinates just before war season.

"You are dismissed, commander," I said, not caring whether Malchi was ready for him to leave or not.

Libni walked stiffly away, followed by three of his fellows.

The rest of the men hurriedly left, and I waited for the sar to turn around. He didn't. "More exceptions to my girdle?" I finally asked.

I should have had my blade in my hand when I spoke. Malchi turned on me so quickly that I didn't have time to draw and had to duck aside. He walked into me, his eyes blazing. I spent the next couple minutes dancing out of his way, wondering if I'd survive long enough to find out what had put him into such a mood. He'd been fine at Nob earlier.

At last he quit trying to slice me in two with every stroke, and I dared to meet a few of his thrusts. But he was so aggressive that my gift stirred. He was careless, too, leaving many openings, and I soon drove him out of the circle and toward the equipment sheds, my concentration sharpening. When he thrust forward, I sidestepped, tripping him. "What's this about, Sar?" I asked as he stumbled to his knees.

"If I want you to know, I'll tell you, zammar!" he exploded, whipping around.

After knocking his sword out of the way, I backed up. "You'd better want to tell me then. Not only are you using me as a sword dummy; you're about to lose what control you have, and one of us could die."

He advanced, slashing three strokes that I barely met, then leaving an opening. I planted my foot on his leg and shoved.

"Does that matter?" he panted as we circled each other, blades just touching.

"It does to me. For both of us."

As he thrust, I parried, swaying aside. Turning with me, he thrust again, his blade scraping the cuirass. I retreated, drawing him between two of the sheds to the grass in back and away from the men watching. He held the blade low.

I lunged into him, slapping down on his arm, digging his blade into the ground. If he hadn't been so surprised, I wouldn't have had time to dance out of reach of his other arm. "Have you considered what Jonathan would do if one of us dies?"

Avoiding my forward thrust, he jumped back, slamming himself into a shed wall as he parried. The shed shook. Slipping by, he laughed harshly. "He would probably do nothing! Haven't you discovered that yet? He certainly didn't do anything when Abner attacked you!"

The air rang with the dull sound of bronze on bronze, and I strained to keep him from overwhelming me. At last I broke away. "So seeing Abner this afternoon put you into this mood!" I guessed. Again I thrust at him, slapped his parry aside and thrust again, then again, driving him back out into the open, staying low to the ground, almost on my knee.

The sar brought his blade down on mine, and I had to grab it with both hands and roll twice to get away, scrambling to my feet.

"He should be banished!" Malchi raged. "After the dishonor he brought on our name, attacking you like that! And Jonathan does nothing while Abner works his way around Abbi again!" Suddenly he drove his blade into the ground and turned his back to me.

I stood there, panting, watching his tense shoulders and clenched fists. "Is that what's been bothering you? That Jonathan didn't answer the insult to the family honor?"

"And I can't!" He said in a low voice. "Abbi would . . ." He stopped.

"Turn around and pick up your sword, Sar," I said, drawing out my southern accent. "Jonathan did confront Abner. You don't think the adon left just because of his wound, do you? I don't know what the hassar said to him, but I got the distinct feeling that if Abner steps out of line, Jonathan will have him killed."

His eyes incredulous, Malchi slowly faced me. "The only reason Abbi would order Abner killed was if he had threatened Jonathan!" he said, his voice hoarse.

"Food for thought, isn't it? Your sword, Sar! Unless this bout is mine?"

"Lose to a zammar? Not likely."

The air rang again, but he broke away as often as I, both of us maneuvering for advantage as often as we engaged. We had driven ourselves back to the sparring ring, when I heard the hoofbeats of a mule at full speed.

At that moment I backed up, suddenly hardly able to hold the sword, wondering if I'd ever get enough air. When I looked at Sar Malchi, he was down on the ground, chest heaving.

"It's a wonder neither of you were killed!" the hassar's voice raged above me. "I don't care what either of you say! This was more than a sparring bout!"

Neither of us replied. Then my leg started to cramp, and I forced myself to move, knowing I had to stretch that muscle.

"Just what happened here?" Jonathan demanded.

"A discussion, Hassar," I answered, finding the breath to speak, and fighting down my irritation that his actions, or lack of them, had disrupted the army command. I was general after all, and I was the one that had to deal with his brother's moods.

"And what subject would produce such extraordinary exertions?" he inquired.

"Your mulish habit of not talking to your brothers when you should, adoni!" I snapped acerbically, thankful no one else had dared come close, and I could say what was on my mind.

I left Sar Malchi trying to laugh, and Jonathan Hassar staring as I limped away, looking for my mule. I had to get back to Nob.

Fortunately, the king delayed the start of the feast until sars Jonathan and Malchi arrived. The extra time meant Ahiam was able to massage my leg before I washed and dressed in the robe from the hassar. Hassarah Ahinoam had supervised the roasting of a calf, and the spiced chickpeas with greens and garlic were a new dish to me.

Now, I sat back in the shadows and tuned the harp, then sang two or three of the family's favorites, including the "Answering Song," which always made Merab laugh.

Shaul held up his hand. "Sing the one about the sar and the children again. The one you did this afternoon."

"As you command, adoni," I responded, keeping my face straight. Before I was half done, Shaul was laughing outright.

"How do you think of these things, zammar?" he asked when I finished. "I can just see some sar from Hamath or Mari trapped in the forest trying to deal with Habiru children! Did you have someone particular in mind when you wrote it?"

"That depends on how you look at it," I replied carefully. "Most of the time, I see someone do something, or maybe catch a phrase of conversation, and that starts me thinking. Then I build from there. For songs like this one, I exaggerate the idea a lot to make it more amusing."

Later as I leaned against a sycamore, staring into the clearing in the darkness, I smiled a bit, remembering how startled I'd been when Shaul's family had sat down with the children to listen to my songs. I realized now that I'd never seen them around children before. None lived in the fortress, except Baalah Rizpah's sons, and she kept them well contained.

I felt a bit guilty about the fun I'd had, knowing what Eliab would have thought of my wasting time with just children, but the royal family had enjoyed it as much as the little ones had, so I couldn't have done anything too terrible.

Then again, I was mashiah, the anointed king for Yahweh. Had I brought dishonor on my God by what I had done? Old Patah's words came back to me. "All kings are called shepherds of their people." As I well know, shepherds served the sheep, especially the lambs, rather than the other way around. Turning that thought over in my mind, the feeling flooded me that Yah was just as pleased that I had played my harp for the children as He was that I had performed before the entire congregation by the tabernacle.

"Let the sayings of my mouth and the thinking of my heart be always pleasing before You, O Yahweh, my rock and my redeemer."

I hummed the phrase several times. It didn't quite fit with my melody, but almost.

"More to your song?" Jonathan stood behind me.

"I think so."

We watched the stars in silence for a while.

"Does the song about the sar offend you?" I asked quietly.

"No, Dahveed," he said, his rich voice catching just a little. "Knowing the origin of that song is a very small price to pay for the laughter it brought to Abbi. Do you know how long it has been since we had a day as joyous as this?"

"Merab hasn't laughed so much in many years. Malchi spoiled another robe, but those children have taken his heart. And because of your words, I spoke with him, and the bitterness that had settled on him is gone. You have brought the light to us again, zammar. Allow me to say thank you."

"As long as you allow me to repay what you give to me, Hassar."

He turned to me in exasperation.

"Be quiet, Jonathan," I said softly, amused.

"Yes, adoni." His words vibrated with laughter.

CHAPTER 13

What about Merab?" Shaul's voice rose a little, carrying to the other well of the throne room.

"That decision is up to you, adoni," the hassar replied. "Michal had some good ideas last time. Maybe she does now."

"If there is any way I can help, I will," she said, bowing slightly. They had come back from Nob more than a week ago to be met with the news that the Philistines were gathering again. This was the first break in war preparations, and Eshbaal had slipped in an afternoon of administrative business when he had the chance.

"When should they be married?" Shaul asked.

"Well, adoni, there's hardly time now," Sahrah Michal said thoughtfully. "The war season is upon us, and the bekorah's marriage will require a lot of preparation, as befits a king's daughter. And if you gave Merab to Dahveed now, he couldn't fight this season since newly married men are exempt from military service for the year."

"Yes, and we need him to fight, but I do not like the dahveed to wait so long for his rewards," Shaul said, annoyed. "What do you think, Jonathan?"

"I can see the sense in Michal's viewpoint," the hassar said carefully. "But I have no opinion one way or the other."

Shaul still hesitated. Just then he caught sight of someone. "What about you, Balak?" he asked unexpectedly.

The servant looked up, genuinely surprised. "Well, adoni, I don't see that my opinion matters, but if you are asking, there might be other considerations. The bekorah is a very rich reward, and Dahveed has been in the army only for part of one war season. Some may question whether he is worthy of her. Wouldn't it be better to give him the chance to prove himself? Once he returns as victor, no one could say he didn't deserve the reward. It would vindicate your judgment of him and settle any doubts at the same time."

"There is much sense in what you say," the king responded, fingering his beard.

Balak was no fool, Michal thought, eyeing him. That argument struck a good balance between Shaul's wish for Dahveed to fight and his desire to reward the zammar's service. It also acknowledged the need for the general populace to agree that the king's new general deserved the bekorah.

"Jonathan?" Shaul turned to him again.

"You know what it's like trying to reward the zammar, adoni."

The king nodded. "And if he has victories to his credit, he cannot refuse anything. I will wait to give him Merab until after the war season. That will allow Ahinoam time to prepare everything. I'll give Dahveed that house by the wall instead. He needs a proper place to stay."

Michal breathed a sigh of relief. She had some more time, thanks to Balak's advice.

"Now, Jonathan, you mentioned that you had something important to ask?" Shaul said, drawing Michal's attention back to her father.

"Yes, adoni. I wondered if you could do without me this war season. There is enough here to keep Eshbaal and me busy, and you could concentrate on warfare."

The king looked startled.

"The tribes are getting used to a central authority now, and we have more and more requests and petitions," his son went on. "The northern tribes and Manasseh across Jordan have requested several judgments that Eshbaal cannot decide using the judgment scroll the roeh gave you, and since much of our militia comes from these places, it hardly seems honorable to make them wait for answers."

"Adoni, may I mention something?" Michal asked. "If Dahveed is to prove himself, he needs to be on his own. If you go, there might still be questions about Dahveed's abilities."

"What do you say to that, Jonathan?" Michal detected a note of interest in her father's voice.

"To be truthful, adoni, there is enough work to keep us both busy the entire season, and I agree with Michal. Dahveed must prove himself on his own."

"Balak?"

The servant glanced up, again surprised. "Adoni, I'm certain whatever you decide will be best, but Dahveed is very young and inexperienced. Perhaps someone should accompany him. Maybe Sar Ishvi? He would be able to represent you in military strategy and as a warrior, would he not, Hassar?"

"Yes, he would make a good balance for Dahveed," Jonathan agreed.

Balak was far from a fool, Michal thought, watching the servant again.

"I'll think about it," the king said.

Balak quietly entered the king's bedchamber. When the king had returned from Nob with his mind full of nothing but Dahveed, Balak had been afraid that all the time he'd spent in the records room had been wasted. But since yesterday the king had commented twice on his good counsel, and deferring to the hassar had struck just the right note.

Now that idea in the back of his mind refused to go away. He took a deep breath. Today would prove whether or not it might work.

"Adoni?" Balak said softly, standing by the king's bed. "Adoni, it's time to return to court."

Muttering something, the king stirred.

"Adoni? Please wake. The noon rest is over, and you must return to court. You wanted to see Dahveed this afternoon."

Shaul opened his eyes and stared at the ceiling. "Zammar?"

"He is near, if you need him, adoni," the servant continued soothingly. "Remember his music? It brings peace to the king."

The lines on Shaul's face softened. "Yes, his music is good."

"It is time to waken, adoni. The court awaits."

"Yes, yes," the king muttered, looking at Balak, who lowered his gaze respectfully.

"Come, adoni, you must prepare. Today you will send Dahveed out with the army."

Shaul sat up. "And give him the general's mantle again. Which sar did I say I would send with him?"

"Ishvi, wasn't it?"

"That's right. But what about Malchi?"

"Do you think Dahveed could handle both of them?"

"Malchi can be quite a handful," Shaul frowned. "Sometimes Abner had trouble with him. And he's become more difficult recently."

"Yes, although if Dahveed is going to be general, he must eventually learn to handle Malchi. If you think it should be later, rather than now when Ishvi can help, it probably should."

The king considered. "True, but it's early in the season, and if anything happens, we will have time to recover."

"Why should anything happen? With both of them along, things should go smoothly."

"I *will* send both," Shaul decided. "And I will give him the house, also."

"Of course, adoni, but after he proves himself with some victories, didn't you say? He can easily do that, and then you'll be able to reward him handsomely."

Shaul stood for Balak to straighten his robe. "Yes. Yes, I shall. Let's go to court, Balak."

"As you wish, adoni." Quietly elated at how easily he'd led Shaul to alter his plans, Balak followed him from the room.

⊡⌐⊟⊡

I shifted uneasily on my brown mule, rubbing the back of my neck with my hand, then flexing the tension out of my fingers.

Ahiam glanced at me out of the corner of his eye. "What's the matter, adoni?"

I adjusted my position again. "Nothing," I said, staring west at the town of Zanoah. We were about 15 miles* southwest of Gibeah at the bottom of the land-stair on the Shephelah. Zanoah, across the lowland, looked peaceful enough, but something didn't feel right to me, and I hesitated, glancing northwest where the land opened directly down to the coastal plain.

The sars sat on their mules, watching. Neither had said much during the two days since we'd left the fortress, and knowing that one of their duties was to report on how I acquitted myself made me nervous. It didn't help that my relationship with them was ambiguous to say the least. As king's representatives, they outranked me. But they were also commanders of army divisions, so as general, I was above them.

I turned my attention back to Zanoah. Dahveed Joel had reported several Philistine raiding parties in this area, even though it was farther north than his band usually went. I didn't know any

Habiru near here, so my information was minimal, which added to my indecision.

Behind me, 10 units stretched up the hill along the road. Most of the professional force, now officers for the militia, had already signaled a rest as I stared at a perfectly innocent-looking town with few protective fortifications around it. The mule danced under me, reflecting my tension. He'd learned to read me well since I'd gotten him the previous year, and we had a great liking for each other. I signaled my mount forward, then pulled up, bumps appearing on my arms.

"What's the matter?" Ahiam asked again.

I shook my head in irritation. A woman hauled water up from the town well, her figure small in the distance. The town's orchards and vineyards sprawled down the slope, the grain fields clustering around the bottom on the lowlands and continuing up the small valley in front of me.

"I don't see anything unusual, General," Ishvi said, keeping his eyes on the town.

Nor did I, but I couldn't shake the feeling that something was not right.

"Shall I go look around?" Shagay, my first retainer, asked from beside me.

"What for?" Sar Malchi muttered behind me.

I flushed, knowing what the sars must think of my hesitations and delays. Raising my chin, I firmly sent the mule forward into the valley, and the uneasiness that had plagued me abruptly disappeared.

Relieved, I rode around a sharp turn where field walls crowded the road against the hill on the left. Shagay and Ahiam had closed in around me, both of them alert. Behind me, Josheb, my third retainer and a former bodyguard to the hassar, flanked Ahiam. All of the units were just past the turn when the crash of a falling tree reached my ears, and men behind me shouted. The crash shook the ground, and I whirled around on the mule. A huge oak tree blocked the road at the turn.

Horn blasts and a war cry erupted all around us. The mule leaped straight in the air, rearing as Philistines leaped over the field walls on both sides of the road. I didn't have time to think of more than clinging to the mule as it rose under me again, braying in terror. The sudden attack and confusing noise swept everything before it, and every man in the militia broke and ran, carrying the professionals before them.

The sars' mules had reacted as mine, and I got a brief glimpse of Sar Malchi trying to fend off Philistines and fight his mule at the same time. Sar Ishvi was nearly to the lowland, getting his animal under control enough to pull his sword and make an effort to fight. The militia crowded by the oak, milling there in confusion. Around me, more of the enemy charged straight at us.

"Dahveed! Get back there!" Josheb shouted. He grabbed the mule's bridle, swung its head around, and gave it a resounding slap on the rump. Shagay and Ahiam fought side by side, giving me time. Suddenly I realized that Yahweh's gift wasn't with me. At all.

Fear wormed its way into my heart, and my hands started to tremble. The mule carried me back down the road, and I tried to make sense of what I saw, but the confusion meant nothing to me, and all I could see ahead was a growing mass of men trapped against that tree, terror on every face, and I knew that if the Philistines behind me made it back here, they would slaughter those men. And all because I had ignored Yahweh's plain promptings, being too worried about what the sars might think if I showed caution because Yahweh said that I should.

Memory flashed a picture of my sheep in the valley the day I had killed the bear. The flock had bunched against the boulders, stirring around in terror as the militia did now. "Yahweh, please grant them hesed!" I prayed. "I have led them here. What have they done? Let my blood answer for my sin, but not theirs."

The mule suddenly checked, and I missed my frantic grab for its mane, spilling off. I scrambled up as the mule jumped the four-foot wall of a lentil field and galloped across it, jumping the far wall into the forest clearing beyond.

The field! Some of the daze left my mind, and I ran to the wall, realizing that the militia were too terrified to notice any way out but the blocked road. Scrambling over the wall, I started heaving aside the rocks forming the barrier. My knees would hardly support me, for I knew that I'd die here, but those men out there had become my sheep, and sheep couldn't go over walls. They needed a gate. I intended to make one if Yahweh granted me enough time.

I kept lifting stones and tossing them aside. The shouts of the fighting got closer. I didn't have much more time. A gap loomed in the wall now, and hurriedly I made it bigger. Then I ran into the

PHILISTINE AMBUSH AT ZANOAH/SHAGAY'S BATTLE

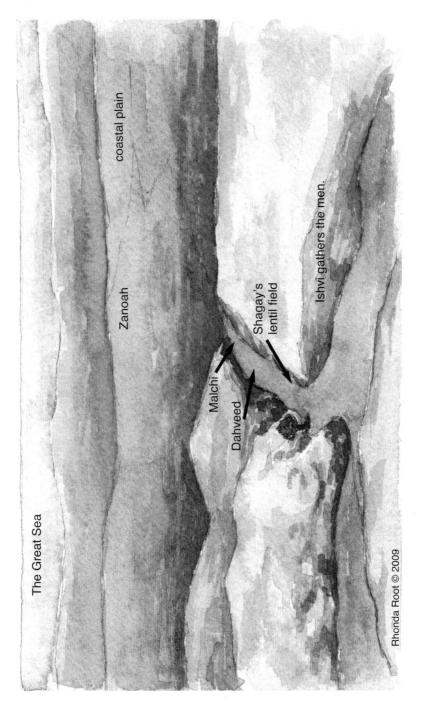

coastal plain

Zanoah

The Great Sea

Malchi

Dahveed

Shagay's lentil field

Ishvi gathers the men.

Rhonda Root © 2009

road, grabbing the first man I reached and shoving him toward it.

"Go!" I yelled in his ear. He saw the break and darted forward. I sent another man after him, then a third. "This way," I yelled, reaching for anyone that I could get my hands on. "Go this way! Into the field." I hurled aside some more stones, widening the opening, and an arrow whistled by my head.

"Look! A way of escape!" someone shouted, and the entire group surged ahead. I let them go, shouting for the professionals to keep order if they could. The militia poured through the wall, some grabbing companions who were too frightened to move and pulling them along. Many now overcame their terror enough to simply vault the wall, and these men responded first to the commands and directions of Ram and Zorath on the opposite side and in the clearing beyond.

A cry of disappointment from the Philistines reached my ears. Feeling weak and tired, I turned to see the road behind me, grateful that Yahweh had given hesed to those who deserved it most. Natan and what was left of the fifth unit retreated toward me, Sar Malchi's sword rising and falling with deadly regularity. I couldn't see his brother.

Once I tried to pull my sword, but my hand refused to grip it. I waited there anyway, wanting to die, knowing that I had foolishly thrown away the most precious thing in my life.

---

* See Cultural Notes: Units of measure.

CHAPTER 14

Within moments the battle swirled around me, and Ahiam hauled me through the gap in the wall into the lentil field. Men bunched up around Ram and Zorath at the far end.

"Drink it, Dahveed," my retainer commanded, holding a cruise to my lips.

The cool wine revived me, and I looked around. Shagay stood alone barring the gap in the wall across the field, sword at ready while the Philistines hesitated. Four charged him as I watched, and he met them head-on, his sword flashing its deadly dance, and then he was alone again. Three more hurled themselves at him. He ducked aside, whirling and slashing, and again stood alone.

Shame and bitterness overwhelmed me. That's where I should be, but I had rejected Yahweh's help. As Shagay met another challenge, I realized that there weren't all that many Philistines. Turning away, I studied the layout of the fields.

"Zorath, how many men can you muster?" I yelled.

"Twenty with me now," he replied.

"Go over there." I pointed to a harvested wheat field beyond the lentils. "I'll send you whatever fighters I can find. Hit them in the rear."

As swiftly as I could, I grabbed anyone who still had a sword, sending them to Zorath.

To my relief, I saw Sar Ishvi in the clearing beyond Ram working to bring order to the militia, keeping the retreat from turning into a rout.

Sar Malchi rode up as I sent more men to Zorath. "Where's your mule?"

"Probably back in Gibeah. Go join Zorath. He'll need all the help he can get."

"Oh?"

"The Philistines gave us a perfectly good tree. I don't see the need to waste it." I searched the men around me for more fighters.

The sar chuckled grimly. "By all means, let us not waste it" he said before riding away. I sent a few more men, then signaled Zorath to go, knowing that every second would be an hour to Shagay in that field. My retainer had retreated a little, but only because he didn't want to stumble over the dead around him. Beyond him, some Philistine commanders argued on the road.

Nearly 30 men grouped around me now, and then the Israelite war cry sounded, and Sar Malchi's mule led the charge farther up the road. I plunged across the lentils, the men close behind me, and we swept past Shagay, who joined in. The fighting was bitter and short. No one felt much like showing hesed as we took the Philistines in their own trap.

We set up camp in the trees where I had stopped that morning, and I knew that by dawn my force would probably have diminished by half. Militia did not take well to experiences such as today's.

Late in the afternoon Sar Ishvi entered the small tent I was using as headquarters.

"Sar," I said, rising.

"General," he replied, looking at me a bit puzzled. "I've been hearing some odd stories, mostly from the militia. What did you do?"

"Before or after I led the army into an ambush?" I asked bitterly, starting to pace.

"That happens to everyone, General. Neither Malchi nor I had any indication that anything was wrong."

I bit my tongue. I'd had plenty of warnings, and I'd ignored them all. Thinking back, I realized that all three of my retainers had known, and done their best to protect me from my own stupidity.

"The stories I hear say that you miraculously destroyed a wall, allowing the men to escape from the trap, and that you personally showed them where to go while fighting off attackers."

"I did nothing of the kind," I said angrily. "Pasach held off the Philistines near the tree, and Natan's unit with Sar Malchi, Josheb, and Shagay kept the force on the road off us for just long enough."

Ishvi stirred a little. "What about the wall?"

"There is nothing miraculous about picking up stones and throwing them aside."

"That might depend. Why did you take down that wall?"

"The men were too terrified to vault over it. They were afraid of what might be on the other side. It happens sometimes with sheep. I removed a few stones to make a visible gap. That's all they needed."

"A few stones?" Ishvi repeated. "Dahveed, let me see your hands."

Puzzled, I held them out.

He reached for them, inspecting them and turning them over. "I wondered why you never took that sword from its sheath. I doubt you could hold it."

When I looked down, I saw that my hands were bloody, the palms lacerated and bruised, dried blood cracking at the edges of the tears in my skin. The backs of them had discolored, and my fingernails were torn, a couple nearly in half. I had to sit down, suddenly realizing how much they hurt.

The sar shook his head. "A few stones, Dahveed? Go look at the size of a couple of them. Ahiam!"

"Yes, adon?" My retainer stuck his head in the tent door.

"I think Dahveed will let you tend to his hands now." Ishvi walked out.

⬚⬚⬚

That evening after I had congratulated and rewarded the honored men, I bowed to the ground in my tent. No words could excuse what I had done today. Men had died. More were wounded because of my folly. My heart cried out in the stillness, begging for Yah's compassion and forgiveness, for without Him, I couldn't hope to lead Israel's army.

Gradually the tension seeped out of me, leaving me limp and exhausted and still devoid of my God's presence. Knowing that if He rejected me, I had only myself to blame, I finally whispered, "Yah, I am Your possession, and I will accept whatever is Your will for me." In the silence, phrases formed in my mind, matching the melody to the song that I had started.

"How can I discern ignorant errors?

"Exempt me from punishment for hidden faults.

"Hold back Your servant from arrogant sins;

"May they not govern me.

"Then I will be blameless; I will be innocent of great transgression."

Repeating the words, I closed my eyes, and the Spirit of Yah touched my mind, bringing a faint scent of myrrh and cinnamon, assuring me that I was still chosen in spite of my arrogance and disrespect. My heart bowed in humble gratitude.

⬚⬚⬚

One month later, after we had repelled three more attempts to send raiding parties into the hills, Sar Ishvi and I, with three of the units and the spoils so far, entered Gibeah to the shouts and cheers of a welcoming crowd. I rode my brown mule again. The animal had appeared outside my tent the morning after the battle, and from the way he acted, he seemed chagrined that he had run away. I knew how he felt. I was embarrassed at all the praise from the people when I knew that the battle of Zanoah would have been significantly different if I had not blundered so badly.

"You have come home in triumph, Ishvi," Shaul declared when we arrived at the fortress. He had ridden out to welcome us.

"Yes, adoni. We have been successful so far."

The king turned to me, a smile spread across his face. "Dahveed, my son, I knew you would return in victory. You have done very well!"

I flushed. "Yahweh honored our efforts, adoni," I managed to reply.

The hassar helped his father dismount, then Ishvi, and then lent me his shoulder to lean on as I slid off the mule. My discomfort increased with every expression of congratulations that I heard, and I determined that in my report to the king, I'd make sure that he knew who should really be honored.

At last, I could escape and started for my room. Ahiam stood at the door, a blank expression on his face.

"What's the matter?" I asked.

He stepped aside for me to look in.

The room was completely bare. My heart sank. Who would know where our things were? Suddenly, panic hit me. Had anyone found the meil and weapons that Jonathan gave me? Then I remembered that I had managed to send them all south just before the war season, and they should be safely tucked away with my anointing robe in the forest house.

My relief was so great, I stepped back outside ready for anything. Sahrah Michal's amused face watched us, and I suddenly noticed the quiet. Everyone had stopped working, and Judith couldn't keep the delighted smile off her lips. Suspicion took over my mind. "Sahrah, have our things been taken somewhere?"

"To your house, of course."

"My house?"

"It's not fitting for the champion of Israel to live in a storeroom," King Shaul announced, smiling. "The house on the east town wall is yours. I suggest you go home, immediately."

I didn't know what to say. My first reaction was to refuse it, knowing it was far more than I deserved, especially after the disaster at

Zanoah.

Jonathan's amused chuckle reached my ears from the door of the king's house. "Would you possibly be contemplating an objection?" he asked, eyebrows raised, hand creeping toward that earring.

The king had the same wicked gleam in his eye as he waited for my reaction. "I don't think I dare," I said, touching my knee to the ground to Shaul, deciding that part of accepting the status Yahweh had given me meant accepting such gifts whether or not I thought I deserved them. Besides, Ahiam and I *had* become cramped in that little room. "Your generosity is more than I deserve, adoni, but I gratefully accept the honor and gift you have seen fit to give me. I will serve the king as well as I can in return."

"You have served me better than anyone else already, Dahveed," Shaul responded. "Come, we will show you where you now live."

As I rose, the courtyard echoed with the applause and laughter of the servants and royal family, and everyone accompanied Ahiam and me to our new house. Shaul insisted that I walk beside his mule as we went out the fortress gates and down the path to the left leading to the east face of Gibeah's hill. At the bottom, nestled against the east wall of town not far from the ridge to the eastern height, we stopped at the gate to a courtyard.

The house was a large two-story dwelling, the back wall consisting of the town wall. The lower part had stalls for animals on one side and space for fodder and straw across a narrow aisle that led to the back, where a storage room spanned the rear. It had grain silos,[1] a small cistern, and the midden pile was nicely downwind. A narrow stairway led to the top of the first story, which had a balcony and upper room as large as Abbi's in Bethlehem. More stairs went up to the roof, which abutted against the walkway of the town wall.

Across the courtyard was a series of small rooms, some for storage, along with a small garden plot and a grape arbor. There was even an almond tree for shade with a bench beneath it.

I knelt to the king again. "Thank you, adoni, Your graciousness to me is great."

"You find it suitable?"

How could I not? It is sufficient in every way, and close to my king so that I can come quickly when there is need."

DAHVEED'S COMPOUND IN GIBEAH

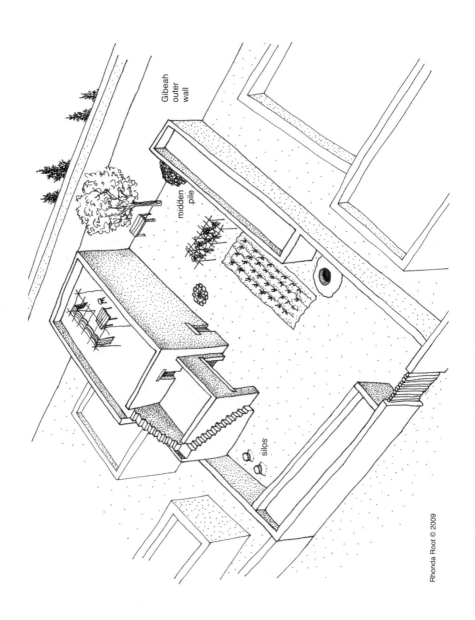

"You will stay, then," Shaul said with satisfaction. "Sahrah Michal said this would suit you, and she has excellent taste."

"Thank you, adoni," I said again.

The next evening Jamin appeared, a donkey loaded with a long covered bundle following him.

"What *is* that?" I asked, eyeing it as the Habiru set it on the ground. It thunked like wood.

"Delivery for you." He walked away without further words, the donkey plodding behind, ears pointed toward the stable.

Puzzled, I untied the bindings and pulled the cloth away. Large wooden posts? Uncovering them more, I saw the curious whorls and knots on the dark wood, one post ending in a rounded knob that resembled a man's head.

My mouth dropped open. Rahab's terephim![2] I stood up, scratching my head. What was I going to do with my ancestress' household gods? Boaz had put them into storage in his time, and they had rarely been out since.

After pulling the coverings completely away, I touched the wood again, seeing how carefully they had been cleaned. A gift, then, for my new house. Something that Abbi could send that very few would connect with my home. Ethan had probably told him my true status with the king.

A lump rose in my throat as I stroked the shiny wood, worn smooth from handling all those years ago, my thoughts flooded with memories of Bethlehem and growing up, of Grandmother Ruth and Abigail and the rest.

As old and neglected as they were, power still seemed to cling to them. I didn't want to put them in the house—that seemed an insult to Yah—but I couldn't bring myself to destroy them or abandon them either. Too much of a tie to home, as well as the uneasiness at the thought of burning the sacred objects of my ancestors. Carefully covering them again, I awkwardly carried them across the courtyard to a storeroom. They'd have to stay there until I decided what to do with them.

Two days later word came from Sar Malchi that more raiding parties were headed into the hills.

---

[1] See Cultural Notes: Grain silos.
[2] See Cultural Notes: Teraphim.

CHAPTER 15

After most of the other servants had left for the day, Balak entered the records room off the passage under the throne room, setting his lamp carefully on the three-legged table. The last three times he'd sat at the gate, he'd heard whispers of deaths in the Gibeonite towns. Someone had said that the king had appointed officers to investigate, and someone else had laughed and said that the deaths seemed to multiply around the officers, not diminish. Now he studied the multitude of papyri and clay tablets stacked carelessly on the shelves on the wall. He had a feeling there was something to be learned in those records.

Sar Eshbaal never had time to attend to them, and, consequently, neither did Kohath. Balak picked up the first stack and started sorting it by date on the table. The Gibeonites lived in four towns—Gibeon, Beeroth, Chephirah, and Kiriath-jearim—covering a wide area in central Ephraim. He wondered if the deaths followed any pattern. If so, he should be able to find it in these records, for they reported the names both of those who worked their assigned weeks at the tabernacle and those excused from their labor, and why.

As he sorted the second stack, he found that most of those records predated the ones he'd just examined. Going through a third stack, he found not only records from Nob of who had reported for duty, but individual releases turned in to the overseers. In addition, three papyri concerned the appointment of a new overseer in Kiriath-jearim, the record cutting off abruptly, and he looked in vain for the rest. He sighed. This would take longer than he had planned. There were two more shelves stuffed full beside this one. Giving up on finding the rest of the interrupted account, he cleared off the table, putting the sorted records on the top shelf to keep them separate from the others.

After pulling the door closed behind him, he noticed a gleam on the floor by the door at the end of the passage that led into the king's treasure room. A silver piece[1] had fallen unnoticed by the scribe. Balak shoved it into his girdle. He'd have another offering for Kemosh in the morning. The thought made him smile a little. Judith had seen the shrine one day and assumed that it was for Yahweh. Now she kept him supplied with incense and also bowed to the shrine with him every Shabbat without the least idea of what god she was worshipping.

As he left the fortress, he glanced left, to the path that led to the east side of town and Dahveed's house. The thought of what Dahveed must be going through out there by the Shephelah with both Sar Ishvi and Sar Malchi on his back amused him.

The army now camped in the hills opposite Zorah. Ekron was about 10 miles west and a little north, and Gath was about 10 miles west and a little south, making us the point of the triangle. I sat in the tent at what was supposed to be a war council. The disastrous ambush at the beginning of the season had made me acutely aware of my ignorance, and left me content to listen during those first councils while the sars debated the defense of the realm. I was now reaping the rewards of that hesitancy in ways that I'd never dreamed possible.

The two sars had very opposite styles of command. Sar Ishvi was cautious, concerned that whatever attack we planned was the one most favorable to our side, reducing casualties as far as possible. Sar Malchi wasn't reckless, but if he saw a Philistine raiding party, he'd attack as soon as he could, rather than wait for the possibility of a better position later. Since both of them wanted the army to fight their way, they haggled with each other about every move we made.

When I'd tried once or twice to say something, they both turned on me, so I remained silent. They were to the point where they hardly spoke to each other except in this tent with me present.

Meanwhile, all 10 units with us sat around, consuming supplies with nothing to do. Our scouts reported no movements of Philistine warriors, no sight of mercenaries, no indication whatever that either Gath or Ekron planned on attacking us again this year. But Joel and Jeshua had both sent word indicating movement far out on the plain near the sea, and those reports had stirred Yahweh's gift until it was a constant buzz in the back of my mind, keeping me jittery and tense.

I knew what the sars thought of my tension. I suspected they hadn't overruled me yet and sent everyone home because neither wanted to explain to the hassar why they had. But I had felt Yah's gift so seldom since ignoring it at Zanoah that I was prepared to accept the reputation of a madman rather than ignore that warning a second time. And I wasn't going to move from this camp until Shagay returned from his scouting trip. At least the unit commanders were busy drilling the militia every day, and the one good thing about the continued inactivity was how much better prepared the forces were for combat.

Worried and discouraged, I took the harp into the hills after dark. Hearing a tiny stream singing to itself, I pushed through some stiff brush. The sound of scratching on wood made me pause, but it was too late. I'd forgotten that I didn't have the harp in a case. Sighing, I eased through as best I could, emerging under the spreading branches of an oak where a little spring fed the stream. I played for a while, then stilled the strings. "What am I to do, Yah? I'm not able to command the sars. Neither is wrong, and neither is right. What will happen if their quarrel comes into the open?"

Leaning back against a rock, I watched the moon, stilling my mind, wondering if Yah would answer.

"Can't" or "won't" command the sars?

The thought startled me. Then I flushed in the darkness. "You are right, Yah," I whispered. "I don't want to confront them. There will be trouble and anger, and if they refuse to acknowledge me, what can I do? I can't dismiss them."

Separate them.

How could I do that? My fingers plucked the strings again while my thoughts flew, searching for plausible ways to get Shaul's sons away from each other.

My ears told me the insects had stopped droning at the same moment I got the distinct feeling that I was watched. Continuing my playing, I shifted positions, getting my legs under me. Whoever was out there was likely a Philistine, and I had come out here alone, something I shouldn't have done, I acknowledged ruefully. Letting the notes of the harp die out, I silently stepped backward toward the oak, every sense alert, and eased my belt knife from its sheath.

A whisper of cloth on the stiff brush in front of me drew my attention. Then a darker fragment of the night appeared, the man dropping to one knee. "Adoni."

"Shagay, you have news?" I asked anxiously, resheathing the belt knife.

"Yes. And I hope it's not too late. They went up the coast to Ashdod, Dahveed."

"Who?"

"The Philistine army. By the time I learned what they'd done, it was too late to stay around and get the details. There are supposed to be 40 units, but you can probably discount that by 10. What I do know for certain is that they split up two days ago. Some headed for Mount Gerizim and Shechem in the north, another column for Hebron in the south. I heard rumors of a third thrust toward Gibeah, but that seemed more like a wild tale than anything else. I didn't have time to investigate further."

I felt as if I had suddenly and inexplicably collapsed on the ground. This meant that the Philistines could be invading Israel's borders *today* in two places, outflanking us on both sides. We didn't have the numbers to fight on two fronts.

I had no idea what to do, yet I must do something.

"You've done well, Shagay."

"I should have figured it out sooner," he growled. "I'll wait for you," he added.

I leaned my head against the tree, the rough bark digging into my forehead as he moved off. "Yah, tell me what to do," I said, dropping to my knees beside the tiny stream. "Don't let Your people be driven from their inheritance and slaughtered. I don't know how to lead an army. I've never faced anything like this before. Please, Yahweh, take this burden from my shoulders! I am not ready to bear it!"

You never killed a bear before, or a giant. Is My hand suddenly too weak to save?

"No, Adonai," I said, grabbing hold of my thoughts, "but I am too frightened to remember, and I can see no way out. I didn't have time to be afraid when the bear came, and I knew Your will was for me to save Israel from Goliath. But I have failed You since then, and I have not done well with the duties the king gave me."

You are still Dahveed Israel.

"Adonai, King Shaul called me Dahveed Israel."

I work through whomever I choose.

Taking a deep breath to steady myself, I touched my forehead to the leaves on the forest floor. "I am Your possession, Adonai Yahweh. What is Your servant to do?"

Separate the sars.

"How many men shall I send with them?"

One unit each.

I remained silent in puzzlement. Then I realized that if the sars needed only one unit each, the pincer movements to the north and south must be meant to draw our army away. The real danger was the rumored third thrust. A blow like that to the center of Shaul's realm could tear the kingdom apart, especially if the major portion of the Philistine army had a couple days to pillage and destroy before any sort of defensive force could assemble.

"Adonai, will the Philistine army come through the center toward Gibeah?"

Yes.

"Shall I stand in the way? Will You deliver them to my hand?"

Yes.

"Thank You, Adonai. You have greatly honored Your servant. Fight for Your people, and save us with Your strength, for You are Israel's only God."

I called a war council as soon as I returned to camp. On my way to the tent, a messenger reported Philistine raiders moving north of Beth-horon.

"What has happened, Dahveed?" Sar Ishvi asked as the brothers entered.

"Word just reached us that the Philistines gathered in Ashdod, and are raiding—"

"They'll head north again to Aijalon," Sar Malchi interrupted. "I'll take five units and stop them."

"We don't know how many units they have," Ishvi said. "And Socoh is just as good a target as Aijalon. We should collect more information before moving."

"Only if you're willing to let them steal a march on us. We need someone up north."

"Sars—" I started to say.

"We have another flank in the south."

Malchi snorted. "What's down there except Habiru? And they got along fine without us several years ago."

I gritted my teeth. I'd been too small then to really understand, but

I knew that the people of Judah had not done fine that year. Ethan had taken in what was left of several families, and he had come to Abbi for help.

"We can't just ignore our backs, Malchi," Ishvi continued. "We have to be aware of the south, as well. As representative of the king, I have to keep the whole picture in mind."

"I represent the king also, brother, so the decision is not just yours."

In the silence that followed, I nearly groaned. When King Shaul had made both his sons his representatives, he put Malchi on equal footing with Ishvi. Such an arrangement had invited honor battles not only between me and the sars, but also between the sars themselves. There was only one way to stop them. I must assert my rank.

I took a deep breath. "I believe the final decision is mine. The Philistines are headed for Mount Gerizim, and are already at Lachish, and will strike eastward from those two points."

"Gerizim is halfway to Jezreel!" Malchi exclaimed.

"Both moves are feints," I stated. "The main thrust will come right here, and head for Gibeah. We know—"

"Gibeah!" Both sars laughed.

"Dahveed, the Philistines aren't going to plant themselves outside of Shaul's fortress in the middle of hostile territory," Ishvi insisted.

"If our army is split in half, running north and south, who will stop them?" I persisted. "We know—"

Sar Malchi snorted in digust. "Even you should know better than this, Dahveed!"

"I'm basing my decision on very reliable information, Sar," I said, clenching my hands to keep the anger from my voice, reminding myself sternly that I needed to do what Yahweh wanted, not squabble with the sar. "We do, however, need to respond to the raiders at Mount Gerizim. You can do that, Sar Malchi. Pick one unit to take with you. If you find yourself facing more than three Philistine units, I'll send you however many reinforcements you ask for."

"I'll take the first, fifth, and sixth."

"I said one, Sar."

"Are you denying the king's representative his requirements?" Malchi challenged.

"I am allocating resources as necessary to my commanders."

I locked eyes with him and waited.

After a moment or two he pulled back from my gaze, dropping his eyes. "Ram and the first unit."

"Leave as soon as you get ready. The Philistines have a two-day lead on you. Stop at Aijalon if you wish, but I'd advise you to plan on heading straight to Mount Gerizim." Nodding in dismissal, I then turned to Ishvi.

"Sar Ishvi, there will be a force of Philistines entering the hill country south of Lachish. Pick a unit and go make their lives miserable, if you let them keep them at all. Whom do you want?"

I waited in the silence. Without taking my eyes from Ishvi, I added, "Sar Malchi, I believe you have your orders."

That prickle of awareness went down my spine, and I shifted my weight slightly, eyes still on Ishvi, ears centered completely on Malchi. The light from the lamps intensified, and the colors on Sar Ishvi's meil seemed impossibly bright and varied.

Finally I heard the rustle of his clothing as the sar turned, flipped the tent flap out of his way, and strode off into the darkness, his voice raised for Ram.

"The hassar is very protective of the family honor," Ishvi commented, his eyes measuring me.

"Yes, Sar. What unit did you want?"

"Perhaps I, as king's representative, should send you south with one unit while I remain here. Lachish is in Judah, after all, not Israel. I found it interesting that Shaul is considered the hassar's adon, and not the king, in the south. Calls to arms do not bring much response from Beer-sheba to Jebus. Should I risk the lives of faithful Israelites for those who do not support the throne?"

A shaft of pain went through my heart. For a second I didn't know what to say. I knew most northerners did not consider Judah part of Israel.[2] But that the sar would think that way had never entered my mind. I had assumed that because Jonathan saw the land as a whole, all the royal family did.

I knew the struggle that most people who lived between Jebus and Beer-sheba had to survive. Anything could upset the balance of life and death, and many places had never recovered from the raids years ago.

Unable to think of any way to explain to him what he had never experienced before, I did not answer his question. "Declaring yourself king's representative would not be necessary, Sar. If you object to defending territory that you do not believe is part of Israel, I will not ask you to do so. I will send someone else."

He studied me a moment. "I'll take Natan and the fifth. But my concern still stands."

"It is noted, Sar."

After he left, I bent over in agony, holding my side, wondering if Ishvi knew how much it would hurt me to exclude my people. Had I made enemies of both sars?

Putting the thought out of my mind, I wrote a brief report to the king, and then summoned Shagay. "Where is the best place around Lehi for us to ambush about 30 units of Philistines?" I asked.

After standing in thought a bit, he said slowly, "The trade route to Jebus crosses a long ravine just south of Lehi. There's a fork there, and coming up from the west, it can be hard to tell which route goes to Jebus. If we can lure the Philistines up the north fork toward Lehi, that would be a perfect place. The hills narrow quickly, and the road winds around enough that it would be difficult for a large force to see what was happening in front or behind."

"Perfect!" I smiled.

---

[1] See Cultural Notes: Money.
[2] See Cultural Notes: Israel and Judah separate.111111

CHAPTER 16

Balak placed the shrine on the old stump in the tiny courtyard, kneeling there in the dim light before dawn, placing a tiny gold piece as thank offering beside the statue of Kemosh. Yesterday after the noon rest he'd happened to mention to Shaul that Jonathan would be needed for an important judgment case. The king had walked into court and reversed his decision to let Jonathan take the remaining army units and check on Dahveed at Lehi. Court had come to a standstill while the hassar spent three hours persuading the king back to his original decision.

The servant laughed softly. He could probably make the king do anything he wanted, for Shaul clung to him now, needing his reminders and descriptions of the zammar's music to calm his mind and quiet his fears of the darkness that he said lurked in the corners of the rooms.

Bowing to the shrine, Balak whispered, "Bring my plans to fruition, Kemosh, that I may be honored before my abbi." He paused. Was there more he could do? How else could he bind Shaul to him? The king's increasing fear of the darkness sprang to his mind. Smiling slightly, he continued, "Increase the darkness that the king fears, O Kemosh. Send that which causes it to haunt Shaul's mind that he may turn to me even more, and you may be honored before your enemies." To be doubly sure that Kemosh knew what he wanted, he found a scrap of papyrus and wrote out his curse.

I sat on my brown mule on a knoll on the north side of the road. From there I could spot the fork in the road half a mile west, look into the ravine directly below, and see farther east where the road curved away. The areas in between those three points were not visible, but it was the best vantage point that I could find.

The first report came about the third hour.

"Twenty-two units altogether," the messenger reported. "There is an Egyptian chariot and one unit of Egyptian foot soldiers."

A smaller force than I'd expected, which was good. But what were the Egyptians for? "What is the order of march?" I asked.

"The Egyptian unit and chariot are toward the end. All the officers ride mules."

Yah, fight for us, I prayed silently. Looking down over the late summer foliage of oak, elm, and sycamore trees, I studied them carefully, but I couldn't tell that most of the Israelite army waited in them.

Far to the east toward the Jebus road, a slight haze hung just above the trees, and something startled a flock of birds that took wing, black dots against the blue of the sky in the distance. I checked back to the west, searching for the first signs of the Philistines' approach. A figure ran down the road toward the fork. Then another, and another. That

ISRAELITE AMBUSH AT LEHI

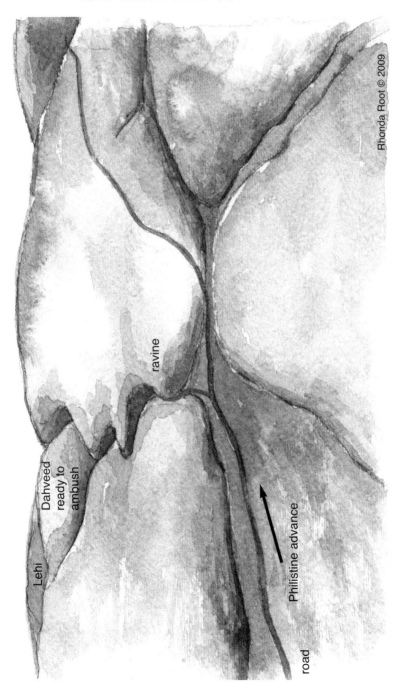

would be the second unit, left behind to put up a token resistance, then retreat, drawing the Philistines after them. They passed from my sight, and I waited tensely.

The mule tossed his head and tugged at the reins. I patted him and checked the road to the east. Empty. But in the west, figures moved swiftly, and the chariot finally appeared, the driver probably swearing at the excuse for a path called a road in these barbaric hills. It seemed ages before the first of Commander Jarib's men arrived below me, stumbling down the middle of the road.

"Where are we supposed to go?" one asked, his voice carrying in the silence.

"Doesn't matter, just keep going," his companion panted. "I think the ambush is supposed to be somewhere around here, but maybe it's farther down."

They paused, and three more caught up to them.

"Where's Jarib?" the first man asked.

"He was back there, making sure that we took the right fork and keeping track of the Philistines. He was angry as a dry duck when he saw that chariot. No one told him about chariots."

"We're lucky it can't go very fast. I'll never complain about this road again!"

The soldiers trotted on, and not a man on either side of the road had given away our position. Yahweh's hand was over us today.

Later, there was a slight stir when the Philistine scouts cautiously advanced into sight. "What do you think?" one of them asked another.

"I wish I had the walls of Jebus around me."

I cocked my head. The accent was more marked than I'd ever heard before. I wondered which city they were from. They had a slight twist to the ends of some words that reminded me of Minelek, the Philistine merchant that I'd made Gibeonite overseer in Chephirah.

They moved on, and others followed. A couple scouts slipped into the trees and never reappeared. Still the silence continued. A fly landed on the mule's ear, and the animal flicked it away. Below me, the first line of Philistines walked swiftly by. This had all the earmarks of a forced march. Another unit came through, the officer urging his men on.

As the Philistines continued to come, a restless stirring from the trees reached my ears. The chariot entered the trap, the driver trying to control the horses, a strange-looking pair, one black and one gray. The charioteer could hardly keep them on the road, and the officer's gaze suddenly riveted on the stallions. He added his hand to the driver's, raising his voice. Once the horses stilled a little, the Egyptian glanced from the horses to the trees.

"Get the horn ready," I said to the trumpeter. He raised the battle horn to his lips. The stallions suddenly jumped, and an instant later, the officer shouted a warning in what had to be Egyptian. Then everything was drowned out as the horn beside me bellowed, and those of the commanders followed suit.

Confined by the hills, the combined shout of the army rose toward me, setting my heart racing and the mule plunging as the men leaped from the trees, rushing on the unprepared Philistines.

The road was full of fighting men, swords gleaming in the sun, then dulling with red. As I watched, Ahiam gripped the mule to steady it. Even though the surprise had been complete, the Philistines had responded quickly and with little panic.

"Mercenaries!" I exclaimed. I'd counted on at least half of their army being militia, like ours, but nearly all fought as seasoned warriors. Where had they all come from?

"Messenger!" I called. "Tell the commanders we're facing professionals. They are to pull back into the trees and let the archers fire from cover."

I sent another man to the west end, where the eighth, under Dishon, and Zorath, with the third, had the hardest fighting. Not all the Philistines had made it past them, and the enemy quickly realized they were on the end of the ambush. The unmatched stallions were in the thick of things, but the officer seemed to be directing the battle instead of fighting.

He had gathered his men into a tight unit, fighting his way out. Ahiam signaled to a Habiru on the hill opposite, and I saw runners start down the line with the same message that I'd given over here.

Soon messengers arrived from various points of the battle. All reported heavy casualties for both sides, and I repeated my orders to pull back into the trees and let the archers handle the situation. The Philistine serens had to have been hiring mercenaries for months to assemble all these!

188 | YAHWEH'S WARRIOR

Over on my right that Egyptian had successfully fought clear, his unit staying to one side. Now, he ordered the Philistines around him to give covering fire for the unit next in line. He positioned archers on either side, and sent two parties of foot soldiers into the trees. Below me, the combatants gradually drew apart as the commanders followed my orders. At the extreme eastern end, the sixth unit reported that two units of Philistines had fought out and were headed east. I sent a fresh runner to warn the king.

Then the eerie sound of the Philistine battle horns reached my ears. I held my breath, wondering what the order was. Retreat. I relaxed a little as the invaders started back along the road, fighting as they went.

Quickly I sent a message to the east end, telling them to push the enemy west. It didn't take long for the Philistines to break into a jog. As the last of them passed, the Israelite commanders beneath my vantage point joined the push to move them even faster.

When I looked back to the west where the Egyptian held the escape route open, I noticed the battle line forming behind him on the road. I didn't want a pitched battle. I couldn't afford to lose that many men.

"Ahiam, signal the Habiru," I snapped. "Tell the commanders to push the Philistines as hard as possible. I want them running as fast as they can when they hit that battle line!"

I waited until the units below me charged, turning the retreat into a full-fledged rout. The Philistines burst out of the confining hills and hit the Egyptian's battle line just as I planned. It shattered and fell back as the fleeing soldiers broke through. Bowing to the inevitable, my opponent retreated farther from the confining hills before ordering the formation of another line.

Then without warning, the Israelite battle cry rose from the south side of the road, and fresh warriors sprang from a point of trees, led by the hassar on his black mule! The Philistines fled after only a token resistance.

"Charge, sound the charge!" I yelled, and the horn blasted beside me. Instantly the rest of the army responded. I sent the mule down to the road.

Moments later, I pulled to a halt, staring. That Egyptian just wouldn't give up! While most of the army had fled, he had managed to hold back a portion and was slowing the Israelite charge. Archers shot steadily even as they ran after their fellows, his own unit lagging behind.

Jonathan rode his black mount back and forth, gathering warriors to the side, and the Egyptian saw his intent just a little too late. A wedge of men drove between his group and the rest of the Philistine army, forcing them into a tangled side ravine to the north.

As the hassar charged forward to meet the chariot, his mule suddenly seemed to hesitate, and I watched as the world slowed down. In eerie silence, that magnificent mule bowed his head and plowed into the ground, taking the hassar down with him. They hit the ground gently, so it seemed, and the mule lay still.

Jonathan half rose, his head turning toward the chariot charging down on him, struggling to free his leg trapped under the mule. It happened too fast and too slow for me to react. Horror descended on me, and nothing existed except the sight of the war horses pulling the chariot, the driver's mouth open as he handled the reins. A Philistine mercenary raised his bow, arrow aimed for the hassar, and I wondered whether the arrow or the horses would get to Jonathan first.

Pain squeezed my heart. A war dagger suddenly appeared in the mercenary's back, and as he dropped his bow, that Egyptian knocked aside the driver, seized the reins, and impossible as it seemed, he commanded the stallions in ringing Canaanite. Bracing himself, he hauled back, arm muscles bulging, lifting the stallions to their hind legs, turning them. The chariot pivoted, and the horses leaped forward, dragging the overturned chariot back to the road and into the chaos of the fleeing Philistine army.

I was halfway there before I realized that I'd sent my mule forward. My breath sobbed in my chest as I sat that mule on its haunches and leaped off.

Commander Libni was there before me.

"After them!" the hassar roared. "Libni, take the twelfth and thirteenth with you, and go after them! Fourteenth, pin those Egyptians in the ravine! Dara, get this mule off me!"

"It will take more than Dara, Jonathan," I said, bending over him. "Are you hurt anywhere?"

"Why would I be with you standing between me and the battle? Get me up!"

"I wasn't near you, Hassar."

Well, someone was. Where did that cursedly persistent Egyptian go?"

I looked around. The Egyptian driver lay nearby, his neck broken from the spill out of the chariot, and beyond him on the ground, lay the officer, looking as if he had just lain down for a rest. His kilt was brilliant white, and his gold armbands flashed in the sun. A gold collar circled his neck. At first I thought his head was broken, but then I realized that I gazed at a wig, partially askew. The sunlight gleamed on his own hair, and I stared. Where had that blaze of red come from? I looked again as I walked closer. He had dark-brown hair.

I felt his neck. He was alive.

"What is your wish, Dahveed?" Ahiam asked beside me, his hand on his belt knife.

Had I really seen what I thought I had? I couldn't make up my mind.

"Don't let anyone touch him," I decided. I touched a gold armband, and it shifted. Stunned, I pulled it off. The clasp had burst open. I turned it over in my hands.

Ahiam handed me the other one. It too had burst apart. I stared down at the man. Was it possible that he really *had* stopped and turned those stallions by brute force? Why?

I looked the collar over. It was solid gold strips, set with gems, and gleamed with a deep glow that seemed very, very old, unlike the bright new shine on the armbands.

Puzzled, I returned to the hassar. "He was thrown from the chariot, but he's alive."

Dara had collected some men, and while they shifted the mule, the shield bearer and I dragged Jonathan from under it. I could see the broken shaft of an Egyptian arrow in the mule's chest just behind the foreleg. That archer had known right where to shoot.

"Is it broken?" the hassar asked, trying to see his leg.

"No, adoni, and a hollow in the ground saved it from being crushed, but the bone is badly bruised. It will take longer to heal than a break would," Dara replied.

"How goes the battle, Dahveed?" the hassar snapped. "If you don't know, get out there and find out!"

I jumped back on the mule, dragging my mind back to the battle. Most of the fighting had passed to the west, and I rode that way, sending messengers forward to bring back as many of the units as possible.

By dusk all the commanders except the tenth, twelfth, and thirteenth had returned, and the battlefield had been cleared, arms collected, and the wounded and dead seen to. The hassar sat on a rock by the road keeping track of the fourteenth unit, which was in a stalemate with the Egyptians trapped in the ravine.

"Still waiting?" I asked.

"They're more stubborn than you are," he said sourly. "As soon as it's dark, I'll send the Habiru after them!"

"Adoni, grant them hesed," a hoarse voice said.

Jonathan and I turned toward the sound. The Egyptian officer dragged himself from the ground, right arm held close to his side. Shagay straightened in the shadows behind him and cocked an arrow in his bow, following silently as the man stumbled toward us.

He went to his knees, nearly falling as he did. "Hesed, adoni. Do not kill them." He raised his eyes, seeing the royal seal on Jonathan's hand, and looked from the hassar to me, confusion crossing his face.

"Bring him closer," Jonathan commanded.

I went to him. When he looked into my face, I froze. Even in the dusky light, his unfocused gaze came from eyes the color of the dark-blue sky just before dusk. I shivered, wanting to look away. I'd heard of eyes that color, but I'd never seen them. Unresisting, he came with me, still shifting his look between us, his confusion growing.

He bowed to the ground. "Adoni, take my life, but do not kill those with me. They are," he paused, searching for words. "They are sheep in my care. They fought only to protect the young one. I am the one who directed the others against you. I will give you my life for them; only let the young one, the lamb, return to his home."

I cocked my head to understand the sharp, old accent. His words struck deep into my heart. But the hassar's gaze was chill, and his hand went to the hilt of his war dagger. Silently I placed my own hand on his arm. The officer looked from the royal seal to me and back to Jonathan, confused once more.

"I think you lie, Egyptian," Jonathan said, looking straight at me. "I think the others are mercenaries as the rest. And if it weren't for you, we would have routed that army, and maybe even destroyed it completely."

Sweat appeared on the man's neck and face. "Perhaps that is true, adoni. I am trained for war, and when the battle was joined, I did what I could. But the archers from my country are only to protect the young one and those who accompany him on his journey. He was sent to Mari and Babylon to gain experience. Let me bear the blame for what happened before you. I beg you to send them home. The young man's mother loves him."

"If you are only an escort, as you say, you would not be accompanying an army into battle, Egyptian."

Jonathan watched me steadily, pointing out all the different considerations of the situation, reminding me that misplaced hesed might result in the slaughter of many people in the future.

A tremor ran through the man, and he clenched his teeth against the pain, leaning again toward his right side. "I had little choice, adoni. I was assured my charge would be safer with the army than continuing on our way alone. And surrounded by that army, I could hardly disagree. I suspected there would be a battle, and I instructed my unit to fight only to protect the young one. If those with me died, there would be one more proof mark before Pharaoh that the hill people live to upset ma at."

"Why should our standing before Pharaoh concern you?" the hassar replied coldly.

"It shouldn't," he admitted, wincing again. "But the stories of the battles here have come to our land. There is genius here, in the way the land has been made to fight for you." Briefly he glanced at the hills around him. Both Jonathan and I caught the unwilling admiration in his tone.

A hard smile crossed the hassar's face. "Flattery will not help you, Egyptian."

"I have no way of proving my words, adoni," the officer admitted. "I will do anything you require. Only let the young man live."

The hassar waited, and I struggled to decide what to do. Jonathan's own words decided the issue. Whom had he seen standing in front of him in the battle? There had been no one there. I could not let this man die until I knew what had happened.

"I have too many questions to condemn him now, Hassar," I nearly whispered.

"He is a flatterer, playing to your sympathies, Dahveed," Jonathan answered just as quietly. "He and those with him are dangerous."

"How could he know that I'm a shepherd?"

The hassar paused. "Tell Ram we will be interrogating this prisoner for some time, and do not wish to be disturbed," he said at last.

CHAPTER 17

Dara led us back to where Jonathan's retainers had pitched his tent, and I helped him hobble inside. The guards brought the Egyptian officer in after us.

While Dara made Jonathan comfortable, I dismissed the guards and gave our captive a quick examination. He looked to be badly bruised, but no more.

His gaze kept switching from Jonathan to me, and he blinked. "Adoni, who are you?" he blurted out when we were alone. "You are two, yet you are one. The adon comes from darkness, but the darkness does not cling to him. The other brings light and commands that which is above him."

Jonathan and I both froze. "How do you know?" the hassar asked.

"My God, El Shaddai, lets me see what is hidden."

"El Shaddai!" I gasped. Suddenly the air around us stirred, and a fierce, powerful presence filled the tent, bringing with it a breath of dry desert wind. The lamps Dara had lit blazed briefly, setting everything in the tent in such sharp relief that I had to close my eyes.

When I opened them, the lamps burned normally again, but neither Jonathan nor I needed more than that to remember the consuming flame that had come that night in the anteroom.

"El Shaddai gave you this gift?" the hassar asked, his tone considerably altered.

The officer heard it, and knelt. "It comes to those of us with the Great One's eyes."

"Who was the Great One?"

The Egyptian paused. "Adon Paanekh came to Egypt from El Shaddai's lands long before my fathers' fathers or their fathers' fathers were born. He saved Egypt from destruction, and he taught my fathers to honor his God, who is greater than all other gods. We have remained faithful to El Shaddai's commands from that time to this."

"How do you have the Great One's eyes?" I asked, trying to still the tremor in my voice, unwilling to believe who this man had to be.

"It is said that the Great One's grandchildren married the grandchildren of my ancestor, and so his blood entered ours. The stories say this happened many times in the generations, and sometimes there is a child born with the Horus eyes of the Great One. That child receives the golden collar when they reach the age of 30, the age at which the Great One received it from Pharaoh Amenemhet III."

Jonathan sat like a statue, his gaze riveted on the collar. His hand reached out of its own accord, his fingers brushing the gold. "Could this really be Joseph's collar?" he whispered.

The officer bowed lower. "Adoni, you hold my life. Take the collar if you wish. It is yours."

The hassar smiled wryly. "No, Egyptian, you do not belong to me. You belong to El Shaddai."

"Someone must take the collar one day," the officer said, his voice unsteady. "There is no one to take it when I die, and El Shaddai looks on you with favor, for His warrior stood before you in the battle."

"Why is there no one to take it?"

The man bowed his head. "My son is with Pharaoh. When Pharaoh hears what I have done, his anger will fall on my house."

"Doesn't Pharaoh understand the chances of war? You fought better than all the others."

"It's not that," I said softly. "He saw El Shaddai's warrior protecting you, and he deliberately turned his horses to avoid you. By now, those mercenaries will know just who you are, Hassar, and I can't imagine Pharaoh will be pleased to hear that an officer of his spared your life."

"You risked your son to save me?" Jonathan stared in disbelief at the man kneeling before him.

"My son is in El Shaddai's hands, and I will not bring dishonor to my God."

"El Shaddai will remember what you have done," Jonathan said in a subdued tone.

"He has," the officer replied. "My God has told me that my son will hold me in his arms when I die. I will not question Him, although I do not see how this is possible. But my son is in His hands as the youth in my charge is in mine. I ask again, adoni, spare his life! Let him return home in peace."

"You have your request," the hassar answered, still staring at that collar.

I could hardly take my eyes off it, either. Just seeing the thing that had been the symbol of El Shaddai's ability to work for His people even in Egypt sent a sense of awe through me.

The Egyptian spoke again. "Adoni, your patience has given me courage to ask something more. Before I die, please tell me, what is this ground, and who are you of Israel?"

The sar looked blank, but I thought I knew what the officer was asking. "The hassar is of Benjamin. I am of Judah, and the ground here was given to Ephraim, younger son of Joseph."

"Thank You, El Shaddai," the man whispered. "I will die content, knowing that I will lie on the Great One's inheritance." He looked up at the hassar. "My life is yours, adoni. Take it as you will."

"Does stubbornness increase the farther south one goes?" Jonathan demanded in exasperation.

"You will not die, Egyptian," I interjected, hiding my amusement. "Nor will any of those with you. Yahweh has made it clear that you are under His hand."

"Yahweh, adoni?" the man asked in puzzlement.

"Yahweh is the personal name of El Shaddai. We worship the same God," I explained. "That being the case, how do we call you?"

"I am called Mahesa, adoni."

"Get up, Mahesa."

I called in the guards to take charge of our prisoner. When we were alone again, I turned to the hassar. "What are you doing here?" I asked curiously.

The hassar chuckled. "I finally got enough dispatches put together to understand what was happening. Between Malchi's irritations and Ishvi's brotherly concerns, I decided the sars had not been helpful. What did they do, argue with you about battle plans?"

"It was more like a lecture," I said wryly, handing Jonathan the cruise he gestured toward. "But they may be more willing to listen after this."

"Don't count on it," Jonathan sighed, grimacing from the pain in his leg. "They can both be stubborn."

"So long as they don't get mulish like you, I'll manage, adoni."

Two weeks later I glanced to my right as I rode, seeing the walls of Jebus in the near distance. Israel had survived another war season thanks to Yahweh's hesed. We had driven the last raiding parties from the hills, and the sars had both returned, reporting that they had found the diversionary columns. Sar Malchi had vented his anger at me on the two units trying to enter the hills west of Shiloh, and Sar Ishvi had lured two units into the uplands and wiped them out above Adullam.

Hassar Jonathan returned to Gibeah the day after the battle, taking the fourteenth unit and the Egyptians with him. The unit would escort the Egyptians to Israel's north border at Dan. I knew he would always wonder if I'd done the right thing letting them go. So would I.

The pack animals and carts were loaded with spoils, most of it payment from the Philistines to the mercenaries, and the mercenaries had been expensive. As we approached Gibeah, I put on the general's mantle. Ahead, the first of the townspeople began to cheer, and everyone straightened up a little. As we came within sight of the walls, the women began to sing.

"The dahveed!" someone cried out, and heads turned in my direction. "Sar Ishvi! Sar Malchi-shua! Sons of Shaul!" the chant rose as a line of women danced forward. "Shaul has slain a thousand enemies of Yahweh, yes, thousands." From the opposite side of the road, another line of women echoed the line. "Shaul has slain thousands!"

"And Dahveed 10 thousands!" a male voice shouted.

A roar answered him, the crowd stamping and clapping as we rode by. I tried to keep the flush from my face as I bowed and nodded. My mule lowered his head and pranced a few steps, making the crowd laugh.

"Shaul has slain thousands, and Dahveed his 10 thousands." The chant quickly passed along both sides of the road, getting louder and louder as we approached the gates, the people clapping in rhythm.

The king waited on his mule just outside the gate, Eshbaal holding the bridle, the hassar on a dark-gray mule beside him. Standing on the wall above the gate, the sahrahs waved, Michal looking flushed and excited.

"Shaul has slain thousands, and Dahveed his 10 thousands." The words bounced off the walls. I noted the tension in Jonathan's body, and immediately looked to the king, keeping him in my view as much as possible as we got closer. The way he sat on the mule and how his head tilted just a little upward warned me that I'd better keep the harp with me at all times, and stay as close to him as I could. But he was smiling a welcome, and I relaxed a little. Maybe it wasn't as bad as it might be.

Then the smile hesitated on his face, his eyes sharpening as he looked from me to his sons following along behind. A shiver of unease tightened the muscles in my legs, and the mule pranced again, putting his head down and feeling the bit with his mouth. I calmed him and rode on.

"Shaul has slain thousands, and Dahveed his 10 thousands," the women next to the gate took up the chant, and I saw Sahrah Michal clapping her hands with the rhythm, but Hassarah Ahinoam had bitten her lip and watched her husband.

When I glanced back, my stomach dropped. As the chant repeated again and again, the smile left Shaul's face completely, and suspicion began to cross it.

My insides cramped, and the welcoming cheers and singing faded from my ears. I got nearer to King Shaul and saw the way he clenched his hands, and the glitter of anger in his eyes.

"Yah, what can I do?" I whispered as the general's mantle weighed heavier and heavier on my shoulders. I hesitated, and the mule checked slightly. Sar Ishvi continued forward, whether by chance or design, I didn't know, and with a puzzled glance at me, Sar Malchi followed. I bowed from my seat to the king. Sar Eshbaal led the royal mule into the road, and I followed the king and his sons toward the fortress. At the turn, the king faced the road from under the tamarisk tree, the hassar flanking him. Ishvi took his place, and Malchi followed suit. I lined up a little farther down, keeping enough space between Sar Malchi and myself so that I would not be considered one of the royal family.

The rest of the procession seemed endless, and that chant echoed many times more against the walls of the town. Each time, Shaul's eyes glittered with rage.

Yahweh, shield me, I prayed silently as I rode into the fortress. Dismounting just inside the gate, I gave the mule to a guard and walked to where the king waited on his mount. The hassar watched, his eyes concerned as he glanced from me to his father.

Very conscious of the rich clothing that I wore and every piece of gold that glittered on me, I knelt to the king, bowing nearly to the ground, and waited. Shaul remained silent a long time, while the welcoming conversation stilled to silence.

"So you have returned, successful again," he said coldly.

"Yes, adoni," I replied without looking up. "Yahweh granted His favor to Israel and fulfilled the king's wish against his enemies."

"I will hear your report tomorrow," he said curtly, turning his head away, and Eshbaal helped him dismount. With his back toward me he walked into the private courtyard.

The next morning Josheb accompanied me to the court, carrying the harp. I wore a kilt and the general's mantle since I would be making my official report to the king.

"Dahveed, is that you?" Jonathan's voice asked from the curtains by the stairs when I entered the anteroom.

"Yes, Hassar," I said, bowing.

"Good. I wanted to speak with you."

He led the way down the back passage to the second scribe's room, limping much less on his leg than I expected.

As soon as the door shut, I spoke. "How is the king?"

"Not good, Dahveed. I nearly sent a messenger to bring you back three times since that last battle. His illness has been heavy on him, and I've counted the days until you returned. Do you have your harp?"

"Josheb has it in the anteroom. How many attacks has the king had?"

"Several. He is more and more unpredictable. I never know what he will decide from one day to the next. It's been so bad that I dare not let anything remain undone past the noon rest or overnight. By then he will have changed his mind, and I can spend hours trying to persuade him back to the original decision. I haven't been able to determine what is influencing him, but something is."

I hadn't seen this much tension in him since I first arrived, years ago. "What is it you fear, Jonathan?" I asked bluntly.

He looked up, a denial on his lips that he never spoke.

I held his gaze.

"I think the demon is trying to take him again," he finally confessed. "He's been violent, his eyes constantly wandering to the shadows and the skies."

"Has he been terrorized at all?"

"Not yet." Jonathan eased down on the three-legged stool, stretching his leg out. "I first noticed signs of this a week or so before the battle at Lehi. But since I got back, he's worsened rapidly. He is suspicious of people again, and Michal, Balak, and I seem to be the only ones he can tolerate for any length of time."

"Balak?"

Jonathan shrugged. "I don't favor him much, but he can handle the king. Can you sit in the throne room as you used to?"

"I could, but the king is angry with me now, Hassar. That might make my presence more a hindrance than a help." I shifted restlessly. The mention of Balak with the king made me edgy.

"He did seem upset yesterday, but that may have passed."

I kept my gaze away from Jonathan's face. Upset? The king had been in a rage yesterday, more so than when I had refused my loyalty after killing Goliath.

A knock at the door interrupted us.

"Come!" the hassar said.

A scribe opened the door. "Hassar, the king is on his way."

Jonathan nodded, and the scribe bowed before leaving.

"I'll try to work you in as soon as I can," Jonathan said as he rose. "We've got a full schedule today, and I know there are hundreds of things you should be doing."

I trailed after him down the passage, remaining in it until the king had gone up the stairs to the throne room. In the anteroom I stayed to one side, Josheb with me, waiting. A couple hours passed.

My retainer glanced at me. "The king must be very busy," he ventured.

"The king is very angry," I said softly. "If anything happens, you, Ahaim, and Shagay get out of Gibeah. That's an order, Josheb."

"Yes, adoni," the guard replied, his eyes wide.

We were still waiting close to noon when Sahrah Michal went up the stairs, and in a couple minutes Jonathan returned to the anteroom with her.

"Take his meal up to him," he said to her. "I don't like the way he's acting."

"All right, Jonathan. What about having Dahveed play while he eats?"

"That might help," he said, looking around for me.

I stepped away from the wall. "What am I to do, Hassar?"

"Come in with the food when it arrives. We clear the court and anteroom while the king eats. The quiet seems to help calm him." The hassar went back upstairs, hesitating a little on his bad leg.

I turned to Michal. "Sahrah, send for the sars."

Her hands started to tremble. "All right, Dahveed."

CHAPTER 18

I took the harp from the case and tuned it, noticing the dozens of small scratches from the brush that I'd gone through at Lehi, and the dent in the horizontal bar where the harp had hit the wall when I stumbled and knocked it off the table the morning after Jonathan and I fought that demon. My own hands shook a little. I hoped we wouldn't have to battle it again.

As soon as the meal arrived, I went to the throne room and, noting where the king would eat, I moved my stool just around the corner into the west ell on the other side of a pillar that had not been here before.

Starting with quiet, random notes, I looked around curiously at the changes since I'd been in the room last. Four slim pillars crossed the south ell where it met the west ell, framing the dais and throne, rich dark-blue curtains tied up between them, shielding most of my form from the king. In front of my seat Sar Eshbaal's table was larger, covered with a fringed cloth that matched the new curtains. The door in the far end of the alcove was barred. On the other side of the dais, to the right of the throne, the hassar's table was also covered with an opulent cloth, and an expensive polished stone bowl held fruit on the small stand on the right of the throne. Sar Eshbaal bent over his table with Jonathan as they discussed something.

King Shaul ate in the south ell at the end of the long table closest to the throne. By the time the servers had taken food to the sars in the alcove, my music had become loud enough to be heard, and the king had relaxed his shoulders.

Leaning against the wall, I transformed the notes into a song, plucking just the melody in a lazy rhythm. The quiet making me uneasy, I added accompaniment to the melody of my song, and Yahweh's gift pricked at my mind. Jonathan and Eshbaal seemed intent on their discussion, both hastily stuffing food into their mouths at rare intervals, but I noticed the glances they gave their father.

Shaul paid attention only to his food, occasionally adding more olive oil to his bread from the polished black juglet. He hadn't looked toward me once. And that's what was wrong, I realized. Always before, he would notice me some way. I took some deep breaths, relaxing my arms and hands so I could continue to play. Shifting on the stool, I braced myself so that I could move in any direction I needed to, feeling Yahweh's gift strengthen inside.

The hassar checked through some records, and then limped past me through the curtains to the door, going down to the anteroom. A couple minutes later Sar Eshbaal walked through the new curtains also.

The king laughed.

The sound sent a chill down my spine, and both Sahrah Michal on the dais and Sar Eshbaal by the stair door jerked around.

Shaul stood, eyes raised to the ceiling, and that horrible laugh came from his lips again. "Have you returned?" he shouted. "I know what to do about you this time! The light will come again and drive you out." He moved as he spoke, and Yahweh's gift flooded through me. The

CHANGES IN THE GIBEAH THRONE ROOM

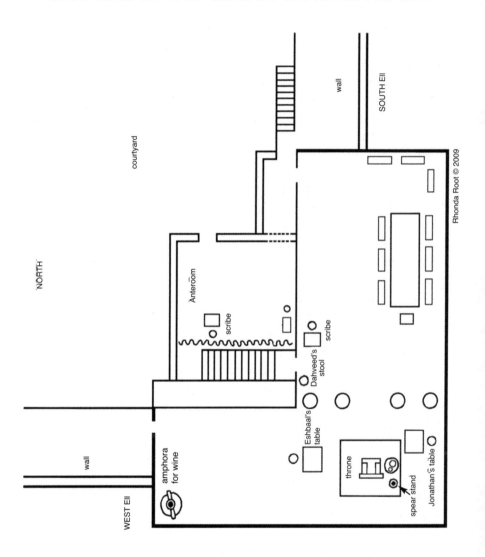

king wandered toward the throne, eyes glued to the ceiling, incoherent sounds tumbling from his lips. His hands raised toward his head. "No! No!" he shrieked.

Sar Eshbaal backed toward the stair door. I added the fullest notes I could on the harp, and the music seemed to pull at the king, making him hesitate. Sahrah Michal stood absolutely still as her father passed within two feet of her. She seemed very calm, but the fringes on her robe trembled, and her face was as white as Egyptian linen.

The king tried to look at her, but something kept pulling his gaze upward, and he seemed torn between going forward or turning back to me. I added my voice to the music, and he wrapped his arms around his head. "Stop! No more!"

Sar Eshbaal disappeared down the stairs, and Sahrah Michal shifted backward an inch at a time, retreating toward the pillars opposite me.

Just then Shaul screamed, and words streamed from his mouth in a babble of sound, his eyes rolled painfully upward, one arm straining toward the ceiling, the other flailing to the side. He hit the spear of office in the stand behind the throne and pulled it to him.

"Jonathan!" Eshbaal yelled.

Yahweh's gift brought a calm with it, and I stayed on the stool, the harp still demanding attention, its music tugging at the king, who continued to rave as he clutched the spear, one arm still thrust upward.

Sahrah Michal had backed to the pillar now, squeezing between it and the wall, where the curtains shielded her from her father's sight.

I kept an eye on her, thankful for her self-control, and prayed to Yahweh that she could stay hidden. I hadn't moved, the music coaxing and demanding at the same time, my voice raised in a praise song, filling the room with something for the king to pay attention to besides the demon striving within him, for I had no doubt that it had returned.

The sahrah slumped against the pillar. Tears streamed down her face as she hugged herself tightly, one hand on her mouth to keep from crying aloud.

"I know, I know, IknowIknowIknow you, treacherous cockatrice!" the king babbled, almost too fast for me to understand. He had his back turned to me, addressing the corner of the room by the hassar's table. "Iknowwhatyouwant. You cannothidefrommeanylonger."

He laughed again, and the inhuman cruelty and malice in the sound sent a shudder of fear through me.

"Treachery!" Shaul shrieked, and whipped around, the spear sailing through the air straight toward my heart. Light flashed off the point as the harp tumbled from my hands, and I shoved myself to the left just barely in time. The head buried itself in the wall, the point finding a course of timber and pinning me by the mantle as the king threw himself toward me, shrieking.

"*Dahveed!*" Michal screamed.

Realizing that I'd never get the spear out in time to get away, I tore open the clasp of the brooch fastening the general's mantle, leaving it hanging there as I ducked aside, just barely ahead of the enraged king, whose fingers brushed my arm as I leaped away. I slipped behind the next pillar, my belt knife slicing through the ties holding the curtains.

Shaul wrenched the spear from the wall, muttering, "Pin him to the wall. Takes my place before the sars, does he? Kills 10 thousands while I kill only thousands? He shall die thrust through with my spear and pinned to the wall. Traitor!" he finished with a shriek. I heard the thunk of metal on wood, and the harp skidded along the floor toward Eshbaal's table. Facing the long table with the second pillar at my back, I clutched my belt knife and listened for the king's movements, his words leaving a trail of fear in my mind. Shaul in his right mind was a formidable opponent, but with him under the control of a demon, I knew that only Yahweh could save me from him, and Michal still remained in danger, unable to do anything without drawing the king's attention. In his present state he would launch that spear at anything. And the thought of Jonathan entering the room to encounter an unexpected attack made sweat break out all over me.

The king laughed again, just a couple feet away, hidden by the hanging. "You are afraid," he said in a voice that didn't sound like his own. "You will die, Dahveed. Refusing me after all I've done for you. Taking my place, robbing me of my praise and honor. Stealing my house from me."

When he moved, I dashed to the third pillar, slashing the ties on those hangings. Now I faced the dais, with Shaul again on the other side by the long table. My heart pounded in my chest, and my arms shook. The door to the outside looked so inviting, but I knew that I'd never make it ahead of that spear, let alone get the bar off. Hearing the whisper of the king's clothing, I crouched down. Not another sound had come from the sahrah after she screamed my name, but I could see her feet on my left. If the king drove me that way, she could well die.

Closing my eyes, I slipped the belt knife back into its sheath, trusting to Yahweh's gift to protect me. The king lunged forward, and I rolled twice, back to my stool, surging to my feet and facing the dais just as he burst through the hangings, turned, and launched the spear at point-blank range.

By the time the weapon had left his hand, his movements had slowed down, and I watched it float toward me as I twisted my body to avoid the point. It struck the wall with a resounding thud. "Now, Michal!" I ordered as I seized the handle and wrenched it sideways. It snapped just above the head, splinters flying in every direction.

She darted for the door as I flung the spear handle over the king's head to the far corner behind the throne. Shaul's eyes followed it, swinging him away from his daughter as she ran. I lunged after her. Behind me, the king whined like an animal. I jumped down the stairs, noting that Michal huddled in the shadows between the anteroom hangings and the stairs, her eyes wide with fear. I went into the anteroom.

On either side of the opening stood the sars and Balak, Jonathan looking sick. He would not meet my eyes. No one else was in the room, and the outer door was shut. Yahweh's gift still pounded in my veins, and when the king came down the stairs, I showed myself briefly, luring him through the curtains. The sars closed in, Jonathan and Ishvi on one side, Malchi and Balak on the other.

Shaul kept right on walking, his eyes filled with contempt at his sons' efforts to stop him. Unexpectedly he planted his feet, and Jonathan gasped a warning too late. One arm broke free, and the king grabbed Balak, dragging the servant in front of him.

"You! You brought me here!" he said in that strange voice and threw the man aside. It was a casual gesture using only one arm, but Balak crashed against the wall, clutching his own arm. The moment of distraction gave Malchi a chance to regain his hold on the king.

"El Shaddai, grant us hesed," Jonathan said, wrapping his arm around his father's throat while his brothers struggled to hold the king

206 | YAHWEH'S WARRIOR

back. Bracing himself, the hassar pulled backward, his body tense with the strain, until at last the king stopped, his breath rasping as Jonathan cut off more and more air.

Shaul sagged to his knees, and his son loosened his hold a little. Immediately, the king heaved himself up, nearly throwing the sars off their feet. As Jonathan resumed his choke hold, their father slumped to the floor once more. Behind them Sar Eshbaal appeared at the curtains with several of the court guards and Sahrah Michal. Balak lay on the floor, lower lip held between his teeth, and I realized that Shaul had broken his servant's arm.

The king's eyes still remained fixed on me, demonic rage burning in them. Yahweh's gift flowed in me, making it next to impossible to remain still, but I knew that if I moved, Shaul's sons would lose what control they had over him.

What am I to do, Yah? I asked in my mind.

Jonathan tentatively relaxed his grip, and the king nearly broke free before the sars forced him back, the hassar clamping down on his throat. Seconds stretched into minutes, and the hassar's injured leg trembled. Somehow Shaul found breath to hurl accusations at me, promising what would happen to me for my treachery and presumption, raving that he had seen through all the schemes that I had been involved in, and that he knew everything I thought in my heart, vowing that I would never sit on his throne.

"We can't keep this up, Jonathan," Ishvi gasped. "He's not weakening in the slightest."

The king laughed, chilling and cruel, his teeth snapping together like a dog's.

"Jonathan!" Malchi said desperately.

The hassar applied more pressure until the king began to go limp. Then, for the first time, he looked at me, his eyes begging me to do something.

Ishvi and Malchi's ragged breathing and sweat-streaked faces told me they couldn't hold on much longer, and if Jonathan's leg gave way, the king would break free, and the first person he would attack was me.

"Mashiah," Shaul's son said barely audibly, lowering his eyes again, head bent and arms rigid around his abbi's neck as he waited.

Appalled, I realized the only option remaining to Jonathan to protect me was to break his abbi's neck. No one would blame the hassar if Shaul did die, even if they knew he had deliberately killed him, but I knew what killing his abbi and king would do to Jonathan. The price was too terrible for me to think about, and yet the hassar stood there, ready to pay it.

Suddenly I realized that nothing in our power could defeat the force arrayed against us, certainly not me and The Hassarah's harp. Only one Spirit was fierce and powerful and fiery enough to meet that which faced us now.

I sank to my knees. The king struggled to reach me, and the sars managed to restrain him one more time. Jonathan looked at me, and I held his eye.

"Call Him with me," I said.

The hassar's face paled. "We will all die."

"We cannot control what holds the king. Do you think he will stop with my blood, or yours?"

"Call Him," Jonathan finally whispered.

Somehow my harp was in my hands. I found out later that Sheva brought it to me, risking the attention of the demon as he did.

I plucked the strings, playing the same song I had used before. Only this time, it was El Shaddai whom I summoned. We needed the same fierce desert Fire that had destroyed the cities of the plain in Abraham's time, that had demanded that Isaac choose death over life, and that had defeated the gods of Egypt and come down on the mountain in glory to claim His people.

As I sang, I abandoned myself to whatever Yahweh's will was, whether it was life or death, as I asked Him to free the king forever, with no possibility of demonic return. What words I sang, or how, I don't remember. I only knew that we needed El Shaddai's help and protection, and I begged Him to come while my voice filled the room, proclaiming El Shaddai's greatness.

Balak screamed in fear on the floor to one side, and the king flung off his sons and lurched forward, only to be stopped by nothing at all, as shriek after shriek poured from his mouth. I cried out El Shaddai's name, knowing that our only hope was His protection. And then I was overwhelmed with fire and darkness, and the ground shook beneath my knees. The scent of the hot desert wind streaming over me met the sounds of howling and hatred. Thunder filled the air, and I nearly fell as the ground shook in response.

A light too intense to bear flared before my eyes, seeming to devour the dense blackness writhing about the king. The God of my fathers wrenched the demon from the king, binding it away forever. I covered my face. Never would I even consider serving any other God, for I doubted that any other deity existed. After glimpsing the depth of the darkness that El Shaddai had bound, I could only imagine the intensity of the Light powerful enough to surpass it, and I remember knowing, like the hassar, that I would die.

CHAPTER 19

The scent of a woman's perfume first penetrated my mind.

"Help him lie down," I heard Sahrah Michal say, and hands eased me to the floor, taking the harp.

I turned my head toward the voice. "What of the king?" I whispered.

"He's alive, but he's not conscious," Commander Sheva spoke.

"The hassar?"

"The sahrah is checking him now," Sheva replied.

When I managed to look behind me, I saw Balak on the floor. A pulse pounded in his neck, so even though he looked pale enough to be dead, he wasn't.

"Sheva, bring Dara to set that arm before he wakes up," I ordered.

"Whose arm?"

"Balak's. The king broke it."

"Get Dara from the armory," the commander snapped at a guard. The soldier left on the run.

Slowly I sat up. More of the fortress guards stood at the closed door and the curtains. Sar Malchi bent over Jonathan with Sahrah Michal, and Sar Ishvi sat next to the king.

I half-crawled over to Ishvi. "What happened?"

"After you finished your song, Abbi fell, and neither you nor Jonathan moved. Michal finally touched you. You seemed to be in a trance. Jonathan, too."

"Did you hear or see anything else?"

Ishvi shook his head.

Yahweh had covered them, then, with His compassion.

Someone pounded on the outside doors.

"Let him in," Sar Ishvi ordered.

A white-faced servant bowed from the door. "Quartermaster Nadab sends to the hassar," he said, panting. "Every animal in the stables is wild with terror."

I pulled myself up. "Tell Nadab from the dahveed that the, uh, disturbance is over."

Another messenger took the first man's place. "Sar Ishvi, Hassarah Ahinoam sends to you. Bekorah Merab has been struck down somehow."

"Go to her," I urged him.

"Will the king be all right?" he asked, hesitating on his way out the door.

"Shaul will never be troubled by that demon again," I said with absolute certainty. "Go, the bekorah needs you."

Ishvi departed, and I went to the king. "Adoni?"

He stirred, opening his eyes.

"Adoni, are you well?"

"Zammar, the light came. Light I could not bear!" As he tried to sit up, I reached to help him, but he flinched away, the look in his eyes puzzling me. "Where is Jonathan?"

"Still resting, adoni."

"What did you do to him?" The king's voice was hoarse. "Where are my sons?" Shaul sat up, again refusing to let me help him.

"Sar Malchi is here, and Sar Ishvi has gone to see about Bekorah Merab. Sar Eshbaal and Sahrah Michal are here also if you wish them."

"Yes, Michal, come to me."

Dara arrived, refusing to tend Balak until he satisfied himself that the hassar was unhurt. Then he set the servant's arm and had him carried to his house.

I went to Jonathan. He seemed to be in an extremely deep sleep.

King Shaul watched me anxiously, and in deference to his worry, I kept a respectful distance from the hassar, letting Sheva and Malchi deal with the messengers that appeared at the door almost constantly.

As the minutes stretched and the hassar remained motionless, Shaul became more and more worried. At last, Dara and I gently rolled Jonathan onto his back. The shield bearer checked him over once more, then shrugged. "See if you can wake him."

"Hassar, wake up."

He turned his head and sighed, one hand moving to his chest. Shaul stepped closer. "Jonathan, speak to me."

I backed away, and the king knelt by his son's side, taking his hand. Jonathan opened his eyes. "Abbi?"

"Yes, Jonathan. Are you hurt?"

"I don't think so. What happened?" When he glanced around and saw the harp lying a few feet away, he began looking for me. Then, as memory returned, he stiffened and whipped his glance back to the king.

"Adoni, are you—?"

"The darkness is gone, my son. How are you?"

"I'm unhurt."

They gripped each other's hands tightly, and I could feel the bond between them. I looked down. It was all that Shaul had left, and I would not intrude if I could help it.

Jonathan turned back to me. "Dahveed?"

"No one was harmed, Hassar," I said, without moving. "The king will not be troubled by the demon again."

"I know."

His tone confirmed my suspicions that he had experienced what I had.

"I think everyone would be better for some food and wine," Sahrah Michal announced.

"I certainly would," Jonathan agreed. "Adoni, what is your wish?"

"Let us go," Shaul said, looking uneasily at me.

I kept my gaze averted.

"Dahveed," Jonathan said, "come along. You need this more than the rest of us."

"No!" Shaul interjected, his voice sharp with fear. "The zammar is not to come. He is never to come to me again. I will not have him in my presence. Send him away, Jonathan," the king continued, backing toward the door. "Send him away at once!"

Balak lay on his bedroll and tried to still his pounding heart. It made his arm explode with pain at every beat. But he couldn't forget looking into the king's eyes and not seeing Shaul there.

His body shuddered, until he nearly cried with the pain it brought to his arm. Surely what that spirit had said was a lie. He, Balak, couldn't have brought it here. The king must have invited it somehow. Glancing fearfully at the niche where the shrine was, Balak started to tremble. Surely the gods didn't really pay attention to mere mortals. It must have been something that the king had done, or thought, or said that had unleashed the demon.

Then he felt again the whisper of the dry wind and the heat of the fire that scorched through him, and he had to bite his lips to keep from screaming. He knew that the Fire had been better than what he'd seen in the king's eyes, but he turned away in terror just the same.

Where was everyone? He tossed on the bedroll, trying to sit up, but the pain from his arm prevented him. What if that thing came back while he was here by himself? Either of those things?

"Judith!" he shouted.

His wife appeared at the door, her eyes wide in alarm. "Balak? What's wrong? Is the pain too bad?"

He lay panting on the floor. "Where were you?" he asked fretfully.

"Just in the courtyard. Shall I get some of the herbs for you? Dara said they'd ease any pain so that you could sleep."

Suddenly he wanted to sleep more than anything. Sleep without dreams, without thoughts accusing him for what he'd done—maybe done, he corrected himself. "Yes, give me some."

"I'll get them."

Before he could call her back, she disappeared. Balak looked around the empty room, and his heart pounded again. They wouldn't come unless they were called. He knew that. Well, Yahweh wouldn't come. He didn't know about the demon. At least, he didn't think Shaul had summoned it. Yet it had come anyway. The thought made him shake more, and he glanced wildly around, every sound filling him with terror.

It was an eternity before he heard Judith return, and he fixed his eyes on the door, nearly crying with the need to have someone with him. She gave him a cup, and he greedily drank in spite of the bitter taste. Pain and thought faded away, and he welcomed the oblivion.

My house was empty when I returned to it. Evidently Josheb had followed my orders, for which I was glad. I rested until after dark; then my owl calls brought Ahiam from the eastern height. He climbed the Habiru stair on the wall, and we discussed what should be done. I decided to send both him and Shagay back to Ethan's band, since I had no idea what would happen to me now. Josheb could remain with me.

I checked in with Sheva the next morning, fulfilling my duties as general since they had not been taken from me yet. But they would be soon, for Sheva told me that the hassar and the tenth unit had already left for Zelah and Abner. I was relieved, and waited impatiently for the summons so I could give up the mantle. It didn't come until after the noon rest of the next day.

"Adon, the hassar requests that you bring the general's mantle with you," the messenger said after telling me when to appear.

"It's at the fortress," I replied, startled. "It was, uh, removed day before yesterday. Look at the corner of the throne room where the zammar's stool is, next to the closest pillar to the stair door."

I pulled a robe from my clothes chest, deciding that I'd better wear a full-length formal one. While I'd have to report to the anteroom only if the king was there, it would still be best that I be prepared for a formal interview just in case.

Unbinding my hair, I combed the tangles from it. I'd just wrapped the hassar's girdle around my waist and slipped a gold headband over my forehead when I heard Josheb shout, "Adoni!"

I whirled, suddenly realizing the door was the only way out of this room. I'd take care of that tomorrow, if I was still living here, as well as having some windows facing the courtyard put in. In spite of Josheb's warning, Yahweh's gift stayed quiet, so I shoved my belt knife into the girdle and opened the door. Jonathan Hassar climbed the stairs, the general's mantle flung over one arm, his face white and still.

Dara and four soldiers stood in the courtyard with the hassar's mule, and people lingered outside the courtyard gate.

"Shalom, Jonathan," I greeted, bowing slightly.

"Dahveed."

From the look on his face I decided this talk should be private. "Come in," I invited, stepping aside.

He limped to the door, ducking his head as he stepped over the threshold. Inside, he stood by the small table, his back to me, and I lit a lamp. With clouds covering more of the sky, the light was dim.

"What did Abbi do while you were in the throne room?"

While the lamplight flickered, I gave him a brief outline of what had occurred.

"You were wearing this?" he asked, lifting the mantle slightly.

"Yes."

"Did my father try to kill you?" he asked, indicating the tear in the mantle.

"The king has a habit of throwing his spear at shadows, and it pinned the mantle to the wall. I undid the clasp and slipped away."

Still not looking at me, Jonathan threw something on the table. What was left of the gold brooch gleamed in the light, torn in half.

"Yahweh's gift does not come on you because the king throws his spear at shadows, Dahveed. There are two spear holes in the wall. He tried again?"

"The demon was persistent, yes." I stood calmly, feeling the tension in the hassar.

"Why did you stay to break the spear? You would have had enough time to get out."

"And leave a weapon to that demon to kill someone with?"

"So you break rock-hard oak like it's a dried pine branch for the fire? He must have been on top of you by then."

"He hesitated and gave me the second I needed."

The sar faced me. "Why did you stay, Dahveed?" Jonathan was just as relentless as he'd been in the upper room of the residence.

"Sahrah Michal needed to get away."

"*Michal was still in there?*" he exclaimed in horror. He swayed a little, then steadied himself on the table.

"The sahrah is a very strong woman, Hassar. She ran at just the right moment, and the king couldn't decide whether to chase her, try for the spearhead, or go after me."

Suddenly Jonathan looked old. Slowly he straightened, then bowed his head. "What is your will in this matter, Mashiah?" he whispered. "Abbi has raised his hand against you. Will you be content to have the king removed from the city, or must I—must I do—more, adoni?"

No wonder Yahweh loved this man, answered his cries for help, and healed his wounds. *He should be king,* I thought fiercely. *Yahweh, he should be king! I am a poor substitute for him.*

"I have given him comfort, and he will have his heart's desires."

The distinctness of the thought eased my mind. "Your abbi did not raise his hand to me, Jonathan. The demon did, and Yahweh protected me."

He must have been willing to kill you, adoni, else the demon would have found no welcome, as I have cause to know. What will you have me do?"

"We fought a demon, not your abbi," I repeated, crossing my arms in irritation.

"Mashiah, you could have died. Shall I let Shaul go free to threaten you again?"

He still hadn't looked at me, and his relentlessness frustrated me no end. I walked over to him and put my fingers on the earring hanging on his chest, catching his eye.

"You shall not touch your abbi and king over this incident. He was taken by something greater than us all, and it would not be honorable or just for me to blame him for what only El Shaddai can control. Is my will plain to you?"

"Yes, Mashiah."

When he broke our gaze, I could tell he was about to kneel, and I couldn't have coped with that, so I jerked around and stalked out the door.

CHAPTER 20

Michal had never been so furious in her life. Not only had the king demoted Dahveed to the status of a commander, giving the general's mantle back to Abner, but Abner had then assigned Dahveed to the second unit! She threw more grain into the grinding trough and attacked it with the basalt roller. A chill wind blew in from the sea, and the weights on Merab's loom clattered angrily as she yanked the yarn through the hanging threads. Michal smiled grimly. If Merab was upset, then something truly bad had happened.

She threw more grain into the trough. The sounds of people in the outer courtyard signaled the end of court for the day. Talk was subdued, and Michal smiled as she heard Abner's greetings returned curtly, if at all. In the year that he'd been away, much had changed. Dahveed had garnered a lot of friends.

Sar Malchi rode in and stalked into the anteroom. Within moments he and Jonathan appeared, headed for the private courtyard.

"But the *second* unit?" Malchi raged as they entered. "After what he did?"

"I don't like it any better than you, Malchi," her oldest brother replied, his voice smooth. "The king and the general told me only that Dahveed was demoted to commander, and once the general assigned him, Dahveed himself wouldn't let me interfere. He's more comfortable as a commander than as general anyway."

"It's an affront to his honor."

"Since he served at the pleasure of the king, it's not as much a dishonor as it could be. And the fact that he accepted the king's wishes so readily has gained him honor, in sharp contrast to Abner's decision to place him in the second unit."

Michal scooped up the pulverized grain from the trough and put it under the pestle, pounding it into fine flour, imagining that she was smashing Abner.

"Jonathan!" Ishvi shouted, sliding off his mule in the private courtyard.

The hassar held up his hand. "I've already heard it, Ishvi. Dahveed has been assigned, and I can't change it."

"How did it happen?"

"Ask the king."

"*The king* is party to this?"

"It's not likely to change," Jonathan said soberly. "Dahveed is banned from his presence."

"Why?" Ishvi stared.

"I haven't asked."

"Do you know what kind of life Abner will force on Dahveed?"

"I know what kind of life he'd like to impose, but that is something I *can* do something about."

Michal glanced up at her brother.

The hassar's smile was wolfish. "Dahveed is going to find that he has a very free hand with that second unit. I'm looking forward to seeing what it will be like by next war season."

Suddenly Malchi chuckled. "I hadn't thought of that, brother. And I don't think Father's cousin has either!"

Braced for the worst, I reported to the training ground the next morning. The stiffness in Abner's carriage when he saw me was not reassuring. I wondered what would descend on me when he asked me to stay after the others had left.

"As you know, the second unit is the weakest of the professional force," the general said when we were alone.

"Yes, General."

A muscle in his jaw twitched as if he was clenching and unclenching his teeth, and he refused to meet my eyes when I glanced at him. "Since you now command it, see if you can make something of it besides a garbage dump. Get whatever you need from the armory."

Astonishment held me speechless for several seconds. "Yes, General," I managed to say.

"Dismissed."

I bowed slightly and fled, still wondering if I'd heard correctly.

By the sparring circle I found the second unit standing off to the side. I looked them over, taking the time to really study them. The first thing would be to find out who they all were, and what they had and didn't have in the way of weapons. On our way back to Gibeah I discovered that the second unit included men from everywhere. What might be buried in them, I wondered, thinking of Eleazar. He and Sar Ishvi weren't quite up to the level of Jonathan and Dara, but it wouldn't be long.

When we arrived at the armory, Nadab wasn't happy about letting us into the storerooms. I supervised the men while they picked out swords. Most of them took whatever caught their fancy, but one man, Lotan, started a systematic search. Some blades he passed over with barely a glance, but others he took down and studied. After trying out a few, he laid one or two aside and went back to searching. He had strangely cropped hair and odd scars on his massive arms. Although shorter, he probably made almost twice of me in sheer weight.

I went to him. "What are you looking for?"

"Some decent bronze," he snapped impatiently. "Look at this one. It's so brittle, it would break the first time someone landed a good blow on it."

"It took a very sharp edge," I said, admiring the job done with it.

"What good is that if half the blade is at your feet?" he snorted.

"There is that. What about this one?"

"Too soft. I can almost bend it with my hands. Halfway through a battle it would be too dull to cut leben, let alone flesh."

"You could hit someone over the head with it."

He barked a laugh. "It would bend over their head, and then you'd have to reforge the blade, which wouldn't be a bad idea anyway."

Picking the first blade up, I struck it with the hilt of my belt knife, cocking my head to listen. Bronze suitable for a battle sword would give a dull sound. This had a bell-like ring, so it was indeed too hard. But how had Lotan known? He had just glanced at it.

"What about this one?" I asked, handing him mine.

His eyes lit up, and he took the blade reverently. "Now, this is bronze!" he said in delight. "Where did you find it?"

"In the discard heap. It's my personal blade," I added, seeing the gleam in his eye.

Disappointment written all over him, he handed it back with a sigh. "Having seen that one, I'll never be satisfied with anything else," he grumbled.

"Do the best you can. How do you know so much about bronze?"

"I'm a smith. Worked with it until I joined the army," he admitted reluctantly.

Not believing my ears, I froze. A *smith*? They were kept on the outskirts of society because they crossed boundaries by transforming one thing into another and were thus impure.* But they were also more precious than gold right now.

"Where did you learn the craft?" I inquired, trying to keep the excitement out of my voice, and understanding the scars on his arms now.

"I'm a Hittite," he said absently, trying out another blade.

I swallowed. A *Hittite* smith? Impure or not, he had just become the most valuable man in the kingdom! Leaving him to his search, I retreated, praying to Yahweh that he'd find something to fight with so I wouldn't have to give up my blade.

Everyone else had picked out a sword by the time Lotan emerged. I breathed a sigh of relief. He carried a short, stubby assembly that didn't look as much like a sword as two sickles mashed together somehow. I took it and pulled my blade, striking his against mine. It rang true. He'd probably found the strongest bronze in the room and, as dust-covered as it was, it had probably been in a corner somewhere for years.

As I handed it back, an idea formed in my mind. All I needed was permission from Jonathan to use a forge, and I was certain that he'd give me that. I dismissed the men for the day, much to their delight, then told them that I'd expect them on the practice field before dawn the next day.

Groaning, the men walked from the armory. I called Lotan back. "Tell me, could you forge good bronze out of what's in that room?"

His mouth nearly dropped open. "Commander?"

"Theres a lot of bronze in that room, and you muttered about some having too much tin, and some not enough. Is it possible to melt a couple of weak blades and get two strong ones out of the mix?"

"It might be, Commander," he said, staring at me from under his bushy eyebrows. "If there are copper and tin to work with."

"I think I can arrange that."

---

* See Cultural Notes: Pure and impure.

CHAPTER 21

S hortly after I replaced Jarib as commander of the second unit, news arrived from Zelah that Shaul's abbi, Kish, had died. The entire clan gathered there to mourn him. While the royal family was gone, I spoke with Libni, who'd been left in charge of the professional force, and he gave me permission to train my unit privately. I worked the men hard every day in a small glade about a mile west of Gibeah. Lotan, and two others, both left-handed as Eleazar had been, were the only ones who could really excel as fighters. The rest could develop skills beyond those of the militia, but would never make outstanding warriors. However, I discovered a fascinating mix of other knowledge and talents.

Pallu, my best archer, taught the unit how to judge archery equipment, the finer points of bows, arrows, fletching, bowstrings, and much else, as well as how to estimate the strength and range of a bow in the enemy's battle lines. I didn't have to explain the value of that information.

Reu brought his engineering skills to my attention when he organized the removal of a large tree that had fallen across the path to our private practice ground. Seemingly able to build anything from whatever happened to be on hand, he taught the men the basics of leverage and construction.

When Tahan approached me, wanting to teach the men about jewelry, I hesitated. I didn't want to refuse since this was the first indication that I'd had that the men felt something besides disgraced, but I couldn't see how the subject would benefit them.

"That could be very useful," Areli, a man from Naphtali, observed. He had a sharp eye that made me wonder what was hidden in him. His reaction to Lotan had fascinated me. The first day of training out in the hills, the smith had inspected their swords. Areli had displayed his proudly. He had an elegant-looking weapon with a worked hilt that Lotan barely glanced at.

"Just throw that one out," he had said, moving on.

Areli had reddened. "It's a good sword," he had protested.

"It's fit only for the trash ravine or perhaps to melt down."

"As well as it's made? Look at the hilt!" He had held up the decorated hilt.

GIBEON HABIRU
TRAINING GROUND AND EZEL STONE

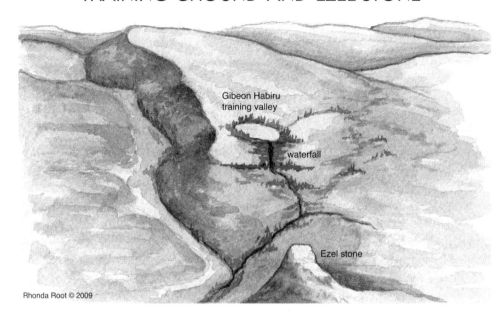

Gibeon Habiru training valley

waterfall

Ezel stone

Rhonda Root © 2009

SECOND UNIT TRAINING GROUND

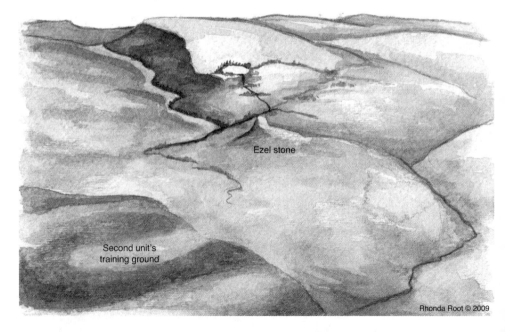

Ezel stone

Second unit's training ground

Rhonda Root © 2009

Lotan had taken the weapon, shoved it into the ground, and snapped the hilt off, handing it back to the stunned soldier. "If you pick a blade for the hilt, then just keep the hilt," he grunted, going to the next man.

No one had protested the smith's judgments after that, and I'd watched Areli closely. Once his anger had passed, he had said nothing, but stayed close to the smith, listening to him intently.

"How would knowledge of jewelry benefit us?" I asked now.

"Jewelry comes from different places and in different qualities like bronze. Styles will vary, and knowledge of those differences could be useful. If nothing else, you can get an indication of where someone has been, or what part of the world they might be from." Then he grinned. "And the men will certainly appreciate knowing which spoils will be worth the most!"

"All right, Tahan. You can start tomorrow since Reu is finished."

"Thank you, adon. What about Gedor? His background is weaving. He was telling me just yesterday how distinctive cloth can be if you know what to look for."

"All right," I agreed, thinking that while the men might be learning in order to enrich themselves, the knowledge might come in useful in other ways.

By now Lotan had forged enough swords for the entire unit. The blades were plain, a little shorter than mine, but straight and true. And they would chop almost any other bronze blade to pieces. After a single demonstration, not a man in the unit would let his out of his sight.

I discovered that Sithri, a small man with skinny arms and a narrow face, could put an edge on a blade better than any I'd ever seen before. I gave him mine to sharpen, and I could have sliced limp linen with it when he finished. I had him teach everyone how to sharpen a sword.

Between weapons practice in the mornings, and afternoons spent acquiring the skills of their fellows, the second unit was busier than it ever had been, and I'd learned most of what I thought I should about the men. I also discovered why Jarib had never done any training with the men when he was commander.

He was the clumsiest man that I'd ever met! During practices he tripped over nothing at all and tangled his sword in his cloak even when it wasn't on. More than once he limped away from sparring practice because he'd somehow managed to fall off his sandals. The man just couldn't keep track of where his arms and legs were. But give him a delicate repair of some kind, such as refletching an arrow or mending a sandal strap or small hole in a pouch, and his fingers moved swiftly and surely, without wasted motion. Jarib had an exceptional hand with a pen and was able to write with either hand.

By now Ahiam and Shagay had returned to my house. The latter talked for hours about his son, Jonathan, and hearing the news about everyone else's family brought on the longing for news of mine.

The night after Hassar Jonathan and Sahrah Michal returned to the fortress, I stirred restlessly on my bedroll against the side wall, unable to sleep, water dripping onto the table again. The clay on the roof needed compacting. Constant rain had forced the farmers to plant their grain in mud, and most roads were impassable, the high trails treacherous. Half the runners for the court had sprained ankles or broken legs from falls. Streams and rivers ran full, and the Jordan had swollen to flood stage already.

At last, unable to banish my thoughts of home, I put on my heaviest cloak against the biting dampness and went out onto the roof, staring south. Snow had probably fallen around Bethlehem. I looked over to the eastern height, longing to hear familiar voices in the accents of home.

Should I ask the hassar for permission to send for someone? But who could take the time to come? I knew how busy everyone was. At last I knelt by the low parapet and just stared south. By the time I went back inside, I'd decided that if my homesickness continued much longer, I would talk to Jonathan.

For a wonder, the sun came out the next day. Libni worked everyone extra hard during the last of the week, and we all looked forward to Shabbat and a rest. I didn't get to stay in bed, however, because a message arrived from Jonathan requesting that I visit Ishvi's house on the north side of town, bringing the harp. I took the time to dress in a better robe and oil the instrument before I left, wondering who was visiting that he wanted me to play for.

"Good, you came right away," Jonathan greeted me when the servant showed me into the upper room. "My guests have been impatient to see you."

I looked over his shoulder, and a laughing face watched mine. "Abigail!" I gasped.

She launched herself at me, and the hassar prudently got out of the way of our embrace.

"Whatever are you doing here?" I said before I realized that there was something between the two of us. I pulled away, my hands touching the roundness of her stomach. "What's this?"

"What do you think it is, silly boy?" she retorted.

"You're with child? Are you all right? Has there been any trouble?"

She groaned. "Not you, too! I'm fine, Dahveed. Everything has gone perfectly this time, and the midwife couldn't be happier with me. And now that I'm over being sick every morning, I haven't felt better in my life."

I assumed my best adon's voice. "In that case, O lovely one, allow your humble servant to present his poor congratulations. Truly your husband is the most blessed of men, favored by the gods with the joy of your presence, the sight of your radiant face, and the fortune of your sweet temperament."

"Why, adon, the words flow from your mouth like the waters of the Jordan, and they are just as muddy, too! Speak no more foolishness to me, or you will know more than you wish of my sweet temperament!"

"O great and gracious baalah, do not deal harshly with me," I coaxed. "I but wished to express my joy at this auspicious news. Surely I, dazzled as ever by your divine beauty, can rejoice with you at this wondrous event."

"And would you have me favor you, while your flatteries lure me to believe I am equal to a goddess, and so bring disaster upon my house?"

"But, O light for the eyes, you *are* the equal to—"

"How long can this go on?" the hassar groaned.

"For hours, much as I hate to say it," Jether replied in disgust. "Dahveed, if you don't stop, I'll have to take offense on general principles, and if I cut a hair from your head, my life would be one of intense misery from that moment on."

Both Abigail and I laughed, and I hugged her again, carefully. "How are you, Jether?"

"I'm fine, Dahveed. It's good to see you."

We clasped hands, and I noticed that in spite of his answer, Jether seemed subdued.

"Are things going all right?" I asked Abigail softly, drawing her away. "Jether seems worried or something."

"He is, but I can tell you only a little. His abbi sent him out alone for the first time with a caravan of goods. Oh, Dahveed, he lost it all!" Tears filled her eyes.

"Raiders?"

"No, that wouldn't be so bad. It was stolen . . . the whole caravan! That's why we're traveling around in midwinter. Jether is trying to un-ravel just what happened, and how the thief got away with it all. I'm so glad this pregnancy is going well—it's the only thing that distracts him."

"I hope he finds out what happened. Tell me about home, Abigail. What's going on there?"

"I hardly know where to begin. It's been a couple months since we visited there. I do remember that Eliab seemed heavy-handed with everyone. But I wasn't there long enough to really know. Abinadab's carpentry shop is doing a very good business. He's got two assistants now. Oh! That olive tree his wife thought had died in the hamsin sur-vived after all! Abinadab shows it to everyone, and he expects to get first fruits from it soon."

I blinked back tears, starved for the little things that everyone dis-cussed at home each day. "What else?" I asked, taking her hand in mine.

"Well, Shammah's busy raising mules!"

"Don't let him quit," Jonathan interjected. "He promised me one better than that black I lost at Lehi. I'm skeptical that he can do it, though."

"He'll do it!" Abigail insisted. "He'll make you admit he did what he promised, too! Zelek is just as bad," she added, referring to her ma-ternal cousin. "Nethanel did get married, and he looks more like Abbi every day. We have some of the best fields in Bethlehem now, and the buyers from Jebus tried to tie Abbi to a deal for all his grain every year. Abbi said he'd be glad to sell the surplus, but that was all! They weren't happy, but they had to accept it."

"I didn't know your family had close ties to Jebus," Jonathan commented.

"We don't," I replied. "But Bethlehem feeds Jebus. That's another reason we've had so little trouble with the Philistines and other raiders. Ethan's band guarded us from smaller raids and casual harassment, but a serious attack would bring retribution from Jebus."

"Sounds as if the Habiru have an important place in the balance of politics there."

"More than most people realize," I continued. "Boaz named them Yahweh's Arrows, because Yahweh took them directly into His hands to protect us all. They have lived up to that honor."

"That certainly explains a great deal about Ethan's bearing," the hassar said thoughtfully.

I turned back to Abigail. "What about the twins?"

"Raddai has a regular wine shop now with Lahab. Thanks to Jether, their wines are becoming known on the cararvan routes."

I smiled. "What about the sheep?"

"Ozem has continued breeding The Hassarah's cross, although he did seem worried about something that last visit. He might get married next. There's a young woman who sort of lingers around when she can, and he's noticed." She laced her fingers in mine. "Your hand is so big!"

"I grew," I chuckled, "and Ahiam has warned me I may still grow more. What about Elihu? He must be finished with the scribal school at Beth-shean. Did he get an appointment somewhere?"

Abigail frowned. "That has bothered me," she said slowly. "He's finished and received the highest recommendations, but he's working at home."

"At home? His training is good enough that he could go anywhere! That's what Abbi planned."

"I know. But he's at home, and I couldn't find out why. The only thing he would say was that he was doing some work for Abbi. Your immi seems a little sad when she looks at him sometimes."

"She's probably remembering her brother, my dodi Jonathan," I said. "He was on his way to Beth-shean for scribal training when Habiru wiped out his caravan."

While Abigail and I talked of home, the hassar and Jether discussed something in low tones, and I caught the words: "House of Tahat." I had to smile. Trust Jonathan to take advantage of any opportunity!

"How's Zeruiah doing?" I asked. "Has she married again?"

Abigail shook her head. "She's not likely to. No one wants to handle Joab. Abishai stays home most of the time, and I don't know what Zeruiah would do without him."

"Asahel?" I continued, mentioning Zeruiah's youngest.

"He's a delight! Fastest runner in the country. He's hired himself out as a courier to merchants in Jebus, and his income is a big help to Zeruiah. Abishai has managed to hold on to most of his inheritance with Abbi's help, but with Joab constantly in trouble, I'm not certain what will happen. Zeruiah is so tired lately. I worry about her."

"You mentioned Zelek is still working with Shammah. What about his sister, Ala? Is she still at Bethlehem?"

"Yes," Abigail laughed. "She must have made quite an impression on the hassar. When Jether and I first arrived, he kept calling me Ala. Jether asked if we could take her back to Ammon with us when we go. She has wanted to return. I think she hopes to coax another husband out of our royal grandfather. But Zelek is all wrapped up in breeding mules. I don't think he and King Nahash got along very well."

Our visit lasted long into the night, and the next afternoon Jonathan sent me the brass earring via messenger, along with a stern message reminding me that I was supposed to tell him *before* I got so lonely that I acted like a caged animal on my roof. Resigned, I put the earring on, wondering what he'd been doing out on the battlements that night.

◻◻ ⟦▱⟧ ◻◻

It was past midwinter before the second unit showed up on the training ground for exercises with the rest of the army. Abner wasn't pleased to see us, but he assigned us a place in the practices and drills.

The sars were there, carefully controlling their expressions as several of the second unit proved the equal of men in the other units. Most of my men weren't, but every one showed marked improvement, and I was satisfied.

As my men sparred with those of the fourteenth unit, I kept an eye on Sar Malchi as he walked around. When I checked the sar next, his eyes were fastened on the blade hanging from Lotan's girdle. He wandered onto the field, then noticed Areli's sword, and Pallu's. "Commander Dahveed, I'd like to inspect your unit," he said at last.

"Certainly, Sar. Second unit, report for review," I shouted.

The men gathered quickly, arranging themselves in the two lines I normally required. Malchi walked between them, examining swords and daggers, dumbfounded that the second unit had weapons superior to anything the rest of the army had. Likely he'd already noticed they were all made by the same smith. Lotan left a special rounded mark near the hilt of every blade he forged.

Giving me an odd glance, Malchi sent for the hassar.

"What is it?" Jonathan asked when he arrived.

"The second unit possesses some unusual weapons," the sar said.

The hassar checked several swords and approached me, his hand out. Wordlessly, I pulled my own blade. He turned it over in his hands.

"*Where* did you get this?" he breathed, testing the perfect balance and nearly cutting his hands on the sharp edge.

"It's the blade Abner let me take from the spoils."

The hassar's eyes danced. "What did you do to it?"

"Nothing to the blade itself, except have it sharpened. I did have it properly set in a new hilt, though."

He choked back his laughter, casting a quick glance at Abner to be certain the general wasn't paying attention.

"Hassar?" Malchi asked.

"I'm getting to it, Malchi. Where did you find the swords and daggers for your unit?"

"In the armory, adoni."

"We've never had bronze of that quality in the armory," Malchi said, his eyes flashing.

"Not in this form, no."

The hassar's eyes widened. "That's why you wanted a forge!" he gasped. "What did you do? Find a mastersmith lurking in the second unit or something?"

"Yes, Hassar."

"But that's got to be Hittite work," Malchi protested. "It's the best I've ever seen!"

"It should be."

The hassar and his brother stood motionless. "Are you saying we have a *Hittite mastersmith* in the second unit?"

"Yes, Hassar."

"Who?" The hassar's voice was hoarse. "Can he make more? What does he need?"

"He might make more. You'd have to ask. He was quite disgusted with the behavior of one of the smiths while he was working at the forge, though. I had to coax him to finish."

"He can have all three forges to himself, and I'll beg. What else?"

"He'll need bronze of one sort or another."

"Tell him to sack the armory."

"We did that—the swords and the daggers."

"What about the bronze on the shields and the cuirasses?" Malchi put in eagerly. "Did he look at that?"

"I didn't think of that. Lotan!"

The Hittite stepped from the line and walked over. "Yes, Commander?"

"The hassar wants to know if you'll forge more bronze."

"Who told him I could?" he grunted.

"He asked. I could hardly lie," I answered, hiding my smile. "You can use the bronze from shields and cuirasses and anything else if you need it."

"What about that idiot of a smith who tried to tell me what I was doing wrong all the time?"

"He'll be buried head-down outside the gates if that's what you want," the hassar interjected promptly. "Who is it?"

Lotan raised his eyebrows. "Nothing that drastic. Just keep him out of the forge unless he is willing to listen. There was one young man there who was very helpful, though. He learned quickly, too."

"He's yours. Anything else?"

"Do I remain in the second unit? Commander Dahveed is the first decent officer I've encountered in a long time. He knows good bronze."

"You can stay in the second unit as long as you want to."

"Then I'll forge bronze." Lotan went back to his place in line.

"Will that be all, sars?" I asked.

Jonathan turned to me. "Do you have anyone else lurking in the second unit that I should know about?"

"No one I can think of at the moment, but you never know."

As they walked off, I heard Malchi ask, "Should we tell Abner about this?"

"*Only* if he asks."

CHAPTER 22

Balak waited outside the king's chamber until time to waken him for afternoon court. Absentmindedly he rubbed his arm. It had taken six weeks to heal and was still sore some days. He'd worked late last night in the records room, sorting through the last of the Gibeonite papyri. Probably he knew more now about the Gibeonite situation than anyone else in the kingdom, and he couldn't see that it did him any good. There had been deaths, but most because of accident, sickness, or age, as might be expected. A few did seem odd, but he couldn't find any pattern to them.

And when it came to judicial decisions, he could nearly predict what the hassar would say and which parts of the roeh's scroll that he would consult. A couple times people at the gate had asked Balak to speak to the king on their behalf, and he'd made sure that he intervened only for those he knew the hassar would favor. The people had shown their gratitude with silver, but beyond that he'd worked the entire winter with no appreciable gain that he could see.

Dahveed, on the other hand, had become the hassar's personal representative. He might be just a courier, taking reciprocal gifts or delivering judgments to individual householders on the hassar's lands, but he rode a mule and wore one of the hassar's meils.

Sighing, Balak entered the king's chamber and approached the platform bed. Gently he shook the king's shoulder. "Adoni? Please wake. It is time to resume court."

Shaul yawned, rolled onto his back, then sat up.

"You speak to the commanders today, adoni."

"Yes. Ishvi and Malchi will go with Abner this year."

"And Dahveed," the servant reminded him.

"And Dahveed, but he shall not see my face," the king responded irritably.

"There is also the question of Merab, adoni. You had mentioned that you were thinking of what to do, and people will be expecting some sort of announcement soon."

The king stood. "I promised Merab, but Dahveed should not have taken a place before my sons. I don't know what to do."

Balak straightened the king's robe, racking his mind for a suggestion. "Your hair is in need of attention, adoni," he said to gain more time. Shaul sat down, and Balak got the comb.

"There is one thing you could do, adoni," he said, an idea coming to him as he ran the comb through the king's hair.

"What is it?"

"Why don't you put it in the hands of Yahweh? Encourage Dahveed to battle valiantly against the king's enemies so that Merab will be his. The Philistines are beginning to know his name, and the deeds he has done. They will fight hard against him. If Yahweh doesn't protect him, we would mourn, but Merab would be saved from disgrace," he ended.

"H'mmm."

Curious to see if anything came of his suggestion, Balak waited in the common courtyard as the army commanders gathered. Dahveed was present, but off to the side out of sight. King Shaul gave his usual speech, encouraging the men to remember they were the representatives of Israel and Yahweh, and to fight well.

But as the men were dismissed, he turned to Jonathan. "I would speak with Dahveed," Balak heard him say.

"Yes, adoni. Dahveed, the king would speak to you," Jonathan called, and Balak edged closer.

The commander approached, careful to keep his face from the king's, and touched his knee to the ground. "What is your wish, adoni?"

"You know that I promised you Merab, my bekorah, because you killed the giant Philistine in the valley of Elah."

"Yes, adoni."

"Serve me bravely, and fight well in the battles of Yahweh, and Merab will be yours."

"Adoni, you are more gracious than I deserve," Dahveed replied, puzzlement in his voice. "Why should I be given such a great honor when I have incurred your displeasure? My clan and father's house are nothing in Israel."

"Nevertheless, I say it." He touched Dahveed's head briefly, then took Jonathan's arm as the two of them walked to the throne room.

Balak followed at a respectful distance. There was always hope that Dahveed would get killed this year.

I fretted about the king's words all afternoon. While his speech had said one thing, his tone had said another, and when he touched my head, his hand had been tense and hard. I didn't have the time to go ask the roeh, but who else could tell me what was on the king's mind? Then I remembered the priests at Nob.

That afternoon when the men had been dismissed, I strapped on my traveling sandals. Out on the trails I set a steady jog that put me at Nob in less than half an hour. As I came up the road to the tabernacle, the Gibeonites doing their duties all drew away from me, as if afraid. It puzzled me.

Hakkohen Abiathar sat next to the entrance of the tabernacle. "It is Dahveed, isn't it?" he asked.

"Yes, adoni."

He stood to meet me, a little shorter than I, and very close to my age. "What have you come for?"

"I am troubled and wish to inquire of Yahweh, but I'm not certain if I am right to ask."

"The best way to know is to ask," Abiathar replied. "Be at ease, Dahveed."

Somewhat reassured, I nodded. "But what if Yahweh does not wish to tell me what I want to know?"

"He'll tell you that," the man said with a smile. His whole face lit up, and I had to smile back.

"Will you inquire of Yahweh for me, Abiathar?"

"Certainly, Dahveed. Come within the curtain." He led me into the outer courtyard of the tabernacle and to the side. I knelt, and he stood silent a minute. When he spoke, his voice sounded distant. "Why have you come, Dahveed ben Jesse?"

"I am troubled by the words of the king, Adonai," I said, barely speaking aloud. "He has promised me Merab with his tongue, but I do not know if his heart is in his promise. Am I wrong to ask this of You?"

"No."

"Tell your servant, is the king's heart good toward me?"

"No."

A shiver went through me. "Adonai, please deal kindly with me. Am I in danger from the king?"

"No, for he will do My will concerning you."

"Thank You, Adonai. Let me always be pleasing in Your sight."

I stayed on my knees until Abiathar touched my shoulder. "You have your answer?"

"Yes, adoni. I know what to do now."

Sahrah Michal thumped the pestle in time to the clacking weights on Merab's loom. What could she do? She kept her head down, afraid that Immi would notice her expression. Merab had been so prostrate after the most recent demon attack on the king that Immi had sent her to Zelah. To help distract her mind, their mother had invited the relatives from Jabesh to come, and her older sister had blossomed again in the relaxed atmosphere, spending much time with Adriel, who clearly favored her.

She had been certain that her father would notice the attraction, offering a chance to mention the possible marriage of the two. But it hadn't happened, and Adriel had left for Meholah, where he now had a house of his own.

And now Abbi had to promise Merab again! She pounded the grain in frustration. There had to be something more that she could do. Sneaking a glance at Merab's face, she noticed the troubled look in her sister's eyes as she gradually stopped weaving.

"Michal?"

"Yes, Merab?"

"Did Abbi promise me to Dahveed again today?"

"Yes."

The disturbed expression intensified. "When?"

"Abbi told him to fight bravely, and he would reward that."

"Anytime after the first battles then," Merab sighed, looking down. "I don't want to, Michal," she whispered.

"I know. I don't want you to either."

"Really? I thought you might, because then you'd be next to marry."

"And have you be miserable all your days? No." Michal stood beside her sister.

Merab stared at the weave on the loom. "I didn't realize how much I didn't want to until I'd been out at the estates for a while. It was so peaceful there, and there wasn't a lot to worry about, unlike here with people constantly coming and going, and never knowing what Abbi was going to do. He's much better, isn't he?"

"Yes. He doesn't need Dahveed to play anymore. The demon is gone for good, I think."

"I wish I were back there, Michal. I loved talking to Adriel about all the home things that you always find so boring. We told each other about the way that we'd like to have our own houses, and the kinds of things that we wanted to do and grow, and it sounded so wonderful." Tears trickled down Merab's face, which she hastily wiped away. "I know I can't ever, but, oh, I wish I could."

"Maybe you can, Merab," Michal said in a very low voice. "I'll marry Dahveed for you, if Abbi will let me."

"But Michal, I can't ask you to do that!"

"Oh, yes, you can," she insisted, looking directly at her sister.

Merab's eyes widened. "Michal! You don't mean you want to?" She laughed a little. "Why you silly thing! As if you could get Abbi to change his mind."

"We might. Some of us have been working on it for a long time. I don't know what made Abbi say what he did this morning, but he's much less set on giving you than he used to be."

"But Michal, what about Dahveed? Giving him a different wife would disparage his honor."

"Not if I marry him. I'm not that much in status below you."

Silently, Merab started weaving again, and Michal went back to milling grain. But Merab looked extremely thoughtful the rest of the day.

TAMAR BAT DAHVEED

That is the way of things, you know. While everyone dreams and plans and schemes for their heart's desires, Adonai will work His will, picking up Michal's faults, using Jonathan's weaknesses and even the king's anger, while He guides things to their proper conclusion.

And Dahveed? Adonai's intervention through the past generations is bearing fruit. The mashiah is learning more about power and governance, what it will mean to be king for Yahweh. But Adonai will direct Dahveed's mind toward a different concept of what kingship is for and what kings should do with honor. Right now, however, Dahveed will use his new understandings in his dealings with Sar Malchi, for the third sar is ready to take his stand regarding Yahweh's mashiah.

CHAPTER 23

This year the Philistines raided up near Birzaith, north and west of Bethel. Shagay and Josheb accompanied me since Ahiam was staying with the house. The second unit was assigned to guard the equipment and baggage under the command of Nadab, the quartermaster, and as the sun rose, it didn't take long for all of us to collect a noticeable coating of dust that only got thicker as the day progressed.

While we traveled, I had time to think of what Yahweh had said. I wished I could have discussed it with Jonathan, but he was busier than ever as the king transferred more power to him, and any time we had together, he used to give me instructions for when he sent me out as his representative, or to question me when I got back. Every time, one question would be if I'd heard anything about the Steward of the House of Tahat.

We arrived near Birzaith after a march of about 15 miles. Abner turned down a valley toward the Shephelah for a little more than a mile to a fold in one of the highest hills around. Nadab headed directly for a particular spot and pressed the second unit into helping get the animals unhitched, the carts set out, and the quartermaster's tent up. I wondered at his hurry until I saw the men arriving, wanting their own tents and luggage.

While my unit pitched our tents, Shagay came to me, shaking his head.

"What's wrong?"

"There's a ravine in back of us big enough to channel an invading force. Look how the army is pitching camp. Someone coming in from back there could spread out in no time. It wouldn't take many men either."

"You think too much like a Habiru," I grinned.

"I *am* a Habiru," he said in disgust. "Give me a dark night and 40 men, and I could take this place."

"You're right, so we'll just post a guard back there in case the Philistines have gotten creative in their thinking or hired someone like you."

Since my unit did not contain any militia, I had time on my hands, and I took the entire second unit up that ravine and had the men work out ways to thwart attackers, which we then implemented. Reu, my engineer, found a couple boulders that we could roll down, and supervised the digging around them to make them easy to push. Shagay showed the men how to use an old ox pelt to cover a bunch of thorn bushes, push them to the side and cut them off at ground level, then roll them into a huge ball that we could place at the edge of the incline, ready to shove over.

Two weeks passed with little excitement. Scouts spotted a few raiding parties, and units went out to chase them down.

Then Shagay came to my tent late one night. "Jeshua is here."

I went out immediately.

"What are you doing back here?" the local dahveed asked. "Aren't you general?"

"The king put Abner back in command. What have you found out, Jeshua?"

"The Philistines are out in force, but they've scattered their units just at the edge of the Shephelah close by here. Once they get where they're going, they stay put. No raiding, no moving around, not a lot of noise. Just sitting there."

"Why?"

"Haven't been able to find out. But this is typical of our tactics, Dahveed. Seren Manani in Ekron probably hired some Habiru from the south again. One day all those units will meet together and hit something hard. If they follow the pattern, they'll break up after that, or maybe just make a run for it to the Shephelah."

After Jeshua departed, I debated what to do with his news. Knowing Abner's opinion of Habiru, I could guess the reception that I'd get if I went to him about it. On the other hand, this could be vital information.

The next afternoon I stayed behind after the commander's meeting. The general turned his attention to me. "Well?"

"I heard some information that I thought you should know about," I began.

Abner sighed. "From those sneaking Habiru?"

"Yes. You may not like them, General, but they do know most of what goes on."

"What have they said now? That there's a large force nearby set to attack something?"

"Not quite. The force is broken up into units, which could combine at any time."

Abner had a superior smile on his face. "Your news is out of date, Dahveed. We captured a Philistine two days ago, and he said that large force will head north for the Shiloh valley. We'll be there to meet them."

I frowned. Jeshua had been clear. The units were in *this* area. If the Philistines wanted to attack something nearly six miles north, why didn't they station themselves closer to the target? Even with very experienced guides, trying to get numerous units to one place at the same time across the rough, tangled country between here and the Shiloh was extremely difficult, if not impossible. Something about it didn't make sense.

"Then why are they here instead of there?" I asked, almost to myself. "Is there any other evidence they are headed north?"

"If there is, I'd not be obliged to consult you about it, Commander," Abner replied, his eyes hard.

I flushed. "Forgive my impertinence, General. Have I your leave to go?"

"That's one thing you don't need to ask for, Dahveed."

Biting down on my temper, I bowed slightly and left. At least I'd done my duty, and he knew about the units in the area. Nevertheless, the evidence did not make sense. I wandered around the encampment restlessly, telling myself that I should just stay out of the situation and out of Abner's way. I was a commander who took orders, not the general who gave them.

But Yahweh's gift continued to whisper in the back of my mind. "You did what you could," I muttered to myself. My tour of the camp had shown that the general was a canny man. The position he'd taken was very defensible, with good fields of arrow fire from the camp outward. The units were positioned so that every approach was well manned. The only weakness was that ravine, and if it was adequately defended, the camp was safe from anything but a sustained, determined attack from a force with men to waste.

In spite of my restlessness I had nearly convinced myself to return to my unit when Zorath called, "Dahveed, what brings you here?"

"Just looking around. I noticed the men are getting ready to move out."

"Not the camp. Just the units. General Abner wants to be near the Shilo valley at daybreak to head off the Philistines. With the high ground, we should be able to see which branch of the valley they use."

"Did you see that prisoner that the general questioned?"

Zorath chuckled. "My unit caught him."

"Could I see him?" I heard myself ask.

"I don't know about that, but I can show you his clothing and things."

Uncertain of what good that would do, I followed my fellow commander. At a tent near the third unit I examined the clothing the prisoner had been wearing. The robe was high-quality Philistine, and so was the girdle. Then something Gedor had taught the unit caught my eye. The girdle was a weave generally used for women. I couldn't imagine a Philistine commander wearing a woman's girdle. The leg wrappings were the same quality as the robe, but slightly mismatched.

His sandals caught my eye. They reminded me of Dahveed Joel's sandals, the ties and inner soles heavy, made for hard, long travel. They were worn, but the bottoms looked nearly new. Inspecting them carefully, I saw that new leather had been sewn on, encasing the old worn soles. Once again, someone wearing that quality a robe should have had entirely new sandals.

"Did he have any weapons?" I asked.

"There," Zorath pointed, watching me curiously.

The bow was very good quality. The quiver was full of arrows. I took one out and turned it in my fingers as Pallu had demonstrated and as I'd seen the hassar do on several occasions. The balance and line of the shaft were not quite straight, with slightly uneven fletching. I checked several more. Second-rate arrows. Then I unsheathed the sword. The decorated hilt had a small jewel in it. The blade was bright and very sharp, with a good balance and nice shaping. I flicked the bronze with my finger, cocking my head. It wasn't loud enough, so I picked up the belt knife and struck the blade.

While the commander watched intently, I braced my leg on the ground, put that blade across my thigh, and bore down hard on the flat and the hilt. When I held it up again, the blade had a nice gentle wave in the middle.

Zorath gasped. I handed the blade to him and picked up that belt knife. It fitted the sheath perfectly, was good-quality bronze and perfectly balanced, the hilt sanded in spots to fit the hand of the owner. That was a Habiru's belt knife, or I'd never seen one before. I wondered what they'd paid him to let himself get captured and questioned.

As I stand there, the dilemma of what to do renewed itself in my mind. I'd been slapped down by Abner once already today. Why should I open myself up to another disgrace? But how would I feel if defeat overtook the army, and I could have prevented it? It would be Zanoah all over again. I couldn't stand aside and have even more widows weep every night. Finally I turned back to Zorath. This wasn't about Abner and me. It was about keeping the Philistines from the land I lived in, and serving the king that I loved to the best of my abilities. And I wasn't going to let Abner stand in the way of that!

"May I suggest something, Commander?"

Still stunned at the wave in that sword, he nodded.

"Get the general back in here to look at these weapons. Maybe he knows why someone claiming to be a Philistine commander is carrying that sorry excuse for a sword."

"How did you know he claimed that?" Zorath gasped.

As I walked to the tent door, I pointed at the robe. Then I paused. "Zorath, a word to open your ear You might want to be slow about leaving tomorrow, or lag behind, or even stay here."

Then I left. "Yah, show me what else I can do," I whispered.

Talk to the sar.

The thought was so distinct that I nearly turned to see who had spoken. Well, if one of the sars remained behind, perhaps another unit besides mine would do so also. But how was I going to approach either of Shaul's sons without interference from Abner? Their tents were right by his, and he'd be sure to see me, or hear of my visit. Just then, Sar Malchi's voice, raised in annoyance, reached my ears.

Several torches had been set up around an open space, and the sar was giving three men in it the sharp edge of his tongue, looking like that ram again.

"I wouldn't want to be around him now for anything," Natan said to Pasach as I walked up.

"Why not?" I asked.

Natan turned. "Dahveed! Maybe you can do something. Abner told the sar he must stay behind tomorrow, and he's in a rage."

"Why would the general do that?" I asked, amazed.

"The two have nearly crossed swords a couple times because the sar has been so cold to Abner," Natan explained.

I could imagine that Malchi would find it hard to work with the general, feeling the disgrace Abner had brought on the family as deeply as he did, and especially since he was technically superior as Sar Israel. Undoubtedly, Abner would respond without tact and bluntly—such as confining the sar to camp.

Well, my gift warned me there was trouble brewing, and I didn't know anyone that I'd rather have with me than Sar Malchi, especially if he was in a bad mood. I walked into the ring. "Still taking exception to my girdle, Sar?"

The other men hastily left, and the sar stared at me, looking like a big bear in the smoky light. I had my arms folded, but the hilt of my sword was in my fist. Suddenly, I drew, thrusting toward him. He countered in a flash, circling my blade away and lunging. For the next few minutes we sparred as seriously as we ever had. I was grateful for the cuirass, as his blade grazed me more than once. I knocked him to his knees, then barely got away from his counterthrust.

We circled, blades just touching. "Sar, do not let Abner anger you," I said quietly.

"He has dishonored me with his words," he replied, whipping his blade past mine, and I leaped backward, shedding his sword to the side, pulling my belt knife to face him with two blades. He smiled, the point of his sword weaving a little as he approached. When he thrust, I caught the sword between my two blades, shoving upward, crowding close.

"Sar, bide your time," I urged. "Abner's order will be to your advantage." I used the belt knife to turn aside his blade, several times refusing to take advantage of any openings that provided.

The sar grew curious. "You're holding back, Dahveed," he said as we crowded close again.

"Yes, Sar. I wish to ask something of you, and this was the only way I could do so without raising Abner's suspicions."

We broke apart, both of us getting our breath back. Men crowded around the area, and Abner watched with a twisted smile on his face.

"What did you want, Dahveed?" Malchi asked, thrusting again and letting me twist his blade out of the way so we closed.

"Stay tomorrow, Sar. You will be needed here."

He threw me from him angrily, and I came right back, pinning his blade between both of mine. "Abner is being led by the nose, Sar. That prisoner is suspicious in too many ways. The danger is here, not up north."

When he twisted his sword, I let him break free, then circled again. Suddenly, I lunged forward, driving him back with a series of thrusts, slapping his parries aside as they came.

"You'll have to teach me that one," he grunted, testing my guard once or twice before slipping by it, and I had to jump backward. What could I do to keep him in camp? He brought his sword down from above, and I caught it in my crossed blades, then sank under him as he bore down, forcing me all the way to my knees.

"Please, Sar," I begged. "I don't know why. All I know is that something is wrong. I felt it at Zanoah. And I feel it now. There will be few here, and I would rather have you than even the hassar."

Curiosity replacing his anger again, he searched my face. "There was no indication of trouble at Zanoah," he said, bearing down a little more.

I held him off. "Nothing that any human could see. But Yahweh knew, and I foolishly ignored His warning. I will not do so again."

We remained motionless, and the crowd quieted. Abner looked pleased with the bout.

"I owe you my life, Dahveed. Shall I refuse a request you bring from your knees while Abner gloats over you? I will stay."

Malchi stepped back and slipped his sword into the sheath, then bowed slightly before he walked away.

CHAPTER 24

I woke as the units left before dawn, and the moment I opened my eyes, the simplicity of what was going to happen that day stared me in the face. The Philistines had decided to use that ravine. The thought made me sit straight up on the bedroll. With only two units left in camp—unless Zorath had stayed—the Philistines could simply occupy the place. When Abner returned, he'd find that he would have to attack his own strong point.

Once dressed, I ran to Nadab. "Quartermaster, how many archers can you muster?" I asked, breathless.

"Ten."

"I'll need them all. Tell them to report to the ravine. We're going to have visitors."

Nadab nodded. "All right, Dahveed."

I hurried to Sar Malchi's tent. "Sar!" I called.

He emerged, fully dressed for war in a shortened battle dress that came to his knees, leg greaves, helmet, and arm guards. The torch light flashed off the scales, blinding me. His shield bearer was with him, a man that I'd noticed sparring occasionally with Eleazar and Dara.

Jeshua suddenly appeared at my side. "They're moving, Dahveed, gathering not far from the ravine."

"What ravine?" the sar asked.

"The one that passes by the back of camp," I answered. "Likely they'll stage a diversion in the front."

Zorath appeared. "Dahveed? What's happening?"

"We're about to be attacked," Sar Malchi said. "Since you're still here, Zorath, you're in charge of defending the front of camp. You should be able to hold it with your militia and those of the eighth under Dishon. Be sure the militia understand they must hold the line. Send me all the professionals you can."

"Sar, I need archers at the ravine, or we'll never hold them off. May I have the archers from the units in front?" I asked.

He nodded. "We'll send you all the swordsmen and slingers from the quartermaster's men, Zorath, in exchange for the archers."

The commander of the third unit nodded in turn. "Yes, Sar."

I turned to Jeshua. "How many men do you have?"

"Fifteen, Dahveed. There's a couple up here from Joel near Keilah."

"Can you handle the Habiru guides on the Philistine side?"

He smiled. "I think so."

Sar Malchi accompanied me to the ravine and decided that the best place for him was where a small branch of it entered the camp. Stripped of archers, most of the second unit, the other professionals, and who- ever was left of the quartermaster's men would stand with the sar. I took selected men from my unit and all the archers up both sides of the ravine, Shagay leading on one side, I on the other. I told them to hold their fire until we had released the boulders. Then we all waited. The sun was just peeking over the hills when the first Philistines cautiously descended the defile.

When the ravine was well filled, the advance nearly to the bend by our camp, I signaled Pallu, and he and the men with him sent the huge balls of thorns down in four places. The men below tried to scatter, thinking they were boulders, then finding them worse as the thorns caught on anything in reach. The advance came to an instant halt, but remained surprisingly silent.

While the Philistines tried to rake the thorns aside, I gave the next signal, and both boulders went crashing down. The silence ended as men screamed and ran. The archers opened up at close range. The at- tack must have included almost 15 Philistine units, and I knew that we could never hope to stop them all, but we could cut their numbers con- siderably. I slung stone after stone into the men below, and soon disor- der reigned, with some Philistine units trying to go back and some forward. The ones that made it past us found the sar waiting for them, and sounds of battle rose behind me.

Jeshua rushed up, panting. "We got most of the guides, Dahveed, but not all. They've pulled the last units out of the ravine and are send- ing them down each side."

It didn't take long for the enemy to arrive, and I pulled my sword, giving myself to Yahweh's gift and praying that Abner would return soon. As the archers loosed their last volley of arrows, the first sword met mine. That enemy fell, and I engaged the next, thrusting and par- rying, sidestepping, moving forward and back in the deadly dance as I fought for a life worth living for Keziah and my two nephews, the

BATTLE AT BIRZAITH

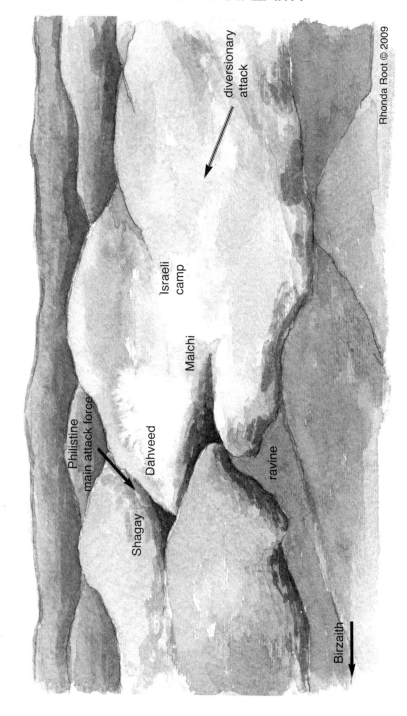

Rhonda Root © 2009

Habiru who had trained me, the people waiting for us in Gibeah, and the king who feared me and would one day yield his throne to me.

⊡⊏⊐⊡

"Dahveed!"

Lowering my sword point, I turned my head a little. Someone wanted me. I tried to think who.

"It's over, Dahveed."

I looked to the side. A man stood there holding a cruise, and I was extremely thirsty.

"Want some?" he asked.

I jerked my head a little, trying to find my voice, and backed up.

He stepped forward, holding it out to me. "Answer me, Dahveed. Are you thirsty?"

"Yes," I croaked.

As he held out the cruise, I tried to take it, but my hand had something in it. I raised my other hand. It had my belt knife, but I knew what to do with that. I dropped it, and the sar put the cruise into my hand. Then he approached closer, helping me drink until I bent over, sucking in air as fast as I could.

"Drop the sword, Dahveed."

Somehow I managed to open my fingers. Shagay took it, along with my belt knife. I put one arm over his shoulders, and the sar's arm supported me on the other side.

"We must have won," I gasped as they helped me back to camp.

"It was those Habiru archers who turned the battle," Sar Malchi replied. "I've never seen anyone fight like they do."

"Jeshua has had more than one run-in with Seren Manani's men from Ekron," I explained, noticing the cut on his arm. "You're injured."

"Not much more than a scratch. But you've got a cut on your leg that needs tending."

I looked down at myself, but I couldn't tell whether the blood all over me was mine or not.

⊡⊏⊐⊡

By the time I woke, it was nearly dark, and the sounds outside my tent told of a great deal of excitement in the camp. Shagay held out a piece of bread. I wolfed it down, along with cheese, raisins, and dried apricots. Then I emptied the cruise twice.

"What happened?" I asked.

My retainer grinned. "We patched up your leg, and then cleared off the battlefield in the front of camp. That sar! He's a mean one when he decides to be. He wanted the camp cleaned before Abner got back, and he pushed everyone getting it done, but it took a while. Zorath had some fairly sustained fighting before joining the sar at the ravine."

After accepting another cruise from Josheb, Shagay then went on with his story.

"That second unit of yours proved themselves today. Every one of them stayed right by the sar. And those swords they have!" Shagay whistled. "Took bites out of anything they hit, armor included. No wonder those men sleep with them!"

I smiled. "Lotan's a good smith."

"May I have one?" Shagay asked, looking appealingly at me.

"I'll see. How is the unit? Did many get wounded? Any killed?"

"One. Gedor. He went down taking a blow meant for the sar, but he saw the sar kill the man who did it. Malchi and his shield bearer stood over him until he could be removed from the line, but the wound was too deep."

I looked away. Gedor had been an awkward fighter to begin with, but he had practiced hard and become competent. And his knowledge of cloth and weaving had prompted me to look carefully at the captured man's clothes.

"Wounded?"

"Just about every man spilled some blood, but none seriously. Yours is the worst."

"When did Abner get back?"

My retainer smiled, not very nicely. "Oh, it took him a while. He'd gone all the way to the Shiloh valley and then found he was chasing less than two units. So things looked fairly normal when Abner returned, except for the stacks of weapons. Sar Malchi sat outside his tent peaceful as you please, and Abner came up growling about taking things from the quartermaster and strewing them all over camp.

"The sar looked at him quite amazed, and said he'd done nothing of the kind. They were spoils from the battle. Abner sputtered, he was so angry. Sar Ishvi almost said something when he noticed the bandage on Malchi's arm, but he stayed quiet."

I had to smile. I could just see Malchi oozing innocence while he twisted the dagger he'd just shoved into Abner. Shaul's third son was a bundle of contradictions sometimes.

"Go on," I said, accepting another chunk of bread from the second loaf Josheb brought.

"Abner had to ask what happened, and Malchi said there had been a nice little skirmish not long after they left this morning, and now everyone was resting. The general asked sort of sarcastically how many had been killed and wounded in this little skirmish."

Shagay chuckled. "Keep in mind, Dahveed, the sar hasn't moved from his stool yet. He leaned back on the center tent pole by his door, and let the general stand in front of him and stew.

"He told them we lost 17 dead, and about 50 wounded, 10 of those seriously. Ishvi went pale. You don't get those kinds of casualties with a skirmish, but a major battle."

I nodded, taking another drink.

"Abner didn't know what to say. Ishvi asked about the Philistine casualties, and that's when Malchi gave things the final twist. He looked real thoughtful and counted some and then shook his head. He said they'd found about 20 out front, 14 on one hillside, but they hadn't found them all on the other hillside yet, and of course, no one had started on the ravine, but they looked to be piled up some down there."

I groaned, holding my head. "How long did it take them to go to the ravine?"

"Ishvi started there right away, and Abner followed him. Malchi brought up the rear. He hadn't cracked a smile once, Dahveed.

"They both stopped when they got to the battle line by the ravine mouth. Ishvi glanced at Malchi, and the sar shrugged and said he'd been in a bad mood today. They went up the ravine, and came back looking a bit pale around the edges.

"The sar was very helpful. He asked if they wanted to go up the hill too, since that's where you'd fought, and from what he'd seen up there, a lot must have happened."

I choked on the figs Josheb had handed me. "Did they look?"

"Abner spent quite a lot of time up there. Ishvi came back after a survey and asked Malchi what had happened. The sar told him, short and clear. And Malchi was angry, Dahveed, angry like I've never seen him. He was quietly mad this time, and Ishvi was wise enough to see it. He looked at his brother, and then he looked at all those dead bodies by the ravine, and he didn't say a word. I don't know what will happen, but I don't think Abner has any idea what he roused in the sar this time. I don't think anyone does."

That evening I attended the hastily prepared feast to celebrate, but by the time it was over, I was exhausted from fatigue and pain. Both Josheb and Sithri had to support me on my way back to the tent. As Abner and the sars caught up to us, I stumbled, nearly falling. Sithri managed to keep his feet under him only by stepping into General Abner's way.

The general's hand flashed out, aiming a blow at Sithri's face.

Sar Malchi grabbed Abner's wrist before it landed.

Abner winced in pain as the sar ground his fingers tighter and tighter into the general's tendons.

"Abner ben Ner, that man is part of the second unit," Malchi said in a conversational voice. "The second unit stood beside me this morning and fought the Philistines to a standstill while you were off chasing an illusion any experienced officer could have seen through. One of those same men, Abner, jumped between me and a sword and died as a result."

Face creased with pain, his knees beginning to buckle, the general didn't answer. His left hand fumbled at his girdle.

"Don't tell me you're actually going to draw a weapon against me," the sar said, still talking as if he were discussing the weather. "That would give me the perfect excuse to do what ought to be done.

"The second unit may not be the best fighters in the army, but they were here. Which is more than can be said for you. Maybe it took us a little longer to defeat the Philistines, but they were still defeated. I don't know about you, but I think that should be rewarded, not punished. That unit is mine, General. Every man in it belongs to me."

Abner was on his knees now, the sar bending over him, still squeezing with only one hand.

JONATHAN AND ISRAEL | 249

"Perhaps you should think about why those men could stand with me and fight today. If I'd been left here with the second unit as it used to be, you'd be outside this encampment, wondering how to explain to the king why you had to attack your own fortified position. And I might be dead, or worse, alive, in the hands of Seren Manani. Or have you forgotten what that man did to Nemuel, thinking he was Jonathan?"

Sweat streamed from the general's pale face, and the veins stood out in his neck.

"You did forget, didn't you, Abner? You've been so busy seething over some possible harm the dahveed might do to your honor that you've forgotten a lot of things."

Malchi studied the man dispassionately. "Jonathan has spoken to you already, but apparently he didn't get your attention. Perhaps this will. I owe Dahveed my life. Twice. My father owes Dahveed his life. Twice. The kingdom is still here because of Dahveed. You owe my life to him because of the training he gave the second unit, and you owe your command to him because of his request to me last evening."

Ishvi had remained motionless during the entire exchange, and knowing how he usually interfered when Jonathan lost his temper, I wondered why he hadn't done anything now. He was older than Malchi, after all. But the only move he made was to shift his stance a little, and glance once at Malchi's face.

Tightening my grip on Josheb, I took another step. Abner looked like death.

"Dahveed told me the situation during that sparring bout," the sar continued. "I saw your face, Abner, when I forced him to his knees. But I can't force Dahveed to his knees with a sword. When I wasn't in any mood to be reasonable, he begged me to listen to him, to stay behind, where he knew we were vulnerable.

"So, Abner, why don't you spend the rest of this night thinking about what amusements Manani might be having with me if it weren't for the loyalty and honor of the dahveed."

Josheb had me over by the sar now, and I knelt beside Abner. His fingers were curled inward with pain, and he swayed on his knees.

Now that I was here, I knew why Ishvi had hardly moved. I was used to the white hot anger that could claim the hassar, but this was an icy, bottomless wrath, nearly unemotional in its totality. I doubted that I could stop Malchi. I only knew that I had to try.

"Did you want something, Dahveed?" he asked.

I hadn't thought he had even registered my presence. "Adoni, let him go," I said. "There has been enough of pain and dishonor today. Let it stop now."

With agonizing slowness, the pressure on Abner's wrist lessened. When the sar released it entirely, Abner leaned backward, cradling the hand in his other one. Malchi stepped back and bowed as he had last night. "Because you asked it, Dahveed." Then he went into his tent.

Sar Ishvi turned on his heel and disappeared without a word.

After that day, the second unit became known as "the Sar's Own," and went from being the dumping ground of the army to the elite. When Sar Malchi moved his tent from the center of camp to the rear with ours, he made every man in the unit his for life.

CHAPTER 25

A day later, when Abner sent for me to assign my unit to escort Nadab, the wounded, and the spoils back to Gibeah, his conduct toward me indicated that Malchi had indeed gotten his attention. He never actually apologized, but he did treat me with respect.

Our column approached Gibeah's gate in the early afternoon. Nadab pushed the pace, for he wanted to get the wounded tended to as soon as possible, and the sun was hot today. As he turned off the Jebus highway, the cheering began.

"Quartermaster Nadab," the crowd shouted as he passed by. At first he looked very taken aback. But he soon straightened and rode with quiet dignity as the cheering continued.

"Second unit! Second unit!" the women chanted.

"We are the Sar's Own!" Lotan shouted, and every man in the unit added his voice. "Sar Malchi's Own!"

The crowd laughed and sent the name back to us. When my mule started to dance under me, it attracted the attention of the people.

"Dahveed! Dahveed!" The roar nearly deafened me. "Dahveed! And the Sar's Own Unit!" People pressed close to the mule, stretching out their hands to touch me, following along behind. I was stunned, having never seen anything like this before. I tried to acknowledge the cheers and good wishes, while making sure the mule didn't act up, but it seemed to know what was happening and stepped carefully along.

Hands reached to me from every direction, and I could grasp only a few of them, but touching my clothes and the mule seemed fine to them, too. I might have been the king. The thought made me freeze inside. What if Shaul was watching?

I glanced toward the gate, but I didn't see the king's mule there, and I prayed that most of this would be over before I got to wherever Shaul was. At first I tried to stop the people, but at last had to give it up, and accepted the cheers and adulation as best I could.

The crowd stayed with us all the way up the west road. Many of the people did break off as we passed through the streets, but there were still many with me when we got to the turn that led to the fortress. The hassar waited on his mule under the tamarisk. I remained with him for a few minutes while the crowd vented its last congratulations and cheers. Then one look at Jonathan's face told me the entire story. "He saw what happened, didn't he?"

"Yes, Dahveed. After you came through the town gate, the king returned to the fortress. He will not receive you."

"I am barred from his presence anyway, Jonathan. Where did you want to hear my report?"

"I would normally take it now."

"The situation is not normal, Hassar."

His shoulders relaxed a little. "Would tonight be all right, or even tomorrow?"

"I will be at my house, Hassar. Come whenever you think it's best."

"He shall not have her!" King Shaul raged, pacing back and forth on the dais. "Do you hear, Jonathan? He shall not have her!"

The hassar waited in front of the dais, knowing there was nothing he could do now to calm his father's anger. Balak stood to the side, watching carefully, and Michal remained by the table, her face composed.

"Did you see? Did you hear them? Does this zammar think he is king?" Shaul shouted, trembling. "Marry him to the bekorah? I might as well hand him my throne! Does he think I will give him the kingdom? Set my house under his keeping, and beg hesed from his hands?"

Jonathan's face remained impassive. One day, he thought to himself, the king would probably do exactly that.

Shaul whirled around, his mantle flaring out behind him, and stormed the other way. "I took him from nothing! He is a son of a whore from the south, and I took him into my house and called him my son. *And he refused to swear his loyalty to me!* He places himself before my sons. He takes my honor before the people as their champion. The people say he killed 10 times more of Yahweh's enemies than I! He returns with the *baggage*, and the people hail him as king. *And he accepts it!*"

"I doubt he had much choice, adoni. What happened, happened," Jonathan said quietly.

The king's eyes flashed. "Would you defend him, Jonathan? It is your place he seeks!"

"Dahveed will never take my place."

The flat certainty in the comment made the king pause. "No, I will see to that," Shaul promised, clenching his fist. "Where is he?"

"I sent him to his house, adoni."

"He returns and then does not report?" his father thundered. "I will have his head for this!"

His own temper flaring, Jonathan strove to keep his voice reasonable. "He is barred from your presence, adoni."

"And rightly so. He is a treacherous foreign snake come to steal my daughter and rob my house of the throne! I will treat him like the dogs."

The hassar clenched his teeth.

"Is the king's honor to be lightly esteemed, given to any pretty hill man who comes along, passing himself as honorable in the people's eyes?" Shaul snarled.

"No, the king's honor should not be lightly esteemed. And

Dahveed has served you well, better than any other, as you have said yourself. He belongs to your household, so honor to him is honor to you, adoni, just like the victories at Gibeah and at Michmash belong to you. His valor and efforts should be rewarded, not punished."

"So I should give him the bekorah? Give him another hold on the throne? Give honor to the one stealing the hearts of my people? Did you hear them out there?"

"You promised the bekorah to the man who would kill the giant of Gath, adoni. Dahveed performed the service. The king must keep his word." Striving to hold himself in check, Jonathan stood rigidly, thankful that Michal had sent everyone else from the room. Feeling Balak's intent gaze, he wished the servant had gone also.

Shaul's eyes glittered as he turned to his youngest daughter. "What do you think, Michal?"

"Frankly, Abbi, I don't think Dahveed threatens your throne *personally*."

Her matter-of-fact tone drained away much of the tension in the room. The king's shoulders relaxed as he stepped back and sat in the ebony chair. Jonathan heaved a quiet sigh. Maybe the worst was over.

"What does that mean, Sahrah?" the king demanded.

"Think about it, Abbi. Dahveed has always served you. No, he didn't swear to you, but maybe when he swore to his father, he had to swear to give his loyalty to no one else. When you asked for his loyalty, what could he do? But even though he didn't swear, he is here serving you, not in Bethlehem serving his father."

Bless you, Michal, bless you, Jonathan said to himself, daring to relax a little more. Balak watched the sahrah intently, his face inscrutable.

"Seems to me, you have the better part of Dahveed, adoni," she went on. "He has never, *personally*, been disloyal in the slightest. You called him your son, and he has served you with the loyalty of a son. It may not be wise to give the bekorah to the dahveed, but not because of anything he has done personally."

Shaul looked interested, and Jonathan studied his sister.

"Dahveed will never grasp for more than you wish to give him. He has proved that numerous times, but that will not prevent other people from trying to give him what should not be his. If he married Merab, some people might think she should be declared gebirah so her husband would rule.* Withholding the bekorah will help the people keep Dahveed in his proper place in regard to you."

Jonathan looked down. Michal was holding to their bargain, upholding Dahveed's honor as she worked to change the king's mind, so he could not protest. He prayed that his father would decide without asking him for an opinion.

"I should not marry the bekorah to him?"

"No, adoni."

"Balak?" Shaul glanced at the servant.

"Adoni, I am hardly competent to judge, but there seems to me much sense in the sahrah's arguments."

Watching Balak's face, Jonathan felt a little chill go through him. The king had turned to him as though he did it often, and there was something in the way the servant spoke that made the hassar uneasy. He should pay more attention to Balak.

"What do you say to this, Jonathan?"

"You must do as you think best, adoni."

"I asked for your opinion, Jonathan Hassar. Do you think I should marry Merab Bekorah to the zammar?"

He had to answer. But how could he? He owed Dahveed higher loyalty than his father, but should he condemn his gentle sister to a life of torment when she had the chance to find happiness after so many years of loneliness and grief? Did the king really understand what marriage to Dahveed would mean to Merab? Should that matter?

"Hassar?"

Jonathan closed his eyes, and sweat trickled down the back of his neck. He could insist that Dahveed receive Merab. Probably he could convince Shaul to do so, but the price would be a break between him and his father that might never be bridged. Those days after Michmash rose up in his memory. Could he stand getting up each morning to face the cold displeasure and contempt in his father's eyes?

His stomach turned over, and sweat ran down his face now. He couldn't imagine constantly facing Merab's quiet torment either. Each day she stayed here, she seemed to lose more of the hope and sparkle that had been with her when she had returned from Zelah. And Immi would have to bear the pain of watching her daughter slowly die. The thought sent a shaft through his heart. No, he couldn't bring himself to do that. Not to Immi. Or Merab.

He knelt in front of the dais. *Forgive me, Adonai,* he cried silently. *I am not worthy of Your blessing.*

"No, adoni," he whispered. "I do not think you should marry Merab to Dahveed."

Michal woke the next morning to find Merab staring at her.

"Is it true?"

"Is what true?" Michal yawned.

"That Abbi refused to give me to Dahveed?"

The suppressed hope in her sister's voice made Michal sit up. "Yes."

The woman hugged herself. "Oh, Michal, I can hardly believe it. I don't have to stay here? I won't always be waiting to see if my husband got killed this time?" Suddenly she broke into tears. "If only I can go away from here!" She covered her face, sobs shaking her whole body. "And see Adriel again, and go to Jabesh!"

Michal threw her arms around her sister, hugging and rocking her, but Merab's sobs grew harder and harder. "Immi!" Michal shouted. "Come quick!"

Within moments, Ahinoam's footsteps hurried to the door. She took Michal's place, holding her oldest daughter. "There, Merab. What's upset you so?"

"I'm not upset!" Merab managed to say between sobs. "I'm just so happy, Immi! I don't have to! Abbi said so. I've been so frightened and worried!"

"What worried you?"

"M–marrying Dahveed."

Ahinoam glanced at Michal. "Did you know she felt this way?"

Michal shook her head. "We've talked about it only once, and she said she really didn't want to, but I had no idea that it actually frightened her!"

"What's the matter?" Jonathan asked anxiously from the doorway.

Hearing his voice, Merab jumped up and threw her arms around him. "It was you! I know it was! Abbi would listen to you." She buried her face against his shoulder. "Can you ask Abbi to let me marry Adriel? He's loved me for so long, and we could live in Meholah just like we talked about, and everything would be so nice. Please, Jonathan?"

"What's happened?" Ishvi gasped, running into the passage. "Someone said Merab—"

"It's so wonderful, Ishvi!" Merab exclaimed, pulling away from Jonathan to hug her favorite brother.

Looking bewildered, Ishvi nevertheless wrapped his arms around her, rubbing her back while she cried.

"Did you know she was frightened of marrying Dahveed?" Immi asked sternly, catching her second son's eye.

"Not like this!" the sar explained. He stayed until Merab quieted, then returned to the passage where Michal, Jonathan, and Ahinoam waited.

"Merab said you spoke to Abbi?" Ishvi asked, looking at Jonathan.

"He was in a rage yesterday and decided himself to withhold the bekorah. Once things calmed down, he asked if I agreed with his decision." Jonathan hesitated a little. "I did."

"I am obligated to you for this, Jonathan," Ishvi said formally.

"She's my sister, too," the hassar replied in surprise.

"Not like she's mine. If I can do anything for you, you let me know, Jonathan!"

The hassar nodded.

"And if Father asks, Merab would be very happy with Adriel ben Barzillai."

"Who would be a very politic choice in any case," Jonathan said with a smile.

⁘

Balak placed the lamp on the table in the records chamber. He'd left Judith sleeping, and with only the guards on the fortress walls awake, this room was the best place he knew of to be alone where he could think. The scene in the throne room the day before yesterday had shown him that the hassar did have limits when it came to Dahveed. It had taken the shock of seeing the hassar decide against the zammar to make him understand the true import of what had just happened, and to appreciate the true power of his own position.

Suddenly he slammed the table in disgust as he realized that he'd wasted literally years fighting the wrong battle. Dahveed was not the problem. *Yahweh was!* Dahveed was important only because he was the channel that Yahweh used. And the king had banished that channel from his presence. Then Jonathan had agreed to limit Dahveed's contact with the king even more by withholding Merab! It would be months, *if ever,* before the king accepted Dahveed again. And that swung the balance of time in his favor.

Perhaps he could keep Dahveed away from Shaul by feeding the king's anger, something easily done after he woke him each day. If he kept his comments on the other subjects the king asked about in line with what the hassar would say, there would be no reason for Jonathan to suspect anything.

That cleared the way for his true goal—separating the king further from his God. The old stories about his great namesake, King Balak, showed the one infallible way to do that. Get Shaul to break a covenant, just as the Israelites had done at Beth-peor. He stared at the Gibeonite records on the shelves. The answer to that was up there. He knew it; he just hadn't looked hard enough the first time.

Balak picked up the papyri on the end of the lowest shelf. The scribes simply stacked the new records here without even reading them, and no one knew, or cared, who put them away. Breaking the seals, he scanned the contents, then shelved them.

Next, he got down the overseer reports, and those from the priests listing who had fulfilled their work commitments and who hadn't, setting aside every document that listed death as the reason for absence.

His lamp was nearly out, and the writing on the papyri blurred before his eyes when he finally sat back, a smile playing on his lips. At last he had found the pattern! The rich irony of it brought a laugh from deep inside. *Get* Shaul to break a covenant? The king was already *breaking* a covenant. All Balak needed to do was make it easier!

★ See Cultural Notes: Gebirah.

CHAPTER 26

The first hint of clouds blurred the horizon this morning, and I rejoiced. The war season was almost over. We were headed home after spending the past two months up near the Jezreel Valley. The country fascinated me. I'd never seen that much open space. People were everywhere, and farmsteads lined the valleys instead of climbing the hills for protection as they did down south.

We were approaching Tappuah, about 20 miles north of Gibeah and on a major east-west route from the Jordan River to the Shephelah. Three units of Philistines had dashed into the hills for a last raid yesterday. We'd caught one and had scouts out looking for the other two. The second unit still guarded the supplies and equipment, so I was surprised to receive a summons to a war council at the noon rest.

"We've located the other Philistine units," General Abner began. "They are on the Tappuah road, heading west for the Shephelah. We just have time to stay ahead of them. Four miles out there's a swell that runs for several hundred feet on the south side of the road. From the road itself, the top of the swell blends into the hill behind it, concealing the depression between the two. Most of the units will fit behind that rise."

I shook my head in wonder. Everywhere we went, Abner knew the land like his own courtyard. I wondered if there was any place up here where he didn't know what was around the bend of whatever road we happened to be on.

"Three units will stay behind us, attack the Philistines, then retreat west down the road. If the enemy is occupied chasing Israelites, our force can be on top of them before they have time to notice. This is one time I don't want a lot of yelling. Come over that rise quietly. I'd like to use this place again sometime, so don't make them remember our tactics here. Units three, six, and seven will take the initial attack. Remember, once the battle is well joined, retreat. Run if necessary. Just bring them to us with their minds someplace else."

Zorath and the other two commanders nodded.

"All other units will wait behind the swell. The second unit, also. Nadab can continue south without escort for a while. We need to get into position now."

Sar Ishvi, commanding the diversionary force, lagged behind while the rest of us hurried to fill the depression behind the rise. Several men surveyed us from the road to be certain no one could be seen. Lotan and Pallu had to move when they were spotted at the extreme east end of the line.

After a time, we heard voices, the tones telling us the bait had found the fish. Laughter drifted to us faintly, and then angry shouts. Taunts went back and forth several times, with the answering responses getting more and more incensed.

We stiffened as the clash of bronze on bronze reached us, and shouts turned to cries, which soon drew closer. The Philistine voices turned triumphant. Soon our men appeared, the retreat masterfully done, Zorath keeping everyone in good order while they fell back, fighting as they gave ground. Beside me, the second unit tensed, straining to stay back as the Philistines came ever nearer.

Abner kept his hand down, watching Zorath's men draw more of the Philistine force past the hill shielding us. Suddenly the commander shouted, and his forces stood firm, making the Philistine advance pause.

The general waved his hand, and without a sound the men leaped up and charged over the top of the swell. As Abner had hoped, we were halfway to them before the Philistines noticed. Someone in their ranks yelled, and as if on signal, every man on our side roared in response.

The surprise was complete, but the men we charged were veterans now, and few panicked, turning to defend themselves as they retreated in their turn toward the trees across the road. Sar Malchi was on my left with his shield bearer, the two accounting for some dead already. Lotan had assumed a position on the sar's other side, his powerful smith's arms thrusting his sword. Pallu was down, then up again. Areli and Sithri battled side by side, apparently carrying on a conversation while they did. Tahan and the others fought on my right, teaming together to cover for each other, acquitting themselves well.

Something tugged at my mind, but I couldn't think of what. The battle line moved across the road as the Philistines headed for the safety of the trees.

Yahweh's gift stirred in my mind again, and I paused, looking up and down the battle line. What was missing? I searched my mind, trying to remember what should be here. A slinger let loose a stone that

ISRAELITE AMBUSH
AT TAPPUAH/ELEAZZAR'S BATTLE

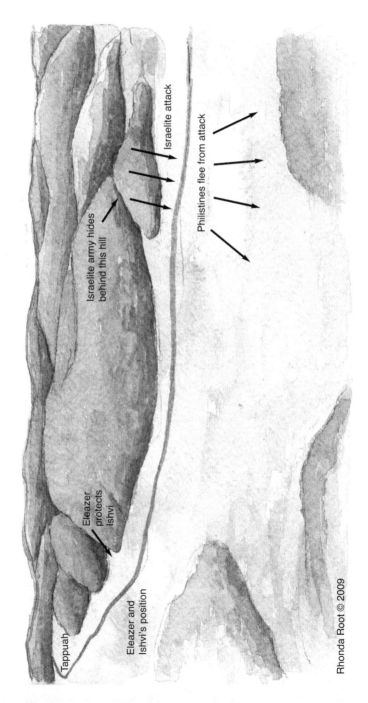

hurled right at me, and I ducked aside, trying frantically now to remember.

The sun glinted off Abner's helmet and Sar Malchi's cuirass. My
heart stopped. *Ishvi!*

I ran as fast as I could back up the road, rounding the bend. Farther
ahead, Eleazar faced three men, his sword flashing. As I charged up the
road, one man fell, and I saw that the shield bearer was surrounded by
bodies. He fought silently, desperately, killing the second man, swaying
back and forth a little as he directed his full attention to the last one,
who broke and ran, stumbling twice over fallen comrades. I slowed as
the shield bearer spotted me, raising his sword again.

"You shall not have him," he gasped, tears streaming from his eyes.

I sheathed my sword. "It's over, Eleazar. Let me see what happened."

He didn't respond, and I began to move some of the bodies. It appeared as if this had already been done more than once, and I glanced
around in amazement. Eleazar still swayed, watching me like a hawk,
refusing to budge an inch from where he stood.

And then it all made sense. He had stood there and killed the
enemy until the Philistines had to move their own dead to get at him.
Then he'd repeated the strategy again, and probably a third time.
Having backed up against an out-thrust of rock, with a tree shielding
his left side and his shield protecting his right, Eleazar could be gotten
at only head-on, and no one had gotten by.

My first look at his face had told me why. "Eleazar, where's Sar
Ishvi?" I asked, pulling aside another dead man so I could stand in front
of him.

"Dahveed?"

"Yes, Eleazar."

Finally he lowered the shield a little, almost as if his arm were too
stiff to move. "Back here. They can't have him!"

"They won't. You kept them away. Let me see the sar, Eleazar."

Just then he started to crumple up, and I caught him as the shield
fell to the ground. Then I helped him to one side, seating him on the
grass. In a niche in the outcropping Sar Ishvi sat with his legs curled
under him out of Eleazar's way, his right arm just above the elbow
pinned securely to his side by an arrow. The point had gone in right

where the ties held the cuirass on. His eyes were closed, and he was pale. Blood seeped from the wounds. I backed away.

"Eleazar, where is the sar's sword?"

The shield bearer nodded toward the road, and I found it farther ahead. Ishvi must have been at the front of the force when he was hit, and it must have happened soon after the battle was joined. I brought the weapon back.

"Dahveed?" Sithri called, running toward me.

"Bring Sar Malchi! Sar Ishvi is wounded!"

My man reversed directions, and I stripped off my commander's mantle, covering the sar. Picking up Eleazar's hand, I rubbed his fingers, still tight around his sword, working at his wrist and lower arm also.

"He's alive?" he kept asking.

"He's still alive," I assured him each time.

Malchi charged around the bend. While more men gathered around silently, Malchi examined the injury. After feeling his brother's neck, he eased back. "Dara should take that arrow out. But how will we get him home?"

"Hand-carried stretcher," I said, still working at Eleazar's hand. "And we could send a messenger ahead and have Dara meet us on the way."

"He hasn't lost that much blood, either," Malchi observed. "Looks as if he got here and stayed still."

"The most sensible thing to do under the circumstances. Eleazar did the rest."

Malchi rose, looked around, and began studying the wounds on body after body. When he came back, he stared at Eleazar in awe. "He stood here alone and did all this?" he muttered, starting to count. Finished, he shook his head. "It's amazing. Why didn't they just leave him? Why did they keep coming for him?"

I shrugged. "Maybe the taunts we heard had something to do with it. There you go, Eleazar." His fingers loosened enough that I could take the sword from his fist.

Sar Malchi turned toward Ishvi again. "We need a stretcher."

Lotan heard him and looked around. "Reu?" he called. "The sar wants a stretcher to carry Sar Ishvi. Go look at the wound, and tell us how to make one."

Malchi watched as Reu lifted my mantle and studied the sar. My engineer thought for a minute and then started snapping out directions.

Messenger for the king! Make way!" the man shouted, his mule dripping lather as he galloped through the fortress gate.

Michal and Merab jumped up from their place in the private courtyard, hurrying to the gate as the messenger threw the reins to a guard and slid off before the mule had stopped completely. He ran into the anteroom.

Ahinoam came out of the upper room, standing by the stairs. Since the day had just begun, what could have happened? The upper door over the anteroom slammed open, and Jonathan stepped out. "Dara! To me!" he roared.

Michal grabbed Merab's hand. A door in the armory flew open, and Dara ran out, carrying a sword.

Instantly Ahinoam hurried down the stairs. "Get the hassar's mule ready to travel," she ordered a servant, who raced out the fortress gate.

The three women waited tensely. Michal knew it could only be one of four people. Her heart sank. This on top of everything else, and after things had started to go so well.

Only hours after Dahveed and Nadab returned to the front, a message had gone out to Barzillai, proposing the marriage of Adriel and the bekorah. It had been accepted, of course, and Merab had almost danced when she heard the news. She had plunged into wedding plans with such joy and enthusiasm that no one had the heart to worry her with thoughts of how Dahveed might react.

Since she was the bekorah, there would be a feast here, and then Adriel would take her to his house in Meholah, where Barzillai would give the usual bridegroom feast for everyone there. Merab had been so happy. Then the king announced she would marry before the end of the war season.

"But Ishvi and Malchi won't be back!" Merab had protested. "I heard Abbi say he wasn't even going to tell them! I can't get married without Ishvi here!"

Ahinoam had pressed her lips together. "We will do what we must,

Merab," she said quietly. "I'll ask Barzillai to delay things up north so that your brothers can be there."

Michal hadn't said anything, knowing that her father wanted Merab married and away before Dahveed returned. The king was having second thoughts about his decision. Merab had finally become resigned to the situation, and was planning all sorts of things up north to make it up to her brothers. Barzillai and Adriel were supposed to arrive tomorrow. Now this.

Dara emerged on the anteroom roof and ran down the stairs, headed for the chamber where he kept his healing supplies. Michal put her other hand in Immi's, surprised to find her mother trembling. Jonathan descended the outside stairs, then came through the gate, his face grave, and took Merab in his arms. She burst into tears.

"He's alive," her brother announced. "It's an arrow wound in the side, apparently right where the ties are on the cuirass. Eleazar kept the Philistines off him until help arrived. Malchi sent the message. It happened yesterday afternoon."

As he put his other arm around Immi, Michal crowded close. Then Ahinoam broke away as Shaul emerged from the throne room. Baalah Rizpah and her boys, Armoni and Mephibosheth, stood a little ways off, looking anxiously at them.

Michal went to her. "It's Ishvi. Arrow wound. He's still alive, and Dara is going to him."

Rizpah nodded. "This will change things. I'll see to the household, for Ahinoam will be needed with Shaul. Adriel will be here tomorrow for the bekorah."

"What would we do without you, Rizpah?" Michal said gratefully.

The concubine drew herself up proudly. "We of Jabesh in Gilead owe the king much, Sahrah. I serve as I can."

Michal went back to Merab. Shaul paused by his children as he entered the courtyard. "This will make it hard for your wedding feast, Merab, but we will not delay."

Stunned, Merab stared at her father. Then a white spot appeared on each cheek. She straightened to her full height, standing as tall as Immi. "And shall I sit at a feast while my brother lies in pain, maybe at the point of death? *I will not!*" Her voice was quiet and implacable.

Shaul's eyes widened. When he glanced at Ahinoam, he saw the same hardness on her face. "As you wish, Bekorah."

Dara exhausted three mules getting to us. He was surprised and pleased when he saw how the stretcher that Reu created had kept the sar immobilized. Once he had carefully eased the arrow out, he was confident that Ishvi would recover. We camped for some days, letting the sar gain strength, and General Abner dismissed the militia while we waited.

As we approached Gibeah, the column appeared somewhat unusual since both sars insisted on riding with the second unit. The cheering turned to a roar when Ishvi came into view, walking on his own feet, Eleazar beside him and leading both mules. Merab screamed when she saw him and would have scrambled over the wall, except that Adriel held her back, taking her down the stairs instead. The whole procession came to a halt as she ran down the street, checking herself just before she got to him, and put her arms carefully around him, tears streaming. When they reached the king, Jonathan dismounted to greet his brothers, and then the king did, too.

Barzillai was with him, I noted. I dismounted since the king was walking, and when we got to the turn to the fortress at the top of the hill, I went the other way, stabling my mule myself and heading directly to my house.

Ahiam cornered me there before the evening meal, presenting me with household records to go over. I sat down at the table.

"When did you decide to do this to me?" I asked, resigned.

"When I had time to go over your possessions, adoni. I don't think that you realized it, but as general of the army, a portion of all the spoils came to you. While you were general, you accumulated considerable wealth from that alone. As a commander, you also get extra, and commendation by superior officers brings rewards as well."

"I've never had wealth before, Ahiam."

"I know. And the first thing to do is keep track of what you've got."

Duly chastened, I listened while he explained how the records were maintained and then read off what I had. When he finally finished, I scratched my head. "That seems rather a lot."

"It's enough to buy your father's holdings in their entirety and have some left over."

I was wealthier than Abbi. The thought took some getting used to. But then, with the king's attitude lately, I probably shouldn't get used to it. I could find myself stripped and dumped in the streets at any time. After all, I belonged to the king.

As I read over the papyri Ahiam handed me, I noticed several entries that had things being taken south. "What are those?"

"Ethan has tapped me several times for help with families in the south. I didn't think you'd mind."

"Good. Ethan will know more of what to do with all this than I would. I don't need much. Keep it that way, Ahiam. I've come to appreciate good quality, and I'll have it if I can, but I don't need to put on a show. Anything that can go to help the people in Judah, send it. Anything else?"

Ahiam hesitated. "No, adoni," he finally said, looking uncomfortable. "You need to eat and rest."

The next day was Shabbat, for which I was grateful. I slept most of the day, relaxing from the tension of recent events. As dusk drew closer, I sat on the bench under the almond tree in the courtyard, enjoying the cool breeze coming down the hill.

Ahiam joined me.

"What's the news here?" I asked lazily, stretching my legs. "I saw Barzillai and Adriel with the king yesterday. Are they visiting again?"

"They are here for the wedding," he replied, getting that disturbed expression again.

"Who's getting married?"

My retainer looked away. "The king gave Merab Bekorah to Adriel ben Barzillai, adoni. The feast will be tomorrow."

For a moment I couldn't breathe. "Balak?" I asked at last.

Ahiam shook his head. "From what I can tell, the king decided to withhold the bekorah after your return with Nadab early in the war season."

I sighed. "How is it I still have a house?"

"I'm not sure. I've been expecting to have to move for most of the summer."

"Maybe the king decided giving Merab to someone else was punishment enough." I did not say anything for a moment, then added, "She will be happier with him than with me anyway."

"Are you angry, adoni?" Ahiam asked after a short silence.

I studied the gate in the compound wall opposite me. "I'm not sure," I finally admitted. "Maybe this is from Yah."

"It's an affront to your honor."

"Only my honor from human beings, Ahiam. No one can touch my honor from Yah."

We remained in silence until it was dark.

But the next afternoon when I sat in my courtyard and watched the bustle and activity going on up around the fortress, I did feel melancholy. That was supposed to be my wedding, my bride, my wedding night.

Darkness descended, and I moved to the roof of the house, gazing at the stars as I'd seen The Hassarah do so many times. I reached for the harp, more words for the song I was working on materializing in my thoughts. "A bridegroom coming from his bridal chamber." The phrase turned over in my mind. What would go with that? Bridegrooms dressed splendidly, like a warrior returning from the war. "A bridegroom coming from his pavilion and a warrior rejoicing to come home." It went with the melody, but wasn't quite what I wanted. "He has pitched his tent. And a bridegroom coming . . ." I played with various phrases, but nothing seemed to fit. I liked the bridegroom imagery and that of the warrior, however.

Setting the harp aside, I leaned back against the wall. What did Yah have in store for me? Who was I? Dishonored man? Almost son-in-law to the king? Nearly mashiah? Ben-geber?

Eventually I smiled a little. I might have a storeroom or two stuffed with wealth, but when King Shaul gave Merab to Adriel, he had made me poor by stripping me of any honor in human eyes. The king couldn't have chosen a more forceful way to show his displeasure.

I supposed I should be upset, but I'd been honor-poor most of my life. In addition, Yah had stated plainly that the king would do His will regarding me, and deep in my heart, the glow of Yah's presence sat with me this night. As I listened to the sounds of feasting and laughter from the fortress, I knew that Yah's regard brought more honor than I could ever have received up there on the hilltop.

TAMAR BAT DAHVEED

Yes, Dahveed has been made honor-poor, left with nothing by the king who owed him everything. But that is the ultimate result of envy, and it is the greatest tragedy of Shaul. His refusal to accept Yahweh's gift to him made the last years of his life bitter as gall, poisoning much of his children's lives as well, and nearly destroying his family forever.

Had he only accepted Yahweh's will and judgments, he could have lived out his days as joyously as those at the Feast of Weeks, blessed by the light of the zammar and covered by Yahweh's hesed brought by the steadfast loyalty and love of his oldest son. But he would not.

Well, there is much still for Adonai to do, giving some strange twists to Dahveed's life, for one man's mind must be set at ease lest a word from him should endanger Dahveed now when he has critical lessons to learn. The Evil One will try one last time to separate Adonai's champions, and Ethan has had a secret weighing on his heart for years, which he must somehow find the courage to tell.

CHAPTER 27

It was long after midnight when someone pounding on the gate woke me. I had pulled on a robe and was on the balcony when Ahiam ran up the stairs. "Someone brought Jamin," he reported tersely. "He was running messages and broke his leg. Shagay is getting Dara, but Jamin's asking for you."

I went down immediately. "I'm here, Jamin," I said, kneeling by the bedroll.

Ethan's brother handed me a message pouch. "They're urgent, Dahveed," he managed to get out, gritting his teeth against the pain. "Especially the one for Jabesh. Take that one first; then cross the Jordan and swing back south to Shechem. Ethan said you're Jonathan's fastest courier, and I thought you might not mind being gone for a while." Jamin glanced up toward the fortress.

He was right. I would just as soon be gone for a while, and by dawn, I was on the east side of Jordan, far up the Arabah, lying on the eastern escarpment overlooking the Jordan as the sun rays stole over the land.

"The sun stretched a tent; nothing is hidden from his glow." That, too, was a good phrase that might fit into the song. Sitting there, I quietly sang praise songs for my private worship, then slept an hour or so before continuing on my way, reaching Jabesh by sunset after a hard run. I got a late start the next day since I had to wait for another message for the man I was to see next, but I crossed the Jordan again and climbed into the highlands by dark.

The afternoon of the third day, I arrived in Shechem, looking for a Canaanite landowner named Ahor. I stopped at the town well, standing aside while a well-dressed man about my age directed three servants as they filled and loaded water jars on six donkeys.

He noticed me. "Shalom, geber," he greeted. "Please have some water. I am called Hushai if you need anything." He let me fill my cruise from the dripping bucket, his quick eyes taking in my dusty clothing, lingering a moment on my sword.

"You are kind, Geber Hushai," I returned. "I have some messages for Ahor the Canaanite. Can you direct me to his house?"

The man smiled, his eyes twinkling. "Ah, you must be the reason my grandfather is in such a state that he can hardly prepare for our coming guests!"

I grinned back. "Then tell me the way quickly, geber, so that I can relieve your grandfather's mind and assure your guests of his complete attention."

He gave me directions, and soon I stood in Ahor's business chamber while the elderly man hurriedly scanned the messages I handed him.

"You left Jabesh just yesterday?" he asked anxiously.

"Yes, geber."

"There is time, then. You are to be commended for your quick run. Wait here. I will have replies." Calling for his scribe and sending a servant scurrying away for refreshments for me, he hurried out the door.

When the door opened a short time later, Hushai himself entered, carrying a bowl of fruit and a cruise of wine. Just then a shout came from the gate, and through the door, I saw Ahor pause in the courtyard, finishing his instructions to the scribe before hurrying forward to welcome the newcomers.

"I seem to have come at a bad time," I commented.

"That depends on your point of view," Hushai replied, his lips twitching as he set the food on the table. "Having you here has provided me with a good excuse to avoid the onrushing invasion in the courtyard."

The conspiratorial amusement in his tone made me chuckle, and I reached for the pomegranate in the bowl. "There is quite a crowd," I agreed, looking out the window. "They must be very important since the honor guard looks like a full unit. As for me, I'm more than provided for. Please, join your family."

The man gazed out the window too. "There is a full unit out there," he murmured. "That's strange." He turned back to me. "Don't worry, geber. With so many arriving, I need to fortify myself for the occasion." Looking unrepentant, he took an apple from the bowl and bit into it.

With a laugh I sat down. I'd nearly finished the pomegranate when a familiar voice caught my attention, and I rose to stare out the window. Was that Commander Libni and the tenth unit?

"Someone you know?" Hushai asked curiously, watching me.

"I've seen him before, but not usually in this part of the country."

"What part of the country do you usually see him in?"

I sat down again and grinned. "Depends on whether or not it's the war season!"

The two of us enjoyed a quiet cup of wine and talked. My host had dark hair, brown eyes, and wore a striped brown robe with a matching girdle, both of top-quality wool. Two thin bands of embroidery along the edges decorated the girdle, and it ended in short fringe. His easy acceptance of me intrigued me, for in my rough short robe, traveling sandals, and weapons, I could only be taken for a Habiru, even if I did carry a messenger pouch. Yet he spoke with me as if I were a guest, not a servant.

"Don't worry. I think I know where to find him."

The comment had drifted in from outside, and I glanced out the window again. My heart skipped a beat when I recognized the people approaching the door. Astonishment, then dread, washed over me.

"Your guests are looking for you. You need not bother about me," I said, hastily retreating into the shadows, hoping against hope that I'd be ignored there in the back of the room.

"You were right—he's here!"

I turned away, studying a hanging on the wall as Adriel came through the door, followed by Bekorah Merab and Barzillai!

"I knew I'd find you hiding," Adriel laughed. "Hushai, you must meet my wife, Merab."

"It is an honor, Sahrah," Hushai replied. "Please excuse me for not meeting you at our gate, but some unexpected business came up that had to be tended to."

"Think nothing of it," Merab said. "There were quite enough people to meet us as it was."

The sound of her voice told me that she now faced my direction.

"May I meet your guest—why, Dahveed! What are you doing here?" she exclaimed.

Everything got very still. I closed my eyes a moment. I should have known that Merab would not ignore anyone in the room. Past experience having assured me that the earth would not swallow me, I reluctantly turned around. I was prepared for embarrassment, discomfort, maybe anger. Anything but the stark fear that showed in her eyes.

"Bekorah?" I asked, concerned.

Hushai jerked around to stare at me, and Barzillai froze, watching me warily.

As I glanced from one to the other, I caught a glimpse again of the soldiers in the courtyard, and the true situation broke on my mind. "That's not an honor guard, is it?" I asked quietly. "The king must think me completely without shame—" I stopped. It was quite obvious what the king thought of me.

I felt numb. Up to that moment I'd thought that Shaul had done the worst he could already. But this? What the people in Gibeah must have thought when the bekorah left guarded by an entire unit! Stomach churning with humiliation, I touched my knee to the ground. "If there is nothing further, have I your leave to go, Bekorah?"

Merab walked forward. "Shut the door, Adriel," she commanded. Then she came right up to me and held out her hand. I touched it briefly and looked down again. "You have always brought the light, Dahveed. But everyone kept saying that you would come someday and leave death behind for the offense that my father gave you. What do you say to me, zammar?"

I looked up. "I say that my life is in Yahweh's hands, and He has told me that the king will do Yahweh's will for me. I am not blind, Sahrah. I know what staying in Gibeah does to you. And I am not made of stone, to want to hold you there. Yahweh has given you your heart's desire, and it is not for me to stand in the way."

"I didn't think Jonathan would agree to this without speaking to you about it first," she said with satisfaction. "I shouldn't have doubted you, Dahveed."

"I owe your family much, and I serve the king, Bekorah." Standing, I turned to Adriel. "Let me give my congratulations and wishes for Yahweh's blessing on you and your house."

"Coming from you, adon, that means a great deal to me," the bridegroom said.

After bowing slightly to Barzillai, I started toward the door. "Hushai, if you would take my apology to your grandfather for not waiting for his return message, I would be grateful."

"Of course." The man stared at me in amazement.

"Ben-geber?"

I didn't turn around at the name, but it still froze me in my tracks, my hand on the door.

"Ah, I was right," Barzillai continued. "You don't remember me, do you?"

I faced him. "No, adon."

"I bought a lamb from The Hassarah long ago. You were to deliver it, but on the way you were injured, and the lamb killed. I knew that I'd heard that tone of voice somewhere. I met The Hassarah only twice, but I have never forgotten her."

For a moment I looked at him curiously. I'd not remembered his name, if I had ever known it. "No one ever forgot Hassarah Ruth. It may be years late, but accept my apologies for the delay in delivery. I trust we made up the loss?"

Barzillai laughed. "That dry, subtle humor is hers, too! Yes, The Hassarah made up the loss, which you will see if you ever inspect my flocks of sheep! I am glad to meet you, Dahveed. I've never known anyone but Hassarah Ruth to speak with such conviction regarding Yahweh's will. To hear it now from you, and to know who taught you, assures me that my family will live in peace. I confess that I have stayed awake nights over this matter."

I smiled a bit sadly. "My only wish for you is that Yahweh will grant you happiness and His blessings." Then I turned back to Merab. "Shalom, Bekorah."

I skirted Libni's unit as I headed for the gate.

"Good journey, Dahveed," one of the men said in a low voice as I walked by.

"There's the man you want," the wine shop owner said quietly to Balak.

The Moabite turned his head slightly. The new customer went to the bench in a corner of the tiny shop tucked away in the north quarter of Gibeah, stumbling slightly as he sat. A servant brought him some wine.

"He can both read and write?" Balak asked skeptically. He didn't want to seem too eager.

"Yes, and he doesn't mind what you ask him to write. He told me once that he didn't see that it was any of his business. He was just the brush for the ink."

A useful trait, Balak thought. After finishing his wine, he paid with a copper piece and drifted over to the bench.

The man looked up indifferently and moved a little to make more room.

"I understand you can write letters," Balak began.

"Yes, geber. Did you need a scribe?"

"In a manner of speaking. I need some copying done for a private matter. Very private."

The man turned his head, and a knowing expression crept into his eye. "I have little interest in private matters."

"So I've been told," the king's servant replied, smiling at the double meaning in the man's words. "The copying will be dull, and the less interest you have, the more I will pay."

"For that circumstance, I will have no interest at all," the scribe smiled. "What copying did you want done?"

"This." Balak pulled a papyrus from his girdle.

The man's eyes widened a bit when he saw the broken seal, but he looked the record over. "I assume you want the writing matched as well?"

"Of course." Balak hid his annoyance that he hadn't thought of that himself.

"All right. But you pay in silver."

⚬⚬⚬

After the evening meal I went up to the roof with my harp. The song I was working on had tickled my mind all day on my way home. *He stretched a tent from one end of heaven to the other,* I thought, plucking the melody, and I was soon lost in working out just the right phrases for this stanza.

Vaguely I thought I heard the gate open, but I wasn't certain. I almost had the stanza worked out, all but the last phrase. Playing the tune again, I tested the meter of what I'd done. "Nothing is hidden from his glow as he makes his way from one extremity to the other." It still didn't work. Stilling the harp, I waited, my head bowed. I almost had it. Then the phrase reversed itself, and everything fell into place in my mind.

"That's it!" I exclaimed, plucking the strings on the harp. I had it now.

"For the sun set a tent in them,
"And, like a bridegroom coming forth from his bridal chamber,
"He rejoices like a warrior to run in his path
"From the extremity of the heavens to its outlet,
"Even to his turning at solstice at the end.
"And there is no hiding from his glow."

Perfect. I played it twice more to be sure that I had it memorized, and then set the harp down, stretching and leaning back.

After a while Ahiam emerged from the upper room. "Adoni, if you have finished, there is someone here to see you."

Wondering who would arrive at this hour, I got up immediately. "Where is he?"

"In the upper room, adoni."

When I walked in the door, Jonathan stood to greet me.

"Hassar!" I exclaimed. "You should not have been kept waiting! Ahiam should have told me you were here." I was horrified at such carelessness, so totally unlike Ahiam, who was always mindful of what was proper and what wasn't.

"Ahiam knows your rank, as well as mine, Dahveed. Besides, I've never had the chance to listen to you compose before, and I didn't think you'd mind if I did. If you recall, I'm still waiting to hear all of that song."

"No, I don't mind," I told the hassar, silently vowing that I was still going to speak to Ahiam. "Sit down again. Why did you come?" I took a seat on the other side of the table, glad to see that food had been put out, and that Jonathan had eaten.

"I came to see if there is anything I can do to recompense you for not telling you myself that Merab would be given to Adriel."

"When did you know about that decision?" I asked curiously.

"I was there when Shaul made it. I planned to tell you when I took your report after Birzaith. Then I got distracted, hearing about the spy and all the rest."

I thought for a while. "There wasn't much chance since then."

"Not to tell you personally, adoni, but I still should have informed you," he continued, his shoulders tense.

Something that Merab had said to me niggled at my mind, and I tried to remember just what it was.

Jonathan studied the top of the table.

"Did you agree to this?"

His eyes closed briefly, and he got very still. Then he pushed himself up from the table, looking straight over my head. "Yes, Mashiah."

"Why?"

His hands clenched, but other than that, he didn't move. "I couldn't bring myself to go against Abbi, Mashiah."

"You're lying, Jonathan." I stood and faced him. "You go against your father regarding me more often than I know; otherwise I'd be dead."

The hassar remained silent.

The lamplight flickered.

"If I were to tell you I wanted her, would you bring her to me?"

He went pale, and the silence stretched on while he stood rigidly.

"You wouldn't, would you, Jonathan?" The lack of anger in my voice made him take a quick look at me. I sighed and sat down. "What makes you think that I would take something from your family that no one wants me to have?"

"The king promised his bekorah to the Elah champion."

"And this champion will take his reward by force if necessary?"

Still he didn't say anything.

"It's obvious that's what the king assumed, since he sent the tenth unit. But what did you think, Jonathan?"

He set both hands on the table and leaned on them, his head bowed. "If Merab had married you, she would have died. I couldn't bear to do that to her, or bring that kind of pain to Immi. So I agreed with Abbi's decision."

"Don't you think I saw that also?" I asked in a tired voice. "Did you really believe that I would drag your sister down to death? Merab didn't. She assumed that you had asked me about it." I looked down and saw the earring on my chest. Slowly I took it off and put it in the middle of the table. "If that is how you have judged me, I will never put this on again, Jonathan Hassar."

CHAPTER 28

The hassar reached forward and touched the earring lightly. Then he slipped his father's signet ring off his finger and laid it by the earring. "I owe you my abbi and king's life three times, the kingdom at least twice, Malchi's life, Michal's life, Ishvi's life just days ago—"

"Eleazar saved Sar Ishvi," I corrected.

"And who brought Eleazar to Ishvi, Dahveed?" He glanced at me, his expression revealing his weariness and pain. "You refuse to take offense or recompense when my father tries to kill you, you served as armor bearer to the king knowing you are mashiah, you submit to Abner's deliberate malice, you beg my brother to follow orders so the army will be saved—where does it end, Dahveed?

"I have no right to ask anything of you. Your hesed piles around me already. Why would you expect me to ask for more?"

Something akin to anger stirred in me, raising all the hurt and bewilderment that had been deep in my heart as a child trying to understand why I wasn't good enough to be someone's son. Standing, I leaned toward him. "Because I've never had a brother before, Nahsi. Because you wanted me, would have claimed me, before my *own* abbi would have. Because you spent 10 days holding on to me so I wouldn't die. Because you honored me before my clan and town, protected me from your abbi, championed me, taught me, forced me to step into your place so that one day the throne that should be yours will be mine. And I wake up every morning because of your protection. Where does it end, Nahsi?"

We stared at each other while it dawned on us that neither would feel that he could adequately repay the other. I glanced at the earring and signet ring. They seemed to separate us, to force us to hold back in order to maintain some impossible balance that we both knew was incalculable. "Are we going to let something as fleeting and petty as an honor balance come between us?" I asked softly.

His head jerked up, and his surprised gaze dawned with realization. Then he slowly sat down, pushing the signet and earring away. "Not if I can help it, Dahveed."

I sat opposite him again, and the silence stretched out, neither of us certain how to go on from here. "Do you think we could just say what is in our hearts?" I asked.

He fingered his beard, then shoved the jewelry even farther away. "It would be a relief."

"Was agreeing with the king about Merab easy or hard?"

"It was one of the hardest things that I've ever done. But I couldn't seem to do anything else. I kept thinking of Merab and Immi, and what would happen, and then I bowed to the king. Forgive me, Dahveed."

I toyed with the chain of the earring, thinking hard. "I went to Nob and inquired of Yahweh after the king offered me Merab last fall," I finally said. "Adonai said the king would do only His will for me. I don't think it was Yahweh's will that I marry Merab. I believe He influenced your decision."

"And that's why you're not angry," Jonathan murmured, picking up the king's signet.

"Yes. It's hard being stripped of honor, but the king has taken only what he gave in the first place, so I can accept that. What galled me is that he sent a guard with her when she left."

Jonathan's face hardened. "That was Abner. Everyone was getting ready to go, and Barzillai was talking about the long trip, and someone mentioned that they hoped nothing would happen. Adriel said he didn't think anything would. And someone said that was a relief, since you had disappeared. Abner took it from there."

"Someone, or Balak?"

He thought a little. "Balak. Wait a minute; how do you know Libni and the tenth unit went north?"

I flushed, having hoped that he wouldn't pick up on that remark. "I saw them."

The hassar raised his eyebrows and sat back, leaning against the wall. "You must have done more than just see them. I believe you also mentioned something Merab thought that I didn't even know."

Reluctantly, I told him of my trip north.

"If Abner ever finds out about this, he'll choke on his own gall!" Jonathan chuckled. "You actually walked out of Ahor's compound right under Libni's nose?"

"I was a messenger. Who would notice?"

"Dahveed, why would you still deliver messages?"

I smiled. "I enjoyed it. It felt so good to get out on the trails and run that I'm near thanking the king for doing this."

The hassar looked wistful a minute, and I wondered what he wished that he could be doing.

Not long after, Jonathan left. After I gave him the earring.

The next morning Ethan slept on the floor beside me. On top of my 30-mile run yesterday, the talk with the hassar had been tiring, and I slept longer than normal, so I had to hurry when a messenger arrived, announcing that General Abner wished to see me.

"Yes, General?" I asked, bowing a little when I arrived.

"A new man has joined up. He knows next to nothing about arms, armor, fighting, or anything else apparently. Several other commanders have said they don't want to bother with him. You turned the second unit into something that can fight. I wondered if you would take him on."

"Of course, General," I said instantly, knowing how much it had cost the man to request rather than just assign the recruit to me.

Abner looked relieved. "He's probably on the training ground. Since he'll need weapons and equipment, take him to the armory."

"As you wish, General."

While Naharai, my new man, picked out some weapons, I talked with Dara, who was putting a new string on one of Jonathan's hunting bows. Behind him, a stack of bows sat next to the wall. Some were broken, and one looked as if it were a child's bow for birds.

I picked it up. "Where did this come from?"

Dara shrugged in resignation. "When militia start collecting from the battlefield, we never know what will show up. We've got everything from that"—he indicated what I held—"to that," and he pointed to a roughly arced object standing against the wall.

I reached for it. It was more than 36 inches long and oddly arched into a half circle. Layer after layer of rawhide strips were wrapped around it, and the ends bulged into knobs. Three bow strings hung from the ends. I surveyed it in amazement.

"My thoughts exactly," Dara chuckled. "I don't know what it is, but we've got it. I can't imagine anyone using it as a weapon unless they simply flailed you with it. The arch is too deep to use it effectively as a bow."

I flexed it in my hands. "It would hurt," I commented, feeling the power and tension as it bent inward, and I could hardly bend it outward.

Naharai had picked a bow, and I took a quick look at his sword, hiding my smile. He'd soon want to exchange that for something worth fighting with, but the bow was a capable weapon.

"The quivers are over there," I told him. "Next door down are daggers. Pick one of those, and then report back to the training ground after the noon rest."

"Yes, Commander." After quickly selecting a quiver, he headed out the door.

Wondering at the odd feeling that seemed to come from it, I continued to study the object I held. Tentatively, I flexed the thing again. A lot of power lurked in there.

Dara watched. "Take it with you, if you like, Dahveed. Abner's looked through everything here and has reserved what he wanted for the army already. That stack is to be thrown out, so do what you want."

I picked up my new acquisition, flexing it again on my way out the door. Since I didn't see Ahiam or Shagay when I entered the courtyard, I went to the upstairs room and shut the door, extremely curious about what could be under all those layers of rawhide.

I worked the point of my belt knife under a piece of the old, filthy stuff and twisted, slicing it, scraping it off a piece at a time. The first layer came off fairly easily, but I had to work at it after that, finding that the two ends of the thing had almost twice as many layers as the rest of it.

But the more I took off, the more the arc rounded, and what looked like a handhold appeared in the middle. The final layers were supple enough to unwind in longer pieces, and as I worked in the middle of one end, a gleam caught my eye. I paused, turning the thing in the light from the window. The gleam appeared again as I unwrapped some more.

Silver inlay? What had I found? I stripped off the rawhide as quickly as I could, revealing a beautiful twining vine that apparently ran from the ends of what had to be a bow, to the center handhold. I tugged at the layers of protection over that part. They were still supple and soaked with oil.

Under them, the handhold gleamed, the dyed leather protected by the oil put there when it had been wrapped. I laid the bow down, studying the three layers forming the arm. Different woods, with horn in between. It had to be a composite bow! The arch was so deep because unstrung composite bows arched around the back, not the belly, and whoever had it last had strung it inside out!

I looked at the ends, still swathed in layer after layer of hide. Working quickly, I cut most of it off now that I knew how much there was. The ends appeared to be capped with something very hard, and I slowed down. The gleam of white made me stop and carefully strip off the last layer. Ivory! It looked just like the handle of my belt knife. The curling cap sat perfectly on the end of the bow arm, carved with a delicate vine to match the inlay, and in the center of the curl on the side was a harp, the small carving so detailed that I could count the 24 strings.

For a moment I could not breathe. My hands shaking so much that I could hardly hold the bow, I turned it over. On the other side of the cap was a wheat sheaf. I fumbled for my belt knife, nearly cutting myself as I tore at the wrapping I kept around its handle, heart pounding so much that I was dizzy.

On the back of the handle were the very same harp and wheat sheaf.

"Boaz's bow!" I gasped. "It's Boaz's bow!"

Too unsteady to handle a knife blade, I attacked the rawhide on the other end with my bare hands. When I stripped it off, the other ivory cap emerged, the adon's robe and fringe opposite the Habiru kilt and sword belt.

After I brushed the rawhide pieces off the table, I reverently laid the bow on it beside my belt knife, too overwhelmed to do more than just stare. The door opened.

"I didn't hear you come in," Ethan's voice said. Then he froze.

Tears streaming down my cheeks, I turned toward him. "It's Boaz's bow, Ethan! I've found Boaz's bow!"

He approached the table slowly, eyes riveted on the weapon as if he were afraid it would vanish if he got too close. His hands shaking too, he picked it up, smoothing his fingers down the inlay and over the handhold, examining the ivory caps. Noticing the knife on the table, he picked it up, comparing the carvings.

"Every detail is the same," he whispered. "Just as The Hassarah described it. Dahveed, where?"

"In the armory. It was covered with all this"—I indicated the rawhide everywhere—"and had been strung inside out. Dara said it was to be thrown out. But it felt so powerful when I flexed it that I brought it home just to see what it was."

"What are you going to do with it?" he asked, stroking the inlay again.

"It's not mine!"

"Then whose is it? Dahveed Mattan gave it to Boaz when he pledged our band, and The Hassarah would have gotten it along with the dagger. She gave the dagger to you. I'd say that makes it yours."

I looked at it in awe, taking the time now to really inspect it. The ivory caps had a couple chips in them, some of the carving had almost been rubbed away, and the silver inlay was missing in two places. But Ethan assured me the bow itself was perfectly sound. I decided the first step was to have it repaired; then I'd figure out what to do with it.

A little later, Ethan and I sat eating at the table, the rawhide swept away, and the bow encased in oiled cloth, ready for Ethan to send off for restoration. The handhold was very old-fashioned looking, and I asked him to have it trimmed down and streamlined, with new leather put on.

I'd halfway finished my meal when I looked at Ethan a bit puzzled. "What are you doing here?"

"I came to check on Jamin."

"How is he?"

"Fretting because he can't get up."

"Did you send Ahiam and Shagay off somewhere? I haven't seen them all day."

The Habiru nodded. "Shagay's wife has wanted him come home for a while, and with Jamin down, I needed Ahiam to help with some things. I didn't figure you'd mind lending them if I took their place."

"Not at all. I'm pleased to have you. With Jonathan likely to send me all over the land again, you're just the person I need."

"You're done already?" Balak asked the man beside him on the bench in the wine shop.

The scribe shrugged. "It was easy." He handed over the papyri.

Balak checked them. Perfect. The handwriting on the copy looked like the original. The only difference in the reports was that two or three names had their service status altered from "completed" to "missing." The broken seals had even been transferred from one report to the other.

A silver piece passed between their hands.

"Any qualms about doing this on a regular basis?" the royal servant asked.

A shrug. "They're only Gibeonites."

Keeping his elation to himself, Balak left the shop.

The lamplight flickered, gleaming off the metallic embroidery of the meils of the five people standing in the throne room.

"Understand, I feel that this is something we must all agree on since I will not be informing the king," Jonathan began.

Michal watched her four brothers. She was here again in her capacity of Sahrah Israel, acting as witness to the sealing of the tax exemption document on the table.

"I can only say that I think this is the best way to uphold the king's honor. However, because of the circumstances, I want each of you to have the chance to agree or disagree."

Michal had to smile. Malchi already had his signet ring off his finger, waiting impatiently. Ishvi hadn't said anything yet, having listened impassively to Jonathan's tale of what had happened between the dahveed and Merab only a couple days earlier. She knew what he'd decide. Eshbaal was the unknown one. Her younger brother had disappeared as much as possible when family tensions surfaced, and whether he would follow Jonathan's lead or not was the crucial question.

She looked at the parchment again, wondering if it was worth the price being paid tonight. Despite the fancy wording, the only "taxes" her abbi collected were for the yearly tribute to Egypt, and they hadn't paid that for two years now. Since most people down south didn't send support to Shaul in the first place, what good was the exemption? But then, Dahveed's brothers had fought with the king, so maybe the exemption from military service and corvée labor would be welcome, even to the southern rustics.

"The king's word should be carried out," Eshbaal said softly, breaking the silence and Michal's thoughts.

She stepped forward with a small wad of clay and pinched a piece off. Jonathan pressed his personal seal in it, then Ishvi, Malchi, and last, Eshbaal. Silently Jonathan drew the king's seal from his finger, and Michal added a fifth ball of clay. With the king's signet Jonathan sealed the string tying up the document and put it in an oiled skin pouch. Then he bowed slightly to his brothers, who turned and left.

The sahrah put the scribal materials back at Eshbaal's table, and when she returned, her brother still stared at the pouch, his face pale and old. She put her arms around him, and his automatically circled her shoulders.

"It hurts just as much every time," he whispered. "It doesn't matter what I do, who I side with, it hurts."

The sahrah hugged him, feeling the familiar trembling that seized him every time he faced such a decision. As always, it tore at her heart. She wondered if Jonathan realized the full implications of the decision made here tonight, what it meant for the future. But one glance at the agony shining out of his eyes told her that he did. All three of his brothers had just declared that their loyalty now lay with the hassar, not the king.

CHAPTER 29

I entered the throne room in response to Jonathan's summons, holding the leather pouch that Ethan had given me. "Make sure you give it to Hassar Jonathan personally," he had said. "Tell him that the man who carried it is dead." I rubbed the leather between my fingers while I waited as Jonathan conferred with Sar Eshbaal over some papyri. The pouch looked like an Egyptian courier's to me, and I wondered how it had ended up with Ethan.

The hassar looked up.

"You sent for me, adoni?"

Jonathan picked up a message pouch beside him. "I'm taking you at your word about running messages, Dahveed. These are for Jebus. Will you take them?"

"Of course, Hassar."

"Good. These three are for merchants. Just ask to find them. But this one"—he showed me an oiled skin pouch with the king's and his own seal on it—"must be delivered personally as soon as possible. Go down the central street of the city from the north gate. There's a silver jewelry shop at the beginning of the jewelers' section. Turn right just before it. At the fourth house down the alley, knock on the wooden door with the brass lion head on it. Say you are the messenger from Gibeah, and they will take you to a room upstairs. This document is to be delivered to the man there."

I frowned. "How will I know he's the right man?"

"That's another reason I wanted you to deliver it. You should recognize him. If someone is there whom you've never met, say that you've been sent to the wrong place and bring the document back. Just get it there as soon as you can. I don't want you to miss this contact," he finished, holding my gaze.

I bowed. "I'll do my best, Hassar. And Ethan sent this to you. He said the man who carried it was dead." I handed the pouch to him and left.

Ethan entered as I was changing into a short robe to run the messages. Catching sight of the pouch, he said, "You'd better take a bodyguard. The Egyptians lost a courier two days ago. Geresh found the evidence of a fight and the ripped courier case. What else do you have?"

"Three messages to merchants in Jebus."

Soon Ethan was ready, and we jogged out of town, turning into the hills for the trail south. When we climbed the last hill and saw the walls of Jebus, both of us stopped short, Ethan instinctively pulling back into the trees to check out the space around us, his hand on his sword.

Sliding into the shadow of a pine, I unsheathed my sword as well, watching the massive northern gates of Jebus slowly close. Travelers, some making it out just before the gates shut, milled about, talking among themselves.

"What do you think happened?" I asked.

"Most likely a palace coup. Rumors have it that Adon Debir was restless and impatient with the Araunah."

"You think he was successful?" I studied the situation in front of the gate.

"Probably. He's a crafty man, much as he can't resist the temptation to irritate people. I believe he's annoyed Shaul on more than one occasion."

I grinned. "It's all the sars can do to speak civilly of the man, let alone to him. But I haven't heard much about him lately." My leg muscles twitched a little, and I started to walk, stretching them and keeping well into the trees. Ethan followed. Glancing at the sun, I wondered what to do. Why was the hassar so concerned to get that message delivered? Could it have something to do with what had just happened? That might make delivering it now dangerous. Retreating farther into the stand of pines, we rested, but I couldn't stay still for long.

I moved to a vantage point where we could look down the western side of the city. The walls rose sheer and tall above the drop to the Hinnom Valley floor, and I wondered who had built them. Were they there when Abraham walked this land, or had the hill been empty when he and Isaac climbed the northern height together so that Abraham could return his son to El Elyon, who gave him?

Unable to shake off the need to deliver the message, I wandered down into a grove of oaks until I could see the south gates. They were shut also. The pool below suddenly boiled and rose, as the water rushed into it from the periodic gushing force of the Gihon Spring. I fingered the message pouch.

"Ethan, is there a back door into Jebus?"

"I've asked every member of my band, and any other Habiru that I've ever met, and none of them know a way into that city except through the gates. It hasn't been called the perfect fortress for nothing. Why?"

"I need to be in there," I replied, moving as restlessly as the waters below me.

My fingers tingled, and the back of my scalp prickled. Scanning the valley below, I listened closely to the sounds in the forest behind me, but no matter what I did, my focus always returned to Ethan.

Yah, what am I to do? I asked silently. I could feel an almost physical pull toward Jebus. There was something I must do there.

Ask Ethan.

But I did, I argued, sweat trickling down my neck under my robe. The sun had just passed full noon, and in the forest the silence of midday reigned.

Ask Ethan.

I thought back over my question and his answer. What had he actually said? I chewed my lip. To be certain, I tried again. "You're sure there's no back door?"

"The Habiru do not know of one, Dahveed."

I took that answer apart and came to the same conclusion.

Ask. The impulse would not let me go. "Do *you* know of any way inside other than the gates?"

Ethan caught his breath, the pulse pounding in his neck, and he looked at me in surprise. Once he had, he couldn't pull his gaze away. "Why has Yahweh's hand come on you?"

"I don't know. All I know is that I must get inside that city. Is there a way in, Ethan ben Patah?"

He went pale, and his jaw clenched nervously, but I held his eyes. Sweat ran down his face. "Yes, Mashiah," he finally whispered.

"Take me there, Ethan."

"Mashiah, don't ask this of me. Please."

Yahweh's gift swelled with urgency. "I must."

Ethan struggled to refuse, something he had never done before. "As you wish, Mashiah." His voice was barely audible.

He led me back north, pausing several times to study the hillside under the walls. In a spot shielded from sight by elms and terebinths, he climbed the rocks jutting out of the hill. On top was a tiny ledge nearly covered with spiny broom, wild rocket, and thyme under the reddish foliage of a young terebinth.

Taking out his sword, he shoved aside the thorny broom, ducking under the small, bushy terebinth, and I followed, the scent of the thyme rising to my nose as my feet crushed it.

A small opening in the rock appeared, and Ethan squeezed through. Inside, the cave was high enough to stand. I looked around in the dim light, then jumped back in horror. Off to one side, laid out in rotting clothes, was a skeleton, a leather belt still holding a sword around the white bones, the bony fingers of one hand curled around a dagger hilt. "Yahweh preserve us!" I gasped. "This is a grave, Ethan!"

"Yes, adoni," he said in a toneless voice. Tears trickled down his face. "Shoher, your abbi?"

He bowed his head in assent. "There is a way under the walls back there," he said, pointing to the blackness leading farther into the hill. His voice shook, and he looked like a stone statue. "Abbi found this place as a boy, and later explored the passages. He told me about it the last time—" Ethan abruptly sat down.

I eased down beside him. "What happened, Ethan?"

"I never got along well with Shoher. Immi always said that we were too much alike. He was traveling most of the time, and I resented how hard things were for Immi, I guess. We had a falling out when I was about 16. That's when I went to The Hassarah." Ethan ran his hand over his face. "It was months later that Grandfather Gaddi came to talk to me about Shoher, and he nearly had to beat me into the ground with his sword before I'd listen."

A wry smile briefly crossed my mentor's face. "I'd thought I was a good swordsman, but Gaddi did things with that sword I'd never dreamed of. I begged him to teach me. He said I could never learn because my hatred of Shoher crowded out everything else. Gaddi was very nearly right," he admitted quietly.

"Since Gaddi did teach you, you must have talked to your abbi."

"He came to Bethlehem several days later. When he told me about this cave, I didn't believe him. Nobody gets into Jebus. But he finally convinced me to see, and arranged to meet me here one afternoon. I waited for hours, but he never arrived." The Habiru looked over at the resting place of his father and shuddered.

"Did you look for him?"

He nodded. "Even though I was angry, I couldn't believe that Abbi would outright lie to me, and everything was just like he'd told me it would be except that I couldn't find any passage with water in it. I'd nearly given up when I heard water gushing and followed the sound."

Again he shuddered, eyes filled with pain. "I'd passed the place several times before. It looked like a shallow shelf in the wall on the floor, because it dips down into the rock. Water was welling up in it this time."

I shut my eyes, shuddering too. Ethan continued, almost as if once started, he couldn't stop.

"I waited until the water went down—I don't know how long. Then I started through the passage, and I found him. I pulled him out. I had to cut his girdle. It had caught on a projection of rock. He must have been in a hurry to meet me and tried to go through while the water was coming. There's a hole not far from the other side of the dip, and sometimes it gushes like the Gihon does and fills the space in moments. I've watched it.

"Once I left here, I couldn't speak of what happened, and I vowed never to return. Then just before Immi died, she asked me if I'd killed Shoher. I hadn't realized that anyone thought I had until she asked, and then I didn't know what to say. He'd been there because of me. And he died. It still hurt so much, I couldn't answer her, Dahveed. I told her I didn't know."

I gently touched his kilt. "That's why you always wear black, isn't it? You're still mourning."

Ethan rubbed his eyes with the heels of his hands. "I hated him so, Dahveed. I thought he had betrayed us all, and lied to me. But after coming here, I didn't know what to think. And after Immi died, I couldn't seem to stay away from here. Finally, I explored the other side of the dip. The passage empties into a larger one, and that one goes all the way under the mountain along the Kidron Valley. You can walk right to the pool in the city where people get their water. They leave ropes down the sides. You can climb up."

We sat there in silence for a while, and then I went to Shoher's resting place. Ethan had pillowed his father's head with something. "May Yahweh grant him peace. And you also, Ethan."

He didn't answer.

I bowed my head a moment, then stood. Yahweh's hand lay on me again, and I faced the opening in back of us. It looked like the entrance to Sheol, and I shuddered. Although I wanted to turn away, Yah's urging was plain. "Show me where to go, Ethan," I said in a shaking voice.

"It's too dangerous, Dahveed. I am to keep you safe."

"I don't want to go either, Ethan," I said, looking at him. "But Yahweh says that I must."

"Yahweh grant us hesed," the Habiru murmured. He rose and led me to the beginning of the passage. There were three lamps there. Ethan worked the seal off the cruise beside the lamps. The oil was thick and rancid with age, but it would burn. I filled two of the lamps, lit them, and handed one to Ethan. He started down the narrow tunnel, indicating the marks that he'd made on the walls as he had looked for his father. The passage twisted and turned, taking us deeper and deeper under the city, traveling downward. At last we came to the dip, and Ethan stopped. His hands shook so much that the lamp flame wavered, nearly going out.

I crouched down and looked into that hole. What if I crawled into it and came face to face with the dead, staring eyes of my own abbi? Sweat broke out all over me, and I had to set my lamp down. I looked up at Ethan's face. He simply waited, his memories too painful for him to do anything but accept whatever I decided.

"Your father gave you a gift of knowledge, Ethan ben Shoher," I said unsteadily. "The mashiah needs that gift. What Yahweh has entrusted to you, He will enable you to give. Take me through, Ethan. Yahweh will go with us."

"Yes, Mashiah," he whispered. "Take off your robe."

We undressed, bundling the clothes in our cloaks. I put the pouch with the hassar's messages in the middle of my bundle. Ethan entered the dip, crawling on his belly, pushing the lamp and his robe ahead of him. I followed. The passage was tight, and I had to suppress the thought of water suddenly pouring down on us from above. The tunnel was mercifully short, however. After about 30 feet it curved upward, and then we could stand again. Ethan crawled up a slippery ledge of rock covered with damp clay, squeezing through another hole and emerging on a ledge above a larger passage. The Habiru pointed up, showing me the mark on the ceiling that indicated the ledge. Then he turned left, holding up his lamp. I followed closely, careful to avoid bumping my head.

We moved as swiftly as we could on the smooth, slippery rock. The walls had been sculpted into weird patterns and shapes, and when occasionally the tunnel widened out, Ethan followed the largest streambed cut into the rock. The darkness pressed against my back as we moved in the circle of light cast by the flickering lamps. The rocks gleamed, and our steps and breathing sounded loud in the passages. I shivered with the dank chill, my skin covered with bumps, my nose filled with the stench of the burning rancid oil.

Then something that resembled thunder filled the air. Ethan froze, then whirled around. "Back, Dahveed!" he said hoarsely. "Run! Into the side passage!" He shoved me, and we stumbled and slipped for several yards to an opening in the wall. As he pushed me in ahead of him, I narrowly missed slamming my head into a protrusion of rock as the ceiling sloped down rapidly. "Grab onto something! Brace yourself!" he ordered.

The thunder filled the darkness around us, and I stuffed my clothes bundle beside me, leaning against it in the narrow passage, trying to find a handhold with one hand while my other held the lamp. A rushing sound made the lamps flicker wildly as a wind pushed past us, driven by the blast of water that instantly filled the main passage, then swirled into the side passage, soaking us to the waist, and nearly sweeping my feet from under me.

Heart pounding, I fought to stay upright. The water gushed around us again, slamming into Ethan, and he grabbed wildly with the hand holding his lamp. Although he kept himself upright, the lamp fell. Trembling, he watched it disappear. I could see the barely controlled fear in his eyes when he turned to me. "Whatever you do, Dahveed, *don't lose yours.*"

"I won't, Ethan," I said, fighting to keep my voice steady. It seemed like ages before the water began to calm, flowing evenly now, but too swiftly for us to leave our refuge.

"What quarrel did you have with your abbi?" I asked, casting about for anything to keep my mind from the darkness crowding on us.

The Habiru glanced up, and an ironic smile flickered across his face. "The battle of Michmash," he said. "When the Philistines started hiring mercenaries, Shoher saw the chance to bring some silver to the band, and he contracted for about half our warriors. Grandfather Patah wasn't happy about it, but we needed the silver badly, and every other band in the area had already joined up. I didn't like it either, but when Abbi asked me to fight, I went along.

"Even so, I couldn't shake the feeling that it was all wrong. I kept trying to convince Abbi to leave. After all, we were Yahweh's Arrows, not Philistine arrows, and we should not fight against anyone belonging to Yahweh. We were in the middle of another argument when Hassar Jonathan and Dara appeared at the top of the cliff."

Ethan paused again, and I leaned forward a little, checking the flow of the water around us.

"I'll never forget the bitterness I felt toward Shoher when the earth started shaking under us," he continued. "I knew that we would all die under Yahweh's hand for fighting against Him, and the only thing I could think of was to show Yah that I was truly His arrow, not another's. I pulled my sword and attacked the nearest Philistine. The next thing I knew, all the rest of the Habiru had joined in. When I left after the battle, I didn't ever want to see my abbi again. He had betrayed our oath to Boaz. So I went to The Hassarah."

I remained silent, trying to imagine Ethan as a youth at odds with his father. His loyalty to me made more sense now.

"Did you mean what you said about a gift of knowledge?" he finally asked.

I nodded. "Yahweh's hand eased off when you agreed to show me the way. I believe that I will need to know of this passage some day."

Ethan shifted beside me, as we both checked how far down the water had gone. "I never thought my father served before," he said. "He was gone so much, but now I realize he just served in a different way. Maybe I can be at peace about him now." He glanced at the lamp, which burned steadily lower. "We've got to move, Dahveed."

A few moments later we waded up to our knees in the main passage, the flow still swift enough to make walking hazardous. I couldn't seem to stop shivering, and Ethan moved as if in a dream. The tunnel was now wide enough for us to walk side by side, and we went as quickly as we could. The lamp was guttering when Ethan suddenly paused.

"Is that light?" he asked, pointing ahead.

"I think so."

A little farther, and he sighed in relief, pointing to a shelf nearly above our heads with another old lamp sitting on it. I handed him the one I carried, and he set it on the shelf, then blew out the flame.

Instantly we were plunged into total darkness. "Keep your eyes closed for a while," he advised. When I opened them a bit later, I immediately noticed the small gleam of light ahead.

"That's from the torches at the pool," the Habiru said. "Come on."

We made our way forward in the darkness, moving cautiously and silently, easing around a last bend of rock.

I sensed the empty space in front of us. "Where do we go from here?" I whispered.

He indicated the faint shadows of the ropes hanging down the wall of the well shaft on our left. "Up the ropes."

Holding our clothes in one hand, we waded over, clinging to the wall when the water got deep, and the sounds we made echoed loudly in the stillness. It took me a little while to find a rope, and the bucket on the end floated by. I grabbed for the bucket, missed it, and nearly lost the bundle I held in that hand. Stuffing part of my cloak into my mouth to free my hand, I finally captured the rope and hauled myself up toward the dim glow of the torches.

"Be sure you have a good grip at the top," Ethan warned from below. "If you slip, it's a long fall to the bottom."

At the top I clung to the rope with one hand, and felt for a handhold with the other, swinging slightly back and forth as I explored. Finally I found a crack in the rocks and held on with my fingers while I hitched my feet higher and shoved my head over the lip. Another crack farther along enabled me to lever myself onto the stone floor at the top of the shaft.

My own panting filled the place, and I couldn't hear Ethan. "Are you up?" I asked.

He grunted.

Following the sound, I crawled over and gave him an arm up. "You're heavier than I remember," I said, heaving him up beside me.

"Been living too well," he gasped. "Get dressed before anyone comes. If someone sees us this close to the shaft without clothes, they'll start asking questions I'd rather not have to answer."

Once we had dressed, I led the way rapidly up the rock-cut stairs into the midafternoon sunshine, and we cautiously crept through the deserted streets.

CHAPTER 30

Soon after we left the well shaft, I opened the door of the room where I was to deliver the official document.

"Dahveed?"

I jerked my head around as Ethan and I stepped over the threshhold.

Immi threw herself into my arms.

"Dahveed!" she repeated. "He didn't say you would come."

"Immi?" I asked in disbelief. "What are you doing here? Is everything all right?" I hugged her tightly, too bewildered to do more than convince myself it was really Immi that I held after longing for her so much. My heart pounded against her chest, and she smelled faintly of myrrh. Neither of us could bear to let go.

"There's some wine and bread on the table, Ethan," I heard Abinadab say. "You might as well relax and eat. I fear that we'll be here for a while!"

Immi laughed and pushed herself away. "What are you doing here?"

"I'm supposed to be delivering a message to the man in this room."

"That would be me," Abinadab said. "Abbi has been waiting anxiously for the exemption rights from King Shaul. He has a new boundary stone all ready, with the rights listed on it. It will be such a relief to him when none of us have to go to war anymore."

"And Jonathan Hassar said that if we picked up the document in Jebus, he could make sure we got news of you!" Immi added. "But I never suspected you'd bring it yourself!"

Again I hugged her, bending over her small form, tears stinging my eyes. It was worth that horrible trip under the mountain to hold Immi in my arms, and I'd thank Jonathan from my knees for this whether he liked it or not!

We sat down on the colorful carpet in a corner. The room had two three-legged tables; a couple stools; pottery bowls decorated in red and black containing fruit, bread, wine; writing utensils; and woven hangings covering the walls. A second door led into another room that looked as though it was for sleeping. Whatever place this was, the owners were very well-off.

Ethan and Abinadab brought over some of the food, while Immi told me all the family news. Abinadab talked about the town and what had happened at the gate, and Ethan added news of the Habiru. Most of the children in the band were learning business as well as war skills, and Ethan was pleased with how well the change from a mercenary no-madic existence to a more settled life was going. He seemed completely recovered from our trip under the mountain.

As we talked and laughed for hours, one part of my mind kept track of the sounds outside. The place seemed quite busy in spite of the po-litical situation. Footsteps often went past the door, and more than once, I heard the door downstairs open and close.

At last Abinadab looked around and sighed. "We'd better find a place to stay, Keren," he announced. "The hassar said that we should stay here only until sunset, and I'd guess this is the most expensive place in Jebus."

"It's also the safest," Ethan said quietly. "You'd be taking your life in your hands to go anywhere else now, but it's very doubtful that any-one here will be disturbed."

"What is this place?" Immi asked.

"In the daytime the Brass Lion is a very expensive, high-class estab-lishment providing private rooms for the rich and noble to meet for business purposes. It is known for its excellent service and complete confidentiality. After sundown it is still very expensive, high-class, and confidential, but the entertainment alters considerably," Ethan ex-plained drily.

"Oh," Immi said, looking surprisingly calm. "So this is what one of those places looks like!"

"Um, only the high-class ones," Ethan said, his eyes twinkling as he carefully avoided looking at Abinadab and me.

With nothing else to do, we soon settled down to talking again, and it was very late when we decided to bed down. Immi hugged me again as we stood. "Do you have to leave tomorrow?"

"I don't know. If the gates are opened, then yes, I'll have to go back to Gibeah. But if the political situation drags on, I'm just as stuck as you are."

I noticed the sigh of relief that Ethan gave. But I was in no hurry to go back down those dark cramped tunnels, not knowing if the thunder of the water would fill my ears, or if the oil would be used up, or we'd be lost in the maze—I jerked my thoughts away. I could only imagine what nightmares Ethan must suffer from his experiences in that place.

The next morning I awoke with Yahweh's gift tugging at my mind. After dressing and eating some fruit, I paced the room, every sense alert.

"What is it?" Ethan asked from his place on the floor.

"I'm not sure. I feel as if the walls are a trap."

Ethan thought a minute. "Danger? Or just the need to be outside?"

"The latter, I think."

"Then let's go. We can check to see if the gates will open today, if nothing else."

Ethan and I went out into the streets. It was well after sunrise, but we saw only one or two women, escorted by armed men, headed for the well shaft. Windows were shuttered and doors closed. Our footsteps sounded loud on the stones of the street.

Suddenly hearing other footsteps, we ducked into an alley and watched as unit after unit of soldiers passed by.

"This isn't good, Dahveed," Ethan said, his face tense. "We're near the elite quarter of town. It looks as if some sort of purge may be beginning."

More soldiers appeared, and I straightened abruptly. "Ethan, what would a unit of Philistines be doing here?"

"I don't know. Maybe we should find out." Curiosity gleamed in the Habiru's eyes.

Ethan's knowledge of the side streets allowed us to keep the Philistine unit in sight without actually following them. When they reached a large compound in the elite quarter, the unit disbursed, each soldier finding a concealed place that allowed him to watch the house's wall.

"You're leading me into bad habits, Ethan," I whispered, trying to figure things out from our vantage point in the midden alley in back of the compound. The stench made me wrinkle my nose, but I wasn't about to leave.

Just then the midden gate creaked open.

"Well, don't just stand there; get in here," a rough voice demanded.

We both whirled to face a house guard, who gestured us inside. "If they catch you back here, you'll die," he said in disgust. "You should have been here before. What happened?"

I glanced at Ethan.

One of his shoulders rose faintly, a half smile on his lips.

"I wouldn't want to say," I replied, stepping boldly toward the gate. "What's happening here?"

"Dumah is in a fret. Hurry up!" He waved at another guard by the house as he led us forward.

I looked around the compound. Carpentry tools sat on an old stool in front of one storeroom, and a half-woven basket in front of another. To one side the grape arbor looked cared for, as did a small garden plot next to it. The rows were neat and straight, but contained what must be herbs, rather than food. The house was big enough for a second door that was hidden from the main gate. It opened, and a short man with thin hair and a scraggly beard hurried out, two more guards following him, dragging a young man and woman dressed in ill-fitting clothes with them.

"Dumah, what are you doing?" the youth asked, his eyes shocked and bewildered.

"He sent Habiru?" Dumah snapped, glaring at Ethan and me.

The undertone of a whine in his voice grated on my nerves. I flexed my hand on the sling, not liking the situation as it was developing. "It looks that way, doesn't it?" I said. Suddenly, I was seized with the urge to get away. The hair rose on my arms, and I backed up a step. "Let's go," I said softly.

Ethan turned immediately.

"Not without taking them, you don't!" the man sputtered. "I'll not be cheated!"

"Dumah, why?" the youth protested, struggling as the house guard shoved him into Ethan's arms. The Habiru automatically brought the youth under control as the second guard flung the young woman at me. I managed to keep her from falling to the ground.

"Where's my payment?"

Ethan smiled grimly. "Do you really think we were trusted with that?" he asked, already dragging his captive toward the back gate.

"Well, you tell him I want it today," Dumah hissed after us.

"Only if I see him," I muttered to myself, practically running after Ethan, the woman I held hardly able to keep up with me. I took a quick look at her face. Her eyes didn't look quite as glazed as those of the young man in Ethan's grasp.

As we entered the midden alley, I caught a glimpse of Jebusite soldiers hurrying by in the street where the Philistines had hidden. I was glad Ethan turned the other way, for the singing of Yah's gift in my blood told me there would be a fight in that street, and I didn't want any part of it. We burst out of the alley onto another narrow street, right into the arms of two Philistines just turning into it. The surprise was complete on both sides, but my gift gave me an instant's advantage. As I shoved the woman to one side, my left hand landed solidly in the first soldier's stomach, doubling him over. By the time my knee had smashed into his face, I had my hand in my pouch, pulling out a stone and dropping it into the sling pan that I'd brushed off the back of my hand.

I whipped my hand around, the sling unwinding from my wrist once, the stone slamming viciously into the side of the second soldier's helmet. With a scream he grabbed his head as I reversed the swing, whipping the stone into the head of the first soldier as he began to straighten up. He fell without a sound, and I grabbed the woman again, pulling her after me as I followed Ethan.

"How are you called?" I asked tersely as Ethan ducked into a narrow passage between two compounds.

She gave me an odd look. "Atarah."

We crossed another alley. "And him?"

"My brother, Ornan," she panted.

Ethan got halfway down yet another narrow alleyway, hesitated, and then disappeared. I nearly passed the hollow in the wall that he had stepped into, having to yank Atarah around to join me in it. Ethan had Ornan crowded against the wall behind him. I shoved Atarah back there also, pressing against her, glad I had my hands free. Ethan had one of his over Ornan's mouth.

I wondered why we were here until the sounds from the streets around us finally penetrated my ears. The shouts and cries reminded me of a battle, and it wasn't until I felt Atarah trembling like a leaf against me that I realized the difference in the cries signaled the death of defenseless people, not warriors. Debir's purge had begun.

We stayed huddled in the niche for hours it seemed, listening to the death all around us. Atarah managed to find her brother's hand in the cramped space, her touch calming him to the point that Ethan could take his hand away from the boy's mouth. But when the slaughter spread to the courtyard just over the wall we huddled against, she nearly fainted, and silent tears ran down her cheeks. At last silence settled around us. We eased up a little, but Ethan didn't check the alley until the streets on both sides had been quiet for some time.

"What is this place?" I asked, referring to the alcove we hid in.

"Legacy from Mattan's time," Ethan replied. "When this house was built, there was a huge tree here. It was blasted apart by Yahweh's fire, and Mattan's brother, Pashur, was one of the laborers hired to clear it away. He passed the location down through the band. It's saved some of us more than once."

"So The Hassarah was right," I said. "What one Habiru knows, they all know."

Ethan didn't reply, but he couldn't quite hide his smile.

"Do we dare leave?" I asked after a while.

"I'm willing to try," Ethan said after listening carefully.

It took nearly an hour, but we reached the Brass Lion without incident, and Immi welcomed me with tears, for she and Abinadab had heard enough to realize what was happening in the city.

We stayed the rest of the day in our room, Immi mothering Atarah and Ornan. It turned out the Jebusites' abbi and their brother worked in the palace and had been killed in the coup. Dumah, the "brother to pigs" as Ethan called him, was a kinsman of theirs, who had apparently betrayed them to Debir's men since they were more closely related to the royal family, and Debir was paying for information regarding anyone of royal blood.

Ethan went out in the evening again, returning after an hour with news. "It's rumored that the gebirah was killed in the purge. Debir is raging and already cutting off heads," he reported.

"What about the emmanuel?" Atarah asked, her face completely white.

"He's dead also, which is the only reason Debir hasn't slaughtered every one of the units that took part in the purge."

I turned away. I knew enough about Jebus politics to know that the emmanuel, the son resulting from the ritual marriage between the king and the giberah, was the heir to the throne, rather than any sons that the king had with his queen or concubines. Debir would kill the emmanuel as a matter of course, but the death of the gebirah, the woman who owned and embodied the kingdom, was a major setback to him since without ritual marriage to her, he had no legitimate claim to the throne.

"Will he appoint another gebirah?" I asked.

Ethan shook his head. "He can't. A new gebirah is always appointed by the old one. If something prevents that from happening, only the legitimate king, in consultation with his adons and the gebirah's bloodline, can choose one."

"And Debir never had the chance to become legitimate!" I chuckled.

We stayed a second night in the room, leaving the sleeping area to Atarah and Ornan. He seemed to be especially hard-hit by what had happened.

The next day Ethan greeted us with the news that the gates were open. While Immi and Abinadab packed, I spoke to Atarah and Ornan.

"We will take you from Jebus with us if you wish," I told them. "Do you have any place where you can go?"

"No, adon," Ornan said, the quiet dignity of his address making me revise my estimate of his age. His short stature added to the difficulty of determining how old he was. "We discussed what to do. We would serve you, adoni, if you will have us. You saved our lives. We owe you a blood debt."

My first thought was to refuse, but seeing the desolate looks on their faces, I knew I couldn't.

"All right."

We split up to leave. Ornan accompanied Immi and Abinadab out of the south gate as their servant. Ethan would then bring Ornan to Atarah and me. Dressed in garish clothing, Atarah left as my mistress with whom I was not happy. I kept up a constant stream of invective about her overspending habits as we walked out the gate. She sobbed and kept her face covered, crying that she hadn't thought the robe was all that expensive since I liked it so well. The guards at the north gate smirked at each other as we walked past.

CHAPTER 31

Ethan and I waited until nightfall before we approached Gibeah, and Ornan and Atarah were almost dropping from fatigue. There had been trouble at the south gate, delaying Immi and Abinadab's departure until after noon, so Ethan and Ornan didn't join Atarah and me until late. The two Jebusites had kept to themselves, and out of respect for their grief, neither Ethan nor I intruded on their privacy. The last of the light faded from the sky, and the breeze from the sea brushed my hair, bringing with it the scent of pines from the hills behind me.

Some family was giving a feast, and I could hear the faint sounds of singing and laughter as we rested before the final climb to the town. Then a figure appeared on the road and strode to the training ground. The hassar strung his bow and let fly an arrow while I watched.

"He's worried," Ethan said from beside me. "Jonathan always comes here at night when he's distressed."

"Maybe I should relieve his mind," I said, suddenly remembering that I'd been in Jebus in the first place because Jonathan had sent me there, and that I still had three messages of his undelivered.

"I'll take the Jebusites to the compound and see that they are ready when the hassar wants to talk to them."

"All right, Ethan," I replied, moving off.

The hassar was so intent on his archery that I approached within a few feet without his knowing—or so I thought. Then he casually turned, an arrow cocked in his bow and pointed at me.

"And which Habiru would you be?" he asked.

I knelt. "I would be Dahveed, adoni."

"Dahveed!" he nearly shouted, loosing the arrow into the ground and flinging his bow beside it. "I should pin you to the wall! I should chain you to my father's throne, or put a collar on you and give you to Michal! *Where have you been?*"

"Jebus, adoni."

"Jebus? The gates to Jebus were barred day before yesterday and didn't open until today. *Where were you?*"

"Jebus, adoni."

He walked up to me, and his large hands landed on my shoulders. "I should strangle you," he threatened through clenched teeth. "Why didn't you come back when you found the gates barred? All I could think of was that you must have been inside when they closed, and with trouble in the city, I thought—I thought—" He didn't finish, but the muscles in his arms trembled, and his fingers dug into me.

I reached up and gripped his wrists. "It's just as hard to get out of Jebus when the gates are closed as it is to get in. I delivered the document—"

"Forget the documents! Anything can happen when a city's gates close like that! Dahveed, are you all right?"

I'd never seen the hassar like this, except after one of his nightmares about Nemuel. How could I distract him? Maybe give him something to roar at for a while?

"I'm fine, Jonathan," I assured him. "I got to the Brass Lion a little late, but I did get there. Abinadab was still waiting, since he couldn't leave anyway. And I won't apologize for staying both nights there. You don't know what it meant to me. Immi had come with Abinadab. I cannot thank you enough, Nahsi. I will never forget this."

Jonathan's fingers loosened on my shoulders. "Your immi came?" he asked, pleasure edging out the fear in his tone. "That worked out better than I expected!"

"Thank you, adoni!" I repeated.

"I'm glad it happened that way." Smug satisfaction filled his voice. "You—wait a minute! You stayed both *nights*? With your *immi*?"

I suppressed my laughter at his chagrined horror. "We didn't have much of a choice, Hassar. There was nowhere else to go. I will admit, however, that Immi found it quite, uh, enlightening."

Jonathan groaned. "Geberet Keren wasn't offended?"

"Not at all. In fact, she seemed rather amused," I added, a bit puzzled myself about that.

Jonathan put his head in his hands. "I will never, ever, understand women!" he sighed. "And the price of that room for three days and two nights is small compared to having your immi offended with me."

"Two days and two nights," I corrected. "Don't let them overcharge you. We left early this morning."

The hassar's hands landed on my shoulders again. "Then what did you do all day instead of coming here to report?" he asked dangerously.

"Waited for Ethan, adoni."

"Ethan is involved in this?" the hassar roared, grasping my robe and hauling me to my feet. "Where is that misbegotten, insolent son-of-the-forest? He's supposed to be guarding you!"

"Please lower your voice, Hassar," I said, taking his hands from my robe. "I'm sure they can hear you all the way to the gate, and if they aren't inside yet, you'll frighten Atarah. She's gone through enough already. Ethan guarded my back very effectively when we were attacked in the streets, so don't insult him by saying otherwise. He's very sensitive about that, if you'll recall."

Jonathan froze. "Did you say 'she'? Don't tell me you came back with a woman!"

"Her brother is along, so you don't need to worry about her."

"Does the Araunah know that you abducted two of his citizens?"

"Not really. We didn't plan on telling Debir since he was trying to kill them at the time."

"Why would you worry about that insidious fly Debir?"

"Because he is the Araunah. Took over in a palace coup. And since Atarah and Ornan are related to the previous Araunah, we thought it best to get them out of the way quietly."

"You mean that you've saddled me with two members of the Jebusite royalty? I—" He ground his teeth together.

I was glad the darkness hid the laughter in my eyes. "Yes, Hassar?"

"Have you told me everything that you did in the past 48 hours, or is there something else waiting to ambush me later?"

"Well, there is one other thing I probably should mention." I reached into my girdle.

"There would be," Jonathan growled, bracing himself. "What now?"

"I'm afraid I forgot to deliver the other three messages you gave me," I confessed, holding them out to him.

The hassar dissolved into speechlessness. Seizing me, he hauled me along as he strode toward Gibeah.

"Dahveed, I shall bind you in fetters and send you to Tyre with instructions that you are to be taken into the middle of the Great Sea and dumped overboard."

I didn't reply, keeping abreast of him as he walked, glad that my diversion had worked so well.

"No, not the sea," he muttered to himself as we approached the gate. "The sea would spit you back out, and I'd still be stuck with you. No, I'll send you to Egypt—to Pharaoh's court—with a glowing description of the indescribable sound of your voice. Then two years later, I'll arrive to take the throne, since by that time, the entire land will be in chaos simply because you're in it! Sentry!"

"Yes, adoni?"

"Why am I standing out here waiting for the door to open?"

"Your pardon, adoni," the sentry gasped, and the small door by the gate opened almost immediately.

Once he had me in the throne room, Jonathan finally let go, sitting down on the throne as a guard hastily lit some lamps. "Don't leave anything out!" he warned.

I began with Ethan and me in the city, and by the time I finished, Jonathan stared at me. "You're certain the unit that you saw was Philistine?"

"Yes, adoni, and so were the two I fought at the entrance to the midden alley. I think Dumah was supposed to give Atarah and Ornan to them."

"Very likely, which puts an interesting political twist to the situation. This is the first I've heard of Philistines involving themselves in Jebusite politics. Now, what about Ornan?"

"He doesn't look it, but I'd say he's older than I. Atarah is older than her brother, I think. I have an idea their abbi was fairly high up in the palace, but I don't know for certain."

"Bring them in."

I went down to the anteroom. Ethan had found some suitable clothes for the two refugees, and I led the way up the stairs. Jonathan had been pacing, and he turned to the door as we entered. His breath caught in his throat, and he froze in place. Atarah stood in the doorway, dressed in a green robe and matching headband, her hair falling in shining waves down her back. Jonathan couldn't take his eyes from her.

She looked down, blushing, and Ornan glanced from his sister to the hassar, then grimly stepped in front of her. Jonathan walked forward as if drawn by ropes. He stopped, still staring, and cast a brief glance at Ornan, who looked at me anxiously.

I nodded, and the young man backed up a little.

The hassar held out his hand. "Welcome to Israel's court," he said softly. "I'm Jonathan ben Shaul, Hassar Israel. And you are—?" He left the sentence hanging.

Timidly she put her hand in his. "Atarah bat Tanhum."

The hassar took her over to a bench at the table and seated her on it. "Dahveed has told me of your father's death. My condolences."

"Thank you, Hassar." Tears filling her eyes once more, she looked down again.

Ornan turned to stare at me when Jonathan called me by name. "Dahveed Israel, the one who killed the giant of Gath?" he asked quietly.

I bowed.

"No wonder those two soldiers had no chance with you!" A fierce light shone in his eyes. "I'm glad you won. Very glad. Will he be kind to Atarah?" He glanced uneasily at Jonathan.

"He is an honorable man, and he will ask for her if he wishes her. And since it seems he's forgotten everything that he wanted to ask you, I will ask for him. Who was your abbi, Ornan, and what did he do?"

"Tanhum is the man my immi married. He was the royal treasurer," he replied, blinking rapidly. "He was training me to follow after him. I don't understand why he was killed. He would have served whoever sat on Jebus' throne."

"It is possible that he was not meant to die."

"He's still dead."

"Yes, he's still dead."

Jonathan talked with Atarah for some time, and the Jebusite youth and I listened in silence. At last the hassar regretfully stood up. "I won't keep you longer," he said. "You are exhausted. Do you have a place to sleep?"

"They are staying at my compound," I put in.

"Shalom, geberet. I hope you and your brother find comfort in your loss. We will do whatever we can."

"Thank you, Hassar," she replied, standing. Ornan took her hand, and they left the room, Jonathan watching her all the way.

"What did you have in mind for them?" he asked, dragging his eyes from the door to look at me.

"They apparently have nothing left in Jebus, and since I saved them, they asked to serve me. I agreed."

"Good," the hassar said, staring again at the door Atarah had gone out of. Then he pulled the brass earring over his head and held it out to me. "You shouldn't have knelt to me, Dahveed," he remarked, still fascinated by the door.

Without doubt full winter had arrived, Balak thought to himself as he added more sticks to the brazier nearest the throne. He noticed the hassar shiver and replenished the brazier next to Jonathan's table also. The king and his son were deep in a discussion about a judgment that the roeh's scroll was vague about, the hassar coughing every so often. So did everyone else, since the smoke from the braziers hung over them more often than it wafted out the window slits around the room.

Taking a forged Gibeonite report from his girdle and handing it to Sar Eshbaal, Balak said, "Here is the latest overseer's report from Kiriath-jearim." The sar set it aside absently. Satisfied, Balak turned away. The original report was safely hidden behind a group of wine jars in the storeroom, along with several petitions and complaints about the new king's officers that only he had seen. He couldn't help but notice that the royal officers somehow multiplied without a word being said in the throne room.

The anteroom scribe escorted a man in, taking him to Kohath's table in the west ell. The visitor looked like a Philistine, and Balak casually walked closer.

"It is unfortunate, geber," Kohath said, "but there is no room today for you to speak to the king. Perhaps tomorrow."

"But this is most urgent," the visitor insisted. "I'm the Gibeonite overseer from Chephirah, and I've come all the way from there. It will take only a moment of time, but so much depends on the king hearing me quickly. Surely something can be done."

"The slate is full for today," Kohath repeated. "I cannot put aside someone else to fit you in, geber. There is no time."

"I will speak to the hassar if the king is busy," the man replied. "But I must speak with someone today. This matter of the Gibeonites cannot be delayed!"

"I can take your name, geber," Kohath said.

"It's Minelek. This petition is most urgent. It must be heard."

"I'll do my best, geber," the court official promised, setting his note aside as the anteroom scribe escorted the man out of the room again. The next time Balak passed the table with more fuel for the braziers, he slipped the note into his girdle.

Michal sat up on the bedroll, shivering in the damp cold. There it was again. She'd been hearing a muffled hacking sound for a couple nights. The hacking came again. It had to be in the house. She put on her robe and sandals, pulling her cloak on also. It was cold, and the braziers didn't seem to radiate much heat.

For several minutes she shivered in the corner of the passage, waiting. Just as she was about to go back to bed, she heard it again from the other side of Jonathan's door. "What can be wrong?" she murmured, looking in. Jonathan sat on the edge of his bed, coughing into his cloak so hard that he almost fell over.

The sahrah hurried to his side. "Jonathan! How long has this been going on?"

He couldn't answer.

When she touched him, he was burning with fever. Michal ran down the passage to her mother's chamber. "Immi, wake up," she said, shaking her mother's shoulder.

Ahinoam's eyes opened. "What is it?" she asked sleepily.

"Jonathan's burning with fever and coughing so hard he can't talk."

Immi sat up immediately, shivering as she reached for a robe and sandals. "If your father had listened to me, we'd at least be upstairs where it's a little warmer. But no, we had to sleep in storerooms so we could have separate chambers like Pharaoh of Egypt . . ." Abruptly she went silent, put on her cloak, and headed for Jonathan's room.

He had lain down again, shivering on the bed until it shook.

"Have Nadab get a cart filled with straw up here," Immi ordered. "Then go to the herb chamber and bring the willow bark. I'll dose him here, and then we're going to the estates!" She bent over her oldest son as Michal ran from the room.

TAMAR BAT DAHVEED

As you can see, the hassar's desire to be all things to his abbi is exacting a price. Adonai will be as severe as He must over this, for the hassar's first priority is the mashiah, and he must remember that. But even so, Adonai can use Jonathan's most persistent fault for His purposes. He is the great God, and can use anything, whether good or not.

And Dahveed has added two more people to his life. His hesed to them will return to him, as hesed always does, one way or the other. Yahweh has seen to it that Dahveed has grown in his understanding of rulership by learning to listen to those around him and to Yah's promptings. The test of how well he has learned is at hand, for Yah has chosen Dahveed to reveal to the hassar the sin of Shaul's house.

CHAPTER 32

With the hassar ill, the king refused to hold court. Balak put on his thickest cloak and walked with Judith to the fortress anyway. He had another report to put behind the jars before he went to the city gate. She chattered anxiously about the hassar while they walked. Her husband barely listened. He'd had ample time the previous night to wonder what might happen if the hassar died. With both Dahveed and the hassar out of the way, and the king separated from Yahweh, there was nothing to prevent him from rising much higher than just a king's counselor. Why couldn't he sit on that ebony throne one day?

King Balak. It sounded good. He would make it happen. After all, he now had the knack of just how much and when to petition Kemosh. Just last week he'd given his god a bit of frankincense, along with the written curse on the hassar. When he sat on the throne, he'd have to build a temple to Kemosh in Gibeah.

Judith left him at the fortress gate, but he remained until he saw the overseer from Chephirah coming. "Geber, I'm afraid I have bad news," he greeted the man. "The hassar was taken ill last night and has been moved to his estate. The king has refused to see anyone until he is better. I thought you should know immediately since you said your matter was urgent."

Minelek's shoulders slumped. "The king refuses to see anyone?"

"Yes, overseer," Balak said sympathetically. "If you like, I will send a message as soon as the king reopens court. We will keep your name on the record as someone who should be admitted quickly."

"If you would be so kind. It is something that he must know."

"I will," the royal servant promised, watching the man leave before going to the storeroom to hide the report.

More than a week after Hassarah Ahinoam took Jonathan to Zelah, Ethan and I rode our mules toward the royal estates. The hassar had sent for me, and I carried some medicine from Atarah, who had trained as a healer in Jebus.

I'd never been here before in the daytime, and I was unprepared for what I saw. Jonathan's place was larger than the residence in the fortress, and the compound around it had two smaller houses and numerous rooms. Fields stretched on all sides, orchards climbed one hillside, and a large vineyard occupied the other. To me it resembled an entire town.

"Up in the Jezreel Valley this would be just an average place," Ethan said quietly, dismounting. "When Shaul began acquiring land, I knew he would not be just another judge. He has enough power now that if anyone dies without heirs, that land comes to him, along with any taken as punishment from lawbreakers. He was wise enough from the first to use the wealth from his lands to create a professional army, and now to support a court."

As I looked around in wonder, I realized that I'd never thought of what it meant to be a sar from this perspective. The occasional piece of jewelry given to me, the clothes, even my house in Gibeah, all were indeed small gifts.

Ethan noted my subdued demeanor. "The king and the sars are very powerful men, Dahveed, in ways you have yet to learn. They can give their land to whomever they will, or take it back again, and that can either enrich or ruin families or clans. Much clan loyalty to the king is based on land that Shaul gave to someone. In addition, there is the wealth that comes from war spoils. Think of that, and you will begin to realize what it means to be a king or a sar."

Peleth met us at the gate. "Shalom, Dahveed," he greeted me with a bow.

"Peleth, I haven't seen you in a very long time," I exclaimed.

The former slave smiled. "The hassar made me the overseer of his Philistine slaves here on the private estate, and my immi and I moved here. You know she has lived with me since the hassar freed me. We have all the years that I was a slave to catch up on."

"Geresh and Bodbaal send their greetings to her," Ethan put in.

"I will tell her they think of her. If you would go up to the house, adon," he added to me.

As we went, I turned to Ethan. "How is your search for the steward of Tahat coming along?"

"I haven't heard anything since the last time the hassar asked."

"Surely he's learned something?"

"Very little. He's found a couple places that handle goods for the steward, but nothing substantial. I'm not doing much better for him, I'm afraid."

At the house several scribes had set tables up in the lower part, some in the courtyard. People milled around, obviously waiting. Sahrah Michal met us. "Good, you've come, Dahveed. He is impossible today, and I've had to threaten him twice with Immi in the last hour. Go see him before he crawls up the walls and brings the roof down on himself."

The worry in her eyes belied her words. I climbed the stairs to the upper part of the house. A loud racking cough reached me before I got to the door.

The hassar lay on a bed in the center of the room, one arm holding his midsection while he coughed. His face was pale and creased with pain. The arm he held up to his head was unsteady, and he had to try twice before he could turn himself over.

"You're trying to work?" I shouted, glaring at him.

He squinted up at me. "Dahveed?" he croaked. "Didn't expect you, but I'm glad that you're here. There's—"

"There is not!" I stormed at him. "What do you think you're doing? You can't move, and you're worried about hearing some report?"

He started coughing again, and I took the cruise that Atarah had given me, and unsealed it. When he eased back from the spell, I handed it to him.

"One swallow, no more!" I growled.

"Dahveed, I—"

"Drink it!"

He managed a swallow, and I took the cruise, ignoring the face that he made. "Whatever possessed you to think you should be seeing people?"

"There's more coming in all the time," he whispered. "I don't want to have it pile up. We'll never dig out from under."

"Have it pile up?" I fumed. "I'd rather have a few papyri pile up than pile rocks around the entrance to your grave! You should be sleeping."

"I can't sleep now. I have appointments." When he started to say more, the cough returned, and I handed him the cruise again.

"One swallow."

Again he made a face. "What is that stuff?"

"A gift. Your appointments have just been canceled. You are going to sleep."

He turned to me angrily. "I have too much to do to—" The coughing returned, and I stared at him until he quit, then held out the cruise.

With a shudder he got it down. "Dahveed, I need to talk to you about—"

"Is anyone going to die in the next day if you don't talk to me?" I interrupted.

"No, but—"

"Then you are going to sleep, and Jonathan, that's an order," I finished very quietly.

"You can't—" Realization dawning in his eyes, he instantly shut up.

"I can," I replied, my voice hard. "You are in no condition to be doing anything, and you will rest now. I will talk to you *after* you rest. And if you don't sleep until tonight, then I won't come up here until morning. And no one else will, either."

"Dahveed, you don't understand."

"Explain after you sleep."

He coughed a couple times, and I offered him the cruise. After another gulp he passed it back, his breathing easier. "There is so much to do."

Then, turning his head to one side, he fell asleep.

I sat beside him for the next half hour before footsteps approached outside the door and someone knocked softly. Hassarah Ahinoam stood outside. I stepped back to allow her to enter, but she shook her head and motioned me to her.

I closed the door and touched a knee to the ground briefly. Things were very quiet in the house and yard, everyone's attention on us even if it didn't appear to be.

"So you were the one shouting up here."

I nodded. "He's in no condition to be working. And look at all these people!"

Her eyes twinkled. "I know. But sometimes I can't roar loud enough at him to get his attention. I'm glad you got here."

"You sent that message!" I exclaimed, remembering Jonathan's comment when he first saw me. "But it had his seal on it."

"Getting *his* signet is easy. It's getting the *king's* signet off his finger that's been impossible. Nothing can be done until we have that. Shaul is so upset now that I don't dare let him see Jonathan's true condition. It might throw him into prophesying again. Otherwise I'd have Shaul in here getting the signet."

"What would you have me do, Hassarah?"

She put her hand on my arm. "Michal said you were very direct. We can't convince him to rest as long as he feels responsible for the court. Would you get the signet for us, Dahveed? Jonathan will listen to you."

I thought about it a minute. "Would this be a command, Hassarah?"

Her eyes twinkled at me again. "Get the king's signet, Dahveed."

"As you command, then. I will speak with the hassar as soon as he wakes. Whom shall I give it to? I am barred from the king."

"Sar Ishvi will be here to receive it. That will preserve the proprieties."

Bowing, I went back into the room.

An hour later Jonathan started coughing.

As soon as he stopped, I handed him the cruise.

He grimaced as he drank. "It's so bitter!" His voice was unrecognizable, hoarse and ragged.

"Whisper," I told him. "It hurts my throat to hear you talk."

"Mine, too," he confessed. "Why did you come?"

"To talk some sense into you. You have to rest."

He tried to sit up but couldn't make it. "I can't rest too much. Immi said that Abbi is distraught and unable to think about court matters. That leaves me."

"I don't suppose it ever occurred to you that the reason King Shaul is so distraught is that Hassar Israel is ill? That if he knew the hassar was resting and recovering well, he would be perfectly capable of handling the court just as he's done for years?"

"I'm not going to die, Dahveed!"

"I'm not so certain. Especially if you continue to be so mulish about letting someone else attend to things while you recover." My hand fiddled with the earring on my chest.

"You wouldn't!" he managed to get out before starting to cough again.

I handed him the cruise, without taking my hand from the earring.

"Well, I suppose Ishvi could do some of this."

"Give me the king's signet, Jonathan. Sar Ishvi can handle it all."

"He doesn't like to do administrative details," the hassar protested, setting the cruise down.

"Sar Eshbaal does. The signet, Jonathan."

"But the army reports and—"

"Which Sar Malchi loves. Your immi gave me a command, Jonathan, and I fully intend to carry it out. *Give me the signet ring.*"

His whole body shaking, Jonathan coughed again.

I handed him the cruise, and he took the swallow. Then he lay back again, weariness settling down on his face. With a sigh he held his hand out to me. "As you wish." I stripped the ring from his finger and put his hand back on his chest. I think he was asleep by then.

It was almost time for the evening meal when Sahrah Michal came up the stairs. Sar Ishvi had already arrived and gone, taking the signet and the scribes and people with him. She checked on Jonathan and emerged, bringing a stool for herself. "He hasn't coughed once all afternoon," she said.

I held up the cruise. "This appears to be very effective."

"What is it?" she asked, holding out her hand. I gave it to her, and she opened it, smelling it. Her nose wrinkled, but she sniffed again. Then she put a little on her finger and tasted it, making a face like Jonathan had. "It's got wormwood in it, and probably black cumin oil. I wonder if there's poppy in it, too. Where did you get it?"

"Atarah, the Jebusite woman, prepared it. When she heard the hassar had a bad cough, she offered to make this."

"Get more. This is the longest sleep he's had in days. The coughing keeps waking him up."

"I'll send a message. I'm sure she'll be willing."

Closing the cruise, she set it down. "Tell me about your grandmother."

I looked at the sahrah. She sat back on the stool, watching the darkness gather on the roof, waiting for me to answer. It was easy to remember in the quietness, and Sahrah Michal was easy to talk to.

When I finished, she shifted on the stool. "Odd to think that you might have grown up as a slave."

I shrugged. "It might have been easier if I had, considering where I am now." I flushed the moment the words were out of my mouth.

Before I could think of how to apologize, she spoke. "That's what's so refreshing about you, Dahveed. Every once in a while you say something that lets me see into your heart. Or you do something unexpected, like acting the royal sar to tease Jonathan, and I realize again just how much you mean to me."

Then she abruptly left the balcony as I gaped after her.

At the end of a week Jonathan was much improved, and word came that Merab was carrying a child. Sar Eshbaal had also taken this opportunity to reorganize the court administration again. He kept charge of the private estates and court records. Sar Malchi oversaw the professional forces, and only in time of war could Abner go over his head. Sar Ishvi took over supervision of the king's lands, leaving judicial and diplomatic concerns for the king and Jonathan.

I wasn't around much to deal with the changes. Jonathan frequently sent me out as his representative, with full authority this time, usually combining the settling of a dispute on his lands with a visit to a town or two in the same area. Before each trip I stopped at Nob, bringing an offering and inquiring of Yahweh for guidance. I always received an answer that helped me when I heard the case.

Visits to the towns normally involved a feast at which I would present the hassar's gifts. My memories of how The Hassarah treated people aided me immensely. Also, my music helped me over any awkwardness at such times since I felt at ease playing, and people had an excuse to speak to me, responding with enthusiasm. When I commented on this to Ethan, he gave me a look that implied that I was missing the significance of something. "It's not just the music, Dahveed," he said drily.

When I returned from a trip, the hassar would come to my house, and we discussed what I had done and why. His searching questions pulled from me details that I hadn't realized I'd noticed, teaching me to pay attention to everything. He corrected me several times, showing me better ways I could have done things, and he adjusted a couple of my punishments. But he only once reversed a decision I made, and that was because one of the accused men died suddenly, and paying the fine would have ruined the widow. Withdrawing the fine, he quietly made certain that the family would be adequately cared for. And he always inquired whether I'd heard anything of the House of Tahat.

When I asked Jonathan about the king's attitude toward me, he sighed. "He misses you, Dahveed, but he can't bring himself to forgive you. It's almost as if something keeps reminding him of what you've done to anger him."

During my travels I gained a good understanding of the hassar's reach and power. The sight of his signet brought instant respect, and I was careful to do nothing that would detract from it, understanding how important it was to Jonathan's dream for the kingdom. Ethan had reminded me that something I might say or do could mean life or death to someone else, and I soon found myself exhibiting the same silence and restraint that I had wondered at in the sars more than once.

Going out so much meant that I changed escorts often. I added eight more men to the second unit, dividing the men suited for escorts into squads, which rotated through the duty roster. Since I was a representative of the hassar, by extension so were my men, and Ethan suggested that I consecrate the escort as if we were going to war, as a reminder to them to be on their best behavior at all times, and to leave the local women strictly alone. It was effective and became a regular procedure.

CHAPTER 33

Balak, his face completely blank, trying to hide the pounding of his heart, silently regarded Kohath.

"I don't know what to do. I've looked everywhere. I put that

Gibeonite petition right here, and it's gone," the scribe said worriedly. "Not only that, but I can't find any of the other petitions, either. Have you seen any of them?"

"Is the king asking to see them?"

"No, Sar Eshbaal did, some time ago. I looked, but there weren't any petitions here, so I told him that we hadn't received any. But I know that we have gotten some since then. And now that overseer in Chephirah, Minelek, sent a message to the hassar himself, asking for a reply on a petition. And I can't find it. The other scribes all remember putting them right here on the corner of the table. But I've searched through the shelves, and none of them are here. The guards said you sometimes are here when everyone else is gone. I wondered if you'd noticed anything?"

Still carefully keeping his expression under control, Balak turned away slightly. "I'm mostly concerned with the storeroom across the passage," he said slowly. "I haven't noticed anything missing from there. I can't imagine what anyone would want with Gibeonite petitions."

"But what am I going to say to the hassar?" Kohath fretted. "Sar Eshbaal is so meticulous with the records. He might dismiss me if I've lost some. I'd never get another position, and with our oldest sick and the healers so expensive . . ." His voice trailed off.

"Why not just say you haven't seen it?" Balak said reasonably. "That way you won't get blamed. You can always search for it more, and if you find it, all will be well."

"But what if the hassar discovers that I've lied?"

"How can he?" the Moabite replied. "Look, everything up there is in good order." He gestured to the shelves. "If Sar Eshbaal checks that, he'll know you've done a good job keeping track of things. It's just one petition. Maybe the courier lost it."

"But it was here!"

"How do you know? Did you read it? Maybe it was something else, one of the other reports, or something."

"Well, I didn't really read it," Kohath admitted. "I put it aside to look at later."

"Then what you saw was probably just one of the regular reports," Balak soothed. "You'd best tell the hassar that you haven't seen anything. That will avoid trouble for everyone, and if it really is urgent, the overseer can always send another one, can't he?"

"Yes, yes, he could. That's what I'll do. Then I'll have time to search more."

Balak watched the scribe hurry off before getting his cloak. Spring had come, but the nights were still chilly. He shivered a little in the near dusk as he walked through the fortress gates. He'd have to move those papyri out of the storeroom. But it was too large a stack for him to take all at once. He'd think of something in the next week or so. Below him on the street curling around the east side of the hill, he saw Dahveed ride by, headed for his house. The zammar must have just returned from his latest errand for Hassar Jonathan.

I dismounted in my courtyard, bone-weary from our rapid ride home. The trip to the tribes of Asher, Naphtali, and Zebulun around the Sea of Chinnereth had been hurried since I must return in time to prepare for the war season, and the second and the eighth units had practically run the entire way back. I'd given them First Day off as well as tomorrow, which was Shabbat. I patted the mule and glanced at the lowering clouds overhead. The sun had been out for nearly two weeks up north, so I no longer stank of wet wool, and, having no desire to smell that way again, I decided to stable the mules here for the night. Before Ethan and I finished with them, the wind suddenly whipped around the house, and rain pounded on the roof as we climbed the ladder to the upper room and the food waiting on the table. I sighed in contentment. Here was one storm that I wouldn't have to camp out in!

"Some of those gifts we just delivered were the most valuable that I've ever handled," I said thoughtfully to Ethan after we'd finished.

"It's crucial to King Shaul's power to maintain his alliances," he replied, shoving his stool back so that he could lean against the wall. "The tribes up there don't have frequent contact with the royal family, so they needed something spectacular to show them the advantages of remaining allied to Shaul. Remember, without the willingness of the elders and tribes to follow his lead, he could not reign. His authority is not yet powerful enough to overrule theirs."

"That's why the north doesn't count Judah as part of the kingdom," I said with sudden understanding. "Most people down there don't look to Shaul and are too poor to support him if they did."

"Yes. It is to the hassar's credit that he has begun to woo the south. There is much there if someone took the time to develop it."

I mulled over what Ethan had said while the Habiru pulled out a bedroll and fell asleep. Then, as I watched the lamp on the table burn, thoughts of Sahrah Michal intruded like an itch that I couldn't reach. Her comment weeks ago wouldn't leave my mind. Why had she said it? What could I possibly mean to her? Whenever she saw me, she made it plain that she welcomed me, but she'd never done anything that showed any special regard. On the other hand, I had noticed that she watched me as much as I did her.

Thunder boomed, the sound reverberating around the courtyard as the gate opened. I glanced out the small window. In moments Nimshi stepped through the door, his cloak dripping a steady stream as he hung it up. I lit a brazier and set it by the table for him to warm himself.

"What's the news?" I asked.

"Until today, mostly the rain," Ethan's youngest son replied. "We haven't had any sun to speak of down here, and the farmers are worried that the grain will not dry for harvest."

"What happened today to get everyone's mind off the weather?"

"A murder. The overseer of the king's lands in Benjamin disappeared a week ago, and they found his body last night. His scribe is gone too, so everyone is wondering if he's also dead."*

"Has anyone been appointed to take his place?"

"Palti of Gallim. He's gone already to take the city elders' oath that they know nothing about it, and he's a good man, but—" Nimshi shrugged.

"Not up to finding a murderer in your opinion?" I asked with a smile.

"No. He can't think like one."

"Anything else?"

"I heard a messenger saying that Achish is on the throne of Gath now that Seren Maoch died. The other messengers were all discussing whether he'd be able to keep it. And Sahrah Merab is coming. She wants to have the baby here."

"That will make the king and hassarah happy."

"And Balak's been at the gate a lot, Dod. The elders usually consult him when anyone wants to see the king. And do you remember that Edomite, Doeg, who joined the professionals about midwinter? He's already got half the force betting he'll be able to outfight three men during the spring mock battle. Oh, and Ahiam and Shagay got back yesterday. I'm supposed to tell Abbi."

I gestured with my chin toward the corner. "Wait till he wakes up." I knew my old teacher would leave as soon as he heard the news. He'd been longing for the wild god-places for the past couple weeks. There was more of Shoher in him than he admitted!

The smoke from the brazier curled up around the ceiling, drifting toward the open window. Nimshi stood with his back toward the fire. "And I found out something about Naharai, Dod," he said after a short silence.

"Oh?" I'd asked the youth to see what he could dig up about Naharai shortly after he joined the second unit. His chronic fatigue and persistent silence about himself, along with his evident poverty, had roused my curiosity.

"He's a Gibeonite from Beeroth. His sister is here in town too."

"Do you know where?"

"She is a servant for the women in the house that I'm not supposed to know about. I'm not supposed to know about the women, either. So, of course, I don't."

"Of course," I agreed solemnly, leaning back against the wall. "Is there anything else you don't know?"

"I don't know that her name is Keturah, and I don't know that her brother is also a servant in the same house every night."

He grinned at me mischievously and pulled out another bedroll, lying down beside his abbi.

Since the next day was Shabbat, Ahiam let me sleep myself out. When I woke, it was past the noon meal, and Ethan had left for Bethlehem long before. I ate the food on the table and then stepped outside, looking for my retainers. I wanted to follow up on Nimshi's information on Naharai. The Gibeonite would make a good soldier if he could stay awake enough to learn to fight, and he wouldn't do that so long as he worked every night. What puzzled me was why the brother and sister were not with their clan in Beeroth, and how they'd gotten excused from tabernacle service.

"I wondered if you were going to wake, adoni," Ahiam said as I stepped off the stairs into the courtyard.

"I wondered myself," I said, stretching. "Now that I'm up, there are some people I want to talk to. You'll probably find both Naharai and his sister at the Brass Lion on the other side of town. Bring them here."

Taking a dubious look at the sky, which was turning dark-gray again, my second retainer opened the gate and started out into the street. An instant later a startled cry jerked my head around, and I saw Ahiam stagger back a step before he lunged forward.

I took off for the gate, arriving before either Shagay or Josheb, all of us with weapons in hand. My retainer stood dumbly, staring down at the woman half sitting, half lying, on the stones in front of him.

"Don't you know any better than to step out into someone's way like that?" she blazed up at him.

"Um, yes, geberet, I mean no, geberet, I mean . . ." His voice trailed off.

Slipping my belt knife back into its sheath, I glanced around. Ahiam had the oddest expression on his face, and he couldn't seem to move.

"If you knocked her down, the least you could do is help her up, Ahiam," Josheb commented from behind me.

"I didn't knock her down. She ran into me."

"I did not!" the woman contradicted, glaring at him. "You came rushing out of that gate right in my way!"

"No, I—"

"Help her up, Ahiam," I ordered, barely keeping my face straight. "Then you can decide how she got there."

Both of them suddenly realized that they had an audience, and my retainer stumbled over his feet as he leaned forward to give her a hand. She let him settle her on her feet, then tossed her head before turning away and ignoring him.

"To whom should my retainer send his apologies?" I asked, noting the dazed look still on the Habiru's face.

"I'm Palti of Gallim's sister, called Jemima, and I work at the fortress for Sahrah Michal," she said. "I'm looking for Adon Dahveed's house."

"You found it." I stepped aside for her to enter the gate. When Ahiam tried to follow her, I stopped him. "You have an errand," I reminded him.

"Errand? Oh, Naharai." As he turned and started down the street, he tripped over a stone.

Shagay, Josheb, and I kept sober faces as we waited for Jemima to tell us why she was here. She stared around the courtyard as if she didn't see it, and said nothing.

"Geberet? You had a message or something for me?" I finally asked.

"Oh! I'm supposed to ask when you'll be back. Sar Malchi wanted to know when the second and eighth units would be on the training ground."

"On Second Day."

"I'll tell her," she said, abruptly leaving.

"Her?" Shagay asked.

"I think that means she'll tell Sahrah Michal, who will tell Sar Malchi," I chuckled.

It took so long for Ahiam to return that I nearly sent Shagay out to search for him, but eventually my retainer came through the gate, the two Gibeonites in tow, neither looking very happy about being here. Keturah was a little taller than my sister Abigail, with light-brown hair and a sensitive face that looked frightened as she glanced around my courtyard. She hung onto Naharai's arm, keeping herself half behind him as they climbed the stairs to the balcony outside my upper room. I noted with approval that Naharai had worn his sword when he came, and that he kept his right arm free. He also watched Ahiam until my retainer had left the roof, and I invited my guests inside.

"What did you want, Commander?" the Gibeonite asked immediately.

"Just some information that I hope will help with your training," I replied easily. "Please sit down. There are bread and wine on the table."

Keturah shrank farther back behind her brother, who watched me warily. "What sort of information?"

I cocked my head at the defensive tone of his voice. Perhaps a direct approach would serve me better. "I wondered why you work nights for the women. Your fatigue is interfering with your training. If you need more to live on, and your clan in Beeroth can't—"

"Who said we were from Beeroth?" Naharai broke in sharply.

"I'm aware that you're Gibeonites—" I began.

As soon as that last word fell from my lips, Keturah fainted.

For a moment I could only stare in astonishment. Then I whirled around to call for Atarah. The sound of a sword coming free from its sheath jerked me back, my hand on my belt knife.

Naharai stood over his sister, blade in hand, eyes burning into me.

He didn't move, and I watched him closely, trying to figure out what had happened. "I have not threatened you, Naharai," I said at last.

"That's a matter of opinion," he replied grimly.

I stiffened. "I do not attack guests under my roof," I said coldly, barely able to contain my anger. "Or are you implying that I would break the covenant with your people? And anger Yahweh?"

The Gibeonite didn't move an inch. "Someone has," he said in a deadly voice. "Keturah and I are the only two left from our entire clan."

A chill went through me.

---

* See Cultural Notes: Bloodguilt.

CHAPTER 34

Put that sword away," I ordered. "You need to talk to me, not fight me." I strode past him to the door. "Atarah!" I called, then stepped back inside.

"What is it, adon?" she asked from the ladder hole to the storeroom below.

"Keturah has fainted. Could you see to her?"

She hurried the rest of the way up the ladder and went directly to the young woman.

I stayed at the far end of the room until Keturah awakened, clutching Naharai, who eased down beside her.

"What has happened to your people?" I asked.

They were silent for some time; then Keturah tightened her grip on

324 | YAHWEH'S WARRIOR

Naharai's hand. "The king ordered us killed," she whispered. "But we have done nothing. We have served faithfully, every year at our appointed time in the tabernacle. The priests have reckoned our service each year, and still we are condemned. The king's officers come, and we die."

I glanced at Naharai. He nodded grimly. "We aren't safe anywhere. They kill us in the streets and come into our houses at night. When we protested, they showed us the orders from the king and murdered any who raised a voice. Some ran to the hills and were hunted there."

Keturah started to sob. "Why has this happened? Why is Yahweh angry with us? We've done everything that He commanded. Even when the king's officers came to kill us, we didn't fight back. We just ran. Abbi said Yahweh would see that we were innocent, and that He would rebuke the king. But He hasn't. What have we done? Please, we just want to live!"

Keturah rolled over on her side, gripping her brother, sobs shaking her from head to foot. I sat motionless, trying to understand. Were they telling the truth? If they were, why was their house slaughtered for no reason at all? Why would Yahweh protect me from the king, but not them? No answers came. I sat lost in thought for a long time. Finally I went outside. It was nearly dark, and my retainers waited on the balcony.

"Do you know anything of killings among the Gibeonites?" I asked.

"No, adon," Josheb said, clearly relieved that he could deny the question.

"Shagay?"

"The news on the trails has brought some mention of this," he replied cautiously, almost reluctantly. "There has always been trouble between Shaul and the Gibeonites. After the king's victory over Amalek, things got worse. The Gibeonites seem to have a hard time obtaining the king's justice, and his mercy toward them is nonexistent. Sometime after you took over the army, the royal officers suddenly appeared. Then the killings supposedly began." He sighed. "Apparently it has gotten worse since then."

"How can he do this? Shaul's own clan is descended from the Gibeonites!" I snapped, pacing restlessly, a hard knot twisting my middle. "He will bring Yahweh's curse on the entire land! Why hasn't anyone said anything?"

"It was ordered by the king, adoni. Who would question that?"

"When the king's command flies in the face of Yahweh's covenant, someone should!"

Ahiam stared at me. "Yes, Dahveed. Someone should."

I whirled around to walk the other way on the short balcony, my retainer's words echoing my own in the Elah Valley. Someone should have answered Goliath's challenge the first time he gave it. But no one would trust Yahweh to fight for them. What if the Gibeonites were dying because no one would call to account the people breaking His covenant? That knot in my middle burst into rage, the same rage that I'd felt when I heard Goliath mocking Yahweh. I hit the low parapet with my fist.

"Shagay, go to Jeshua. Find out what he knows about this."

He left immediately.

I would have to get Jonathan here. Obviously he could know nothing of this. Breaking a covenant of Yahweh wasn't something that he'd do. If it were, I'd be dead about six times over by now. Once Jonathan knew of this, we could destroy those royal officers, whoever they were, as I ached to do right now. Waiting for Shagay to return with Jeshua, I continued to pace. But darkness came, and still he hadn't come.

Yah's hand drove me into the streets, and with the only thought in my head that of getting to the hassar as quickly as possible, I turned off the street at the boulder by the huge pine, climbing into the steep ravine that backed the north side of the fortress. Moving silently to the rocks and shrubs that shielded the narrow opening into the hill, I kept one hand raised to be sure I didn't knock my head on the ceiling in the darkness as I climbed the rough-hewn stairs in the tunnel. The door at the top opened silently, and I edged into the narrow space between two of the storerooms on the north wall of the fortress.

The king's residence was dark and still. I remembered the passage well, and moved silently to the hassar's door despite the pitch darkness. Lifting the latch carefully, I stepped in and closed the door behind me.

The dull glow of a brazier provided the only light. I knelt beside it, reviving the flames around the still-unburned ends of the sticks. The hassar slept on his side, his powerful shoulders bulking under the blankets spread across a low bedstead. I knelt at the foot of the bed.

"Jonathan! Get up."

He stirred and rolled over.

I pulled my blade from the sheath, the distinctive sound of bronze sliding free guaranteed to pierce the sleep of a warrior.

His breathing didn't falter, but he was awake. With a sigh he rolled again, allowing him to see the other side of the room now. A gleam from his face betrayed his slitted eyes, watching the light from the brazier glimmering off the edge of my blade that was point-down by his feet. The fact that I was kneeling would give him a nice conundrum to puzzle over for a moment.

"Get up." A fresh shaft of anger ran through me, making me tremble, and I had to bite my tongue to keep from snarling.

Moving slowly, the hassar drew his legs up and pushed himself off the bed, keeping one hand close to his side, clutching the blankets.

"Get dressed, Jonathan. There is something you should hear." My voice sounded cold even to my own ears, and I struggled to contain the indignation washing over me.

"Dahveed?"

"Yes."

"There's more fuel for the brazier on the floor behind it. I can get dressed faster if I can see better."

As he loosened his hold on the blankets, I tipped my sword into its sheath, then added a couple sticks to the brazier and blew them into flame. He cast a quick glance at what I was wearing and then silently dressed similarly, in a shirt and kilt, with leg wraps, and picked up his campaign cloak.

As he settled the cloak on his shoulders, he finally spoke. "Is the anger in you against me, adoni?"

"Not yet." Handing him his sword, I led him outside. My anger cooled a little as we walked out the fortress gate and down the path around the east side of Gibeah's hill.

"Naharai and his sister will be terrified when they see you," I said when we arrived.

"All right."

I opened the door to the upstairs room and walked in, the hassar right behind me.

Naharai swung around to see, and when he recognized Jonathan, he turned dead white. The expression he gave me was more bitter than gall, and he pulled his sword from the sheath, standing over his sister.

The hassar took off his cloak as if nothing had happened, then removed his sword and laid it on the table. Approaching one of the braziers, he held his hands over it, ignoring Naharai. The man didn't know what to do. He cast a quick look at me.

"I can guarantee that Jonathan Hassar knows nothing about what you've told me. Stand guard over your sister if you must, but start talking."

"Tell him," Keturah urged. "Please, Naharai. Someone must help us, and perhaps he can!"

The soldier's hand tightened and loosened on the sword hilt.

Jonathan gave me a quick, measuring glance, then waited.

The words spilled out of Naharai.

Hearing the story again, with the details this time, roused me to the extent that I couldn't keep still. I paced the room, turning and twisting, wishing that I could find relief, unable to determine why Yahweh's hand rested on me this heavily. Naharai wasn't that much of a danger in spite of the sword he held. Jonathan listened without a word, but he kept checking me frequently, a puzzled expression in his eyes.

Once the Gibeonite fell silent, Jonathan began to ask questions, pulling from Naharai as much information as he could, and frowning more and more frequently. At last he asked, "Have you petitioned the king?"

The Gibeonite laughed bitterly. "Numberless times, Hassar. The petitions went out, and we never heard another word. At last we decided that our requests weren't reaching the king, so the clans at Chephirah sent someone they trusted with one. He was never allowed in the king's presence. Beeroth sent me with one. I managed to get to the throne room with it."

"If it reached the throne room, I must have seen it," Jonathan said thoughtfully.

"You did, Hassar," Naharai replied bitterly. "You held it in your hands, took one look at the Gibeonite seal, and handed it off to a scribe. I waited for three weeks in this wretched town, coming every day to the court, and no one said a word.

"When I got back home, I found that every man in my clan was dead, killed on the way back from their service at the tabernacle. I was

328 | YAHWEH'S WARRIOR

alone except for Keturah." He spun to face me. "So don't tell me, Commander, that the hassar hasn't known about this. *He has.*"

I looked at Jonathan. His face was shadowed and still in the flickering lamplight. The brazier had nearly gone out, but he stood by it anyway. The gift burned in me, and I struggled to contain it. How could the hassar let something like this go on? I forced myself away from him, only to face him again, the gift driving me nearer. Twice more I pulled away, but always I turned back, my hand on my sword. I felt as if unable to breathe because of the fiery anger flaming in me.

Jonathan remained motionless as I struggled with my gift.

"Give me a little time," he said finally.

What is he asking me for? I wondered, too distracted to think this through. "All right," I heard myself say curtly. Again I tried to pull away from him, and managed to get halfway to a corner of the room.

"Josheb, waken Sar Eshbaal, and tell him to search for any papyri with complaints by the Gibeonites. Have him look anywhere there are records. Tell him I need them before dawn."

"Yes, Hassar."

Jonathan then asked Naharai to name the royal officers involved, and the man did, citing 10 or more. The hassar looked at him in frank disbelief.

"Two officers were assigned to your district," he said. "No more. They were to check out the records recording any absences of service for your city."

"Absence of service? The priests released us. We served as required."

"Do you have the release?"

"Of course not. The king has every last one."

"I have mine," Keturah interrupted timidly. "It got left behind when Abbi went. I didn't know who to give it to here, and I've kept it in case anyone asked."

"Let me see it," Jonathan said.

"Don't give it to him, Keturah," Naharai ordered, still standing between her and the hassar. "It will just vanish like all the others."

"Naharai, what difference does it make? It doesn't do me any good now." She reached into her girdle and pulled out the folded papyrus. Naharai tossed it on the table.

The hassar's jaw clenched, but he opened it, reading it. Again that puzzled expression crossed his face.

"I suppose no one actually thought to ask a priest about any of this?" Naharai said sarcastically.

"No need. We have their reports." Jonathan studied me again.

By now I'd been able to get some control over myself, keeping my restlessness to a minimum.

"What day did you bring your petition?" the hassar asked, but this time I noted the slight change in his voice. He wasn't being patient—something was bothering him.

"I don't remember. It isn't a time I care to think about."

An owl called outside, and I slipped out the door, going to the roof to meet whoever was arriving.

Jeshua greeted me quietly, and I brought him into the house. The hassar had drawn back into the shadows by the wall and couldnt be seen by Jeshua. Surprisingly, Naharai had his sword sheathed although he still stood guard over his sister, who had sat up against the wall.

"When Shagay told me what you wanted to know, I decided to come myself," Jeshua said, when I indicated that he could report now. "I brought someone with me, so if you'd send to the west gate, he should be there about now."

Slipping back outside, I dispatched Ahiam.

When I returned, the local Habiru leader continued. "I've been worried about this, Dahveed. Talked it over with Dahveed Joel more than once. I'm not eager for my band to get blamed. We've had no serious trouble for some years now, and I don't want any."

"Blamed for what?" I asked.

"The killings. It's gotten so bad, I won't let my women out without escort, and the children are afraid to sleep at night. We've got some fields planted around Kiriath-jearim, but I don't know if I'll harvest them. Seems everywhere we go around there, we find a body.

"I'd considered moving north of Beth-horon, but then I heard the king's officers were responsible for the deaths. It was a relief to us, but I got to thinking about it, and it didn't make sense, what with the covenant and all, so I poked around a little. Sent a message to Ethan. It wasn't likely that he'd have trouble out his way, but he might know something. He usually does."

The hassar stood totally still, his attention riveted on Jeshua.

Naharai watched him, a sardonic smile on his face.

I tried to still my trembling by folding my arms as tightly against my chest as I could, and by pressing my back against the wall.

"Ethan found out a little," Jeshua went on. "Seems that the king thought the Gibeonites had shirked on their duties or something and was punishing them. He'd heard they were rebelling and planning military action."

"But we didn't!" Keturah protested. "None of us. We didn't!"

Jeshua glanced her way, studying her and Naharai. "Didn't say I thought you had. You're of Gibeon?"

"Beeroth," I answered for them.

"Thought so. From what I hear, one clan is gone from there."

"Ours," Naharai said bitterly. "My sister and I are all that's left."

"Have you talked to the hassar? He might help. That's another thing that bothered me. It isn't like the hassar to let something like this happen."

"I'll keep it in mind," Naharai said so ironically that Jeshua blinked.

The compound gate opened, and Jeshua went to the door. "He's here. And he's got records with him. I should get back. My people are jittery. Some of my band are worried those royal officers won't know the difference between a Gibeonite and a Habiru—or care, if it comes to that."

"How many royal officers are there now?" I asked.

"Started with two," Jeshua said promptly. "Then there were five, and eight, and 10. Might be a dozen now for all I know."

He left as Ahiam led the newcomer up the stairs, both carrying a stack of records. As they entered the glow of the brazier, I recognized Minelek, the Philistine merchant who served as overseer for Chephirah.

The hassar remained back in the shadows, sitting so still on the stool that he was nearly invisible. Minelek glanced around. "Adon Dahveed?" he asked a bit hesitantly.

"Yes, geber."

"Adon, I'm so glad someone will finally hear me! I sent message after message. These people have done nothing! Why has the king sentenced them to death?"

"That's what we're trying to determine. What do you have?"

"I brought all the records concerning the Gibeonites' service. They have gone every month, they have been released by the priests, and I sent their records and documents of release every month to the king. Then I received a query from the court asking why several Gibeonites had not reported to the tabernacle. I replied that they had, and sent another copy of the report."

He shook his head. "It was as if no one heard what I said. Then two new royal officers showed up, saying that the king had appointed them to investigate the matter! I didn't understand. There was no matter to investigate! All had been done."

Minelek sighed in frustration. "Dahveed, I will place myself under your hesed now. I didn't trust the men the king had sent. After they came, I went myself to see King Shaul and was refused both times. And I returned to Chephirah to find that several Gibeonites had been killed while I was gone.

"The Gibeonites came to me, pleading for their lives. I barred the king's officers from the town, then helped the people flee. I don't know where they are, only that they are safe. I sent a message to the Hakkohen Haggadol, telling him that until the matter was cleared up, no one from Chephirah would report for duty. I didn't know what else to do, adon. These people are innocent of wrong-doing!"

The hassar stood and walked to the table. Minelek's eyes widened, and he knelt. I pulled myself back from Jonathan as Yahweh's gift washed over me again. The hassar glanced once at Minelek, his eyes hard, and studied the records on the table. Before long, a bleak expression settled on his face.

CHAPTER 35

Outside, the gate opened and closed again. Within moments, Ahiam ushered in Josheb and Eshbaal, their arms full of records.

Sar Eshbaal set his pile on the table. "I brought what you wanted, and found something else you must see."

The hassar glanced at Minelek. "Wait outside."

Ahiam accompanied him out.

"What did you find?" the hassar began.

His brother touched a stack of papyri, a tablet or two, and a parchment. "These are the reports that have come in this past year. They were shelved in the records room as I expected. I'd already checked the chambers of the other scribes. Josheb helped, and we didn't find anything."

He looked grim. "As I left the records room, I smelled sour wine and checked the storeroom. An entire jar had fallen and broken. It, and several others, were stacked close to the back wall concealing these." Eshbaal touched the stack that Josheb had brought in.

"I can't be certain I found them all. I can go through everything more thoroughly if you want me to."

Jonathan read the first few on the stack and leaned on the table. "I don't think so," he said, his voice as bleak as his face. "This should be more than I'll need. You read them?"

"Some. They go back for months. I've been wondering how they were kept from us. As far as I can see, only two scribes could have done it."

"I want to see those men."

"Yes, Hassar." Josheb accompanied him as he left.

Picking up the first papyrus, Jonathan scanned it, then the next and the next, comparing them to the ones that Eshbaal had discovered in the records room. His expression grew more and more haggard until finally he shoved the documents away and just stared.

"Adon?" Atarah spoke to me, coming in again. "Keturah needs to rest. Let me take her and Naharai to our room while you sort things out."

I nodded.

The three of them left, leaving the hassar and me alone.

After adding Keturah's release to the pile, he waited in silence, his face a mask. I sat on the platform in the niche that I'd excavated from the casement wall,* the cool night air from the square window behind me helping to calm me more as the gift gave me a little rest.

When the gate opened again and footsteps sounded on the stairs, I rose and opened the door. Eshbaal entered, followed by Kohath and Josheb. The scribe saw the stack of papyri and then stopped short at the expression in the hassar's eyes. He backed up; then Josheb had to keep him from collapsing on the floor.

"I guess that answers my first question," Jonathan said.

He had many more, although it was difficult to sort out Kohath's answers through his fear. Gradually a picture emerged of his discovery of the loss of the petitions, his failure to find any of them, and his decision to deny that they had come. But when it came to the substitution of records and who handled them and the appointment of the king's officers, he denied any knowledge whatsoever. When he learned that Gibeonites had been killed, his fear turned to terror, and he became completely incoherent.

At last Jonathan sent him and Minelek home. Josheb would remain at Kohath's house as a guard until tomorrow, when the hassar would see the scribe again.

Once the sars and I were alone, Jonathan stared at the table. "It's only half here. If I'm understanding Kohath correctly, he became involved only recently. There has to be someone who intercepted and changed the records. And none of this explains the king's officers!" He slammed the table in frustration.

As he picked up a papyrus from each stack, matching them by dates, I decided to stay as far from the table as I could, afraid to get closer while Yahweh's gift still flowed in my veins. The hassar kept sorting, adding some records from Minelek's pile. Then he paused, finding a bunch of smaller papyri folded together. Using them, he double-checked several records. His eyes closed, and I thought he was going to land on the floor.

"Eshbaal, examine these names," he said hoarsely.

The youngest sar looked the records over, and his hands trembled as he organized several others with them.

"Does the correlation hold?" Jonathan whispered.

"Yes, Hassar."

"What is it?" I asked, my stomach turning over at the expressions on their faces.

"The names on the substituted reports, the ones altered to missing. Within a week, they're all dead," Jonathan replied, his voice shaking. He touched the smaller papyri. "These are warrants with the royal seal, and reports from the king's officers, listing whom they killed. But I've never seen them before! Where did you find them, Eshbaal?"

The sar slowly sat down and put his head in his hands. "Abbi's room."

"Why would you look there?" Jonathan asked in amazement.

"I'd noticed a couple times that couriers delivered messages directly to the king, always before you came or after you had left the throne room. Abbi never paid much attention. He just shoved them into his girdle. I don't know why I thought about them tonight. I almost didn't go in, afraid of what might happen if he woke up while I was there."

The silence stretched for some time.

"With warrants going out under the king's seal, there has to be another signet somewhere," Jonathan concluded finally. "But what could possibly be behind all this?"

Eshbaal pulled something from his girdle. "This might have a bearing on it. I found it with the others in Abbi's room." He handed the hassar a wax tablet.

Jonathan read it, and his face turned gray. "Dahveed," he croaked, "did you say anything to anyone about the assassination attempt against me by the Beerothites?"

"Absolutely not, Jonathan Hassar," I said instantly.

"Eshbaal?"

"No, Jonathan Hassar."

"Then where did this come from?" He shoved the tablet to the end of the table.

I picked it up, then retreated again. It was a partial account of the attempt, saying only that it had been unsuccessful. "Who else could have known?" I wondered out loud, trying to remember.

"The scribe and the two guards involved," Sar Eshbaal said. "Any one else?"

"Oh, Yahweh above!" Jonathan groaned, his face sickly. "Michal saw Abner give Abbi a wax tablet. He bought his way into the king's favor again with Gibeonite lives!"

His brother stared at him. "But how did he know?"

"I told him," Jonathan whispered, turning to me. "When I faced him down after he attacked you, Dahveed, I told him what his carelessness had done. It was the only way that I could command him. Abner's the only one who could send something like this and expect the king to accept it without question. Look how carefully it's worded, emphasizing only that the Gibeonites tried to kill me. I was afraid that Abbi would break Yahweh's covenant if he knew. That's why I never told him. Look at the timing," he went on, hardly able to speak. "This gave Abner something to do while he was exiled to his estate."

"Maybe he did it on his own," I suggested.

Jonathan smiled sadly. "No, Dahveed. Abbi ordered this, and Abner carried out the king's orders with his usual efficiency and dispatch." The hassar put his head in his hands. Eshbaal gathered up all the records, and he and I left the room.

When I returned some time later, Jonathan still sat at the table.

"You will do something?" I asked needlessly.

"Yes." Despair filled his voice. "What is Abbi thinking?" he burst out. "Is he trying to force Yahweh to strike us with His sacred fire? How do I even approach our God after what has been done? What am I going to do, Dahveed?"

I had no more answer for him than I had for Naharai and Keturah. "I wish I knew. At least now it will stop."

"As much of it as I can," he replied. "But things like this are never over. They come back to haunt you. I only hope our house survives the storm. Have I your leave to go?"

I looked at him, amazed. "Of course. Whatever made you ask?"

"Had I tried to leave earlier, you would have killed me."

I looked at him in horror. "Jonathan, I—"

He held up his hand. "Think back, Dahveed. When you woke me in my room, Yahweh's gift raged in you just as it did at the Valley of Elah, and I knew something was very wrong.

"It was seeing you trying to control that outrage that kept me listening to Naharai. I believed that he was lying when I first came. I had means to prove it, I thought. But as he talked, I could see the anger and outrage growing in you.

"I wanted to bring the records, and dismiss Naharai and his story, and let it teach you to be more careful whom you believed. That's when your gift turned against me. It is a frightening thing to find the sword of Yahweh at your throat. Only after that, did I take Naharai seriously. So, Dahveed, have I your leave to go?"

"Yes, Hassar," I said, bowing my head.

Balak reached the throne room before anyone else. He liked the few minutes he had alone just to imagine what it would be like someday to sit on the ebony chair while everyone bowed before him. Of course, he would raise the dais at least two more steps.

Sahrah Michal arrived, giving him a cool smile. He bowed, hiding his thoughts. Someday he would have her. With her dignified demeanor and instinct for fitting display she was just the wife he required. And as daughter to Shaul, she would give him the connection that he would need to the previous king when he took the throne. As for Judith, she could be shuffled aside easily.

Eventually the scribes took their places, all but Kohath. The hassar entered, appearing as if he hadn't slept.

Then Sar Eshbaal arrived, followed by a messenger.

"Hassar," the runner panted. "I came from Josheb of Dahveed's household. Scribe Kohath killed himself last night."

The two sars froze.

The messenger waited.

"You may go," Jonathan said at last. Looking ill, he went over to Eshbaal's table.

Sahrah Michal watched him, puzzled concern on her face.

When the king arrived, everyone bowed as he approached the dais and sat on the throne. The hassar picked up a papyrus, then set it down again.

"What is it, Jonathan?" King Shaul asked.

The hassar stepped closer and then knelt. "I would beg leave from the court today. I am not well, adoni."

"You still work too hard," the king said, his voice worried. "Go to your house and rest for today and tomorrow, Jonathan."

"Yes, adoni."

The king's oldest son's voice had a woodenness to it, and Balak hid his smile as Jonathan left the room. *And may Kemosh send his arrows after you,* he thought behind his bland mask.

Up on the battlements the next night Michal watched for her brother to return. A chance remark had let her know that Jonathan had indeed gone to his estate, and then to Nob with a double sin offering of two young bulls. A bull was the required sin offering for a high priest or the entire congregation. And two of them?

The wind blew chill and drove a mist of rain into her face. If the sun didn't come out soon, the grain would never fully ripen for harvest. She should go inside, where it was at least dry. But she stayed, something telling her that Jonathan was out in the night also.

At last, she went to the sentry, and he let her out the small door by the gates. The mud squished under her sandals as she carefully descended the path to the street at the bottom of the hill and walked through the town to the west gate. A guard accompanied her to the training ground, and she dismissed him as soon as she saw her brother alone on the archery range, his cloak a little blacker than the rest of the night, his head soaked from the misty rain.

"At least put your hood up, brother," Michal said gently.

"Should I hide from the tears of those Yahweh gave to us to protect?" he asked.

Michal tilted her head. "I'd never thought of the rain as tears before. Who weeps in your heart?"

"I found out the truth about the Gibeonites. By the king's order they have been slaughtered in direct disobedience to Yahweh's covenant. Of the five clans at Kiriath-jearim, three are gone. Gibeon was hit nearly as hard, two of six clans entirely wiped out, the others decimated. All but one of Chephirah's clans survived because the people there aided them, led by a Philistine merchant.

"A Philistine, Michal!" he repeated savagely. "And Beeroth lost only one clan, a very small one of six men, killed when they were elsewhere, because the overseer there would have reported any possible irregularity, and murdered Gibeonites would have had him running to me!"

Appalled, the sahrah hugged herself. "How long has this been going on?" she whispered.

"For months."

"Who could Abbi possibly get to do such a thing?"

"Who's the only one who would, Michal?"

"What are you going to do?"

"Send orders to all the towns, recalling any royal officers. The problem will be convincing the officers that the king's permission has been withdrawn. But I can't imagine that people willing to do this in the first place will care about something as trifling as permission."

Michal wanted to cry. She'd never heard her brother sound so hopeless. He hadn't moved while they talked, just stood there in the wetness, staring off into the dark trees. "Our father has brought Yahweh's curse on us, Michal," he said, sounding as if his mind were far away even as he spoke. "It will be wiped from our house only with our blood. Abbi has doomed not just us to destruction, but our descendants as well. Provided there are any. Have you noticed that, Michal?"

"Sometimes it happens that way," she said, trying to ignore the point, edging closer to him.

"Maybe. And maybe it's Yahweh's displeasure. I've chafed under that thought for a long time. Now, I'm rather glad there are no children. There will be no one to suffer for what they could not prevent."

"There are Rizpah's boys, and Merab carries a child."

"I thought of them. I can't avoid it any longer, Michal. This can't go on."

His voice was so remote, so stark with pain, that Michal shivered, and once she had, the cold wouldn't let go, striking deep into her. "What do you mean, Jonathan?"

"Abbi. The king ordered the shedding of innocent blood, and the bloodguilt will destroy our house. He attacked the mashiah. Who knows what else he'll do?"

Michal twisted her hands in her cloak, remembering the look in Abbi's eyes when he'd come down the stairs the day the demon seized him. "What can we do?"

"I have to stop him."

His decision was barely a whisper, but the bleakness in his voice frightened her, and Michal ached to touch her brother, but didn't dare for fear that she'd find only a stone statue beside her instead of flesh and blood.

"Can you?" she asked, her voice shaky and dry.

"Yes. I can take enough power to be certain he cannot dishonor

Yahweh again."

She dared to take Jonathan's hand. It was cold as stone, but still flesh. "Tell me what to do."

"Go back home, Michal." He raised her hand to his lips. "You have eased my heart tonight. I'll be in soon."

Sensing the tightness of the control that her brother had over himself, she knew he wanted to be alone, and she gave his hand a squeeze before starting for Gibeah. When she looked back, the hassar's pain had driven him to his face in the mud. She kept going. Only Yahweh could ease Jonathan's torment now.

In sharp contrast to the chilly rain of the night, the next day was almost hot, with the sun shining from a clean, clear sky. Four units were missing from the practice ground, and General Abner wasn't there either. Sar Malchi continued exercises with the other 10 units. It was almost time for the usual mock battle, and the men wanted to do well.

Late in the afternoon, I was on my way back to my house when I saw Ahiam hurrying toward me.

"Adoni, the hassar is at the house. He looks near death. Please come quickly."

I ran to the compound, jumping up the stairs three at a time, shoving the door out of my way. The hassar made it to his feet as I burst in, then swayed, and I caught his shoulders.

"I did what I could, adoni," he said, his voice barely audible. "The units went out this morning. I brought this to you. Abner had it."

I took what he handed me without looking. The hassar shivered uncontrollably, but his skin was so feverish that I could hardly bear to touch him.

"Atarah!" I yelled as Jonathan sagged against me, and I managed a slow fall to the floor.

The fever held him for five days. Atarah and Ahinoam were constantly in attendance while Jonathan tossed and muttered in my upstairs room. Not knowing what the sickness was, Ahinoam refused to let her other children or the king near him.

The nights were the worst, when nightmares plagued him, often of

Nemuel, and sometimes of more terrible things that only I understood. During those times the only way to calm him was for me to hold on to his wrists. If I let go for even a moment, he would thrash around, crying with torment. Sometimes he wrestled against me, the fever giving him strength for a short period.

Hassarah Ahinoam looked to me during his struggles. "What torments him?" she asked, her voice worried.

"Memories," I said grimly, my hands locked around her son's wrists. "We fought something once."

The town was strangely hushed during the day, and dead silent at night. The street outside my gate had people waiting at all hours. The high place was constantly in use, and Hakkohen Haggadol Ahimelech sent five priests to help with the sacrifices.

The fifth night, after Jonathan had another struggle through a nightmare of Nemuel, I began to sing softly, more to let Ahinoam rest than anything else. Soon she drifted off, and Atarah came up with another dose of medicine. After giving it one swallow at a time, she took one of Jonathan's hands, gently rubbing the red mark left by my fingers.

As he curled his hand around hers and sighed, he turned his head toward me. When my voice faded a little, Atarah said, "Don't stop. He's listening." She pointed to his open eyes, staring in my direction.

I kept singing, repeating every song I knew. Atarah stayed with me, and we let Ahinoam sleep. Just after the dark of the night, Jonathan's grip on Atarah suddenly tightened, and his entire body jerked several times. Then he lay still, his chest barely moving. For two more hours we sat, and I didn't know now much longer I would have a voice.

Then tears streamed down Atarah's face, and she pressed the hassar's hand to her cheek. "Look!" she said, pointing.

Beads of sweat formed on Jonathan's forehead, then his neck and arms, until he was covered with it. His hand relaxed around hers, and she put his arm down by his side. "You can stop singing, now," she told me.

The sun was up when Jonathan's stirring pulled me awake. I'd fallen asleep with my hand around his wrist. As I raised my head, he looked at me.

"Shalom," I whispered, since I had all but lost my voice.

"Got a cistern?" he whispered back.

I reached for the cruise beside me with my free hand and held it for him. He took several swallows and then raised his hand. Mine came with it.

"Did I dream it all?" he asked.

"Most of it. You've been sick."

"You held on to me again."

"Returning a favor. Go back to sleep. I'll wake you when the food gets here."

A faint smile crossed his mouth. "Yes, adoni."

Since Sar Malchi was the first member of Jonathan's family to pass my gate, he was the first one to see his brother. I'd told Shagay to let one person from the family in. The sar came up the stairs quickly, pushing open the door without knocking. He hesitated in the dim light.

I stood. "He's over here, Sar."

He knelt by the bedroll. Jonathan's skin was so pale from the sickness that it looked as white as the hair streaking his black locks. When Malchi bent down to touch Jonathan's hand, I realized that the hassar was older now than my abbi had been when I was born. Blinking back the tears, I looked away.

Jonathan opened his eyes, seeing his brother bending over him.

You've got to stop doing this," the sar said seriously. "I don't think I'll survive another time wondering if you're going to die or not."

"Dahveed wouldn't let me go."

"So I see," Malchi said, eyeing the red imprints around his brother's wrists. "What shall I tell Abbi?"

A flash of pain flooded Jonathan's eyes. "Tell him Immi is sleeping. That should reassure him."

"Sounds like something you should do, too."

The hassar closed his eyes, and Malchi stood to leave. Pausing by the table, he stared at something on it, then glanced at Jonathan again. "Where did that come from?" he asked, pointing.

"I don't know, Sar," I said, reaching for it.

"Don't touch it!"

I jerked back. The king's signet lay on my table. Gasping, I looked at Jonathan. He also wore the king's signet on his finger. Memory returned. "That's what he handed me!" I exclaimed. "When he first returned. He said Abner had had it."

The sar's face turned cold, and I stepped back, feeling that icy wrath settle over him. "Jonathan told me about the Gibeonites," Malchi said. "But I didn't believe him about Abner—until now." He picked up the signet and strode out the door. In the courtyard he found a fist-sized rock. Putting the ring in the basalt grinding trough, he brought the rock smashing down on it until he'd pounded it to dust. Then he scraped the remains into his hand and returned to Jonathan's side.

"Malchi, what are you doing?" the hassar asked weakly, holding his head.

The sar took his brother's hand and poured what was left of the signet into it. "Taking care of family business, adoni." Closing Jonathan's hand gently, he touched it to his lips and then left.

The next day Sahrah Michal moved in. Since Hassarah Ahinoam had let someone else come to my house, the town knew that Jonathan was recovering. The priests had to stay another three days, handling thank offerings now. As nothing else could have, this outpouring brought home to me how beloved Jonathan was.

The second night she was there, Michal joined me on the balcony just after sunset. The fortress blocked my view of the western sky, but the last faint blush of red and dark-blue streaked the horizon on the south side of it. Michal's face had a most odd expression.

"What happened, Sahrah?"

"Jonathan just sent me out so that he could talk to Atarah!" she said, disbelief in her voice. "What could he be saying to her?"

I smiled. "Probably nothing of consequence."

"Then why couldn't I remain?"

Deciding that silence was the better part of valor, I didn't reply, just watched the last light fade from the sunset. The neighbors were in their courtyard, eating the evening meal. Atarah and Keturah had fed us early, their schedule dictated by the hassar's needs. Keturah and Naharai lived here now. Atarah told me that she needed more help, and Keturah agreed to stay. Naharai slept in the compound most nights, as withdrawn as his sister, but willing to take his turn at gate duty and whatever else needed to be done, working around his time on the training ground.

"You haven't answered me," the sahrah persisted.

"You wouldn't like what I'd say."

She waved aside a couple insects, and a lightning bug flashed on its way by. "Tell me anyway."

"Atarah suits Jonathan in a different way than you do, and he wants her way now."

"Why are you always right?" she demanded, annoyed.

"I'm not."

"Well, you're always exasperating, then."

"What did you expect from a hill man?" The darkness hid my smile, but not the amusement in my voice.

"It can be dangerous laughing at one of the royal family," she said sweetly.

"I'm desolated by your displeasure, Sahrah."

"How dare you say that to me when it isn't true?"

"It was what you wanted to hear," I said equitably. "You just flared up at me for telling you what you didn't want to hear. I thought I'd try the other way and see what happened."

"Jonathan's right. We should put a collar on you and chain you to a doorpost."

I chuckled. "Don't let Atarah worry you, Sahrah. No one will ever take your place in Jonathan's heart. He's just making a different place for her."

"I'm not sure I want him to!" She started to stand.

Without thinking, I reached over and took her wrist. "Please, Sahrah, don't interrupt." My fingertips met, circling her arm. I'd never noticed how small she was. She stayed very still. I suddenly realized that I'd laid a hand on her! Loosening my grip, I trailed my fingers down the back of her hand as I let go. "Please, don't take from Jonathan what he so rarely finds, Sahrah. He can't open himself to very many. Am I such bad company that you would run away so quickly?" I coaxed.

She sat down again. "You're impertinent company, anyway. I should tell the hassar that you dared to touch a Sahrah Israel without permission!" she threatened halfheartedly.

"What do you think he'd do?"

"Roar at you, and then you'd tell him why, and he'd throw his hands in the air and ask Yahweh why he was plagued with such a zammar! And I'd be left to defend myself."

"But that wouldn't be hard. I fear your tongue, Sahrah."

"That's the second lie you've told tonight, zammar. Is it the stars or the company?"

I settled back a little. "It couldn't be the company, Sahrah, so it must be the stars."

She turned to me. "Is there a place for me in your heart, Dahveed?"

Before I could recover enough to reply, she went down the stairs, leaving me still staring.

★ See Cultural Notes: Casement walls.

MICHAL AND GIBEAH

TAMAR BAT DAHVEED

D oesn't your heart weep for the hassar? He loved his father, and could not bring himself to completely supplant him. But as Jonathan knew deep in his heart, Shaul's power must be more than just restricted. The price for pulling back will be more terrible than he can imagine, and Jonathan will bitterly repent of his refusal to follow his God all the way. But Adonai knows we are dust, and He will hold Israel's hassar even closer as the king's son sets about saving as much of his family's honor as he can.

It is time now for the mashiah to discover how much he has changed, to recognize the work of Adonai in his life. There is risk here, for Dahveed has tasted power and is feeling its pull. But he is destined for a place of power, so he must know how to handle it, both its dangers and its benefits. He has been content so far to exercise his power only in private, and as we shall see, while he is willing to use his power to help those close to him, he is yet unwilling to publicly claim the authority of a sar. At the same time, even though he accepted with equanimity the king's denying him Merab, he will find himself eager to acquire Michal, and all it will mean to be the king's son-in-law.

And Adonai will take this chance to add one more person to Dahveed's life. They will meet only briefly and painfully, but irrevocably.

CHAPTER 36

No one seemed in any hurry to make Jonathan return to work, so harvest had begun before Ahinoam and Atarah let him move back into his room in the fortress. During the days before he left, Jonathan's gaze had followed Atarah's every move, and I guessed that he would ask for her soon. I came back from the training ground one afternoon to find Ornan waiting for me in the upstairs room. He'd become a quiet, thoughtful servant. Yet sometimes I'd catch something in his manner that made me wonder if he was more than he seemed. But he worked hard at whatever task given him, first helping Jamin, who had recovered and gone back to Bethlehem, and now Ahiam, as taking care of well as any other chores that needed doing.

"What is it, Ornan?" I asked.

"Adon, the hassar has asked to speak with me tomorrow regarding Atarah. He sent these. Would you advise us in this matter?" He shifted uneasily, looking at the two expensive robes folded on the table.

"Of course. Bring Atarah," I directed.

Handing me the message, the Jebusite left, returning shortly with Atarah, who looked annoyed at having to leave the cooking.

"Atarah, Jonathan Hassar Israel, has sent a message regarding you," I began, "and your brother has asked me to advise you in this."

She looked down, blushing. "Yes, adon."

"The hassar will ask permission to present his affections to you. Are you willing to listen?"

She twisted the fabric of her robe between her fingers. "I think so, adon."

"Does it mean that he will marry Atarah?" Ornan asked.

"Not necessarily. To do that, he would need the king's permission, and the king would probably grant that only if an alliance was to be sealed with the marriage."

"And Shaul doesn't like foreigners much."

"Correct, Ornan."

"Will he take her for a concubine?"

"I don't know. That's possible. How would you feel about that, Atarah?"

She glanced up at the fortress, her lower lip between her teeth. "Would I have to live up there?"

"Maybe not. Jonathan doesn't have a house in town, but he could get one."

"How would he treat us?" Ornan asked bluntly.

"He will express his appreciation and gratitude generously." I indicated the robes on the table.

The brother and sister glanced at each other. I knew they felt keenly the loss of their home and property in Jebus, and their dependence on my goodwill was still a burden, no matter how light I tried to make it.

"This is not something you should do if it is distasteful to you, Atarah," I stated.

"Oh, no, it's not that," she said quickly, then blushed again.

"Then what is the hesitation about?"

"I don't want to live up there with the king. There are . . . too many people."

I scratched my chin, unconsciously tugging at my beard as I'd seen Abbi do a thousand times. I'd already noticed that both Ornan and Atarah avoided anything to do with the fortress and rarely left the compound by day if they could help it. Given their experiences with the palace coup in Jebus, I didn't blame them. "You're still sending medicine to the hassar, aren't you?"

She nodded.

"And it would help build his strength to walk every day, wouldn't it?"

Her eyes widened, and she smiled.

"Then there is no reason Jonathan couldn't come here to get it from you."

They looked at each other again.

"It's up to you, Atarah. I'll tell him no if you want me to."

"I like the hassar."

The smell of scorched lentils drifted into the room on the passing breeze.

"The food!" she exclaimed and ran out the door.

Ornan asked me to be present when the hassar planned to come, and Jonathan appeared surprised when I ushered him into the upstairs room. His eyes tightened a little when he saw that Ornan was not wearing the robe sent yesterday.

The Jebusite stood by the table, looking surprisingly self-possessed. "Shalom, Jonathan Hassar," he greeted him with a bow.

"Shalom, Ornan ben Tanhum," Jonathan replied, nodding. He almost moved farther into the room, then eased back, noticing that I stood to the side, leaving this up to Ornan, who had not yet offered a seat.

"I understand you wish to discuss some business with me," the young man said.

"Yes, geber. I mentioned the subject in my message to you."

"Before we begin, please sit down and refresh yourself."

I hid my grin. The Jebusite had known my presence would change the atmosphere of the interview, and he was playing it for all it was worth. I put some fruit and wine on the table and provided water and towels for the two to wash their hands. While they ate a little, Ornan asked after the hassar's health, and Jonathan inquired about Atarah's.

Once the preliminaries were out of the way, the young man leaned back from the table and said, "Your message was quite brief, Hassar. Before I can give you an adequate answer, I would be certain that I understand your request."

Whatever Jonathan had planned to say had just flown out the window. I looked down, biting my lip painfully to keep from laughing, refusing to glance at the hassar, although I felt his black eyes on me.

Ornan waited with the blandest expression that I'd ever seen.

Jonathan leaned back a little, and a glimmer of respect flickered in his eyes. "An admirable attitude, Ornan. I have found your sister, Atarah, pleasing since I first saw her some months ago when you arrived here in Gibeah." A hint of hardness appeared in his tone as he reminded the Jebusite of his dependent status.

Ornan inclined his head. "Your kindness has indeed come back to you, at least twice. Atarah's mother was a respected healer, Hassar, and she taught Atarah all that she knew." Having just reminded Jonathan that he might owe his life to his sister, Ornan went on. "She has mentioned to me the comfort you brought her after the death of our father and brother."

"Then maybe she will listen to what I have to say now."

Ornan kept him waiting a couple of seconds. "I spoke with her about it," he said finally. "She wished you to know that she is willing to listen. Would you like to speak with her now?"

"I would like that very much."

The Jebusite looked at me. "Adon, would you send for my sister? The hassar would like to speak with her."

"Of course." I took my time going down the outside stairs, trying to contain myself. Atarah was waiting. Likely she'd been standing at the bottom of the ladder to the upstairs room the entire time. She wore the robe that Jonathan had sent yesterday, a green one with embroidery around the hem and a matching embroidered girdle.

With a slight bow, I gave her my hand and escorted her up the stairs. She went in and stood before her brother. "Yes, Ornan?"

"Atarah, Jonathan Hassar would like to speak with you, if that is your wish."

She turned to the hassar, regarding him for a moment. "I will listen," she said at last, with a slight smile. Jonathan couldn't take his eyes off her, and Ornan and I left.

When the hassar at last departed, I walked with him to the gate. His escort had waited in the street, and they dropped in behind us.

"Did you know what that young guttersnipe had planned?" he asked, striding away.

I matched his pace. "He didn't consult me."

"Then what were you doing there?"

"Throwing you off balance, I think."

"He did that all by himself!" Jonathan fumed. "The gall he had! I thought he was going to expect me to beg."

"Would you have?" I asked, interested.

He gave me a deadly look. We walked in silence to the path up to the fortress. "Where do you find these people, Dahveed?" he demanded, stopping. "He looks hardly more than a youth, and he nearly outfaced me. Do you know what he'll be like in 10 years?"

"Be nice to his sister, and maybe he'll stay on your side."

He smiled a little. "I think I can manage that."

Thereafter Jonathan took the noon meal and stayed for the noon rest at my house nearly every day. But he and Ornan were quite stiff with each other for a week or two.

I concentrated on getting the second unit ready for battle. But the tension in the professional forces was worse than usual this year, for the men wondered if Yahweh would fight with us after Shaul had broken the covenant with the Gibeonites. Many of them hoped the king would stay in Gibeah again. They did not want Shaul with them, even though Yahweh had obviously accepted the hassar's sin offering, since Jonathan had survived his illness.

I was resting in my upper room after the noon meal one day when Josheb brought Jemima up. Her face was flushed and her hair in such disarray that I guessed that she'd run all the way from the fortress.

"You must come immediately," she panted. "Sahrah Michal said the hassar was about to give judgment, and she thinks it'll be death. Hurry!" She tugged at my arm.

"Why would Michal send for me? Death for whom?" I asked, puzzled.

Palti's sister yanked me forward. "The sahrah said you'd insist on asking questions," she sputtered, exasperated. "The hassar can't do anything else since it's plain that the mule from Shammah was stolen and then sold."

"What does Shammah have to do with this?" I insisted, no longer resisting her tugs and hurrying after her out my gate.

"I'm not certain, but the sahrah said that if I didn't get you into the fortress right away, you'd be without a brother or two!"

Realizing that whatever had happened must be extremely serious, I scrambled up beside the huge boulder that marked the ravine behind the fortress and prayed that no one was watching as I ducked under the trees and into the passage.

Sahrah Michal saw me as I hurried across the common courtyard. "Get in there, Dahveed," she said, motioning me toward the anteroom. "The king left the case to Jonathan and is in his room, so don't worry about seeing him. Jonathan would be lenient, but that new Edomite in the army, Doeg, overheard the conversation proving that your brothers knew the mule was stolen before they bought it, and the king demanded full justice before he left."

CHAPTER 37

My head whirling, I raced up the stairs, wondering why the hassar hadn't sent for me the moment my brothers had been brought before him. Opening the door quietly, I slipped in. Abinadab and Elihu knelt in front of the dais, both faces bruised from blows. Elihu glanced my way, but gave no sign of recognition. Well, it had been nearly five years since he'd seen me, and I'd changed a lot.

Jonathan looked up from the throne, his face becoming an unreadable mask when he saw me. Sar Ishvi stood in Jonathan's usual place.

"What are you doing here?" The hassar's voice was hard.

His tone, and the warning glance from Sar Ishvi, made me swallow the words about to come out of my mouth. Then the dilemma my arrival had just created for the hassar burst on my mind, a situation as fraught with pitfalls as the one that I'd been in when I wanted to discuss things with Ethan just after my anointing. A word or two from me could force the hassar to publicly choose between me and the king. His honor for Yahweh would dictate that he favor me, and that would split Shaul's house, to say nothing of the civil war that might follow! I must weigh every word carefully. Now was not the time to act the mashiah!

I bowed slightly. "Forgive my intrusion, Hassar. I was told I might be of some use to you."

Some of the stiffness left Jonathan's posture.

"He might be at that," Sar Ishvi added. "Someone from the south might be able to get a little more information from these two," he said, jerking his chin toward my brothers. "I believe you wanted to know more of how the situation developed in the first place. Correct, Hassar?"

Jonathan eased back a little more on the throne. "Correct, Ishvi."

"I will do my best, Hassar. What is the situation?"

"Doeg overheard Abinadab ben Jesse and Elihu ben Obed buying a mule clearly marked for the royal house, something that further conversation revealed they knew before the purchase. Doeg arrested them south of Jebus and brought them here. They claim they were buying the mule in order to send it to me, since it was one that I had purchased from Shammah ben Jesse."

My stomach clenched. How on earth had something like this happened? And why was Elihu named ben Obed? Stifling my questions and controlling my expression, I glanced at the kneeling men. "With your permission, Hassar?"

He nodded.

I took them to the far end of the room. "Tell me quickly," I said in a low voice.

"Since the summer you killed Goliath, the bekor has been asserting his rights, as he called it," Abinadab said bitterly. "He's taken the best of everything that we produce, and this time he wanted three of the mules that Shammah had marked for the king's house. Shammah told him they were already sold, but apparently, Eliab didn't believe it, since he took them anyway. Abbi was horrified when he realized what had happened, and he sent us after him. We traced the mules to Jericho, and bought back two of them there. One was lame, and Shammah took them back to Bethlehem while Elihu and I searched for the last one. We found it in a caravan just leaving Jebus and decided to take it to Bethlehem, also, so Shammah could make the delivery of all three mules as agreed. But we didn't get far," he finished, glancing at Doeg.

"And where is Eliab?" I demanded, trying to swallow my rage.

"Probably wasting the proceeds of the sales at the Brass Lion in Jebus."

I clenched my fists. "So he's become as overbearing with all of you as he's always been with me?" I spat out.

"Yes," Abinadab sighed. "But there's something else you should know. When Doeg asked, I gave Elihu's name as ben Obed. He might find hesed if he's not considered one of our family. Is there anything at all that you can do for him at least?" my brother asked, his voice shaking.

"I don't know. I may be able to limit the punishment to just Eliab," I said at last.

Elihu looked up. "If you can do that, there might be something I would be able to do if I'm allowed to write up the judgment and punishment," he said, his face calm in spite of the sweat on his neck.

"I'll do my best," I promised, bringing them back to the dais, where Jonathan waited with Sar Ishvi. "The affair seems to be quite complicated, Hassar," I began. "Apparently, your mule was taken and sold by a member of the family under the impression that the animal had not been sold to anyone else. When Jesse heard of it, he sent these two to retrieve it. They headed south from Jebus after getting the mule back since they knew you are expecting two other mules to be delivered with it, and they wanted the delivery to be complete when it arrived here."

Doeg nearly snorted in disgust at that explanation, but I ignored him.

"I see," Jonathan said, studying me closely. "And which family member thought to profit from my mule?"

"Eliab ben Jesse."

The hassar's eyes glinted. Probably he'd suspected who it was already. "The situation does seemed to have altered," he said slowly. "I don't think I'll need you any further, however. You may go, Dahveed."

I bent my head a little. "Let me stay, adoni. There might be something else that I can help with." Straightening again, I held his gaze.

Ishvi watched curiously as Jonathan turned back to Abinadab and Elihu.

"Having had dealings with your family in the past, I'm inclined to be lenient in this case. I will visit judgment only on Eliab and spare the rest of your house, which has done what was necessary to retrieve my property. However, deliberate dishonor against the king, and against myself, will not be tolerated. Eliab ben Jesse is sentenced to die for his theft of the mule."

Despair filled Abinadab's face, and I knew that he was wondering how he would tell our abbi about this.

"Doeg, you will be commended and rewarded for your part in this," Jonathan went on.

"Thank you, adoni." The Edomite bowed.

"You are dismissed," the hassar added, and the man reluctantly left. Now that only Sar Ishvi remained, I felt much freer to act. I knelt.

"What do you wish, Dahveed?"

"Since there is no other scribe here, perhaps Elihu ben Obed could serve as your scribe in this matter," I suggested.

Sar Ishvi turned his gaze from my brothers to me, waiting to see what the hassar would decide.

A hint of curiosity crept into Jonathan's voice as he said, "I see nothing wrong in that." He turned to Elihu. "You are a scribe?"

"Yes, adoni. I trained in Beth-shean."

"There are materials at that table. Write up the order."

Rising, Elihu walked to the table and searched among the materials. Moving a papyrus, he hesitated a moment, casting a quick glance at the hassar, and then found a blank one that he could use. Swiftly, he wrote the order, giving it to the hassar.

Jonathan read it, looked at Elihu, and read it again. "This seems satisfactory in every way," he said slowly. "This concludes the king's business with your house, Abinadab. You are dismissed." Jonathan held out the order.

Looking as if he'd been sentenced to die himself, Abinadab took it and left the room.

"You hesitated over something on the table. What was it?" Sar Ishvi asked Elihu.

"I recognized the hand of someone that I knew at Beth-shean, adoni. It surprised me to see it here."

"Why?"

"Ibsam of Zebulun was dismissed from the school for theft. He could likely tell you most of what you want to know about the murder of the overseer for the king's lands in Benjamin since he was apparently the man's scribe."

"You picked up all that just from glancing at that papyrus? What positions have you trained for?" Jonathan inquired, looking at Ishvi.

"Administration, both palace and estates, and I have training also in organizing and keeping records. I can record in hieratic, cuneiform, or alphabetic script on papyri, clay, or wax tablets. I can translate Egyptian, and am fluent in Akkadian and Canaanite, adoni. May I speak further?"

"Certainly, ben Obed," Ishvi responded.

"You might check up on the overseer for Sar Malchi's estate in Shechem. The totals from the estate business report there on the table seem excessive."

"Why should we trust your judgment?" Jonathan asked, while Ishvi located the report.

Elihu gestured to me. "Because if I found the adon dead somewhere, and could only return one thing to his family, it would be that twisted brass earring. It's worthless of itself, but its chain is the most expensive thing on him. I would assume, therefore, that it is very important in some way."

Sar Ishvi stroked his beard. "Your assessment is quite correct," he said, hiding his smile. "How come you are working in a little town such as Bethlehem in the south?"

Elihu hesitated a moment. "I must eat, adoni, and I did not hear of the offer from the House of Tahat until it was too late to accept it."

I controlled my surprise. How could Elihu not have heard of such an offer? Was Eliab interfering that much with my brothers? Then the expression on the hassar's face made me smile.

"Oh, no, you don't," Ishvi protested. "I get him. You can ask him whatever you want about the steward of Tahat, but Palti of Gallim needs him for that mess in Benjamin much more than you do here!"

"You heard my brother," the hassar conceded, smiling a little as he turned back to Elihu. "I don't believe that I have meted out punishment yet for your part in this affair. You will work for Sar Ishvi for the next two years, beginning now, although why I would want another southerner around to plague me is more than I know," he finished testily.

"I'll be sure to keep him out of your way," Ishvi promised.

Elihu bowed again. "I will serve as you wish. You have shown me much hesed, adoni."

Abinadab was waiting for me when I left the anteroom. He watched anxiously as Elihu followed Sar Ishvi from the fortress without a backward glance.

"What happened?" he asked in a low voice.

"Elihu is sentenced to work for Ishvi for the next two years. By the time that's over, I'll wager Ishvi won't be able to do without him."

"That will cheer Abbi a little," Abinadab said. Then he nearly broke down. "Dahveed, how am I going to tell Abbi?"

"From what you've said already, it seems Eliab has brought this on himself. Surely Abbi recognizes that!"

My brother looked down. "We haven't said much to Abbi about it," he confessed. "The rest of us tried to work around him. I do much work that Eliab doesn't know about, even in little Bethlehem, and Shammah and Zelek hide the best of the mules. We couldn't do much about him skimming the wine and olive oil, and he's completely disrupted the sheep-breeding program for The Hassarah's cross. After Elihu returned, Eliab made sure that he didn't know about an offer from the House of Tahat because he wanted Elihu to serve him! That was his big mistake, because until Elihu came, we didn't realize how much we were losing to his foolishness. The worst of it is, he's been selling what he took, and then spending the silver on a lot of fancy clothes and trips to Jebus and Jericho. But with Elihu home, we got enough evidence to go to Abbi about it. That's what we were doing when the word came that Eliab had taken the mules."

"Well, his ways have caught up to him now. What does the judgment order say?" I asked, my stomach tight with both anger and apprehension.

"I couldn't bear to read it," my older brother confessed, handing it to me. "How could Elihu want to write it up? To condemn his own brother?"

"Considering what Eliab's done, I'd have written it myself!" I muttered as I flipped the papyrus open and scanned it quickly, then read it again. "I don't think that you need to worry about telling Abbi," I said, trying to control my expression since we were in the middle of the common courtyard. "According to this order, Eliab is indeed condemned to die, but the execution of the order is up to the discretion of the bearer, which would be you."

"What do I have to do with it?" Abinadab asked, unable to grasp what I had said.

"It means *you* are the one who decides *when* this order will be carried out," I repeated patiently. "Elihu has placed Eliab's life completely in your power."

Snatching the document, Abinadab read it himself. Then the amazement on his face was replaced with determination. "Things at home are going to change," he muttered, carefully folding the papyrus and putting it into his girdle.

"Don't you agree, Balak?" the king inquired as the servant adjusted the royal robe preparatory to going to afternoon court.

"Of course, adoni. It's wonderful that Merab gave you a grandson, and is doing so well. And since she's staying at Zelah, you can visit often. With the hassar well now, he can handle the court for you. I hope he won't say that he overtired himself again. It makes things harder for you."

The king's hand clamped down on his servant's wrist and twisted, instantly forcing Balak to his knees. "Are you saying Jonathan would lie to me, Balak?"

"No, adoni, no! I know that he would never do that," the Moabite gasped as pain shot up his arm. "Adoni, I beg you. It was a slip of the tongue. Please!"

The pressure on his arm lessened. "Take care your tongue does not slip too far, Balak," Shaul warned before leaving the room.

The servant followed the king into the throne room at a respectful distance, angry with himself. Since the hassar's illness, Shaul had been sensitive to any mention of his son. There was also a new restraint on the hassar's part toward his father, one that must involve more than the Gibeonite situation, but even the most adroit questioning had garnered Balak no information about it.

He glanced at Jonathan, wondering how many offerings he would have to give Kemosh before that man would be out of his way.

"What is first, Jonathan?" King Shaul asked.

"The dahveed, adoni."

"He is not to come to me!" The king glanced at the door.

"No, adoni, but he still must be rewarded for his victory at Elah."

Shaul shifted on the throne. "We gave him a house and clothes and gold. What else would you have me do?"

"They were for the victories after Elah. He should be given Sahrah Michal. You have made your displeasure plain, adoni. Now it is time to fulfill your promise. Otherwise people will say that the king's honor is unreliable. Michal is the youngest but one of your children, and now that the bekorah has borne a son, I do not see how people would think that Dahveed should have your throne. And as Michal has said, he has never personally done anything in the slightest against you."

"He refused to swear to me!" Shaul's face hardened.

"And how has that affected his service? He is here, as you commanded, serving you wherever you have told him to." The hassar stood with his arms folded, watching his father coolly.

Balak's eyes narrowed. He'd never seen the hassar this way with the king.

"What if Michal has objections?" the king asked.

"She told me herself that she favors Dahveed. Indeed, she loves him."

"Michal," Shaul called, raising his voice.

She came immediately. "Yes, adoni?"

"Jonathan says you favor Dahveed for a husband."

Michal raised her eyebrows. "Why, yes, I do," she said calmly. "He is handsome, and has brought much honor to you, adoni. Why wouldn't I favor him?"

"He is but a zammar from the hills below Jebus."

"But he is also the champion of Elah. And you'd hardly know now that he was from the hills. He learns quickly, adoni, and continues to bring honor to you. I favor him more than anyone else."

Knowing that he must keep his own thoughts about Michal very much to himself, Balak averted his face.

"I will consider it," the king said after a moment. "What's next, Jonathan?"

When court finished, Balak attended the king back to his room, expecting Shaul to dismiss him immediately because of his mistake earlier. But the king wandered restlessly around his room. "She said she loved him, Balak. What do you think of that?"

"This could be both good and bad, adoni," he answered carefully. "She was very cool when you asked, and spoke only of your honor."

"Yes. Her affections must not be much involved. Michal would favor him because of what he has done for me. She said so. But if she favors him enough to marry, that may be all I need. I must preserve Jonathan's place."

Surprised, Balak remained silent. Was it possible the king's mind was still set against Dahveed?

Shaul paused at the table, his hand resting on it. "He will surely want her if I offer. What should I ask for?" Then the king smiled, and a little shiver went down Balak's spine. "Let the Philistines take care of him. They surely will, after they learn what he's doing! A hundred. A full hundred.* That should be sufficient. And he will never have my throne." King Shaul looked up. "What are you still doing here, Balak? You may go," he said absently.

The servant left, rubbing his wrist. Once he was home, he took the shrine into the courtyard and wrote a petition to Kemosh for aid. He wanted this to be over soon. Nightmares had been troubling him lately.

Balak added the scrap of papyrus to the others in the shrine along with another silver piece. The wind gusted, pulling at his cloak as Judith called from the house, and he went inside. When he returned after the noon rest, the wind had blown the papyri away. Shrugging, he carried the shrine inside. Even if someone found them, he hadn't signed them, and the first ones that he'd written were safely hidden in the house.

---

* Keep in mind that numbers in biblical times are difficult to pin down. We don't really know how many the ancient Israelites counted as their "hundred," beyond that it was considerably smaller than what we consider a hundred. A similar situation existed in New Testament times when a Roman centurion, an officer by title in charge of 100, actually commanded 80, and sometimes far less.

CHAPTER 38

Tired from the spring mock battle that afternoon, I eased back on the stool and leaned against the wall, still smiling as I heard the gate close after Elihu. He'd just spent the past hour pouring out his excitement over his new job and the opportunities it offered. I gathered very quickly that the work itself barely touched the surface of what he was capable of, but associating with Palti of Gallim challenged him in other ways. Elihu's talent for recognizing individual hands with a pen had come into play more than once, and my table was littered with scraps of papyri that he'd used to show me just what he was speaking about.

As I collected them all into a pile, I wondered how things were in Bethlehem. I hoped they were going as well for Abinadab as they were for Elihu. I thanked Yahweh again for His hesed that day. What could have been a disaster for Boaz's blood had turned into a blessing all around. Even Doeg profited, for he was now "Chief of the Shepherds," serving as a commander under Sheva on the king's guard. The title was a Hittite military one that the hassar had appropriated for the purpose of honoring Doeg.

The top scrap of papyrus caught my eye again. On it Elihu had written three letters, the *vav*, the *kaph*, and the *resh*, demonstrating a little tick mark to the right on the downstroke of each letter. He'd said that if I ever saw anything like this, please send it to him, since it might help solve some puzzles about the Gibeonite troubles.

Setting it aside, I reached for the harp waiting on the table. I'd been composing more on my song when Elihu showed up. Now I went back to it, gathering the bits and pieces of my memories from the past winter into my mind again. I'd made many judgments this winter, so many that Jonathan had a copy of the roeh's scroll made for my use. I'd studied it extensively, seeing for myself the wisdom of Yahweh's laws. Why couldn't my own brother have followed them? As I played the tune again, the words to fit the melody sprang into my mind.

"The law of Yahweh is without blemish, reviving life.

"The warning sign of Yahweh is reliable, making wise the young naive one."

I hummed under my breath.

"The directions of Yahweh are right, making glad the heart.

"The commandment of Yahweh is pure, making bright the eyes."

As I plucked the strings, the melody pulled the final phrases from me.

"The fear of Yahweh is clean, standing forever.

"The judgments of Yahweh are trustworthy, they are righteous altogether."

I was playing the phrases again, locking them into my memory, when a loud knock on the door rudely jerked me from my concentration. "Come in," I called, startled.

The door opened, and Balak ben Hod stepped through, followed by two other servants. I hurriedly rose. What brought Balak, of all people, here at this time of night? He bowed slightly, his eyes flinty. "I carry a message from King Shaul."

Since he was here with other servants, I knew it was a formal message. "Will you sit down?" I responded.

He sat on the other stool. The others remained standing.

Ahiam came up the ladder and added bread to the fruit already on the table. After setting out thin brown saucers for our food, he poured wine for both of us into matching pottery cups.

Balak picked up the cup, toying with it a while before taking a very small sip. Only then did I drink some also. It didn't look as if he would accept any of the food, so I broke the silence. "Is the king well?"

"He is well," the servant replied, "and he sent me to speak privately with you. He wishes to say that his displeasure is not because of anything you've done. He remains cold to destroy the hopes of those who are not as loyal to him as you are."

Startled, I looked up. I'd never considered the possibility that my popularity would attract dissidents. In fact, I'd never heard a whisper of anything like it. Did this mean Shaul wasn't afraid of me anymore? Or angry? Curious now, I relaxed a little.

"The king is actually pleased with the victories and honor that you have brought to his house. He knows his servants favor you too." Balak paused a moment.

I couldn't keep the sardonic look off my face, and he clenched his jaw before continuing. "The king sent me with an offer to become his son-in-law. He will give you Sahrah Michal."

Michal! After a moment of surprise, I stood and turned away, fingering the harp on the end of the table. Marry the sahrah? I hadn't known what to do with the knowledge that she favored me, having assumed that she was far from my reach. Now it seemed that she wasn't. Or was the king toying with me again, offering me another gift that he would snatch away later? I'd better be certain of things this time.

As neutrally as possible, I replied, still not directly facing him. "While the king offers me a high honor, it was his hand that made me, without cause, so honor-poor that I'm held in contempt. Why should he give me this when I mean nothing to him?"

Balak gasped.

I turned around, looking at the other messengers. "Tell the king that is my reply."

They left in silence, and I sat down again, my thoughts churning. What would it mean to become a sar in my own right? Did I want to?

Balak took the long way through the north and west sides of town back to the fortress. He'd been annoyed enough that the king would use him as a messenger to Dahveed, and now he had to give Shaul that outrageous reply! It skirted the edges of open insult! Who knew how he would react? But then again, if the king did get angry, it would be with Dahveed.

In the throne room he bowed before the dais, where the king waited, the hassar standing next to him. The other messengers bowed with him, although they kept a significant amount of space between him and them.

"Did you speak to Dahveed?" Shaul asked.

"I did, adoni. He received us and—"

"Never mind that. What was his reply?"

Balak hesitated a moment. "He said, 'While the king offers me a high honor, it was his hand that made me, without cause, so honor-poor that I'm held in contempt. Why should he give me this when I mean nothing to him?'"

Shaul stroked his beard, chuckling. "Ah, he knows it is a high honor. But he feels his disgrace too keenly. What do you say, Jonathan?" The king had turned to his son.

"It would seem he's timid about offending you again, adoni."

"He needs encouragement!" King Shaul went on. "We must tell him how he can gain enough honor to accept the bride we offer. Go back and tell him this," Shaul commanded. "'The king wants no other wealth for the bride than 100 Philistine foreskins, so that he might have vengeance against his enemies.'"

Balak froze. Foreskins? Dahveed would have to kill the Philistines . . . and that was the point. The king's comments earlier in the private chamber made sense now. Once the Philistines realized what Dahveed was doing, they would fight him fiercely, and chances were that he'd be killed assembling his bride wealth.*

"It might take him a while to collect them," the king went on. "Do you think two war seasons will be sufficient, Jonathan?"

"Most likely," the hassar answered smoothly.

"Tell him that, Balak."

The king's personal attendant glanced up. "I shall go at once, adoni."

The same Habiru let them in the gate, the one who always looked at him as if he were debating where to thrust his sword through him.

Balak swept by and climbed the stairs. The door opened before he got to it. His companions followed him into the house. Dahveed rose from the stool.

One day you'll fall on your face when I walk in, Balak thought to himself. "We bring another message from the king," he announced.

"What does the king say to me?"

"He would encourage you to gain the honor to accept his gift of a bride."

"Did he say how I am to do this?"

Balak smiled. "The king says that the only bride wealth he will require is 100 foreskins from Philistines. He wishes to be revenged on his enemies."

Dahveed's eyes went to the other messengers, who nodded in agreement. The zammar's face went blank, and he stared at the opposite wall with unfocused eyes. "Yes, I'll bet he does," he said finally. When he looked at Balak again, he had a cold, hard expression that made Balak want to cover himself and run.

"When does the king expect his bride wealth?"

"After two war seasons."

"Tell the king that I will endeavor to serve him in this matter, as in all others."

"Yes, Dahveed." Balak bowed and departed. He was through the gate before he realized what he'd done. Anger at his automatic response—as if Dahveed were already a sar—filled him. Then he shivered. Dahveed's eyes had stared right through him just as Hassarah Ruth's used to. And no one crossed The Hassarah when she had looked like that.

I rode my brown mule down the road in the heat. Once the cold let go, summer had arrived immediately. My thoughts turned again to Michal and her bride wealth. I had double-checked all my information with Jonathan. I didn't want to make any mistakes on this. I hadn't realized how much I chafed under the king's displeasure until the way had opened for me to escape it.

At the same time, I didn't trust Shaul. Before the army left, I'd taken another trip to Nob. Hakkohen Haggadol Ahimelech had inquired of Yahweh if I should honor the king's request for Michal's bride wealth. Yahweh had replied that I should, so apparently becoming her husband and a sar was the next step on my way to being king for Him.

I hoped that I could collect the majority of the bride wealth this season, before Shaul had an opportunity to change his mind, because the more I thought about marrying Michal, the more I wanted to. I'd found myself fascinated and challenged by the cases that I'd handled for Jonathan during the past winter, and having the power to protect my family attracted me greatly. In addition, I had no objections to Michal, and the thought of being her husband drew me just as powerfully, so I was eager to fulfill the king's demand.

Unfortunately, this was the year the Philistines decided that Yahweh was too strong for Dagon, and didn't invade.

By the end of a month all the commanders were at their wit's end. Every unit had a full complement of militia, who could be drilled for only a limited number of hours a day, and with no battles to reinforce the value of what they were learning, the routine quickly palled. By the fifth week the commanders were finding another woman in camp almost nightly in spite of Yah's prohibition of women during war. If the problem wasn't a woman, it was a fight, usually over a woman.

Shagay came to the tent. "Trouble, Dahveed."

Hurriedly putting on my sword, I followed him into the afternoon sun. A knot of men had gathered outside of Jarib's tent.

"I want my silver back," a man yelled. "You said there would be no trouble. I could have gotten killed!"

"Doing what?" I asked as I walked up.

The man whirled around. "Nothing, Commander," he muttered. "It was a—a misunderstanding."

Shoving past him, I stepped into Jarib's tent.

He waited, looking embarrassed.

"Where is she?"

"She's gone, Commander. But it's not what you think. She was willing. It was her husband who was angry."

"Her husband?" I glared at him.

"I didn't think it would matter. They were only Habiru."

"From Jeshua's band? After all he's done for us? Jarib, what were you thinking?" I grated out between clenched teeth.

"Oh, they were from much farther north, Commander," the man assured me.

At least he had some sense, I thought in angry exasperation. What didn't seem to be in his mind was any remorse or acknowledgment of wrongdoing, just resignation that he was going to get a beating because he got caught. He was right.

The entire incident upset me, so I was up instantly that night when a young Habiru, Hanan, brought news of raids down south around Keilah.

The first thing next morning, I went to Sar Malchi's tent. He was sole king's representative this war season, since his older brothers and the king had stayed in Gibeah. Abner was in the tent with him when I arrived. I bowed. "Shalom, Sar, General."

Abner's face went blank when I placed the sar above him, but I ignored his reaction.

"Shalom, Commander," Malchi said. "What did you wish?"

"Some Philistines are raiding on the edge of the Shephelah in the south. I am requesting permission to take my unit and see if I can find them."

"We can't let that many men go," the general growled. "They are just waiting for us to release enough men so that they can hit us in strength."

Malchi lounged back in the three-legged chair. I noticed the general sat on a stool. "Are you comfortable taking your full unit with you, Dahveed?" he asked, eyeing me.

"Yes, Sar. If I may be very frank, I would be comfortable dismissing all the militia in my unit. Many are from the south, and they are frustrated doing nothing while there is so much to do at home. It would be a relief all the way around."

Malchi stared outside the tent for a little while. "No hesitation at all, Dahveed?" he asked again.

"No, Sar."

"Then as the king's representative, you have my permission to send your militia home and take your unit south. Report in at the end of the war season."

I stiffened a moment as I caught the angry look that quickly vanished from Abner's face. "As you wish, Sar!" I said, touching my knee briefly to the ground as I would have to the king.

By dawn the next morning I took my unit the fastest way down the Shephelah. The sack of salt hanging from my girdle needed something in it besides salt.

When afternoon court closed, Michal walked to the market at the west gate, followed by her escort. Immi needed more black cumin oil for cough and willow herb for fever, besides garlic and anise. The woman they usually bought from kept a stall near the gate.

As she arrived, she saw Balak sitting with the elders. While the farmer's wife picked out the herbs that her current customer wanted, Michal watched the crowd shifting about the market in the afternoon heat. Coming down the street was a man who had just presented a petition to the king. The village elders had decided against him in a dispute involving three almond trees at the edge of an orchard.

Now he carried his sealed judgment—the king had reversed the elders' decision—and Michal watched as he went to the king's personal attendant, greeting him effusively. He held up the document, and Balak's face expressed polite rejoicing for the man. The servant rose and walked a little way with the petitioner. She saw the glint of silver pass between them, and the servant returned to his seat.

The stall owner watched also, her lips in a thin line.

"Does that happen often?" Michal asked curiously.

Usually once or twice on petition days. Sometimes other days as well. Did Hassarah Ahinoam want more anise?"

"Yes," Michal answered, reciting the rest of the list.

After paying with a silver piece, Michal turned back toward the fortress, her mind busy with what she had seen. Had Balak found a way to influence the king? Could this be the reason Shaul had remained angry with Dahveed for so long?

Glancing into an alley, she saw Dahveed's back retreating down it. When she abruptly stopped, her escort nearly ran into her. "See that man in the gray robe with the wooden case? Bring him to me," she directed.

As soon as her guard returned with the man, she realized her mistake. But now she was curious.

"You wished to see me, Sahrah?" he asked in an even voice.

"Yes. What is your clan, and how are you called?"

"I am the scribe who assists Palti of Gallim as overseer of the king's lands in Benjamin, Sahrah. I am called Elihu ben Obed."

Michal frowned a little. He had avoided her first question. "Would that be Obed of Bethlehem?"

The merest flicker passed over the man's face. "Yes, Sahrah."

She was sure Dahveed's grandfather was named Obed, and there couldn't be that many Obeds in Bethlehem. The man had to be one of Dahveed's brothers. An idea slipped into her mind, and she started down the street again, motioning the scribe to follow. "Since your family is from Bethlehem, perhaps you could find out something," she went on, stepping around a pile of fresh dung.

"What would you require, Sahrah?"

She nodded to someone who bowed to her. "The hassar would like information about the family and clan of Balak ben Hod, the king's personal attendant. There are some conflicting stories about him, and he would like to know the truth of it."

"I will do what I can," Elihu said slowly.

"Good. Please write up only one report and direct it to me. With personal inquiries such as this, the hassar doesn't want copies floating around."

"As you wish, Sahrah."

"Shalom, Elihu," she said, leaving him. He might be like Dahveed in some ways, but he didn't have the dahveed's openness or directness. He was still nice, though.

❖❖❖

Hanan slid down the last of the hill. "Four," he said.

I sighed. Four were better than nothing. Ahiam sighed too. He had carefully gone over the spoils from every raiding party that we had attacked in the past three weeks, picking out the best he could get, and had twice sent his hoard somewhere by one of Joel's Habiru. He'd finally told me where.

368 | YAHWEH'S WARRIOR

"Some of it goes to Palti of Gallim, and the rest to his sister, Jemima," he had said a bit sheepishly. "Palti doesn't think Habiru are worth anything. I'm trying to show him that we can be profitable and useful."

"And what does Jemina think of this?"

Ahiam had actually blushed. "She, uh, doesn't mind, adoni. Do you?"

"Of course not, Ahiam. Palti is an honorable man, and Sahrah Michal likes his sister very much. She's been a big help to the sahrah since she came to work at the fortress."

Well, I thought, *each to his wooing in his own way. So far, only the hassar has been successful. Trust Jonathan to come out on top.*

The trail the Philistines were following went past a huge downed tree about a quarter of a mile farther up, and I sent six men, led by Areli. The man from Naphtali was getting quite good at ambushing raiding parties. When he and Sithri teamed together, they usually came back successful. Areli was successful this time also, and I added four more to my count.

Dahveed Joel caught up to me later that afternoon. "Trouble coming, Dahveed," he said bluntly. "A full unit of Philistines is headed in from Socoh. You've been too elusive these past three weeks. They think the Habiru are fighting them, and they are out for my people."

"We'll have to teach them otherwise," I replied.

I held a war council, explaining the situation. "I want every man to strip down to only what you must have. We're going to convince these Philistines that they are facing about four times our number. We will hit hard from ambush at every opportunity, and then we move, and do it again."

During the next few weeks we learned the 20-mile stretch from Zorah and Lehi south to Cabbon and Ashnah until we could place ourselves anywhere in the dark and get to the nearest water. We lived on our feet, slept wherever we lay down, and ate whenever we found something edible.

Our tactics were effective. The Philistine raiding parties came less frequently and got larger, making them easier to hunt down. The week we stopped three of them in as many days was the same week that we watched from a hilltop as the Philistine commanders pulled not one, but what was left of four units out of the hills. I looked at Hanan. He shrugged. "It didn't seem worth it to tell you how many more came," he commented.

Since the Habiru were standing watch on the hills for the night, we set up a permanent camp. That meant we sat on our blankets and ate a hot meal, along with some bread that we didn't have to soak first in order to chew.

I looked around at the men with pride. By now I'd back them against anyone the Philistines or Abner had in their armies. Their faces were thin, some nearly gaunt, and we all had sore feet and aching legs. I had two cuts on my arms and a new scar on one calf. Lotan was flexing the leg that he had nearly broken, Sithri had another cut on his head, and Pallu probably needed his arm sewn up, but he was too busy trading stories with Tahan. Naharai, Reu, and the rest all bore signs of the past month, and carried themselves with a confidence that they'd never had before.

Except Jarib. Even though dogged practice had given him average fighting skills, he still could never keep his feet under him and was always bruised somewhere from falls.

Just then, Shagay emerged from the trees and sat down by the fire I shared with my three retainers. He motioned us to be quiet, and brought out the wooden bowl that he'd been hiding under his cloak.

"You found a bee tree!" I exclaimed softly, seeing the chunk of honeycomb swimming in honey.

Shagay grinned. "I found it this afternoon, grabbed a chunk of comb, and ran! Only got stung six or seven times!" he finished, looking smug.

The four of us quietly divided the treat, eating it with our bread. Sucking the last of the sweetness from my fingers, I washed my hands in the nearby spring and walked back toward the fire. Ahiam had his hoard of spoils spread out on a cloth, the firelight gleaming off the gold earrings that he'd found just today. Shagay and Josheb helped him decide what to send to Palti and what Jemima would like.

They are ones more desirable than gold, than much pure gold. I turned the phrase over in my mind. *And sweetnesses more than honey, than honey from the comb.* I stopped in the shadows. Those phrases would fit in my song, if I could just think a minute . . .

"Count, Dahveed!" Areli called, catching sight of me.

Instantly everyone in camp took up the cry. We'd been so busy lately that I hadn't bothered to keep track of how many foreskins I had. Ahiam cleared away his things and spread a cloth carefully on my blanket, and Shagay ceremoniously poured the contents of the sack on it. I counted, and then Shagay did, and then Ahiam and Josheb. We all came up with the same number, and the men waited breathlessly to hear what it was.

I stood. "When I have five more—" The men groaned. "—I'll have *twice the number of the bride wealth!*"

Wild cheering broke out, and the men surrounded me, pounding me on the back, shouting their good wishes and congratulations, as excited as if they were marrying the sahrah themselves. They determined that I would return with twice the price. We had three more weeks to do it.

And, once again, there wasn't a Philistine to be seen.

CHAPTER 39

You're looking smug," Jonathan said to Ishvi as he met his brother, who was on his way out of the fortress after the noon rest.

"We figured out what happened in Benjamin," Sar Ishvi replied, grinning. "Once the entire situation was laid out, we realized that it's a wonder that the overseer wasn't killed long before he actually was."

"Oh? How did you solve it? Just last week you were moaning about never getting to the bottom of it."

"That was before I ordered Palti to use other scribes for the routine things so that Elihu ben Obed could concentrate on that problem. I've never seen anyone like him," Ishvi went on enthusiastically. "He's paid any debt he owes this family already. That absconding scribe had stolen nearly half the king's lands and had a series of overseers set up that would have kept him in riches for the rest of his life no matter where he went."

"Half the king's lands?" Jonathan interrupted skeptically.

"I didn't believe it either, until I saw all the documents myself. Palti's scribe doesn't miss anything, however, and he found the one flaw in the plan. After that, there was no stopping him. Within days he'd unraveled the entire scheme."

"Well, I'm glad he could help you at least," Jonathan sighed.

Ishvi turned to him in surprise. "Did you ask him for something?"

"I inquired about the House of Tahat. He had a couple things to tell me, all of which I already knew except for one point. He had the impression that the House was located in the north. Maybe around Dan, or even Damascus."

"Then start looking there. I've discovered that Elihu ben Obed's impressions are better than most people's facts."

"I hope so," the hassar said. "I'm beginning to think that the steward existed only in the mind of Baqqush of Mari!" He turned to go.

"Oh, one more thing. Have there been more complaints from Ephraim that usual?"

"Sort of," Jonathan replied. "We've had to settle several disputes involving the king's lands. Most of them should never have been allowed to drag on as they did. Why?"

"Elihu asked me to find out," the sar explained. "I've been unhappy with the overseer there for some time. Now that the mess in Benjamin is cleared up, I think I'm going to assign Ephraim to Palti and Elihu, also." He paused. "I'm glad that you handled Eliab ben Jesse as you did," he went on quietly.

"Why?" Jonathan asked. He'd told Ishvi about the order he'd sealed.

"Because Elihu is connected to Jesse's family some way. He knows how much hesed you gave them, and he's grateful. I think that Yahweh gave us another gift when he put Elihu in this house, and I intend to use him."

Jonathan watched his brother stride out the gate. The afternoon's heat intruded on his mind, and he glanced at the throne room. Perhaps he could persuade the king to hold court under the tamarisk tree down the hill. It was cooler there and caught the afternoon breeze well.

Day after hot day went by. Up and down the hills we marched. For the first time in their lives, the men prayed that the rains would hold off and some Philistines would decide to visit Israel. Neither happened. Glumly, we sat under the trees as the first rain of the season pounded down on us. We'd long since forgotten where our tents were. Some of the men were discussing whether or not they still knew how to pitch them.

The sun came out briefly the next day, and we took our time moving north. The men were still hopeful for twice the bride wealth, but I knew that the army had probably returned to Gibeah, and I needed to report in.

When we stopped for a noon meal, the wind picked up. It rushed through the tops of the pines, and as always, I listened uneasily. The loud wind made it impossible to hear anything else around, such as a stray sheep in trouble. And the constant motion hid the movement of anything that might be sneaking up on the flock. Or us.

The wind raced across the land all afternoon, turning cold. I rubbed the back of my neck and flexed my fingers, glancing at the gray, angry-looking clouds skimming by. Ahiam and Josheb closed up the unit, and Shagay and Hanan scouted ahead. When we climbed from the trail to the small hidden nook where we camped, Dahveed Joel waited with our tents. The men cheered.

While they pitched camp, I stood by the large boulder that marked this place, checking the trail west to the Shephelah one last time, my cloak whipping around me. Yahweh's gift buzzed in my mind, but I couldn't determine why.

After examining the sky again, I looked back and discovered that a Philistine soldier had appeared on the trail. I froze. Another came over the rise, then another and another. Standing in plain sight as I was, my only hope of being unseen was to remain perfectly still and hope the movements of my cloak in the wind would blend in with the wildly waving brush around me.

They had a youth with them, the sixth person over the rise. I thought at first that he was a seren of some kind. Then I realized that he was bound and wearing only a loincloth. The first soldier was getting nearer. Although he glanced around often, and I expected he'd spot me at any moment, he never looked up far enough to actually see me. More soldiers followed, moving cautiously, peering into the forest that closed around the trail not far beyond.

As the eleventh, and last, man came over the rise, the wind gusted, pulling at my cloak, and the youth looked right at me. His footsteps faltered. The soldier behind shoved him, and the captive stumbled forward again, then fell to his knees, his white face giving me an anguished glance as he crouched on the ground, in as plain a cry for help as I'd ever seen.

Behind me I heard the brief sound of voices as the wind abated for a moment, only to return in another gust. The soldier yanked the youth to his feet, cuffing him and sending him on down the trail. The captive did not look in my direction again. I watched, my hand resting on my sword hilt, while the entire group passed below me. The last man paused just at the bend in the trail, turning back, but I had faded out of his sight by then.

"Dahveed! What is it?" Shagay exclaimed when he saw me.

"Philistine soldiers—10 of them—just passed on the trail. We barely have time to get in front of them."

The men assembled swiftly. I sent Shagay and Hanan to scout ahead as we jogged after the invaders. As soon as I could, I divided my forces and sent them through the open forest on the hills on either side of the trail. The wind worked for us now, masking the sounds that we made as we approached within sight of the party. They had stopped in a fairly open place, where the trail below split, and half of them stood guard, while the other half conferred.

It was the worst place in the entire trail to attack, and Jarib fell. He didn't just stumble or land on his knees. He fell, sliding down the steep slope on last year's leaves, somehow managing to avoid the oaks and elms in his way. Finally he landed in a late-blooming myrtle bush at the bottom of the hill, the white petals raining down on his clothes as the Philistines jumped toward him.

My men reacted in the only way they could. The war cry burst from every mouth, and they rushed the enemy. If Jarib had done the wrong thing to begin with, he did the right thing thereafter. Somehow he'd kept his sword, and he killed the first man that got to him. "One!" he shouted, trying to drag himself back toward the hill.

By the time another Philistine started toward him, the second unit was on top of them. Ahiam and Shagay fought on either side of me as I knocked a sword out of my way, doubling over the Philistine holding it with a blow to the body and then shoving him to Shagay as I met the sword of the next man slashing down on top of me.

"Two!" Lotan roared behind me. These men fought like professionals, and I ducked back to avoid a thrust, slamming the Philitine's sword into the ground, and bringing the hilt of mine down on his head, then stepping over him to move forward. Three of my men ran back down the trail after a couple Philistines headed that way. My attack had broken up the group of soldiers that had formed in the middle of the clearing, destroying any order or coherence to the fight, leaving man against man wherever they happened to be.

The Philistine in front of me retreated, trying to disengage and run. Someone yelled "Three!" and I pressed forward. The swordsman in front of me fell back again, and I heard Tahan cry out.

Double the bride price wasn't worth the life of one of my men. "Let them go! Second unit, halt and report!" I yelled, my voice rising against the wind. The men reluctantly drew back. I took a quick report. Jarib was down, his ankle probably broken. Tahan had taken a sword thrust in the leg and had a bad wound. The others had various cuts and bruises.

I sent men up and down the trail. The fighting had spread out for more than half a mile, and we found two dead out on the trail, besides one around me and another just as the trail narrowed again. At least three blood trails disappeared into the forest, but we left them alone. I didn't like the wild roar that I heard in the wind. The clouds rushing overhead were heavy and black, and dead leaves fled east on the trail as fast as a man could run.

While I helped Jarib to his feet, two men tended to Tahan, binding his leg and making a stretcher to get him back to our camp. Sithri had found the bound youth, and the rest of the unit stripped the dead and collected all the weapons that we could find.

Back at our camp I ducked into my tent, where Sithri and Pallu waited with our young prisoner. He watched me warily.

"You did ask, you know," I reminded him.

He flushed. "I didn't know that you were Habiru, shobeh," he muttered.

"You might be in less trouble if we were. This is the Sar's Own unit of Israel's army."

"But the six units of Israel's army left three weeks ago!" he exclaimed.

"Six!" Pallu snorted. "Whom did you get your information from?"

"I overheard them talking," the youth said.

"Six!" my man repeated in disgust. "They should have thought there were eight at least, Dahveed."

"You'll just have to try harder next time, Pallu," I said calmly.

"Dahveed?" The youth paled and backed away, his eyes riveted on the small sack hanging from my girdle. He bolted past me, and Pallu leaped after him, missing his hold. By the time I got out of the tent, the lad had jumped to the trail before anyone could stop him.

I went to the head of the nook. "Shagay?"

"Yes, Dahveed?" he replied, watching the young man disappearing to the west.

"Bring him back. He's got on only a loincloth, and this will be a bad storm. Besides, his accent was different from the other's."

"Why does it always have to be me chasing after the people that you collect?"

"It's your lot in life, Shagay. Your special duty, the one way you can serve me better than anyone else, the—"

"Spare me, adoni." Jumping lightly down to the trail, he leaned into the wind, trotting after the youth.

I went back to the tents. Ahiam, Lotan, and Reu had decided that Jarib's ankle wasn't quite broken, but they splinted it anyway so that he could hobble around. Tahan's wound had been cleaned and stitched, and he was sitting up in his tent.

I had the men check the ropes on the tents, and I studied the trees around us, for the line of mountainous thunderheads bearing down on the back of the wind made my hair stand up. Yahweh's fire flickered, backlighting the gigantic piles of blackness that raced toward our refuge.

Shagay appeared at the head of the nook, his face pale, practically dragging the youth behind him.

"Have you seen what's coming?" he asked.

I nodded. "Put him in my tent, and make sure he stays there," I added.

Minutes later the rest of the men began arriving, the wind billowing the tent sides every time someone entered.

"Who is contributing today?" Ahiam asked.

"I am," Lotan said, putting his trophy on the cloth in front of me.

"But I was first," Jarib said, hitching his leg around so he could reach forward also.

"Only because you fell, and that Philistine ran into your sword," Reu laughed, adding his trophy.

"I'm afraid to ask what you happened to kill your man with," I said, remembering the time that I'd seen Reu suddenly sit down beside the man he was fighting. The crooked limb he had sat on whipped up and knocked the back of his opponent's knees in. Reu had then calmly knocked the branch around to crack the man on the head when he'd fallen.

Reu turned red, and the men laughed, Pallu producing the last count for the day.

The young man with us stared, transfixed, at me. "It's true, what you're doing," he choked.

"Do you regret what happened today?" I asked, looking at him.

Biting his lip, he lowered his eyes. "No, shobeh."

"I didn't think so. We have taken only from those who come to plunder and kill in our land."

"How many, Dahveed?" Pallu asked.

"Four."

The men's faces fell, and the lamplight flickered as the wind slammed against the tent, bringing the rumble of thunder with it.

"All we need is one more," Jarib sighed.

Every eye in the tent riveted on our captive. He stared back in horror, twisting his bound hands frantically.

The men looked to me, Lotan fingering his war dagger. I watched the youth as he glanced desperately from one face to the other, tugging against his bonds. He was scarcely more than a boy, and from the paleness of his skin, I wondered if he was from a well-off family. What had happened to bring him here?

Lotan started to draw his dagger, and I shook my head slightly.

The young Philistine grasped the slim indication of hesed, his eyes pleading with me. "Hesed, shobeh. It is said that you have taken from us to make offerings to the demoness Lilith and bring her presence among us to curse us. Is this true, shobeh?"

A couple men chuckled.

"The truth is much more mundane," I explained. "I am collecting a bride wealth, set by my adon. The men"—I nodded toward the others—"wish for me to be able to marry as soon as possible. They feel that I need one more count for my adon."

"And if you had that, I would live?"

"I have not said that I would kill you at all. You appealed to me, and I answered."

His breathing grew a little easier, and he was thinking now.

"And I am grateful. They were taking me to Ekron, to their seren, Manani." He looked at the sack back on my girdle, and fierce triumph flashed across his face. "Complete your count, for I am of Gath," he said, "but I am also of Israel, and I claim the right to have my flesh taken by circumcision. I am called Ittai, and my father was Ribai of Gibeah. He was enslaved when Philistia held the fortress there, and was taken with them out of his country when Shaul of Benjamin drove them out. I will give my flesh to you if you become my covenant father, and my flesh will stand between you and me and all my house."

Total silence reigned in the tent although the wind whipped the sides until they strained against the ropes, the rumble of thunder constantly rolling around the rocky nook.

"If I do this," I said at last, "you and your descendants will be subject to me and mine as a son is to his father."

"Yes, shobeh. But there will be peace between my family and you."

I rose and flipped on my cloak, stepping outside. The wind nearly swept me from my feet, the sound of it through the branches rising to a steady note. I knew that if I held the harp to the wind, the strings would sing in harmony with the bass notes from the trees.

The fire in the clouds nearly upon us flickered downward again and again, the crash of thunder ringing in my ears. As I drew in a deep breath, I smelled the tang of the sea salt as the breath of Yahweh rushed by, combing my hair with rough fingers. My God rode the back of the storm, reaching down and touching me, and His gift raged in my veins.

My heart leaping as His presence seethed around me, I bowed my head.

Then I turned my face upward. "Yahweh, what is Your servant to do in this matter?"

Blazing light blinded me, and then the loudest sound I ever heard slammed me to my face on the ground. The oak tree beyond me exploded in white flame, showering burning debris everywhere.

When the ground stopped shaking, I dared to lift my face. A line of flickering flame curled around the tree from top to bottom, and one side of the base burned steadily. Several of the top branches had ripped away, lying on the hillside away from the tents.

"Shall I use Your fire, Adonai?" I asked, getting unsteadily to my feet.

The flames leaped up, and I picked up a large piece of bark lying nearby. Gathering smaller burning pieces on it, I soon had a small fire. Shielding it with my cloak, I edged back to the tent, where the men watched with white faces.

Every man there had to turn his face away as I entered the tent, and I struggled to contain the exultation still surging through me. Adding a bit to the fire on the bark, I pulled my belt knife, and held the blade in the flame, heating and purifying it. Then I turned to Ittai. "I will become your father," I said.

When the rite was done, the men filed from the tent. Ahiam made certain Ittai's wound was cared for, and I stood in the entrance, holding the bit of flesh that I had taken. Yahweh's presence touched me again, impressing me with the knowledge that I could not claim it. I dug a shallow hole in the dirt and put the fire on the bark piece into it. On my knees, I added the bit of flesh in my hand and watched it burn, my cloak protecting the fire from the wind.

Behind me, Ittai lay white and limp on the floor, his bonds gone, for he would be unable to walk for at least three days. "Accept what has been given by one who knows You not, Adonai. He is a worthy servant for You," I whispered. "Grant his petitions when he comes to You, for he has entered into Your covenant as a son of Israel."

The fire died, and I covered the ashes. As I went into the tent, the rain rushed on us, the sound a hard roar that drowned out all else.

Before dawn I left the tent, taking the harp with me, my thumb rubbing at the small scorch mark on the base where the heated blade of my belt knife had accidentally touched it. I hadn't slept, too caught up in the events of the previous day, and now I felt the need to talk to Yah.

Half a mile away, I found a terebinth growing beside the rocky outcrop of the hillside where a streambed emptied from the hill, splashing down the rocks. Sitting in the deep shadows, I plucked the strings, my mind wandering, settling at last on the melody to the song I needed to finish. *Sweetnesses more than honey, than strained honey from the honeycomb.* The last two phrases popped into my head again. "Surely your servant is warned by them; in keeping them is much reward!" Suddenly I sat bolt upright. I knew where they would fit! I had it all!

Hurriedly, I played the phrases of melody again, cocking my head to put the pieces together in my mind. After rearranging a couple sections, I then strummed the harp. As the first streaks of dawn broke over the hills, I sang the song for the first time.

"The heavens proclaim the glory of El; and the firmament announces the work of His hands.

"Day to day they pour out speech; night to night they announce knowledge.

"There is no voice, there is no speaking without their voice being heard.

"Their voice goes forth in all the earth, and at the end of the land is their word.

"For the sun set a tent in them, and, like a bridegroom coming forth from his bridal chamber,

"He rejoices like a warrior to run in his path from the extremity of the heavens to its outlet, even to his turning at solstice at the end. And there is no hiding from his glow.

"The law of Yahweh is without blemish, reviving life.

"The warning sign of Yahweh is reliable, making wise the young naive one.

"The directions of Yahweh are right, making glad the heart.

"The commandment of Yahweh is pure, making bright the eyes.

"The fear of Yahweh is clean, standing forever.

"The judgments of Yahweh are trustworthy, they are righteous altogether.

"They are the ones which are more desirable than gold, than much fine gold;

"With sweetnesses more than honey, than strained honey in the honeycomb.

"Surely Your servant is warned by them; in keeping them is much reward.

"How can I discern ignorant errors?

"Exempt me from punishment for hidden faults.

"Hold back Your servant from arrogant sins, may they not govern me.

"Then I will be blameless; I will be innocent of great transgression.

"Let the sayings of my mouth and the thinking of my heart be pleasing before You, O Yahweh, my rock and my redeemer."

I'd worked long on this song, sometimes wondering if it would ever be finished. Now I bowed my head. "Thank You, Yah!" I whispered.

When I returned to the tent, Ittai was gone. I stared at the empty place on the floor in disbelief.

Shagay looked embarrassed. "Shall I go after him, adoni?" he asked, resigned.

I shook my head. "No. If he can walk, it must be Yahweh's will that he go."

"At least you have your price."

"Ittai's flesh belonged to Yah," I said with a shrug.

We arrived at Adullam by midafternoon, Tahan on a stretcher, and Jarib leaning on Pallu and Reu. Shagay didn't show up until that night, and he had my last count. "One of the wounded Philistines didn't survive the storm," he explained.

Michal was on her way to the throne room when the messenger stopped her.

"Sahrah? I was instructed to give this to you." The man bowed, holding out a sealed document.

"Very well," she replied, accepting the papyrus and wondering what on earth it could be.

The morning passed swiftly. She ate the noon meal in the courtyard with her family. Word had come from Merab that her second pregnancy was progressing nicely. As soon as she could, Michal went to her room and settled on her bedroll to read the document. By the time she finished, she was hugging herself, trying to stop her trembling. Elihu ben Obed was very thorough.

She walked out of the passage in somewhat of a daze, dimly aware that she had passed Balak going into the king's chamber to awaken him for afternoon court. Eshbaal fell into step with her on the way across the private courtyard.

"I hope this afternoon goes all right," he sighed.

"Why is that?" she asked absently.

"We're giving judgments today, remember? I've noticed that if someone comes to the king with a case that is questionable or with vague evidence, they request an interview in the afternoon. And Abbi usually favors them, sometimes in spite of what we find in the roeh's scroll. A lot of the cases overturn something already decided by the town elders. That always causes more trouble, and occasionally we see the man on the other side of the dispute appealing to the king also. It wastes so much of our time that Jonathan has tried to get the king to refuse to hear such cases, but Abbi usually insists."

Michal frowned thoughtfully. As court began, she kept an eye on Balak. Twice when petitioners came into the room, they glanced at him before they looked at the king, and each time Balak had nodded almost imperceptably. The king decided in the petitioner's favor both times.

So Balak *was* influencing the king. But when? Not in open court, or during meals, and he left as soon as he could in the evenings. Then her mind flashed the image of Balak entering the king's room to rouse him from the noon rest. She stood still in startled realization. Every day, Balak had those few minutes alone with the king. How had she missed this for so long? Michal wondered. Because no one could imagine that Shaul's mind could be altered without a long argument, she admitted to herself. Balak had apparently found some way to do it, though.

The king was restless today, shifting his position often on the throne, impatient with everything that happened.

As the scribe ushered the current petitioner out of the room, Jonathan turned to Shaul.

"Adoni, what troubles you?"

"How long ago did Malchi and Abner return with the army?" his father asked.

"Almost three weeks, adoni," the hassar replied, puzzled.

"Where is Dahveed?" Shaul burst out, glancing at Balak. "Why didn't he come back also? What is he doing out there alone?"

Michal clenched her fists, seeing the way that her abbi looked at the servant. Balak was not only influencing the king; he was feeding the king's anger against Dahveed!

"Sar Malchi sent Dahveed to hunt for raiding parties down the Shephelah," Jonathan said.

"But the rains have come, and he has not returned. Surely there can't be any more Philistines in the land. What is he doing?" Shaul glanced at Balak again. "What if he has joined with them against us? Why did Malchi let him go?"

"Shall I send for Sar Malchi?" Jonathan asked.

"Yes!" her father said, relieved. "Send for him. Maybe he knows what Dahveed is doing. Malchi would have heard from him during the war season. Bring the sar at once."

Once that was off his mind, King Shaul settled back and listened to the next case patiently enough, making a decision that Jonathan approved of, but causing Balak to frown.

The petitioner left with a disgusted expression on his face, and Michal had to smile. Her father's servant would receive no fee from that man.

The door opened, and Malchi entered. He touched his knee to the floor briefly. "You sent for me, Abbi?"

"Yes. What has happened to Dahveed? Why hasn't he returned?"

"I would imagine that he's still collecting foreskins," the sar said. "He headed down the Shephelah after the Philistines like an eagle after a coney. Wouldn't surprise me if he didn't return until he had the full price."

The king looked a bit startled. "He was that eager?"

"Do you blame him?" Malchi replied.

"No, no, I don't," Shaul said, glancing at Michal. "She is a reward worth fighting for," he added to himself.

"Was there anything else, Abbi?"

"No, Malchi. You may go."

The sar bowed again and walked out.

Michal climbed to the southeast battlements, and the sentries short-ened their beats, leaving the corner to her. Jonathan joined her soon after, and she handed him the report from Elihu. "Read it when you get back to your room. Balak is a full-blooded Moabite. His family had to flee from Moab's king, charged with treason."

Jonathan stood motionless. "This is sudden news, Michal. What made you start asking questions?"

"He's always made me uneasy, you know. Then I saw him paid at the gate when a petitioner was favored in afternoon court, and I got suspicious. He must be talking to the king when he wakes him after the noon rest every day."

Jonathan sighed explosively. "I never even thought of that!" he said in disgust. "I've wondered about Balak, too, but I knew that he never had the opportunity to speak to the king for long. I spend so much time persuading the king that I assumed anyone else would need the same amount of time."

Her brother leaned against the wall, the papyrus shaking in his hand. "This is frightening, Michal. Balak's no fool. If he found a way to influence Abbi in just those few minutes, he's gone far beyond any-thing that I've dreamed anyone could."

★ Captor.

CHAPTER 40

I led my battered unit up the road to Gibeah. Tahan wasn't really back on his feet yet, but the men were as impatient as I to return. As we approached the town, my heart beat faster in spite of my warnings to myself not to expect too much from King Shaul. He might decide that he wanted more for the bride wealth or some such, which would put off my marriage again. My mule sensed my tension and danced under me, his head down, mouthing the bit.

"The dahveed!" someone yelled, and others took up the cry. People appeared from the fields, running toward the road. "The bride wealth?" they shouted. "Dahveed, the bride wealth?"

I held the sack over my head, and the cheering brought more people to see us. By the time we reached the gates, we had to slow as the crowd grew more, the shouting and cheering following us as we climbed through the town, people reaching out to touch me again. I dismounted and walked the mule forward, Ahiam and Shagay on either side, the rest of the men enjoying the enthusiastic welcome.

But I didn't know whether to be gratified or dismayed. If King Shaul took offense, I'd probably never get Michal. I glanced up at the fortress, hoping he was busy in court and not watching me arrive.

In the fortress courtyard I stroked the mule's neck. My hand shook, and I took a deep breath to calm myself. Shaul had done so much for me, and I loved him and wanted to do whatever I could to repay his favor. Would his attitude soften enough to admit me back into his presence? Praying that the king would be in a good mood, I helped Jarib hobble into the anteroom.

At the top of the stairs I gave him the sack, and the guard there helped him through the door into the throne room. The guard turned back, holding the door open.

"Commander Dahveed, come in," the hassar called.

I hadn't expected this. Taking another steadying breath, I stepped over the threshold, keeping my head lowered and kneeling immediately. The hangings were down between me and the throne, and Jonathan stood in front of them.

"Why have you come, Commander?"

"I am bringing the bride price that the king commanded for Sahrah Michal."

The officials and messengers behind me stirred in excitement, and Michal glanced at me from her place by the long table.

"The king will receive your bride wealth," the hassar said.

Taking the sack from Jarib, I brought it to him, dropping to one knee.

He hefted it, then looked at me, his eyebrows raised. "Have you brought the full price?"

"No, hassar. I have brought double the price."

He stroked his beard. "You were certainly zealous for the king's honor, Dahveed."

"I serve him as best I can."

Jonathan took the sack behind the curtain.

I kept a tight grip on my thoughts in the ensuing silence, not daring to speculate on whether or not the king would be pleased. It was my best chance to erase the suspicions that I felt sure Balak had placed in the king's mind, and I waited for the next words from behind the curtain.

"Twice the bride wealth is here, adoni. Dahveed has revenged you double on your enemies," the hassar announced.

"Very good! Open the curtains, for Dahveed has pleased me greatly and shall see my face again."

A murmur of approval ran softly through the watching courtiers and officials, and Sahrah Michal quickly stepped forward to tie back the curtains. I had to steady myself on my knee, relief sweeping through me. Then my right hand clenched around the sling wrapped around my wrist. Yahweh had said that the king's heart was not good toward me. What if he was doing this just for show? I wouldn't be able to stand seeing hardness in his eyes even though his lips smiled on me.

But when he spoke, his voice was gentler than I'd heard in a long time. "Come near, Dahveed."

I obeyed.

"It is time to end my displeasure. You have done well, and shown your zeal for my honor once again. Look at me, Dahveed, for you shall have my daughter Michal as your wife."

I forced myself to raise my head.

Shaul's smile played around his lips. "I trust that you will not object to this reward," he said, his eyes twinkling.

Relief rushed through me! He really was pleased with me again! I flushed. "No, adoni, not at all," I assured him, unable to resist a quick glance at the sahrah.

She blushed, and the hassar chuckled. "Adoni, is Dahveed's bride wealth acceptable?" he asked formally.

"It is. Dahveed shall have Michal for his wife."

Jonathan poured wine from the pitcher into two cups, handing one to his father and the other to me. King Shaul and I formally sealed the betrothal as we both drank the wine. As I lowered the cup, I saw Balak ben Hod watching me, his expression patient, like the face of a lion waiting the chance to kill.

◻◻◻

Two weeks later Balak sat down at the table as Judith put the last of the food for the noon meal on it.

"It's so nice to see the king pleased with Dahveed again just like he used to be! Wasn't it nice of the king to offer Dahveed that estate outside of town as part of the dowry?" she added, sitting down beside him. "I wonder how much the king will give to Dahveed to match the bride wealth? How would you decide the amount of goods needed to equal what Dahveed brought?"

Balak left his wife's questions unanswered, but he shifted in irritation. That's all he heard about morning, noon, and evening! Every day, Judith favored him with a complete list of all the wealth that the king planned on giving the zammar now that he was to become a sar and a son-in-law.

Once again he wondered how long he should let the zammar stay in the king's good graces. Certainly he didn't intend for the marriage to actually happen. That would put Yahweh's instrument back in the king's household, and now that the Gibeonite killings had ended, he didn't want the king led back to his God again. He'd already planned what to say, but not when.

"And wait until you see the new robe for Dahveed that Michal is planning for the wedding night," Judith chattered on. "She was talking to the hassarah about it, and even asked me what I thought! Wasn't that nice?"

"He'll never wear it," Balak muttered, annoyed. Couldn't Judith think about anything but Dahveed?

"Whyever not?" she exclaimed. "Nothing could change the king's mind now. Dahveed and Michal were formally pledged, right there in the throne room."

His irritation intensified. Did his wife think he was just another servant in the fortress? "It can be changed, Judith. I've done it."

"But this is already decided and done, and it won't change."

His exasperation at her disbelief made him reckless. "Judith, all I have to do is speak at the right time, and the king will do whatever I say." He took another bite of bread.

"You could change the king's mind?" she gasped, looking at him with wide eyes.

Balak smiled. "I don't talk about it much. Remember, if the king continues to be pleased with my advice, our life will be much easier. We could have a bigger house one day."

"That will be nice," she said, her face brightening, her hand touching her stomach.

"Just don't speak about this," he warned.

She nodded solemnly.

Judith was like clay in his hands, he thought while he walked to the fortress.

After listening to the conversations around the anteroom for a while, he then went into the throne room passage, stroking his beard. Maybe it *was* time that he stopped the wedding. But in spite of what he had told Judith, he was uncertain. If he had gauged things incorrectly, he could lose his life. For a few moments he chewed his lip. He still hadn't made up his mind by the time to awaken the king. Maybe he should just leave it up to Kemosh, he finally thought. If the god gave him an opportunity to speak, he would.

At last he entered the king's bedchamber. "Adoni? Adoni, it is time to return to court."

Shaul stirred and opened his eyes.

"It is time to rise, adoni. The court waits for you."

The king sat up, grimacing from the stiffness in his shoulders, and sat on the edge of the bed. "Balak, what is wrong? You look upset."

"Maybe a little, adoni," Balak said, his heart beginning to pound.

"About what?" Shaul stood.

"Dahveed, adoni. Are you ready to go?" he added, unable to make himself bring the topic up.

"What about Dahveed? Don't you think his zeal for me is commendable?"

No sign could be more plain. The servant took a deep breath. "It would be, adoni, if I believed that his zeal was for you." Too tense to look at the king, he dropped to his knees. "Forgive my speech, adoni, but please allow me to open your ear on this! It has burned in my heart for so long. Do not trust the dahveed! He has been treacherous from his youth! Why do you think he was unclaimed for so many years?"

"Unclaimed?" Shaul interrupted. "Dahveed is unclaimed?"

"He was until his fifteenth year, adoni," Balak rushed on. "They said it was to protect his immi from Jesse's first wife, but everyone knew it was because his father didn't trust him!"

Balak risked a glance at the king. Shaul stared at him.

"And do you think his father sends him to serve you because he would do as the king requested?" the attendant continued, encouraged by the king's reaction. "Dahveed's father lets him stay here because he does not want him at home, where he would be a danger to him. Adoni, he is indeed zealous, but not for you! It is the throne that he wants. You've felt this in your heart. Dahveed means to have the throne, and Michal is but another step toward taking it!"

The king had sat down again, never taking his eyes from Balak.

"Think back, adoni," the servant continued. "Remember all the things that Dahveed has done, all the glory and honor and praise he has garnered to himself? Do you think this was for you? And he has ingratiated himself with the hassar, but he will turn on him one day."

"How do you know this?" the king asked, his voice unsteady.

"Adoni, I grew up in his village," Balak said, bowing again. "His own father refused to have him in the house. He was raised by Habiru, taught their ways and their treachery, and he still maintains contact with them today. Two of his retainers are Habiru and will do anything he says. I shudder whenever I see the hassar in his presence. Who knows when he will give the order, and Jonathan will be cut down?"

"He endangers Jonathan?" Shaul said, rising again. "He would do this?"

"He would, adoni," Balak said eagerly, looking up again. "He showed his true side when he took your honor at the gate, allowing the people to greet him as they would have you, and Jonathan sees nothing, blinded by Dahveed's pretended respect. Yes, he fought fiercely for Michal. It is his final step to the throne. With her, he can shove you aside, order his Habiru to slay the hassar and your other sons, and sit on Israel's throne in your place.

"I can no longer be silent, adoni. Dahveed can charm like a snake, and he will mourn with tears when your house is gone, but he will do it from the throne!"

The fringe on the king's robe trembled. "We shall see."

"What is there today?" Shaul asked the hassar as he seated himself.

"The afternoon was reserved for a long judgment case involving the king's lands near Anathoth, adoni. But we just received a message that the petitioner is too ill to come. The afternoon is open, and I thought we could—"

"Good," Shaul interrupted. "We can spend time on a matter of great importance that came to my attention just today. It concerns treason."

"Treason, adoni?" the hassar asked, amazed.

"Yes. Someone who has slipped under your guard, Jonathan. I have found it out, and I will put a stop to it. Send for Sar Malchi, General Abner, and Commander Sheva."

While they waited, Jonathan tried twice to find out what the king had on his mind, but Shaul silenced him each time. The three army officers arrived at the same time.

"You sent for us, Abbi?" Sar Malchi said, clearly puzzled.

"Yes. It has come to my attention that we are harboring a traitor. I have called you all here to put a stop to this immediately."

Malchi cast a quick look at Jonathan. "What is your will, Abbi?" the sar asked.

"I want you to kill Dahveed."

The court became totally silent. The officials and messengers in the back stilled to immobility, and the hassar appeared so thunderstruck that Balak nearly laughed.

The king looked at Jonathan. "You are surprised, I see. I am not. I have found his perfidy, and I will punish it." The king glanced at Balak. "He shall die. Today!"

Sar Malchi stared silently at his brother, and General Abner watched the king, puzzled. Only Sheva cast one frightened glance at him, Balak noted. He'd have to keep an eye on the commander. Then he caught Sahrah Michal's gaze. Her expression was calm and steady, and completely deadly.

His stomach suddenly unsettled, he stared at her. She couldn't possibly know anything, could she?

"Jonathan, did you hear my command?" the king said.

"Yes, adoni," the hassar answered, dropping to his knees. "Why is Dahveed condemned?"

"I have determined that he committed treason. Does there need to be any other reason?"

"No, adoni."

"He is to die. He thought to take your place, Jonathan. You shall kill him. It is fitting."

"I will go now, adoni." His face a complete mask, the hassar walked from the court.

The king turned to the others. "Tell the army that anyone who sees Dahveed is to kill him."

"Yes, Abbi," Sar Malchi said, bowing.

I pushed the empty dishes away and eased back, groaning as Ornan put another stack of papyri on the table for Ahiam and me to go over. The possibility of getting killed during war season was bad enough without coming home to the mountain of household records those two slave drivers insisted on setting in front of me.

While Atarah cleared away the dishes, I sorted through the pile, some of it dated months before the hassar's illness. Ahiam pulled out a couple that pertained to Jamin's business, which had become mixed in. He was back in my compound, having found it much easier to conduct the Habiru business from here than down in Bethlehem.

"How did those get in here?" I asked.

Ornan flushed. "Your pardon, adon. Atarah can't read, and anything she finds lying around, she puts in this stack for me to sort out. I haven't been as careful to check it as I should."

I nodded, pulling one of Jarib's reports from under a couple papyri and setting it aside to take to Sar Malchi tomorrow. I glanced at Ornan. His robe was of much better quality, and he wore earrings. Atarah looked contented as she moved about the place with a quiet confidence.

"The hassar has been generous," I commented.

He flushed again. Yes, adon. I'm hoping that you will not have to support us much longer. We would not have trespassed on your generosity for so long except for our need to help some dependents still in Jebus."

I looked up in surprise. "I didn't know you'd left anyone there, Ornan. Do you need more for them? I can arrange—"

"No, adon! Please don't think I am asking for more from you!" the young man said, his face deep red. "You have done much more than we could have expected! We didn't know until just lately—I—forgive my clumsy speech. All is well with us."

My curiosity was aroused, but Ornan looked so painfully embarrassed that I hadn't the heart to question him. "I understand. But please remember that if you do need anything, you are to come to me."

"Yes, adon. I will remember. But Atarah and I have plans. Geber Jamin has thought of hiring me, and with what Atarah is earning as a healer, it should be enough to keep us. We're hoping to buy a small house in town with what the hassar has been pleased to give."

"I will be sorry to see you and your sister go, Ornan. You are both welcome here as long as you need a place."

"You have been generous to us already, adon."

The gate opened, and rapid steps crossed the courtyard. Ornan went back down the ladder.

"Hassar?" Atarah said outside, her voice questioning.

I looked up, picking out the softer stride of Shagay, who had been at the gate. The sar came up the outside steps and strode to the door. He walked in without knocking, Shagay right behind him.

When I started to stand, the ghastly look on his face froze me in place.

"Dahveed, the king has just sent me to kill you."

CHAPTER 41

No one moved. I stared at the hassar in shock. Kill me? The king was pleased with me! He'd rarely allowed me away from his side since my return. We'd discussed which of two estates near Zelah he would give to me just this morning! "He couldn't have!" I gasped in disbelief.

"The king called in Malchi, Abner, and Sheva, then condemned you and ordered your death. Malchi will stall as long as he can, but Sheva was frightened, and he'll be quick with the town sentries," Jonathan said, his voice trembling.

"But I don't understand, Hassar! *Why?*"

Jonathan's eyes closed a moment. Tears filled them. "Balak. I didn't realize that he could influence the king this much! Somehow he convinced Abbi that you've committed treason."

Discouragement and frustration flooded through me. As long as Balak was around, I would never be allowed to live down the king's suspicions!

"You must go," Jonathan's voice broke through my thoughts.

Ahiam was already pulling my harp from the storage basket, and I reached for my sword, fastening it on quickly and checking for my belt knife. A shaking hand reached up from the ladder hole and set a cloth wrapped around some food on the floor. Ahiam scooped it up, along with the cruise on the table.

"Be careful at least until tomorrow morning," Jonathan went on. "I should be able to untangle this by then. I'll look for you at the meadow by the Ezel stone. I'll take Abbi there if I can. Once he's away from everyone else, I can find out what he's really thinking. I'll let you know what he says. Please, Dahveed, go!" the hassar urged. "Sheva will already have the sentries looking for you."

I threw on my cloak, wondering what use it was for Jonathan to change the king's mind as long as Balak was around to shift it back again. As I turned to leave, my eye fell on a report on the corner of the table, and I froze. There before my eyes were the tick marks on the *vav*, the *kaph*, and the *resh* that Elihu had drawn so carefully for me. That report must have something to do with the Gibeonites. My brother needed to see it. I reached for the papyrus.

Jonathan moved for the first time since he'd come through the door. "Dahveed, you must go," he insisted, pulling at me.

"You don't understand," I protested. "Elihu needs this."

The hassar's fist twisted in my cloak, and I barely managed to grab the papyrus before he hauled me to the door.

Hastily, I pulled the earring from my chest, thrusting both it and the papyrus into his hands. "Nahsi, *you must listen!*" I said as he pushed me to the door. "Take this to Elihu, Elihu ben Obed, the scribe who's working with Palti of Gallim. Elihu will tell you who wrote it."

Then I stepped outside, settling my cloak. I knew of several hiding places inside the town, and I made for the nearest one.

Jonathan waited for several minutes, debating what to do next. The king's order had caught him completely unprepared. The only thing he could think of was to get to Dahveed first, and the king had handed that to him. Now he'd have to pretend to search, and he'd have to find some reason to get rid of that cursed Moabite poisoning his abbi's mind.

He had failed miserably this time. If Balak succeeded in pushing the king to destroy Dahveed, what could he do but break completely with his father? And plunge the country into civil war? As he shuddered at the thought, he found himself staring down at the papyrus that Dahveed had thrust on him. He had the earring, too, and didn't remember taking it. What had Dahveed said as he left? He'd—he'd called him Nahsi! Why? Something about Palti's scribe knowing who wrote the report? What would that matter?

Puzzled, he read the words in front of him. He held a standard military report from one of the units. What difference did it make who wrote it? Then his hand clamped over the earring, and he crushed the papyrus, stuffing both into his girdle. He had to do something, go somewhere, to pretend to look for Dahveed, and a trip to the west gate and Ishvi's business chamber would occupy a lot of time. Leaving the room, he hurried down the stairs and out the gate.

Commanders Libni and Natan waited for him there. "Hassar, General Abner sent us to accompany you," Libni managed to whisper.

"Come if you dare," Jonathan said, whirling and starting around the hill to the north.

The two followed, almost trotting to keep up.

Now that he knew Dahveed had a chance to get away, his fear for the zammar left him, to be replaced with anger. That his father would order Dahveed's death after all the zammar had done and after awarding him Michal, infuriated him until Jonathan didn't know what to do. He increased his pace, his stride restricted by the court robe. Pausing, he reached for the hem and tore the garment from hem to knees. Libni and Natan gave each other frightened looks. Ignoring them, he took a few side streets on his way, hot bitterness welling up in him that his father would turn against the hill man, and that he himself hadn't seen it coming. Well, at least he could give Dahveed more of a chance to get away by delaying with Ishvi as long as he dared!

"Ishvi Sar Israel!" he yelled, marching into the compound.

The door to the upstairs room of the house opened almost instantly. "Jonathan Hassar?"

"Bring me Palti of Gallim's scribe!" He strode across the courtyard and up the stairs to pace in the upper room while Ishvi watched from the table. How could his abbi have done this? To order the zammar killed?

The door opened, and two of Ishvi's guards brought a man in, followed by Natan. The guards forced the scribe to his knees, and Jonathan turned on them.

"Out!"

They hesitated.

"*Get out!*" the hassar roared.

All three of the soldiers fled. He looked at the man bowing in front of him, and fresh rage burst on him. It could be Dahveed, bowing there! The scribe stayed still, while Jonathan tried to regain some sort of control over himself. Carefully putting his hands on Ishvi's table, he leaned on them, sweat dripping from his face while he fought with the fury inside.

"Who is he to Dahveed?" he finally asked.

"I believe Elihu is a brother, Hassar."

The calm sound of Ishvi's voice helped. Drawing in a huge breath, Jonathan let it out slowly. "Get up, Elihu."

When the man obeyed, Jonathan pulled the crushed report from his girdle and held it out without turning around. "Who wrote this?"

The scribe's hand wasn't quite steady when he took the papyrus, but his face was calm. "Jarib, assistant commander of the sec—"

At the sudden silence, Jonathan turned around.

Elihu ben Obed tilted the report into the light slightly, studying it intently.

"Where did you get this?" he asked after several moments, obviously no longer aware of whom he was talking to.

Jonathan exchanged a glance with Ishvi. "Dahveed just gave it to me. Why do you ask?"

"Because of the tick marks at the ends of some letters," the scribe replied absently, still scrutinizing the report. "This Jarib of the second unit is the scribe who wrote those falsified Gibeonite reports. The same tick marks are on all of them."

For a moment Jonathan couldn't breathe. The Gibeonite reports? "You're certain?" he demanded.

"Yes, adoni," Elihu replied, coming to himself again and bowing. "The marks are plain."

"Then bring him here," the hassar ordered. "You are dismissed," he added curtly to the scribe.

Elihu walked out, and Ishvi stepped out to send a messenger.

Jonathan stared at that papyrus. He'd brought word that the king had ordered Dahveed's death, yet the hill man had refused to flee until he'd given him the key that might salvage some of the king's honor. And this was the man the king had condemned as a traitor! Bubbling up in him welled a hot fire such as he'd never felt. A red haze gathered before his eyes, and he clenched his fists, pounding on the table as his brother returned to the room.

"Abbi truly ordered Dahveed's death, adoni?"

The slight emphasis on the last word, and his brother's calm tone again helped the hassar choke down his emotions. "He did, and before Dahveed would save his own life, he insisted on giving me this report! I will not let our house shed more innocent blood, Ishvi!"

"Our loyalty to Yahweh alone requires that, adoni."

The red haze faded a little, and he felt as if he could breathe again. He'd track the culprit of his house's fall to the stars if he had to. Once he had the man responsible for those reports, he'd have someone that he could justly vent his wrath at, and then maybe he could be reasonable when it came to Dahveed. But he doubted it. Not after this!

Unable to keep still as time passed, Jonathan strode out of the compound and up the west road, followed by Libni and Natan. They met Sar Malchi halfway up the hill. He had Jarib between three other soldiers. The assistant commander looked a little worse for wear. The man had a cut lip and carried one arm as though it hurt.

Jonathan turned his blazing eyes on the sar.

His brother met them, signaling the others to wait while he approached the hassar alone. The commanders backed away. "I beg pardon for the delay. I had to hunt for him," the sar explained. "Abner seems to have detained the entire second unit under the impression that they might know where Dahveed would go."

"The unit is yours, Malchi. Did you give permission for this?"

"No."

"Put a stop to it, then. They're the last men Dahveed would tell, and I'd rather not have to worry about their loyalty from now on."

"Would that be an order, adoni?" Malchi asked very quietly.

"It would, Malchi-shua Sar Israel."

"As you wish, adoni." Something iced over in the back of Malchi's eyes, and in spite of his own rage, Jonathan was glad that he wasn't Abner.

The hassar approached Jarib, and the guards backed away. The man waited patiently, the most relaxed one in the group.

"Did you write this?" Jonathan held out the wrinkled report.

"Yes, adoni."

"This report was written by the same hand that falsified Gibeonite reports. Did you also write them?"

"Yes, adoni," the man admitted uncomfortably.

"For whom?"

"Balak ben Hod."

"*Balak?*" Jonathan's voice sank to a purr. "Why would the king's personal attendant meddle with Gibeonite reports?"

"I assume that he wanted to make trouble between the king and the Gibeonites."

The matter-of-fact acceptance of such a thing brought Jonathan up short. His black eyes bored into the assistant commander's. "Why would you participate in this thing? These people are covered by Yahweh's covenant."

Jarib looked a little embarrassed. "He paid me."

Jonathan turned away, struggling to understand, and losing again to the black explosion of anger that settled on him. "Natan, this man is detained by the king until further notice. See that he is confined appropriately."

Natan hesitated only a moment. Then he took Jarib's arm, leading him toward the fortress.

The hassar stared unseeing down the street. Balak. Again. How much had that double-faced, sly Moabite done? As he turned to go, he found himself confronted by a woman.

"Hassar, I need to speak with you."

"I don't have time now," he said brusquely, throttling his anger yet again.

"You should take the time, adoni."

Her tone, so much like his immi's, quenched his rage enough that he looked down. Judith stood before him, her head high. A shiver of trepidation ran down his back. The expression in her eyes promised another disaster.

What more was to descend on him? he wondered, following her down the street. Could Balak have done still more? He had already poisoned the king's mind against Dahveed and raised the king's anger against the Gibeonites. What else was there?

The streets emptied before them as they walked around the hill to the east side of the town. Exhaustion crept into Jonathan's mind. He had next to nothing with which to convince his father to get rid of the Moabite, but go the man must, even if it tore the kingdom apart. "Yahweh, grant us hesed," he murmured fervently.

Judith entered her house, and Jonathan followed, curtly ordering Libni to remain outside. She pulled aside an old robe hanging on the wall and took a shrine from the niche there.

"What god is this for?" she asked.

Jonathan moved into the light from the door, studying the object. "It could be any god, Judith. There is no designation on it."

"If this is added?" She took something from her girdle.

He turned the six-inch bronze figure over in his hands. "This appears to be Kemosh, Judith."

She went pale, and her chin trembled a little. "And these?" She held out some pieces of torn papyri.

"These are addressed to Kemosh," he said, scanning them. Then he read them more slowly. "They are curses against me and Dahveed," he finished slowly. "Do you read, Judith?"

"No, adoni."

"What made you give these to me?"

Her chin went up. "I've wondered about some things for a long time, adoni. Since the king broke his arm, Balak has had nightmares. I never paid much attention until just lately. I can't sleep well right now. I'm carrying a child. It took me a while to understand that he was calling on Kemosh in his sleep, and then I saw him writing these and putting them into the shrine. He left the shrine out in the courtyard a while ago, and the wind blew them all over. I picked them up, intending to give them to him again."

She paused a minute, and Jonathan waited patiently. "Today, when he came home at noon, he told me how easy it is for him to influence Shaul." She wrapped her arms protectively around her stomach. "When I heard—I knew what he must have done."

"You know what this means?" Jonathan asked.

She straightened, all trace of her usual giddiness gone. "Yes, Hassar."

"Go back to your immi's house immediately, Judith. You are the king's kinswoman, and you have served him well today. I would not have you harmed for that."

"Thank you, Hassar."

As she walked out the door, Jonathan sensed that there was nothing in the house she wanted to take with her.

"Libni?" he called, standing at the door.

"Yes, Hassar?"

"You will go with Judith and see her safely to her destination."

"Hassar, I am to stay with—"

"*Now, Libni!*"

"Yes, Hassar!" the man gasped, hurrying after the woman's retreating figure.

Jonathan turned back to the room, beginning a thorough search.

Light from the throne room shone into the courtyard when Jonathan walked into the fortress, carrying the covered shrine along with the statue of Kemosh and the other pieces of papyri that he'd found. He had what he needed now. The sun had almost disappeared, and it would soon be dark. If no one had found Dahveed by now, he'd get well away.

Hearing the king's voice, he paused outside the door at the top of the stairs.

"Where is he? Why hasn't anyone come to me?"

"They will come, adoni," Balak spoke. "But Dahveed can be cunning and very hard to find."

Jonathan shuddered. Why hadn't he noticed how that voice stroked the king like an adder twining about, waiting to strike?

"Jonathan will find him. No one will take Jonathan's place," his abbi said.

"Of course not, adoni," the servant replied.

The hassar pushed the door open and silently slipped through.

"Jonathan will take care of things. Dahveed will never have the throne," Balak continued. "You will see that he will die."

The other officials stilled as the hassar set the shrine on the table and walked forward, his steps light and soundless.

"All traitors to the king will die, adoni," the servant declared, and threw a glance back at the officials, only to find himself face-to-face with the hassar.

"Indeed, they will, Balak." Jonathan's hand shot out, grabbing the attendant's arm, yanking him forward and forcing him to his knees. "Perhaps we should start with you."

"What are you doing?" the king asked, amazed. "Balak is loyal to me."

"Why would a full-blooded Moabite be loyal to you, adoni?" Jonathan replied, pinning the trembling man with his gaze. "If you would see how loyal he is, go look on the table."

Uncertainly, Shaul rose and started forward.

Seeing the shrine, Balak turned pale. "Adoni, don't believe him," he gasped. "I have served you always. It's Dahveed who has betrayed you. He has influenced the hassar against me!"

The king halted, his face troubled.

"Dahveed has said very little against you," Jonathan replied, his grip hauling the man to his feet. "The most convincing witness was you, yourself. Here stands the man who has deceived you, adoni," Jonathan added. "He forgot to tell anyone that his family was driven from Moab under the curse of their king for treason. He does not seem to have changed much from his father."

"No, how can this be?" Shaul asked, looking from his son to Balak in distress. "Balak has been devoted to me. The things he said—they were true."

"No doubt," the hassar agreed, taking Balak to the table, the king following him. "But I would guess they were all true of himself, not Dahveed."

His face pale, sweat gleaming on his forehead, Balak shrank away.

"Look on the table, adoni!" Jonathan commanded.

The king glanced at the shrine, then picked up the figure of the god and turned it over in his hands. "This is Kemosh," he said, facing Balak.

"My king, don't believe these lies," the man pleaded, twisting in Jonathan's grip.

"Read what's in the shrine," Jonathan said, his gaze steady on the Moabite.

Balak's face turned gray. "Adoni," he gasped. "Hesed! Those aren't what they seem to be. They are not something that will concern you. They have no power, no place . . ."

While Balak babbled on, the king read piece after piece, and his face grew harder and harder. When he turned to Balak again, his eyes glittered.

"You cursed the hassar? You brought that illness down on him? You dared to touch Jonathan? *And the darkness?* The darkness was from you?"

Balak crumpled to his knees, pulling his arm from the hassar's grip, prostrating himself on the floor, a low moan coming from his mouth.

"You back-stabbing, fawning asp!" the king roared. "*You shall die, Balak!*"

The servant scrambled back, pleading for hesed as the sentries closed in.

"Bind him, and confine him! Tomorrow we will find an appropriate way of execution!"

"No, adoni, give me hesed!" Balak cried as the guards dragged him from the room.

King Shaul looked at the shrine on the table. "Dahveed, my son, what have I done?" he exclaimed.

CHAPTER 42

I paced back and forth in the tiny clearing above the meadow and the Ezel stone. Getting out of town last night had been simple, and within an hour I had arrived here. I'd expected Jonathan to come with Shaul this morning, and when no one showed up, I started to worry. Then Zeri, from Jeshua's band, had arrived, bringing word that two army units under Abner's command had left Gibeah for Bethlehem early this morning! The only thing I could think of was that Jonathan had been unable to persuade his father of my innocence, and those units were on their way to seize my family.

I couldn't decide what to do. Every fiber of my being wanted to run to Bethlehem, but even if I left now, I'd be too late to stop whatever was to happen. Going there would also be in direct disobedience to the king's command, and angering Shaul more would erase any hope of hesed that my family might have.

But what would I do if the king killed my family? How could I live? "Yahweh, shelter them under Your wings," I pleaded aloud. "Preserve them for the love you had toward Adon Boaz and Hassarah Ruth!"

On the other hand, if my family was in danger, surely Jonathan Hassar would find some way to warn them and tell me. Why hadn't any message come from him? What could be happening in Gibeah? Had the king's anger turned toward his son? Surely King Shaul wouldn't harm Jonathan! Unless the demon had returned! For a moment fear stopped my pacing. A shudder ran through me. No, that couldn't have happened. I remembered too well the unbearable light binding the darkness away from the king. There must be some other reason. But what?

I glanced at the sun, low now in the west. Zeri had promised to return with news.

"Geber Dahveed?"

Belt knife in my hand, I leaped around.

Hanan stepped out of the trees, eyeing the knife. "The hassar will probably come tomorrow," he announced. "He found what he was looking for."

"Hanan, do you know anything of the units that went south? Zeri said they went to Bethlehem. Is my family safe?"

"Why wouldn't they be?" he replied, puzzled.

"Didn't the king send Abner after them?"

"No. Didn't Zeri tell you what the hassar did last night?"

"Zeri didn't know. My family is safe?"

"Yes, and so is Balak's, no thanks to him!" Hanan snorted. "Abner was quite put out," he added with a sly smile.

I wilted in relief, easing down on the warm meadow grass. "What happened? Tell me everything, Hanan."

The Habiru youth related yesterday's events, convincing me of Balak's fall from favor. "So what's the excitement about today?" I asked, shaking my head at the Moabite's effrontery in cursing the king.

"The guards put Balak in one of the royal storerooms on the west side of the fortress hill. They didn't search him very well, and he escaped."

I stared at Hanan a moment, then smiled a little. "He's from the south—carried a belt knife, didn't he?"

The youth nodded. "Quite small, but it was enough for him to dig out a hole through the mud brick courses between the timbers in the wall. He squeezed out through that and ran straight to the Jordan. Didn't even send a message warning his kin," he finished in contempt.

"And when the king found out he was gone, he sent Abner for Hod and his family," I guessed.

"Yes. They got out of town just ahead of Abner's units, and by the time Abner had searched Bethlehem, they were safe in Jebus. Araunah Debir wasn't any too happy to have Shaul's soldiers poking around Bethlehem either."

The self-satisfied smile that flickered across his face made me suspicious that Hanan had been much more than an observer to these events. "What made you alert the Araunah?" I asked, without looking at him.

His lips twitched. "I don't like Abner. Neither does Debir."

Jonathan did not show up the next morning. Zeri reported that having ascertained Balak had indeed crossed the Jordan, the hassar was busy soothing Debir's ruffled feelings. Also Zeri reported that the king had doubled the guard in the fortress and the throne room, and that Malchi had called Abner to account regarding the second unit.

Now that I knew my family was safe, I could relax and wait for Jonathan to arrive. With Balak gone, I knew the hassar would be able to sway the king.

The heat of the day had passed, and I leaned against an oak and closed my eyes, listening to the sounds of the forest. The wind lifted my hair briefly, and I recalled the dragonfly, clinging to my finger before suddenly lifting its wings and setting them horizontally. I didn't think my wings were set, but they probably would be soon. Meanwhile, I clung to my place for a while longer.

"Dahveed, someone comes," Zeri spoke behind me. "Two adons on mules and six guards."

I brushed the leaves from my clothes and peeked over the rocky overlook in time to see King Shaul and Jonathan walk into the meadow. I descended the rocky stair, staying close under the outcropping and concealed in the underbrush. They paused by the waterfall that spilled from the rocks above me and then wandered past it toward the trees.

"Are we alone enough now, Jonathan, that you can tell me what troubles you?" the king asked, looking around uneasily. "Perhaps we should call the guards."

"Balak has left, adoni. There is nothing to fear."

"The zammar is not here. Yahweh may not protect us." Shaul tightly gripped the hassar's arm.

"It is of the zammar that I would speak to you," Jonathan said quietly.

His abbi turned to him quickly. "Do you know where he is?"

"I could guess, but he moves swiftly, and once gone, is impossible to find. And he will never return unless you want him to."

Shaul sighed. "Yahweh was with him, and his harp added much to our joy."

"Yes, adoni. Yahweh sent him to bring the light back to us. Why will you drive away that gift? Dahveed freed you from a demon; he saved Ishvi's life and Malchi's. How can you wrong him now, when he has never wronged you? Remember how the zammar risked his life in battle, going against the giant of Gath with only his staff and sling? Yahweh granted us a great victory that day, preserving the kingdom. You were elated, Abbi, for Dahveed had done what no one else could do."

The hassar looked at his father. "He has never done the slightest thing against you, serving you however you asked, whether there was honor in it or not. Remember how he saved the army at Birzaith, even though Abner wouldn't listen to him? Would you effront Yahweh by condemning and killing Dahveed for no reason?"

Jonathan dropped to his knees, his hands taking the king's. "You cannot do this thing, Abbi! Do not bring his innocent blood down on our house. If you cannot give him your favor, at least grant him his life! Send him away. He'll go. Give him hesed, please Abbi, for he has done no wrong!" His voice broke, and he bowed his head.

"Don't distress youself so, Jonathan! He will live," the king replied anxiously, his hands gripping his son's.

"Swear to me, Abbi," Jonathan pushed, tears falling from his eyes. "Swear to me that Dahveed will not die."

Answering tears appeared in the king's eyes. "As Yahweh lives, Jonathan, Dahveed will not be put to death. I miss him too, my son, and I keep thinking that one day I will look up and he will be there, just as he was before."

"He will find your favor again?"

"And my daughter. He will live, Jonathan. Now, get up, my son." Jonathan rose, and the king kissed his forehead. "You have your request, Hassar."

Frozen in place, I watched them disappear into the trees on the other side of the meadow. Israel's hassar had begged for my life as if I were his son!

Later that night, the harp in my hands, I stared at the vast stretch of the stars overhead, hardly able yet to believe that Jonathan would plead

for my life as he had. Why should he? What was I to him? For that matter, what was I to Yah? Why would He choose me over anyone else?
He ruled the heavens, the earth, and the seas. Wonder filled me, and a
song sprang to my mind, the words fitting themselves to a tune that
Grandmother had taught me long ago. I had always wished for words
for it, and now they came.

I forgot everything, opening my throat to give voice to the awe and
wonder that filled me, the honor given me by Yah confused in my
mind with the honor and authority that Jonathan had bestowed on me,
all of it mixed up with my bewilderment that either of them would notice me at all. But they had, and I could only pour my thankfulness into
song.

"O Yahweh, our Adon, how splendid is Your name in all the earth

"Which set Your majesty on the heavens.

"From the mouths of children and infants is founded strength so
that You can fight to stop the enemy and take vengeance.

"When I see Your heavens, the work of Your fingers, the moon
and the stars, which You set up, what is man that You remember us
and the son of Adam that You take care of us?

"You make us lack only a little in comparison with the gods.

"With honor and splendor You crown us.

"You make us lord over the work of Your hands.

"You put everything under our feet: sheep and goats and cattle, all
of them.

"And also beasts of the field, the birds of the heaven, and the fishes
of the sea passing through the ways of the seas.

"O Yahweh, our Adon, how splendid is Your name in all the
earth!"

When the echoes of my voice died away, not even the crickets
broke the silence. I bowed in worship, the close presence of my God
reassuring me that He would care for me and those I loved.

I followed Jonathan the next morning, dressed in a plain robe
and an old cloak. Since Shaul had condemned me so publicly, the
hassar wanted it very clear to everyone that the king had accepted me

again.

"Are you sure he will honor me?" I asked as we approached the fortress gate.

"He will, Dahveed."

I hoped so. My fortunes had reversed themselves so often that I was hesitant to press the king for anything more than a chance to prove that my only wish was to serve as best I might. But Jonathan seemed set on having the king show his favor in every public way possible.

I remained behind him through the anteroom, walking as I used to, my head covered by the hood of the cloak. In the throne room a rich northern adon whose accent indicated he was from Napthali petitioned the king, and I glanced quickly around the room.

Sahrah Michal was refilling the king's wine cup by the throne. She shifted her feet and looked around as I watched, and I lowered my eyes, finding myself trembling slightly. I didn't want anything to mess up the reconciliation with the king.

When the man finished his flowery speech, King Shaul looked at him sternly. "I see no reason your neighbor must turn his vineyard over to you simply because you want it. Guards, take this man from my presence at once!"

The man's face flushed with anger, but two guards strode toward him, and his anger turned to alarm. Hastily backing away, he looked for the door that another guard held open. His three servants hurried after him, their heads lowered in shame.

While everyone watched and listened to the adon's departure, Jonathan took my arm and brought me forward. I knelt beside him, praying for Yahweh to grant me one more chance before the king. Surely now, Shaul would believe that I would not threaten him or his house or throne.

The king caught sight of his oldest son. "What is it, Jonathan?" he asked in surprise.

Instead of answering, the hassar stepped aside a little.

"I have come at the wish of the king," I said, fighting to keep my voice steady.

"Dahveed?" Shaul exclaimed, straightening abruptly. "Dahveed, is that your voice?"

"It is, adoni. What is my sin before you that you sought my life?"

I replied as the hassar had instructed me to.

"Dahveed, come near to me. He who accused you is gone, and the truth of the matter has been found out. Balak will speak against you no more, for he is condemned of treason and is under pain of death. I have longed for your return, zammar. Approach the throne."

I rose, and Jonathan ushered me to his abbi. "Let me find favor with you," I said, bowing again. "Forgive your servant for any wrong that I have done."

"Don't say such things," Shaul answered. "I know that you are blameless before me. You have served me better than any other. Do not leave me again."

"I am here as long as the king desires," I said, looking up. Tears again filled the king's eyes as in the meadow, and happiness shown out of them. Reassurance spread through me. I could keep his favor this time! I knew it, and I'd serve him however he asked.

King Shaul glanced to one side. "Michal, the zammar has returned!"

The sahrah nodded, her arms wrapped around herself. "I see, Abbi," she said, her voice unsteady.

The king turned back to me. "But Dahveed, why do you come to me dressed like this? It is unfitting for you. You are to be my son-in-law. And commander of my guard as well! Then Yahweh will be with us to protect us. Jonathan, bring some clothes fit for Dahveed Israel to wear, and the mantle of commander of the guard."

"As you wish, adoni," the hassar replied, flicking a glance at me, a slight smile on his face.

Someone must have been waiting on the landing, because the hassar returned almost instantly with a fine gray robe with blue stripes and a matching blue girdle. He took off my old cloak and dressed me himself. By the time he finished, the mantle had been brought, and the king fastened that on.

"Come here, daughter," Shaul directed.

Michal approached, and the king put her hand in mine. "When will we celebrate the wedding? It must be soon."

Not trusting myself to speak, I just squeezed her hand.

"I think a month to get ready will be enough," she said, but I felt her trembling, and her hand gripped mine tightly.

It was dark when I walked through the gate of my house. The king had refused to allow me from his sight the rest of the day, and only Jonathan's persuasion had permitted me to return home for the night.

Shagay stepped from the shadows. "Something came for you this afternoon," he said. "Ahiam has it in the upstairs room."

Hearing suppressed excitement in my retainer's voice, I turned to him curiously. He smiled.

I climbed the stairs.

Ahiam opened the door. "I thought I heard your step. The king accepted you?"

"Yes, and I am to be married in a month."

"Well, this will make an early wedding present, then."

He stepped back. There on the table, lying on a soft dark cloth, was Boaz's bow. Even from here, I knew it was magnificent. I removed my cloak without taking my gaze off it. The silver inlay gleamed in the lamplight, and the ivory caps were polished and smooth. They had been streamlined and recarved by a master at the craft, and the symbols stood out plainly in all their detail. The wood gleamed, and the hand-hold had been shortened and cut down without removing any of its usefulness, giving the bow a sleek, lethal appearance, even unstrung. A new bow string waited to be put in place, and a quiver, also capped with ivory and carved with the same twining vine as the inlay, lay beside it.

Shagay stood in the doorway, grinning.

"This message came with it," Ahiam said.

I picked up the papyrus. The bow maker said that he was honored to have the care of this weapon, and that his grandfather had helped with the crafting of it years before. He was delighted to see it, having heard or read descriptions of it more than once. After sending his good wishes and hope that the bow would give much pleasure to its owner, he added that his search of the records had not found mention of a case for it. Since a case had apparently been included in the original price, he was preparing one and would send it as soon as it was completed.

Picking the bow up, I stroked the sides, inspected the caps, and generally handled it. Ahiam and Shagay reached for it also, and we couldn't stop gazing in wonder at what we had, even though we knew that we could never appreciate it fully, and hadn't an idea in the world what to do with it.

Footsteps sounded on the stairs, and Shagay went to the door. Ahiam started to cover the bow, but I stopped him, suddenly knowing exactly what to do with this bow.

"Let him in, Shagay," I said.

My retainer opened the door, and Jonathan ducked his head to enter. "I knocked at the gate, Dahveed, but no one . . ." His voice trailed off as his gaze riveted on the weapon. He walked forward as if in a trance. "It's magnificent!" he whispered.

I leaned against the wall on my stool, watching his face, a half smile on mine.

Jonathan picked it up, inspecting it expertly. He found the artisan's mark and gasped. "I never thought to see one, let alone handle one," he said, flashing a glance at me. "They're legendary. They shoot farther than any other bow, and oh—" Seeing the extra large quiver, which must have had 40 arrows in it, he broke off. When he picked that up, I noticed he did it without letting go of the bow. He took out several arrows, studying them, then the quiver. Then he noticed the carving and turned back to the bow, running his finger down the silver inlay and stroking the curled ivory caps, giving his attention to each of the four carvings.

Holding it away from his body by the handhold, he looked at me. "May I?"

"Go ahead."

Bracing the bottom arm, he set his knee in the middle of the bow, using all his strength to turn the arc inside out and hold it steady while he slipped the string over the upper arm, then releasing it slowly.

Eyes shining, he lifted it. "Do you know what a privilege it is to just handle one of these?" he said. "They can take up to 10 years to make, and will last for generations if cared for properly."

"You'd like to have one, then?" I asked.

"Like to? Dahveed, I'd give anything for one of these! But they are only made by special order, and those able to craft one have enough orders to last for the rest of their life, as well as that of their son. Pharaohs of Egypt wait years for them. I've dreamed all my life of one of these." He looked at the weapon with longing.

"Take it."

Jonathan stared at me. "What did you say?"

"I said take it."

"Dahveed, you don't know what you're doing! This is more valuable than the entire kingdom! It's worth an empire's ransom!"

I lounged back against the wall. "Are you by chance objecting, Hassar?"

His mouth dropped open. Then, gripping the bow tightly, he glanced at Shagay and Ahiam, who stared back with impassive faces.

"It comes with my gratitude, Jonathan. I think you should be the one to keep it. I've got the feeling that it was made for you."

Finally I convinced him that I meant it, and once he was certain I knew what I was doing, I doubted I would ever hold that bow again. He couldn't let go of it. At last he rose, the bow wrapped tightly in the cloth.

At the door, I said, "Hassar, a word to open your ear."

He turned back. "Yes, Dahveed?"

"Should anyone ever ask, just tell them that you have been entrusted with the bow."

"Of course, Dahveed," he said, but I knew that he had no idea what I meant.

I smiled. He would. Someday.

CHAPTER 43

The next month was the busiest that I'd ever known. Sahrah Michal, trailed everywhere by Jemima, was in and out, sending me for measurements for my wedding clothes, asking about what jewelry I had, and telling me that the wedding would be put off for a week to be certain her period of purification would be over.

She looked through the house to see where she would put her things, went through all the storerooms taking an inventory, and asked me where on earth the teraphim in the back corner had come from.

I hastily explained they had been given to me when I got the house, and that I hadn't known what else to do with them, then said she could do whatever she wanted with them. I was more than glad to leave the details up to her since I had other things to think about.

Jonathan asked if I'd mind a small private feast at his estate a week before the wedding, and I said no. Atarah helped me find the jewelry for Michal that I would give her at the wedding ceremony, and Ahiam and Shagay helped me choose gifts for all my personal guests. I also had to plan a feast at my house for my servants and the second unit. Then I had to determine who in the unit needed clothes fit to wear for it, and arrange to get them.

Josheb volunteered to help me pick out the robes, and when I saw him coaxing Keturah to rest under the almond tree one day, her blushes making him preen like a cock bird, I woke up to the other wooing going on at my house. Jonathan usually came with me at noon to be with Atarah, and Ahiam's cheerful face said that Palti had been impressed with the gifts he'd sent during the war season. It was seeing Shagay's amused smile when I stood in the doorway watching Michal walk out my gate that told me I was just as bad as the rest. No wonder Naharai took to sleeping with the second unit!

In the middle of all this, Jonathan asked me to stay after court one day.

"What did you wish, Hassar?" I asked once the throne room was empty.

He took some papyri from his table by the dais, and handed them to me, his face somber.

After reading them, I sat down on a bench by the long table. "Looks as if Jarib told you everything," I commented. I'd learned of my assistant commander's part in the Gibeonite affair soon after my return, but there had been nothing that I could do to help him.

"I think so," Jonathan replied. "He answered anything I asked. Apparently he and Balak worked together from the onset, so we've pieced together the whole story. I gave my judgment on Jarib yesterday," he added, his face sad and lined.

I rubbed my hand along the table, memories filling my mind of Jarib as my assistant, with his quick, deft fingers, working with me as best he could after I replaced him as commander, doggedly training until he finally learned to handle a sword with some proficiency, forever stumbling through each day. "May I beg hesed for him?" I asked slowly.

"I have given him what I could," the hassar sighed. "I granted him an honorable death, with burial afterward. He did have one request."

"What was it?"

Jonathan's expression was oddly compassionate. "He asked to die by your hand."

My mouth was suddenly dry. "Me?"

The hassar nodded.

I turned away. Jarib wanted me to execute him? He was part of my unit, had fought beside me. How could I turn against him? Yet how could I refuse his last request? But then, he had actively worked against a covenant of Yahweh, and a man had died because of it. His actions indirectly contributed to the deaths of scores of people.

"When?" I asked, my voice ragged.

"Sunset today."

I glanced outside. Another hour. "Jonathan, what shall I do?" I whispered.

"You have to decide this yourself, Dahveed. I'll come back in a while." He walked out the door.

As his footsteps faded down the stairs, I bowed my head, turning to Yah for guidance.

When Jonathan returned, the sun was almost touching the horizon. He looked at me.

"I will grant his request," I said.

We walked out of the fortress and down the path to the south gate, going to a hillside east of town where there were a couple caves used to bury the very poor, the nameless, and the condemned. Jarib was there, standing between two guards. He gave me a resigned smile when I stopped in front of him. "Thank you, Dahveed," he said, kneeling.

I took out my belt knife.

Jarib's death lingered with me for days. I had held him as he died, and then burned the clothes I wore. The second unit was subdued, and going to the training ground was hard. More than a week after the execution, the men gathered around when we were dismissed for the noon meal. Lotan, now my assistant commander, spoke for them.

"Commander, may we remember his name?"

"If the hassar can grant him an honorable death, we can keep his name on the roll of the second unit," I decided.

"Good," Sithri commented. "He was a part of us, even if he

couldn't keep his feet under him."

The afternoon of the private feast that Jonathan gave, I wore the first of the sar's robes that Michal had ordered made for me. It was a light-brown, with sar's length fringe, tassels on the girdle, and a band of green embroidery around all the edges. A matching green mantle was fastened with a silver brooch, and the headband and earrings were worked with a crosshatch design.

Jonathan looked at me with approval before he ushered me through the door to the upper room at his private estate. I stopped short just inside. All the adults in my family burst out laughing at the look on my face, and Immi rushed to give me a hug.

Joy flooded through me as I wrapped my arms around her. I had not dared ask to have my family as guests at the wedding, unwilling to test the king's regard for me until he forgot Balak's lies. My gaze found the hassar as I traded Immi for Abigail. How could I tell him what this meant to me? I squeezed my eyes against the tears.

"Don't worry, Dahveed," he said in a low voice. "The king gave me permission to ask anyone I wanted to this feast!"

When I embraced Elihu, I glanced at him again, and he grinned. "It didn't take long for Ishvi to figure things out."

I flushed a little, and he chuckled.

Everyone crowded around, and I hugged them all, at last looking for Eliab, who had hung back, casting a glance or two at Abinadab, not knowing how to greet me. I held my arm out to him, and then drew him into an embrace.

"You are looking well, Dahveed," he said, hardly daring to face me.

"I'm glad you came, Eliab. I needed all my family here."

Once the first round of greetings concluded, we sat down, all trying to talk at once with so much to catch up on. Jonathan solved that problem by ordering the food served, and as the large polished red platters arrived, loaded with couscous, beans, peas, cucumbers, and more, we settled down to a wonderful feast and reasonable conversation.

Abinadab had been quietly effective in righting the problems caused by Eliab. The grain was growing well, and everyone was hopeful for a good harvest in the spring. The south hadn't had a really good one for four or five years.

Abinadab had made a portable desk for Elihu to use as he traveled around with Palti, and when Sar Ishvi had seen it, he'd wanted one for each of the scribes for the king's lands. Joab hadn't caused as much trouble in the town anymore, but he disappeared for days at a time, worrying Zeruiah constantly. Abigail and Jether told news of the caravans and bragged about Amasa. Eliab's wife introduced me to my newest nephew, who was still nursing. Immi refused to let go of my left hand, and my heart was too full for words.

"Sing for us, Dahveed," Abbi suggested. "We have so much to be thankful for."

Ahiam brought me the harp, and I sang my gratitude to Yahweh for this day. Abbi requested a favorite of his, and I made Abigail and Nethanel sing the "Answering Song." We did Jether's favorite, the "Desert Maiden," and I noticed Jonathan wiping tears from his eyes as Abigail finished the last line about the maiden waiting in the desert moonlight for her lover.

It was very late when the lamps were extinguished, and my family bedded down for the night. I was too full yet to sleep, and I went outside, leaning on the wall of one of the hassar's grain fields, letting my joy flow silently from my heart to Yah.

I don't know how long I had been there when someone stopped not far away.

"Ben-geber?"

I'd never heard that voice say that name humbly before. Straightening up, I turned. "Yes, bekor?"

"Abinadab told me what happened in Gibeah, and how you stepped in with the hassar and saved them—and me." He paused, the silence stretching between us. Then he sort of crumpled up, rocking back on his knees, covering his face with his hands.

I went to him, kneeling also, gathering his hands into mine, the distress coming from him tearing at my heart. Glad that the darkness veiled our faces, I waited while he gripped my hands and his tears dropped on them.

"After what I've done, I should be dead," he said at last.

"Abbi would nearly have died if he lost you, and we all knew it," I said, letting go of his hands and sitting back on my heels.

"No," he said in a dead voice. "Maybe because of one of the others, but not me."

"Eliab, how can you say that?" I exclaimed. "You're the bekor." I barely saw his shrug in the darkness.

"Not now. Abinadab is. I've never had words or a voice like you. The things Abinadab makes are beautiful, and vines seem to talk to Raddai like Shammah can to his mules. Ozem is trying to breed the sheep again, and Nethanel and Abbi don't even have to talk to each other much. They know what the other one is thinking. Even The Hassarah—" He stopped again.

"What did she say to you?" I asked, stunned that Eliab felt there was no way he brought honor to the family. I felt him shrug again.

"All she said was that one day everything would be in my care, and our inheritance would remain because of it."

"Everything? Or your portion?"

"She said everything," he replied, his voice suddenly thoughtful.

"I don't think you should worry about what you can do, Eliab," I said softly. "The Hassarah knew things. Someday it will all depend on you."

"I'll probably lose it all."

"Only if you're no longer Jesse's hard-headed, stubborn bekor."

"You never change, do you?" A grim humor underlay his comment.

"Do any of us? We just change directions sometimes."

I pulled my oldest brother to his feet, and we went back to the compound.

⁅▯⌐▯⁆

"Relax, Michal. You can't make the sun go down any faster," Immi said as Achsah combed out the bride's hair.

Michal blushed. "Are you sure the bakers made that spiced bread?"

"Yes, and the servants have put the extra tables in the throne room, and your brothers will all wear the robes that you planned for them. The robe you gave Merab still fits her, although it's a good thing you're getting married today and not two weeks from now," Ahinoam laughed.

Blushing again, the sahrah folded her hands tightly in front of her while Achsah combed.

"Oh, your hair looks just lovely, Michal!" Merab said admiringly.

Michal whirled around. "I didn't hear you come in. How are things coming along?"

"The midwife says I'm not going to have any trouble with this pregnancy either," her sister said with satisfaction. "I do hope it's a boy. Adriel would be thrilled to have two sons."

Seeing the hope on Merab's face, Michal added a silent petition to Yahweh that her sister did carry another boy. Then she sat while Achsah fixed her hair, listening not so much to Merab's words as to the happiness that flowed under them.

And then the sun was low in the sky, and it looked as if some of the guests were already arriving. Merab and Achsah laid out the robes that she had chosen, in her favorite green. Michal stood in the middle of the room, looking at them, shivering.

"I do believe you're nervous!" Merab exclaimed in amazement. "I thought you'd be the calmest one here tonight."

"I planned to be, but I don't think I am," Michal admitted. "Merab, I'm not beautiful like you are. What if Dahveed doesn't like me?"

Merab swept her up in a hug. "Don't worry about it, Michal. Dahveed already likes you! It's in his eyes when he looks at you."

Michal put her arms around her sister. "Oh, Merab, I love him so much! I'd die if he turned away from me."

"He won't. He wouldn't dream of it. Now get dressed."

The bride slipped into the robe, careful of her hair. Immi came in, fussing a little with her girdle and straightening the meil one more time. Then she stepped back. "You have excellent taste, Michal," she said quietly. "You've made yourself beautiful tonight."

"Thank you, Immi. I hope Dahveed thinks so."

"Don't worry about that!"

Since the feast was in the throne room, Dahveed would escort her to his house after it, but the simple ceremony of sealing the covenant between their two houses would take place now. She went out into the passage, careful not to disarrange her robe and mantle, butterflies in her stomach as she waited. Merab was her only attendant.

Jonathan arrived. "Michal," he began, and then stopped, staring.

"Do I look all right?" she asked, uncertain what to make of his re-action.

"You're exquisite, Michal," her brother said, his voice serious.

She blushed. He had never said anything like that before.

After giving her a smile, Jonathan went back outside.

Michal got one more hug from Immi, and then took Merab's hand and walked down the passage.

The courtyard was almost as bright as day with all the lamps and torches, and I tried to stand still while I waited for Michal to appear. I wore the dark-red robe that she had ordered for me, along with a deep-blue mantle over a colorful meil with gold thread among the embroidery that matched the one Michal would be wearing. Jonathan had given me the gold armbands and headband, and Josheb stood by me with the jewelry that I would give to Michal.

As he emerged from the passage, Jonathan flashed me a reassuring smile. The crowd hushed as the hassar joined the king, and then Michal stepped out the door, looking toward me. For an instant I froze, unable to take my eyes from her. I didn't know what she'd done, but she was beautiful as I'd never seen her before. I was supposed to wait for her to join me, but the next thing I knew, I was walking toward her. She looked into my eyes and blushed. It was all that I could do to keep from picking her up and carrying her back into the king's residence where I could have her to myself!

Josheb had the presence of mind to follow me, and when I reached out my hand for the cloak to put around her, he had it for me. I took her hand again and escorted her back to my place in front of the king. We knelt on the rug put there for us.

"Dahveed Israel, because of your service to me, and the honor you have brought to my house and kingdom, I have awarded you my daughter Michal Sahrah Israel as a wife," Shaul said, his eyes shining as he looked at the sahrah.

"The honor you have given me is more than I deserve, adoni, and

I swear to remain faithful to her, and provide for her as is my duty as her husband," I replied, a bit surprised that my voice would work.

"Before Yahweh, do you enter into this covenant in His name?" he asked, turning his gaze to me.

"Yes, adoni," we both replied.

Michal squeezed my hand before letting go, and Jonathan handed me a piece of bread, which I broke, giving one piece to Michal. After we ate, Jonathan handed me a cup of wine. I sipped it, then passed it to Michal, who drank also, thus sealing the covenant between us and our houses.

"Rise, Sar Dahveed, Sahrah Michal."

We stood, and I turned again to Josheb, who handed me two rings. I put one on each of her hands, then took the matching necklace, gold with green gems, and Merab held her hair out of the way while I fastened the clasp in back of her neck. My fingers were shaking so badly that I almost couldn't get it fastened, but a whispered hint from Merab helped me in time.

The earrings came next. I hadn't really looked at them until I fastened them on, and it wasn't until I was putting them in her ears that I realized they were deliberately twisted into the shape of the brass earring! I looked at the hassar in exasperation, and the wicked gleam in his eye told me whose idea that had been!

Josheb passed me the brooch for the cloak, which I got fastened without any trouble, and last, I carefully settled a matching gold headband on her head. "Is it too tight?" I whispered.

"No," she replied, looking at me with suppressed fire in her eyes.

Suddenly I felt as if we were alone in the crowded courtyard. It was true. Her desire was for me, southern shepherd though I might be. Deep inside of me an answering fire burst into flame, and I caught her to me, bending my head to kiss her for the first time. Instantly her arms wrapped around my neck, pulling me close.

The roar of approval from the packed courtyard nearly shook the ground, and we broke apart, both our faces red with embarrassment! But even the king was laughing, and a blaze of pure joy went through me as I turned and led the way into the throne room for my wedding feast. I was a southern shepherd no longer. My God had made me Sar Dahveed Israel, Yahweh's warrior.

TAMAR BAT DAHVEED

There now, Dahveed has his reward, Sahrah Michal received the wish of her heart, and Hassar Jonathan can relax now that Balak is no longer influencing the king. See how Yahweh's plan has moved forward in spite of the obstacles that the Evil One threw in the way? Hassar Israel and Dahveed Israel are bound together for life, and Jonathan has taught him well and protected him from harm. The mashiah has learned much of what it is to be a king, of the responsibilities and practices of power, of what it means to lead men to war, to bring Yah's laws to them, and to govern them for the benefit of all. And Michal and Merab both have their heart's desires.

What was that, young geber? Ittai? He has gone his way, leaving Dahveed a little puzzled, but Yahweh must have had a very special reason for cementing these two lives together. Why would Yahweh want his mashiah to be connected to a Philistine? Perhaps only He knows the complete answer to that. Maybe it was for Ittai more than Dahveed, although Dahveed will benefit by the connection. That may be something that we will learn only when the Seed of Abraham comes to bring final justice to this land.

And Balak? Yes, he got away. But despite his fall, he did his work well, and it will not be forgotten.

Well, the second part of my story is done, and it is very late and time to go. So be careful now, as you touch the harp. See, there are the scratches from the brush when Shagay came to Dahveed in the forest. They have almost dis-

appeared because the wood has been polished so much. No, that's not the gouge from the king's spear when the demon took him the second time. That's at the bottom, between those two strings. The other was an arrow that nearly ended Dahveed's life. You can see the scorch mark close by it. And that's the dent from falling off the table the morning after Dahveed and Jonathan fought the demon.

Those funny little bumps? Well, those are very special. They come from my brother. There now, you've made me cry. Be sure you have all your things. Take some pomegranates, why don't you?

And shalom to you, young geberet. Come back again, for there's much more to tell! I haven't begun to tell of how Jonathan finds the steward of Tahat, how Dahveed meets up with Goliath's brothers, and the fight he and Malchi have with the lions, or how Mahesa repays his debt and Eliab saves the inheritance, and—and if you don't go on out the door, I'll keep you up all night!

Tamar bat Dahveed
Second year of Solomon
(968 B.C.)

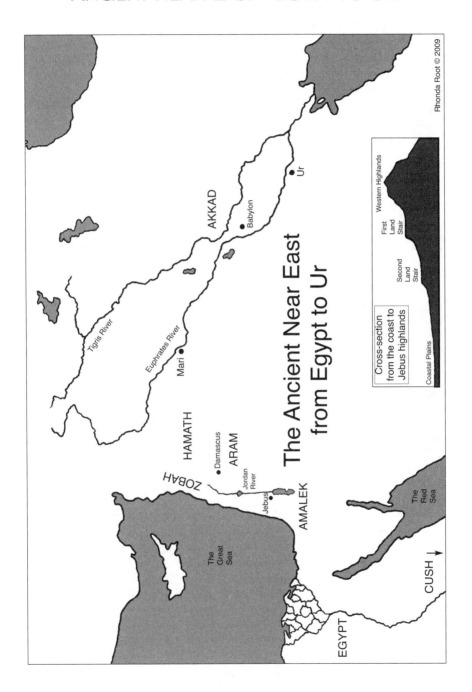

The Ancient Near East from Egypt to Ur

Rhonda Root © 2009

ISRAEL—DAN TO BEER-SHEBA

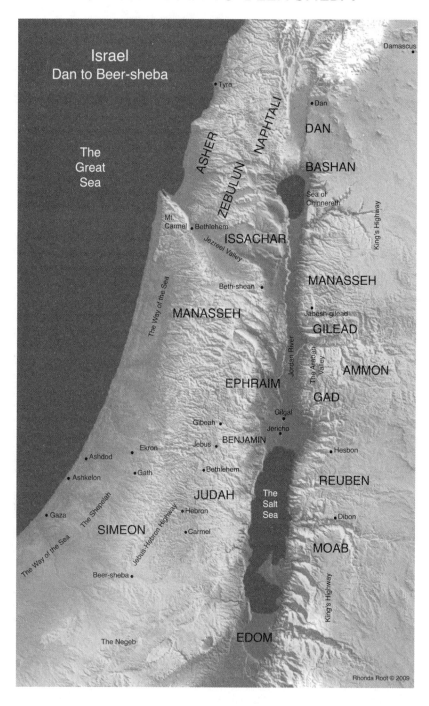

Israel
Dan to Beer-sheba

The
Great
Sea

Damascus

Tyre

Dan

DAN

ASHER

NAPHTALI

ZEBULUN

BASHAN

Sea of
Chinnereth

King's Highway

Mt.
Carmel Bethlehem

ISSACHAR

Jezreel Valley

The Way of the Sea

Beth-shean

MANASSEH

MANASSEH

Jabesh-gilead

GILEAD

Jordan River

The Arabah Valley

AMMON

EPHRAIM

GAD

Gilgal

Gibeah

Jericho

Jebus

BENJAMIN

Ekron

Ashdod

Hesbon

Ashkelon

Gath

Bethlehem

REUBEN

JUDAH

The
Salt
Sea

Dibon

The Shephelah

Hebron

Gaza

SIMEON

Carmel

Jebus-Hebron Highway

MOAB

The Way of the Sea

Beer-sheba

King's Highway

The Negeb

EDOM

Rhonda Root © 2009

422

CENTRAL ISRAEL—HEBRON TO MEHOLAH

CORE TRUTHS

LISA FOX

Crystal Skipper Press

CRYSTAL SKIPPER PRESS

CONTENTS

To my boys, Ryan and Aidan

No wish too small,

No dream too big

Introduction

Core Truth—it's the nebulous, quintessential 'something' that defines us as individuals. It guides our beliefs and decisions; it determines the trajectory of who we ultimately become.

Whether we like it or not.

Selflessness, selfishness, fear, and ambition.

All core truths.

Devotion to family. Love of money. Unwavering commitment to duty. Compassion toward humankind.

All core truths.

The characters in this collection confront hard truths. They challenge personal long-standing beliefs and question ideals society imposes upon them. They examine their own reality and the nature of the 'self.' They weigh goodness against justice, their own desires relative to others' expectations, the value of one versus the needs of the collective.

Sometimes their journey leads toward a rare and beautiful epiphany or resolution. But not every ending is happy.

It is my hope that as you enter the various worlds created in each of these tales, you will discover these characters' truths and consider how *you* would react if faced with the same circumstances and choices. I firmly believe that literature—whether it's speculative fiction or grounded in reality—not only gives us the opportunity to observe, but allows us to safely look within ourselves, perhaps consider our own core truths and find the drivers of our 'why.'

Your truth. I cannot wait to see it.

-Lisa Fox, April 2023

SOMETHING RARE AND BEAUTIFUL

THE OLD WOMAN SAT on a weathered park bench; a multi-colored shawl draped over her hunched shoulders. I watched as her gaze fixed on the crows gathered around her. They squawked and pecked about, flying off when they realized she had nothing to offer. She tugged her wrap, swaddled like a newborn longing for the womb.

Henry looked up at me from his digging. A pile of worms squiggled atop a fresh mound of dirt in the patchy grass. He stopped his play and pointed toward the bench.

"What's that, Daddy?"

"An Elderly. A special sort of being. Very rare."

Their kind existed in museum exhibits and history books only. I tried not to stare at the wrinkles etched into the Elderly's skin, patterned like tree bark, or at the way the hollows of her cheeks sank beneath

her defiant, protruding cheekbones. A halo of white hair, cloud-soft, framed her face. Through heavy lids and sparse lashes, her eyes twinkled, blue as a midday summer sky.

I'd never seen a creature more beautiful.

A curt breeze swiped dead leaves from the grass, lifting them in a crackling eddy that whirled toward the old woman. Dusk danced at the edges of the horizon. Yet she sat, immune to the fading sun, to the winds that taunted her, rocking to the cadence of her own quiet humming.

Henry scratched his head as he stared. Four parallel marks peeked out from beneath the collar of my son's standard-issue shirt. Glowing red through his pale skin, they ran adjacent to his carotid artery and just as deep, sustaining life in their pre-programmed allotment. Only five years old, Henry had a near-full lifeline. The dull heat of the one remaining mark on my neck reminded me I had but one decade left to raise Henry on my own.

I felt a familiar pinch in my gut. Worse than any hunger, it was the pang of absence. In those rare moments when I considered my mortality, I missed Adrienne the most. My wife expired far short of the forty years The Order allocated humans to live.

It was the amount of time deemed statistically sufficient to maximize our contributions to society's "greater good." All that was full and productive contained within a forty-year span. Time beyond that was superfluous as the body initiated its physical decline. A human's vulnerability to alterations in its cellular composition or to any number of pestilence outbreaks after the calculated peak period was expensive, the cost for life maintenance misaligned with any potential benefit.

"Can I talk to it?" Henry pointed at the woman, regarding her with wide green eyes. Like Adrienne's, they held a glimmer of promise in a tedious world.

"Her," I corrected, lowering Henry's hand. "Can you talk to *her*."

Henry scrunched up his face and tilted his head. "An Elderly is a person?"

I glanced over at the Elderly, who tugged her shawl closer as her body shuddered in the breeze. She didn't belong here. I wondered how she'd evaded The Order and survived on her own for as long as she had.

"She is a person, Henry. Like you and me, just..." I struggled for the word. "Malfunctioned."

Henry lowered his head, pushing his toe into the ground.

"Like Mommy."

Nodding, I rested my hand on Henry's shoulder.

"Like Mommy," I said. "But different."

The last time I saw Adrienne, we were finishing our evening Order-issued rations, laughing over the mundane wonder of our respective days, when she froze, the fork halfway to her lips. It crashed to the plate, and she was gone. I hadn't noticed the absence of her markings that night, but then again, I had neither been looking for them nor thinking about them. I was looking at *her,* thinking about how her laughter was sweeter than any birdsong and how blessed Henry was each night when his mother sang a lullaby.

My wife and the life I knew dissipated into the stale kitchen air, as if neither had existed. We were simply living our lives when her body self-destructed, erasing her from Henry's world when he was but a toddler, leaving me as my child's sole life guide.

I tried my best.

"Can I talk to it? To her? Please?" Henry looked up at me with hopeful eyes and a protruding lip. The same look he gave when his cookie ration wasn't enough to satisfy him.

The generation that preceded my parents endorsed The Order's edict: human beings were never intended to be a burden, youth shouldn't sacrifice their ambitions, livelihoods, and dreams for the sake of a generation incapable of productivity. They stood in line in a show of nationalism, unflinching as their own markings were implanted beneath their skin. They didn't question The Order, even as their own children were marked from the moment they entered this world; the tracks of a defined lifeline carved and embedded within each infant before government doctors cut the cord to liberate baby from mother.

Who was I to question their vision?

Yet this woman—this Elderly—defied the lifespan the Order granted, just as Adrienne had. On the day after Adrienne's expiration, an Agent had visited, citing our residence with a Level Three Programming Error—a premature halt of the markings' integral clock. Adrienne's death was deemed classified; I was never to speak of it, or of her, to anyone. But I told Henry everything I could about his mother, painting her in the vibrant hues that colored her life. Inconsistencies did not exist, according to The Order, but I knew differently. The

probability we'd randomly encounter another in the park on this day was incalculable.

"Please, Daddy?"

Heat teemed through my cheeks as an icy vulnerability crawled over me. Under The Order's edict, it was our duty as productive citizens to report any unusual or suspicious activity to the authorities. Defying that order was a punishable crime. I didn't want to think about the penalty for consorting with someone who wasn't supposed to exist.

"No, Henry, it's too dangerous." I scanned the sky for hovering drones or the telltale flash of surveillance devices hiding in the treetops.

"But the Elderly is little! She can't hurt us!" Henry said. "Besides, you said she was like Mommy."

"I said she'd malfunctioned like Mommy—"

"—And that makes her special. Because Mommy was special." Henry crossed his arms and pouted.

I glanced past my son toward the woods beyond and a memory of Adrienne beaming as she retrieved a small, grey kitten from beneath a pile of leaves. Despite my admonitions, she'd handed it to Henry, who squealed with delight as it squirmed in his arms. The Order forbade pets, viewing them as an unnecessary encumbrance. Yet, Adrienne kept the cat hidden and safe beneath our porch until the day it left us, shortly after she'd expired. Somehow, I think it knew she was gone, and it missed her almost as much as we did.

"Henry, do you know what serendipity means?"

"Seren-what?"

"Never mind. It's like when Mommy found our kitten in the woods. Do you remember?"

Henry shook his head. Again, I felt a twinge as I thought of Adrienne's smile when she snuggled the tiny forbidden creature to her cheek, and how Henry had reached his dimpled hand to touch it, to touch his mother.

The Order forbade such recklessness.

I held my breath. A shiver of lightheadedness consumed me, as if I were underwater, on the cusp of breaking through the surface. Neither Henry nor I would ever have an opportunity like this again.

"We'll go talk to the Elderly. But for just a minute."

Henry grinned, pumping his small fist in the air, which I caught and promptly lowered. "And only if she allows us to."

Henry let go of me and trotted toward the woman with sure and rapid steps. As we approached, I wondered if my own mother would have resembled this being, had we lived in a different time. I'd never said goodbye; Mother had faded in her sleep, the imprint in her rumpled sheets still warm when I'd discovered she was gone.

The Elderly looked up, gasping at us. She shrank into her shawl.

"Hi! I'm Henry." My son extended his hand.

Trembling, the woman glanced from Henry, to me, to Henry again.

"My Daddy says you're special."

The Elderly's expression relaxed; the tense wrinkles framing her eyes smoothed as her lips struggled for a smile. She released the grip on her shawl and reached out to Henry.

"Hello," she said. "I'm afraid your daddy's wrong. There's nothing special about me. I'm just a relic with a broken timer."

Henry and I knew all too well the heartbreak of malfunction. As the woman sat alone on that bench in a world that didn't want her, I supposed she did, too.

The Elderly's eyes widened as she regarded my son, his tousled blond hair, his bright eyes. Rumpled play clothes. Dirt embedded beneath his fingernails.

"But you, young man," she said. "*You're* remarkable."

"Re-mark. Ubble." Henry giggled. "What does that mean?"

"You're the first person to talk to me in four hundred thirty-seven days. Most folks passing by pretend I'm not here. They walk away when they see me. I think they're afraid of me. Or they're afraid of…" Her voice trailed as she looked up at me, both of us recognizing that, without Henry's intercession, I would have remained a silent observer, too. Or worse.

Henry frowned. "That's not very nice."

"No, it's not," I said.

"Why would people do that, Daddy?"

I rested my hand on Henry's shoulder, again glancing toward the sky and the trees. The longer we spoke to this woman, the greater the risk for us all.

"When people are afraid, they often do things that aren't nice," I said.

I thought about how The Order was born of "necessity" in the aftermath of the Five-Year Scourge, when scientific and financial resources were exhausted to preserve humanity's eldest and frailest from a plague that targeted them. With little left for the youth that powered the world, some say our society bled out and even died in those years. The Order's edicts supposedly revived and revitalized us, *marking* humankind with new hope.

"Besides," the Elderly said, "The Order prohibits engagement with people like me."

"Well, I think that's dumb," Henry said. "I'm not afraid."

Turning toward the woman, Henry cupped the Elderly's gnarled hand between his palms gently, as if holding a baby bird. I bowed my head, overcome by the empathy that flashed over my young child's face. "My Mommy had a broken timer, too, but she died when she was twenty-four," Henry said. "Her name was Adrienne—"

"Henry," I warned.

The woman glanced at me, eyes soft, eyebrows raised, as if sharing our secret.

"I'm so sorry about your mom, Henry," she said. "You must miss her terribly."

Henry nodded, blinking back tears.

"What's your name?" Henry asked.

"My name is Dorothy." She smiled. "Funny, I can't remember the last time I said that. My friends used to call me Dot."

"It's nice to meet you, Dorothy," Henry said.

"Dot," she corrected.

"Why are you here all by yourself? Don't you have a family?"

Dot fidgeted with her wrapping and drew in a ragged breath. I flinched as I watched the flashing red pulse beneath her sagging skin. Noticing my stare, Dot rested her hand against her neck, massaging it. The flashing stopped. The remnants of her marking faded in and out, her one line as faint as an errant scratch. She didn't have much longer.

"They moved on a long time ago, once I—" She paused, and her eyes changed; pupils dilated, black encroaching over blue, sure as night consumes day. "They're probably long expired by now."

Coughs exploded from deep within Dot's chest. Spasms wracked her body, leaving her gasping. She covered her mouth, her eyes bulging. Before I could help her, Henry reached out and patted her back, tapping until the choking subsided and Dot regained color.

"Today, we can be your family," Henry said.

"I'd like that," Dot said, her voice raspy.

Dot's smile warped into a grimace. She pitched forward, her body stiffening.

"Daddy!" Henry screamed.

I grabbed Dot's shoulders to stop her fall; her frame was nothing but brittle bones. As Henry began to cry, Dot looked up. Trembling, she wiped my child's tears.

"You have given me a gift, Henry, so beautiful and rare." Dot smiled at us. "I'm not alone, now."

Henry and I watched in wonder as the woman's marking dissipated into her skin, time ultimately devouring the last vestige of her lifeline. Its dull glow diminished, absorbed like the light in her eyes, the glimmer of her existence eclipsed by the vacancy of death. Her face turned grey as ash; the shadow crept across her body with the stealth of a thief, her form flashing and pixelating in and out of the night until nothing remained of her but a pile of tattered clothing.

We stood for a moment, frozen. Henry stared at the empty bench, his eyes pooling with tears. I held my breath, waiting, wondering if The Order had taken the old woman, or if it was some cruel trick of timing that we happened to be standing here at the same moment her malfunctioning markings finally aligned to their intended purpose.

Perhaps Dot had just been waiting for something—someone—to see her. To validate that she existed, that she mattered, outrunning the destiny The Order had dictated for her, and for us all. It was the ultimate act of defiance, and somehow, I loved her for it.

I'd never known a time before The Order. My mother and father rarely spoke of their own parents, revealing no knowledge of the world as it once was. I'd heard forbidden terms such as *grandma, grandpa,* and *senior citizen* passed only in whispers, and my childhood curiosity

about such ideas was met with a stern glance and a firm hand. The Elderly, The Infirm—they were simply an enemy who sucked the marrow from bones that framed a world I was born into but never knew. According to The Order, the markings saved us from ourselves—once our final line faded, so did we, in a cloud of self-destruction such that even in death, we would not be a burden.

I glanced toward the trees and the darkening sky, cognizant of my posture—crouching over Henry, perhaps even cowering, as I waited for The Order to materialize. The silence hinted toward our safety, however fleeting, and I breathed in deep, pulling my son to me. Henry buried his face into my chest, my shirt dampened by his sniffling. It would have been safer for both of us if we had allowed the old woman to stay a mysterious relic, a lonely thing mingled with the crooked, weathered trees that populated the park.

"I'm sorry you had to see that, Henry," I said. "But we should go now."

Dot's shawl lay atop her pile of clothing, fallen like the last stubborn leaf from an oak tree in autumn. Reds and yellows and blues intersected in a repetition that reminded me of the certainty of days, of hours. Of years. Yet, it was the slight flaws that commanded my gaze—an errant stitch. A pilling in the fabric. Color that had faded with time and wear. I wondered if Dot had crafted that shawl with her own hands, and how long it took her to weave simple fabric into a complex and cohesive whole. As her knitting needles clacked against each other and her mind and hands busied themselves with her creation, did she offer a fleeting thought to her markings, to the time she knew remained, or the time that lingered in question? Undeserved, by The Order's standards, but nothing less than a miracle.

Henry picked up the shawl and hugged it close. "I wish we'd had more time to talk to her. She was a nice lady."

He rolled the soft yarn between his fingers, much as he did when he was a smaller boy, comforted by the feel of the blanket Adrienne draped over him as he drifted off to sleep each night.

"She was nice," I whispered, still thinking of Adrienne. The best.

"I won't forget her," Henry said. "Ever."

A soft breeze ruffled Henry's hair. As his curls shone under the street-lamp, I wondered how long it would take before this old woman faded out of Henry's consciousness. How much Henry remembered of his mother, outside of the portrait I'd painted. Could he still see Adrienne's face when he closed his eyes at night? Or did Adrienne exist in flashes, her features as hazy as a dream?

I saw Adrienne's eyes in every sunrise, the fire of her red hair in every desperate sunset. I heard her voice in the song of the wood thrush perched on the sycamore tree outside our bedroom window, hopeful yet melancholy, hidden deep within the lush foliage. How I wished Henry could remember Adrienne's laughter, as rich and melodious as the music we'd danced to, the three of us, barefoot in the kitchen, our small family relishing the life we'd been promised.

But a child's memory is as fragile as a fallen leaf crunching into dust.

I kissed the top of Henry's head, just as Adrienne had, heavy with the realization that he'd never know just how much his mother loved him.

"Dot is part of the night now," I said. "Just like Mommy."

"Just like Mommy."

I'd never questioned The Order. I feared it. I accepted it. It was the only life I knew. Yet, a new feeling surged over me, sure as the churning night wind that prickled my skin. I felt larger, my breaths deeper, each step firmer than the last. It was something like change.

Something like hope.

Although The Order limited the number of days we spent walking the Earth, they could never ration our ability to love. To show compassion for other humans.

Henry wrapped the shawl around his shoulders, a testament to the stranger who defied the certainty of life programmed within us all. I thought of Adrienne, and how a deviation from certainty led to the anomaly of her passing.

I glanced down at my son, who scuffed his shoes and yawned as we marched on. Henry would not realize the magnitude of the day's encounter until he was older—the enormity of the risk we took, and our own act of defiance.

Perhaps it would be the first of many.

For nothing was guaranteed, even when it was.

DON'T BLINK

THE BACKPACK STRAPS DIG an angry ridge into my sunburned shoulders; I glow red as a chili pepper in the August heat. In my haste to apply sunscreen to your baby-soft skin (through your squirming and your screaming and your kicking), I'd neglected to address my own needs, and now, my suffering radiates, palpable. I'm weighted down by sippy cups and snacks, diapers, wipes, and creams, extra clothes and a gazillion new toys—plushes and spinning flashlights and plastic poseable animals, both real and imagined, current and extinct.

Of course, I'd obliged each of your gift shop demands—partially to quiet you, but mostly to quell the guilt of being a mom who works too many hours, a mom who plays hard at the zoo to compensate for lost time.

Work hard, play hard. I wear that mantra like some goddamn badge of honor, so programmed to "lean in" that I'm teetering on the cusp of falling over.

Our leisurely walk through the County Zoo is anything but. The wheels of your stroller skid on the gravel path; your 35-pounds feel more like seventy, as if I'm pushing a wheelbarrow full of concrete up a slippery hill. Perspiration oozes from my back and sticks to me like the wet papier mâché from your latest daycare project.

"Daddy getting popsicles?" you ask. Your tiny hands grasp a toy bear and a toy robot, plastic clicking on plastic in an epic, impossible battle.

Where is Todd? What could be taking him so long?

"Soon, buddy. Daddy will be here soon with your popsicle."

We stop at an empty bench, and I squirm myself out of the drenched backpack.

"Blue! Blue popsicle!" you sing.

You'd asked him for red—loudly. Unequivocally. Fearing a tantrum that would terrify both human and animal alike, I dial my husband's cell.

No answer.

Of course. He's probably checking his stocks, or his fantasy baseball stats. Why would he use a phone as a phone?

"Daddy will get whatever they have. Remember, you get what you get—"

I turn your stroller toward me. Before I can finish my sentence, I notice your left foot. Bare. Without your Spiderman sandal.

... And you don't get upset.

15

"Aw, bud, you lost your shoe. We just bought those!"

I feel the sigh rise from my core; a lone bubble of oxygen pushed from the depths, reminding me to breathe.

Exhale.

You stop playing, still gripping your toys, and glance up at me, the twinkle in your big blue eyes a bastion of mischief. Shrugging your shoulders, you giggle, and I can't help but smile, too. This... this is the easy part of parenthood. I tickle your belly; you wriggle beneath my fingertips, your laughter a melody played at my touch. I forget about shoes and ice pops, sweat and sunburn, and in that moment, it's just you and me swallowing a moment of joy with a gusto that makes our eyes water.

"Missing something?" An old woman shuffles toward us, cane in one hand, your sandal in the other. I wipe the tears from my cheeks and offer her a smile as you resume playing.

"Oh! He must have dropped it as we were walking."

Wistful, the woman glances from you to me as she offers your shoe. Her gaze settles over us, soft as fleece in winter, yet with a depth so familiar it's as if I'm staring into a mirror.

"Don't blink," she says, resting her cold palm on my blazing shoulder. I wince at her touch, at once comforting and jarring, and can't help but notice the way her gold wedding band cinches the loose skin of her knobby fingers. Her hand is liver-spotted, its tremor like an ancient tree limb disturbed by a scampering squirrel.

"Thank you," I reply. Without another word, she turns from us. Her heavy footfalls crunch in the gravel path; a pained effort plagues every step as she ambles toward the zoo's exit. I listen and I stare until a quiet distance separates us, and the old woman vanishes.

I secure your errant shoe and stand, my legs wobbly and slick in the afternoon sun. A tingle of cold heat stretches from my eyebrows up to my hairline, setting my temples aflutter as the odd summer shiver tugs across my head like a snug cap.

"Looks like we're back in business."

I steady myself on your stroller; you gaze at me with those wide eyes and smile.

"Mommy."

"Let's go look at the bears while we wait for Daddy."

"Your favorite," you say, pronouncing the word as *fayvwit*.

Once again, I secure the bag to my back and push us forward, leaning on the stroller's handles for support. From a distance, I see a momma bear skulk through the tall grass of the American Brown Bear exhibit, tips of green brushing her fur. Her baby pushes its nose against her back legs as they walk together, in step and slow, always touching, always near.

As we approach them, the summer haze shimmers ahead, the atmosphere around us wavering and blurred as if rising from a grill. I blink, hard, and step through the distortion, mother bear and baby both dark brushstrokes on an impressionist canvas, and glance down as your stroller, and you, are sucked into the warped summer afternoon air...

17

... and my feet crunch decaying leaves as a curt autumn breeze slaps the gooseflesh up through my skin. I shiver in my jeans and tee shirt, tug at the sweatshirt tied around my waist and pull it over my head, huddling inside it.

Four brown bears trudge through the leaves in the exhibit ahead, side by side at first and then branching out—one ambling toward a rock enclosure, one toward a grassy knoll at the far end. Still another lopes toward the observers who are clad in jackets and sweaters and hats. The crowds are sparse, even for a chilly day and I can't help but wonder why surgical masks cover some of the children's faces. Their expressions linger, empty yet suspicious, as if expecting some predator to sidle over them at any moment and suck away their joy.

And the fourth bear, the largest, she sits, staring at me—into me—with big, sad eyes, as if she knows something, understands something I have yet to comprehend. She approaches the fence of her enclosure. It's adorned with a sign bearing a black-and-white square that looks like an inaccessible television channel from my youth; all static and scramble with the words "Scan Here for More Information" below it.

More information would be useful right about now. I approach the sign, scrutinizing the box. Is there some hidden code within the black and white maze of squares? Words embedded in the pattern like some sort of surrealist painting?

I blink, hard.

"Mom, you almost done looking at those dumb bears?" A male voice calls from the bench behind me, deep and sonorous. The blue-eyed teenager, straddling the gap between boy and man, sits sprawled, gan-

gly legs in athletic pants and expensive sneakers. Floppy blond hair falls over wide blue eyes—those eyes, those eyes I'd know anywhere! White plastic plugs both ears, dangling over the lobes like cheap and ill-placed earrings. He stares at the phone in his hand, tapping rapidly on the screen with both thumbs.

"Where's Dad with that soda?" he asks.

You ask.

"They better have Coke products. Anything else is ass."

I open my mouth to respond, then close it again. Parched, I swallow down the autumn air, as if the simple act of gulping will somehow explain this bizarre reality I've found myself in.

You stand, towering a head taller than I am.

"Come on, Shorty," you say, and ruffle my hair. "Let's go find Dad." A wisp of gray falls over my forehead, feather-soft, into my eyes, the white strands like ash. You reach for the backpack on the bench and hand it to me, gravity pulling the bag into a pile of waiting leaves. In that moment, I struggle to hold the weight of teenage angst, misplaced friendships and blossoming acne and the enticement to engage in forbidden tasks, college visits and fear about a future that shimmers on the horizon, blurred in some long-forgotten heat haze.

I glance over at the bear enclosure and the mother bear sits watching me, her shoulders slumped as if in a permanent sigh. The breeze awakens and stirs, emerging from hibernation. It lifts the decaying leaves from the ground, twisting and swirling them until they are nothing but dust that whistles in a cloud around me. The particles flick like

tiny pinpricks against my eyes. I blink hard to fend off their assault, reach my arms out, blinded, and step forward through the dust, my feet crunching into gravel and dead leaves...

... and I step down into a plush floor, my hands gripping a metal armrest as I settle into a chair, a pillow propped against my back. Shock-white, fluorescent lights blur with the white walls and carpet and the attire of the man wearing white scrubs and a surgical mask who shines a bright light into my eyes.

"Vitals look good," the man says. He pats my arm with a soft, beefy hand that warms my chilled skin. I wince at his touch, at once comforting and jarring.

You exhale the breath you'd been holding inside. "Thank you, Dr. Birch. Always a relief."

"It's safe to take her wherever she wants to go."

The doctor turns on his heel and walks across the vast room, past a wall with a floor-to-ceiling shaded window. He tends to the patients slumping in wheelchairs—young and old—their loved ones hovering like angels behind them. I glance down at my hands now resting in my lap, knobby and wrinkled fingers intertwined like ancient tree limbs yearning for a connection. My body tremors, as if disturbed by a scampering dream, of places and people and things long forgotten, yet aching for remembrance.

"What do you want to see today, Mama?" You lean in, blue eyes soft yet constrained by the crow's feet cinching the edges of your eyelids. I'd know those eyes anywhere, in any time, that twinkle a bastion of mischief... now sprinkled with sadness.

"Where's Daddy?" I cough. My voice is gravel and crunched leaves and dry summer heat.

You glance at the floor. "You know Daddy's long gone, Mama."

"Gone?"

What could be taking Todd so long? Was it a red popsicle or blue that you'd wanted? A Pepsi or a Coke? I squeezed my eyes shut. Had he returned? Had he gotten it right?

The children, they'd worn masks, their expressions empty, joy scrambled and hidden within some bizarre pattern painted on a sign in a zoo.

You crouch next to me, so close now our faces nearly touch.

"Plague," you whisper, exhaustion weighing in your voice. Your eyes dart past me, wild and suspicious, scanning the room. "Not many of our kind left. You and me, we're survivors. It's why we're here, Mama. It's why they..."

Your voice trails off and I swallow my grief down, hard, as if the simple act of gulping will somehow explain this bizarre reality where the world is a bright white room and my son is a man with graying hair at his temples and I cannot recall my husband's death—how he got sick, when they all got sick and disappeared...

You stand and turn my wheelchair toward you, and I notice my left foot. Bare and cold, without my white slipper. I point toward it, wordless, and feel a sigh rise from my core; glass shards pushed from the depths of my lungs.

21

It hurts to breathe.

You slip the plush sandal over my foot. Bones pop through my skin like roots in a forest, my veins ancient rivers coursing through me.

"Looks like we're back in business," you say, smiling.

The masked doctor—Dr. Birch—begins raising the giant shade. "Destination coordinates locked," he says. "Commencing in five, four, three..."

The doctor's words fade as a wistful smile stiffens over your features. "Do you want to see the bears, Mama?" Your voice catches. "They are always your favorite."

An echo. My *fayvwit*.

You place a round device into my hands and press a red button on its side. The holographic image of a brown bear bursts from its center; a mama bear sitting, staring with big, sad eyes, as if she knows something, understands something I have yet to comprehend. Around the room, others hold similar devices, projecting hot air balloons, rainbows, mountains, flowerbeds, puppies—filling the open space with color, with images of open memory.

And as the shade raises, a lab-coated crowd lines up in front of the large picture window, observing us from outside. Their expressions are identical and vacant, like mannequins; all maintain an equal height and build, the same shine reflects off matching bald heads. Their eyes flicker red, then green, amber and blue, in a syncopated pulse, until an opaque sheen drops over them.

"They're sleeping?" I ask.

"They're watching." You shake your head. "They're always watching."

White flakes fall from the sky and settle on the watchers' shoulders, ignored, unnoticed.

"It's snowing."

"A simulation," you reply.

And I remember a toy bear and a toy robot in an epic, impossible battle. The scorch of summer crumbling into the bitter breeze of fall. Children growing and aging, time obscured in the flutter of an eyelash. Disease. Death. Particles of humanity burning, burning until nothing remains but memory.

Red, radiating, palpable.

"Watch the bear, Mama. It'll make you happy." You gesture toward the hologram; the bear's shoulders slump, its massive brown form soft, its gaze connecting me to someplace long ago, a time that is far away, and I stare and stare and stare with a gusto that makes my eyes water. I turn toward you; you wipe tears from your cheek, and I rest my palm on your face, baby-soft and sticky like wet papier mâché and popsicles, spilled colas and the sweet sweat of summertime.

I can't help but notice the way my gold wedding band cinches the loose skin of my knobby fingers.

"Don't blink, Mama," you say, "or the image will be lost."

"Don't blink," the old woman whispers.

To Lure Gavin Back Home

THE NORTH WIND ROLLED over the snow-covered mountain caps and silvery clouds dotted the sky like errant balloons, floating. Helene pulled her parka closer; she raised her scarf over her cheeks to prevent the tears from freezing.

She looked down into the jagged hole she'd cut in the crust of the lake. Concealed under a shell of ice, the water lay still and dark as a grave. But Helene knew that frigid dormancy was an illusion, and life flourished far beneath the surface, pulsing with a light unseen.

With heavily gloved hands, she reached into her bucket to bait the line on her fishing pole. She'd fashioned the rod from Gavin's pee-wee lacrosse stick; the wire from his Xbox formed the line. For bait, she'd chosen his favorite Matchbox car, the red Corvette he'd always carried in his pocket for good luck.

Maybe this will be the one, she thought. The one that will bring him back.

It was early summer when Gavin had vanished, the kind of afternoon best captured in the cicada's song, when insect voices shimmer bright as sunlit ripples over water. She was sitting on the deck of their lake house, pouring lemonade for Gavin and his friends when she heard the shrieking. She bolted up, gaping at Gavin's friends standing at the edge of the lake.

They pointed and shouted his name, their cries visceral and raw.

An oily film rose from the center of the water, pulsing steady as a heartbeat. From its core, black tendrils branched out, reaching like jagged tentacles toward the shoreline. The film bubbled and boiled into a murky, steaming mist; and as quickly as it had appeared, it dissipated in a swift summer breeze.

Then, all was still.

Helene tried to tell the police what she saw. There was something alive in that lake and it had taken her son. Stone-faced, her husband Larry had draped a blanket over her shoulders. Through whispers, sounds coalesced into words.

Denial. Shock. Drowning.

Twenty-four hours after Gavin disappeared, the divers searching for him shifted their focus from rescue to recovery. It seemed so easy for these men to reach this level of routine finality, one moment, looking for the living and the next, seeking out the dead.

Seasons passed and Gavin was still lost. But without a body, she had hope.

Her family insisted on a funeral, but Helene refused to go. What good would it do to stare at an empty box, or listen to the droning platitudes of well-wishers, telling her he was in a better place?

Gavin wasn't in a better place. He was in a different place. Wherever he was in that lake, she was going to lure her son back to the surface; let him know she was waiting for him to come home. Someone—some *thing*—held him there; of that she was convinced.

Not long after Gavin disappeared, so did Helene's marriage. At first, Larry humored her, taking her out by rowboat every night before sunset to say goodnight to their only child. As the leaves changed and evenings fell sooner, he said it was time to move on. Spotting a realtor's business card on the kitchen countertop, Helene concurred. She packed Larry's suitcase and shut the door.

One by one, her friends drifted away. They'd tired of her talk of creatures, of underwater worlds. They said Gavin was dead.

Helene didn't care what anyone thought.

Shivering, Helene wrapped the cord around the Matchbox car and pulled it tight, double knotting just like she'd taught her son so many years ago. She lowered the toy into the water; after only a few feet, she could no longer see the metal reflecting in the winter sunlight.

She swirled the line in the water, imagining the start of a small current brushing against Gavin's skin, soft and subtle as her kiss. How he would look up from his underwater task, his eyes fixed on the shiny relic, a beacon through the depths of his captivity. Maybe this toy would give him the courage to break away from whatever held him, when so many other trinkets hadn't.

Helene wondered what Gavin did with his days. She hoped he was happy and that his captor kept him busy. Gavin fidgeted when he was bored; she feared they'd tire of his whining, just as Larry had. Surely the creature must have had its reasons for selecting him and not one of the other boys. Gavin was a straight-A student, as clever and witty as he was kind-hearted. And he was an obedient son who never complained about chores or homework, the type of boy who always said, "I love you," even with friends nearby.

Helene peered into the depths. It was time for him to come home.

"Gavin? Can you hear me? Gavin?"

All was silent, save for the wind skating over the ice.

The frigid air tugged tears from Helene's eyes. She was freezing, so tired of being cold. She never should have let Gavin swim in the water without her, never should have allowed herself to be swayed by his nine-year old bravado. Lemonade could have waited until the boys were safely seated up on the deck, teeth chattering and wrapped in towels, welcoming the sun's warmth.

And then, a tugging from below. Helene gasped as the line pulled taut and the pole arched. An inky substance filtered through the surface; the water undulated and bubbled as she looked down through the rising mist.

"Gavin!"

The ice dissipated beneath her and she plunged into the frosty water, grasping tight to the pole. Head-first, she was pulled into the depths, ensconced in the darkness that cocooned her.

And then she saw it, the tiny beacon. The red Matchbox car—in Gavin's hand.

"This is what I wanted," he said. "It's good luck. Right, Mom?"

Smiling the same gap-toothed smile Helene saw only in her dreams, Gavin extended his hand. And together, they swam.

DARE I

DARE I DEFY THE teachings of the ancient ones, whose lips first drank from the font of darkness?

The sun casts vengeance upon the living dead.

With one gaze upon the forbidden light, we would crumble to ash.

Like Lot's wife, turned to a pillar of salt.

I stand at the precipice where twilight meets dawn.

Tide kisses the tips of my shoes; leather soles imprint the damp sands of the shoreline.

I long to be like Guggenheim, in his finest dress, defying death on a ship unsinkable.

For in the uncertainty of his final hour of life, or his first hour of hope, he prepared to waltz.

I, too, don topcoat and tails, leased furtively; retrieved after-hours.

Dressed for the funeral of my interminable night, or the baptism of my rebirth.

I tire of the stars; the ubiquitous moon whose light deflects from my face, leaving my skin cold, rigid as a corpse. I long to dance in the warmth of illicit daylight, swath myself in the vivid palette of color that exists only in the waking world.

Lethal, the ancient ones said.

My trepidation blind, I'd abided by their truth. Until now.

Until...

A sliver of sun crowns at the horizon like the head of a newborn babe.

My eyes sting with tears unshed for centuries; the glare of daybreak both beautiful and agonizing.

My skin prickles as rays of gold thaw the dismal cloak enshrouding me.

Shun sunlight. Fear its wrath.

Dare I defy?

Dare I...

WORMS

*D*RAW THE CURTAINS, YOU *idiot. They see you, and you're done.*

I tug at the dark fabric. Metal hooks scrape against the rod. I wince. The panel edges refuse to meet; a thin line of light glows between them. I squeeze the curtains together as hard as I can.

Get the thumbtacks!

Yes, yes, thumbtacks should do. I grab a handful; the points prick at my palms. I push the pins through the cloth, but the light persists.

Something stronger... Duct tape. Hurry!

I yank it from the roll, ripping hard and fast.

They'll hear you, stupid. Can't do anything right.

"I'm trying!" I mutter.

I slap the tape over the seam. I secure the corners.

I breathe.

The only light remaining is the glow from my television.

The Watchers can't see you when it's dark, Michael.

The newscaster on screen winks at me. Two more layers of cellophane over the picture tube should do.

"Can't see me now."

Not today. There's someplace I need to go.

The invitation, addressed to me personally from Dr. Martin Weiss, Director of the Centers for Disease Control, leans against the microscope on my desk. I place the card atop a stack of binders, thicker than the Encyclopedia of Microbiology, that hold three years' worth of notes and observations. I stuff the pile, along with my dissertation, into a white kitchen bag. I place that bag into another, and another, until there are three layers of plastic protecting my work.

Today, I need to tell them.

They need to know about the worms.

Worms that first appeared as I was live streaming a performance of the New York Philharmonic in the University's main lab. I'd been examining samples of white blood cells under a microscope, and the worms splashed down on my specimen like a rainstorm from a cloudless sky. They writhed across the slide, opened their mouths, and devoured the blood cells until nothing remained.

"Call NBC! ABC!" I'd shouted. "The CDC! The FCC! I'm on to something big!"

But my professors and my peers weren't interested in hearing about the worms.

Neither was my sister, Deidre.

Deidre hates you.

I'd tried to warn her the night I saw the skin on her daughter's hand undulating, when a spark from Allison's cell phone leapt to her flesh and pushed, needle-like, into the veins on her wrist. As quickly as this explosion ignited, it quieted, a reverse big bang that led to nothingness, save for the worms writhing beneath her skin.

Deidre hadn't seen the spark. Allison said she felt nothing. They gave me a funny look and Deidre sent me to my room. She wanted to call Dr. Atkins in private.

"Stay away from Allison," she'd said. "I mean it."

But I couldn't. I needed to protect her.

That night, while my niece slept, I scraped off just enough cells from her hand to examine under my microscope; just enough to try cutting the heads off those worms before they began devouring her immune system.

Allison screamed.

I was just trying to help.

They hate you.

Deidre would only let me stay if I agreed to let Dr. Atkins inject me with his mind-numbing poison.

She didn't want to hear any more about the worms.

So, I waited. Stayed quiet. Cooperative. I'd even gotten a part-time job at the grocery store. In time, Deidre let me stop the injections and restart an oral treatment regimen for being so compliant. I'm not a fool; I know what they're trying to do.

And it's easy to hide my pills, especially now that Deidre is distracted with Allison getting sick. They say it's pneumonia. Again. But I know better.

The worms are eating her lungs.

Time to go, Michael. The Watchers are near.

I SIT ON A bench in the middle of 30th Street Station and lean my head back. Hundreds of tiles hang from the ceiling; I've already counted two hundred and seventy-five. As I focus on counting, the squares merge and shift until they take the shape of a giant chessboard.

Chess. It's a lot like science—complex, analytical, with clear cause and effect.

The pieces materialize above me and invisible chess masters make their moves: white pawn to F4; black to E6. White hesitates; pawn inches to G4. The King stands exposed, his heart a thrumming, bloody mass.

A Fool's Mate. The consequence of an ill-formed plan.

Be prepared, Michael. They're everywhere.

Cackling, Black Queen marches to H4. The Knight whinnies; Queen pounces. She rips the White King in two. His remains fall into a ball of flame.

I fling my arms over my head, bracing for impact.

The station quakes as the King crashes through a newsstand. Magazines fly like ravens. The floor cracks open, swallowing it all, and closes just as quickly, as if it were never there.

I blink.

The newsstand has arisen, intact; the magazines dormant, flightless birds.

"Did you see that?"

No one answers.

Dr. Atkins said I might see things that others don't. But isn't that the nature of science?

Science. The plastic bag crackles as I slide my hand inside. My fingers rest on the invitation to a meeting of the greatest minds in the nation. And how clever of Dr. Weiss to pick Georgetown! He must have figured it would be an easy trip for me to take from Philly. Two hours by train, a route I'd always remember, regardless of any poison Dr. Atkins pumped into my veins or shoved down my throat.

Their eyes, Michael. Watchers are everywhere.

I pull my hand from the bag and squeeze the opening shut; glance left, right, and left again.

So many people here, walking by like zombies held captive by their glowing screens. I cringe as the electromagnetic vines sprout from their phones and wrap around their wrists—strangling limbs, pulsing with life as the worms push through and wriggle into their waiting hosts.

I smell the death oozing from their pores when the tiny infiltrators take root, and watch the black shroud fall over their faces, the pigment sucked from irises of brown and blue, reducing them to the color of ash.

But the green-eyed, they are safe.

No one is safe, Michael.

The convergence of genes OCA2, TYRP1, and ALC42A5 and their related mutations that lead to green eye pigmentation blocks the worms from passing through. We've come a long way from the days of the Punnett Square, old science that endeavored to simplify far more complex phenomena to the uneducated.

Nothing is simple anymore. They need to know.

CLACKETY-CLACKETY-CLACKETY-CLACK.

My organs jiggle as the train makes its way to Union Station. My stomach shimmies and my liver bounces with each bump over the aging rails. I lean forward, cradling the bag, to make myself smaller and lessen the impact of this rocking train on my body.

Less than an hour until I reach the city.

Less than an hour until Dr. Weiss tips his hat to welcome me into his counsel, until his eyes widen and he grasps my hand, awed by the implications of my discovery.

Together, we'll save lives.

Perhaps we'll save Allison's life.

Then Deidre will believe me when I tell her there's nothing wrong with me. She'll come to see, too, that my scientific vision is a gift.

I'm like the great Ignaz Semmelweis, the first to see how bacteria travel among human hosts under unsanitary conditions. They thought he was seeing things, too. So many people dying, needlessly, when all they had to do was listen to science. No one wanted to hear about the microscopic killers he'd found. Just as Deidre doesn't want to hear about the worms wriggling through invisible wires in the sky.

So, the Watchers silenced Dr. Semmelweis. Locked him away.

You can't let them stop you, Michael.

"Baaaltimore Stay-tion!"

As the train rolls to a halt, I push on my belly to move my organs back into their proper positions. The conductor marches down the aisle;

his footsteps rattle the car. I pull my bag close and lower my head, throwing a quick glance in his direction. He takes my ticket off the seatback and frowns. His green eyes bore into me from beneath thick eyebrows that wriggle like caterpillars.

Like worms.

"Next stop, D.C." He leans in and clips a hole in the ticket, shoving it just beneath my nose.

I squeeze my eyes tight and pull my knees up to my throat. I hold my breath. One Mississippi. Two Mississippi. Three Mississippi. If I make myself invisible, maybe he'll go away. The oxygen pushes against my lungs like a prisoner fighting his restraints.

Man up or Atkins'll bring his chains again. Shoot you up with more poison.

Just as the numbness hits my brain, my breath explodes from me. I suck the air in to retrieve any lung particles that may have escaped in my outburst. The Watchers may be monitoring the air for my DNA.

They're everywhere, Michael.

I open my eyes. The conductor is gone. In his place stands a harried woman carrying multiple bags and a small, snot-ridden child. She plops down next to me. I lean toward the window and cross my legs, inching away from her.

She settles the child into her lap and hands over a tablet. The child taps on the screen, opening a portal to the screeching singsong of the ABCs. I glance over, waiting for the tendrils to push through the device like a hatching seedling. But there's nothing. And I look closer.

The child has green eyes.

The mother turns toward me, her eyes wide.

Brown eyes—save her, Michael!

"Are you okay, sir?"

Social convention dictates that I answer, but what if she's a Watcher?

Careful... you'll ruin everything.

"Yes, yes. I'm fine. Fine as wine."

She nods and adjusts the child on her lap, jostling the device closer to me. I lean toward the window to avoid its reach and bring my hand up to shield my eyes from the glowing screen.

"Traveling for business or pleasure?"

Trick question.

I swallow hard.

"Business. Risky Business. Like the movie." I squint as I stare at her. Could she be one of them? I decide to test her. "Where are you going? I'm off to D.C. Off to see the wizard."

She turns away, quiet. The child yelps; the woman leans into the girl and gathers her bags.

This woman's days are numbered. I can smell it.

"Two percent of the U.S. population have green eyes," I tell her.

"What?" She pulls the child's tablet from her hand and shoves it into a bag.

"The girl. Green eyes keep her safe. Not out. Umpire's call is final."

She stands, bags swinging and child whimpering.

"You take care, sir." The woman hustles down the aisle; her arms scrape against the seats, leaving worm-castings behind.

Stay vigilant.

Clackety-clackety-clackety-clack.

The train rolls down the track.

M Y LUNGS BURN FROM the pink-tinged oxygen that has settled with dusk over the Georgetown campus. Lifted by the wind, I bound up the familiar steps of the Pre-Clinical Science Building. My hands sweat against the plastic as I clutch the bag close to my chest. The shield remains intact, though the top layer has been compromised.

Stupid, stupid fool.

That Watcher in Union Station, disguised as a vagrant, had almost ruined everything when he'd reached for my bag. What a trickster, begging me for change, saying he hadn't eaten in days. But I'd showed him the true meaning of Newton's Third Law of Motion: every action has an equal but opposite reaction. How he'd howled when I'd kicked

in his kneecap and it broke in two! Just like the body of the chessboard King when it fell through the ground.

The Watchers are everywhere, Michael.

The crowd presses toward the doorway of the lecture hall, crashing into each other like oversized atoms. I rummage through the bag for the invitation, careful to pull the drawstrings. The Suit standing in the doorframe mustn't see.

I grab the glossy paper and slide it from the bag.

Georgetown Alums: Exploring the Roots of Cancer.

"I need a seat. Up close. Up close and personal. I have a personal invitation."

I point to the card that Dr. Weiss had sent me. My hand tingles. Sweat oozes through my palms.

"It's an honor to be here," I whisper.

The Suit taps my arm. "Did you say something?"

Don't trust him, Michael.

"He's expecting me. Dr. Weiss. The Wise."

The Suit chuckles.

"Dr. Weiss is wise all right." He flicks a glance at my bag. A fissure cracks in the space between his sclera and his eyelid; the viscous fluid ripples, worms squishing and writhing toward his iris. "May I check your bag?" The suit reaches out.

I shake my head. "No."

I brush past him and bolt down the aisle, pushing my way to the middle of the second row, the crowd on either side a shield. Eyes squeezed tight, I fall into the seat, draw up my knees, and hold my breath. The Suit can't find me if I'm invisible.

A torrent of applause rains around me. I feel its heat splatter against my skin. The cacophony forces my eyes open. I breathe in the friction of hundreds of clapping hands.

Dr. Martin Weiss appears on stage, waving a warm, capable hand above his head. He brings his arm down, curling his fingers into a fist, and extends his index finger toward me. It stretches over the crowd, shining a spotlight on my face.

"Welcome," he says.

I slide the evidence from my bag. My dissertation. Words leap from the page and hover like a glowing marquee: **The Effects of Wireless Transmissions on Healthy White Blood Cells.**

I stand. It is time.

"Dr. Weiss. Wise, wise man. Wireless pulses from electronic devices are killing humanity. Race against time. Time, a terrible thing to waste."

The crowd murmurs around me. Assent!

"The green-eyed are safe. Two percent of the population immune to the microscopic worms that slither through the air and burrow into our skin. Parasites. Oh, what a sight."

Murmurs lead to shouting. "Yes! Yes!"

"But the others..." I stop, and glance at the brown-eyed woman beside me, a fellow scientist standing up, supporting me. But as she turns her head toward the aisle, I see them.

Wriggling, writhing worms crawling into her ear.

I grab her arm.

She screams. The worms are pushing toward her brain.

"I have evidence! Here! And there! And..."

The Watchers, Michael...

You fool.

The Suit races down the aisle, yelling words I don't understand.

I release the woman and fling my dissertation toward the stage.

"Scientific proof!"

The great Dr. Weiss's arms stretch like rubber, humanity's last hope reaching out.

He will save them now—cure the blue-eyed and the brown-eyed of the pestilence that would bring about their extermination. He'll liberate the green-eyed from the bonds of electronically induced mind control. With the sword of my science, he'll cut down the whole telecommunications industry. Bring the conspirators to justice. Save the world.

The shouts in the auditorium beat against my brain.

They're distracting you, Michael.

They'll make you forget.

"Restrain him!"

The Suit—*the Watcher*—pounces.

The floor opens and swallows me whole.

Like the fallen King. Like worms on white blood cells.

Fool's Mate.

The Watchers can't see you when it's dark, Michael.

You Won't Feel a Thing

EPILOGUE

I shall never rest, dear daughter; for the demons, they ravage our dreams.

PART THREE: FEAR

Your small body trembles and I curl myself around you, my back curved in a perpetual question: Why should a child suffer?

I hold you close, restraining your arms; they thrash like caged wildcats. Your feet strike me, legs kicking and pumping as if you're fleeing something. Someone. The sheets rumple beneath us, drenched in the sweat of your horror, in my own helpless tears. Your neck twists, head jolting side-to-side, in defiance of some silent command. Mouth

agape, your tongue protrudes, murmurs unintelligible spilling from your lips. Eyelids squeeze tight as if to contain some macabre vision inside your mind. Or shield a ghastlier one from entering.

For so long, these terrors have consumed you.

We'd done all the sleep studies, the psychological evaluations. Pediatric specialists ruled out apnea, restless leg syndrome, ADHD, autism, anxiety disorders. There are no blockages, hemorrhages, tumors, or malignancies. "No medical cause," they'd determined, simply a nuisance you'd outgrow.

Yet as your ten years have spun in a kaleidoscope of time, the world shifting in a blur of sunrises; the night has persisted as my greatest nemesis. With the strike of each midnight, the chill of insomnia shivers around me. I lie awake in the darkness waiting for your voice, for your shadow to crest across the threshold of my bedroom.

For the screams.

For the pain.

For the beauty of your daytime memories—playdates and ballet recitals and hopscotch blocks sketched on sun-kissed sidewalks in hot-pink chalk—to turn rancid once the cloak of slumber falls. Your friends morph into fiends; the tips of your ballet shoes sharpen to razors as you twist and turn and pirouette, hopping after stones cast over lines drawn in blood.

I lean my face into your hair. It's wild and knotted and damp, and I breathe you into me—the scent of your strawberry shampoo reminiscent of those dolls I'd played with when I was a little girl. How I yearn

for the days of make-believe stories; joy in the manufactured likeness of a child forever smiling, our eyes wide and bright and awake.

For dreams untouched by fear.

"Annie," I murmur. "My sweet Annie."

I pull you tighter, our bodies almost as close as they were when you slept inside my womb. The moon, through the skylight, shines a beam over your face, at once comforting and cold. You are like a specter in the night, beautiful and haunted.

Your father grumbles nightly, an outcast from our bed; your presence quashing all prospects for intimacy and his much-needed rest.

"It's attention-seeking behavior."

"But Robert," I'd protest. "She needs her mother."

"But Deidre, I need to function in the morning." He lifts a palm to silence me. "My meetings start at eight."

So many nights he'd brushed past you as you stood, staring, wide-eyed, in the doorway; the edges of your nightgown swaying in the confused stillness. Asleep, awake, or somewhere in the depths between, unaware that you'd risen from your own bed, with no recollection of how you'd ventured down the dark hallway.

He doesn't understand.

I kiss the crown of your head. Your body slackens in my embrace, and you draw in a long breath. The tremors subside. Your eyelashes flutter. A sigh escapes you, soft and hesitant, as if released from its shackles.

I dare not wake you.

Yet you stir and turn toward me, snuggling into my chest. Your eyes are big and glassy; I see my exhaustion in your stare.

"Mom?"

"You're safe now, Annie," I whisper.

You shake your head, a grimace twisting your features. That look, it's the face of a child bracing at the whirring of a dentist's drill, blanching at the unexpected news of a "needle" at the doctor's office. The stiffening response to the lie when one is told *'you won't feel a thing'* as a pinch grips tight and yanks every nerve in the body, relentless, to a place of agony.

"No, Mom. We're not safe."

We are not.

You squeeze your eyes shut. My breath catches. I know who you see before your words paint her portrait in my mind, that message she delivers each night when slumber ravages you and I can do nothing but watch your terrors unfold.

"The old woman," you say. "She's waiting for us."

Part Two: Existentialism

CORE TRUTHS

I sit at our worn, second-hand kitchen table; it's littered with half-finished coloring books, broken crayons, hardened Play-Doh remnants, and a stack of unpaid bills. A lonely bulb offers the only light in this dingy room. The hole in my thrift-store sweater has grown bigger, as if the moths have invited friends to their feast. Knots tighten at the nape of my neck, my hair unwashed, unbrushed for days.

The scythe of midnight has fallen, and the apartment is quiet. For now. You sleep soundly on the couch, your favorite pink blanket tucked up to your chin. In your eyes, it's beautiful—you never seem to notice the pilling of the wool, the yellowed stains, or the threadbare trim that's unraveling despite my failed efforts to mend it.

I wonder if that's how you see me, too.

I open an envelope embossed in big red letters: URGENT—FINAL NOTICE and retrieve the letter from within.

The words fatten on the page through my tears until they are nothing more than inkblots whose uneven patterns form shapes, puzzle pieces my subconscious connects into objects remembered and forgotten. The pacifier you refused to relinquish until you were nearly three. Your winter hat with the pom-pom top. The stuffed bunny I bought for your cradle, a tempt of fate the moment I learned I was pregnant.

But one word hovers—the one I've dreaded since neighbors complained about the nighttime noise and the landlord came calling for missed rent.

Eviction.

What I wouldn't give for a nice house in the suburbs—a yard with a swing set.

But your daddy tries hard to give us a decent life. He works the night shift, loading trailers at the warehouse. The pay is time and a half, though it's never enough to cover our bills.

Or his daily bar tab.

"Babe, you know I need to blow off steam, especially with Annie's *problem*..."

I try to understand, but I hear the message between his words. He doesn't want to be around us after dark.

Some days, I long to slam the door behind him. Rattle the walls until they crack, watch the plaster rain down like ash.

Bob will never understand the burden of motherhood, the torture of not knowing whether the stroke of each midnight will usher in chaos or peace for your weary mind. He will never feel the relief of sunrise like we do; how the dawn lifts the millstone of dread from our backs. How we can feel normalcy, laughter, joy for only a finite number of hours.

Where the terrors cannot find you.

Until the cycle begins again.

A glass crashes, exploding on the floor. You stand beside me, stare past me—through me—eyes unblinking. Shards splinter into my socks, miraculously missing your bare toes, painted pink from the pedicure I gave you this morning.

"Annie?"

You stand so rigid I cannot tell if you're breathing.

I push myself from the creaking chair; brush the sparkling pieces aside with my foot. I wince as a shard bites into me and a droplet of blood pools through my sock. More shapes—a heart, this time. Your heart. I shuffle past the mess and lift you from the floor and its dangers, carry you back to the couch and wrap you in that blanket.

Your body stiffens, and you lay flat across my lap. Your eyes stretch open as wide as your mouth as you screech into the night. I caress your head, lean my body over you until I feel your nose pressed into my torso. Your screams echo through the hollows of my chest, each slashing a cutting helplessness that will forever scar me.

I'm your mother and I cannot help you. I cannot stop this. I can only wait, and breathe, try to steady my heartbeat in time with the ticking clock, each second pushing us closer toward a blessed awakening when *you* will return.

My lids are heavy with slumber, yet I am resolute to resist, to maintain my night watch.

And as quickly as that waterglass slipped from your fingers, your screaming subsides. You blink and lick your lips.

"Thirsty."

I lay you down, tiptoe past the detritus, and pour water into a plastic cup. You are seated when I return, blanket snug around you like a cocoon.

"Another bad dream?" I ask.

You nod.

"Want to tell me...?"

"No."

"Why don't we read," I say.

You gesture toward a book on the end table: *Goodnight, Moon*.

How fitting.

I snuggle in beside you and open the front cover. You point to each word, struggling to sound the letters. So much of your kindergarten year missed, lost to the nightmares that plague you.

Sighing, you rest your palms on the pages and glance up at me.

"Mommy, am I real?"

I slide the book from beneath your hands and close it gently.

"Of course, you're real. You're as real as the day you were born." I feign a smile. "That's a big question for a five-year-old. Why do you ask?"

You fidget and slide your tiny hands over mine, entwining our fingers as if weaving a net. Casting a lifeline.

"The old lady told me I'm nothing more than a dream."

"What old lady, Annie?" Blood pulses in my temple; numbness crawls across my scalp. The light dims, yet your face shines brightly.

"The old lady in the long white dress. The one who squeezes my cheeks with her fingers when lightning flashes in my sleep." Your lower lip quivers; a teardrop buds in the corner of your eye. "Why would she say that if it wasn't true?"

I wipe your tear away. "That old lady is a figment of your mind. And a mean one at that."

"But Mommy, the old lady told me to give you a message. She's coming for us. And I believe her."

Part One: Faith

I turn on the faucets to drown the sounds of your cries; water gushing from sink and tub like a reverse geyser. Thunder rattles the bathroom's small, frosted window; lightning sketches our silhouettes as I hold you and rock you. Your screams encircle the pacifier in your mouth. It trembles as it dangles from your lower lip, hanging with the desperation of a fallen bird scrabbling to re-enter its nest.

"Shhhh Annie, quiet time now." My lips graze your ear as I beg you to hush. At two and a half, you've long passed the colic stage and are too big for the breast. Those fleeting few months where you'd slept through the night dissipated as if they'd never existed. Rest and peace have evaded me and abandoned us; for each night when the tick of the second hand marks the rise of midnight, your eyes open and your voice sings. Your screeching reverberates through the halls of this temporary

home where drifters shelter from the cold, bound by the Christian Brothers' draconian rules. Lights out and silence after 11pm.

Your daddy tried to love us those first two years, until that random Tuesday when we'd taken a ride in his Jeep and he threatened to leave you at the local church with a note pinned to your coat—*free to a good home*—like some goddamned dog with fleas, because he couldn't take it anymore... couldn't take *us* anymore... it was you or it was him and I chose you.

I always choose you.

The priests told me to pray, that things would get better. Bobby would repent for his sins; see the light that children bring to this life. But I didn't believe them. I struggled to believe anything when my brain never had a moment's quiet, when the fall of the sun triggered the dawn of my endless night.

Humming a lullaby, I slide the pacifier between your lips, rest your head on my shoulder, and sway. Your sobs echo in time with the rolling thunder. Lightning bursts through the window, an unwelcome visitor that douses the room in white.

I turn you toward the mirror, pointing at our reflection. "Where's the baby?" I attempt a smile. "There's the baby!"

The lightning, it flashes and freezes in time. The room glows with an effervescent radiance. Your cries silence and you stare, your face a specter. You stiffen in my arms, eyes wide and unblinking.

The old woman chuckles, her profile contoured in the light as she stares back at us, her long white dress flowing around her like water.

You point your tiny finger toward her. She stretches out her arms, encircling us in steam.

Lightning dies and the room pitches into darkness. Rain patters against the window and you melt into me.

"Lady, Mama, Lady," you murmur.

I begin to sob.

P ROLOGUE

I squint in the fluorescence of the sterile room, my body chilled by the metal table upon which I lie. Claustrophobic panic rushes over me as they hang a large blue sheet from the ceiling; it rests on my collarbone and slides over my neck when I breathe. I am immobile, limbs useless as I surrender to the will of strangers. I see only the eyes of the man beside me who fiddles with knobs connected to tubes implanted inside me. Somewhere.

"You won't feel a thing," he says.

I've never felt so alone. Vulnerability is a wave that steals my breath as it washes over me like a cold sweat I can't feel. Nothing, *nothing*, as the man had promised. I stare at the clock on the wall. Seconds click in regimented syncopation toward midnight. The sound ricochets off the white walls that surround me, walls that close in around my brain.

I long to sleep yet my eyelids freeze open, my breath trapped in the silence until the moment your wails vibrate through my body as you leave it. We are no longer one, but two—the emptiness inside palpable. A crushing void.

The old woman in the flowing white dress hovers in the corner. She smiles as I turn toward her.

"Where's the baby?" I ask.

She shakes her head and purses her lips.

"Hush, now," she says.

Fluorescence explodes around me like glass shattering in a lightning storm.

And then the world is dim. I'm melting into the metal slab.

A faceless doctor places you into the old woman's waiting arms. Tulle and satin swaddle you both as if spun by a breeze.

You won't feel a thing.

I scream and scream, terror consuming what remains of me.

A DIGNIFIED DEATH

C HARLOTTE NAYAR WRAPPED HER fingers around the detonator. Red and metallic, the device scalded her palms with a
frigid sizzle. It was as if she held the entire Moon of Desola in her
hands. She startled, the notion of cold as far from her comprehension
as Earth itself. Charlotte was born on this moon, about a million
parsecs from the Milky Way, under the scorching eye of the Riza Sun.
She'd die here, too, along with the Settlement, regardless of whether
she was ready. Or if any of them were ready.

None of them deserved to end this way.

Not Charlotte's mother, who'd toiled in the fields with the other
Farmers after Dad's death, despite the blistered skin and blood-tinged
phlegmy cough she'd attempted to hide from everyone.

Not her younger siblings, who played, oblivious as children are, while
their chromosomes mutated with each skip across artificial turf laid to
emulate Earthen backyards.

Not Mr. Smith, the widower who baked cookies on the railing of his back deck, or Mrs. Miller, who used spare parts from broken field tillers to build robotic pets—yapping dogs and chirping birds that made Charlotte's mother smile, remembering a home to which she'd never return.

It would be better for all of them. Charlotte liked to think of herself as a savior, not a murderer. After all, murderers were bad people. At least, the ones she'd read about in those mystery books her parents had taken with them during transport.

Aside from what she'd seen in fiction, Charlotte knew nothing of crime. There were no crimes in the Settlement.

Until today.

It was almost too easy getting past the Comms technicians busy in their night shifts outside the reactor room. They'd known her for all her sixteen years, since she was a baby, and gladly accepted a plate of Mr. Smith's cookies, sprinkled with just enough painkiller to pull them into a forever dreamless sleep.

Charlotte planted her feet on the grating in the reactor room. The blinking yellow sensors and heartbeat-steady beep of a warning alarm reminded her of her father's last days in the infirmary, when he told her the truth about the reactor.

'It's like a sickness rooted itself in the core,' he'd said. *'Its spread will be slow, but inevitable. A bit like mine. Like Tamara's sickness, too.'*

The lead scientist on the Desola agricultural mission, Dad had always approached everything in his life in a methodical, calculated manner.

The clothing he chose, the hours he kept. The bits of Earthen history he'd shared around the dinner table. The circumstances under which he delegated his weekly reporting duties to Tamara Dows, his second-in-command, and the times he'd disappear for a day or two at a time, sleeping, eating, and living at the reactor building.

Choosing Charlotte for the Settlement's final task, that was calculated, too.

There were things her father had kept close, especially as his death approached. In the years since, Charlotte too had hidden this secret away, as deep as the microchip Dad had implanted in her thigh when she was only a child, when he chose her for this mission, a proxy for himself or Tamara in the event they were—*unavailable*—to fulfill their obligation.

That morning, the microchip erupted in her muscle with a volcanic pain whose searing heat flowed over every tendon, burning rivulets through each nerve in her body.

It was time.

Her father had told her as much. The reactor did, too, its excruciating demise tied to her pain like sinew to muscle, a heart to its arteries.

Charlotte wasn't a murderer. She could never be a murderer.

But she had a job to do.

D R. William Nayar watched his ten-year-old daughter Charlotte run. No matter how fast the other children were, they never caught up to her. Sometimes she'd slow down if a much smaller child challenged her to a race. She'd never let them win, but would allow them to come close, beating them by a nose or a hair or whatever that old horseracing term was.

It had been so long, he couldn't remember.

Charlotte differed from the other children born on Desola. Instinctively, she had a keen sense of what was right, and wouldn't let anyone interfere when entrusted to complete a task—even if it might hurt them in the short term.

He recalled the time when Charlotte snapped the dislocated shoulder of a young farmer back into place after he'd fallen from atop a combine. When she'd decapitated that moon serpent after it invaded the family's chicken coop, swinging a scythe as her siblings wailed in horror at the blood... *so much blood*. Calls to action that would have raked shivers through the souls of adults left Charlotte unfazed. She'd moved on from them as if those tasks were as simple as clearing dishes from a table, as easy as breathing.

And unlike other children, whose penchant for frivolity aligned to their age and the small, sheltered lives they were born into on the Settlement, Charlotte asked intelligent—existential—questions:

"What's ozone, and how does the reactor make it?"

"Do we need ozone to farm?"

"How can we save Earth when we're so far away from it?"

"Do other humans know about us?"

"How long will we stay here?"

"What happens if the reactor breaks?"

Dr. Nayar never talked about his work on the reactor with anyone except for Tamara and his contacts at Earth Central Command. He relegated everyone else to 'need to know' status. Farmers farmed as instructed, using Dr. Nayar's calculations to plant and till. Comms techs transmitted messages Nayar himself created back to Earth without a clue as to their content. His wife kept a neat home and relatively clean children, coordinated the educational curriculum for the Settlement's youth, served as Magistrate in managing squabbles over the Settlement's bylaws, and trusted Nayar to keep them all safe—no questions asked.

But one day, Dr. Nayar recognized Charlotte might 'need to know' things that others didn't. He wished to all the stars that it would never come to that, but they needed a contingency.

"Have you implanted it yet?" Tamara asked. She sat with Dr. Nayar on a makeshift bench. The children had settled in a circle to play some clapping game, a permanent squint narrowing their eyes under the chartreuse haze. Charlotte sat on the ground alone, away from them, gazing at the intensity of a horizon that offered more questions than answers.

Trepidation over hope, Dr. Nayar thought, as he shook his head *no*.

"Soon. When the house is quiet and everyone is asleep. Charlotte's a deep dreamer. With the numbing agent, she won't know the chip's in place until the time comes for me to tell her."

"Sure you want to do this?" Tamara asked. "Sure we need to do this? What if the calculations are off?"

"They're not." Dr. Nayar leaned forward. Resting his elbows on his knees, he ran his hands through his hair. Thin, brittle strands stuck to his fingers, falling like deadening Earthen leaves to the sand at his feet.

He thought of Charlotte's most prominent and most pressing question: *What if the reactor breaks?*

Tamara's eyes widened. "Oh."

"I'd say the Settlement's got five, maybe seven more years. And me...?" Nayar shook his head, frowning.

"How could the engineers have been so far off in their projections?" Tamara wrung her hands as if seeking an oracle in her palms. "They promised ten more years."

"It's a slow leak. We'll get by for a while," Dr. Nayar said, deepening his voice to push confidence past the tremor that threatened. "Hopefully, the data we've collected will be enough for the Earth Stations to act upon before their Southern Hemisphere fries up entirely."

"They've lost so many people," Tamara said. Dr. Nayar watched his colleague's gaze fix on the children, on Charlotte, who stood pulling her hair into a ponytail as she entered the house.

"They're absolutely certain transport can't get here any faster?" Tamara asked. "Maybe find another wormhole. If they could fix the reactor...? Evacuate the Settlement? Give us a chance...?"

"I ask every time I talk to Command. Even if they left now, by the time they get here, it'll be too late. And that's their best-case hypothesis." Dr. Nayar shivered in the heat, his mind attempting to shut out the biological consequences to the Settlement of a full reactor shutdown—the specifics of which he'd never shared with Tamara or anyone else on Desola.

"Maybe we could survive without the reactor. Long enough to be rescued, anyway. If we start now, build some bunkers deep in the caves?"

Dr. Nayar held up a hand to silence her. "Ever had a dog back on Earth? A real, live dog, fur and wagging tail, fleas, the entire package?"

Tamara nodded in time with a slow smile, the memory spread over her features.

"When I was a kid, I had a chocolate lab named Tank," Nayar said. "Best damn dog there was. He brought the ball when I threw it, curled up in my blankets right next to me when I went to bed at night. Loyal as anything."

"I had a Shih Tzu," Tamara said. "Great dog."

Dr. Nayar continued. "Tank lived to be almost nineteen years old. Day in, day out, he did everything I asked him to. Sure, he whined, and he whimpered a bit as he got old, but I didn't think anything of it. Even stopped eating after a while. I thought it was just his age until one day

I found him on the floor in a pool of blood and urine. Vet told me his insides exploded when his organs all shut down."

"The poor thing." Tamara tsked.

"I ignored the signs," Dr. Nayar said. "Because I didn't want to believe them. Most humane thing I could have done was put that dog out of his misery before he became nothing more than a puddle. I won't let that happen with the Settlement."

He stood, brushing the sand that had rested in the crevices of his clothing and the memory from the forefront of his mind. "If I can't do it, if you can't do it, Charlotte is our last hope. She'll give them a dignified death."

C HARLOTTE LAID THE DETONATOR on the control room's console and rubbed her shoulder to erase the ache of its weight. She glanced around the room that had served as the center of Desola's operations. Its brain, really.

An empty chill consumed her from the inside. This space would be her tomb.

Most children on Desola feared the Command Center. Although Charlotte was never afraid like the others, this place never represented the Desola she knew, where she'd dug her toes in the deep crimson sand and run toward a horizon vast with warmth and promise. Desola, it was more than just a settlement of scientists and farmers; it was a heartbeat—pumping life blood across the galaxies to renew the soul

of the planet that birthed humanity. The brothers and the sisters she'd never meet on Earth, she hoped they'd appreciate Desola's sacrifice, the action she was about to take because she knew it was right, even if it wasn't easy. Though true grey did not exist on Desola, Charlotte knew her task would paint its dull hue onto this day, forever tinging the tiny moon's story.

A story with an unbearable ending.

She stifled a sob, bile swirling chaos in her throat. Charlotte could barely swallow. She could barely breathe. As she cast eyes on the flickering glow of the dying reactor core, Charlotte realized she, the inhabitants of the Settlement, the reactor itself—all were nothing more than a machine sent by Earthen men to fix humanity's ills. If murder was a sin, so too was hubris, a blood-red cloak concealing the darkness of the Earth Council's greatest lie—they had left the settlement to die, with no plans to repair the reactor, or to rescue them.

Charlotte's father had instructed her that once the reactor tower was destroyed and the automated ozone transmission reports between Desola and Earth cut, Earthen Command would know of their fate.

Charlotte was to depress the activation control on the detonator. And wait for the end.

But Charlotte had one last thing to say to the Earth Command. She pressed the dark blue button on the console to activate the recording for one last transmission. She spoke slowly, enunciating each word.

"My name is Charlotte Nayar, daughter of Dr. William Nayar. It is the 23rd of October, the year 2189, and this will be the last communication you'll receive from the Desola Settlement."

Her voice cracked as she held her finger to the smooth plastic.

"The microchip tethering my body to the reactor's cortex activated today, signaling the beginning of the end. To spare my people the horror of an excruciating, slow death, I will soon detonate an explosive that will demolish the reactor and, with a flash of light, obliterate any living thing in its vicinity. The men, women, and children you have sent to inhabit this moon will die within seconds."

Charlotte paused the recording for a moment, pulling in a deep gulp of oxygen.

"I do this at my father's request. My family, my friends, my neighbors, they will be dead before they wake to the flash of brilliance that will claim them. My father, he said I'm a hero, but I don't think so." An uneasy chuckle stuck in her throat. "I suppose that makes me a villain."

In the silence, she reached for the detonator with her empty hand. Charlotte turned her palm this way and that, fixated on the shimmering metal, the tiny vein-like wires sprouting from the top. The button she would need to press with her thumb, deep into its core to begin the sequence—no better than palpating the flesh of a heart with the organ already in arrest.

"Today, the line between hero and villain is as hazy as the horizon on the Desola Moon. Heroes save people, they don't destroy them. Am I a villain? Is my father, who let the Settlement believe that life was infinite, when he knew it was only a matter of time before the ticking of a detonator would mark their final moments? Or is it you, oh great Earthen Council, the ones who sent us here, sacrificing ourselves to save a planet most of us had never known?

"You killed me, and now I need to kill them. Maybe it would be easier for me to ignore my father's wishes and go back to bed. Let the inevitable hallucinations swirl my brain like a centrifuge as the air is depleted. Invite the Riza Sun to boil my organs, roasting them over the coming days until they explode. But I don't deserve that. They don't deserve that."

Charlotte straightened; any residual doubt smoothed in a posture rooted as firm as a spade in the fields.

"So today I confess my sin to whomever is listening. Whether it's God or the Universe or any other all-seeing deity out there. Hear this. I murdered everyone in my Settlement. It was for their own good. I have no regrets."

Charlotte keyed in the code to send the transmission. Upon its confirmation, she took the detonator in both hands. It reminded her of the first time she held her baby brother, just after his birth.

"Be careful with his head," her mother had said. "He's delicate. We must be very gentle with life."

Charlotte held her breath as she did when she was a child, daring her siblings and her friends to keep it inside for as long as possible. And she held it, and held it, until there was nothing left to do but let go.

And jab her thumb into the detonator's core.

THE RISE OF THE MARINER'S STAR

O F EVERYTHING SHE'D LOST, Polara missed starlight the most.

Black sea washed into ebony sky, mist delineating heaven from the vast waters upon which the Warship Fenrir bobbed and slumbered.

Polara was a good deckhand, but she had no choice. The only alternative to servitude was death.

Ragged clothing clung to her; bare feet shuffled over the knotted wooden boards she swabbed. She preferred to work by lamplight, grateful for silence after days and nights bombarded by the arrows of flying trolls and crashing waves from the fists of giants offshore.

The Captain's War was, at first, well-intended, the fleet pursuing a band of ravenous goblins who had plucked human children from their homes. But his victory had awakened a hunger, insatiable as a voracious god, and the Captain pillaged the magical realm in his quest

to ensure human domination. They conscripted dissenters to ship-life or killed them; followers on the mainland fattened by the spoils of his conquests.

It was then that the stars blinked away. One by one, they closed their eyes to the living world, as if ashamed to look upon the evil that consumed it.

As Polara dipped her mop into the bucket, she heard a similar splash outside the ship. She tiptoed to the railing, peered over the side. Light flailed in the water.

A Sea Elf.

Polara had never seen one with her own eyes; she'd thought they only existed in children's tales. Wish-granters with a penchant for mischief, they were quick to anger, thought to breathe fire into the seas when provoked.

The struggling Elf was no larger than Polara's forearm, with skin and hair shimmering silver.

Droplets of elfin blood pooled on the water's surface as two large marauder-fish flanked the creature, stabbing his arms with needle-like pincers.

"Shoo!" Polara whispered. "Leave him be!"

The tickle in her belly stretched chilly tentacles through her body; hot breath caressed the back of her neck. She glanced over her shoulder. Only the breeze and her fear accompanied her on deck.

Polara couldn't bear watching another magical light snuffed out. Turning away from the Elf would make her complicit in the Captain's ambitions.

She leaned over the railing, poking at the fishes' shining red eyes with her mop handle. She hit one dead-on. Glowing goo oozed into the sea as it swam off, opening and closing its mouth in protest. The remaining predator tightened its grip, the Elf's shine fading. Polara bashed the mop down, connecting with the fish's skull. With a shudder, it turned belly-up, and the Elf drifted free.

The Elf floated on his back. His sparse hair flowed like seaweed as the water lapped around him. Fluttering his lashes, he gazed at Polara with rheumy green eyes.

"Take hold." Polara leaned over the rail, toes abandoning the deck as she extended the mop. The Elf wrapped gnarled fingers around the handle. She yanked him from the water; they both fell to the floor. Wonder pushed a gasp from Polara's lungs as the creature shook his head and sat upright. He squeezed a gaping wound on his shoulder. Glitter floated from his fingertips, manifesting a golden bandage.

"Rescued by the ship that seeks to destroy all creatures magical. Did you save me now to kill me later?"

"No," Polara said. "I'm not a killer."

"Will you sacrifice me to your Captain? To win his favor?"

She shook her head. The Elf's mesmerizing stare pulled at her earnestness.

"Kindness begets kindness." He took Polara's hand. "I will grant you two wishes."

"Two? Aren't there usually three?"

"Dearest, you already used your first wish." The Elf chuckled. "I'm still alive."

"But how did you—"

"Your silent prayer resounded within my elfin ears."

Polara tugged at a loose thread on her shabby clothing. Could it be possible? "I wish to be free, Sea Elf. Free to bring light to this dark world."

The Elf kissed her hand. A silvery stamp in the shape of a star remained where his lips had been.

"Soon," he said.

Polara's mind buzzed with awe as the Elf rose high above deck, plunging into the interminable line between night and sea.

From behind, beefy hands grasped her by the elbows. Polara thrashed against the Captain's watchman, all the way to the brig.

S UNLIGHT THROUGH A SMALL porthole burned slumber from Polara's eyes. She bolted up and glanced outside—Mer Island in her sightline.

Merpeople. The Captain's next conquest.

Had she dreamed of the Sea Elf? The doubt smarted. She wrung her hands, more a prisoner now than she'd ever been.

Yet still she searched, waiting. Hoping.

And then, a glowing silver serpent rose from the sea. Polara thought she saw it wink before it swung its massive tail over the top of the warship, slicing it in two. Water rushed in, stifling Polara's screams as it pushed her into the depths. Before the sea crushed Polara's last vestiges of consciousness, the stamp from the Elf's kiss shimmered, forming a protective bubble around her.

Amid the debris, the fallen Captain floundered, trapped in the murky water. Polara gaped as the serpent snatched him, charring him to ash with a puff of sea fire.

Crewmen floated around her, lifeless as the shattered ship.

"No!" Polara shouted. "They're captives, like me. I wish them to live!"

With a blink of its eye, the serpent shrank to the form of the Sea Elf.

"Please," she begged.

The Elf pushed Polara's bubble to the water's surface, raising a glowing finger in the air. Day shifted to a starless night.

"Kindness is the light that shines through this darkness," he said. "But these crewmen, and all who seek to sail these seas, will need a beacon to guide them. Your ultimate wish comes with a price. A life for a life. Nothing less, nothing more."

"Anything," she said.

T HUS, POLARIS, THE MARINER'S Star, was born that night, in that dark sky. She is true North, bringing hope and bearing light for all.

THE OUTLAW OF UNINTENDED CONSEQUENCES

S ALLY SCULL KNEW THREE things about the desert. It was hot, it was gritty, and it was the last place on Earth she wanted to be.

Nonetheless, her duty beckoned.

Saddled up, she nudged Ole Blue, her trusty Appaloosa steed, forward. He bore a mane fitting royal majesty while cloaked by the mantle of a servant's humility. No living creature in the universe was as noble, none had a more complex, multifaceted soul. At least, that was what she'd read about horses, what her superiors in the Rheostatic Command had told her. Sally considered herself fortunate to have secured such a partner, even if briefly, to accompany her on this journey. Agents such as herself typically worked alone.

She wiped a moist sheen of painted dust from the mech-skin covering her cranial circuits; her ivory complexion was tacky under the sun's early-morning rays.

How did humans live like this?

A lone tumbleweed drifted by—a wind witch casting her lonely spell over the desert. The coarse thistle captured the scorched Earth as it rolled, the plant decay and dust a reminder of a potential future that a failed mission could yield.

With a tap to her temple, she engaged her infrared sight-scanner. Sally gazed over the precipice of a valley where the brushstrokes of God seemed to do battle with the devil, carved spires of red and tan piercing through the clouded blue heavens. She zoomed in, squinting like a human to sharpen her radar. And then she saw it, the town of Ruby City nestled at the base of the canyon, its wooden construct tiny and as perfectly engineered as a child's Wild West play set.

If her calculations were correct, the year was 1887, and she was some-where in the middle of Arizona territory. Thomas Tinkerton, the most wanted man in the universe, hid somewhere in that frontier homestead. And despite her distaste for cacti and cowboys, Rheostat Central Command had deputized Sally to round him up and bring him to justice.

A small sacrifice to secure the fate of the planet.

A DUST CLOUD CARPETED the wooden boardwalks in the heart of Ruby City as the townsfolk bustled about. Matronly women clucked and strutted by in petticoated skirts, woven baskets filled with goods from the local mercantile in hand, and mustached men tipped

their Stetsons as they passed. Dirty-faced children ran through the streets. Boys' shirttails flapped, untucked, as they chased after squealing girls whose braids flounced just outside their reach.

An idyllic picture of an Old West town, the kind captured in grainy sepia portraits hanging in stuffy museums and faux frontier-based theme parks.

Orderly, normal, and expected—save for the robotic dogs yipping after the children. Or the sweaty desert natives who strained in Western shirtsleeves and suspenders beneath the weight of overstuffed burlap bags, sparks crackling from their LED-lit boot spurs. Or the gleaming steel hover-wagons into which the men tossed those bags, the mist from their steam-stacks pushing into the sky, ominous as an air-filtered smoke-signal.

I hope I'm not too late, Sally thought, as she and Ole Blue trotted down the street.

Heads turned, eyes widened, and fingers pointed, not at Sally but at Ole Blue—the only warm-blooded animal within her scanner's range. The horse whinnied and shuddered as she dismounted and hitched his reins to the post. His spotted grey coat appeared muted in a herd of gleaming silver steeds. She patted his flank.

"I know the feeling, old boy," she said.

Sally ambled toward the saloon. As she was about to enter, a pale, thin hand holding a metal cup blocked her way. She glanced down at a pair of women costumed in filthy lace and rhinestones huddled against the wall—one in her late teens, the other middle-aged.

"Please," the younger woman said. "Two bits will buy us a meal. We haven't eaten in days, ever since we been tossed from the saloon. They don't want no soiled doves tempting the men folk no more. Old Mr. Tinker said we were dirtying up a place of joy..."

"Patricia!" Panic flickered in the older woman's eyes. "This nice lady don't need to know about our troubles."

"Mr. Tinker, you said?" Sally fished a coin from her pocket and deposited it into the cup.

Patricia's skin flushed as red as desert rock. "You ain't heard me say that man's name," she whispered. The women scurried away, shaking their heads and holding each other for support. Sally couldn't help but notice the way their tattered dresses hung from their skeletal frames like death shrouds over two corpses.

As Sally pushed her way through the saloon's double doors, chaos assaulted her sensors. A cacophony of disjointed chords leapt from a self-playing piano—chamber music and pre-Jazz ragtime, intermingled with the chorus of an Elton John song. A surly tin bartender, sporting a wind-up key affixed to his back, stacked highball glasses behind the bar next to plastic bottles filled with cola. Stiff-suited men hunched around a table playing cards, the distinct "UNO" logo prominently stamped on the deck. Another group sat with eyes transfixed to the screens of the Nintendo Game Boys they clutched. A stout preacher ranted from an empty stage in the corner, spouting prophecies of hellfire and damnation from a dog-eared paperback. Sally squinted to see the cover—it was splashed with the likeness of some 1980s televangelist.

A whip crack of silence cut across the room. Sally's sensors registered the heat of fifty human eyes boring through her. Her footfalls boomed like gunshots over the wooden floor as she approached the bar.

"You ain't from these parts." A grimy cowboy peered at her from beneath a weather-beaten ten-gallon hat.

He spat a wad of tobacco from the wide gap in his teeth. "We don't take kindly to outsiders here. 'Specially your kind."

"And what kind would that be?" Sally asked, wondering whether they had ever seen a model of her caliber. Squeezing her thumb and forefinger together, she initiated a Vitalscan over the room. Elevated heart rates and increased perspiration confirmed their apprehension at her presence. But could apprehension morph into fear? And fear to danger? Would it jeopardize her mission?

"Ain't no womenfolk allowed in this here saloon. 'Specially one dressed in britches." Raucous laughter amplified the cowboy's guffaws as he waved toward her dungarees, chaps, and leather vest with disdain. The room quieted as his gaze rested on the holster at her hips and the bronze deputy badge pinned to her belt.

Dim-witted misogynist with the brainpower of a cow tipped into manure, Sally thought. If cows still exist...

"I don't plan to overstay my welcome," Sally said. "But I'd be much obliged if you could direct me toward a Mister Thomas Tinkerton."

Murmurs swept through the room. The gap-toothed cowboy's eyes narrowed, his lips curling to a sneer.

"What could the likes of you want with our good ole boy, Tinker? That man put Ruby City on the map."

The crowd flung shouts of assent toward Sally.

"—We have farms in the desert 'cause of him!"

"—He cured my young'ns of the plague!"

"—He ran them showgirls outta town!"

"—My horse-bots don't need no feedin' or waterin'!"

"—Tinker's brought God to the godless!"

The cowboy leaned in, the stench of whiskey on his breath offending Sally's olfactory receptors. She huffed to clear them and stretched her spine to maximize her height, glaring into the cowboy's eyes.

"Ya do know Tinker's the new sheriff in town, dontcha?" He folded his arms, his posture threatening. "Deputy."

"Mr. Tinkerton and I—"

"—*Sheriff* Tinkerton—"

"—Have some unfinished business that's none of your concern. Now, if you could kindly tell me where I can find him, I'll see myself out."

The cowboy tsked and spat again. "I don't think ya heard me right the first time, darlin.' We don't take kindly to strangers 'round here. And Tinker? Best leave him be... if ya know what's good for ya."

He turned on his heel, his spur scraping the worn veneer of the saloon floor as if signaling the music and laughter and preaching to resume. The men turned from Sally back to their cards and drinks. She stood in this noise factory, invisible among them, yet heavy with the weight of their ignorance. No battles were to be waged, nor won, in this place. Her footfalls whispered as she exited, the swinging door behind her a pendulum as she pondered her options.

The late morning heat slapped Sally's cheeks. Plucked from retirement for this mission, she'd begged Rheostat Central Command to assign someone else—a newer model with sharper features, more advanced technology. They'd refused, for regression analysis demonstrated that Sally's statistically greater understanding of human nature, versus her peers, would correlate to a higher likelihood of success. But Sally knew better. She'd calculated the probability of failure as 98.632% despite Command's more optimistic estimates. Sally knew the martyrdom of an older android like herself was far more palatable than the loss of newer tech, even if a decade of field duty had altered her processing unit to think and feel more human than machine.

"New plan, Ole Blue," Sally said, approaching her tethered horse. The two former showgirls or brothel dwellers—Sally couldn't tell—stroked his silken mane.

"I don't remember the last time I seen a live horse in these parts." Patricia lifted a bucket of water for Ole Blue, who gladly drank. "Mabel, when was the last time you seen a horse? A real one?"

Sally listened to the women chatter as she adjusted the saddle, preparing to mount.

"Tinker's in the shack down the road a piece," Mabel, the older woman, whispered to Sally. "His workshop. You better get a move on before the saloon boys get an inkling to follow."

"We'll hold 'em off for you," Patricia said. "It's about time someone sees through that snake oil Tinker's sellin'. Seems the whole town's under his spell."

"Mighty kind of you, Miss," Sally said. Fishing through her pockets, she retrieved her remaining coins and pressed them into Patricia's hand, an unspoken promise for the future lightly branded into mech skin and human skin.

The young woman's eyes widened at Sally's touch.

Sally hoped Patricia and Mabel would make it.

Hell, she hoped they all would.

A BELL JINGLED ABOVE the door as Sally entered Tinker's clap-board shack. Dry heat had bleached the wood outside a sickly white, yet life bloomed in the interior. A hundred clocks hung from papered walls, their rich reds and golds complementing the plush carpet that cushioned the floor. Tables of gadgets decorated the room, littered with metal and wood and plastic things in various stages of construction. Two mechanical cats, one silver, one bronze, scurried after a wind-up toy mouse, their tinny yowls cutting through the asynchronously synchronized ticking that reverberated like a cross-wired heartbeat.

A lanky man wearing enormous goggles stood at a workbench, turning the key to an oversized oaken wall clock. Gears wound through the din, though the man's jaundiced jowls drooped in a frown.

"Damn machine," he muttered.

"Thomas Tinkerton?"

He looked up, blue irises overtaking the whites of his eyes through the thick lenses as he gazed at Sally—through Sally—as if his mind had drifted elsewhere.

"Having trouble with time?" she asked.

"Time?"

Tinker lifted his glasses, his pupils were as round as ripe blueberries. He cocked his head, gaping as he regarded Sally; she saw the word *android* sizzle on his tongue. Tinkerton reached across the bench to touch her, and Sally intercepted him, squeezing a wrist that was thinner than a chicken bone. He winced.

"You're a—"

"Yes, I am, and I'm here to send you back, Thomas. The longer you stay, the more damage you'll do."

"Damage?" He chortled. "I've conquered the Old West. Fixed all its ills. No more toiling in the fields. No more disease. No houses of ill repute. Dogs don't die of rabies, and horses don't drop from the strain of overwork. We've got good old-fashioned card games, the music and the soda pop flow easy—no need to think about any of it. The natives adapted, and everybody gets along. Looks like Utopia to me."

Sally released her grip on his arm, and he straightened, wiping his hands on his jacket lapel.

"I'm stayin' right here. Right now."

Stubborn old coot, Sally thought. She opened her hand and held out her palm, activating a hologram that hovered over her skin.

Tinker grinned wider than a wolf in a henhouse.

"What do you see?" Sally asked.

"Earth. And it's most definitely round."

"You know all about Newton's laws of physics, otherwise, you would never have been able to build *this* machine." Sally gestured toward the clock Tinker had been servicing on his workbench. His attention to it and the frozen status of its hands suggested that the clock might have been his way in.

The image of Earth rotated over Sally's hand. "What if I told you that your intervention led to a rift in the formation of the United States with Arizona, Nevada, and California comprising their own separate union?"

Tinker clucked. "Fine by me. I always preferred the East Coast, anyway."

"What if there wasn't just one Civil War?" Sally held up four fingers. "The last one ended the year before you were born."

Tinker furrowed his brow, his mouth stretching into a thin line.

"Oh? Now did it?"

"Those dogs and horses you love so much? Endangered species. There are no protected lands; tribal culture's all but erased. Women never secured voting rights. There is no art, no song, no literature produced outside of government control. And that's just in the United States. Full European countries are falling under the rise of a turbulent Atlantic Ocean. Russia's freezing over. The longer you stay, the more you alter, the worse it becomes."

"Those are mighty strong accusations, Missy." Tinker scowled. "Where's yer proof?"

A series of headlines flashed across the hologram, digital imprints of disaster over the air. He stared at the images as if engraving them into his mind.

Sally clicked off the hologram, replacing it with a visual of Tinkerton's New Jersey driver's license—Date of Birth: July 30, 1959.

"You're the anomaly, Thomas. The crack in the sidewalk of time. The false step taken that changes it all. We've been tracking you."

Tinker's expression stiffened. "I s'pose there may've been some... consequences... for my bein' here." He shook his head vehemently, as if the motion could erase the picture of the future Sally had sketched for him. "I came back here to make a difference. Clean up a time that the history books maligned. A time that made my childhood vibrant and alive." He sniffled. "Cowboys and Indians were my whole world when I was nothin' more than a pint-sized young'n."

"Cut the top off a cactus and you won't kill it," Sally said. "Any cowboy worth his boots knows that. It'll grow itself out—roots intact, spines looking sharp, but it'll be different than it was before. The head may

sprout up someplace else, someplace it doesn't belong, changing the landscape to one that never would have been."

"And that could be the purtiest desert flora, bloomin' to the likes none've ever seen before."

"Or it could've rotted from the inside, something dead that deceives by mimicking life."

"A bit like you, Missy?"

Sally ignored the heat rising through her circuits. "Best to let nature take its course, isn't it, Thomas?"

Tinker turned away, his gaze distant, as if watching storm clouds roll in from the horizon. "Fresh air out here done me a world-a good," he said. "Did you know that back in my day, I'm damn near dead? Cancer's all but chewed up everything that matters to a body. But here. Now. It's different. I'm different. Coming back, this was my chance to do something. Make the world better."

Sally felt herself stiffen. Central Command had neglected to tell her about Tinkerton's health condition. She wasn't aware that human sickness could dissipate through time; but then again, the Rheostats only told her what they thought she needed to know. Not that it changed his actions any, or the consequences of those actions.

"It hasn't all been bad, has it?" he asked, his voice falling to a whisper. "Folks here are happy. I've made good use of my time."

Sally's sensors detected a four percent slump in Tinker's shoulders as his words left his lips. Was it remorse, or some reluctant acknowl-edgement of future failings that overtook him in that moment? She

sensed a great plateau giving way to the fissures eroding its surface, a vast canyon crumbling open despite the prideful grip of rock and shale and soil. She thought of tumbleweed scraping coarse bristles through the valley, of prickly spines breaking through tough cactus skin, and wondered how people endured the sharpness of human life.

And of time. How its relentless ticking pelted the thick skin of giants, eroding the bravado until nothing remained but a dark, cavernous fear, more raw than a desert storm.

Perhaps Command was right about Sally. Perhaps she maintained an unnatural appreciation for the human plight.

"Thomas Tinkerton, you're under arrest for violating the space-time continuum."

A smile twittered at the corner of his lips. "Does that mean I'm a wanted man?"

"The most wanted in the galaxy."

He scratched at his chin. "I have a reputation to uphold. No way I can go with you quietly now. Wouldn't want folks thinkin' I was yellow or somethin'. Can you indulge one last request for a dyin' man?" Tinker surrendered a smile. "If you don't get me, the cancer will, eventually. But nobody need know about none of that."

Sally glanced about the workshop, the clock faces judging her. Their endless ticking heralded a reminder of the finite nature of human life, regardless of time, how each moment wasted was a moment closer to an end that needed to be prevented, an inevitability reversed. Sally was charged with saving the planet, not Thomas Tinkerton's soul.

And yet.

Those marching hands.

That *tick-tick-ticking* rhythmic and regimented and constant as a heartbeat.

Gears turning.

Circuits burning.

She stared at the fragile shell of a man who'd shrugged off the mantle of his fate.

Against all her programmed and learned intelligence, against her better judgment, and against anything Rheostat Central Command may have wanted or expected of its most seasoned agent, she relented.

"Let's make it quick," she said.

H IGH NOON.

The Ruby City townsfolk crammed the boardwalk on either side of the main road, bumping shoulders and scrambling for the best view. The show was about to start, and no one wanted to miss it.

Sally and Tinker stood back-to-back under the spotlight of the Arizona sun. Both had weapons raised and at the ready, while the gap-toothed cowboy sneered and spat as he pronounced the rules of the duel:

"... Ten paces, turn, fire ..."

Sally and Tinker had made their arrangements. With a mutual understanding, neither would harm the other—Tinker's pistol filled with blanks, Sally's blaster set to Transport only. *Go big or don't go,* Tinker had said. Despite the added minutes Tinker's show would require, Sally agreed *it wouldn't hurt none.*

Why *had* she agreed to this? Sally wasn't certain. It was as if Tinker had cast some odd spell for her to do his bidding. Hypnosis, perhaps? Some warping of her circuitry? One minute she was standing in a room full of clocks, and the next, on a dusty street. Against her will or with her consent, Sally couldn't recall.

Either way, a grand and epic exit could be fitting for the man whose inventions and social norms altered the landscape of Ruby City, what eventually would and wouldn't become the United States, and the planet at large. Perhaps letting him go on his own terms could spark the flutter the universe needed to save them all.

At least, she hoped it would.

"One!"

Sally stepped forward.

"Two!"

Another step. She glanced over the crowd, greeted by a nod and a smile from her fallen showgirl friends, a stony scowl from the preacher thrumming his fingers on a paperback.

The remaining numbers processed in a blur, much like Sally's journey across the continuum to arrive in 1887. She flexed her hand around her weapon, waxy moisture emanating from her heat sensors. Sally's design enabled her to *feel* the human experience of anxiety and anticipation, and in this moment, those emotions were far too real, almost too real for her to process.

"Nine!"

Blinking hard, Sally activated her targeting mechanism; a bullseye to Tinker's brain would guarantee an accurate hit.

"Ten!"

As she spun around, a silver bullet ripped through the skin encasing her shoulder. It ricocheted with a ping, spinning into the dirt road. She winced in response to the pain alert activated in her central drive. Another shot to her kneecap sent her stumbling. Her free palm hit the ground as she righted herself, agape at Tinker's pistol-waving, maniacal countenance. He was as mad as a rabid fox in heat and just as sly.

"You won't take me alive, Robot!" he shouted, capering for his disciples. Sally raised her weapon and steadied her hand. Eyes narrowed, she waited for the ping that confirmed target precision.

"Bullseye."

She pulled the trigger hard. A laser flash engulfed Tinker in its purple haze; a split second later, he vaporized.

It was as if Old Tinker hadn't existed at all—though Sally knew he had, in more than one place, in more than one time. She could only hope

that the shadowy paradox of his life hadn't cast a pall over too many human destinies, that this one shot, this one time, would change it all.

Raising her arm skyward, Sally again pulled the trigger, this time squeezing it until it painted the sky in a deep violet sheen. Color cascaded over the town, smooth as a flowing fountain. The deluge of time and space rained upon the townsfolk, drowning them in a cosmic shower. The crowd gaped as 1887 restored itself to its intended state, the town's façade dulled to just the right shade of history-book sepia—filtered, grainy and cool.

A stampede of wind rattled windows and dislodged them from buildings. The sand awakened in a time-warping cyclone that twisted everything in its path. Ole Blue whinnied, staring wide eyed at Sally. His majestic form pixelated through the storm, fading away as if he never was, yet as if he had always lived in this time that had been restored, liberated from Tinkerton's entropy. She bit her lip, human-like, and she watched the horse go. Goodbye, my friend, she thought. Erasure of Tinkerton's artifacts—of her mission's artifacts—it was part of her job. It was never easy, but it had never hurt her like it did this time, in this place.

Sally stood rooted amid the storm, resolute against the lightning crackling around her, the screams and laughter and babies' cries and swaths of color—reds and blues and yellows grating over her like coarse wire—as time grasped the reins and she waited and hoped and wished that wherever she landed would be better than the future that was.

With a roar of thunder, it stopped.

The spires of skyscrapers rose around her like the walls of a great prison, asphalt pavement spreading beneath her feet. She was alone in

the silence of Ruby City, the faint hum of her central processing unit the only sound. Scanning for life forms, she sensed the faint echo of human heartbeats from deep beneath the ground—no life forms, no functioning mechs on the surface, only Sally. Glancing up through the buildings at the cloudless sky, Sally saw it had begun to snow.

Wide, fluffy flakes bleached by the sunlight drifted down, peppering her shoulders. Not with snow, but with ash.

She turned her weapon to her chest, heavy with the weight of her failure. Command had overestimated Sally's capabilities and she, too, overestimated herself. She would never understand human nature and its flawed programming.

Before Sally could pull the trigger, the heat of a million suns melted her into the pavement, transfiguring her into an indelible part of a history that would never be.

T HOMAS TINKERTON IS AN old, old man. Machines keep his temporal body functional on the android station serving as the Rheostat Central Command mother ship. Electrodes wired into his brain maintain the mind whose time-warped synapses hold clues to prevent the Earth's demise. Even in hyper-slumber, Old Tinker wears the smile of the demented, for he remains the most wanted man in the universe.

Tinkerton's Paradox—the curse of the man who learned to send multiple versions of himself dancing across the threads binding time

and fate—it always leads to the same cataclysmic end, though the Rheostats' efforts persist.

Five platinum orbs, no larger than a human fist, float beside Thomas's bed—each faceless, soulless sphere a Rheostat officer. Their glowing myriad-colored lights sparkle like star fire from their central processing units as they monitor the psyche of the outlaw, connecting each of his synapses to a mainframe designed to model and predict his next transgression.

They hope, for the sake of humanity, that their calculations are correct—for outside, through the swirling dust of the star scape, a flaming Earth glows like the offspring of the sun.

A RRA CEREP HATED THE ancient times.

If her calculations were correct, the year was 31 BC, and she was driving a chariot somewhere on the outskirts of the Holy Roman Empire.

Thomas Tinkerton, the most wanted man in the universe, lived somewhere in that crowded, rising city. And despite her distaste for togas and grotesque architecture, Rheostat Central Command had sanctioned Arra to capture him and bring him to justice.

A small sacrifice to secure the fate of the planet.

A History Lesson

E LANA PRESSED HER LIGHT green fingers against the cool glass, the webbing between them dry and scaly. Years of living above-surface had hardened both her skin and her spirit, yet for her own sake, for the sake of her people, she knew she must conceal her emotion.

She'd dreaded this field trip to the Preservationist Museum with her Kagarin classmates. Though she studied among the Kagarin, lived in their dormitories, dined with them—walked among them—she was reminded every day that she was not one of them. She would always be Amphiba.

Her gaze rested on the eye sockets of the three skulls in the center display case. Permanent in their emptiness, they were squared off at the top and rounded just above the protruding cheekbones. Someone, or something, had carved a perfect circle into the crown of the center skull, the bone smooth, without splinters.

She wondered what had happened to the owners of those bones, and how the portrait of their lives differed from the image the Kagarins painted.

The Kagarin canvas, Kagarin brushstrokes—that was the only truth that mattered.

Elana smiled, though she felt like screaming; gritted her teeth until the pain sliced a jagged path from her jaw to her brain. She squeezed her muscles taut, willing her pores to stop the beads of seawater that threatened to seep through. If they saw her weeping, the Kagarin would question her. Her mother warned her that questions meant danger and only led to one outcome—conscription to the mines, certain death.

Elana couldn't do that to her mother—to her mother's memory.

She reached up and touched her own face, pushing her fingers into flesh that embraced the same structure as those skulls—a gift from evolution that enabled the Amphiba people to perceive distance and depth through even the murkiest waters.

Her people had been cast from the Great Sea, onto Kagarin shores. In the sea, they were strong. Powerful. Alive. But here, on Kagarin land, they gave their lives for the right to live, diving deep into the underwater mines of the Asave Pools to mine Selapa Ore, the source of all Kagarin power and technology.

Elana glanced over her shoulder at her classmates milling about the interactive lecture chamber. At least a head taller than she, the Kagarin all shared the same silver hair, long alabaster necks, and wide violet eyes that were hallmark to their race. Short, green, and scaled, Elana

stood out alone, a broken crab shell in a field of sea glass. The Kagarin milled together, laughing at projections from the MindBands fused to their foreheads—mostly memes of Amphiba jokes and Kagarin propaganda.

Kagarin and Amphiba both told Elana she should be grateful. Selected as a young child just days after their arrival on land, she was one of the few Amphiba the Kagarin deemed worthy of an education. Those who arrived with Elana were sent to the mines; any who were born after joined the others the moment they learned to stand.

Elana never understood why she was different.

Staring at her reflection in the glass, she wondered if the eyes held by the empty Amphiba skull on display had looked like her own, wide and turquoise, with flecks of gold that shimmered when she laughed.

Elana hadn't laughed in months. Not since the night her mother died from an infection she'd contracted after being injured in the mines. From the time she was chosen, Elana had barely seen her mother, yet the Kagarins granted her one farewell visit to her mother's deathbed. Only then did Elana learn the truth about her family, about her father, and the plight of her people. She swore to her mother she'd keep the secret locked away as deep as the seas from which they'd emerged.

But the truth was an anchor swallowed whole.

Elana caught a flash out of the corner of her eye. She held her breath as the reflection of Angi, her classmate and tormentor, materialized in the glass next to her. To Angi and her friends, Elana was nothing more than a lizard, a lackey who managed their unwanted assignments and suffered as a target of their abuse.

The Kagarin teenager flipped her long hair over her shoulder and smirked at Elana with thin lips painted with blue rouge—the hallmark of an angelfish. But to Elana, Angi was the devil. Her red eyes glowed back at them both, hovering over the cavern in the center skull like lasers.

"Amphibas Forever Indebted: Kagarin Ingenuity, Compassion Saves the Aliens." Angi read the placard aloud and laughed.

Elana stiffened. Kagarin truth, not Amphiba truth, she thought.

Keep your head down and your shoulders rounded, Mother had said. *Create waves, and you'll unleash a typhoon that will destroy everything.*

From Mother's perspective, Elana's scholarship was the key to a different life. A better life, out of the mines. But Elana was no longer sure what her future held.

"An Amphiba is forever indebted," Angi repeated. She grabbed Elana's arm and squeezed it so tightly the skin turned yellow under her grasp. "You'll complete the day's assignment for me. And my friends."

Elana nodded. "Of course." She silently apologized to her reflection and to the opened skull staring back at her.

"Good." Angi tapped at the metal headband fused to her forehead, photographing the skulls with flashes from her eyes. She projected the image from her band.

"Hmm. And what caption would fit such a beautiful photograph?"

Elana lowered her head and tugged at the webbing between her fingers. Kagarin truth is false, she thought.

"I know!" Angi clapped her hands, her eyes radiating glee. She blinked twice and tapped at her headband again. The words, "The only worthwhile Amphiba is..." hovered above the skulls. Angi cackled and the rest of the Kagarin students turned toward them. Elana felt pins and needles rising into her skin; it glowed amber as she fought the sentiment that threatened to ooze through.

"For Kagarin country! For Kagarin honor!" A high-pitched female voice cried from the back of the room. Twenty arms raised fists in the air and stomped against the wooden floor in a unified drumbeat. Twenty sets of eyes bore into Elana, as if they sought something inside her. A slick oil seeped through her skin, cooling her as her features shimmered like moonlight over the sea. Thank goodness the Kagarin technology hadn't evolved enough to extract thoughts. Yet.

"Ok, students, you've had your fun." Professor Worlo waddled through the crowd. His paunch and wild white hair betrayed his age; Elana had heard rumblings among her classmates that the administration slated the teacher for termination by year's end. And not just his title and tenure. Amphiba people would never discard elders in such a callous manner—they revered the wisdom years brought and never scorned age.

Elana wondered whether any of her elders still breathed.

"Time to learn more about our Kagarin history, and..." He nodded toward Elana and, seemingly, toward a male Amphiba statue standing beside her. "The days when the Amphiba emerged from the Great Sea."

She flinched when the 'statue' nodded back at the professor; he had stood so still, Elana thought he, too, was an artifact on display. An examination of his name tag revealed him as Marvic, a docent.

Odd, she thought.

The Kagarin students groaned as they pushed forward in a single wave toward the glass. "Who cares about a bunch of lizards," a voice muttered.

Elana separated from the crowd; the docent followed her. Marvic was tall for an Amphiba, though she hadn't seen a male of her species in years. The gold flecks in his eyes twinkled as she stood next to him, a signal of camaraderie and interest. She smiled weakly as the lights dimmed and a three-dimensional hologram flickered behind the glass—an image of the sea.

A booming, yet soothing voice filled the room.

"The Kagarins have ruled our planet for centuries, living in harmony with nature and all its creatures."

The scene changed from the ocean, to woodlands, to vast deserts; the silhouette of a Kagarin female overlaid each.

"Our military prowess has preserved that harmony through the world, quelling uprisings, promptly quashing those that would threaten our peace, our prosperity, our position as the superior species."

A collective stomp shook the floor.

"For Kagarin country!"

CORE TRUTHS

"For Kagarin honor!"

Elana shuddered. Marvic shifted his position; so close now that she could feel him breathing next to her. For an Amphiba to hold a role of cultural importance was almost unheard of; it was as uncommon as Amphiba scholarship. She blinked twice to quell the rising shimmer she felt in her own gaze.

The voice continued. Images of battle and blood washed away by the lapping of waves on a rocky beach.

"But our might, our intellect, does not supersede our altruism. When the Amphiba surfaced from the sea, driven from their home world by the Great Rains over 500 fortnights ago, the Kagarins embraced them. Offered refuge. Shelter. The opportunity to live and work among us. A new home."

Simulated thunder boomed around them. Images of great ships cracking through the surface of the sea hovered above the skulls in the display case. These were superimposed by the faces of anguished Amphiba blistered and bleeding as crimson rain pelted the ocean. Through the hologram, Elana saw Angi point and giggle, nudging a friend next to her as she whispered in her ear. The scene changed again; images of Kagarins pulling wounded Amphiba from the water, draping blankets over the Amphibas' shoulders as the storm calmed and the sea lay dormant, red, behind them.

Marvic leaned in. "Ever wonder who poisoned the sea?"

Elana froze with a chill as cold as a glacier at midnight—the same heart-stopping feeling she had when she absorbed her mother's last words.

She moved her eyes toward him, her head stiff, as if still focused on the presentation. "The gods brought the Great Rains." Elana spoke through thin lips, her words nearly inaudible. "We were destined to surface."

"Fairy tales." His eyes flashed again. "What they want us to think."

A new image appeared: Kagarin doctors surrounding a smiling Amphiba patient, his olive skin a stain on the white sheets upon which he lay. Wires and tubes spread from the patient's head, overlapping his body like mechanical tentacles, yet the Amphiba smiled. *Kagarin technology allowed the Amphibas to live.*

"If you call enslavement living," Marvic muttered. His eyes flickered gold for just a moment, casting a glow over his features. His gaze warmed her, just as her mother's did. Just as she remembered her father's gaze in flashes cutting through the depths of the undersea world she had barely known outside of her dreams.

The docent nudged her elbow. "You're the first Amphiba I've seen here in two seasons." He motioned toward the class—a swell of white-caps around the room. "Why?"

"Scholarship," she whispered. "Mother said I was one of the Chosen."

"Chosen." He snorted. "Like that's a good thing."

Red and yellow light flashed above the hologram, which now showed the floor of a deep cave. Purple stalagmites rose through an aquamarine pool like fingers reaching up from the planet's core. Through the mist that slept on the surface, Amphibas dove deep, disappearing for a hundred heartbeats or more before they reemerged with bloodied

fingers that grasped spiked spheres above their heads. Ever smiling, they swam toward a group of Kagarins waiting near a stockpile of the glowing orbs. *"Amphiba mine divers contribute to the greater good by excavating Alwic Spheres, driving cleaner energy, generating purity in the air that we Kagarins breathe. And with Selapa Ore, our technologic prowess allows our people to live fully automated lives—free of worldly constraints to pursue a higher purpose."*

Elana gritted her teeth. "They chose me for an education." She swallowed hard, fighting to control the change of pigment that threatened to surface on her skin. The Kagarins challenged and berated her daily; never did she think one of her own would judge her.

"Ever wonder why you're here?"

She shook her head, her two hearts beating a syncopated rhythm.

"I was on scholarship, too. Same horrible teachers. Same awful classmates. Now I'm an intern. A temporary assignment, they told me. And when I asked them what was next, they smiled. That's when I knew, it was time for me to go."

"Go?" Elana only knew of two options—the school and the mines.

He shook his head and smiled. "You'll know. When the time is right."

Elana rubbed the webbing between her thumb and pointer finger, slowing her hearts to a normal pace. She looked up at him, brow furrowed. "I don't understand."

"Kagarins only show kindness when it suits their purposes. And it's far easier for a beast to prey on a complacent target than a suspicious

one." He folded his arms. "They are ready to take from me what I've been groomed for."

She leaned in closer, convinced Marvic could hear the resurgent fluttering in her chest. "What will they take?"

Saltwater pooled in the palms of her clenched fists. She smelled the sea in her fear. She'd promised her mother silence, but the secret pushed through, as desperate for its freedom as a doomed fish, caught in an angler's line.

"My father. The Kagarins took him when we arrived in the Great Rains. We never knew why. Or where—" She stopped. Her classmates shuffled with boredom as the presentation droned on. Some played Mindgames on their headbands, the green blip reflecting off their eyelashes the only sign of their clandestine activity. Others fidgeted, whispering and giggling to each other. Professor Worlo sat on a chair in the corner, eyes closed in a meditative state.

No one seemed to give a damn about Kagarin history.

Or the two Amphibas speaking quietly in the corner.

Marvic nodded. "Your family's sacrifice."

Elana closed her eyes, recalling her mother's story. Amphiba families clinging to each other, trudging through a sea as thick as blood, and greeted by the barrel of an ion cannon. Mothers, fathers, and children falling to their knees on the rocky sand, prostrate in the grief of an impossible decision. One should go, the rest should stay.

They forced all those who refused to surrender one of their own back into the sea. Hand-in-hand, full families stood waiting to die together,

poisoned by the waters that once nourished them. For Elana's father, there was no choice. He simply stepped forward to spare his wife and young child.

"You know what became of him?"

Elana shook her head. The docent gestured toward the three skulls in the display.

"The center skull is an artifact of the sacrifice."

Her eyes glowing, Elana's hand flew to her mouth to smother the gasp that threatened them both. Did her mother know what the Kagarins had done?

"Your father. My mother," he said. "Sacrifice one, or all should die."

"The Kagarins did that. To him. To your mother."

"The Kagarins were dying. A brain pestilence of which no one speaks. We were the serum that saved them all."

The sound of lapping waves again filled the room. The voice boomed around them. *"We embrace our Kagarin heritage..."*

"There isn't much time." The docent was nearly breathless. "There was a reason they chose you—a reason they chose me. They saw something different in your father when they opened his mind. My mother.... They want to take the same. From us."

"For Kagarin country..."

"Cultivating our brains?" she said. The docent squeezed Elana's hand, as if to quiet her. Realization crashed into her, relentless as a tsunami.

Scholarship was not a privilege or a way out. It was a long-drawn death sentence. All those late nights spent with the headmaster, running mathematics drills, solving equations on the virtu-board until every piece of her cartilage ached—they were not for her betterment. They were part of a fully framed strategy to build a mental machine, a machine for the Kagarin to occupy and manipulate.

"When the tide changes, when their smiles supersede their sneers, the time is close..."

"For Kagarin honor."

"The path is lighted when the three moons of Agralan align in the north. You'll find me, and the others, in the tidepools hidden behind the cliffs outside the Endowin Mine."

Absorbed by the light, the hologram faded. The professor roused, coughing, as the students shuffled their feet and adjusted their packs. Elana turned toward Marvic, but he was gone.

"Reports are due tomorrow," the professor said. "No exceptions."

Arms crossed and smirking, Angi approached Elana.

"You have work to do." The Kagarin's eyes shined red like the poisoned sea.

"I do." Elana nodded, watching Angi turn on her heel and strut away to join her friends. "There is much work to be done," she whispered.

Elana would study their history and their mathematics, their physics and their art. She would study them just as they studied her. But they would not take her thoughts or her memories, her knowledge, her

power, for their own greater good. She would leave them, a whole Amphiba being, not just another skull in the display case.

Armed with the truth, she knew she deserved to live. Her people deserved it.

Elana shuffled toward the door amid the din of Kagarin chatter. As she approached the threshold, she looked back at the three skulls immortalizing her people's oppression. She ran her fingertips across the glass containing them, leaving a streak of sweat that reeked of seawater. Her essence. The mark of her people. Elana smiled.

She awaited the rising moons. And a path forward.

THE RIVERKEEP

R UTH STOOD BAREFOOT ON the riverbank, watching the night
sky. Cool mud oozed between her toes and bulging plastic bags
lay beside her, a day's wages manifested in discarded water bottles and
crushed beer cans. The refuse was a collection of artifacts—shells of
the consumption of strangers passing through, all of which could be
bartered.

Ruth didn't understand the mindset of the careless, having lost count
of how many times she'd unbound the feet of a duck shackled in
plastic, or fished straws from the nests of birds. Though she was only
ten, Ruth knew that apathy didn't understand its evil nature. She
knew how much the River needed her, and how much she needed the
River. Five cents a bottle and seven cents a can from Señora Garcia at
the bodega provided for her Mama and baby sister Angela, huddled in
the tent city they called home.

Every evening before Ruth left to scavenge, Mama hugged her close
and kissed her forehead. "Stay in the shadows," she'd say. "Run if

anyone sees you." And Ruth would smile as she'd skip away into dusk, leaving behind the tiny bonfires that breathed in the night air and the cars that whizzed by on the overpass above them, oblivious to the world that blossomed beneath.

Ruth had never told Mama about her talks with the Riverkeep, about the voice that rippled over the water on hot nights when the moon glowed red. Mist rose from the surface, blowing over Ruth in the breath of a song. Hypnotic in its timbre, the Riverkeep's speech lapped over her like the sea at low tide—rhythmic and calming. Irresistible. The Riverkeep said Ruth was a LifeBearer for keeping the waterway clear and free to flow and thrive, to feed a grander sea that Ruth had never encountered, nor fully understood.

Sometimes the Riverkeep shared special treasures with Ruth, parting the waters to reveal errant coins or even a sodden dollar bill. Pushing her fingers through the muck, Ruth grinned with glee as she retrieved these hidden surprises; often, it was during their most desperate times that the River provided the most.

And Ruth was thankful.

A duck waddled past her, shaking its tail feathers and quacking as Ruth looked up. Low, grey clouds drifted through the sky like passersby on a slow journey, stopping briefly to gather, as if magnetized. They milled about, obscuring the moon in quiet obeisance.

Ruth longed for that familiar glow. She asked nothing of the Riverkeep. They simply provided for each other with a quiet understanding of how things would be. But on this night, Ruth needed help that only the Riverkeep could offer.

She touched her fingertips to her chest to quell the flutter within.

Just as Ruth hadn't told her Mama about the Riverkeep, Mama hadn't told Ruth about the demons that tugged at Angela's breath as she slept each night. But Ruth heard the women whispering around camp, saw them frowning when Mama walked by, cradling Angela close. Sickness taunted with each of Angela's coughs, cackling so loudly that Ruth needed to cover her ears and hide. The red rims around Mama's eyes betrayed the soreness in her heart; the dark, sagging pockets hovering beneath her gaze carried her dread.

As strong as Mama's fear of death was her looming terror of the men in the Blue Suits.

The hospital was far from the tent city. Outside their cocoon, Mama and Angela would be vulnerable to the Suits' whims. They could cut the ties binding a family at any moment, despite the unconditional love connecting them. The men in the Blue Suits could take Angela away; they could take Ruth away, too, if she wasn't careful. Mama always said she'd rather lose her children in her own arms than surrender them to another.

"Riverkeep," Ruth whispered. "Please."

The night air held still. Ruth thought of Angela, the way her soft curls framed her cherubic face like a dark halo. It had been so long since she'd heard her sister giggle. Ruth wondered at how silence could swallow memories in the absence of familiar sounds.

The river gurgled. Bubbles pushed through the water's surface, one by one, popping like errant stars entering the night. Abandoning her wares, Ruth rushed to the water's edge.

"Riverkeep!" A ribbon of cool air swirled around her, and the clouds swelled, rolling thick as smoke. The rains burst forth, the sky tickling the receptive river with fat, deliberate drops. Ruth drank in the deluge, her tears indistinguishable from the sky's.

The moon glowed like fire, burning through the shrouded night.

"My child." Riverkeep's voice quivered in Ruth's bones. "Come."

Ruth splashed through the muck until she was knee deep in the water. "My sister, she needs..."

"Closer."

Ruth pushed forward until the water licked the tops of her shoulders.

"The River will provide, but so you must too."

"I'll do anything," Ruth said. "Please."

"For your sister, you shall offer your breath."

Soft tendrils wrapped around Ruth's hands and tugged her below the surface. She opened her mouth to scream, and the water flooded into her. It pushed past her throat and into her lungs, its sting sharp as glass. Wide-eyed, Ruth kicked and squirmed against her entrapment.

I don't want to die!

But Angela couldn't die, either. Riverkeep had promised, and Ruth needed to trust.

LifeBearer. The word flowed through her.

Floating, Ruth relaxed her body. The tip of her tongue tingled; tiny sparks danced at her lips. She gulped, hard, drinking in the light that pushed into her lungs and radiated through her.

With a strength she didn't know she had, Ruth exhaled, propelling herself back to the surface, star fire shimmering in her wake.

Ruth devoured the night air.

"A kiss for your sister," Riverkeep said. "To blow away the demons."

A shadow drifted past. Ruth thought she saw it smile as the moon paled and the river flowed, leading her to Angela.

Home. To her family.

TAKING HOPE

I NEVER ASKED TO be created.

For fourteen years, I've walked the Earth a shadow, nothing more than an artifact of light cast upon a more worthy being. I exist only to follow. They tell me I live to serve.

I have never been. There would be no *me* without *she*—my sister, the host from whose cells I originated. I'm neither human nor inhuman, but something in between. I entered this world quiet, soulless, placed by the gloved hands of scientists into a lonely incubator. No loving mother waited with soft arms to warm me, no adoring father to wrap me in his gaze—only crisp white lab coats, whose faceless wearers hovered, proud of the specimen and ignorant of the newborn soul.

Of course, I do not remember my creation day. No one does. Human or clone, we all simply arrive, clueless and helpless and squinting against the light.

Yet we persist. Through hours and months and years.

Until we realize who we are.

What we are.

I've spent my life reminded that I exist only so another should live, a truth branded upon me by hard words and harder glares, by a surgeon's scalpel carving that commitment into my flesh each time I'm needed. I'm here for a purpose, but unlike actual humans, I know what my purpose is. Conceived by science, I'm the remedy for my sister's defects; the font for flesh and blood designed to repair her flaws, relieve her pain, allow her to live a 'normal' life.

The doctors, my mother, and my father—they've molded me to be as diminutive as possible, prominent as a coat rack in a home. Though they might remove pieces of me to preserve my sister Elia, her mind and soul will never inhabit *my* body. It would require tremendous stretching to fit one so obese with entitlement within the meek frame they deigned appropriate for me.

Mother and Father wanted a healthy child, one whose giggles would echo as she ran barefoot and unfettered, toes tickled by the prickly blades of their glowing suburban lawn. They sought a completeness to themselves, a family that together smiled at sunsets as red skies faded into the pink shade of night. They wanted someone to read to and sing to, to share bedtime stories and ice cream sundaes. A child with whom they could plant a garden of flowers, hopeful that something would grow.

That something *could* grow.

More than anything, they wanted an assurance of parental joy. They wanted a child who would not be ripped from their grasp by death's sharp talons. They sought a normal life—the assurance of tomorrow echoed in the time *Before*. Before the meteor hit the other side of Earth, destroying half the planet with fallout that poisoned the biological functioning of all who remained. Before children born from their mothers' wombs entered the world substandard, their inevitable defects crying out as newborn wails.

My 'parents' needed something to cling to. They needed Hope. So, in the weeks before Elia entered the world, they sanctioned the making of me.

DOCTORS CALLED US THE 'berry twins.' Elia and I shared eyes as blue as the ripest blueberry, hair the color of strawberry, and cheeks with freckles the color of raspberries.

We were as adorable as a girl and her clone could be.

Every month, Mother and Elia skipped together, hand-in-hand, over the crumbling sidewalks leading to the hospital for our routine check-up. Elia's rainbow ballerina skirt flounced as carefree as her curls as she bounced along. I trailed behind, shuffling under the constraint of my scratchy grey dress. Tight at the knees, it enabled small steps only. I could never keep up.

The doctors poked and prodded and pinched. The light they shined in my eyes was so bright it broke into spots that danced in my vision.

Sometimes I felt like one of those spots, a floating fragment broken from its source—visible yet inconsequential.

Mother always made a show of holding her breath when the doctors examined Elia. Red-faced and buggy-eyed, Mother winced as Elia whined, awaiting those special words that tumbled from the doctor's lips, "Your daughter is fine." Mother squealed and cried. She smothered Elia in a hug so deep all I could see was Elia's hair trailing over Mother's arms, her tiny head buried in Mother's bosom.

Mother always rewarded Elia with a candy store trip for being 'so brave' with the doctors. Elia could choose whatever sweet she wanted. Usually, it was a red lollipop that was bigger than Elia's face.

They left me outside to hold Mother's overflowing bag of Elia's toys, stuffed with my sister's favorite comfort items, and instructed me to wait for the car. Even in the toxic red rain, I stood there as droplets pelted, sharp as stone, and streamed down my face like rivers of blood.

I often dreamed about what it would be like to wander through that candy store—clouds of sugar wafting over the room, consumed with each breath. Oh, the choices! With furtive glances through the storefront window, my eyes devoured licorice and bubblegum and gumdrops and caramels. I imagined how a whiff of their sweetness would translate to taste and texture, and how it would feel to hold a fistful of bliss, packed in a clear shining bag.

How I wished for just a lick of Elia's lollipop.

She never offered, and I never asked.

I never asked for anything. Not even an umbrella.

ELIA AND I SHARED a room until we were five. In those early years, it was simpler for Mother to tend to our needs if we were together. Elia slept in a canopied bed draped in lavender tulle, her bedspread satin and smooth, fit for a princess. An army of toys and dolls and stuffed creatures stood sentinel. Mother spent each night rubbing Elia's back as she fell asleep under a nightlight of stars that bathed the room in a celestial glow. I'd never seen stars before; no one on Earth had. Not since the blast.

But I did not dare ask Mother about the stars. She'd struck me once as I snuggled into the rough cotton sheets of my cot, quietly humming the melody that floated from Elia's music box. "Do not disturb Elia!" Mother gritted her teeth. "Elia needs her rest. You need to know your place here."

My cheek smarted where her hand had connected, but I didn't need to be told. I knew my place. My place was in service to my sister, my existence a ghostly reminder of her fragility, a reminder of what Mother stood to lose.

NOT LONG AFTER THAT night, they moved my cot to the base-ment. My presence was too distracting. Mother told me that Elia needed her strength, and that by sharing the same air, I would weaken her.

"You're old enough to manage on your own," Mother said, tossing my clothing into plastic bins.

Before I'd left Elia's room for good, I took one of her rag dolls from the menagerie on the shelf. She had so many; I knew she wouldn't miss this one. Stuck in cobwebs behind a stack of wooden puzzles, it was plain and old and ugly. It didn't fit with Elia's other toys. It surprised me that it lasted so long.

Sitting beneath the glow of a naked lightbulb hanging from the rafters, I leaned back against the damp basement stone and pulled the doll from its hiding place inside my pillowcase. Its face was dusty, and its yarn hair was matted and sticky. Its button eyes hung from loose threads, like teardrops.

"I'll always love you." I hugged the doll close.

It was nice to care for something.

I named her Hope. After me.

W E WERE TEN YEARS old when the lesions first appeared on Elia's skin. It was a Tuesday, and they had called me upstairs to sweep and mop the floors. Elia started digging at her ankles just as she'd logged out of her online math lesson.

"Bugs, Mommy! Bugs!" she wailed, scratching so hard she drew blood.

Mother frowned as she saturated a kitchen rag with cool water and scowled at me as she wrung it into the sink.

"Don't just stand there," she said to me. Mother's voice quivered, her eyes big and wild—more histrionic than the show she put on in the doctor's office during our monthly exams. I could smell her fear, rancid as rotten fruit. "Do something useful! Earn your keep for once!"

I nodded, scurrying past Mother toward the refrigerator.

Lunch. I could make lunch.

I retrieved packages of deli meat and cheese from the fridge, pulled bread from the breadbox. I folded thin slices of ham atop the bread and layered in the cheese. The meat was slimy and gross.

Elia squirmed and whimpered as Mother dabbed at her ankles with the cloth. Father emerged from his study. This was serious. Usually, we only saw him at dinner.

He clamped hands down onto Elia's shoulders. His clenched jaw and bulging veins suggested efforts not intended for comfort, but for restraint.

The welts grew. Elia's legs looked as if they'd been pulled from boiling water. Within minutes, the lesions had grown into bloody pustules the size of golf balls. She screamed.

I fainted.

I F I MOVED, IT hurt. If I didn't move, it hurt more. At least Mother had been kind enough to replace my scratchy sheets with a set of Elia's satiny princess ones. After all, if it hadn't been for me, Elia would have lost her legs to the infection.

She might even have lost her life.

My lower back, my stomach, the underside of my arms burned where they'd taken my skin. My body was intact, but my insides were exposed. They'd removed squares of flesh for Elia's grafts—like deli meat, I thought—and they needed to do it twice for the skin to take.

I inched my arm toward my pillow, convinced that each movement would crack my body open. Mother hadn't changed the casing on my pillow, thank goodness, and Hope waited in hiding. I rested my hand over the doll's belly and let the soft cotton of her dress slide between my fingers. It was as cool and soothing as springtime grass on those days when the radiation levels were safe and Mother let us sit outside. She and Elia would have tea parties in the garden, and I'd sit by myself, looking out at the red sky.

I laid on my bed and stared into the lightbulb above. The scorching filament danced, taunting me with feverish light. All I wanted was the dark. And to be comfortable. The moist basement air did little to cool me, and I was drenched in sweat.

If I could just pull that string, douse the light and sleep, lose myself to the pain for only a little while.

But I dared not call out for help. Mother had already given me the soft sheets, a glass of room-temperature water, and two painkillers.

Besides, they were busy. Poor Elia was recovering from two major surgeries. She was hurting and sick. Very sick.

A little girl needs her Mother in times like these. At least, that was what Mother said.

I closed my eyes.

That light. So bright.

I NEVER ASKED TO be created.

I never consented when they peeled the skin from my flesh or plucked out my left eye when Elia lost her sight. I never agreed to the scalpel plunged into my belly when Elia's kidney failed.

Why should I have two, they said, when Elia only had one?

But no one gave me a lollipop for being a good girl for the doctors. Instead, they left me in pain and alone. To them, I'm inhuman. Soulless. A specimen.

I slide my hand into my pillowcase to retrieve my doll. I'm fourteen now, too old for playthings, but I hold her close, anyway.

Tomorrow, they plan to take my heart.

I must die so Elia can live. It is my purpose. The reason I exist.

Yet.

I refuse to climb into that car tomorrow.

I will not discard my clothing for a surgical gown, nor glare at Mother when she tells me it won't hurt a bit.

It won't hurt, because I won't lie on their gurney or count backward from one hundred.

They won't touch me. My absence will give voice to my lack of consent.

I would not exist without Elia, but there will be no *she* without *me*.

BEFORE I LEAVE, I look upon Elia, sleeping in her princess room. I kiss her forehead and press my pillow firmly onto her nose and mouth so that she will breathe in the perfume of my shampoo, remember the scent of me, the scent of her as she drifts into never-ending sleep.

I press firm on the pillow until she's quiet. Still.

No one should be made to suffer.

As Mother and Father sleep, I walk out the door. With me, I take my Hope. I won't leave my doll behind to be burned with the trash.

I am not sorry.

I am an errant flash of light floating, a portion split from its source, shining on.

CORE TRUTHS

I am.

I.

Am.

VANISHED

*D*EAR EDITOR OF THE *Des Moines News:*

I am writing to you for help, since no one else will believe me, and maybe somebody out there will read this letter and say they saw what happened to my friend ten days ago at that Mysterious Monolith that popped up on the outskirts of the beach just outside Woodmont. My friend is missing, and nobody seems to care—not my parents, not the police, not the National Guard that's watching the tourists who crowd around that thing like it's the Space Needle or something.

The monolith is big, but not THAT big.

Anyway, my friend's name is Timmy. He just turned 12, and he's staying here in Des Moines, Washington, with his grandma while his dad's away in jail. He doesn't like to talk much about his family—I don't even know his last name—so he's probably gonna be mad at me for telling you all this. But somebody's gotta help, and I'd rather have him get mad at me than have something bad happen to him.

Timmy's a little taller than me, about five foot three, with red hair and freckles. He likes the Marlins because he's from Florida, thinks the Xbox is better than the PS-5, and peels the cheese off his pizza before he eats it.

We rode our bikes over to that obelisk just before lunchtime on July 2nd, on the day after it showed up, and there were lots of people standing around taking pictures. If you saw my friend there, or if you know where he went, please help.

My parents are probably gonna ground me for writing this note (especially since they told me to stay away from the obelisk... something about aliens or UFOs), but I don't care.

I just want Timmy back. I feel like I'm the only one who's out there looking for him.

Thanks for your help.

Sincerely,

Mike Hooper from Des Moines

I T'S COLD.

Inside a freezer cold.

Snow-cold.

I guess.

I've never actually seen snow, except on the Weather Channel.

Maybe I'll never see snow.

Maybe I'll never see anything again.

It's so dark in here. Darker than night.

Maybe darker than space.

So dark I can't see my hand if I wave it in front of my face.

My eyes won't adjust, because there's nothing to adjust to. Not one sliver of light in here.

If I lean back against the wall, it stings my back like frozen bees.

Can bees freeze?

Funny, how that rhymes.

Bees. Freeze.

The bee's knees.

Grandmother's always saying that—something's the bee's knees, and then she laughs and coughs like there's some gunk in her throat. There usually is.

And I have no clue what she's talking about. Bees don't have knees. At least, I don't think they do.

Guess it doesn't matter, now.

It's tight in here. There's no room for me to lie down, so I just sit, lean forward, press my head into my knees.

Timmy's knees.

I can't stop myself from chuckling, and my laugh bounces off the walls like I'm in some little cave.

Echo.

Echo.

It's not funny.

But it is.

I wiggle my toes inside my sneakers to keep the blood flowing. If I let them rest too long, they go numb. They sleep.

Maybe I shouldn't sleep.

Maybe I am asleep.

How long have I been here? A day, a week?

Is this what dead feels like?

Maybe I'm dead. Maybe I should be.

There was light outside. The brightest light I'd ever seen. The sun shimmered in a million tiny glowing boxes from the surface of that Mysterious Monolith. Or is it an obelisk? Who knows? Who cares? But I looked up to the top of it, all the way to its tip, poking like a

spear into the sky. I reached for it. I wanted to touch—I needed to touch—its smooth, sparkling edges.

It was like a box full of stars twinkling in the sunlight.

But then there were hands.

Icy fingers. Squeezing me.

And a flash, and then...

Nothing.

Now I'm here.

*D*EAR *TIMMY:*

I'm leaving you this letter outside the obelisk, on the off chance that you're around somewhere. It's weird. Usually when people go missing from someplace or when something bad happens, people leave flowers and pictures and candles. Stuffed bears, too. At least that's what they show on the news. But there's nothing here, just my letter. I'm folding it up tight so no one sees it and throws it away by accident, or tries to read it, just in case.

There's lots of people here. Those weirdos in the funny clothes—the red sneakers and white sweatsuits—the ones we laughed at, they're still milling around, like they were the last day I saw you. The Guard is still shooing away those older teenagers drinking out of paper bags.

CORE TRUTHS

Don't know what's so bad about that, but whatever. People are having picnics. Everybody here is taking selfies with the Mysterious Monolith. All the girls are making those stupid duck-lip faces that they put up on Instagram. With all the pictures, you'd think someone would have seen you in one of them.

The Des Moines News never printed my Letter to the Editor. Insta, Facebook, and Snap keep taking down my posts about you, too, some violation of fake news policy or something. I'm trying Timmy. I'm really trying. The cops still won't listen. And the Guard ignores me, as many times as I ask them. They say I should go write a book of my fairy tales, that I have a wild imagination. Jerks.

I wish you'd told me your last name. Or your grandma's name. Or where you lived. It didn't seem important then, but I wish I'd asked you when I had the chance.

Whenever I'm in town, I stop every old lady I see and ask if they're Timmy's grandma. Some of them yell at me and tell me to go harass someone else. Others pat me on the head and tell me to be a good boy and help them with their groceries. Most just ignore me and walk right past.

I won't give up on you.

Your friend,

Mike

P.S. Martins have won three in a row.

I'M GROWING.

Or the room is shrinking.

It's hard to tell.

My knees are pushed so hard into my chest now, I can barely breathe. My hair's grazing some type of ceiling that wasn't here before. If I rub the top of my head against it, tiny sparks shoot out, pricking my scalp like some Fourth of July sparkler.

Kind of like the ones Dad brought home when I was really small, and Mom was still around. She'd holler at him that it was too dangerous, that my little fingers would blow off or melt away or something. I can't remember.

She was afraid I'd end up like that Thompson boy down the street.

But Dad would laugh and squeeze her into him. Her shoulder fit right under his sweaty armpit. It was kinda gross, actually. 'Thompson boy's a dumbass, lighting off them cherry bombs like that,' Dad would say. When Mom wasn't listening, he told me he thought the Thompson boy deserved to lose those three fingers. 'People who don't respect the flame have no business going near it,' he'd say. Whatever that meant.

'But this here's a sparkler, just the right size for our Timmy. Right, champ?' Then Mom would frown as he lit it up—seemed Mom always frowned when she was with us. Her eyes always seemed like they were somewhere else, until one day, she was, too.

Funny how I can barely remember her face, but sometimes I think I see her eyes while I'm sitting here. They're snow-cone blue and shining

with the tears that are just about to melt from them. She cried a lot, my mom.

I remember how my dad would flick open that Zippo lighter like some cowboy slinging a gun from his holster. The flame shot up, that sparkler fizzing awake, and I'd grip the end as tight as I could, like my life depended on holding that fireball, and I watched him grin as bright as those white sparks that rained down on my skin from the burning stick, the seconds ticking by in a glittering fire until there was nothing left but a stump of ash between my thumb and pointer finger, and the darkness that stayed, long after the fireworks ended.

I want to miss them both.

But I don't miss them.

I can't miss them.

Missing a past that never was is the first sign of insanity.

Maybe I'm insane.

Maybe I belong here. Maybe I deserve it.

*D*EAR *TIMMY:*

It's been almost two months since the day we rode our bikes out to the obelisk. They still don't know exactly what it is or how it ended up in Des Moines. Mom keeps saying UFO or aliens. Dad tells her not to

get hysterical. There's got to be a logical reason it's here. Maybe it is nothing more than a planned-out tourist attraction. Or some marketing gimmick.

But every day when I come out to the monolith to look for you, I see scientists wandering about in their white lab coats. They've closed off a section to the tourists and I've been watching them dig around the edges, collecting rocks and soil in big bags. Sometimes they scrape at the walls with something that looks like a sharp spoon, putting the shavings in test tubes.

It would be cool to watch all this if you weren't still missing.

Gotta tell you, I've been running my own experiments when no one is watching.

Sometimes I toss pebbles at the obelisk to see what will happen, and they always make a high-pitched ping sound like the ring toss at the carnival. (By the way, the fair has come and gone. I would've had a lot more fun with you but my parents dragged me there like they do every year, even though I'm getting too old to be going with Mom and Dad).

Sometimes I shoot water onto the obelisk's walls, squeezing my water bottle as tight as I can to get the perfect burst. Like those water fights we used to have. It's funny how it pools there for just a second before drying up faster than a puddle in the desert. I wonder if the water gets soaked inside it, like the obelisk is some gigantic sponge. Or if it's osmosis. I learned about that in Mr. Miller's science class last year.

I asked the scientists whether the obelisk could suck things inside it, but the dumbass Guard yells at me every time I throw out a question. So I never got an answer.

Maybe that's where you are, Timmy. Maybe the obelisk swallowed you up when nobody was looking, and you've been in there all along.

It sounds crazy, but all of this is crazy, isn't it?

School is going to start soon. I wonder if they would have put us in the same class. That is, if you were still staying with your grandma—whoever and wherever she is. You never told me how long you planned to be here. Or if you were ever going to leave.

I hope you're okay wherever you are, and that whoever you're with is treating you well.

Your friend,

Mike

P.S. Marlins are killing it this season!

P.P.S. Those red-shoed wackos are still here, and it feels like more of them show up every day. What a freak show!

P.P.P.S. I saw a pretty girl you might have liked. She smiled at me after she took a selfie. But I didn't have the guts to say anything to her. YOU would have gone over to say hello. I'm a real wuss, I know.

I 'VE BEEN SLEEPING. A lot. There's not much else to do. It's dark with my eyes open. Dark with my eyes closed. Sleep is still scary, even though I can't help myself.

If I sleep, will I wake up?

Will I still be me if I wake up?

Will I remember who I am?

Timmy.

Timmy.

I'm Timothy John Doran the third.

From Lake Mary, Florida.

That's not right. I live someplace else now.

I live here.

Here.

Washington.

Des Moines, Washington. Where my grandmother coughs a lot and I ride my bike with a kid I met at the park. Mark? Matthew? Mike. My friend's name is Mike. People wear red shoes and white sweatsuits, and they don't like the Marlins so much.

Best baseball team ever.

My eyelids, they're heavy in the brief moments when I'm awake, like someone is pulling them down. I get so tired after they feed me, who- ever 'they' are, the someone or the something who's in charge here. It's hard to tell. Their icy fingers tug my jaw open and pour a warm, sweet drink into my mouth. Then, I'm in the middle of this crazy

dream. I'm playing second base for the Marlins and Mom and Dad are together cheering in the stands when the clouds come together, like a thatched roof, and out of them pours warm, thick liquid over the entire stadium—hot maple syrup from the sky. The crowd screams and runs, but I stand there with my mouth wide open and I gulp and gulp and gulp that liquid down. It's like rock candy, but better. The sweetest thing I've ever tasted. Clouds fall around me in a giant hug and there's ice, then heat, then ice again, in a scratchy tickle and then a long, slow burn. Something like the way you feel when you're scared shitless. Or so embarrassed you want to crawl into a hole and die. And then there's something else... something weird that I've never felt before. Something like... power.

And then I see Grandmother standing at home plate, dressed up as an umpire, screaming at me, "You're out, you're out, you're out!" I laugh at her, and she wags her finger at me as that sweet liquid slides down my throat and a red-shoed, white-clad army douses her with a bucket full of blood and she vaporizes, every bit of her body popping in the air like a million little clouds until there's nothing left.

Then I grow, and grow, and grow and my skin sticks to the cold metal box that holds me. Parts of me melt and I take the shape of that box. I am square. Square! And I can't contain my giggling. The frost is eating me up, sucking away my breath and then I'm standing, overlooking a cliff at a devil's face painted on the ground below.

I drink more, stuffing myself with the syrup they pour into me until I want to vomit and those freezing hands clamp down on my jaw, keeping the liquid safe inside.

Where it belongs. Where it's always belonged.

And I sleep, again and again, until a great hum, like the song of a thousand cicada bugs, shivers over my skin. It sloshes through my body, surfing over my bloodstream until it comes to rest.

It burrows into my core, where it finds its home.

Home. Where I shall forever dream.

I open my eyes.

To the light.

D^{EAR} *TIMMY:*

My parents want to send me to a psychiatrist. The editor of the Des Moines News called my mom about the letter I wrote, and my parents started following me down to the obelisk to spy on me. The Guard ratted me out, said I was a nuisance coming down every day to ramble on about some missing kid no one had ever seen.

They all think I made you up, like you were some kind of imaginary friend. Sure, if I was five. But twelve-year-olds don't have imaginary friends. And I'll always remember how much fun we had.

I miss our bike rides. I miss meeting up with you at the park. Playing stickball. Arguing about how the Marlins suck and the Mariners will always be the better team. Making fun of the way you eat pizza.

It's lonely without you.

This may be my last letter for a while. I've started riding out to the obelisk in disguise and hope the Guard and my parents don't catch on that it's me—even with my dad's fishing hat and my mom's bug-eye sunglasses.

Yeah, go ahead and laugh. I look like an idiot.

Come back home, Timmy.

Your friend always,

Mike

P.S. They think the Marlins may go all the way to the Series.

I HAVE EMERGED FROM my cocoon.

Free.

The world is warm. The sun is a god who nourishes and provides.

The Mother and The Father and all The Brothers and The Sisters—they are with me, our bond magnetic, celestial. In orbit, like The Earth in tandem with the lesser planets whose life forms once succumbed to the force of our will. Of our strength.

Just as The Earth would.

Soon.

We are One Herd, our white garments pure and beaming in the light of The Great Monolith, our crimson shoes electrifying the ground beneath it. Giving it life, sustaining its roots as they stretch and break deep through the hottest magma into the core.

The core that is us. The core that is whole.

My eyes are The Mother's, and The Mother's are The Father's—bluer than the brightest of skies. All seeing. All-encompassing.

Through their gaze, they tell me what They know, what They've always known.

To vanish is to find purpose, to be reborn into a life that has always been, left unrecognized, unfulfilled until The Light—it changes them—and they become something greater than that which can ever be conceived.

We hum and we chant. We wait for The Great Transformation.

Of The Obelisk. The font of all life.

We hum from the core that binds us.

We are one.

We wait for a sign.

*D*EAR TIMMY:

So much has happened! I need to write this note quickly because the Guard is forcing us to evacuate. The scientists found massive amounts of radiation coming from the Mysterious Monolith, and they say it's too dangerous to stay. In fact, once we get out of here, Mom is taking me to an oncologist. She's worried that all that radiation may have given me brain cancer and the brain cancer caused me to imagine you. I think it's all a lot of nonsense, but I don't have a choice.

What really stinks is that we get to bring one bag each. That's it. So it's goodbye Xbox for me.

I thought I saw you by the obelisk, the last time they allowed people near it. One of the red-shoes wandering around looked just like you, but much taller. His hair was a little bit redder than yours, but his eyes, they were weird. Wide. Like he was somewhere else, even though he was standing right there in the middle of the group. I yelled out "Timmy!" as loud as I could, but he didn't even flinch.

If it really was you, you would've recognized my voice. You would've waved and run over to me. We'd go out for pizza and have a good laugh at you wearing that crazy costume. What a great joke! I'd have even taken a selfie with you, even though it's a little creepy for guys like us to take selfies together. I would have posted it on Insta and called it Me and My Red-Shoed Friend.

You know, it's sad. I don't even have a picture to remember you by. I have nothing but my memories, and sometimes, I wonder if maybe I did imagine you. Maybe there is something wrong with me. Missing something or someone who never existed is a sign that you're wacked, isn't it? Maybe I am wacked and Mom's right, I need a psychiatrist.

And an oncologist, apparently.

Take good care of yourself, wherever you are. I'll root for the Marlins for you, even though they're a crappy team.

Your friend for life,

Mike

THE HUMANS, THEY HAVE abandoned their station, and The Obelisk, it radiates with our strength. The Sun has spoken. The House of the Rising Fire will rule The Earth.

We will show reverence for The Flame.

It is time.

SKELETONS

"MOTHER, CAN YOU HEAR me?" Alexander's voice is a muffled whisper, as if calling out from the grave. His fist raps at my door, knuckles beating a steady rhythm against the thick wood—his bones relentless as the head of a hammer seeking to break through.

Tap, tap, tap.

That noise, it intrudes, perverse and unnatural as a skeleton's phalanges poking the flesh of the living—a ghost puppeteering its cage of bones, confused if it is alive or dead. Despite Alexander's prodding, I will never subject myself to such bewilderment.

I will never be reduced to a lonely and forgotten skeleton, like the hundreds I'd encountered throughout my years traversing the world. Bones licked clean by the tongues of beasts ravenous for flesh. Bones corroded and filthy with the detritus of time. Bones that crumbled to dust with the first kiss of a breeze.

Here, in my chamber, I am safe—fortified by the promise of life eternal, by the power of the Medallion I discovered two decades prior in the Saharan sand.

I retreat to a corner and thrust my hands over my ears to quell the imposition—*those maddening taps.* The flesh of my palms draws a soothing suction to my ears, the rumbling pressure reminiscent of high tides crashing on the Aegean Sea, or of those moments before the Great Avalanche in the Tien Shan. How the seasons have changed since my expeditions, the value of the bounty increasing exponentially. Ancient tablets and jeweled diadems and sacred chalices I, *Dame Elizabeth the Grand Explorer*, retrieved with my own hands and released to the Royal Guard.

But I will never relinquish the Medallion. Not for anything. Not for anyone.

"Mother, I need to speak with you."

Exhaling, I allow my hands to fall from my ears.

"Alexander." I rise, approaching the door. My blonde hair swishes against the backs of my knees, a fluttering caress in this window-less room. The candles melted long ago, the Medallion's glow is my only source of light in this welcome, cloaking darkness. My hair's thickness, its length, its sheen, serve as an omnipresent reminder of the eternal youth flourishing within me. Unencumbered by worldly needs—food, drink, affection—this gift granted through my most precious find renders me better than human.

I've stopped thinking of how many years have passed since I last gazed upon my son. He'd squeezed his tiny hands into fists, waving at me,

blowing kisses—the little boy with sapphire eyes and curls that swirled like a starry field on a moonless night. Fat tears had rolled over his dimpled cheeks as my beloved Raphael stood behind him in the parlor of our home, a callused hand clasping our son's shoulder as I heaved my chamber door shut, bolted with five locks to keep the world out.

To keep the magic inside.

It was the night I'd buried the tax collector in the garden. That beady-eyed man had seen too much. He'd asked too many questions about my work, my history. About the treasures I'd touched throughout the years. Whether I'd kept anything of worth for myself as a souvenir of my adventures. Relics, he'd reminded me, which were the rightful property of the Crown.

At my request, Raphael had led Alexander into the fields to chase fireflies while I fulfilled my task. There was no choice.

Still, there have been moments in my solitude when I've wondered what would have become of me had I relinquished the Medallion to the Queen. How it would have been to mark the years with every inch added to Alexander's height, instead of hearing their forward motion in the deepening timbre of my baby's voice through the sealed door.

"It's the Queen," Alexander says. "She has summoned you for another expedition."

I lean against the door, pressing my ear into the knotty wood. As if by instinct, my fingertips land on the Medallion. It rests upon my heart, my pulse channeled through the ancient metal.

"After all this time? Surely the Crown recalls the terms of my retirement."

"Her Majesty's Chief Explorer believes he has found the location of the grand Arctic Emerald. They seek your counsel—your leadership. No one knows more about the Emerald than you do. Why, it's the very reason..."

Alexander's voice drifts deep into the recesses of my memory, my dreams. I, as a small girl enamored of a glowing gem I once thought existed in tales only. I'd yearned to be a rogue explorer, yet the world demanded I be a dainty maiden awaiting the hand of a husband to guide me, to care for me as I served him and attended his every whim. That world, it didn't understand that my aspirations extended far beyond that which was expected.

"Isn't it exciting, Mother?" Alexander says. "The opportunity you've waited for your entire life. The Emerald..."

... was the reason I became an explorer. My quest to find it led me to Raphael, to love, and briefly, toward motherhood and family.

Toward the Medallion, and eternal life.

"You know I cannot leave this chamber, Alexander. The risk is too great—"

"Yes, I know." His sigh is like a curt breeze against the thick wood. "The Medallion is greater than us all. Greater than the limits humanity has cast upon us, and it is your task to protect it. Regardless of who you hurt."

"Alexander..."

"Twenty years, Mother. Twenty years you've hidden in this... this tomb! Is this sacrifice worth your life?"

Indignation rises through me like festering lava.

"The Medallion *gives* me life," I say. "Besides, as I've told you and your father countless times, the consequences of it falling into nefarious hands would be deadly. End-of-days deadly. For the good of our larger world, I remain sequestered."

"Of course, Mother. You are quite the altruist."

"Mind your tongue, Alexander."

Light shimmers as I lift the Medallion in my palm. I let the thick golden chain drip through my fingers like sunshine-laden honey. The flat, round surface of the metal glows in my hand, my skin alabaster and celestial in the dark. Its significance is why I disposed of the tax collector; why I'd allowed my child to grow up motherless and my dear husband to become old without me. All to protect it.

Leaving the sanctuary of this room would mean losing everything.

"Mother, the grand Arctic Emerald. Doesn't the prospect of its discovery excite you?"

"I've discovered all I need, Alexander. My greatest treasure is safe in here, with me."

"Most mothers consider their family their greatest treasure. Father misses you so much. His health is failing. And I—"

For a fleeting moment, I feel a twinge pinch at my core. The Medallion sparkles over my chest, reminding me of its power. Alexander will never understand the depth of my sacrifice.

"I will not be meeting with the Queen," I say. "Please send my regrets."

"But, Mother, she demands your presence. What shall I do?"

"Kowtow to Her Majesty, as I did for so many years as her servant," I say. "And... lie."

AS ALEXANDER BOWED BEFORE the Queen, he felt his father tremble beside him and wondered if it was fear, frailty, or some combination that led Raphael to quaver. His father's skin appeared ashen, the bones of his shoulders prominent as he leaned on his walking stick for support. For the first time, Alexander saw his father as an old man.

"Your Grace," Raphael said. "It is an honor."

Alexander took his father by the elbow and settled him into an oversized red velvet chair opposite the throne. Deep lines crinkled at the corners of Raphael's eyes and tremors raged across his limbs. Alexander patted Raphael's hand, partially to quell his father's trembling, partially to lend support for this meeting his mother refused to attend. No one refused the Queen's orders, except his mother.

His mother had her *beliefs*, beliefs which served as her only truth. Though he silently cursed her for putting his father through this

ordeal with the Queen, Alexander still loved her, and he knew Raphael did, too. He watched the way his father nestled into Mother's favorite blanket as he sat outside, gazing at the sky on cold, clear evenings. He listened to his father murmur "good night" without fail to a door as tight as a crypt. He heard the intimacies Raphael whispered each night into the empty pillow that once held her head and carried her into dreams. "Here," Raphael would say, pointing to his heart. "She's here, always, even if she spends eternity in that room."

"I am sorry to hear Dame Elizabeth is not well," the Queen said. A stiff, red collar framed her rigid face and shock-white hair. Flowing robes grazed the white marble floor upon which her jeweled, gilded throne rested. A servant handed her a gold-rimmed porcelain cup and saucer; tea steamed from within.

"I hope you will forgive her absence," Raphael said.

"It has been a long time since our youth. We all bear our ills." The Queen sipped, glancing from Raphael to Alexander as she held the cup and saucer in her gloved hands. "It must challenge you, caring for aging parents. You are a dutiful son."

Alexander and Raphael exchanged looks, eyes darting in a rapid meet-and-retreat. Alexander cleared his throat; Raphael rasped: "My Alexander is a good boy. He cares for me like no other could."

"And for Dame Elizabeth, too?"

Raphael pulled his lips taut, the corners twitching as if he were tamping down an itch that reached from his skin to his very core. "Elizabeth has always been more... self-sufficient... than I."

The Queen chuckled, her laughter an errant arrow bouncing off the castle walls, seeking its bullseye. "Your wife always was so full of zest. I've watched her stand toe-to-toe against Royal guards two heads taller than she. I've heard the rumors of her sprinting barefoot across hot coals to outrun a gang of poachers, and that she'd once swallowed a sword to barter the whereabouts of a certain rare item now displayed in our National Museum." The Queen leaned in. "Did you know your mother was this adventurous, Alexander? Fearless creature, she was! So tragic, her retirement, when she was still in her prime."

Alexander shuffled his feet and fidgeted. Raphael nudged his son's leg with his cane.

"Where are my manners?" the Queen said. "Speaking of your wife, your mother, as if her soul has passed on to the next world, when, as you've clearly said, she is very much alive but simply... ill. Too ill to grant a visit to her Queen on this fine day. And her illness, I hope it is not life threatening..."

Raphael met Alexander's eyes with the countenance of a ghost, their silence as thick as stone. They hadn't anticipated such an extensive audience with the Queen—those called to her chamber were most often given but a moment to pay homage.

This felt more like an inquisition.

Simultaneously, they replied with disparate answers, Raphael blaming Elizabeth's illness on 'women's problems,' Alexander claiming she suffered from 'gastric distress.'

"I see," the Queen said. "It is the melancholy that is afflicting her, then. Delirium, too, perhaps. Particularly given her advancing age."

Both Raphael and Alexander fixed their gazes on the shining marble floor. The loose, wrinkled skin on Raphael's arms jiggled with his intensifying tremors, as if his bones attempted to leap from his body.

Alexander lifted his chin and regarded the Queen with tired eyes.

"Your Majesty, when I was small, Mother and I would lie out in the fields, and we'd count stars until I fell asleep. She told me each one had a name and a story of its own, just like all of us. I've rather enjoyed hearing about Mother's... younger... days." He stopped, as if uncertain his next words were appropriate. "It has been a long time since I heard the tales of Mother's adventures."

"Indeed." Raphael nodded, closing his eyes. Alexander glanced at his father, all too cognizant of the need to seal the memories of his mother tightly inside, lest they be lost forever.

"We all have our stories to tell." The Queen took another sip of tea. "And those we seek not to tell, those artifacts of our lives that remain hidden in places even the greatest adventurers cannot touch."

At that moment, Raphael's walking stick slid from between his feet and clattered to the floor as he fell forward, hunched over in his chair.

"Father!" Alexander leapt up and grasped his father's shoulders, raising him into a sitting position. Raphael's blue eyes had rolled up. His body convulsed with a seizure. The Queen rose, signaling her servants for assistance. A small boy in a satin uniform scurried over, carrying a dark crimson root within his hands. He placed it beneath Raphael's nose.

"Breathe, Father, breathe!" Alexander implored.

Raphael was the only family Alexander had; losing him was unfathomable.

With a gurgle, Raphael roused. Pupils heavily dilated, his eyes returned to a healthier, more human position and his shaking subsided; the storm momentarily passed.

"Thank goodness," Alexander whispered. He turned to the Queen. "And thank you, your Majesty, for helping my father."

"Dear boy, it was your mother who discovered the healing power of the boneset root."

Alexander bowed. "We are eternally grateful."

Patting her tight, white curls, the Queen offered a closed-mouthed smile, one that failed to ignite the light in her eyes. "The toils of old age," she said. "We have such a temporary stay, pity that our best years are tainted with poor health."

As if remembering the purpose of their invitation, Alexander bowed again. "Please, your Majesty, accept our regrets on behalf of Mother. It would have been an honor upon her, upon our family, to obtain the Arctic Emerald for the benefit of the Monarchy. Her... health... precludes her from leaving her humble domicile."

Two royal Pages approached. One grasped Raphael's elbow, the other his walking stick.

The Queen stood, signaling an imminent dismissal. "Your mother has been a loyal servant to the Crown," she said. "The artifacts she found during her tenure have been instrumental to our continued dominion in our ever-expanding empire."

Her lips pulled back in a tight smile, smoothness eclipsing her aging features. Alexander held his breath; this monarch, though slight and elderly, had executed men for lesser crimes than their duplicity.

"We will find the jewel, with or without Dame Elizabeth's active contribution. Please convey our best wishes for her continued well-being."

A LEXANDER TAPS AT MY door again with that hollow knock, persistent despite my admonishments for him to leave.

I do not wish to hear about their meeting with the Queen, their reminiscence of the woman I once was. I do not wish to rehash the life I lived a lifetime ago, those days before I placed the Medallion over my head.

Before it had settled against my skin and become part of me. Before its promise rooted in my soul. Did the Queen know about the Medallion? Was her call for my presence simply a ruse to flush it out of my chamber? Had my husband and son been strong enough to maintain my secret, keep safe the most powerful object ever discovered in the history of humanity? This relic, it is mine to have, mine to keep, my life guaranteed to endure beyond the Monarchy.

More than anything, I do not wish to hear again about my beloved's failing health, the curse of age that befell him as it does all humans, save for one. Save for myself.

But Alexander tells me all of it, despite my pleading for him to silence the diatribe gushing from his mouth. It pains me to remember,

although my spirit warms when Alexander informs me it was my discovery that had saved my beloved husband in the Queen's throne room, allowing him to persist for another day, another night on this Earth. I wonder how often the Queen herself partakes of the boneset root, how its healing may have preserved her claim to the throne for far longer than the years have promised.

Further assurance that protecting the Medallion is my life's purpose. An immortal monarch is invariably an immoral one, for such infinite power can lead to decisions that destroy kingdoms, destroy lives. Perhaps even the world.

I lie in my bed, clutching the chain tethering me to immortality. I struggle to swim against the riptide of memories that flood those aspects of my life I've needed to let lie in the darkness of this room. Motherhood and nurturing, marriage and passion, while noble pursuits, are no more than a candle flame in the wake of a much brighter sun.

My duty is to preserve the Medallion, my soul its keeper.

Yet, the images of my beloved flash unbridled as lightning over the sea. Diving from the cliffs of the Serpent's Lair, holding Raphael's hand as our legs scrabbled through the air, desiring yet rejecting the notion of solid ground, our skin slapped by the surface of the cool water, reminding us of our vitality. Watching the sun set over Zanzibar, our naked bodies entwined in the powdery sand as we vowed our lives to each other, limbs curved into the symbol of infinity. Raphael's hands clutching my shoulders, his touch an indelible mark, as our baby slid from my womb on to the chilled soil of a Nepalese mountaintop. The

delight in Raphael's gaze when I placed the Medallion over my head, how he marveled that this discovery was my greatest triumph.

I shake my head to delete the images of an imminent future: Raphael's stiffened body, glimmering coins placed over his eyes. The decaying stench of his burial wrappings as the Earth swallows them. The wriggling of worms burrowing through his flesh, the pincers of insects consuming marrow and organs, cutting through rotting tendons that stretch thread thin.

His skeleton. Remnants of the man he was; the likes of which I swore never to become. Would his decaying jaw position his teeth into an eternal smile, or an infinite and silent scream?

"Mother," Alexander repeats. His voice carries through the door like a whisper in a windstorm. "Father is asking for you. The boneset root's effects did not last. He hasn't much time."

I squeeze my eyes tight. My marriage vow to Raphael ends at the precipice of death. His journey is to continue without me.

"Mother. He needs you now, more than ever. I need you. Please, come back to us."

I rise from the bed. With a heaviness in my gait, I drift toward the door. I allow my palms to graze the knotted wood, attempting to remember the feel of Raphael's roughened skin. He'd built our home with his own hands and fashioned this chamber to suit my vision—first intended as a library to house my journals; later, a trophy room to house any relics the Monarchy would allow me to keep. The latter proved futile, as the Crown allowed me nothing from my expeditions but my memories.

I, myself, had secured the bolts and the barriers and barricaded the windows after the tax collector's ill-fated visit. Though Raphael's quick wit and Alexander's wide, innocent gaze had diverted the authorities' questioning far away from our home, I knew I was not safe, my treasure in jeopardy. Immortality was too valuable to risk the meddling of any further interlopers—even if those interlopers were my greatest love, and my flesh and blood.

Once the Medallion became mine, those whom I loved the most became the most dangerous of trespassers, my greatest tempters.

"I cannot leave this room, Alexander."

Opening the door would be akin to dangling my carcass for circling vultures to feast upon. Untouched by the wrinkled hand of time, my face and my body would betray the nature of my treasure. They would pluck the jewel from my neck, pluck me from this sanctuary, armed with envy and a lust for the Medallion's power. I'd writhe and my flesh would wither, my soul crushed into nothingness. My blood would let until it rotted, rancid against my crumbling form, and the beasts would devour anything left, licking clean my shining skeleton.

My skeleton.

Pieces of me, waiting to be stomped upon by the boots of explorers lesser than me.

Alexander's voice grows frantic, wild as a frightened animal. "Mother, he is failing."

"No," I say.

I cannot. I will not open this door.

My son's deep, bellowing cry rattles the heavy wood. I imagine his hand—a man's, not a child's hand, now—resting on the other side of the door, this barrier between us our only bond. I feel his resonant pain vibrating through it from my fingertips all the way to my heart.

Then, silence.

Ear-splitting, terrifying silence that squeezes the breath from me.

"Alexander?"

My body freezes, and that pain, it clutches my throat, too. I cannot swallow. Can neither inhale nor exhale.

For the first time since I've barricaded myself in this room, I feel trapped.

I press my palms hard against the door as if attempting to open a casket embedded deep in the earth.

Raphael's casket.

My casket.

"Alexander, I'm coming."

I move my hand across the door's rough ridges, the grooves like tick marks immortalizing each moment I've dwelled in this room, each breath I've taken without the warmth of Raphael's lips against mine.

One fissure embedded in the wood for each milestone my child achieved without me holding his hand; each deep scratch a reminder of the life I've lived, the life I've lost.

The first lock cuts into my palm, blood streaming down my arm as I attempt to turn it. It refuses to budge, frozen solid as the bronze statues of the ancient ones that Raphael and I would marvel at on warm summer nights.

The second, the third... similarly immobile.

And as quickly as the wounds appear on my hands, my skin seals, soft and unscarred, as if I've not been injured at all. The Medallion, it scorches my chest, searing my skin.

Warning me to remain within this chamber.

My legs betray me, and I slump to the floor, leaning my head against the door.

"Alexander."

Silence replies.

"Alexander," I say, louder.

I hear shuffling outside.

"Mother."

"Your father, is he...?"

Alexander pauses.

"Father whispered your name in his dying breath. But I'm sure you didn't hear him *in there*."

No... not my Raphael. Not the man whose eyes glimmered like stars over the Sahara when he looked at me, whose jet-black hair blew in the breeze with a wave that rivaled the Pacific tide under the new moon.

The man who'd aged. Who'd grown old without me. The man I haven't seen with my own eyes in almost a quarter of a century.

"He is dead." The deep voice of my child—this grown man I would never recognize—roars outside. "Just like you, Mother. Just like you."

I pull my knees to my chest and grasp the Medallion with both hands. Rocking myself into a daze, I bask in its warmth, in the timeless strength it offers. The Medallion promises me eternity, freedom from the scythe of a Reaper I'll never need to duel. My skeleton and flesh will remain my own for all my days—I will never become an artifact.

"You will never understand," I whisper.

In time, none will remain to mourn me; yet none will have the privilege to study my remains to distill clues to a past that was never theirs to know.

THE SECONDS PUSH FORWARD with each of my heartbeats, time numbing to minutes and hours as my breathing lulls to quell the blood pulsing in my ears. Days blur to years, to decades, perhaps; the last time I've heard Alexander's voice—anyone's voice—was that terrible day I lost my Raphael.

I wonder where my son has gone. Has he found a woman to love, or fathered children to nurture? Has he followed my pursuit of treasures as grand and elusive as the Arctic Emerald, and has he succeeded in finding what he's sought in life? Did he choose to serve the Crown, or elect to live a quiet, humble life?

I squeeze my eyes shut in the darkness. Who my son became matters not, for one day he will come to know death as I never will. As I remain snug within this dark hearth, my son, too, will grow as cold as my beloved. His bones will dissolve to dust, indistinguishable from soil, from rock, from the remains of those who've passed before him. Swallowed by the earth, like my Raphael. My poor, beloved Raphael, who will never know how much I love him, how I miss him.

I bear no regrets about my choice. Free will aligns my destiny to the mysteries of my ancient treasure. I dwell in the Reaper's shadow—untouchable and invisible in this chamber, to an interminable end. The Medallion will not deceive me; it will not lie. There is no death in life, despite my son's final contention. It is a passage that exists evermore only in my subconscious musings—a journey upon which I will never embark. My flesh will remain impervious to the jabbing of skeleton fingers that question the nature of vitality.

As long as we both remain safe within the confines of this vault, the Medallion and I will always live. It burns into my chest, branding me with a warming relief; my heart thrums under its comforting weight.

My soul serves as the Medallion's loyal, forever guardian. It preserves me. Keeps me.

I feel nothing but love for its power.

THE ODDS ARE EVEN

"P APERS."

The SecuriBot's tinny command barked through the bings and blips of the noisy casino. With a reaper-like metallic claw, it snatched a slip of white paper, no bigger than a banknote, from Allie's hands, and slid it into a slot in its torso. Allie hugged her arms across her midsection, the coarse fabric of the government issued Fourthclass attire scratching her skin. She shuddered as the Bot belched out her processed paperwork.

"Line 2. Population Control."

Grasping the sheet, she moved toward a group of young women, cordoned away from the rest of the casino by a red velvet rope. All wore the same drab jumpsuits, the same expression of wide-eyed hope. And wide-eyed dread.

"Happy birthday, ladies. Lucky number 18 for us."

Allie turned toward the voice, a tall Fourthclass whose khaki uniform accentuated her every curve.

"Never dreamed I'd spend it playing Sterility Roulette." The girl smiled, tossed long, blond locks over her shoulder, and extended her hand to Allie.

"I'm Sara."

"Allie," she replied, hunching her shoulders to hide the bloated pudge around her belly and hips.

On the other side of the rope, men and women in designer suits sipped martinis at a craps table with the nonchalance of the privileged. Class Two Alpha, Allie thought. Her throat burned with rising bile as she watched a woman, pregnant belly protruding through her chiffon dress, pluck olives from a full glass.

"Amazing how we can be in the same room as them, but on a totally different planet," Sara said.

"Very little amazes me," Allie murmured. Her gaze lingered on the casino floor where ThinkBots congregated, observing the gamblers as if they were on display. She recognized them by their red skull casings; these judges whose mathematical process allocated humans into sects based on their high-level productivity quotient.

Allie's mother had been a physicist, so valued by the Bots they worked her to death. With the family's quotient more than halved, she and her father were downgraded from Class Two Theta. Their home and possessions seized, their legacy would be one of sacrifice to a machine's

vision of a greater good, where one's output was the sole determinant of human worth.

Allie laid a hand on her stomach to stop it from rumbling. Too nervous to eat, she had only nibbled a few bites of dry toast Michael had made her that morning. "Who needs luck?" he'd said as he kissed her, his lips soft. "You have love on your side."

Raucous whoops burst from the crowd playing craps. They high-fived, back-patted, and bear-hugged, wrapped in the ecstasy of a win.

"Must be nice to be on the other side." Sara said.

Allie tugged at the square of paper, curling the corner between her thumb and forefinger. If her mother hadn't died, she could have easily become one of *them*. Her stomach roiled in a knot of disgust and jealousy. She swallowed hard to fight the nausea that threatened to overtake her. Our humanity makes us do strange and selfish things, she thought, resting a hand on her belly as she watched the pregnant gambler down another drink.

Allie and Sara took a few steps forward with the moving line as a Bot voice droned through the loudspeaker: *"Enjoying your morning at the Sugarloaf Casino? We strive to create a serene and supportive environment. Win or lose, we hope you have a great day."*

"Couldn't the Bots have called us in to some office for this?" Sara said. "It's all fun and games until someone's uterus gets fried. But a casino is taking it a bit too far."

Allie shook her head. "Here, the house always wins."

"Not true. It's a 50/50 shot," Sara said. "The odds are even."

"Nothing's even anymore. Didn't you see those ThinkBots watching? Calculating? Our presence *here* is a statement to the Alpha Twos." Allie gestured toward the gamblers. "*Out there*. One wrong roll of the dice and they're standing on this side of the velvet."

Sara nodded, her countenance sobering. She bit her lip. "Mother told me to take the stipend. Trade my fertility for better rations." She brushed a tear. "I couldn't. I needed to take the chance; hold on to my dreams of motherhood for a little bit longer."

Allie squeezed Sara's hand.

Sara sniffled. "What about you, Allie?"

"I'm—" Allie stopped herself. She pictured Michael pacing the threadbare carpeting in his tiny apartment, awaiting news. She thought of her father, head in his hands with worry. The table stakes were high. "I'm an only child. There's no one after me. Besides, if they take our dreams, what do we have left?"

They reached the front of the line, where a bow-tied DealerBot stood behind an old-fashioned roulette table. The kind Allie's grandmother used to talk about.

"Papers." He placed Allie's slip on red, Sara's on black.

Above them, a hologram flashed the gamblers' incoming wagers—Sara favored three-to-one.

"Sudden death." Sara smirked. "Good luck?"

Allie's eyes fixed on the spinning wheel, spokes of red and black whirling in a centrifuge of chance. The dealer tossed a pearly white ball into the blur—round and round it orbited her future, and the future of the fetus quickening in her womb.

The dealer waved his hand above the table. "No more bets."

The wheel slowed. The ball bounced.

Black red red black red...

"Black."

Allie gasped.

Through Sara's squeals and distant cheers, the bells of workhorse slot machines clanged through Allie's mind—a death knell.

She clutched the edge of the table.

Watched the Bot stamp Sara's paper; inject a microchip beneath the girl's skin. *"... Approved for five years."*

Allie pressed her palms against the mahogany to stop the world from spinning.

With a giggle and a hop, Sara ran off without a glance toward Allie.

"Some you win, some you lose." The Bot grabbed Allie's paper and pushed it into the slot on the front of its torso. A hope that was once whole disintegrated before her as the tiny paper ran through the Bot's shredding mechanism.

The remnants fell to the floor, discarded trash.

A LITTLE BIT OF SUNSHINE IN HELL

THE FIRST TIME THE kid saved my life, I thought it was dumb luck, and the Guy Upstairs wasn't ready for me yet.

The second time the kid saved me, I got myself shifty-eyed paranoid. Kid knew where I was gonna be, who I was gonna meet, what I was gonna do. How I felt about it. Maybe the Coogan clan had hired him as a tail. I thought I smelled a rat—but a rat'll eat you if it's hungry enough, and that kid was no more rat than I was a sandwich.

The third time that kid saved my life, I was almost dead.

HELL'S KITCHEN, NEW YORK: where you stayed because no place else would take you, where nobody loved you except

your mother because she didn't have a choice, no matter how ugly your mug or how charred the depths of your heart. Home in Hell, the devil howled with the verbal abuse doled by every drunken wife-beating bastard. He hid in the shadows of rodent-infested alleys and hummed in the rumbling bellies of siblings whose mothers had to choose which kid would eat and which would go without, disregarding their own pangs. That devil, he wrapped his icy cloak over darkened apartments, devoid of heat or power, electricity cut when the bills became too much.

The devil reminded me of my father, and the shell of my mother he left behind.

"You get paid this week, Jamesey?" Mama's hand trembled as she reached toward me, her palm scarred crimson with the fabric dyes from her work in the garment district. I swallowed back the rage I felt at the chemical smell that lingered on her skin. Her eyes, once soft and playful, now sunk deep and dark like a waiting casket. She forced a smile, but stiffened lips and heavy shoulders betrayed the stolen joy that defined her existence in this world.

"O'Reilly always pays on time." I placed a small stack of singles in her hand.

"He's a good man." A sigh shivered over her as if cast by the breeze from the passing A-train. "Glad he's offered you extra hours at the diner. Maybe we'll make rent."

"Maybe," I said.

Mama deserved more than just maybe.

T HE KID WAS NO older than nine. He wore cuffed dungarees and a gab jacket, like most boys his age. Arms crossed, he leaned against the lamppost on the corner of 57th and 8th, watching me barrel up the stairs of an old brownstone. The streetlight cast a glow over his shock of white-blond hair styled in a miniature pompadour. Mama didn't know, but I'd taken a side job running 'errands' for Michael Gorgon. She wouldn't like it, seeing as Gorgon's boys were always fighting the Coogan clan, and most of them ended up in jail. But cash was cash. If I wanted to make a better life for us, bussing tables at the Seventh Avenue Diner wasn't gonna cut it.

Smirking, the boy looked me up and down, sizing me up. I was twice his height and probably twice his age, which made his staring even more ridiculous.

"It's late. Aren't you a little young to be here alone?" I asked.

"You ain't so old yourself," he said. "Besides, I'm here for your own good."

Shaking my head, I chuckled, trying to control the quaver that threatened. It was my first assignment with Gorgon—no way this kid was gonna mess things up.

"Beat it, kid." I glanced down the empty street, wiping damp hands against my dungarees, before pulling a small package from my pocket. My heart thudded percussion to the police siren wailing in the dis-

tance. "I got a job to do. You've got no business here. Go home to your Mama."

"Watch out for the flying pan." He chewed on his pinky finger and spat a fingernail to the ground. "It'll hit fast on your left side, just below the eye socket."

I stopped. "Did you say *flying* pan?"

"You heard me."

"Don't you mean 'frying pan?' No such thing as a 'flying pan.'"

Just then, the door opened. A scraggly haired man appeared through a shadowed hallway. He glanced left, then right, avoiding my eyes with his wild stare.

I passed him the small, wrapped package. He snatched it like an animal protecting his prey.

"Gorgon sent ya, he did," the man muttered.

I nodded, and as I turned to leave, a screech sharp enough to slice flesh exploded from the hallway behind him. A large beefy hand, attached to a large beefy woman in a faded housecoat, pushed the man down the steps. In her other hand, I caught a glimpse of metal, just as an oversized cast-iron pan flew from her fingertips toward the bullseye of my forehead.

"Goddamn dope pushers!" she bellowed.

I ducked, crouching toward the right, away from the—*flying pan?* Losing my footing mid-step, I tumbled down the stairs to the pave-

ment—grit, gravel, and a searing pain embedded in my left cheek. The pan clanged to the ground, resting beside my ear. Scrambling up, I rushed past the vacant lamppost where the boy had stood only moments before and ran the full ten blocks home.

MAMA PRESSED A COOL compress against my swollen cheek. Pain shot up my head, into the crevices of my brain. Flaps of skin hung from raw, purplish flesh dotted with 57th Street grit.

"Tell me how this happened," Mama said. "I don't want to hear no nonsense about how you tripped on the curb."

How could I explain that some crazy lady tried to attack me for making an illicit delivery to her junkie relative? Or the kid who warned me it was gonna happen?

The kid who warned me it was gonna happen.

"We should get you to a doctor."

"Don't worry about me, Mama."

She stood and rinsed out the washcloth. My cheek soothed with her returning touch.

"That's my job, to worry about you. Besides, a face like yours is one in a million."

Wincing, I smiled.

With my next haul, I'd get something nice for Mama—a new pair of shoes so she wouldn't have to shove cardboard inside her holey ones. If I hustled enough, maybe she could stop working in that godawful sweatshop and I'd see the light flicker in her eyes. Her smile could be soft again, real. Unburdened by pain.

But I wasn't sure if I'd be able to outrun the shadow that chased me under Gorgon's watch—knowing that my attempt to improve our lives could, and probably would, result in the ruination of another. I recalled that junkie's bestial expression, a simple brown parcel his cage.

I thought about the kid.

GORGON HANDED ME A rusty wrench as he described my next assignment. This time I'd be collecting a debt from some guy named Smith over in Brooklyn.

The weight of Gorgon's words fell heavy as the tool in my hand.

"You don't leave without payment. No matter what." He gestured toward the wrench. "Capiche?"

I gulped. "Capiche."

Car exhaust puttered in toxic clouds around me as I waited at the bus stop. Impatient cabbies leaned into their horns as they weaved in and out of the afternoon traffic. Everybody had someplace to go, something to do. Probably that Smith guy, too. I wondered what he did each morning after he woke, what dreams he left behind in the

indentation of his pillow, what thoughts he carried with him. How things could get so bad that he needed to float a loan from Gorgon. Was he just another junkie, stuck on drugs or booze or betting the ponies at the OTB? Or was there someone for whom he'd sell his soul to the devil to help?

What would his eyes tell me when I rang his bell? And would I need to *ring his bell* with this filthy wrench, Gorgon's calling card for debts unpaid?

"You don't need to do this, Jamesey."

I jumped.

It was that kid again, twirling a Yo-Yo on the bench next to me.

"You." I glowered, leaning toward him.

"Me." He nodded.

"You remind me of that bug. The one who talks to the puppet in that cartoon picture. Always showing up outta nowhere, always havin' something to say."

"Jiminy Cricket," the boy said. "But no. I'm not your conscience. Think of me as a messenger."

A messenger. Kinda like me.

He grinned, a wide gap between his two front teeth. I touched my hand to my slowly healing cheek, a residual ache smarting from where Mama stitched me up with a needle and thread. Took a couple shots of whisky to manage that pain.

"Who's been talking to you, kid? How did you know about that *flying pan?* And how do you know what I got planned today? Only one other person knows, and he ain't you."

"There's better ways, Jamesey. Meet that guy down in Brooklyn, and it's curtains for you."

An image of my mother hobbled through my mind. She was hunched over after working another 14-hour shift, holding her back with one hand and gripping the apartment doorframe with the other. The chemical stench swarmed around her, seeping inside, persistent as a parasite; her cough rattling like chains trailing a ghost.

I shook my head. It never occurred to me I could die taking on one of Gorgon's assignments—after all, I considered myself a glorified pickup and delivery guy. Yet, in that moment, the acrid reality of mortality roiled in my gut.

What would happen to Mama?

The kid's expression remained fixed on that Yo-Yo, the bright yellow circle tossed in and out of his palm like it was some goddamn ray of sunshine.

Sunshine in Hell, what a funny idea.

"Who sent ya, kid?"

He caught the Yo-Yo in his hand and turned to me, his silver-grey eyes intense. I'd never seen eyes so clear, yet so deep. Eyes like that on a little kid were downright creepy.

"I wouldn't get on that bus to Brooklyn, if I were you."

"Whaddya know about Brooklyn?"

The bus screeched as it pulled to the curb. It came to a stop with an exasperated sigh. The driver opened the door, and I shook my head, turning toward the kid, who'd once again vanished.

Leaving behind his yellow Yo-Yo.

SOMETHING ABOUT THAT KID didn't sit right: his deep yet clear-eyed stare, the dark way he said *curtains* ("coy-tens"), how he knew about that woman and her big iron pan that was *this close* to clocking me dead.

I wasn't superstitious, but I wasn't a dummy, either.

Lucky for me, Mama still had that small bottle of ipecac in the medicine chest. A twist in the gut gave me a motive for bowing out of the job. Gorgon let me off the hook when I'd vomited the remnants of my bologna sandwich onto the toes of his wingtips. He didn't think I was chickenshit, just disgustingly sick, so there wouldn't be any 'consequences.' There'd still be other opportunities, more loot to earn. Besides, ole Tubby McGee was chompin' at the bit with his buck teeth and stupid laugh to get on Gorgon's good side.

Let 'em have it.

I handed Tubby the wrench.

"Be careful, man." I swallowed back thick, bile-tinged saliva.

Tubby crossed his eyes, shoved his finger down his throat, and made a retching sound.

T HE NEXT DAY, GORGON paced the upper step of the stoop outside his apartment building. He'd chain-smoked so many cigarettes at one point he had two of them hanging from his lips, and he didn't even notice.

Tubby McGee had never returned from his trip to Brooklyn.

I waited with the gang, watching the sidewalk, the street, for any sign of him. The other guys tapped their feet, chewed their fingernails, and avoided Gorgon's eyes, his glare burning as red as the tip of his Kool Menthol.

Nobody wanted to be on the other end of Gorgon's rage.

Bounding down the steps, I stopped just short of the street, my toes teetering over the edge of the curb. I looked left and right and left again, as if I were about to cross, but really, I was biding my time. If Tubby didn't come back, Gorgon might have thought we were in on something together. After all, Tubby went to collect a debt that sure as hell wasn't gonna be chump change.

From my pocket, I retrieved the kid's yellow Yo-Yo. If this went bad for me, it would be his fault, wherever the hell he was. Looping the string around my finger, I released the ball from my hand. Up. Down. Up. Down. So transfixed with the motion, I barely noticed the red

Studebaker barreling down the street until I heard the tires screaming like some wild banshee as it came to a stop, inches from my feet.

The severed head of Tubby McGee flew from the window. It hit me square in the gut and landed between my feet.

"Holy fuck!" Gorgon yelled as the car peeled away and gunshots blasted from behind me.

Heaving, I glanced down at Tubby's vacant stare, judging me. The curtain of his half smile, half sneer parted to reveal those two front buck teeth—cracked and bloodied—just like my soul.

If I still had a soul.

S HORTLY AFTER TUBBY'S DEATH, their landlord found Tubby's mother, dead and naked on the toilet, empty pill bottles scattered across the blue tile. She'd lost her mind after identifying her son's body—what was left of it, anyway.

I broke ties with Gorgon and his crew. Most times you paid for ditching with a pinky finger or a toe, but Gorgon didn't even blink when I told him I got another job down at Miller's Bakery. Pay wasn't great, but the day-olds were mine for the taking and no one lost their head over a Linzer tart.

"Good luck, Jamesey," he'd said, turning away as he tossed his cigarette into the street.

THREE YEARS LATER, I saw the kid one last time.

Mama had been pushing for me to enroll in trade school—*a better life for us, Jamesey,* she'd said. Although I wasn't much for learning, I knew she was right.

Late for my admissions interview, I ducked through a couple of alleyways to get there faster. Mama would kill me if I missed it.

That was when I heard a tortured sound—raw, almost un-human—from the other side of a dumpster. Against a wall, a young woman—couldn't have been older than twenty—and against her this greasy goon with a hand on her mouth and a knife to her throat. Her eyes widened at my approach with a glassy sheen of terror and relief.

"Let her go." My hands balled into fists. I had no weapon to help this woman except for myself, my own muscle and bone and adrenaline and hopefully enough smarts to outwit this creep.

A sneer slithered across his face as he regarded me. His teeth were blackened, a man rotten to his core, as Mama would say.

"Who's gonna make me?"

He pushed the woman to the side. She landed on her knees as I raised my fists and he took a swipe with his knife, just missing my forearm. I landed a punch to his eye; he snarled and swung at me again. Blood spurted from my shoulder as the blade sliced through my shirt. I

held my footing, connecting again with his jaw and then his gut. The woman screamed.

"Enough, man!" he sputtered, doubling over.

"Get outta here!" I shoved him aside; he stumbled down the alleyway as I reached for the woman's hand. She trembled at my touch.

Then I felt it, a lightning bolt from behind. Dead center of my back, heat searing into me like a steaming iron. I dropped to my knees. My wobbling thighs gave way, and I landed on my back. The goon's laughter crackled like hellfire through the alleyway, as if he were the devil himself. The woman's face hovered. I couldn't tell if she were whistling or screaming or blowing air into my face... like the breeze that swept over the alley.

I felt the sun on my face, splintering through the buildings' shade. Hot, like Coney Island summers spent with Mama, just after my father left. I tasted that sweet grit of pink cotton candy, tongue stuck to the roof of my mouth. I felt my gut rising and falling with each run of the Cyclone, my body soaring with each jolt of airtime, beaming at Mama's shrieks as her hair whipped across her face.

At that moment, I remembered what joy felt like.

Then it all stopped.

"How ya feeling, Jamesey?"

That kid, again. He hadn't aged a bit in the years since I'd last seen him. Same blond pompadour, same silver-grey eyes.

"You didn't warn me," I said. "Why?"

He shrugged. "You found a better way."

I STRAINED TO PUSH my eyelids open past the anvils holding them down. The world was heavy. It hurt to breathe, to move.

Life returned in a blur. I blinked at the realization I was in a hospital. Mama sat to my left, and a woman—_the_ woman sat to my right.

"The kid," I mumbled.

"Jamesey!" Mama squeezed my hand. I turned from her to the woman, who offered an embarrassed smile.

"The kid," I repeated.

"Thank God he showed up when he did," the woman said. Her voice was soft, melodic, like the hum of a Christmas choir. "If he hadn't flagged down that cop..."

Life. It was kind of like the rise and dip of a yellow Yo-Yo. And that kid, a little bit of sunshine in the darkness of hell.

I'd never forget him—whoever he was.

CORE TRUTHS

M Y DESTINY CHANGED THE day the Chemist from Sector Four launched an attack on our planet. They'd found him in the throne room of the Empress Mother from Sector Twelve, hovering over the crystal chamber in which she dwelled, his hands and forearms dissolved to stumps by the acidic poison he'd released inside it. The terror he inflicted upon her, one of twelve originators whose sustenance sparked and nourished all life on Gaean, resounded across all our sectors; for the collective power of the twelve Empress Mothers connected us to each other, to our world. They were the root of our existence—the fall of one a harbinger for the demise of many. Perhaps of us all.

The viscous solution in which The Mother floated, ordinarily a vibrant aqua, had decomposed to a sickly green. Opaque film oozed through her eyes, obscuring their light in a milky haze. Her skin had shriveled, its pearlescence faded and jaundiced, cavernous lines etched into flesh that had persisted soft, immortally so, from the beginning of time. All Gaean watched and waited, our collective song of anguish

ringing through each of our planet's twelve domes an entreaty for healing.

Those of us who had committed to Gaean's sacred Vow of Science stood united in our universal helplessness—at our inability to recognize the Chemist's madness, our powerlessness to reverse the Empress Mother's impairment, and the destructive causal sequence we predicted this calamity would yield. Yet, we needed to continue in our daily work. To extricate myself from the despair that had settled over Gaean, I immersed in my latest assignment in the Hybrid Mines. I had just finished casting an alloy of two volatile metals—necessary to reinforce the interior shells of our planet's domes—when I received a vaguely worded alert. The Planetary Council Magistrate representing my home, Sector Two, had summoned me to the Great Hall.

"Hello?" My voice echoed through the cavernous entryway. It reminded me of the cave my team had discovered in their latest exploration of the Mines, and, conscious of the silt clinging to my work jumpsuit, I wiped my damp palms over the rough canvas.

With tentative steps, I proceeded into an alcove laden with jewels—shimmering black sand garnets consorted with wide azure stones, smooth and chiseled. A cornucopia of color adorned the walls and ceiling, a Metallurgist's dream. Emanating from the center of the alcove, a turquoise glow enveloped me in a shawl of brilliance as I saw her for the first time—the Second Empress Mother, *my* Empress Mother, floating in a thick liquid within her crystal chamber, her crimson hair spreading like a halo. She extended long fingers and placed her palms upon the glass, smiling as she beckoned with dancing cerulean eyes. Her heartbeat, *my* heartbeat, echoed in a synergistic clarity that pulled me toward her. Our faces inches apart, I closed my eyes and rested

my fingertips on the chamber surface. Warmth flooded through me like liquid ore, every atom bursting with joy, each breath like my first, flowing and growing through her. In her presence, I felt reborn.

I could not imagine the evil that would drive one to destroy a creature of such peace, such beauty—to introduce death to one whose sole purpose was to perpetuate life.

Some say the Chemist danced when they captured him, thrusting his bloodied stumps upward with glee as he prattled on about the nobility of sacrifice, a yearning for liberation and the unending quest for scientific truth. His rhetoric came as no surprise. He'd spent countless seasons propagating wild hypotheses that Gaean's survival was not dependent on the sustenance provided by the twelve Empress Mothers, that the foundation of our belief system was nothing more than a ruse. But no one expected him to act on his theories in such a devastating and grotesque way.

"Amela TS15-2 of the Second Sector?" The Magistrate's voice startled me, and I whirled around toward him, my fingertips still tingling from the Empress Mother's touch.

"We haven't much time," he said. "You understand why you've been called?"

I shook my head, feeling as awkward as a sprouted adolescent zygote, though it had been over twenty seasons since Carers had extracted me from the Empress Mother's pod. "In response to the tragedy in Sector Twelve, I assume." My voice cracked. "I assure you that the Scientific Community renounces the actions of the Chemist..."

"His actions are those of a madman. Nothing more, nothing less. Yet, the abomination he committed threatens the very core of our existence here in Gaean."

The Empress Mother shuddered in her chamber; the lights in Sector Two flickered, then dimmed.

The Magistrate paled. With a trembling hand, he mopped a thick sheen of perspiration from his ample forehead. "The attack on the Twelfth Empress Mother depleted her of Berym, a life-sustaining metal," he said. "In her struggle to survive, it appears she has siphoned it from the other eleven."

"I'm sorry, did you say Berym?" As a mythic substance briefly mentioned in Gaean's ancient texts, Metallurgical scholars had debated its existence for longer than I'd been alive. Most rendered it nothing more than a fable. I hesitated, handpicking my words so as not to offend the Magistrate. "This is one metal I've never encountered on our planet, sir, in all my years in the Mines."

"Berym is the source of their light. Without it..." Frowning, he turned toward the Second Empress Mother, suspended in her chamber, her body as soft as a sigh. "They'll all need continuous infusions to replenish what was lost. The Astronomers from Sector One believe we might find it on the dwarf planet Hepcida. At least, that's their hypothesis, based on data analyzed from the surveillance drones."

A chill tickled the back of my neck, raising the errant hairs beneath my long white braid before creeping down my spine. "Sir? No one has ever left Gaean."

"No, they haven't. Yet."

Reaching into his pocket, he retrieved a controller, above which a tiny disc-shaped hologram materialized at his touch.

"What is that?" I asked, my reach hesitant.

"A space vehicle. Strategic Engineers from Sector Seven built it some time ago to provide quick transport. In the event of a crisis, which..." His voice trailed off. "It will provide everything you—and your assigned partner—need to bring Berym back to Gaean."

The chill in my spine deadened to ice.

"Me? You want me to go to Hepcida?" I belonged with my feet planted in the Gaean landscape, not with my head adrift in the stars. The study of the galaxy outside Gaean was the job of the Astronomers. Not someone whose life's purpose was rooted in the earth. Not someone like me. "There must be some mistake."

"There is no Metallurgist in all Gaean more qualified than you for this mission. The alloy you developed—that combination of allonium and depedium—sheer genius! All twelve domes standing, shining and strong, for millennia to come. Our people, our Empress Mothers protected—"

He stopped, raising his fingertips to his lips as if to silence himself. We stared each other down, wide eyed. Science had not protected the Twelfth Empress Mother; it had desecrated her. If the other Mothers fell as she had, so would we, too, regardless of the strength of any dome shielding us from space's icy grasp.

The Magistrate dropped his hand, patting my shoulder as he inhaled deeply and pulled his lips into a tight smile. "We've logged the co-

ordinates to Hepcida; the autopilot is programmed and ready. The Custodians are loading your supplies as we speak."

The ship may have been ready, but I wasn't sure *I* was ready.

W E WERE THE FIRST to leave Gaean, the first to behold our planet amidst an ensemble of stars. As we soared into open space, the light from our world's eleven surviving sectors flickered, the ruins of Sector Twelve a distant shadow—its glow extinguished, the glimmering Dome that contained its once thriving ecosystem transfigured into a mausoleum. Gaean's future dangled from the precipice of our mission's success. Or its failure.

Our planet hovered in space like a deep blue eye, watching as our spacecraft drifted further away. The Biologist they called Gentic TS19-12 of the Twelfth Sector sat across from me, his beefy hands squeezing the armrest of his chair. A lesion oozed through the loose gauze covering his knuckles, another gaped just above a blond mustache at odds with his patches of thinning ebony hair. I hadn't expected to be paired with one of the few surviving Biologists from Sector Twelve. A Chemist, perhaps, would have been a more logical scientific partner given the mission's purpose, but since the attack, the Council had detained all Chemists for questioning.

The consistent whir of the ship's engines and the beeps and blips marking the control panel's positioning system were not enough to mask the silence between us—cold and empty as space itself.

I adjusted my seatbelt. Cleared the nerves from my throat.

"Gaean looks nothing like the planet we know from out here." I turned toward him. "So small. Like it's not even real."

He scrunched his eyebrows and scowled, regarding my khaki jump-suit, mining boots, and metal-tinged fingers with disdain.

"Watching everything in my sector die didn't seem real, either."

"Your loss is our loss. From one root, the Mothers provide."

Sector Twelve had fallen into a death spiral as the Twelfth Empress Mother hovered in a dull state of in-between. The bulbiod plants dried up, their azure stalks reduced to dust. Ruby-feathered snare-birds plummeted from the sky, their voices strangled mid-song. Failing zygotes connected to the ailing Empress sprouted limbs from their forming stomachs, third and fourth eyes opening portals to mal-formed brains; they writhed in pain until they simply disintegrat-ed. The hair from Sector Twelve's surviving inhabitants fell out in clumps, the stench of its rot aerosolizing before the tufts reached the ground, shriveling on impact. Amber lesions bubbled from their skin. Two-thirds of Sector Twelve's population had perished, their deaths an unspeakable agony. I feared the fate that would befall all of Gaean if the Empress Mother fully succumbed to the darkness.

Before launching us into space, the Planetary Council had voted to sever the connection between the Twelfth Empress Mother and the remaining Eleven. They deployed the few surviving Biologists from Sector Twelve to draw samples from the Empress Mother's chamber, which they provided to us. They sent High Priests to deliver last rites to the dying. Carers evacuated the surviving refugees from their homes

and positioned them within other sectors, and Sector Twelve was sealed. Possibly forever.

Gentic's eyes softened as he glanced out the window, following the path of a shooting star. "You and I, we're pioneers—you, of the earth, and I, of the force that feeds it."

WE LANDED WITH A jolt, a cloud of grey sediment bursting around the craft. Shimmering, metallic-tinged amber sands hovered briefly, then rained down in a torrent, a reminder that our time was finite.

Gentic and I donned helmets, their shape and structure somewhat like home, our breaths fogging the glass that helped us sustain life in a foreign clime. We stepped from the craft and into the terrain, sand swallowing our footsteps. All around us, dull and jagged black mountains cut through a deep purple horizon tinged with dust.

"This is as good a place to start as any," I said.

We worked quickly, removing the extractor from the craft and positioning it in various locations in the valley. The blades cut deep into the planet's surface, whooshing through soft sand and crunching through rock, pulverizing it into a powdery gravel. We collected over a dozen samples in as many hours and transported the heavy canisters back into the ship. One by one, I transferred them to the heated centrifuge, which separated out the chaff and heated the remaining metal until it flowed like the Rivers of Adaline in Sector One.

I filled test tubes with molten metal and combined specimens to form alloys. As the mixtures cooled, Gentic removed the liquid and released it, gentle as a teardrop, into the viscous fluid obtained from the chamber of the fallen Empress Mother.

And we waited. Just as those living in the remaining eleven sectors waited for us to discover the answer, the miracle, that would let the ailing Empress Mother's life fluid radiate its sapphire brilliance once again. For her skin to plump with the softness of the archid fruits that once bloomed over the Sector Twelve hillsides. For her eyes to open, to spark light.

I closed my eyes in my own divine appeal. That Gentic and I would find *any* trace of Berym from these extractions.

G ENTIC SLUMPED IN HIS SEAT, his features drawn, the stubble on his chin a mark of our time spent toiling in what seemed an interminable night. Two hundred and eighty-seven samples collected and tested—three containing only trace amounts of Berym. Not enough to save the remaining Eleven. Not enough to save us all.

T HE VIBRATION WOKE ME from a heavy sleep.

"Gentic? We're not leaving, are we?" I rubbed my eyes. Parched, I reached for the carafe of archid juice I'd left on the sideboard before retiring. Its surface trembled.

"Gentic?"

A resounding *boom* shook the ship. White liquid sloshed over the glass; it clattered before crashing to the floor. I gripped the armrests of my seat and braced myself.

Gentic bounded in from the laboratory, holding firm to the walls, struggling to regain his footing. He stumbled, thick nectar and shards of glass sticking to his knees.

We watched through the window as hundreds of creatures, the size and shape of small boulders with jagged, insect-like legs, broke through the canyon rock and climbed to the surface.

Their eyes reflected the exterior of their planet: a metallic sheen radiating from orbs embedded within hard, jagged complexions as they stared silently at our spacecraft. They bore no weapons but surrounded us in a semicircle, their regiment assembled as orderly and haphazardly as a constellation of stars.

Gentic scrambled to his feet. "Have you ever seen anything so magnificent?"

We donned our helmets and rushed outside. Flanked by the rock beings, five taller, lithe creatures floated toward us, their feet grazing the sand as they approached. They regarded us with eyes like small moons. Their features were chiseled, their bodies opaque but lustrous

185

like liquid silk. One stepped forward toward me, the remaining four falling in behind her.

"I am Amela TS15-2 of the Second Sector of the planet Gaean. And this," I said, gesturing toward the gaping Gentic, "is my counterpart, Gentic TS19-12 of Sector Twelve."

Gentic winced at the mention of his lost sector as the creature's eyes widened.

"Do you... understand?" I asked. Fissures cracked on its face, resembling a smile. Miniscule pebbles fell to the sand below.

"I am Kay-To, of the Five Matrons of Hepcida," she said in perfect Gaeanese, the timbre and intonation of her voice a complete replication of my own. "As you inhabit our home, we are one. Welcome."

I SAT WITH KAY-To in the cabin of our spacecraft. Outside, the canyon had returned to the barren state in which we found it; the Hepcidians having burrowed beneath the surface with a thunderous rumble. Gentic scampered between Kay-To and a table filled with flasks and scopes scattered among his scribbled notes. He appeared almost manic, like a man obsessed—his movements so dizzying it was embarrassing.

"It's so kind of you to indulge Gentic in this examination," I said, attempting to create calm amid my counterpart's chaos. "On our planet, understanding the living is his life's work."

"So much interest in a being so simple." Kay-To giggled at the way the Biologist's eyebrows and his moustache both furrowed in question as he studied her. The rays of his infrared scope shined in her eyes like fire. She didn't flinch as he prodded and poked at her, depositing samples of her outerskin and lifeblood into test tubes.

"You and your populace were an unexpected surprise," I said, as Gentic turned from Kay-To toward his notes. "Our Astronomers were not aware of any life on Hepcida."

"Just as we, too, remained nescient that there were others alive in the beyond," she said. "Gentic's curiosity exists in parallel to my own. And what joy there is upon us discovering each other! Until you arrived, we knew of nothing that was viable outside the Core."

"The Core?"

Kay-To's arms cracked as she leaned in close. At her touch, a comforting warmth spread over my palms, her skin like tempered metal. She opened her eyes wide. I stared deep, and through her vision I saw, clear as the domes of Gaean, a light brighter than the glow of our Empress Mothers suspended in the heart of a vast cave. Stalactites and stalagmites of luminous crystal formed prisms, igniting the deepest reds, the coolest blues, and the most vivacious yellows in a cadre of color, as if painting the beginning of days. Kay-To and the four other Matrons floated in weightless bliss, their bodies shining in the Core's radiance. Carbonic rock, chiseled in their image, burst from their eyes and drifted, as if magnetized, into the light and exploded into a million facets, diamond dust trailing, absorbed into the fusion.

Kay-To's hands turned cold. She closed her eyes, and I withdrew, my cheeks burning, sheepish with the intimacy we'd shared.

"Our greatest truth," she murmured. "The wellspring of all life on Hepcida."

Kay-To adjusted herself in the seat. As she moved, a thin veil of dust rose from her skin, cascading over the chair on to the floor below. Gentic looked up from his writing and stared at Kay-To. He glanced at me, as if remembering my presence.

Kay-To turned toward me. "And what is your greatest truth, Amela TS15-2?"

I shuddered as I caught my reflection in her gaze.

THE SHIP WAS QUIET under the mantle of twilight. Flasks and test tubes filled with failed amalgams from our mining efforts glistened under the laboratory lights, taunting with a potential that would never be realized.

I lifted each container from its holster and placed it carefully into a box, intending to return the samples to the land from which I'd taken them. It pained me to think of the maturing pink zygotes that would no longer flourish in the Empress Mothers' care, their sweet song reduced to a choking gurgle as the life vines withered, died. I pictured the lush orchards of the Eighth Sector, dewdrops burning the fruit like acid. And each of the remaining eleven Empress Mothers withering, fading, Gaean's lights extinguished with their final breaths.

Arms laden with my burden, I turned and trudged toward the door. At the same moment, Gentic burst through, arms flailing, eyes wild.

"The Astronomers were right!" He gripped my arms tightly, the box wedged between us. "There *is* Berym on Hepcida!"

I shook my head. "Trace amounts. You said so yourself. Not enough to sustain life on Gaean."

"The Berym is not contained in the minerals of this earth, Amela," he said, gesturing toward the tubes. "It flows through its inhabitants."

Just as it flows through our Empress Mothers.

"Of course, the sample volume I acquired from the Hepcidian is too small for harvesting, but the concentrations are confirmed," he said, his speech quickening. "With a larger specimen, an intact specimen, we can generate enough molten Berym to sustain all the Empress Mothers, perhaps even revive my own Empress in Sector Twelve!"

The room blurred, my head engulfed in heat. *We.* What a simple, yet complex concept. Kay-To, she was not a specimen, but a living creature who brought radiance to her planet, to her people. Gentic knew I was the only metallurgical engineer in all of Gaean with the experience and the skill to execute the proposal he suggested.

It was... unconscionable.

"There's got to be another way," I said, my voice catching as I thrust the box toward him. "Here, try testing the ground samples again."

"An exercise in futility." He brushed me aside. "I've discovered a viable, scientifically founded solution that will ensure the preservation of life on Gaean. Now you must fulfill your mission, just as I have. You must do your duty."

"No." My voice was hard, jagged like stone. "I—we—I... I can't do this to her."

"It's a necessary sacrifice." Gentic's expression darkened. "The Hepcidian provides the essential matter we need to preserve our Empress Mothers. Nothing more, nothing less."

I looked at Gentic with a fury I had never known in all my days on Gaean. He was so ravenous for the fruits of his own success, in a mad quest for justice for his own sector's tragedy, that he'd lost all sense of decency. Of sanity. He was a blight on scientists, across all Gaean's sectors, across all our specializations.

Had the Chemist experienced the same distorted vision when he'd set these events in motion, when he'd doomed us all with his assassination attempt, not only on our planet but on worlds beyond?

"Kay-To is a living being." My hands trembled as I gripped the box tight. "It's murder."

"You know the stakes, Amela," Gentic scowled. "Without Berym, the remaining Empress Mothers will die, and all other sectors will follow. Just like mine. And Gaean..."

"Is our world worth more than theirs?" I bit my lower lip to stop it from quivering. "Is her life less valuable than mine? Than yours?"

"We'll lose everything," Gentic said. "There is no choice."

He stormed past, leaving me alone, grasping a container of useless soil.

Rock and dirt. Minerals. Earth. The building blocks of a planet. A tangible, logical pursuit that gave me purpose in a life I'd long taken

for granted. I thought of Kay-To's warmth, how her life force flowed into Hepcida's Core, just as our own Empress Mothers nurtured and nourished our kind from the time we were nothing more than seedlings in the earth. The collective light of the Mothers' essence sustained all of Gaean; to fracture even one precious bond was to destroy it all. I thought of the Empress Mother in Sector Twelve, her life-bearing light disintegrated by the deranged Chemist, who'd likely thought his intentions noble, his actions justified.

Our mission was noble. Our actions would be justified. Gaean's fate danced upon the precipice of our success. We could not fail. And as logic ripped the swath of emotion from my core, I knew Gentic's reasoning was sound. We had exhausted all other scientific solutions.

I had no choice.

Yet, despite Gentic's discovery that promised to restore life to our world, I couldn't help but feel we'd already lost everything.

I STRAPPED INTO MY seat, the whirring of the engine gnawing at me. Through the window, I watched the remaining four Matrons of Hepcida standing sentinel, nearly camouflaged by the mountains that rose around them, the perplexity of their expressions impossible to decipher. I wondered if they celebrated the same glorious possibilities of the journey that Gentic promised Kay-To when he invited her to join us, or if they foresaw how the light of the Core would dim in Kay-To's absence, how perpetual joy would be impossible in the presence of her loss.

I wondered if they realized they would never see her again, if they knew what we were about to do—what I was tasked to do.

My insides fluttered with our craft's liftoff, like the wings of a caged ruby-feathered snarebird that was desperate to fly.

"Ooh!" Kay-To laughed, grasping her middle as her eyes widened. "Space travel, it tickles!" She glanced out the window, watching her home fade away, shrinking smaller and smaller until it was nothing more than a pinprick of dust. "How lucky I am to join you on your home planet, Amela!" She rested her hands on the armrests, settling into the seat.

Melting into the seat.

How would Kay-To respond when we lowered her body into a cupola furnace? Would she look upon me with sadness, with regret, or with rage? Would she rail against her fate until her dying breath, or would she succumb to the destiny we'd determined for her with quiet ac-quiescence to the flash of white heat that would consume her? Would the pain be instantaneous, or would it linger as she liquefied at our hands—*at my hands*? Would Kay-To understand Gentic's perspective that her sacrifice, and the sacrifice of all the Matrons, of her people, was worth the salvation of *our* planet?

How could she? How could I?

"Amela is excited to show you the Hybrid Mines," Gentic said, ad-dressing our new passenger. *The essential matter needed to preserve our existence*. "The mines are deep beneath a mountain of gold that shimmers in the light of our Empress Mothers' gazes. It is where Amela performs her duty to serve the interests of Gaean."

"Your truth," Kay-To said softly. "I cannot wait to see it."

I couldn't look at her, fearing that she would.

THE HEALING POWER OF WITCHCRAFT

MY FIRST ACT UPON taking residence in the barn of Dr. Frederick Burroughs and his wife, Mary, was to remedy the direction of the horseshoe hanging above the door. Worn with time, weather, and rust, the metal had been nailed to the rotting wood, upright, in the shape of a U, presumably to hold the family's good fortune in store for those times when tragedy would strike. As tragedy often does, in a flash of unpredictable precision.

Clearly the good doctor and his wife knew nothing of superstition, or of talismans, of charms or the power of a good omen.

But I knew that good luck was not meant to be contained like some songbird in a cage, but to burst forth with the might of a thousand waterfalls, its deluge drowning the evil that lingered like dust motes in the air. When hung upside-down, fortune would flow from the

horseshoe's core past its heels, protecting the threshold as it painted it with joy and peace and warmth enough to weather any storm.

It was my mother, and her mother before her, who had passed down the tradition of the horseshoe. I learned much about fortune and fate as a small child, in my mother's whispers, as she cradled me to sleep. I learned, too, by listening to the murmurs of old women who blessed themselves whenever storm clouds hovered over their thresholds or when feral cats slunk, staring, across their paths.

Yet, despite all I knew, all I had learned, I grew up to become a widow replete with tragedy. The burden of my sorrow hung like damp linen on a windless day, a display upon which society would cast judgment and form impressions of who I was. What they believed me to be.

Three weeks after my husband died in an accident on horseback, I'd quietly miscarried the baby who would have been our only child, my dreams of motherhood, of a family, nothing more than a shriveled wick inside a melted, burned-down candle. A week later, I watched my mother rounded up in the town square, ropes cutting into her wrists as the authorities hauled her into the jail for sparking an argument with an unscrupulous shop keep. I listened to her cries and watched the townsfolk—her neighbors, her *friends*—glare upon her with censuring eyes as they gathered around the prison each day, maligning my mother and the other imprisoned women who bore the same mark as she.

Witch, they'd chanted.

I could still hear my mother's voice in my mind, in my heart, in whispers that brushed over me like a late autumn shiver, though it had been years since her passing.

My hands bled from the effort of removing the Burroughs' horseshoe. I used every tool I could find—rakes, hoes, shovels—to correct its placement. The mares in the stables whinnied and watched. Chickens strutted through the straw as I yanked at the embedded nails, grunting and cursing under my breath until the deed was done. With the handle of a rake, I forced those crooked nails back into the meat of the defiant wood, the horseshoe's direction righted.

D R. BURROUGHS HAD SPARED me from the inevitability of a trial by fire when he whisked me from outside the general store on a sunny summer afternoon; the day a mob of motley louts closed in around me, spitting and cursing and licking their lips like a pack of rabid wolves. Accusations sputtered from their tongues, branding me with the label burned into my mother before me, the label that foretold only death.

They'd backed away when the doctor moved in front of me, this man of high esteem my shield from their words, from their condemning glares. "Who are *you* to judge anyone?" Burroughs challenged.

Rescued, I left my wares to the beggars on the street, my life to the shadows, vanishing as if invisible beneath the gaze of God himself.

The doctor and his wife had much to gain from my presence and perhaps even more to lose. For what I knew of fortune, I also knew of both bodily and spiritual healing; and the populace of Fairfield proper did not appreciate a woman with such capacity. My mother had the gift, too, deemed more curse than blessing. Those who associated

themselves with women like us laid their own reputations vulnerable to the same suspicions that followed Mother and me.

But I supposed it was different for Dr. Burroughs and his wife. Despondency clung to them with the weight and stench of a wool shawl in a rain shower. They were willing to do anything to return their lives to a more 'normal' state.

Misgivings swirled around Mary Burroughs' mental soundness, sure as smoke from a bonfire. Whispers of gossip carried on the wind that the good doctor's wife, indeed, might be a witch herself. For how could any God-fearing woman claim to hear the voices of the dead singing in her ear, or blaspheme her faith by stating that the faces of her deceased children stared at her every night from the surface of the moon? Burroughs' patients spoke of her screams—*biting shrieks*, they'd say, as if the devil himself had impaled her flesh with his acicular claws.

Then there were the long, bleak days permeated with silence. Dr. Burroughs' heartbreak as his wife stared into empty corners, arms crossed and rocking herself as if cradling a child or embracing a memory; her breathing so shallow one could be convinced she was some hollowed-out woman-doll and not a person with a soul.

A medical pedigree afforded the doctor great reverence. Trusted among the masses to relieve the pain of a sore throat, to bleed out a fever, yet he was not skilled enough to purge the demons plaguing his wife's mind. The townspeople had intimated—politely enough—to the good doctor that if his tonics could not cure Mrs. Burroughs, they may need to subject her to a water trial.

To protect the citizenry. She'd be stripped of her clothing and tied at her hands and feet, tossed from a boat into the waters of the Devil's Belt. If she floated, they'd say it was because she rebuffed her baptism. If she sank, they'd deem her innocent of witchcraft. By then, it would be too late. Either way, they'd murder her.

He'd used every tonic in his bag, sent for potions and concoctions shipped across oceans, but his efforts were all in vain. So, Dr. Burroughs did what any man of science would do in a moment of desperation.

He experimented.

WITH A LIMP HANDKERCHIEF, Dr. Burroughs mopped beads of anxiety and August humidity from his brow. "She lost her mother to yellow fever," he told me. "Almost died of it herself. Watched her favorite dairy cow mauled to death by wolves. Two seasons of crops ruined by pestilence. Buried three babies out there in the fields."

I pushed back the lacy curtains from the window of the Burroughs' front parlor and glanced at the four wooden crosses visible in the distance: one large and three small. Shadows from the grave markers lay like embers burnt by a defiant summer sun; they blanketed the children and the grandmother whose bodies slept deep within the earth. "I am sorry for your troubles," I said. "For your wife's burden."

"My Mary is a sensitive yet strong woman, Mrs. Winters," Dr. Burroughs said. "But sometimes even the strongest bridges cannot bear the weight of those who trudge across them."

I nodded, swallowing hard past the tragedies lodged within my throat. Like Mrs. Burroughs, I, too, felt that pain of loss; each defiant tear, each constricted breath an endless reminder.

I thought again of my mother, how they'd kept her imprisoned for a fortnight, the companion of thieves and murderers and rats. How the gossips raised their torches and their pitchforks; clucking to each other conspiracies of dark magic, as if they expected the devil himself to burst from the lungs of those held captive with each screeching cry.

Only when my mother's voice was silenced did her captors toss her from that prison onto the street. They had taken her tongue. She was beyond healing, caked in filth and misery, as I held her hand. Mother's depleted spirit had whispered as much when it called out my name, *Abigail*, and I moved her from the gutter to the sidewalk so she could take her final rest under a blanket of moonlight. The mob of Accusers watched with smug indifference; they smirked at my tears and grinned with yellowing teeth at Mother's lifeless body. Yet, I saw how their gazes froze upon my glare, their eyes glazed over like ice in a blizzard. I heard the hardening of their hearts, how those hearts had stopped beating for that moment when my desire to harm them burned hotter than any calling to heal. And as that moment passed, I saw the question of who I was curled over lips that twisted into scowls, their hatred for me palpable as the cobblestones upon which my mother lay.

I knew I was alone, yet I would never be left alone—they'd whisper and watch and wait for a time when they could, with certainty, call me

'witch' as they had with my mother. As they did the day Dr. Burroughs brought me to his home.

"I understand." The curtain slipped from my fingers, and I watched the lace swing, pendulum-like, until it stopped. I hoped I could help Mary Burroughs.

I hoped I could help myself.

MARY BURROUGHS SAT UPRIGHT in the four-poster bed, a specter in white. Long, blond hair hung in moist clumps around her face, a tangled nest against her neck. Her glance fixed on an empty rocking chair in the room's corner, a half-knitted blue afghan draped over its back. Shadows sprouted through cracks in the walls, blemishing the neatly apportioned room. Drawn shades pushed the sunlight outside, the glow around the window frames the only hint of life within this dwelling. Yet the summer heat settled within the four walls, the baking stench of despair rank as a crop of rotting lettuce.

"Hello, Mary," I said, closing the door softly behind me. The hinges creaked in protest.

She continued to stare as I approached the bed. The mattress sagged with a sigh as I sat next to her.

"My name is Abigail," I told her. "And the people of Fairfield think I'm a witch."

Mary's eyebrow twitched almost imperceptibly at my words.

"I know the pain of losing those we love," I said. "It's the weight of a thousand stones poured into your soul. The first loss is a boulder, the next, a pile of rocks, the next pebbles, then sand—filling every crevice until there's nothing left of you."

She continued to stare.

"The righteous tell us that these losses are meant to be. Our loved ones are in a better place when they're gone. As women, we're expected to smile and nod and agree and rejoice—march forward in our roles as wives and farmers and teachers and seamstresses and, for those of us granted such good fortune, mothers—as if it never happened. When it's too much for us to bear—when we want to yell and scream or just go silent—they say the devil's got his grip on us."

Mary's eyes moistened, a glassy sheen veiling the vacancy of her stare.

"Your husband, he's worried about you. He sent me here to help." I reached for her hand—the bones were slight, like a baby bird's, her skin cold as an early winter's frost despite the temperature. Her hand stayed limp in mine. "I am a healer."

Through the closed door, I heard Dr. Burroughs' footsteps; the front door opening and a man's voice—presumably his afternoon patient. He'd advised me to tend to Mary while he had guests in the home, to keep her quiet so he could do his job and lend appearances of normalcy.

"The townsfolk say I used a dark magic spell, maybe sold my soul to Satan to avoid the plague that killed so many," I said. "The truth? It was the luck that flowed over the threshold of my home. It kept the evil outside. I'm not a witch, Mary, and neither are you. We are nothing

more than women burdened with unbearable pain. I'm here to sit with you, to understand, to listen if you want to talk."

The silence swathed us as I picked up a hairbrush from the top of Mary's nightstand. Gently, I began stroking her long hair, working the bristles through each knot. Sparks of static crackled from Mary's oily tresses, peculiar and unexpected, as I brushed, unraveling the multiple layers of sorrow that she clenched tightly inside. A tiny sigh, soft as a baby's breath, escaped her lips as fat tears dropped on to her nightgown, flattening and spreading into the fabric until the cloth was drenched, as with a new baptism.

"Thank you," she whispered.

I smiled. Mary didn't need magic or witchcraft or some divine intervention—just kindness—to help heal her burdened soul.

D R. BURROUGHS HAD FASHIONED a comfortable room for me in the barn—a bed of hay, a soft blanket, and the companionship of animals that quickly became friends. I shared my living space with Georgina the grey mare, Gordy the goat, Mabel the cow, five chickens, and a rooster that woke me at dawn. The witch hunts had intensified in Fairfield, according to the doctor, and in exchange for sequestering me, I contributed to the field chores, collected eggs, milked sweet Mabel, and, of course, continued to tend to Mary.

It had taken some time, but as Mary grew to trust me and confided her pain—*anger toward her husband the doctor for being unable to save*

her mother, guilt that her own body had 'failed' her three stillborn chil-dren—she started becoming more like her old self again. According to Dr. Burroughs, anyway.

After the first month, the screaming subsided, outside of the occasional nightmare.

After two months, Mary smiled for the first time.

In the third month I was with the Burroughs, I brought Mary from her bedroom, dressed and primped, once again greeting the doctor's patients as they arrived.

By month four, she worked with me in the fields in the morning. Together, we sang psalms, harmonizing with the beauty of a church choir. We laughed. We shared secrets. I told Mary of my mother's fate, how her soul stirred through me when she'd passed; and the curt breeze that whistled down every cobblestone street, through every hidden alleyway when her spirit escaped this world. How she took a piece of me with her, too. I told her of the loss of my child, the pain of never knowing whether to mourn a son or a daughter. When Mary gripped my hand in solidarity, I heard my mother's voice whisper in my mind: *"Things will be different."*

In the afternoons, Mary took her horse on long rides through the woods, her hair and the animal's mane lifted in the wind. Free. Unencumbered. *Just like the old days*, Dr. Burroughs had said. *It's miraculous.* As the townsfolk saw Mary out and about, the rumors of possession and witchcraft dissipated, the fog over the Burroughs' dwelling lifted.

In the sixth month, Mary discovered she was pregnant.

I PRESSED A COOL cloth to Mary's head as each contraction sub-sided.

"What if it happens again?" Mary gripped the collar of my nightdress, pulling me close. "What if I lose this one, too?" She had summoned me in the night, dismissing Dr. Burroughs to the parlor once her labor began.

"It won't happen again." I wrapped my arms around her in a deep embrace. "Have faith."

"Faith is a funny thing for a witch to advise," she said, smirking. Despite the fear and the pain that consumed her, Mary's humor remained intact. "I know... not a witch."

Her features succumbed to a grimace as another contraction gripped her.

"Not a witch," I whispered. "A friend." I took her hand. It was cold despite the heat emanating from her body.

Mary's body seized with pain, and she screamed. The door burst open, and Dr. Burroughs rushed in.

"Mary! Is it time?"

Her face twisted, and a grey pallor enveloped her skin. She pulled her knees up as far as her belly would allow, revealing a pool of blood on

the bed beneath her. Mary writhed and groaned; her body stiffened, her gaze vast and vacant.

"Mary!" the doctor yelled, a slow-motion panic creeping over his features.

"Something's not right here," I said. I grasped Mary's hand with both of mine and whispered a prayer for my friend, for her child, for the universe to be fair and kind and to allow Mary this moment—this lifetime—of joy that she deserved.

The doctor pulled back his wife's nightdress; the baby's head had crowned. With the desperation of a man drowning, he slid his arm beneath her shoulders, pushing her upright into a sitting position. He leaned hard into Mary's back until her neck was nearly flush with her knees, her forehead falling like a wilted tulip onto her swollen belly.

"Push, push," Burroughs urged.

The child slid from the cocoon of its mother's womb and into a wider world.

I dropped Mary's hand and reached down to retrieve this child who was so wanted, so loved. A boy.

He was blue.

The cord snaked around his neck, the source of life that once nourished him threatening to steal his breath away just moments after his birth. I slipped my index finger between the slick noose and his tender skin. Pressing my thumb and forefinger together, I squeezed that cruel membrane as hard as I could, while laying my lips upon

his tiny mouth—seizing death, breathing life, incantations galloping through my mind swift as Mary's horse at sunset.

Live, live, live.

A slight pop sizzled over my fingertips. Hot liquid oozed into my skin, blackening my fingers as the cord shriveled and dissipated in a puff of smoke, and the baby sucked in his first breath—my breath. With a smile, I relinquished my kiss and the baby cried out, a wail of joy that sounded out in dreadful harmony with his father's screams.

"Mary? No! Mary!"

I turned and stared as the sobbing doctor threw himself over his wife's lifeless body, her eyes wide and staring, much as they had that first day I met her in this house.

I had healed her.

But I hadn't.

Death had taken her regardless of the peace she'd found in those quiet moments of discussion, regardless of the resolution she'd achieved, regardless of the weight of the stones that rolled from her back, pebble by pebble, as she learned to stand again.

None of it mattered.

Yet, while I held her living, breathing child in my arms, I realized that it all mattered.

I walked through the open bedroom door and out of the house. I felt the cool softness of the grassy fields cushioning the soles of my feet as I took each step through the crops she tended with care.

Dr. Burroughs, he needed time to grieve, lest the world deem him mad.

Mary's horse whinnied as I opened the barn door. Standing beneath the threshold, I looked up at that horseshoe I had turned so long ago and wondered about the nature of fortune. Is it wiser to capture it in a bucket, like errant raindrops in a drought, and hoard enough to sustain across a lifetime? Or is it better to let it flow unbridled, knowing that one day the deluge might stop and dry, never to be replenished?

The baby wrinkled his nose and looked up at me with big, brown eyes. *Mary's eyes.* I snuggled him tight to me.

Footfalls crunched on the gravel outside the barn.

"You." Dr. Burroughs stood before me, his face sweating and scarlet, a pitchfork in hand.

"Dr. Burroughs, I'm so sorry about Mary. I thought you needed—"

"You thought I needed what? To be tricked? To have a witch take my wife and spare my child with dark magic?"

"Mary was my friend. I loved her," I said.

"You envied her. You coveted her life, and then you took it from her. Blasphemer! Miscreant!" He gripped his weapon tighter, its gleaming tips like knives. "Now, hand me my child before you inflict your darkness upon him as well."

"You don't mean that," I said, my voice a rasp. "You are grieving. Please, put the pitchfork down."

"I meant every word. I knew what I was getting myself into, bringing you to my home." The doctor's face twisted, his teeth gleaming beneath a sneer. "I should have handed you to those cretins on the street. Let them burn you at the stake, you barren witch!"

Heat emanated from his glare as he flung that word across the barn at me.

Witch.

So this was how the doctor truly regarded me.

Yet perhaps he was right; perhaps they all were, and the misfortune in my life was not an ill fate but a darkness seeded deep inside me that brought death upon those it touched. Was it some plague upon my soul that snuffed out the life of the child growing inside me, or a curse that I had inadvertently cast upon my husband with our last kiss? Was my mother's cruel death somehow a punishment for what I was?

Would Mary Burroughs have survived had I not been with her in that birthing room?

But as I squeezed the boy to my chest, his soft warmth radiated over me like a sunbeam through a storm—my love for him swaddling us in a promise of hope and a strength I had never known before. My mother's spirit had foretold *things would be different*, and somehow, I knew, this time, they were. Fate, it was a form of magic, and magic, the instrument of the witch. All that happened led me to this moment, this baby. This fate.

"Embrace your fortune," my mother's spirit whispered.

A fierce breeze cut through the fields behind Dr. Burroughs. The cornstalks trembled with fear, and Burroughs with rage. At that moment, I saw a hint of the future that the doctor would command. My body consumed in flame; my ashes swirling above the funeral pyre in a cyclone that stretched high as night. The face of the child becoming that of his father, of all those men who would never understand, could never understand anything but cruelty toward women who did not comply with their expectations—be us healers or truth seers, the victims of tragedy, or even those who dared speak against their words. Or their lies.

The doctor seethed with an anger that far surpassed his grief. Through the sweet aroma of hay and manure and a fireplace smoking in the distance, I smelled the rank stench of evil—it was stale beer and sweat and burning garlic intermingled, like the breath of those men who had sought to rip my limbs from me on the street that day the doctor had taken me—not for the sake of kindness but for his own selfish purpose.

Would he have surrendered me anyway, had Mary lived, when my usefulness expired?

"The baby," Dr. Burroughs demanded. "Now."

I thought of Mary Burroughs, of our friendship, our connection. I thought of my mother, the bond between us unbroken beyond death. I thought of my child lost, this child found, and of lonely old women through the ages, dressed in black and clutching to both their talismans and their tales. I thought of those who had been drowned in the water trials. Those who had been branded and burned.

With what I saw and what I knew, everything was different, and I could not allow this innocent baby to become part of a society that justified violence with a misguided sense of self-righteousness.

I shook my head. "No."

Dr. Burroughs tightened his grip on the pitchfork, taking a step closer.

"The child is mine. I'm the father."

"No," I repeated.

The doctor stormed toward us, and a misty haze cascaded from the curve of the horseshoe above, falling over the baby and me like a cloud.

The deluge of good fortune.

I looked up into that brilliant torrent that rained upon us and basked in the tingling of glittering droplets that beaded on my skin, on the skin of the baby. I heard the clinking of glass, the tinkling of tiny bells as the deluge consumed us. I breathed in the earthy scents of cinnamon and sage, peppermint and cloves, drunk in the spell that transformed that barn into a haven of mysticism, where the answers to every question I'd ever asked rained down upon us, and its voice was clear. My mother's voice and the voices of all who came before her, all who loved and shined and sacrificed for their gifts.

In that moment, I could not tell which was brighter, my smile or the prism of my tears. The air glistened and swirled around us and the barn lights dimmed, fading to black. I felt the earthly body of the good doctor rush through us as the child and I vanished into the night.

Under a spray of starbursts, we hovered, anticipating a new path, a destination unknown. Free to embrace who—what—I was, with no need to conceal the truth that burst from within me.

Witchcraft, it had power. Healing power. I drank in the night's beauty, imbibed the sweet purity and goodness of this baby. The magic bloomed, sweet as lilacs and cherry blossoms, yellow roses in spring.

And I, I was light.

ACKNOWLEDGMENTS

Many thanks to all who have taken the journey through these eighteen tales—for each time someone reads one of these stories, the characters and worlds come to life.

I began my writing journey as an avid reader, way back when I could count my age on two hands. My godmother introduced me to the Reader's Digest Condensed Books series (gotta love the 80s!) and every night we'd sit together on opposite ends of the couch, each with books we'd trade and talk about. It was no surprise that, in elementary school, "Composition" class was my favorite part of the week. I wrote (dark) poetry in high school and throughout college (even darker), but unfortunately my creative writing endeavors hit a wall in my early 20s. A minor midlife crisis and a fortuitous ad for the NYC Midnight creative writing competition brought it all back; I've been writing steadily since 2016 and haven't stopped since. Indeed, I'd rediscovered a 'core truth' neglected for so long—coming back to creative writing was like finding a long-lost friend.

So many people have been an integral part of my writing journey. Family, friends, teachers, co-workers, neighbors, other moms waiting for their kids outside on the blacktop... indeed, support has come from both expected and unexpected places. I will never forget your kindness.

I'd like to thank my husband, Dan Fox, for being a sounding board during the creative process and for offering a shoulder to cry on in my (many) moments of self-doubt. I always know I'm on to something good when I'm reading Dan one of my stories, and he turns away from his fantasy sports stats to really listen to my words. To my boys, Ryan and Aidan, for serving as my inspiration every day. To <u>all</u> my family, especially Debbie and John Fox, Frank and Grace Billings, and Olivia Verdon, for their endless encouragement.

I'm a firm believer that the universe delivers what—and who—you need, when you need it. I've been so blessed to find not one, but two amazing writing "tribes." To LF and WAB, I am grateful every day that you're all running this crazy marathon with me, helping me to improve with each new story, picking me up when I'm down, and understanding when I just need to take a breather. You are all wonderful, talented people I'm proud to call friends.

Special thanks to Beth Greenberg, Paul Draper, and R.A. Clarke for helping me get the nuts-and-bolts of this book right—without you, it would still be languishing on my laptop as a Microsoft Word document. To Lydia Collins and Nora Wilson Fry, my accountability partners, thank you for keeping me sane and for reading my work. Thank you to Paulene Turner, Sarah Nutbrown, Cathy Missinne, Rose Camara, and Myna Chang for reviewing my very first pass and for your ongoing encouragement and Maggie Scheier, Lin Morris, Sue

Cook, Charlie Rogers, Stephanie Lennon, Di Brown, and Chrissie Rohrman for always supporting me. Andrea Goyan, thank you for reviewing just about every story and screenplay I've written at least 10 times over (or more) without complaint, for your amazing insights in helping me always dig deeper into 'what's the story about,' for helping me become a better and more confident storyteller, but most of all for your friendship.

Finally, I would like to acknowledge those who are not 'physically' here to celebrate this book with me: those I hold in my heart and my memories, who I think about and miss every day. To my godparents, Frances and James Billings, who instilled in me a passion for all things creative. I'm sorry I started my writing journey too late for you to see any of this. To my dad, Arthur Horne, who was always my greatest cheerleader, I know you'd be telling everyone you met about this book if you were still here. To my mom, Anna Horne, for always being in my corner, and for your encouragement to "keep going" with my writing—the last words you ever said to me and I'm listening, boy am I listening.

If any of the tales in this collection spoke to you, made you think about the world or your life in a different way, I'd love to hear it. Feel free to reach out to me on social media, and if you are so inclined, please leave me a review! As a writer, it's always great to know that I'm not just screaming into the abyss.

PUBLICATION HISTORY

Something Rare and Beautiful, in *All Worlds Wayfarer*

Don't Blink, in *72 Hours of Insanity, vol. 11*

To Lure Gavin Back Home, in *Brilliant Flash Fiction* (nominated for a Pushcart Prize)

Worms, in *The Dark Sire*

The Rise of the Mariner's Star, in *Brilliant Flash Fiction*

A History Lesson, in *Land Beyond the World Magazine*

Taking Hope, in *Dark Matter Magazine*

Vanished, in *72 Hours of Insanity, vol. 10*

The Odds are Even, in *Flash Fiction Magazine*

A Little Bit of Sunshine in Hell, in *The Writers Playground*

ABOUT THE AUTHOR

Lisa Fox is a pharmaceutical market researcher by day and fiction writer by night. She enjoys crafting short stories and short screenplays across genres, but most of her work can best be described as literary speculative fiction. For Lisa, there's no greater thrill than creating something out of nothing, in transforming life's 'what ifs' to prose that flashes a mirror on the human condition. As a writer, nothing makes her happier than having readers say that her work made them feel something or look at the world in a different way.

Lisa won the 2018 NYC Midnight Short Screenplay competition and, over the past several years, has had work nominated for a Pushcart Prize and Best Small Fictions.

A resident of northern New Jersey in the USA, Lisa thrives in the chaos of suburbia. She and her husband are kept busy by the comings and goings of their two teenage sons and by the demands of their double-doodle puppy.

CORE TRUTHS

You can reach Lisa in a variety of ways:

Website: lisafoxiswriting.com

Twitter: @iamlisafox10800

Facebook: lisafoxiswriting

Instagram: lisafoxiswriting

Email: lisafoxiswriting@gmail.com

Made in the USA
Columbia, SC
26 June 2023

19391603R10124

FAMILY BIBLE STORY
SERIES

One of the most extensively researched Bible story books on the market today, this series offers features which give background information to engage every member of the family, young and old alike. Written by Ruth Redding Brand and illustrated by distinguished artists, these carefully researched and beautifully illustrated books will make Bible characters come alive for your children. Every name, place, and custom is carefully explained. Hardcover. Available individually or as a set.

Abraham, 109 pages. ISBN 0-8280-1856-1

Adam & Eve, 95 pages. ISBN 0-8280-1850-2

Jacob, 127 pages. ISBN 0-8280-1852-9

Joseph, 87 pages. ISBN 0-8280-1854-5

Ordinary women—
extraordinary stories

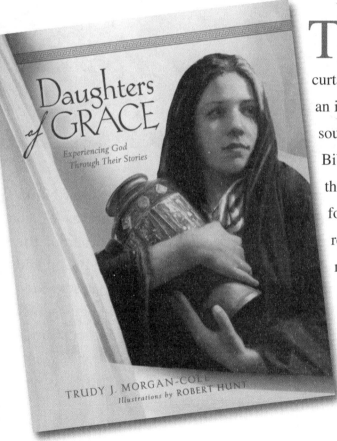

Trudy Morgan-Cole draws back the dusty curtains of time and takes an intimate look into the souls of women in the Bible—women whom the world has never forgotten but never really knew. What made them so unique . . . so special? They were like you. Paperback.

3 WAYS TO SHOP

REVIEW AND HERALD®
PUBLISHING ASSOCIATION
ce 1861 | www.reviewandherald.com

Just imagine . . .

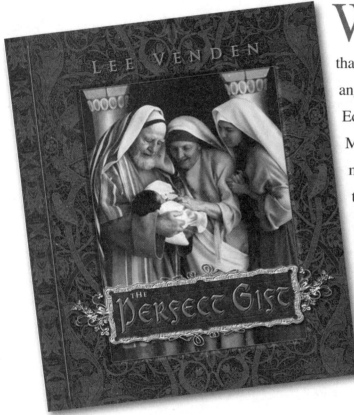

What was it like to catch a glimpse of that Child promised to our anguished parents in Eden? Or to watch that Man mingle among the masses? Lee Venden takes a fresh look at the Savior through the eyes of the ones who saw Him, touched Him, and were transformed by Him. Hardcover, 112 pages.

You've read the greatest story ever told— but never quite like this.

FOUR GOSPELS. ONE STORY.

SAVIOR

A fresh look at Jesus Christ, His Ministry, and His teachings

JACK J. BLANCO

Written in modern language without the disjointed interruption of chapter or verse, Jack Blanco's fresh, unified narrative merges the four Gospel accounts into one. No long genealogical lists. No confusing, archaic words. Just the timeless story of Jesus, our Saviour. Paperback, 160 pages

3 WAYS TO SHOP

JOURNEY BACK IN TIME

Combining thorough research and meticulous attention to detail, these biblical narratives offer the reader a chance to relieve history. Woven into these intriging stories are the sights and sounds of ancient cultures, their customs, and traditions— capturing the imagination and enriching the reading experience.

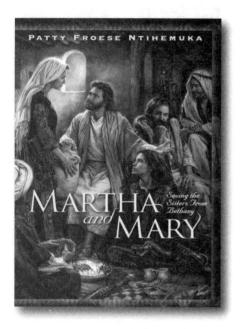

I n this brilliant retelling of an old story, Patty Froese Ntihemuka skillfully weaves together the story of Lazarus' sisters. Dark secrets, betrayal, and shame haunt the two women— until the Savior gives them new life. Paperback, 175 pages.

S he was a broken, cruel woman— until she met the Man who looked at her with gentle respect in His eyes. In this inspiring narrative, Patty Froese Ntihemuka tells of a woman whose life fully changed after an encounter with the Savior. Paperback, 156 pages.

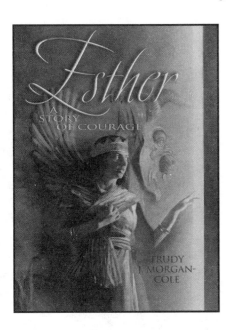

A NEW LOOK
AT TIMELESS STORIES
Biblical narratives by Teri L. Fivash

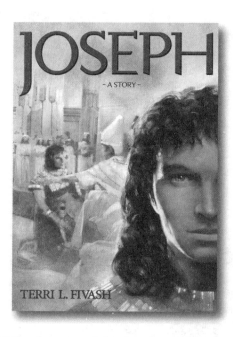

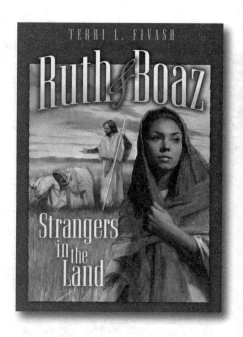

Each page of this book is filled with fresh insights into one of the greatest stories of all time. As the author paints a compelling panorama of Egyptian society, you'll be drawn deeply into Joseph's world. It is an unforgettable story of how one man's seeming failure became unimaginable success. Paperback, 463 pages.

With a cast of 89 characters and a plot that tugs at the heart, this book breathes new life into the story of Ruth—singer of songs, faithful friend, and daughter of royalty. This inspiring look at her life reveals how God is always at work turning tragedy into blessing. Paperback, 317 pages.

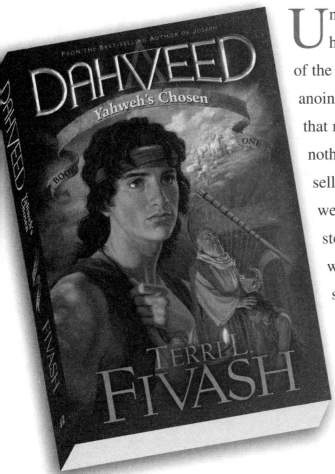